DON'T MISS THE HOTTEST THRILLER OF THE YEAR!

❖❖❖

"AN ENTERTAINING PAGE-TURNER.... The kind of book that hooks you .... Guaranteed to keep readers of suspense thrillers up into the wee hours feverishly reading to discover the outcome."
—*Houston Post*

❖

"HIGH-SPEED STORYTELLING, zigzagging from Paris bistros to the Zurich lairs of the rich and famously evil."
—*Detroit Free Press*

❖

"SPELLBINDING ... and the last line is a killer."
—*Milwaukee Journal*

❖

"A PAGE-TURNING WHOPPER..... A veritable encyclopedia of planes, trains, automobiles, plastic explosives, hairbreadth escapes, and passionate clinches."
—*Entertainment Weekly*

❖

"TAUT AND SUSPENSEFUL ... COMPELLING ADVENTURE."
—*San Francisco Chronicle*

more ...

"IT STARTS OUT WITH A BANG, REMAINS ACTION-PACKED THROUGHOUT.... It's got evil science of a gleaming, high-tech sort; it's filled with stylish European locales, and ... there's a love interest of the sexiest sort."
—*Boston Review*

✤

"HARROWING ... Two pages into the novel, the hero tries to choke a stranger to death. The pace picks up from there.... Expect to see this book tucked into carry-on baggage, propped up on beach blankets, and tossed on poolside tables for months to come."
—*Buffalo News*

✤

"A ONE-SITTING NOVEL ... DELIVERS IN FULL— AND THEN SOME!"
—*Publishers Weekly* (starred review)

✤

"[YOU'LL] BE HOOKED FROM PAGE ONE!... Folsom keeps his complex plot spinning with tremendous brio and momentum."
—*Kirkus Review* (starred review)

✤

"A COMPLEX, LAYERED THRILLER. Each development yields some answers but also deepens and widens the mystery."
—*San Diego Union-Tribune*

ATTENTION: SCHOOLS AND CORPORATIONS

WARNER books are available at quantity discounts with bulk purchase for educational, business, or sales promotional use. For information, please write to: SPECIAL SALES DEPARTMENT, WARNER BOOKS, 1271 AVENUE OF THE AMERICAS, NEW YORK, N.Y. 10020

ARE THERE WARNER BOOKS
YOU WANT BUT CANNOT FIND IN YOUR LOCAL STORES?

You can get any WARNER BOOKS title in print. Simply send title and retail price, plus 95¢ per order and 95¢ per copy to cover mailing and handling costs for each book desired. New York State and California residents add applicable sales tax. Enclose check or money order only, no cash please, to: WARNER BOOKS, P.O. BOX 690, NEW YORK, N.Y. 10019

THE DAY AFTER TOMORROW

ALLAN FOLSOM

WARNER
VISION
BOOKS

A Time Warner Company

WARNER BOOKS EDITION

Copyright © 1994 by Allan Folsom
All rights reserved.

Cover design Steve Snider/Tom Tafuri

Warner Vision is a trademark of Warner Books, Inc.

Warner Books, Inc.
1271 Avenue of the Americas
New York, NY 10020

Ⓦ A Time Warner Company

Printed in the United States of America

First Warner Books Printing: February, 1995

10 9 8 7 6 5 4 3 2 1

For Karen . . .

1

Paris, Monday, October 3.
5:40 P.M.
Brasserie Stella, the rue St.-Antoine.

PAUL OSBORN sat alone among the smoky bustle of the after-work crowd, staring into a glass of red wine. He was tired and hurt and confused. For no particular reason he looked up. When he did, his breath left him with a jolt. Across the room sat the man who murdered his father. That it could be he was inconceivable. But there was no doubt. None. It was a face forever stamped in his memory. The deepset eyes, the square jaw, the ears that stuck out almost at right angles, the jagged scar under the left eye that worked its way sharply down across the cheekbone toward the upper lip. The scar was less distinct now but it was there just the same. Like Osborn, he was alone. A cigarette was in his right hand and his left was curled around the rim of a coffee cup, his concentration on a newspaper at his elbow. He had to be at least fifty, maybe more.

From where Osborn sat, it was hard to tell his height. Maybe five foot eight or nine. He was stocky. Probably a hundred and eighty pounds. His neck was thick and his body looked hard. His complexion pale, his hair was short and curly, black, speckled with gray. Stamping out his cigarette, the man lit another, glancing Osborn's way as he did. Then, putting out the match, he went back to his paper.

Osborn felt his heart skip a beat and the blood start to rise in his veins. Suddenly it was Boston and 1966 again.

1

He was barely ten and he and his father were walking down the street. It was an afternoon in early spring, sunny but still cold. His father, dressed in a business suit, had left his office early to meet his son at the Park Street subway station. From there they crossed a corner of the Common and turned down Winter Street in a flurry of shoppers. They were going to a sale at Grogin's Sporting Goods. The boy had saved all winter for a new baseball mitt, a first baseman's glove. A Trapper model. His father had promised to match his savings dollar for dollar. Together they had thirty-two dollars. They were in sight of the store, and his father was smiling, when the man with the scar and the square jaw struck. He stepped out of the crowd and shoved a butcher knife into his father's stomach. As he did, he glanced over and saw the boy, who had no idea what was happening. In that instant their eyes met. Then the man moved on and his father crumpled to the pavement.

He could still feel the moment, standing so terribly alone on the sidewalk, strangers massing to look, his father staring up at him, helpless, uncomprehending, blood beginning to seep through fingers that had instinctively sought to pull the weapon out but had, instead, died there.

Twenty-eight years later and a continent away the memory roared back to life. Paul Osborn could feel the rage engulf him. In an instant he was up and across the room. A split second later the two men, table and chairs, crashed to the floor. He felt his fingers close around a leathery throat, a stubble of beard at the neck pressed against his palm. At the same time he felt his other hand pounding savagely down. His fist a runaway piston, wrecking flesh and bone, determined to batter the life from it. Around him people were screaming but it made no difference. His only sense was to destroy forever the thing he had in his grasp.

Suddenly he felt hands under his chin, others under his

arms, jerking him up and away. He felt himself hurtling backward. A moment later he crashed into something hard and fell to the floor, vaguely aware of dishes falling around him. Then he heard someone yelling in French to call the police! Looking up, he saw three waiters in white shirts and black vests standing over him. Behind them, his man was getting up unsteadily, sucking in air, blood gushing from his nose. Once up, he seemed to realize what had happened and looked toward his attacker in horror. Refusing a proffered napkin, he suddenly bolted through the crowd and out the front door.

Immediately Osborn was on his feet.

The waiters stiffened.

"Get the hell out of my way!" he shouted.

They didn't move.

If this were New York or L.A. he'd have yelled that the man was a murderer and for them to call the police. But this was Paris, he could barely order coffee. Unable to communicate, he did the only thing he could. He charged. The first waiter moved to grab him. But Osborn was six inches taller, twenty pounds heavier and running as if he were carrying a football. Dropping his shoulder, he drove it hard into the man's chest, spinning him sideways into the others so that they fell in a resounding comic crash, helplessly pinned one on top of the other, in a small service area halfway between the kitchen and the door. Then Osborn was through the door and gone.

Outside it was dark and raining. The rush-hour crowd filled the streets. Osborn dodged around them, his eyes scanning the sidewalk ahead, his heart pounding. This is the way the man had run, where the hell was he? He was going to lose him, he knew it. Then he saw him, a half block ahead, moving down the rue de Fourcy toward the Seine.

Osborn quickened his pace. His blood was still up but the violent explosion had spent most of his murderous rage and reason was beginning to set in. His father's murder had taken place in the United States, where there was no statute of limitations on murder. But was that true in France as well? Did the two countries have a mutual extradition treaty? And what if the man was French, would the French government send one of its own citizens to the U.S. to be tried for murder there?

A half block ahead, the man looked back. As he did, Osborn dropped back into the throng of pedestrians. Better to let him think he got away, calm a little, lose his caution. Then, when he's off guard, grab him alone.

A light changed, traffic stopped, so did the crowd. Osborn was behind a woman with an umbrella, with his man no more than a dozen feet away. Again he saw the face clearly. No doubt at all. He'd seen it in his dreams for twenty-eight years. He could draw it in his sleep. Standing there, the rage started to build once more.

The light changed again and the man crossed the street ahead of the crowd. Reaching the far curb, he glanced back, saw nothing and continued on. By now they were on Pont Marie, crossing the Île St.-Louis. To their right was the Cathedral Notre Dame. A few more minutes and they'd be across the Seine and onto the Left Bank.

For the moment Osborn had the upper hand. He looked ahead, searching for a side street or alley where he might be able to take his man out of public view. This was tricky business. If he moved too fast, he risked drawing attention to himself. But he had to move up or gamble losing him altogether should the man suddenly turn down an unseen street or hail a cab.

The rain came down harder and the glare from the passing yellow Parisian headlights was making it difficult to see. Ahead, his man turned right on boulevard St.-Germain and abruptly crossed the street. Where the hell was he going? Then Osborn saw it. The Métro station. If he got in there, he'd be swallowed up in a moment. Osborn started to run, rudely brushing people aside as he went. Suddenly he darted across the street in front of traffic. Honking horns made his man look back. For a moment he froze where he was, then rushed on. Osborn knew he'd been seen and that the man realized he was being pursued.

Osborn all but flew down the steps into the Métro. At the bottom he saw his man take a ticket from an automated machine. Then push through the crowd toward the turnstiles.

Looking back, the man saw Osborn's running dash down the steps. His hand went forward, his ticket inserted in the turnstile mechanism. The press bar gave, he went through. Cutting a sharp right, he disappeared around a corner.

No time for ticket or turnstiles. Elbowing a young woman out of the way, Osborn vaulted the turnstiles, dodged around a tall black man and headed for the tracks.

A train was already in the station. He saw his man get on. Abruptly the doors closed and the train pulled out. Osborn ran a few feet more, then stopped, chest heaving and out of breath. There was nothing left but gleaming rails and an empty tunnel. The man was gone.

2

MICHELE KANARACK looked across the table, then extended her hand. Her eyes were filled with love and affection. Henri Kanarack took her hand in his and looked at her. This was his fifty-second birthday; she was thirty-four. They'd been married for nearly eight years and today she'd told him she was pregnant with their first child.

"Tonight is very special," she said.

"Yes. Very special." Kissing her hand gently, he let it go and poured from a bottle of red Bordeaux.

"This is the last," she said. "Until the baby. No more drinking while I'm pregnant."

"Then the same for me." Henri smiled.

Outside the rain beat down in torrents. The wind rattled the roof and windows. Their apartment was on the top floor of a five-story building on the avenue Verdier in the Montrouge section of Paris. Henri Kanarack was a baker who left every morning at five and didn't return until nearly six thirty at night. He had an hour commute each way to the bakery near the Gare du Nord on the north side of Paris. It was a long day. But he was happy with it. As he was with his life and the idea of becoming a father for the first time at the age of fifty-two. At least he had been until tonight, when the stranger had attacked him in the brasserie and then chased after him into the Métro. He'd looked American. Thirty-five or so. Well built and strong. Dressed in an expensive sport coat and jeans, like a businessman on vacation.

Who the hell was he? Why had he done that?

"Are you all right?" Michele was staring at him. What was Paris coming to when a baker could be attacked in a brasserie by a total stranger? She wanted him to call the police. Then find a lawyer and sue the brasserie's owner.

"Yes," he said. "I'm all right." He wanted neither to call the police nor sue the brasserie, though his left eye was all but swollen shut and his lip was puffed up and red/blue where the wild man's blow had driven an upper tooth through it.

"Hey, I'm going to be a father," he said, trying to get off it. "No long faces around here. Not tonight." Michele got up from the table, came around behind him and put her arms around his neck.

"Let's make love in celebration of life. A great life between young Michele, old Henri and new baby."

Henri turned around and looked into her eyes, then smiled. How could he not. He loved her.

Later, as he lay in the dark and listened to her breathing, he tried to blank the vision of the dark-haired man from his mind. But it would not go. It revived a deep, almost primal, fear—that no matter what he did, or how far he ran, one day he would be found out.

3

OSBORN COULD see them talking in the corridor. He assumed it was about him but he couldn't be sure. Then the short one walked off and the other came back in through the glass door, a cigarette in one hand, a manila folder in the other.

"Would you like some coffee, Doctor Osborn?" Young and confident, Inspector Maitrot was soft-spoken and polite. He was also blond and tall, unusual for a Frenchman.

"I'd like to know how much longer you intend to hold me." Osborn had been arrested by the Police Urbaine for violating a city ordinance after vaulting the Métro turnstile. When questioned, he'd lied, saying the man he had been chasing had earlier roughed him up and tried to steal his wallet. It was a total coincidence that only a short while later he'd seen him in the brasserie. That was when they'd connected him to the citywide call from the Paris police and brought him to central jail for interrogation.

"You are a doctor." Maitrot was reading from a sheet stapled to the inside cover of the folder. "An American orthopedic surgeon visiting Paris after attending a medical convention in Geneva. Your home is Los Angeles."

"Yes," Osborn said flatly. He'd already told the story to the police at the Métro station, to a uniformed cop in a booking cage somewhere in another part of the building and to a plainclothes officer of some kind who led him through a series of fingerprintings, mug photos and a preliminary interview. Now, in this tiny glassed-in cell of an interrogation room, Maitrot was going through everything all over again. Particular by particular.

"You don't look like a doctor."

"You don't look like a policeman," Osborn said lightly, trying to take the edge off.

Maitrot didn't react. Maybe he didn't get it because English was obviously a struggle, but he was right—Osborn didn't look like a doctor. Six feet tall, dark haired and brown eyed, at a hundred and ninety pounds he had the boyish looks, muscular structure and build of a college athlete.

"What was the name of the convention you attended?"

"I didn't 'attend' it. I presented a paper there. To the World Congress of Surgery." Osborn wanted to say, "How many times do I have to keep telling you this; don't you guys talk to each other?" He should have been frightened, and maybe he was, but he was still too pumped up to realize it. His man might have gotten away, but the vital thing was that he'd been found! He was here, in Paris. And with any luck, he would still be here, at home or in a bar someplace, nursing his wounds and wondering what had happened.

"On what was your paper? What subject?"

Osborn closed his eyes and counted slowly to five. "I already told you."

"You didn't tell *me*."

"My paper was on the anterior cruciate ligament injury. It has to do with the knee." Osborn's mouth was dry. He asked for a glass of water. Maitrot either didn't understand or ignored him.

"You are how old?"

"You already know that."

Maitrot looked up.

"Thirty-eight."

"Married?"

"No."

"Homosexual?"

"Inspector, I'm divorced. Is that all right with you?"

"How long have you been a surgeon?"

Osborn said nothing. Maitrot repeated the question, his cigarette smoke trailing off toward a ventilator in the ceiling.

"Six years."

"Do you think you are a particularly good surgeon?"

"I don't understand why you're asking me these questions. They have nothing to do with what you arrested me for. You may call my office to verify anything I've said." Osborn was exhausted and starting to lose it. But at the same time he knew that if he wanted to get out of there, he'd better watch what he said.

"Look," he said, as calmly and respectfully as he could. "I've cooperated with you. I've done everything you asked. Fingerprints, photographs, answered questions, everything. Now, please, I would like to either be released or see the American consul."

"You assaulted a French citizen."

"How do you know he was a French citizen?" Osborn said without thinking.

Maitrot ignored his emotion. "Why did you do it?"

"Why?" Osborn stared at him incredulously. There wasn't a day when, at some point, he didn't still hear the sound as the butcher knife struck his father's stomach. Didn't hear the awful surprise of his gasp. Didn't see the horror in his eyes as he looked up as if to ask, What happened?, yet knowing exactly what had. Didn't see his knees buckle under him as he slowly collapsed onto the sidewalk. Didn't hear the terrible shriek of a stranger's scream. Didn't see his father roll and try to reach up, knowing he was dying, asking his son without speaking to take hold of his hand so he wouldn't be so afraid. Telling him without speaking that he loved him forever.

"Yes." Maitrot leaned over and twisted his cigarette into an ashtray on the table between them. "Why did you do it?"

Osborn sat up straight and told the lie again. "I came into Charles de Gaulle Airport from London." He had to be careful and not make any changes from what he'd said to his previous interrogators. "The man roughed me up in the men's room and tried to steal my wallet."

"You look fit. Was he a big man?"

"Not particularly. He just wanted my wallet."

"Did he get it?"

"No. He ran away."

"Did you report it to airport authorities?"

"No."

"Why?"

"He didn't steal anything and I don't speak French very well, as you can tell."

Maitrot lit another cigarette and flipped the spent match into the ashtray. "And then later, by sheer coincidence, you saw him in the same brasserie where you had stopped for a drink?"

"Yes."

"What were you going to do, hold him for the police?"

"To tell you the truth, Inspector, I don't know what the

hell I was going to do. I just did it. I got mad. I lost my head."

Osborn stood up and looked off while Maitrot made a note in the folder. What was he going to tell him? That the man he had chased had stabbed his father to death in Boston, Massachusetts, the United States of America, on Tuesday, April 12, 1966? That he saw him do it and had never seen him again until just a few hours ago? That the Boston police had listened with great compassion to the horror tale of a little boy and then spent years trying to track the killer down until finally they admitted there was nothing more they could do? Oh yes, the procedures had been correct. The crime scene and technical analysis, the autopsy, the interviews. But the boy had never seen the man before, and his mother couldn't place him from the boy's description, and since there had been no fingerprints on the murder weapon, and the weapon nothing more than a supermarket knife, the police had had to rely on the only thing they had, the testimony of two other eyewitnesses. Katherine Barnes, a middle-aged sales clerk who worked at Jordan Marsh, and Leroy Green, a custodian at the Boston Public Library. Both had been on the sidewalk at the time of the attack and each had told slight variations of the same story as the boy. But in the end, the police had exactly what they had in the beginning. Nothing. Finally Kevin O'Neil, the brash young homicide detective who'd befriended Paul and been on the case from the start, was killed by a suspect he'd testified against, and the George Osborn file went from a personally handled homicide investigation to simply another unsolved murder crammed into central files alongside hundreds of others. And now, three decades later, Katherine Barnes was in her eighties, senile and in a nursing home in Maine, and Leroy Green was dead. That made, for all intents, Paul Osborn the last surviving witness. And for a prosecutor, any prosecutor, thirty years after the fact, to expect a jury to convict a man on the testimony of the victim's son who had been ten at the time, and had glimpsed the suspect for no more than two or three seconds, would be lunatic. The truth was the killer had simply gotten away with it. And tonight in a Paris jail that truth still reigned because even if Osborn could convince the police to try to track the man down and arrest him, he would never be brought to trial. Not in France, not in America, not anywhere, in a million years. So why tell the police? It would do no good and might only complicate things later, if by some twist of fortune, Osborn was able to find him again.

"You were in London today. This morning." Suddenly Osborn was aware that Maitrot was still talking to him.

"Yes."

"You said you came to Paris from Geneva."

"Via London."

"Why were you there?"

"I was a tourist. But I got sick. A twenty-four-hour bug of some kind."

"Where did you stay?"

Osborn sat back. What did they want from him? Book him or let him go. What business was it of theirs what he had done in London?

"I asked you where you stayed in London." Maitrot was staring at him.

Osborn had been in London with a woman, also a doctor, an intern at a Paris hospital, who he later found out was the mistress of a preeminent French politician. At the time she'd told him how it was important for her to be discreet and begged him not to ask why. Accepting it, he'd carefully selected a hotel known for maintaining its guests' privacy and checked in using his name only.

"The Connaught," Osborn said. Hopefully the hotel would live up to its reputation.

"Were you alone?"

"Okay, enough." Abruptly, Osborn pushed back from

the table and stood up. "I want to see the American consul." Through the glass Osborn saw a uniformed patrolman with a submachine gun over his shoulder turn and stare in at him.

"Why don't you relax, Doctor Osborn. . . . Please, sit down," Maitrot said quietly, then leaned over to make a notation in the file.

Osborn sat back down and stared deliberately off, hopeful Maitrot would pass on the London business and get on with whatever was next. A clock on the wall read almost eleven. That made it three in the afternoon in L.A., or was it two? This time of year, time zones in Europe seemed to jump by the hour, depending where you were. Who the hell did he know there who he could call in a situation like this? He'd only had one encounter with the police in his life. That had been after a particularly grueling day when he'd accosted a careless and remorseless parking lot attendant outside a Beverly Hills restaurant for crushing the front fender of his new car while attempting to park it. Osborn had not been arrested but merely detained and then released. That was all, one experience in a lifetime. When he was fifteen and in boys' school the police had arrested him for throwing snowballs through a classroom window on Christmas Day. When they asked him why he did it, he'd told them the truth. He'd had nothing else to do.

Why? That was a word they always asked. The people at the school. The police. Even his patients. Asking why something hurt. Why surgery was or was not necessary. Why something continued to hurt when they felt it shouldn't. Why they did not need medication when they felt they did. Why they could do this but not that. Then waiting for him to explain it. "Why?" seemed to be a question he was destined to answer, not ask. Although he did remember asking "Why?" twice, in particular: to his first wife and then to his second, after they said they were leaving him. But now, in this glassed-in police interrogation room in the center of Paris, with a French detective making notes and chain-smoking cigarettes in front of him, he suddenly realized that *why* was the most important word in the world to him. And he wanted to ask it only once. To the man he had chased down into the subway.

"*Why*, you bastard, did you murder my father?"

As quickly, the thought came to him that if the police had interviewed the waiters at the brasserie who reported the incident, they might have the man's name. Especially if he was a regular customer or had paid with a check or credit card. Osborn waited until Maitrot finished writing. Then, as politely as possible, said, "Can I ask a question?" Looking up, Maitrot nodded.

"This French citizen I'm accused of assaulting. Do you know who he was?"

"No," Maitrot said.

Just then the glass door opened and the other plainclothes inspector came back in and sat down opposite Osborn. His name was Barras and he glanced at Maitrot, who vaguely shook his head. Barras was small, with dark hair and black, humorless eyes. Dark hair covered the back of his hands, and his nails were cut to perfection.

"Troublemakers are not welcome in France. Physicians are no exception. Deportation is a simple matter," Barras said flatly.

Deportation! God no! Osborn thought. Please, not now! Not after so many years! Not after finally seeing him! Knowing he's alive and where! "I'm sorry," he said, covering his horror. "Very sorry. . . . I was upset, that's all. Please believe that because it's true."

Barras studied him. "How much longer had you planned to stay in France?"

"Five days," Osborn said. "To see Paris. . . ."

Barras hesitated, then reached into his coat pocket and

took out Osborn's passport. "Your passport, Doctor. When you are ready to leave, see me and I'll return it."

Osborn looked from Barras to Maitrot. That was their way of taking care of it. No deportation, no arrest, but keeping tabs on him just the same and making sure he knew it.

"It's late," Maitrot said, standing. "*Au revoir*, Doctor Osborn."

It was eleven twenty-five when Osborn left the police station. The rain had stopped and a bright moon hung over the city. He started to wave at a cab, then decided to walk back to his hotel. Walk and think about what to do next about the man who was no longer a childhood memory but a living creature, here, somewhere within the sweep of Paris. With patience, he was a man who could be found. And questioned. And then destroyed.

4

London.

THE SAME bright moon illuminated an alley just off Charing Cross Road in the theater district. The passageway was L-shaped and narrow and sealed off at both ends by crime scene tape. Passersby peered in from either end trying to see past the uniformed police, to get some idea of what was going on, of what had happened.

The faces in the leering crowd were not what had McVey's attention. It was another face, that of a white male in his early to mid-twenties with the eyeballs bulging grotesquely from their sockets. It had been discovered in a trash bin by a theater custodian emptying cartons after the closing of a show. Ordinarily Metropolitan homicide detectives would have worked it, but this was different. Superintendent Jamison called Commander Ian Noble of Special Branch at home, and Noble, in turn, had phoned McVey's hotel to wake him from a restless sleep.

It wasn't just the face, it was the head to which it was attached that had been the primary source of the Metropolitan detectives' interest. First, because there was no body to go with it. And second, because the head appeared to have been surgically removed from the rest. Where the "rest" was was anybody's guess, but the burden of what was left now belonged to McVey.

What was all too clear, as he watched scenes-of-crime officers carefully lift the head from the trash bin and set it into a clear plastic bag and then place it into a box for transportation, was that Superintendent Jamison's detectives had been right: the removal had been done by a professional. If not by a surgeon, at least by someone with a surgically sharp instrument and a sound knowledge of *Gray's Anatomy*.

To wit: at the base of the neck where it meets the clavicle or collar bone is the juncture of the trachea/esophagus leading to the lungs and stomach and the inferior constrictor muscle (which) arises from the sides of the cricoid and thyroid cartilages. . . .

Which was precisely where the head had been severed from the rest of the body and neither McVey nor Commander Noble needed an authority to confirm it. What they did need, however, was someone to tell them if the head had been removed before or after death. And if the latter, to ascertain the cause of death.

To perform a postmortem on a head is the same as autopsying an entire body except there is less of it.

Laboratory tests would take from twenty-four hours to three or four days. But McVey, Commander Noble and Dr. Evan Michaels, the young, baby-faced Home Office pathologist called from home by beeper to do the job, were of the same opinion. The head had been separated from the body subsequent to death and the cause of death was most probably the result of a lethal dose of a barbiturate, most likely Nembutal. However, there was a question as to what made the eyes bulge out of their sockets the way they did, what caused the slight trickle of blood at the corners of the mouth. Those were symptoms of a lethal breathing of cyanide gas, but there was no clear evidence of it.

McVey scratched behind an ear and stared at the floor.

"He's going to ask you about the time of death," Ian Noble said dryly to Michaels. Noble was fifty and married, with two daughters and four grandchildren. His close-cropped gray hair, square jaw and lean figure gave him an old-school military bearing, not surprising in a former colonel in army intelligence and graduate of the Royal Military Academy at Sandhurst, Class of '65.

"Hard to tell," Michaels said.

"Try." McVey's gray-green eyes were locked on Michaels'. He wanted some kind of answer. Even an educated guess would do.

"There is very little blood, almost none. Hard to assess the clotting time, you know. I can tell you it had been where it was found for some time because its temperature is very nearly identical to the temperature in the alley."

"No rigor mortis."

Michaels stared at him. "No, sir. Doesn't seem to be. As you know, Detective, rigor mortis usually commences within five to six hours, the upper part of the body is affected first, within about twelve hours, and the whole body within about eighteen."

"We don't *have* the whole body," McVey said.

"No, sir. We do not." Responsibility to duty aside, Michaels was beginning to wish he'd stayed home this night, thereby letting someone else have the pleasure of facing this irascible American homicide detective who had more gray in his hair than brown and who seemed to know the answers to his own questions even before he asked them.

"McVey," Noble said with a straight face, "why don't we wait for the lab results and let the poor doctor go home and finish his wedding night?"

"This is your wedding night?" McVey was dumbfounded. "Tonight?"

"Was," Michaels said flatly.

"Why the hell did you answer your beeper? They didn't get you they woulda got the next guy." McVey wasn't only sincere, he was incredulous. "What the hell did your wife say?"

"Not to answer the page."

"I'm glad to see one of you knows which end to light the candle."

"Sir. It's my job, you know."

Inside McVey smiled. Either the young pathologist was going to become a very good professional or a browbeaten civil servant. Which, was anybody's guess.

"If we're done, what do you want me to do with it?" Michaels said abruptly. "I've never done work for the Metropolitan Police before, or Interpol either for that matter."

McVey shrugged and looked to Noble. "I'm with him," he said. "I've never done work for the Metropolitan Police or Interpol before either. How and where do you file heads over here?"

"We file heads, McVey, like we file bodies, or pieces of bodies. Tagged, sealed in plastic and refrigerated." It was much too late for Noble to be in the mood for humor.

"Fine," McVey shrugged. He was more than willing to

call it a night. At first light detectives would be starting in the alley, interviewing everyone and anyone who might have seen activity around the trash dumpster in the hours before the head had been found. In a day, two at most, they would have lab reports on tissue samples and scalp hair follicles. A forensic anthropologist would be brought in to determine the victim's age.

Leaving Dr. Michaels to tag, seal in plastic and refrigerate the head in its own drawer, with a special addendum that henceforth the drawer was only to be opened in the presence of either Commander Noble or Detective McVey, the two detectives left, Noble, for his renovated four-story house in Chelsea; McVey, for his small hotel room in a deceptively small hotel on Half Moon Street across Green Park in Mayfair.

5

HE'D BEEN baptized William Patrick Cavan McVey in St. Mary's Catholic Church, on what was then Leheigh Road in Rochester, New York, on a snowy day in February 1928. Growing up, from Cardinal Manning Parochial School through Don Bosco High, everybody knew him as Paddy McVey, Precinct Sergeant Murphy McVey's first boy. But from the day he'd solved the "hillside torture murders" in Los Angeles twenty-nine years later, nobody called him anything but McVey—not the brass, not his fellow detectives, not the press, not even his wife.

A homicide detective for the LAPD since 1955, he'd

buried two wives and put three kids through college. The day he turned sixty-five he tried to retire. It didn't work. The phone kept ringing. "Call McVey, he knows every way there is to cut up a hooker." "Get McVey, he's got nothing to do, maybe he'll come over take a look at it." "I don't know, call McVey."

Finally he moved to the fishing cabin he'd built in the mountains near Big Bear Lake and had the phone taken out. But he'd barely stored his gear and had the cable TV hooked up when old detective pals started coming up to fish. And it wasn't long before they got around to asking the same questions they asked over the phone. Finally he gave up, padlocked the cabin and went back to work full time.

He'd been at his old nicked steel desk, sitting in the same chair with the squeaky caster at robbery/homicide for less than two weeks, when Bill Woodward, the chief of detectives, came in and asked if he'd like a trip to Europe, all expenses paid. Any of the other six detectives in the squad room would have jumped for their Samsonite. McVey, on the other hand, shrugged and asked why and for how long. He wasn't crazy about traveling and when he did it was usually to some place warm. It was early September. Europe would be getting cold and he hated cold.

"The 'how long,' I guess, is up to you. The 'why' is because Interpol has seven headless corpses they don't know what to do about." Woodward stuck a file under McVey's nose and walked off.

McVey watched him go, glanced at the other detectives in the room, then picked up a cup of cold coffee and opened the file. On the upper righthand corner was a black tab, which, in Interpol circulation, indicated an unidentified dead body and asked for any possible help in identifying it. The tab was old. By now the corpses had been identified.

Of the seven bodies, two had been found in England, two in France, one in Belgium, one in Switzerland and one, washed ashore, near the West German port of Kiel. All were males and their ages ranged from twenty-two to fifty-six. All were white and all, apparently, had been drugged with some sort of barbiturate and then had their heads surgically removed at precisely the same place in the anatomy.

The killings had occurred from February to August and seemed completely random. Yet they were far too similar to be coincidental. But that was all, the rest was completely dissimilar. None of the victims were related or appeared to have known one another. None had criminal records or had lived violent lives. And all were from different economic backgrounds.

What made it even stickier were the statistics: more than fifty percent of the time a murder victim is identified, headless or not, the murderer is found. In these seven cases not a single bona fide suspect had been uncovered. All told, police experts of five countries, including Scotland Yard's special murder investigations unit and Interpol, the international police organization, were batting an even zero, and the tabloid press was having a field day. Hence the call had come to the Los Angeles Police Department for one of the best in the singular world of homicide investigation.

Initially, McVey had gone to Paris, where he'd met with Inspector Lieutenant Alex Lebrun of the First Section of the Paris Préfecture of Police, an impish rogue of a man, with a big grin and an always-present cigarette. Lebrun, in turn, had introduced him to Commander Noble of Scotland Yard and Captain Yves Cadoux, assignment director for Interpol. Together the foursome examined the crime scenes in France. The first was in Lyon, two hours south of Paris by Très Grande Vitesse, the TGV bullet train; and, ironically, less than a mile from Interpol headquarters. The second, in the Alpine ski resort of Chamonix. Later Cadoux and Noble escorted McVey to the murder scenes in Belgium, a small factory on the outskirts of Ostend; Switzerland, a luxury hotel overlooking Lake Geneva in Lausanne; and Germany, a rocky coastal inlet twenty minutes by car north of Kiel. Finally they went to England. First, to a small apartment across from Salisbury Cathedral, eighty miles southwest of London, and then to London itself and a private home on a square in the exclusive Kensington section.

Afterward, McVey spent ten days in a cold, third-floor office in Scotland Yard poring over the extensive police reports of each crime, more often than not finding it necessary to confer on one detail or another with Ian Noble, who had a much larger and warmer office on the first floor. Mercifully, McVey got a respite when he was called back to Los Angeles for a two-day testimony in the murder trial of a Vietnamese drug dealer McVey had arrested himself when the man tried to kill a busboy in a restaurant where McVey was having lunch. Actually, McVey had done nothing more heroic than stick his .38 service revolver in the man's ear and quietly suggest he relax a little bit.

After the trial, McVey was supposed to take two days for personal business and then return to London. But somehow he'd managed to squeeze in some wholly elective oral surgery and turned the two days into two weeks, most of which was spent on a golf course near the Rose Bowl where warm sun filtering through heavy smog helped him, between strokes, muse on the killings.

So far, the only thing the victims seemed to have in common, the only single connecting thread, was the surgical removal of their heads. Something that on first go-round appeared to have been done either by a surgeon or by someone with surgical capabilities who had access to the necessary instruments.

After that, nothing else fit. Three of the victims had been killed where they were found. The remaining four had been killed elsewhere, with three dumped by the roadside and the fourth tossed into Kiel Harbor. For all his years in homicide, this was as confounding and more curious than anything he'd ever encountered.

Then, golf clubs put away, and back in the damp of London, exhausted and disoriented from the long flight, he'd barely settled back on the thing the hotel passed off as a pillow and closed his eyes when the phone rang and Noble informed him he had a head to go with his bodies.

It was now quarter of four in the morning, London time, and McVey was sitting at a writing table in his closet of a room, two fingers of Famous Grouse scotch in a glass in front of him, on a conference call with Noble and Captain Cadoux on the Interpol line from Lyon.

Cadoux, an intense, stockily built man, with a huge handlebar mustache he could never seem to keep from rolling between his thumb and forefinger, had in front of him a fax of young medical examiner Michaels' preliminary autopsy report, which described, among other things, the exact point at which the head had been removed from the body. It was precisely at this same point the seven bodies had been separated from their heads.

"We know that, Cadoux. But it's not enough for us to say for certain that the murders are connected," McVey said wearily.

"The age bracket is the same."

"Still not enough."

"McVey, I have to agree with Captain Cadoux," Noble said genteelly, as if they were talking over four o'clock tea.

"If it's not a connection, it's too damn close to being one to ignore it," Noble finished.

"Fine . . . ," McVey said and repeated the thought he'd had all along. "You gotta wonder who this lunatic is we got running around out there." The minute McVey said it both Scotland Yard and Interpol reacted the same way.

"You think it's one man?" they said together.

"I don't know. Yeah—" McVey said. "Yeah. I think it's one man."

Begging off that jet lag was about to put him under and could they finish this later, McVey hung up. He could have asked for their opinion but didn't. It was they who had asked for his help. Besides, if they felt he was wrong they would have said so. Anyway, it was just a hunch.

Picking up his glass, he looked out the window. Across the street was another hotel, small, like his own. Most of the windows were dark, but a dim light showed on the fourth floor. Someone was reading, or maybe had fallen asleep reading, or maybe left the light on when they went out and hadn't come back yet. Or maybe there was a body in the room, waiting to be discovered in the morning. That was the thing about being a detective, the possibilities for almost anything were endless. It was only over time that you began to get a second sense about things, a feeling of what was in the room before you entered, what you might find when you did, what kind of person was there or had been there, and what they had been up to.

But with the severed head there had been no room with a dim light showing. If they got lucky, maybe that would come later. The room that would point to another room and finally to the space that held the killer. But before any of that, they had to identify the victim.

McVey finished the scotch, wiped his eyes and glanced at the note he'd made earlier and had already set into motion. HEAD/ARTIST/SKETCH/NEWSPAPER/I.D.

6

AT FIVE in the morning Paris streets were deserted. Métro service began at five thirty, so Henri Kanarack relied on Agnes Demblon, head bookkeeper at the bakery where he worked, for a ride to the shop. And dutifully, every day at four forty-five, she would arrive outside his apartment house in her white, five-year-old Citroën. And every day Michele Kanarack would watch out the bedroom window for her husband to come out onto the street, get into the Citroën and drive away with Agnes. Then she would pull her robe tight about her and go back to bed and lie awake thinking about Henri and Agnes. Agnes was a forty-nine-year-old spinster, an eyeglass-wearing bookkeeper, and by no one's imagination attractive. What could Henri see in her that he didn't in Michele? Michele was much younger, a dozen times better-looking, with a figure to match, and she made sure Henri got all the sex he needed, which of course was why she was finally pregnant.

What Michele had no way of knowing, and would never be told, was that it was Agnes who had gotten Henri the job at the bakery. Persuaded the owner to hire him even when he had no experience as a baker. The owner, a small, impatient man named Lebec, had had no interest in taking on a new man, especially when he would have to undergo the expense of training him, but changed his mind immediately when Agnes threatened to quit if he didn't. Bookkeepers like Agnes were hard to find, especially ones who knew their way around the tax laws as she did. So, Henri Kanarack had been hired, had quickly learned his trade, was dependable and did not constantly press for raises like some of the others. In other words, he was an ideal employee and, as such, Lebec could have no quarrel with Agnes for bringing him on board. The only question Lebec had posed was why Agnes had been so willing to quit her job over so nondescript and everyday a man as Henri Kanarack, and Agnes had answered that with a curt "Yes or no, Monsieur Lebec?" The rest was history.

Agnes slowed for a blinking light and glanced at Kanarack. She'd seen the bruises on his face when he'd climbed in, now in the dash lights they glowed even uglier.

"Drinking again," Agnes' voice was cold, bordering on cruel.

"Michele is pregnant," he said, staring straight ahead, watching the yellow headlights cut the darkness.

"Did you get drunk out of joy or misery?"

"I didn't get drunk. A man attacked me."

"What man?" She looked at him.

"I never saw him before."

"What did you do to him?"

"I ran away." Kanarack's eyes were fixed on the road ahead.

"Finally getting smart in your old age."

"This was different—" Kanarack turned to look at her. "I was in the Brasserie Stella. The one on rue St.-Antoine. Reading the paper and having an espresso on the way home. For no reason at all a man flew at me, knocked me to the floor and started beating me. The waiters pulled him off and I ran away."

"Why did he pick you?"

"Don't know." Kanarack looked back to the road again. Night was fading to day. Automatic timers were turning the streetlights off. "He followed me afterward. Across the Seine, down into the Métro. I managed to beat him out, get on a train before he could catch up. I—"

Agnes downshifted, slowing for a man walking his dog. Passing, she accelerated again. "You what?"

"I went to the train window. I saw the Métro police grab him."

"So, he was a crazy. And the police are good for something."

"Maybe not."

Agnes looked over. There was something he was not telling her. "What is it?"

"He was an American."

Paul Osborn got back to his hotel on avenue Kléber at ten minutes to one in the morning. Fifteen minutes later he was in his room and on the phone to L.A. His attorney put him in touch with another attorney, who said he'd make a call and get back to him. At one twenty the phone rang. The caller was in Paris. His name was Jean Packard.

A little more than five and a half hours later, Jean Packard sat down opposite Paul Osborn in the hotel dining room. At forty-two, he was exceedingly fit. His hair was cut short and his suit hung loosely over a wiry frame. He wore no tie, and his shirt was open at the collar, perhaps to purposely reveal a ragged, three-inch scar that ran diagonally across his throat. Packard had been a Foreign Legionnaire, then a soldier of fortune in Angola, Thailand, and El Salvador. He was now an employee of Kolb International, billed as the world's largest private investigation firm.

"We guarantee nothing, but we do our best, and for most clients that is usually sufficient," Packard said with a smile that was surprising. A waiter brought steaming coffee and a small tray of croissants, then left. Jean Packard touched neither. Instead he looked at Osborn directly.

"Let me explain," he continued. His English was heavily accented but understandable. "All investigators for

Kolb International are thoroughly screened and have impeccable credentials. We operate, however, not as employees but as independent contractors. We take our assignments from the regional offices and share the billing with them. Other than that, they ask nothing. In effect, we are on our own unless we request otherwise. Client confidentiality is very nearly religion with us. Keeping matters one on one, investigator to client, assures that. Something I'm certain you can appreciate at a time in history when even the most privileged information is readily available to almost anyone willing to pay for it."

Jean Packard put out a hand and stopped a passing waiter, asking in French for a glass of water. Then he turned back to Osborn and explained the rest of Kolb's procedure.

When an investigation was completed, he said, all files containing written, copied or photographed work, negatives included, were returned to the client. The investigator then turned in a time and expense report to the Kolb regional office, which, in turn, billed the customer.

The water came. "*Merci,*" Packard said. Then, taking a drink, he set the glass on the table and looked to Osborn.

"So you understand how clean, private, and simple our operation is."

Osborn smiled. He not only liked the procedure, he liked the private detective's style and manner. He needed someone he could trust, and Jean Packard seemed to be that person. Still, the wrong person with the wrong approach could send his man running and, as a result, spoil everything. And then there was the other problem, and even to this moment Osborn hadn't quite known how to broach it. And then Jean Packard said the next and Osborn's difficulty was erased.

"I would ask you why you want this person located, but I sense you would prefer not to tell me."

"It's personal," Osborn said quietly. Jean Packard nodded, accepting it.

For the next forty minutes Osborn went over the details of what little he knew of the man he was after. The brasserie on the rue St.-Antoine. The time of day he had seen him there. Which table he had been sitting at. What he had been drinking. The fact that he had been smoking. The route the man had taken afterward, when he thought no one was following him. The Métro on boulevard St.-Germain he had suddenly dashed into when he realized he was.

Closing his eyes, picturing him, Osborn carefully went over Henri Kanarack's physical description, as he had seen him here, just hours ago, in Paris, and as he remembered him from that moment, years before, in Boston. Through it all Jean Packard said little, a question here, to repeat a detail there. Nor did he take notes, he simply listened. The session ended with Osborn giving Packard a drawing of Henri Kanarack he'd made from memory on hotel stationery. The deep-set eyes, the square jaw, the jagged scar under the left eye that worked its way sharply down across the cheekbone toward the upper lip, the ears that stuck out almost at right angles. The sketch was crude, as if drawn by a ten-year-old boy.

Jean Packard folded it in half and put it in his jacket pocket. "In two days you will hear from me," he said. Then, finishing his water, he stood and walked out.

For a long moment Paul Osborn stared after him. He didn't know how to feel or what to think. By a single circumstance of serendipity, the random choosing of a place to have a cup of coffee in a city he knew nothing of, everything had changed and a day he was certain would never come, had. Suddenly there was hope. Not just for retribution but for redemption from the long and terrible bondage to which this murderer had sentenced him. For nearly three decades, from adolescence to adulthood, his life had been a lonely torment of horror and nightmares. The incident unwillingly played over and over in his mind. Propelled mercilessly by the gnawing guilt that somehow his father's death had been his fault, that somehow it could have been prevented had he been a better son, been more vigilant, seen the knife in time to shout a warning, even stepped in front of it himself. But that was only part of it. The rest was darker and even more debilitating. From boyhood to manhood, through any number of counselors, therapists and into the apparently safe hiding place of professional accomplishment, he had unsuccessfully fought another, even more tragic demon: the numbing, emasculating, terror of abandonment, begun by the killer's definitive demonstration of how quickly love could be ended.

It had proven true at that moment and held true ever since. At first by circumstance, with his mother and his aunt, and later, as he got older, with lovers and close friends. The fault in his adult life was his. Though he understood the cause of it, the emotion was still impossible for him to control. The moment real love or real friendship was near, the sheer terror that it might again be so brutally taken from him rose from nowhere to engulf him like a raging tide. And with it came a mistrust and jealousy he was powerless to do anything about. Out of nothing more than sheer self protection, whatever joy and love and trust there had been, he would erase in no time at all.

But now, after nearly thirty years, the cause of his sickness had been isolated. It was here, in Paris. And once found there would be no notifying of police, no attempt at extradition, no seeking of civil justice. Once found, this man would be confronted and then, like a disease itself, swiftly eradicated. The only difference was that this time the victim would know his killer.

7

THE DAY after his father's funeral, Paul Osborn's mother moved them out of their house and in with her sister in a small two-story home on Cape Cod.

His mother's name had been Becky. He assumed it was short for Elizabeth or Rebecca but he'd never asked and never heard her referred to as anything but Becky. She'd married Paul's father when she was only twenty and still in nursing school.

George David Osborn was handsome, but quiet and introverted. He'd come from Chicago to Boston to attend M.I.T. and immediately following graduation had gone to work for Raytheon and then later for Microtab, a small engineering design firm on the Route 128 high-tech hub. The most Paul knew about what his father did was that he designed surgical instruments. Much more than that, he'd been too young to remember.

What he did remember in the blur that followed the funeral was packing up and moving from their big house in the Boston suburbs to the much smaller house on Cape Cod. And that almost immediately, his mother began drinking.

He remembered nights when she made dinner for them both, then left hers to get cold and instead drank cocktail after cocktail until she could no longer talk, and then fell asleep. He remembered being afraid as the drinks mounted up and he tried to get her to eat but she wouldn't. Instead she became angry. At little things at first, but then the anger always came around to him. He was to blame for not having done something—anything—that might have helped save his father. And if his father were alive, they would still be living in their fine home near Boston, instead of where they were in that tiny little house on Cape Cod with her sister.

And then always, the rage would turn to the killer and the life he had left her. And then to the police, who were inept and impotent, and finally to herself, whom she despised most of all, for not being the kind of mother she should have been, for not being prepared or equipped to deal with the aftermath of such a tragedy.

At forty, Paul's aunt Dorothy was eight years older than her sister. Unmarried and overweight, she was a simple, pleasant woman who went to church every Sunday and was active in community projects. In bringing Paul and Becky into her home, she did everything possible to encourage Becky to pick up her life again. To join the church and go back to nursing school and to one day make nursing a career she could be proud of.

"Dorothy is a clerk who works in the county administration building," his mother would rail halfway through her third Canadian Club and ginger ale. "What does she know of the horrors of raising a child without a father? How can she possibly understand that the mother of a ten-year-old boy has to be available every single day when he comes home from school?"

Who would help with his homework? Make his supper? Make certain he didn't fall in with the wrong crowd? Dorothy didn't understand that. Couldn't understand it. And kept on about the church, a career and a normal life. Becky swore she was prepared to move out. There was quite enough life insurance for them to live alone, if frugally, until Paul graduated from high school.

What Becky couldn't understand was that church, a career and a new life weren't what Dorothy was talking about. It was her drinking. Dorothy wanted her to stop. But Becky had no intention of doing so.

Eight months and three days later Becky Osborn drove her car into Barnstable Harbor and sat there until she drowned. She had just turned thirty-three. The funeral was held at First Presbyterian Church in Yarmouth, December 15, 1966. The day was gray, with a forecast of snow. Twenty-eight people, including Paul and Dorothy, attended the service. Mostly they were Dorothy's friends.

On January 4, 1967, at age eleven, Aunt Dorothy became Paul Osborn's legal guardian. On January 12 of that same year, he entered Hartwick, a publicly funded private school for boys in Trenton, New Jersey. He would live there, ten months out of the year, for the next seven years.

8

THE POLICE artist's sketch of the severed head made the London tabloids on Tuesday morning. It was presented as the face of a missing man, and the caption asked anyone with any information to please inform the Metropolitan Police immediately. A phone number was given along with a notation saying all callers could remain anonymous if they so chose. All the police were interested in was information on his whereabouts for a grievously concerned family. No mention was made that the face belonged to a head that had no accompanying body.

By nightfall not a single call had come in.

In Paris, a different sketch had more luck. For a simple hundred-franc bribe, Jean Packard had been able to shake the memory of one of the waiters who had pulled Paul Osborn from the throat of Henri Kanarack while they struggled on the floor of Brasserie Stella.

The waiter, a small man, with slight, effeminate hands and a like manner, had seen Kanarack a month earlier when he had been employed in another brasserie that had closed shortly afterward because of a fire. As he had at Brasserie Stella, Kanarack had come in alone, ordered espresso, then opened a newspaper and smoked a cigarette. The time of day had been about the same, a little after five in the afternoon. The brasserie was called Le Bois on boulevard de Magenta, halfway between the Gare de l'Est and Place de la Republique. A straight line drawn between Le Bois and Brasserie Stella would show a preponderance of Métro stations within the area. And since the stranger did not have the appearance of a man who took taxis, it was reasonably safe to assume he'd either come to each by car or on foot. Parking a car near either café at evening rush hour to linger alone over an espresso was not a likely happenstance either. Simple logic would suggest he'd come by foot.

Both Osborn and the waiter had described the man as having a stubble beard or "five o'clock shadow." That, coinciding with his working-class manner and appearance, made it reasonably safe to presume that the man had been on his way home from work and, since he had done so at least twice, that he seemed to be in the habit of stopping for a respite along the way.

All Packard had to do now was make the rounds of other cafés within the area between the two brasseries. Failing that, he would triangulate out from each, until he found still another café where someone would recognize the man from Paul Osborn's sketch. Each time he would show his identification, explain that the man was missing, and that he had been hired by the family to find him.

On only his fourth try, Packard found a woman who

recognized the crude drawing. She was a cashier at a bistro on rue Lucien, just off boulevard de Magenta. The man in the sketch had been stopping there, off and on, for the past two or three years.

"Do you know his name, madame?"

At this the woman looked up sharply. "You said you were investigating for the man's family, but you do not know his name?"

"What he calls himself one day is quite often not the same as the next."

"He is a criminal?"

"He is ill. . . ."

"I'm sorry. But no, I do not know his name."

"Do you know where he works?"

"No. Except to say that he usually has some kind of fine dust or perhaps powder on his jacket. I remember that because he was always trying to brush it away. Like a nervous habit."

"Construction firms have been eliminated because construction workers do not, in general, wear sport jackets to and from work. And certainly not while they are working." It was just after seven that night when Jean Packard sat down with Paul Osborn in a darkened corner of the hotel bar. Packard had promised to contact him within two days. He was delivering in less.

"Our man seems to work in an area that collects powdery residue where he hangs his jacket during business hours. Scrutinizing the firms within a one-mile radius from the three cafés, more than a normal walking distance from a work day, we have been able to reasonably narrow his profession to cosmetics, dry chemicals, or baking materials."

Jean Packard spoke quietly. His information was brief and explicit. But Osborn was hearing him as if in a dream. A week earlier he had been in Geneva, nervously preoccupied with the paper he would deliver to the World Congress of Surgery. Seven days later he was in a darkened bar in Paris listening to a stranger confirm that his father's murderer was alive. That he walked the streets of Paris. Lived there, worked there, breathed there. That the face he had seen was real. The skin he had touched, the life he had felt under his fingers even as he tried to strangle it, was real.

"By this time tomorrow, I will have for you a name and an address," Packard finished.

"Good," Osborn heard himself say. "Very good."

Jean Packard stared at him for a moment before he got up. It was no business of his what Osborn would do with the information once he had it. But the look in Osborn's eyes he'd seen in other men. Distant, turbulent and resolute. There was no doubt in his mind whatsoever that the man he would soon deliver to the American seated across from him would, very shortly thereafter, be dead.

Back in his room, Osborn stripped and took his second shower of the day. What he was trying to do was not think about tomorrow. Once he had the man's name, knew who he was, where he lived, then he could think about the rest. How to question him and then how to kill him. To think about it now was too difficult and too painful. It brought back everything dark and terrible in his life. Loss, anger, guilt, rage, isolation and loneliness. Fear of love because of the dread that it would be taken away.

Shaving cream covered half his face and he was wiping steam from the mirror when the phone rang.

"Yes," he said directly, expecting Jean Packard with a forgotten detail. It wasn't Jean Packard. Vera was downstairs in the lobby. Was it permissible for her to come to his room? Or was he with someone else, or had he other plans? She was like that. Polite, considerate, almost innocent. The first time they'd made love she'd even asked permission before touching his penis. She had come, she said, to say goodbye.

He wore only a towel when he opened the door and saw her there in the hallway, trembling, with tears in her eyes. She came in and he closed the door, and then he kissed her and she kissed him back and then they were in each other's arms. Her clothes were everywhere. His lips were on her breasts, his hand in the darkness between her legs. And then she spread her legs and he came joyously into her and everything was laughter and tears and unthinkable desire.

Nobody said goodbye like this. Ever had, ever would. Nobody.

9

HER NAME was Vera Monneray. He'd met her in Geneva when she'd come up to him shortly after he'd presented his paper and introduced herself. She was a graduate of Montpellier medical school and in her first year of residency at the Centre Hospitalier Ste.-Anne in Paris, she'd told him. She was alone and celebrating her twenty-sixth birthday. She hadn't known why she was being so forward, except that he'd caught her attention the moment his speech began. There was something about him that made her want to meet him. To find out who he was. To be with him for a little while. At the time she'd had no idea if he was married or not. She didn't care. If he'd said he was married and with his wife, or if he'd simply said he was busy, she would have shaken his hand, told him she admired his paper and left. And that would have been that.

But he hadn't.

They'd gone outside and crossed the footbridge over the Rhône to the old city. Vera was bright and filled with life. Her long hair was almost jet black, and she swept it to one side and tucked it behind her ear in a way that no matter how animated she became, it stayed where it was without coming loose. Her eyes were nearly as dark as her hair and were young and eager for the long life still ahead of her.

No more than twenty minutes after they'd met, they were holding hands. That night they had dinner together in a quiet Italian restaurant just off the red-light district. It was curious to think of Geneva as having a row for prostitutes. Its reputation for chocolate and watches and its aura of sobriety as an international finance center somehow didn't play against the skintight, thigh-slit skirts of street hookers, but there they were anyway, populating the few odd blocks allotted them. Vera watched Osborn carefully as they walked past them. Was he embarrassed or silently shopping or letting life be what it was? All, she thought. All.

And dinner, like most of the afternoon, was more of that same kind of thing, a tender, silent exploration by a man and woman instinctively attracted to one another. A holding of hands, an exchange of glances and, finally, the long, searching stare into the other's eyes. More than once Paul had felt himself become aroused. The first time it happened they were browsing through baked goods in a large department store. The area was crowded with shoppers and he was certain every eye was on his groin area. Quickly picking up a large bread, he discreetly held it in front of himself while pretending to look around. Vera saw him and laughed. It was as if they'd been lovers for a very long time and shared a secretive thrill playing it out in public.

After dinner they walked down the ruc des Alpes and watched the moon rise over Lake Geneva. Behind them was the Beau-Rivage, Paul's hotel. He'd planned dinner, the walk, the evening, to end there in his room, but suddenly, now that it was at hand, he wasn't quite as sure of himself as he thought. He'd been divorced less than four months, hardly time enough to get back the confidence of being an attractive bachelor, and a doctor at that. In the old days, he tried to remember, how did he do it? Get a woman to his room? His mind went blank, he couldn't remember a thing. He didn't have to; Vera was way ahead of him.

"Paul," she said and smiled, tucking her arm in his, pulling him close against the chill of the air coming across the lake, "the thing to always remember about a woman is that you only get her in bed if the decision is hers."

"Is that a fact?" he deadpanned.

"Absolute truth."

Reaching in his pocket he took out a key and held it up. "To my hotel room," he said.

"I have a train. The ten o'clock TGV to Paris," she said matter-of-factly, as if it was something he should have known.

"I don't understand." His heart sank. She'd never mentioned a train, or that she was leaving Geneva that night.

"Paul, this is Friday. I have things to do in Paris over the weekend, and Monday at noon I must be in Calais. It's my grandmother's eighty-first birthday."

"What do you have to do in Paris this weekend that can't wait?"

Vera just looked at him.

"Well, what?" he said.

"What if I told you I had a boyfriend?"

"Do beautiful residents with boyfriends sneak out of town to pick up new lovers? Is that the medical world in Paris?"

"I didn't 'pick you up'!" Vera stood back, indignant. Trouble was, a little smile escaped from the corner of her mouth. He saw it and she knew he saw it.

"Is there an airport in Calais?" he asked.

"Why?" she pushed back.

"It's an easy question." He smiled. "Yes, there is an airport in Calais. No, there isn't an airport in Calais."

Vera's eyes shimmered in the moonlight. A light wind off the lake lifted her hair.

"I'm not sure——"

"But there is an airport in Paris."

"Two."

"Then on Monday morning you can fly to Paris and take the train to Calais." If she wanted him to do this, make him work for her, he was.

"What would I do here until Monday morning?" This time her smile was a little broader. But, yes, she was making him work for her.

"For a man to get a woman into his bed, the decision must be hers," he said quietly, and once again held up the key to his room. Vera's eyes came up to his and held there. And as they did, her fingers reached up and slowly encircled the key.

10

TWO DAYS would not be enough, Osborn decided the following morning. Vera had just gotten out of bed and he'd watched her walk around the foot of it and go into the bathroom. Her shoulders thrown back, unashamedly extending her small alabaster breasts before her, she'd crossed the room with the grace of a barely tamed animal unaware of its magnificence. Purposefully, he thought, she'd put nothing on—not his L.A. Kings T-shirt he'd given her to sleep in but that she'd never put on—nor wrapped around her one of several towels still on the floor, spent trophies of three extended episodes of sex in the shower. It was a way of telling him that the night before had not been a lark and this morning she was embarrassed by it.

Somewhere in the hours before daylight, between the sessions of lovemaking, they'd decided to spend the following day seeing Switzerland by train. Geneva, to Lausanne, to Zurich, to Lucerne. He'd wanted to go on to Lugano on the Italian border but there wasn't time. Save Lugano for the next trip, he remembered musing in the moments before falling into a wholly spent and soundless sleep. That and Italy.

Now, as he heard her step into the shower, it came to him. Today was Saturday, October 1. Vera had to be in Calais on Monday, the third. That same day he was scheduled to fly out of London for L.A. What if today, instead of touring Switzerland, they flew to England? They could have tonight and all day Sunday and all of Sunday night in London or wherever in England Vera wanted to go. Monday morning he could put her on a train to Dover and from there she could take the ferry or Hoverspeed across the Channel directly to Calais.

The sense of it came in a rush, and without thinking more he reached for the telephone. It was only when he was talking to the female clerk at the front desk, and asking how to dial Air Europe, that he realized he was still naked. Not only that but he had an erection, which he seemed to have most of the time Vera was anywhere near. All at once he felt like a teenager on an illicit weekend. Except, as a teenager he'd never had an illicit weekend. Those things had happened to others, not him. Strong and handsome as he was—and had been, even then—he'd remained a virgin until he was nearly twenty-two and a student in medical school. Things other boys did, he'd never done. Though he boasted he had, just to keep from looking the fool. The villain was, as always, the same, the intense and uncontrollable fear that sex would lead to attachment, and attachment, love. And once committed to love, it was only a matter of time before he would find a way to destroy it.

At first Vera said no, England was too expensive, too impulsive. But then he'd taken her hand and pulled her to him and kissed her deeply. Nothing, he told her, was more expensive or impulsive than life. And nothing was more important to him than spending as many hours with her as possible, and they could do that best if they went to London today. He was serious. She could see it in his eyes when she pulled back to look at him, and feel it in his touch when he smiled and ran the back of his hand gently down the side of her face.

"Yes." She smiled. "Yes, let's go to England. But after that, no more, okay?" Her smile left, and for the first time since he'd known her, she became serious.

"You have a career, Paul. I have mine and I want it to continue the way it is."

"Okay—" He grinned and leaned forward to kiss her, but she pulled back.

"No. First agree. After London we won't see each other again."

"Your work means that much to you?"

"What I have already done to get through medical college. What I have yet to do. Yes, it means that much. And I won't apologize for saying it or meaning it."

"Then . . ." He paused. "I agree."

London had been a blur. Vera wanted to stay somewhere discreet, somewhere she would not run into a former classmate or professor—or "boyfriend?" Paul teased—and then be invited to dinner or tea or whatever and have to make excuses. Osborn checked them into the Connaught, one of the grandest, smallest, most guarded, and "English" of all the London hostelries.

They needn't have bothered. Saturday evening was Ambassadors Theatre and a revival of *Les Liaisons Dangereuses*, followed by dinner at The Ivy across the street, a hand-in-hand stroll through the theater district, broken by several giggly champagne breaks at pubs along the way, and finally a long, circuitous taxi ride back to the hotel during which they challenged each other, in sensuous and conspiratorial whispers, to make love without the driver's knowledge. And did. Or thought they did. The rest of their thirty-six-hour stay in London was spent in bed. And it was neither because of sex or by choice. First Paul, and very shortly afterward, Vera, came down with either food poisoning or a violent attack of the flu. All they could hope for was that it was the twenty-four-hour kind. Which it turned out to be. And by the time Monday morning came and they took a cab to Victoria Station, both, though a little weak and shaky, were nearly one hundred percent recovered.

"Hell of a way to spend a weekend in London," he said as he held her arm and they walked toward her train.

Looking at him, she smiled. "In sickness and in health."

Later, she wondered why she'd said it, because she knew she'd put meaning into the words. It was an inflection in her voice that just came out. She had been trying to make it light and funny but she knew it hadn't sounded like that. Whether she meant it or not she didn't know, and she didn't want to think about it. All she remembered afterward was Paul taking her into his arms and kissing her. It was a kiss she would remember all her life, rich and exciting, yet at the same time filled with a strength and self-confidence she'd never before experienced with any man.

She remembered watching him from her compartment window as her train pulled out. Standing there in the massive station, surrounded by trains and tracks and people. Arms folded over his chest, staring after her with a sad, bewildered smile, and with every click of the wheels, growing smaller and smaller, until, at last, she was out of the station and could see him no more.

Paul Osborn had left her at 7:30 Monday morning, October 3. Two and a half hours later he was in the duty-free shop at Heathrow Airport, killing time before boarding his twelve-hour flight back to Los Angeles.

He was looking at T-shirts and coffee mugs and little towels with the London subway system printed on them when he realized he was thinking of Vera. Then his flight was announced and he waded through a sea of milling passengers to the boarding area. Through the window he could see his British Airways 747 being fueled and loaded with baggage.

Turning away from the plane, he looked at his watch. It was nearly eleven and Vera would be on board the Hoverspeed, crossing the English Channel to Calais. By the time she reached her grandmother's, the two would have little more than ninety minutes before she rushed off to catch the two o'clock train to Paris.

He smiled at the thought of her helping the eighty-one-year-old lady open birthday presents and then joke and laugh with her over cake and coffee and wondered if by chance she would mention him. And if she did, how the old woman would respond. And then, in his mind, he saw the succession of goodbye hugs and farewells and chastisements for so short a visit as Vera waited for her taxi that would take her to the railroad station. Osborn had no idea where Vera's grandmother lived in Calais, or even her last name for that matter. Was it her maternal or paternal grandmother?

It was then he realized it didn't make any difference. What he was really thinking about was that Vera would be on the two o'clock Calais-to-Paris train.

In less than forty minutes his bags were pulled from the 747 and he was in the check-in line for the British Airways shuttle to Paris.

11

VERA WATCHED from the window of her first-class compartment as the train slowed and came into the station. She'd tried to relax and read for the few short hours she'd been on the train. But her mind had been elsewhere and she'd had to put her reading material aside. What impulse had caused her to introduce herself to Paul Osborn in Geneva in the first place? And why had she slept with him in Geneva and then gone with him to London? Was it simply that she had been restless and had acted on a whim at the attraction of a handsome man, or had she immediately sensed in him something else, a rare and kindred spirit who shared on many levels an understanding of what life really was and what it could be and where it might lead if they were together?

Suddenly she was aware the train had stopped. People were getting up, taking their luggage from the overhead racks and leaving the train. She was in Paris. Tomorrow she would go back to work, and London and Geneva and Paul Osborn would be a memory.

Suitcase in hand, she stepped from the train and moved along the platform in a crowd. The air felt humid and close as if it were about to rain.

"Vera!"

She looked up.

"Paul?" She was astonished.

"In sickness and in health." He smiled, coming toward her out of the crowd, taking her suitcase, carrying it for her. He'd taken the shuttle from London and then a cab from the airport to Gare du Nord, where they were now. In between he'd booked a flight from Paris to Los Angeles. He would be in Paris for five days. For five days they would do nothing but be together.

He wanted to take her home, to her apartment. He knew she had to go to work, but he wanted to make love to her all the hours between then and now. And after, when she'd finished her shift and came home, they would do the same all over again. Being with her, making love to her, was all that mattered.

"I can't," she told him flatly, angered that he'd even come. How dare he presume upon her like that?

It wasn't exactly the reaction he'd counted on. Their time together had been too close, too perfect. Too loving. And it hadn't come from him alone.

"You agreed that after London there would be no more between us."

He grinned. "Besides a few hours at the theater and dinner, there wasn't an awfully lot to London, was there? Unless you count the throwing up, the high fevers and alternating chills."

For a moment Vera said nothing, then the truth came out. She told him quickly and directly. There *was* someone else.

It would not be prudent to reveal his name, but he was important and powerful in France and he must never know they had been together in Geneva or London. It would hurt him deeply and that was something she would not do. What she and Paul had had, what they had shared in the past few days, was done. And he knew that. Because they had agreed upon it. Painful as it was, she could not and would not see him again.

They reached the escalator and went up and out to the cabs. He gave her the name of his hotel on avenue Kléber. He would be there for five days. He wanted to see her again, if only to say goodbye.

Vera looked away. Paul Osborn was unlike any man she'd ever met. He was gentle and kind and understanding even in his hurt and disappointment. But even had she wanted to, she couldn't give in to him. Where she was in her life, he could not be part of. There was no other way.

"I'm sorry," she said, looking at him. Then she got into a cab, the door closed and she was gone.

"Simple as that," he heard himself say out loud.

Less than an hour later he found himself sitting in a brasserie somewhere off rue St.-Antoine trying to piece the whole thing together. If he had followed his original plans, never taken the shuttle to Paris, in a few hours he'd be landing in L.A., taking a cab back to his house overlooking the

Pacific, getting his Chesapeake retriever out of the kennel, seeing if the deer had come over his fence and eaten his roses. The day after that he would be going back to work. That would have been the natural course of things had he done it. But he hadn't.

Vera, who she was and what she stirred in him, was all that mattered. Nothing else was worth anything. Not the present, the past or the future. At least that was what he'd been thinking when he looked up and saw the man with the jagged scar.

12

Wednesday, October 5.

IT WAS just after ten in the morning when Henri Kanarack stepped into a small grocery a half block from the bakery. He was still disturbed by the incident with the American, but nothing had happened in two days and he was beginning to agree with both his wife and Agnes Demblon that the man had either picked the wrong person or just been crazy. He was bent over collecting several bottles of mineral water to take back to work when Danton Fodor, the store's overweight and nearly blind owner, suddenly took him by the arm and brought him into the back room.

"What is it?" Kanarack said, indignantly. "I'm current with my bill."

"It's not that," Fodor said, peering out through thick glasses to make sure no customers were waiting at the cash register. Fodor was not only the owner but clerk, cashier, stock boy and custodian.

"A man was here earlier today. A private detective with an awkward drawing of you."

"What?" Kanarack felt his heart jump.

"He was showing it around. Asking people if they knew you."

"You didn't say anything!"

"Of course not. I knew he was up to something right away. The tax man?"

"I don't know." Henri Kanarack looked away. A private detective, and he'd gotten this far. How? Suddenly he looked back. "What was his company? Did you get his name?"

Fodor nodded and opened the lone drawer of a table that served as a desk. Pulling out the card, he handed it to Kanarack. "He said we should call if we saw you."

"We, who's we?" Kanarack demanded.

"The other people in the store. He asked everyone. Luckily they were all strangers and no one recognized you. Where he went from here or who else he talked to, I don't know. I'd be careful when I went back to work if I were you."

Henri Kanarack wasn't going back to work. Not today anyway, maybe never again. Glancing at the card in his hand he dialed the bakery and got Agnes on the telephone.

"The American," he said. "He's got a private detective after me. If he shows up, make sure he talks to you. Make sure nobody else says anything. His name is—" Kanarack looked down at the card again—"Jean Packard. He works for a company called Kolb International." Suddenly he got angry. "What do you mean, what should you tell him? Tell him I no longer work there and haven't for some time. If he wants to know where I live, you don't know. You sent some paperwork to me after I left and it came back with no forwarding address." With that, and saying he'd call her later, Kanarack abruptly hung up.

Less than an hour later Jean Packard entered the bakery and glanced around. Conversations with two other shop owners and a young boy who happened to see his sketch by accident had pointed here, to the bakery. There was a small retail shop in the front and behind it he could see an office. Beyond that was a closed door that he assumed led to the area in the back where the baking was done.

An elderly woman paid for two loaves of bread and turned to go. Packard smiled and opened the door for her.

"*Merci beaucoup*," she said in passing.

Jean Packard nodded and then turned to the young girl behind the counter. This was where the man worked. He would show the sketch to no one here. That would be a tip-off someone was after him. What he wanted was a list of employee names. This was obviously a small organization, with probably no more than ten or fifteen people on the payroll. All would be registered at the central Tax Bureau. A computer cross-check would match names with home addresses. Ten or fifteen people would not be difficult to canvass. Simple elimination would give him the one he wanted.

The girl behind the counter wore a tight short skirt and high heels, and had long, shapely legs covered with black net stockings. Her hair was pulled tight in a knot at the top of her head and she wore big loop earrings and enough mascara and eye shadow for three. She was the kind of half-girl, half-woman who spent most of her day waiting for night. A job behind a bakery counter was not high on her list of turn-ons, it just helped with the bills until a better arrangement could be found.

"*Bonjour*," Jean Packard said with a smile.

"*Bonjour*," she replied, and smiled back. Flirting, it seemed, came naturally to her.

Ten minutes later Jean Packard left with a half-dozen croissants and a list of the people who worked there. He'd told her he was opening a nightclub in the area and wanted to make certain the local merchants and their employees got first-night invitations. It was good public relations.

13

McVEY SHIVERED and poured hot water into a big ceramic mug with a British flag on it. Outside a cold rain was falling and a light fog lifted off the Thames. Barges were moving up and down the waterway, and traffic was heavy along the river road beside it.

Looking around, he found a small plastic spoon lying on a stained paper towel and added two scoops of Taster's Choice decaf and a teaspoon of sugar to the steaming water. The Taster's Choice he'd found in a small grocery around the corner from Scotland Yard. Warming his hands on the cup, he took a sip of the decaf and glanced again at the folder open in front of him—an Interpol printout of known or suspected multiple murderers in continental Europe, Great Britain and Northern Ireland. There were probably two hundred in all. Some had served time for lesser crimes and been released, others were in jail, a handful were still at large. Each would be checked out. Not by McVey but by homicide detectives in the respective countries. Transcripts of their reports would be faxed to him immediately as they were completed.

Abruptly McVey set the list aside, got up and crossed the room, his left hand balled up into a loose fist, and began absently to twick his thumb with his little finger. What was troubling him was what had troubled him from the beginning, a gut sense that whoever was surgically removing heads from bodies was not someone with a criminal record. McVey's mind stopped. Why did it have to be a man? Why couldn't it as easily be a woman? These days women had the same access to medical training as men. In some cases, maybe more. And with the current emphasis on fitness, many women were in excellent physical condition.

McVey's first hunch had been that it was one person committing the crimes. If he was right, it narrowed the field from possibly as many as eight killers to one. But his second speculation, or speculations—that the murderer had some degree of medical schooling and access to surgical tools and could be of either gender and with perhaps no criminal record at all—tore the odds to hell.

He had no statistics at his fingertips, but if one totaled up all the doctors, nurses, paramedics, medical students, former medical students, coroners, medical technicians and university professors with some measure of expertise in surgery, to say nothing of the men and women who received some medical training serving in the armed forces, even if they stuck to Great Britain and the Continent alone, the figures had to be staggering. This was no haystack they were poking around in. It was more like a sea of grain blowing in the wind, and Interpol had no vast army of harvesters to separate the grain from the chaff until they finally uncovered their murderer.

The odds had to be narrowed and it was up to McVey to narrow them before he said anything to anybody. To do that he needed more information than he had. His first thought was that maybe somewhere he had missed a connective link between the first killing and the last. If so, the only way to find out would be to go back and start again with the most definitive facts at hand: the autopsy reports on the head and the seven headless bodies.

He was reaching for the phone to request them when it rang.

"McVey," he said, automatically, as he picked it up.

"*Oui*, McVey! Lebrun, at your service!" It was Inspector Lieutenant Lebrun of the First Section of the Paris Préfecture of Police, the diminutive, cigarette-smoking detective who'd greeted him with a hug and a kiss the first time he'd set his size-twelve wing tips on French soil.

"I don't know what it means, if it means anything at all," he said in English. "But in going over the daily reports of my detectives I came across a complaint of simple assault. It was violent and quite vicious but simple assault nonetheless, in that no weapon was used. However, that is beside the point. What caught my attention is that the perpetrator is an orthopedic surgeon, an American, who happened to be in London the same day your man in the alley lost his head. I know he was in England because I have his passport in my hand. He arrived at Gatwick at three twenty-five Saturday afternoon, October first. Your man seems to have been killed sometime late on the first or early on the second. Correct?"

"Correct," McVey said. "But how do we know he was still in England for the next two days? I don't remember French Immigration stamping my passport when I landed in Paris. This guy could've left England and come into France the same day."

"McVey, would I disturb as prominent a policeman as you without doing a little further checking?"

McVey felt the needle and gave it back. "I don't know, would you?" He smiled.

"McVey, I am trying to assist you. Do you wish to be serious or should I hang up?"

"Hey, Lebrun, don't hang up. I need all the help I can get." McVey took a deep breath. "Forgive me." On the other end he could hear Lebrun ask for a file in French.

"His name is Paul Osborn, M.D.," Lebrun said a moment later. "He gives his home address as Pacific Palisades, California. You know where that is?"

"Yeah. I can't afford it. What else?"

"Attached to the arrest sheet is a list of personal belongings he was carrying with him at the time he was taken into custody. The first are two ticket stubs from the Ambassadors Theatre, dated Saturday, October first. Another is a credit card receipt from the Connaught Hotel in the Mayfair district dated October third, the morning he checked out. Then we have—"

"Hold on—" McVey leaned forward to a stack of manila folders on the desk and pulled one from it. "Go ahead—"

"A boarding pass on a British Airways London-to-Paris shuttle dated the same."

While Lebrun talked, McVey scanned several pages of computer printouts provided by the Public Carriage Office, which had answered a police request asking for the names of drivers delivering or picking up fares from the theater district Saturday night, October 1, into Sunday morning, October 2.

"Hardly makes him a criminal." McVey turned one page, then another until he found a cross listing for the Connaught Hotel, then slowly ran his finger down it. He was looking for something specific.

"No, but he was evasive. He didn't want to talk about what he was doing in London. He claimed he became ill and stayed in his room."

McVey heard himself groan. With murder, nothing was ever easy. "From when to when?" he asked with as much enthusiasm as he could muster and put his feet up on the desk.

"Late Saturday evening until Monday morning when he checked out."

"Anybody see him there?" McVey glanced at his shoes and decided they needed to be reheeled.

"Not that he wants to talk about."

"Did you press him?"

"At the time there was no reason, besides he was beginning to yell for a solicitor." Lebrun paused and McVey could hear him light a cigarette, then exhale. Then he finished. "Would you like us to pick him up for further interrogation?"

Suddenly McVey found what he was looking for. *Saturday, 1 October, 23:11. Two passengers picked up at Leicester Square. Delivered Connaught Hotel, 23:33.* The driver was listed as Mike Fisher. Leicester Square was in the heart of the theater district and less than two blocks from the alley where the head was found.

"You mean he's free?" McVey took his feet off the desk. Could Lebrun have, just out of sheer luck, stumbled onto the head-cutter, then let him go?

"McVey, I'm trying to be nice to you. So don't put that sound in your voice. We had no grounds to hold him and so far the victim hasn't come forth to press charges. But we have his passport and we know where he's staying in Paris. He'll be here until the end of the week when he goes back to Los Angeles."

Lebrun was a nice guy doing his job. He probably didn't relish the assignment as Paris Préfecture of Police liaison to Interpol or working under its coldly efficient assignment director, Captain Cadoux, and he probably wasn't crazy about dealing with a Hollywood cop from LaLa Land, or even having to speak English for that matter, but these were the kind of things you did as a civil servant, which McVey knew only too well.

"Lebrun," McVey said measuredly. "Fax me his booking photos and then stand by. Please . . ."

An hour and ten minutes later, Metropolitan police had found Mike Fisher and delivered the bewildered taxi driver to McVey. Whereupon McVey asked him to verify that he had picked up a fare from Leicester Square late Saturday night and delivered said fare to the Connaught Hotel.

"Right, sir. A man and a woman. Amorous bats they were, too; thought I didn't know what they were doing back there. But I did." Fisher grinned.

"Is this the man?" McVey showed him Osborn's French police booking photos.

"Right, sir. That's him, no doubt at all."

Three minutes later the phone rang in Lebrun's office.

"You want us to pick him up?" Lebrun asked.

"No, don't do anything. I'm coming over," McVey said.

14

BY THE time his Fokker jetliner touched down at Charles de Gaulle Airport three hours later, McVey knew where Paul Osborn lived, where he worked, what professional licenses he carried, what his driving record was, and that he'd been divorced twice in the State of California. He also knew that he'd been "detained" and later released by Beverly Hills Police for attacking a parking attendant who had demolished the right front fender of Osborn's new BMW in a restaurant lot. It was clear Paul Osborn had a temper. It was equally true to McVey that the man or woman he was looking for was not severing heads out of passion. Still, a hot head was not passionate twenty-four hours a day. There was adequate time between rages to kill a man, remove his head from his body, and leave the remains in an alley, beside a road, floating in an ocean or tucked up neatly on a couch in a cold, one-room apartment. And Paul Osborn *was* a trained surgeon, wholly capable of removing a head from a body.

The downside of the situation was that, according to the entry stamps in his passport, Paul Osborn had been neither in Great Britain nor on the Continent when the other murders were committed. That could mean any number of things: that he was innocent; that he was not who he said he was, and could have more than one passport; even that he could have done the head in the alley but not the others, which, if that were the case, meant McVey was wrong with his lone killer theory.

So, at this point, he was little more than a stick figure suspect connected to the latest crime only by the coincidences of time, place and profession.

Still, it was more than they had before. Because, so far, they had nothing.

For a moment Paul Osborn stared off, then his eyes flashed back to Jean Packard. They were sitting in the front terrace room of La Coupole, a chatteringly alive gathering place on boulevard du Montparnasse on the Left Bank. Hemingway used to drink here, so did a host of literary others. A waiter passed, and Osborn ordered two glasses of white Bordeaux. Jean Packard shook his head and called the waiter back. Jean Packard did not touch alcohol. He ordered tomato juice instead.

Osborn watched the man walk off, then looked again at

the cocktail napkin Jean Packard had scribbled on and put in his hand. On it was a name and an address—M. Henri Kanarack, 175 avenue Verdier, apartment 6, Montrouge.

The waiter brought their drinks, and left. Again Osborn glanced at the napkin, then, folding it carefully, put it in his jacket pocket.

"You're sure," he said, looking up at the Frenchman.

"Yes," Jean Packard replied. Sitting back, he crossed one leg over the other and stared at Paul Osborn. Packard was tough, very thorough and very experienced and Osborn wondered what he'd say if he queried him about it. He was only a doctor and his first attempt to kill Kanarack, albeit on the spur of the moment and in the heat of rage, had failed. But Jean Packard was a professional. He'd said as much when they first met. Was a killer by trade, as a soldier of fortune against a political or military enemy in a Third World country, any different from a killer for hire in a major cosmopolitan city? The glamour of it might be different, but other than that he doubted it. The act was the same, wasn't it? The payoff, too. You killed; you collected for it. So how could there be any real difference?

"I wonder," Osborn said carefully, "if you sometimes work on your own."

"How do you mean?"

"I *mean*, do you sometimes freelance? Accept assignments outside your company?"

"It would depend on the assignment."

"But you *would* consider it."

"Why are you asking me?"

"Then you know what it is . . ." Osborn could feel the sweat on his palms. Delicately he set his glass down, picked up the napkin it had been sitting on and ran it between his hands.

"I think, Doctor Osborn, that what was promised has been delivered. Billing will be completed through the company. It was a pleasure to meet you and I wish you every good luck."

Putting down a twenty-franc note for the drinks, Jean Packard stood. "*Au revoir*," he said, then, stepping around a young man at the next table, he left.

Paul Osborn watched him go out, saw him pass in front of the large windows overlooking the sidewalk and disappear in the early evening crowd. Absently he ran a hand through his hair. He'd just asked one man to murder another and had been turned down. What was he doing, what had he done? For an instant he wished he'd never come to Paris, never seen the man he now knew as Henri Kanarack.

Closing his eyes he tried to think of something else, to blot it all out. Instead he saw his father's grave alongside that of his mother. In the same vision he saw himself standing in the window of the headmaster's office at Hartwick, watching as his aunt Dorothy, an old raccoon coat pulled around her, got into a taxi and drove away in a blinding snowstorm. The awful aloneness was unbearable. Was *still* unbearable. The jagged pain as brutal now as it had been then.

Pulling himself out of it, he looked up. All around him people were laughing and drinking, relaxing after work or before dinner. Across from him a handsome woman in a maroon business suit had her hand on a gentleman's knee and was looking into his eyes as she talked. A clamor of laughter from another table caused him to turn his head. Immediately there was knocking at the window in front of him. He looked and saw a young woman standing on the sidewalk, peering in, smiling. For a moment Osborn thought she was looking at him, then a young man at the next table jumped up, waved and ran outside to meet her.

When he was ten a man had cut out his heart. Now he

knew who that man was and where he lived. There would be no turning back. Not now, not ever.

It was for his father, for his mother, for himself.

15

SUCCINYLCHOLINE: AN ultrashort-acting depolarizing muscle relaxant. Neuromuscular transmission is inhibited so long as an adequate concentration of succinylcholine remains at the receptor site. Paralysis following an intramuscular injection may vary from seventy-five seconds to three minutes, with general relaxation occurring within one minute.

A kind of synthetic curare, succinylcholine has no effect on consciousness or pain threshold. It works as a simple muscle relaxant beginning with the levator muscles of the eyelids, muscles of the jaw, limb muscles, abdominal muscles, muscles of the diaphragm, other skeletal muscles, and those controlling the lungs.

It is used during operations to relax the skeletal muscles, making it possible to administer lighter doses of more sensitive anesthetics.

A continuous IV drip of succinylcholine keeps the level of paralysis constant over the duration of an operation. A single injection of .03 to 1.1 milligrams (dosage varies among individuals), while having the same effect, lasts only four to six minutes. Immediately afterward the drug breaks down in the body without causing harm or being pathologically apparent because succinylcholine's breakdown products—succinic acid and choline—are normally present in the body.

Hence, a carefully measured dose of succinylcholine administered by injection would cause temporary paralysis—just long enough, say, for the subject to drown—and then fade, undetected, into the body's own system.

And a medical examiner, unless he went over the entire body of the deceased with a magnifying glass, hoping to find a minute puncture wound caused by a syringe, would have little choice but to rule the drowning accidental.

From the beginning, in his first year of residency when he'd seen the drug used and had observed its effects in the operating room, Osborn's fantasy of what to do should the day ever come and the murderer, by some miracle, suddenly materialize before him had begun to grow. He'd experimented with injections on laboratory mice, and later on himself. By the time he'd opened his practice he knew the exact dosage it would take to inject a man with succinylcholine and immobilize him for six to seven minutes. And with no control over skeletal or respiratory muscles, six to seven minutes in sufficiently deep water was more than enough time for that same man to drown.

His attack on Henri Kanarack had been foolish, done wholly out of emotion; the shock of recognition compounded by years of pent-up rage. In doing so, he had exposed himself both to Kanarack and the police. But now that had calmed. What he had to be careful of was that emotions didn't rise again, as they had such a short time ago when he had foolishly solicited Jean Packard. He had no idea why he'd done it, except maybe fear. Murder was no easy thing, but then this was not murder, he told himself, any more than it would have been if a court had sentenced Kanarack to the gas chamber. Which it most certainly would have done had things happened differently. But they hadn't, and accepting that, which Osborn did now, calmly and assuredly, he realized how private a thing it had become between him and this Henri Kanarack and that the responsibility now could never be anything but his alone.

He knew how to find Kanarack. And even if Kanarack suspected he was still being pursued, he would have no way of knowing he'd been found. The idea would be to surprise him, force him into an alley or other secluded area, then inject him with the succinylcholine and get him into a car that Osborn would have waiting. Kanarack would resist, of course, and Osborn would have to take that into consideration. The injection was the key. Once that was done, he would have to be on guard for sixty more seconds and then Kanarack would relax. No more than three minutes after that he would become paralyzed and be physically helpless.

Done at night and planned correctly, Osborn could use those initial minutes to get Kanarack into the car and drive from where the abduction took place to an out-of-the-way spot, a lake or, better yet, a river with a swift current. Then, taking Kanarack, limp but alive, from the car, he would simply lower him into the waterway. If he had time, he would even pour some whiskey down his throat. That way, when the body was eventually pulled from the water, it would appear to both the police and medical examiner that the man had been drinking and had somehow stumbled into the water and drowned.

And by then Dr. Paul Osborn would either be at home in Los Angeles, or airborne and en route. And if the police should ever piece it together and come all that way to ask him about it, what could they suggest? That it had been more than coincidence that the man he'd attacked in the

Parisian brasserie was the same man who'd somehow drowned a few days later?

Hardly.

Osborn didn't know how far he'd walked—from boulevard du Montparnasse to the Eiffel Tower and across the Seine on Pont de'Iena, past the Palais de Chaillot and on to his hotel on avenue Kléber—or even what time it was or how long he'd been sitting at the mahogany bar on the ground floor of his hotel, staring at the untouched cognac in front of him. A glance at his watch told him it was a little past eleven. Suddenly he felt exhausted. He couldn't remember when he'd last felt so tired. Standing, he signed the bar tab and started to walk out, then remembered he'd forgotten to tip the bartender. Going back, he placed a twenty-franc note on the bar.

"*Merci beaucoup,*" the bartender said.

"*Bonsoir,*" Osborn nodded, then smiled faintly and left.

As he did, the raised finger of another customer caught the bartender's eye and he walked the dozen or so feet down the bar to him. The man had been sitting quietly, half staring into his nearly empty drink, his third in the hour and a half he'd been there. He was a gray man with graying hair, nondescript and lonely, the kind who sits in hotel bars around the world unnoticed, hoping for the little action that almost always never comes.

"*Oui, monsieur.*"

"Another," McVey said.

16

"You TELL *me* why!" Henri Kanarack was drunk. But it was not the kind of drunk that messes up a man's mind and tongue so that he can neither think or speak coherently. He was drunk because he had to be, there was no other place to go.

It was a half hour before midnight and he was alternately sitting and pacing in Agnes Demblon's small flat in Porte d'Orleans, barely a ten-minute drive from his own apartment in Montrouge. Early that evening he'd called Michele and told her he had been asked by Monsieur Lebec, the bakery owner, to go with him to Rouen to look over a property where he was considering opening a second bakery. It would be a day, perhaps two, before he got back. Michele was elated. Did this mean Henri was getting a promotion? That if Monsieur Lebec did open a bakery in Rouen, Henri would be asked to manage it? Would they move there? It would be wonderful to raise their child away from the bustling lunacy of Paris.

"I don't know," he'd said harshly. He'd been asked to go and that's all he knew. And with that he'd hung up. Now he stared at Agnes Demblon and waited for her to say something.

"What do you want me to tell you?" she said. "That yes, maybe the American did recognize you and hired a private detective to find you. And that now, since he was in the store, and since that foolish girl gave him the names of the employees, we can assume he has found you or soon will. Assume, too, that he has no doubt reported that back to the American. All right, suppose it's so. Now what?"

Henri Kanarack's eyes glistened and he shook his head

as he crossed the room for more wine. "What I don't understand is how the American could recognize me. He's got to be a dozen years younger than I am, maybe more. I've been out of the States for twenty-five years. The fifteen in Canada, the ten here."

"Henri. Maybe it is a mistake. Maybe he thinks you are someone else."

"It's no mistake."

"How do you know?"

Kanarack took a drink and stared off.

"Henri, you are a French citizen. You've done nothing here. For once in your life the law is on your side."

"The law means nothing if they've found me. If it's them, I'm dead, you know that."

"It's not possible. Albert Merriman is dead. Not you. How could anyone make the connection after so many years? Especially a man who couldn't have been more than ten or twelve when you left America."

"What the hell is he after me for, then, huh?" Kanarack's stare cut through her. It was hard to tell if he was frightened or angry or both.

"They have pictures of what I looked like then. The police have them and they have them. And I haven't changed all that much. Either bunch could have sent that guy to look for me."

"Henri—" Agnes said quietly. He needed to think, to reason, and he wasn't. "Why would they look for a man who is dead? Or, even if they did, why would they look here? Do you think they are sending this man to every city in the world on the off-chance he might bump into you on the street?" Agnes smiled.

"You're making something of nothing. Come, sit here by me," she said, smiling gently and patting the worn couch beside her.

The way she looked at him, the sound of her voice reminded him of the old days when she'd been not as unattractive as she was now. Of the days before she'd purposely let herself go for that very reason, so that he would no longer be attracted to her. Of the days before she refused him her bed, so that after a while he would not want her. It was important that he vanish wholly, to absorb the French culture and become French. To do that he must have a French wife. To make that possible it was necessary that Agnes Demblon no longer be part of his life. She had reentered it only when he had been unable to find work and she'd convinced Lebec he needed another hand at the bakery. After that, their relationship had been totally platonic as it was now, at least as he saw it.

But for Agnes there wasn't a day her heart didn't break at the sight of him. Not an hour or a moment when she did not want to take him into her arms and into her bed. From the beginning she had done it all. Helped him fake his own death, posed as his wife crossing the border into Canada, arranged for his false passport and finally convinced him to leave Montreal for France, where she had relatives, and where he could disappear forever. She'd done it all, even to the point of giving him up to another woman. For no other reason than she loved him so much.

"Agnes. Listen to me." He did not come to sit beside her; instead he stood in the center of the room staring at her, the glass no longer in his hand. The room was absolutely still. There was no sound of traffic outside, no sound of people arguing in the apartment downstairs. For a moment she thought maybe the couple who lived there might have taken the night off from their loud and constant bickering and gone to the movies. Or maybe they were already in bed.

It was then she caught sight of her fingernails, which were long and ridged and should have been cut days ago.

"Agnes," he said again. This time his voice was little more than a whisper.

"What we don't know, we have to find out. You understand?" he said.

For a long time she kept looking at her nails, then, finally, she lifted her head. The fear, anger and rage were gone from him, as she knew they would be. What was there instead was ice.

"We have to find out."

"*Je comprends*," she murmured and looked back at her nails. "*Je comprends*." I understand.

17

8 A.M.

TODAY WAS Thursday, October 6. The morning sky, as predicted, was overcast and a light, cold rain was falling. Osborn ordered a cup of coffee at the counter and took it over to a small table and sat down. The café was filled with people on their way to work stealing a few moments before getting on with the routine of the day. They sipped coffee, toyed with a croissant, smoked a cigarette, looked over the morning paper. A table away, two businesswomen jabbered in high-speed French. Next to them a man in a dark suit, with a shock of even darker hair, leaned on an elbow studying the newspaper *Le Monde*.

Osborn had reservations on Air France Flight 003 leaving Charles de Gaulle Airport on Saturday, October 8, at

5:00 P.M., arriving nonstop in Los Angeles at 7:30, Pacific Daylight time, the same evening. The appropriate thing, as fit into the overall scheme, would be for him to contact Detective Barras at police headquarters, inform him of his reservation and time of departure and politely ask when he could pick up his passport. Once that was done, he could get on with the rest.

It was important he kill Kanarack sometime Friday night. He needed the cover of darkness not just for the act but to prevent Kanarack's body from being discovered too soon and too near Paris. After some simple research, the Seine, his first idea, had become his chosen waterway. It flowed through Paris and then wound northwest through the French countryside for some 120-odd miles before dumping into the Bay of the Seine and the English Channel at Le Havre. Barring some unforeseen complication, if he could get Kanarack into the river at some point west of the city after dark on Friday night, it would be daylight Saturday at the earliest before his body was discovered. By then, in a good current, it should have traveled thirty or forty miles downstream. With luck, maybe more. Bloated and with no identification, it would be days before the authorities determined who he was.

To cover himself, Osborn would need an alibi, something that would place him somewhere else at the time of the killing. A movie, he thought, would be easiest. He could buy a ticket, then make some valid disturbance with the ticket-taker going in, just enough so that later, should the question arise, that person would remember his being at the theater. His proof would be the ticket stub with the time and date of the show. Once having taken a seat in the darkened auditorium, he would wait for the film to begin and then slip out a side exit.

The timing of everything would depend on Kanarack's daily routine. A call to the bakery had established it was open from seven in the morning until seven in the evening and that the last freshly baked goods would be available at approximately four P.M. He'd seen Kanarack at the brasserie on rue St.-Antoine at about six. The brasserie was at least a twenty-minute walk from the bakery, and since Kanarack had left the brasserie on foot after Osborn's attack on him it was safe to assume, as Jean Packard had earlier, that he either had no car or didn't use one in commuting to work. If the last baked goods were available at 4:00 and Kanarack had been at the brasserie at 6:00, it was also reasonable to assume that he left work sometime between 4:30 and 5:30. Though it was still early October, the days were growing short. A glance at the paper predicted that the rain falling now would continue for the next several days. That meant it would be getting dark even earlier. By 5:30, easily.

Osborn's immediate order of business was to rent a car and look for an isolated area on the Seine, west of Paris, where he could get Kanarack into the water without being observed. Afterward he would drive to the bakery and then back again to make certain he knew the way.

Finally, he would go back to the bakery and park across the street, being certain to arrive no later than 4:30. Then he would wait for Kanarack to come out and see which way he went. Up the street or down.

The first time he'd seen him, Kanarack had been alone, so hopefully he did not make it a habit to leave work in the company of co-workers. If, for some reason, he did on Friday night, Osborn's contingency plan would be to follow him in the car until he separated from whomever he was with, and then take him at the most convenient place thereafter. If Kanarack walked with someone all the way to the Métro, then Osborn would simply drive to his apartment building and wait for him there. That was something he did not want to do unless it was absolutely necessary, because there was too much chance Kanarack would run into people he was in the habit of greeting as he came home. Still, if that was the only option, Osborn would take it. What he wished more than anything was that he had more than one night for the run-through, but he didn't, so whatever happened, he'd have to make the best of.

"Hi."

Osborn looked up, startled. He'd been in such deep contemplation he'd not seen Vera come in. Quickly he stood and pulled out a chair for her and she sat down across from him. As he went back to his own chair he saw a clock behind the counter. It read 8:25. Looking around he realized the café had all but emptied out since he'd gotten there.

"Can I get you something?"

"Espresso, *oui*." She smiled.

Getting up, he crossed to the counter, ordered an espresso and stood there while the counterman turned to make it. Glancing back at Vera, he looked past her and then away, concentrating on why he was there, why he'd asked her to meet him when she got off her shift at the hospital.

The succinylcholine.

Twice already that morning he'd tried to have his own prescription for it filled at local pharmacies, but both times he'd been told the drug was available only at hospital pharmacies, and both times he'd been warned he would need authorization from a local physician to get it. A call to the closest hospital pharmacy confirmed it. Yes, they had the succinylcholine. And yes, he would need authorization from a Parisian doctor.

Osborn's first thought was to call the hotel doctor, but asking for succinylcholine was not like asking for an everyday prescription. Questions would be asked; it could become awkward. A nervous doctor might even call the police to report it. There might be other ways, but finding them would take time and time was now his enemy. Reluctantly, his thoughts turned to Vera.

Right away he dialed the pharmacy at the Centre Hospitalier Ste.-Anne where she was a resident. Yes, the succinylcholine was available, but again, not without local authorization. Maybe, he thought, if he played it right, Vera's verbal okay at the pharmacy would be enough. He didn't want to involve any doctor she knew because that person would want to know why. He had a story for Vera, but making anyone else buy it would be complicated and risky.

Hesitating, thinking it through once more, he'd called her at the hospital at 6:30 and asked if she would meet him in a café nearby for coffee when she got off work. He'd heard her pause, and for a moment he was afraid that she was going to make up an excuse and tell him she couldn't see him, but then she'd agreed. Her shift finished at 7:00 but she had a meeting that wouldn't be over until just after 8:00. She would meet him after that.

Osborn watched her as he carried the espresso back to the table. After a thirty-six-hour shift without sleep and an hourlong meeting following that she was still pert and radiant, even beautiful. He couldn't help staring at her as he sat down, and when she caught him she smiled back, lovingly. There was something about her that put him somewhere else, no matter what he was thinking or what else he was involved in. He wanted to be with her and consume her and have her consume him, always and forever. Nothing either one of them could ever do should be more important than that. The trouble was he first had to take care of Henri Kanarack.

Leaning forward, he reached across to take her hand. Almost immediately she pulled it away and slid it into her lap.

"Don't," she said, her eyes darting around the room.

"What are you afraid of? Somebody might see us?"

"Yes."

Vera looked away, then picked up her cup and took a sip of the espresso.

"You came to me, remember? To say goodbye . . . ," Osborn said. "Does he know about that?"

Abruptly Vera put down her cup and stood up to leave.

"Look, I'm sorry," he said. "That wasn't the right thing to say. Let's get out of here and go for a walk."

She hesitated.

"Vera, you're talking to a friend, a doctor you met in Geneva who asked you to meet him for a cup of coffee. Then you walked up the street together. He went back to the U.S. and that was that. Shoptalk between doctors. Good story. Good ending. Right?"

Osborn's head was cocked to the side and the veins stood out on his neck. She'd never seen him angry before. In a way she couldn't explain, it pleased her and she smiled. "Right," she said, almost girlishly.

Outside, Osborn raised an umbrella against a light drizzle. Dodging around a red Peugeot, they crossed the street and walked up rue de la Santé in the direction of the hospital.

In doing so they passed a white Ford parked at the curb. Inspector Lebrun was behind the wheel; McVey sat in the passenger seat beside him.

"I don't suppose you know the girl," McVey said as he watched Osborn and Vera walk away from them. Lebrun turned the key in the ignition and he eased the car off in the same direction.

"You are not asking if I know her, but if I know who she is—correct? French and English expressions do not always mean the same."

McVey was incredulous that a man could talk with a cigarette always dangling from the corner of his mouth. He'd smoked once, for the first two months after his first wife died. He had taken up smoking to keep from drinking. It didn't do much good but it helped. When it stopped helping, he quit.

"Your English is better than my French. So yeah, I'm asking if you know who she is."

Lebrun smiled, then reached for his radio microphone. "The answer, my friend, is—not yet."

18

THE TREES along the boulevard St.-Jacques were beginning to turn yellow, getting ready to drop their leaves for winter. A few had already fallen and the rain made walking slippery. As they crossed the street, Osborn took Vera's arm to steady her. She smiled at the gesture, but as soon as they crossed, asked him to let go.

Osborn looked around. "You worried about the woman pushing the baby carriage or the old man walking the dog?"

"Both. Either. Neither," she said flatly, purposefully being aloof, but not quite sure why. Maybe she was afraid of being seen. Or maybe she didn't want to be with him at all, or maybe she wanted to be with him completely but wanted him to make that decision for her.

Suddenly he stopped. "You're not making it easy."

Vera felt her heart skip a beat. When she turned to look at him, their eyes met and held there, the way they had that first night in Geneva, the way they had in London when he put her on the train to Dover. The way they had in his hotel room on avenue Kléber when he'd opened the door and stood there with nothing but a towel around his waist. "What am I not making easy?"

Then he surprised her.

"I need your help and I guess I'm having a hard time figuring out how to ask for it."

She didn't know what he meant and said so.

Beneath the umbrella he was carrying for both of them, the light was soft and delicate. He could just make out the top of her white medical tunic raising up under the blue anorak she wore. It made her look more like a member of a mountain rescue team than an urban doctor in training. Small gold earrings clung to the base of each ear like tiny raindrops, accenting the narrowness of her face and turning her eyes into enormous emerald pools.

"It's dumb really. And I don't even know if it's illegal. Everybody just makes it seem like it is."

"What is?" What was he talking about? He was throwing her off. What did this have to do with them?

"I have a prescription I wrote for a drug that now they tell me is only available at hospital pharmacies and that I need local authorization for. I don't know any doctors here and . . ."

"What drug?" Concern was written all over her face. "Are you ill?"

"No." Osborn smiled.

"What then?"

"I . . . I told you it was dumb," he started uncertainly, as if he were embarrassed. "I'm presenting a paper when I get back. As *soon* as I get back. For a reason named Vera, I took an extra week off when I should have been back at work. . . ."

"Say what you mean, will you?" Vera grinned and relaxed. Everything they had done together had been rich and romantic and deeply personal, even to helping each other through the private embarrassments of bodily functions when they'd both had the twenty-four-hour flu in London. Aside from their first exploratory conversations in Geneva, little, if anything, had been said about their professional lives and now he was asking an everyday question involving just that.

"I'm presenting a paper to a group of anesthesiologists the day after I get back to L.A. Originally I was to speak on the third day, but they changed it and now I'm first. The paper has to do with presurgical anesthetic preparation involving succinylcholine dosage and effectiveness under emergency field conditions. Most of my experimentation has been done in the lab. I will have no time when I get back, but I still have two days here. And it seems that if I'm going to get any succinylcholine in Paris, I'm going to need an okay from a French doctor before anyone will give it to me. And as I said, I don't know any other doctors."

"You're going to self-medicate?" Vera was astonished. She'd heard of other doctors doing that from time to time and had almost tried it herself as a medical student, but she'd chickened out at the last minute and copied a published study instead.

"I've been doing various experiments since I was in med school." A broad grin crossed Osborn's face. "That's why I'm a little strange." Abruptly he stuck out his tongue, bulged his eyes and twisted up an ear under his thumb.

Vera laughed. This was a side of him she hadn't seen, a silliness she hadn't known existed.

As quickly, he let go of his ear and the goofiness faded. "Vera, I need the succinylcholine and I don't know how to get it. Can you help me?"

He was very serious. This was something that had to do with his life and who he was. Suddenly Vera realized how very little she knew about him and, at the same time, how much more she wanted to know. What he believed, and believed in. What he liked, and disliked. What he loved, feared, envied. What secrets he had he'd never shared with her or anyone else. What it was that had cost two marriages.

Had it been Paul, or were the women at fault? Or was he just bad at choosing them? Or—was there something else, something inside him that festered a relationship all the way to ruin? From the beginning she'd sensed he was troubled, but by what she didn't know. It wasn't something she could point to and understand. It was deeper and for the most part he kept it hidden. But it was there just the same. And now, more than at any time since she'd known him, as he stood there under her umbrella in the rain asking her to help him, she saw him absorbed by it. All at once she felt herself overwhelmed by a wanting to know and comfort and understand. Much more a feeling than a conscious thought, it was also dangerous, and she knew it, because it was pulling her somewhere where she had not been asked, and to a place, she was certain, no one had ever been invited.

"Vera?" Suddenly she realized they were still on the street corner and that he was talking to her. "I asked if you could help."

Looking at him, she smiled. "Yes," she said. "Let me try."

19

OSBORN STOOD near the front counter of the hospital pharmacy trying to read get well cards in French while Vera took his prescription and walked to the pharmacist in the back. Once he glanced up and saw the pharmacist talking and gesturing with both hands while Vera stood with a hand on a hip waiting for him to finish. Osborn turned away. Maybe he'd made a mistake involving her. If he were ever caught and the truth came out, she could be charged as an accessory. He should tell her to forget it, find some other way to deal with Henri Kanarack. Fumbling, he replaced the card he was looking at in the rack and was turning to go back to her when he saw her coming toward him.

"Easier than buying condoms—less awkward, too." She winked and walked past him.

Two minutes later they were outside and walking down the boulevard St.-Jacques, the succinylcholine and a packet of hypodermic syringes in Osborn's sport coat pocket.

"Thank you," he said quietly, putting up the umbrella and holding it so they could both walk under it. Then the rain started to come down more heavily and Osborn suggested they look for a taxi.

"Would it be all right if we just walked?" Vera said.

"If you don't mind, I don't."

Taking her arm, they crossed the street against the light. When they reached the far curb, Osborn purposefully let go. Vera grinned broadly, and then for the next fifteen minutes they simply walked and said nothing.

Osborn's thoughts turned inward. In a way, he was filled with relief. Getting the succinylcholine had been easier than he'd imagined. What he didn't like was that he'd lied to Vera and used her and it bothered him a great deal more than he thought it would. Of anyone he'd ever known, Vera was the last person he'd deliberately use or not tell the absolute truth to. But the fact was, as he reminded himself, he'd had little choice.

Today was not every day, nor was what he doing the stuff of everyday life. Old and dark things were at work. Tragic things, that only he and Kanarack knew. And that only he and Kanarack could settle. It worried him again to think that if things went wrong, Vera might be accused of being an accomplice. In all likelihood she wouldn't go to jail, but her career and everything she'd worked for could be ruined. He should have thought of that earlier, before he'd even talked to her about it. He should have but he hadn't and now it was done. What he had to think about was the rest. To make sure that nothing went wrong, to make sure that both he and Vera were protected.

Suddenly she took his hand and pulled him around to face her. When she did, he realized they were no longer on boulevard St.-Jacques but crossing the Jardin des Plantes, the formal gardens of the National Museum of Natural History, and were almost to the Seine.

"What is it?" he asked, puzzled.

Vera watched his eyes find their way to hers and she knew she'd snatched him out of a dream.

"I want you to come to my apartment," she said.

"You what?" He was clearly bewildered. Pedestrians scurried past left and right and gardeners, despite the rain, were preparing their work for the day.

"I said, I want you to come to my apartment."

"Why?"

"I want to give you a bath."

"A bath?"

"Yes."

A great boyish grin crept over him.

"First you didn't want to be seen with me and now you want to take me to your apartment?"

"What's wrong with that?"

Osborn could see her blush. "Do you know what you're doing?"

"Yes. I have it in my mind that I want to give you a bath, and in the thing they call a tub in your hotel you could barely wash a small dog."

"What about 'Frenchy.'?"

"Don't call him that."

"Tell me his name and I won't."

For a moment Vera was silent. Then she said, "I don't care about him."

"No?" Osborn thought she was teasing.

"No."

Osborn looked at her carefully. "You're serious."

She nodded definitively.

"Since when?"

"Since . . . I don't know. Since I decided, that's all." She didn't want to examine it and her voice trailed off.

Osborn didn't know what to think, or even feel. On Monday she'd said she never wanted to see him again. She had a lover, an important man in France. Today was Thursday. Today he was in and the lover was out. Did she really care for him deeply enough to do that? Or had the lover business been only a story to put him off in the first place, a convenient way to end a brief affair?

The breeze off the river caught her hair and she tucked a strand of it behind her ear. Yes, she knew the chance she was taking but she didn't care. All she knew was that right now she wanted to make love to Paul Osborn, in her own apartment and in her own bed. She wanted to be with him completely for as long as they could. She had forty-eight hours before her next shift began. François, Osborn's "Frenchy," was in New York and had not contacted her for several days. As far as she was concerned, she was free to do as she pleased, when she pleased, where she pleased.

"I'm tired. Do you want to come? Yes, or no?"

"You're sure?"

"I'm sure," she said. It was five minutes to ten in the morning.

20

THE SOUND of the phone woke her. For a moment she had no idea where she was. A harsh glare came in through the French doors partially open to the patio. Beyond them, over the Seine, a midafternoon sun had given up trying to push through a stubborn overcast and vanished into it. Still half asleep, Vera rose up on one elbow and looked around. Bedclothes were strewn everywhere. Her stockings and underwear were on the floor, half under the bed. Then her mind cleared and she realized she was in her apartment bedroom and her phone was ringing. Covering herself with part of the sheet, as if whoever was on the other end might be able to see her, she snatched up the phone.

"*Oui?*"

"Vera Monneray?"

It was a male voice. One she'd never heard. "*Oui . . . ,*" she said again, puzzled. There was a distinct *click* on the other end and the line went dead.

Hanging up, she looked around. "Paul?" she called out. "Paul?"

This time there was concern in her voice. Still there was no reply and she realized he was gone. Getting out of bed, she saw her nakedness reflected in the antique mirror over her dressing table. To her right was the open bathroom door. Used towels lay on the sink and on the floor by the bidet. The bath curtain had come down and was lying half across the tub. On the far side of it, one of her shoes perched ceremoniously on the closed lid of the toilet. To anyone entering now there would be no mistaking that long and forceful love had been made in these two rooms and God knew where else in the apartment. In her life she'd never experienced anything like the past hours. Her entire body ached, and what didn't ache was rubbed raw and sore. She felt as if she'd locked union with a beast and in so doing had unleashed a primitive fury that had built, moment by moment, thrust by thrust, into a gargantuan firestorm of physical and emotional hunger from which there was no escape or release except through complete and utter exhaustion.

Turning away, she saw herself again in the mirror and came closer. She wasn't sure what she saw, exactly, except that somehow it was different. Her slim figure, her small breasts were the same. Her hair, though completely disheveled, hadn't changed. It was something else. Something had gone from her, and in its place something else had come.

Abruptly the phone rang again. She looked over at it, provoked by the intrusion. It continued to ring and finally she picked it up.

"*Oui* . . . ," she said distantly.

"One moment," a voice came back.

He was calling.

"Vera! *Bonjour!*" François' voice bounded at her over the phone. He was up, bright, demanding.

It was a moment before she replied. And in that moment, she realized that what was gone from her was the child in her, she'd crossed a brink from which there was no turning back. Whoever she had been, she was not anymore. And her life, for better or worse, would never again be what it had.

"*Bonjour*," she said, finally. "*Bonjour*, François."

Paul Osborn left Vera's apartment at a little after noon and took the Métro back to his hotel. By two o'clock, dressed in sweatshirt, jeans and running shoes, he was driving a rented dark blue Peugeot down the avenue de Clichy. Carefully following the rental agency's street map, he made a right off the rue Martre onto the highway that led northeast along the Seine. In the next twenty minutes he made three stops at pull-outs and side roads. None showed promise.

Then at two thirty-five he passed a wooded road that seemed to lead toward the river. Making a U-turn, he came back and turned down it. A quarter of a mile later he came to a secluded park situated on a hill directly along the river's eastern banks. From what he could see, the park itself was little more than a large field surrounded by trees, with a dirt road around its periphery. Taking it, he drove along until the road began to curve back toward the highway. Then he saw what he was looking for: a dirt and gravel ramp leading down to the water. Stopping, he got out and looked back. The main highway was a good half mile away and obscured from view by the trees and heavy undergrowth.

In summer, the park, with its access to the river, probably saw heavy use, but now, at nearly three o'clock in the afternoon on a rainy Thursday in October, the area was completely deserted.

Leaving the Peugeot, Osborn walked to the top of the ramp and started down. Below, through the trees, he could just make out the river. The dark sky and drizzle closed everything in, making it seem, almost, as if he alone existed. The ramp was steep and had been worn into ruts by vehicles using it as a portal to a landing at the bottom that no doubt served as a launching place for small boats.

As he neared the bottom and the incline leveled out, he saw a line of old pilings rotting at the water's edge and assumed the site had served as a much larger entry to the river years before. When, or for what reason or in what years, who knew? How many armies, over how many centuries, had passed this way? How many men had walked where he walked now?

A dozen or more feet from the water's edge, the gravel gave way to a gray sand that quickly became a reddish mud just as it reached the water. Venturing out, Osborn tested the firmness. The sand held, but the moment he reached the mud his shoes sank into it. Pulling back, he kicked what mud he could from his shoes, then looked again toward the water. Directly in front of him the Seine flowed lazily, lapping gently in tiny wavelets against the shoreline. Then, less than thirty yards down, an outcropping of rock and trees jutted sharply, turning the flow abruptly and sending it off into the main current.

Osborn watched for a long moment, all too conscious of what he was doing. Then, turning purposefully, he crossed the landing to a stand of trees at the base of the hill leading up from the water. Finding a large branch, he picked it up, crossed back, and tossed it into the water. For a moment nothing happened and it just hung there. Then slowly, the current nudged it forward, and in a few short seconds it was swept down toward the trees and then out toward the main current. Osborn glanced at his watch. It had taken ten seconds for the branch to move away and get caught up in the predominant flow. Another twenty and it disappeared from sight around the outcrop of rock and trees. All told, just about thirty seconds from the time he tossed the branch in until he lost sight of it.

Turning back, he recrossed the landing to the woods on the far side. He wanted something heavier, something that might begin more to approximate a man's weight. In a matter of moments he found the uprooted trunk of a dead tree. Struggling for a grip, he hefted it, then carried it to the water's edge, stepped into the mud once more and heaved it in. For a moment it remained still in the water, as the branch had, then the current picked it up and started forward along the shore. Once it reached the curve of the outcropping it moved swiftly and steadily out toward the main current. Once more he looked at his watch. Thirty-two seconds until it reached mid-river and was swept from view. The tree trunk had to have weighed fifty pounds. Kanarack, he estimated, weighed about one hundred and eighty. The ratio of the weight from the branch to the tree trunk was far greater than the ratio of the tree trunk to what Kanarack weighed, yet both had taken nearly the same time to be swept up and out and then be fully caught up in the current.

Osborn could feel the rise of his pulse and the sweat at his armpits as the reality of it began to set in. It would work, he was certain! Moving sideways at first, then turning, Osborn started to run, hurrying along the riverbank and past the trees to where the land projected farthest out toward midriver. Here, he found the water deep flowing and free of obstacles. With nothing to stop him, Kanarack, physically helpless under the succinylcholine, would float off like the tree trunk, picking up speed as he reached the flow line. Less than sixty seconds after his body was shoved out from the landing it would reach midriver and be caught up in the Seine's main current.

Now he had to make sure. Pushing through a stand of high grass, he followed the river's edge through shrubs and thicket for a half mile or more. The farther he walked, the steeper the embankment became and the swifter the current flowing between the shorelines. Reaching the top of a hill, he stopped. The river kept on uninterrupted for as far as he could see. There were no small islands, no sandbanks, no yawning catch-alls of dead trees. Nothing but fast-moving open water cutting through raw countryside. Moreover, there were no towns, factories, homes or bridges. No place at all, as far as he could tell, from which to see a thing rushing along with the current.

Especially if it were happening in the rain and darkness.

21

LEBRUN AND McVEY had followed Osborn and Vera to the gardens of the National Museum of Natural History. There, another unmarked police car had taken over and tailed them to Vera's apartment on the Île St.-Louis.

As soon as they entered, Lebrun was radioed the address. Forty seconds later they had a printout of the building's residents, courtesy of a computer cross-check with the Postal Service.

Lebrun scanned it then handed it to McVey, who had to put on his glasses to read it. The listing confirmed that all six of the apartments at 18 Quai de Bethune were occupied. Two of the surnames carried first initials only, indicating they were probably occupied by single women. One was an M. Seyrig, the other a V. Monneray. French *permis de conduire*—driver's license—records disclosed that M. Seyrig was Monique Seyrig, who was sixty, and that V. Monneray was one Vera Monneray, who was twenty-six. Less than a minute later a copy of Vera Monneray's driver's license came over the fax machine in Lebrun's unmarked Ford. The accompanying photograph confirmed her as Paul Osborn's companion.

It was at that moment that headquarters abruptly called off the surveillance. Dr. Paul Osborn, Lebrun was told, was under the spotlight of Interpol, not of the Paris Préfecture of Police. If Interpol wanted somebody to watch from across the street while Osborn had dalliance with a lady, let them pay for it, the locals couldn't afford it. McVey was all too aware of city budgets, where management cut corners and where pork-barrel politics vied for every allotted franc. So, when Lebrun apologetically dropped him off back at headquarters a half hour later, all he could do was shrug and head for the beige two-door Opel Interpol had assigned him, knowing he would have to do the legwork himself.

It took a good forty minutes, driving in circles trying to find his way back to Île St.-Louis, before McVey finally pulled into a parking space at the rear of Vera Monneray's apartment building. The stone and stucco structure that ran the entire length of the block was well kept and freshly painted. Service entrances, at convenient intervals along the way, were secured by heavy, windowless doors, making the ground floor at the back seem like a sealed military garrison.

Opening the car door, McVey got out and walked the half block down the cobblestone street to the cross street at the end of the building. That it was raining and cold didn't help. Or that the ancient cobblestones under his wing tips were slippery as hell. Pulling a handkerchief from a hip pocket, he blew his nose, then carefully folding it on the creases, put it back. It didn't help either that he was beginning to think of a warm, smoggy day on the Rancho Park course on Pico across from the Twentieth

Century Fox lot. Tee off about eight when the sun was just beginning to warm things up, and for the next few hours make light with the rest of his foursome, Sheriff's Department homicide detectives playing hooky from domestic chores on their day off.

When he got to the cross street, McVey turned right and walked to the front of the building. To his surprise he was literally on top of the Seine. If he put a hand out he could almost touch the passing barge traffic. Across the river, the entire Left Bank hung under a blanket of clouds that rolled out left to right as far as he could see. Cranking his head back and looking up, he realized that nearly every apartment in the building must have the same remarkable view.

What the hell can the rent cost here? he thought, then smiled. It's what he would have said to his second wife, Judy, who really was the only true companion he'd ever had. Valerie, his first wife, he'd married out of high school. They were both too young. Valerie worked as a checkout clerk at a supermarket while he struggled through the academy and his first years on the force. What mattered to Val was not work, not a career, but children. She wanted two boys and two girls, the same as her family. And it was all she wanted. McVey was into his third year on the LAPD when she got pregnant. Four months later, while he was in the field on auto theft, she had a miscarriage at her mother's house and hemorrhaged to death on the way to the hospital.

Why the hell was he thinking about that?

Looking up, the found himself staring through the filigreed wrought-iron security gate at the main entrance to Vera Monneray's apartment building. Inside, a uniformed doorman looked back at him and he knew the only way he was going in there was with a search warrant. Even with one, supposing he could get in, what did he expect to find? Osborn and Ms. Monneray still in the act? And what made him think either of them was still there? It had been almost two hours since Lebrun and his team had been pulled off the surveillance.

Turning away, McVey started back toward his car. Five minutes later he was behind the wheel of the Opel trying to figure out how to get off the Île St.-Louis and back to his hotel. He was at a stop sign and had made an agonizing but final decision to turn right instead of left when he saw a phone booth on the corner next to him. The idea came fast. Cutting off a taxi, he pulled to the curb. Going into the phone booth, he opened the directory, looked up V. Monneray, then dialed her apartment. The phone rang for a long time and McVey was about to give up. Then a woman answered.

"Vera Monneray?" he said.

There was a pause and then—

"*Oui*," she said.

With that, he hung up. At least one of them was still there.

"Vera Monneray, 18 Quai de Bethune? A name and address?" McVey closed the open folder and stared at Lebrun. "That's the entire file?"

Lebrun squashed out a cigarette and nodded. It was a little after six in the evening and they were in Lebrun's cubicle of an office on the fourth floor of Police Headquarters.

"A ten-year-old kid writing a TV show could come up with more than that," McVey said with an uncharacteristic edge to his voice. He'd spent a good part of midafternoon illegally in Paul Osborn's hotel room going through his things and had come up with nothing but an array of dirty linen, traveler's checks, vitamins, antihistamines, headache pills and condoms. With the exception of the condoms, he found nothing he didn't have in his own hotel room. It wasn't that he was against rubbers, it was just that he'd honestly had no interest in sex since his Judy had died four years earlier. All the years they were married he'd harbored sensational fantasies about making it with all kinds of women, nubile teenagers to middle-aged Avon ladies, and he'd met any number who were more than willing to lie down on the spot for a homicide detective, but he never had. Then when Judy had gone, none of it, not even the fantasies, seemed worth it. He was like a man who thought he was starving and then suddenly wasn't hungry anymore.

Aside from the ticket stubs from the Ambassadors Theatre in London that had sent up Lebrun's antennae in the first place, the only objects of even passing interest he'd turned up in Osborn's belongings were restaurant receipts, tucked in the pocket of his "daily reminder." They were dated Friday, September 30, and Saturday, October 1. Friday was Geneva, Saturday, London. The receipts were for two. But that was all. So Osborn had taken someone to dinner in both those cities. So had a hundred thousand other people. He'd told Paris detectives he'd been alone in his hotel in London. They probably never asked him about dinner. Chiefly because they had no reason. Any more than McVey had reason now to connect him to the beheading murders.

Lebrun smiled at McVey's painful dismay. "My friend, you forget you are in Paris."

"What does that mean?"

"It means, *mon ami*, that a ten-year-old kid writing a TV show . . . ," Lebrun paused just slightly for effect— "isn't likely to be sleeping with the prime minister."

McVey's jaw dropped. "You're kidding."

"Not kidding," Lebrun said, lighting another cigarette.

"Does Osborn know?"

Lebrun shrugged.

McVey glowered at him. "So she's out of bounds, right?"

"*Oui*." Lebrun smiled a little. Veteran homicide detectives should know better than to be surprised at "*l'amour*," even if they *were* American. Or the ramifications of how hopelessly complicated it could get.

McVey stood up. "If you'll excuse me, I'm going to my hotel and then back to London. And if you have any more bright suspects, check them out yourself first, okay?"

"I seem to remember offering to do it this time," Lebrun said with a grin. "You may recall that the idea to come to Paris was yours."

"Next time talk me out of it." McVey started for the door.

"McVey." Lebrun reached over and stamped out his cigarette. "I couldn't reach you this afternoon."

McVey said nothing. His methods of investigation were his own and they were not always entirely legal, nor did they always involve fellow officers—the Paris P.D., Interpol, the London Metropolitan Police and the LAPD included.

"I wish I had been able to," Lebrun said.

"Why?" McVey said flatly, wondering if Lebrun knew and was testing him.

Pulling open his top desk drawer, Lebrun took out another manila folder. "We were in the middle of this," he said, handing it to McVey. "We could have used your expertise."

McVey eyed him for a moment, then opened it. What he saw were crime scene photographs of an extremely brutal murder. A man had been killed in what looked like an apartment. Separate photographs showed close-ups of his knees. Each had been destroyed by a single, and powerful, gunshot.

"Done with a U.S.-made Colt thirty-eight automatic

fitted with a silencer. We found it next to him. Taped grip. No prints. No identification numbers," Lebrun said quietly.

McVey looked at the next two photographs. The first was of the man's face. It was bloated three times its normal size. The eyes protruded from the skull in horror. Pulled tight around the neck was a wire garrote that looked as if it was once a clothes hanger. The second photograph was of the groin area. The man's genitals had been shot away.

"Jesus," McVey mumbled under his breath.

"Done with the same weapon," Lebrun said.

McVey looked up. "Somebody was trying to get him to talk."

"If it were me, I would have told them whatever they wanted to know," Lebrun said. "Just in the hopes they'd kill me."

"Why are you showing me this?" McVey asked. The First Préfecture of Paris Police had a sparkling record as far as inner-city homicide investigations went. They certainly didn't need McVey's counsel.

Lebrun smiled. "Because I don't want you to go running back to London quite so soon."

"I don't get it." McVey glanced at the open file once more.

"His name is Jean Packard. He was a private detective for the Paris office of Kolb International. On Tuesday, Dr. Paul Osborn hired him to locate someone."

"Osborn?"

Lighting another cigarette, Lebrun blew out the match and nodded.

"A pro did this, not Osborn," McVey said.

"I know. Tech found a smudged print on a piece of broken glass. It wasn't Osborn's and we had nothing in our computer that would match it. So we sent it to Interpol headquarters at Lyon."

"And?"

"McVey, we only found him this morning."

"It still wasn't Osborn," McVey said with certainty.

"No, it wasn't," Lebrun agreed. "And it might be a complete coincidence and not have a thing to do with him."

McVey sat back down.

Lebrun picked up the folder and put it back in his drawer. "You're thinking things are complicated enough and this Jean Packard business has nothing to do with our headless bodies and bodyless head. But you're also thinking you came to Paris because of Osborn, because there was the slightest chance he might have had something to do with it. And now this happens. So you're asking yourself if we look far enough, for long enough, maybe there is a connection after all. . . . Am I correct, McVey?"

McVey looked up. "*Oui*," he said.

22

THE DARK limousine was waiting outside.

Vera had seen it pull up from her bedroom window. How many times had she stood in that window waiting for it to turn the corner? How many times had her heart jumped at the sight of it? Now she wished it had nothing to do with her, that she was watching from another apartment and that the intrigue belonged to someone else.

She wore a black dress with black stockings, pearl earrings and a simple pearl necklace. Thrown over her shoulders was a short jacket of silver mink.

The chauffeur opened the rear door and she got in. A moment later he got behind the wheel and drove off.

At 4:55, Henri Kanarack washed his hands in the employee sink at the bakery, stuck his time card into the clock on the wall and punched out for the day. Stepping into the hallway where he kept his coat, he found Agnes Demblon waiting for him.

"Do you want a lift?" she asked.

"Why? Do you ever give me a lift home? No, you don't. You always stay until the day's receipts are in."

"Yes. But, tonight I . . ."

"Tonight, especially," Kanarack said. "Today. Tonight. Nothing is different. Do you understand?"

Without looking at her he pulled on his jacket, then opened the door and stepped out into the rain. It was a short walk from the employees' entrance down the alley to the street in front. When he turned the corner, he pulled his collar up against the rain, then walked off. It was exactly two minutes after five.

Across the street and two doors down, a rented dark blue Peugeot was parked at the curb, the rain beading up in little knots on its freshly waxed exterior. Inside, sitting in the dark behind the wheel, was Paul Osborn.

At the corner, Kanarack turned left onto boulevard de Magenta. At the same time Osborn twisted the key in the ignition, then pulled out from the curb and followed. At the corner he swung left in the direction Kanarack had gone. He glanced at his watch. Seven after the hour and with the rain, already dark. Looking back, all Osborn saw were strangers and for a moment he thought he'd lost him, then he caught sight of Kanarack on the far sidewalk, walking deliberately but apparently in no hurry. His easy manner made Osborn think that he'd given up on the idea he was being followed, that he had taken the other night's attack and foot chase as an obscure incident done by a crazy man.

Ahead, Kanarack stopped for a traffic light. So did Osborn. As he did, he could feel the emotion rise up. "Why not do it now?" an inner voice was saying. Wait for him to step off the curb and into the street. Then gun the accelerator, run him down and drive away! No one will see you. And who cares if they do? If the police find you just tell them you were about to go to them. That you thought you might have run over someone in the dark and the rain. You weren't sure. You looked but you saw no one. What can they say? How could they know it was the same man? They had no idea who it was in the first place.

No! Don't even think it. Your emotion nearly ruined it the first time. Besides, kill him like that and you will never have the answer to your question, and having that answer is every bit as important as killing him. So calm down and stick to your plan and everything will be all right.

The first shot of succinylcholine will have its own effect, putting his lungs on fire for lack of oxygen because he doesn't have the muscle control to breathe. He'll be suffocating and helpless and more afraid than he's ever been in his life. He'd tell you anything if he could, but he won't be able to.

Then, little by little, the drug will start to wear off and he'll begin to breathe again. Grateful, he'll smile and think he's beaten you. Then suddenly he'll realize you are about to give him a second shot. Much stronger than the first, you'll tell him. And all he'll think about is that second shot and the horror of repeating what he's just been through, only this time with the knowledge that it will be worse, much worse, if such a thing were possible. That's when he'll answer your question, Paul. That's when he'll tell you anything you want to know.

Osborn's eyes went to his hands and he saw his knuckles clenched white around the steering wheel. He thought if he squeezed any harder the wheel would snap off in his hands. Taking a deep breath, he relaxed. And the urge to act faded.

Ahead, the light changed and Kanarack crossed the street. He had to assume he was being followed, either by the American or, by now, though he doubted it, the police. Either way, he could let nothing appear to be any different than it had been, five days a week, fifty weeks a year for the past ten years. Leave the bakery at five, stop somewhere along the way for a brief refreshment, then take the Métro home.

Halfway down the next block was the brasserie Le Bois. He kept his pace unhurried and steady; to all the world he was a simple working man, exhausted at the end of his day. Stepping around a young woman walking a dog, he reached Le Bois, pulled open its heavy glass door, and entered.

Inside, the terrace room facing the street was crowded with the noise and smoke of people unwinding after work. Looking around, Kanarack tried to find a table by the window where he could be seen from the street, but there was none. Grudgingly, he took a seat at the bar. Ordering an espresso with Pernod, he looked toward the door. If a plainclothes policeman came in, he would recognize him or her immediately by attitude and body language as they looked around. Plainclothes or not, high rank or low, every cop in the world wore white socks and black shoes.

The American was another question. The initial attack on him had been so sudden Kanarack had barely seen his face. And when the American had followed him down into the Métro, Kanarack's own emotions had been rushing and the place jammed with commuters. The little he could remember was that he had been nearly six feet tall, had dark hair and was very strong.

Kanarack's drink came and for a minute he let it sit on the bar in front of him. Then, picking it up, he took a small sip and felt the warmth of the mixture of coffee and liqueur as it went down. He could still feel Osborn's hands around his throat, the fingers digging savagely into his windpipe trying to strangle him. That was the part he didn't understand. If Osborn had been there to kill him, why did he do it that way? A gun or a knife, sure. But bare hands in a crowded public building? It didn't make sense.

Jean Packard hadn't been able to explain it either.

It had been easy enough to find out where the detective lived, even though his phone number, along with his address, was unlisted. Speaking in English with an unwavering American accent, Kanarack had placed an emotional call to the Kolb International switchboard in New York just at closing. Saying he was calling from his car phone somewhere outside Fort Wayne, Indiana, and was desperately trying to reach his half brother, Jean Packard, an employee of Kolb International, with whom he'd lost contact since Packard had moved to Paris. Packard's eighty-year-old mother was desperately ill in a Fort Wayne hospital and not expected to live through the night. Was there any way he could get in touch with his half brother at home?

New York was five hours behind Paris at this time of year. Six o'clock in New York was eleven in Paris, the Kolb offices there were closed. The New York operator on duty checked with his supervisor. This was a legitimate family emergency. Paris was closed. What should he do? At closing time his supervisor, like everyone else, was in a hurry to leave. With only a moment's hesitation, the supervisor cleared the international computer code and authorized the channeling of Jean Packard's home telephone number in Paris to his half brother in Indiana.

Agnes Demblon's first cousin worked as a fire brigade dispatcher in Paris Central Fire District One. A telephone number became an address. It was no harder than that.

Two hours later, at 1:15 Thursday morning, Henri Kanarack stood outside Jean Packard's apartment building in the Porte de la Chapelle section north of the city. A bloody twenty minutes later, Kanarack went down the back stairwell leaving what was left of Jean Packard sprawled on his living room floor.

Ultimately he'd given Kanarack Paul Osborn's name and the name of the hotel where he was staying in Paris. But that was all. The other questions—why Osborn had attacked Kanarack in the brasserie, why he'd hired Kolb International to track him down, if Osborn represented or was working for someone else—Packard could not answer. And Kanarack was certain he'd been told the truth. Jean Packard had been tough, but not that tough. Kanarack had learned well his stock in trade in the early sixties, taught proudly and with relish by the U.S. Army Special Forces. As leader of a long-range reconnaissance platoon in the first days of Vietnam, he'd been thoroughly schooled in the ways of obtaining the most delicate information from even the most hardheaded adversary.

The trouble was that in the end all he'd gotten from Jean Packard was a name and an address. The exact same information Packard had given Osborn about him. So to his thinking, Osborn could only be one thing, a representative of the Organization come to liquidate him. Even if the first attempt had been sloppy, there could be no other reason. No one else would recognize him or have cause.

The ugly part was that if he killed Osborn, they would only send someone else. That is, if they knew. His only hope was that Osborn was a freelancer, some kind of bounty hunter given a list of names and faces and promised a fortune if he brought any of them in. If Osborn had happened on him by chance and had hired Jean Packard on his own, things still might be all right.

Suddenly he felt a rush of air from outside and looked up. Le Bois' front door had opened and a man in a raincoat was standing there. He was tall and wore a hat and was looking around. At first his eyes swept the crowded terrace, then he looked toward the bar. When he did, he found Henri Kanarack staring at him. As quickly, he looked away. A moment later, he pushed through the door and was gone. Kanarack relaxed. The tall man had not been a cop and not been Osborn. He'd been nobody.

Across the street, Osborn sat behind the wheel of the Peugeot and watched the same man come out, glance back in through the door, then walk off. Osborn shrugged. Whoever he was, he wasn't Kanarack.

The baker had gone into Le Bois at five fifteen. It was now almost a quarter to six. He'd made the drive back from the river park through rush-hour traffic in less than twenty-five minutes, and had parked across from the bakery just after four. It had given him time to canvass the neighborhood and get back into his car before Kanarack came out.

Walking a half-dozen blocks in either direction, Osborn had found three alleys and two deliveryways leading to industrial warehouses that were closed. Any of the five would do. And if tomorrow night Kanarack followed the same route he'd taken tonight, the best of the five would be right on the way. A narrow alley with no doors opening onto it and without streetlights, less than a half block from the bakery.

Dressed in the same jeans and running shoes he now wore, he'd pull a watch cap low over his face and wait in the darkness for Kanarack to pass. Then, with a full syringe of succinylcholine in his hand, and another in his pocket to make sure, he'd attack Kanarack from behind. Throwing his left arm around his throat, he'd jerk Kanarack backward into the alley while at the same time driving the needle solidly into his right buttock through clothes and all. Kanarack would react hard, but Osborn needed only four seconds to complete the injection. All he had to do then was let go and step back and Kanarack could do what he wanted. Attack him or run away, it would make no difference. In less than twenty seconds his legs would begin to lose feeling. Twenty more, and he'd be unable to stand. Once he collapsed, Osborn would move in. If there were passersby, he would say in English that his friend was American and ill and he was helping him into the Peugeot at the curb to take him to a medical facility. And Kanarack, on the brink of skeletal muscular paralysis, would be unable to protest. Once in the car and moving, Kanarack would be helpless and terrified. His entire being would be concentrated on one thing alone, trying to breathe.

Then, as they sped across Paris for the river road and the secluded park, the effects of succinylcholine would begin to wear off and Kanarack would slowly begin to take in air once more. And just as he was feeling better, Osborn would hold up the second syringe and tell his prisoner who he was and threaten him with a stronger, far more potent and most unforgettable shot. Then, and only then, could he sit back and ask why Kanarack had murdered his father. And have no doubt whatsoever that Kanarack would tell him.

23

AT FIVE minutes past six, Henri Kanarack came out of Le Bois and indifferently walked two blocks to enter the Métro station across from the Gare de l'Est.

Osborn watched him go, then clicked on the overhead light and checked the map on the seat next to him. Ten and a half miles and nearly thirty-five minutes later, he drove past Kanarack's apartment building in Montrouge. Leaving the car on a side street, he walked a block and a half and took up a position in the shadows across the street from Kanarack's building. Fifteen minutes later, Kanarack came walking up the sidewalk and went inside. From beginning to end, bakery to home, there had been no indication he thought he was being followed, or in danger. No sense at all of anything other than daily routine. Osborn smiled. Everything was on track and running as planned.

At seven forty, he pulled the Peugeot up in front of his hotel, gave the keys to an attendant and went inside. Crossing the lobby, he checked the front desk for messages.

"No, monsieur. I am sorry." The petite brunette smiled at him from across the desk.

Osborn thanked her and turned away. In a way he'd been hoping Vera had called, but he was just as glad she hadn't. He didn't want the distraction. Simplicity now was everything, and he had to concentrate on what he was doing. He wondered what made him tell Detective Barras he would be leaving Paris in five days. He could have as easily said a week or ten days, two weeks even. Five days had compressed everything to the point of nearly losing control. Things were happening too fast.

Timing was too critical. There was no room for error or for the unforeseen. What if Kanarack became ill overnight and decided not to go to work. Then what? Go to his apartment, force himself in and do it there? What about other people? Kanarack's wife, family, neighbors? There was no room for something like that to happen because he hadn't given himself room. There was no latitude. None. It was as if he held dynamite in his hand with the fuse already lit. What could he do but follow through and hope for the best?

Taking his mind from it, Osborn turned away from the elevators and went into the gift shop for an English-language newspaper. Taking a copy from the rack, he turned to wait his turn at the cashier. For a moment it hung in his mind what would have happened if Jean Packard had not located Kanarack as quickly as he had. What would he have done—left the country and come back? But when? How would he know that the police hadn't made a notation on the electronic code on his passport to alert them if he did come back within a certain time? How long would he have to wait before he felt it was safe to return? Or what if the investigator had not been able to locate Kanarack at all? What would he have done then? But luckily that wasn't the case. Jean Packard had done his job well and it was up to him to follow through with the rest. Relax, he told himself and moved up to the cashier, absently glancing at the newspaper as he did.

What he saw was beyond reason. Nothing could have prepared him for the sight of Jean Packard's face staring out at him from under a bold front-page headline: *PRIVATE DETECTIVE SAVAGELY MURDERED!*

Below it was a subheading: "Former soldier of fortune heinously tortured before death."

Slowly the gift shop began to spin. Slowly at first. Then faster and faster. Finally Osborn had to put out a hand against a candy counter to stop it. His heart was pounding and he could hear the sound of his own deep breaths. Steadying himself, he looked at the paper again. The face was still there; so was the headline and the words underneath.

Somewhere off he heard the cashier ask if he was all right. Vaguely he nodded and reached in his pocket for change. Paying for the newspaper, he managed to navigate his way through the gift shop and then out and back across the lobby toward the elevators. He was certain Henri Kanarack had discovered Jean Packard following him, had turned the tables and killed him. Quickly he scanned the article for Kanarack's name. It wasn't there. All it said was that the private investigator had been murdered in his apartment late the night before and that the police had refused comment on either suspects or motive.

Reaching the elevators, Osborn found himself waiting in a group with several others he scarcely noticed. Three might have been Japanese tourists, the other was a plain-looking man in a rumpled gray suit. Looking away, he tried to think. Then the elevator doors opened and two businessmen got out. The others filed in, Osborn with them. One of the Japanese pressed the button for the fifth floor. The man in the gray suit pushed nine. Osborn pressed seven.

The doors closed and the elevator started up.

What to do now? Osborn's first thought was Jean Packard's files. They would lead the police directly to him and then to Henri Kanarack. Then he remembered Jean Packard's explanation of how Kolb International worked. Of how Kolb prided itself on protecting its patrons. How its investigators worked in complete confidentiality with clients. How all files were given to the client at the end of an investigation with no copies made. That Kolb was little more than a guarantor of professionalism and a billing agent. But Packard had not given Osborn his files. Where were they?

Suddenly Osborn remembered being amazed that the detective never wrote anything down. Maybe there weren't any files. Maybe these days that had to be the private investigator's game. Keep information out of everyone's hands but your own. Kanarack's name and address had been given to him only at the last moment, handwritten and on a cocktail napkin. A napkin that was still in the pocket of the jacket Osborn was wearing. Maybe that was it, the file in its entirety.

The elevator stopped on the fifth floor and the Japanese got out. The doors closed again and the elevator started up. Osborn glanced at the man in the gray suit. He looked vaguely familiar, but he couldn't place him. A moment later they reached the seventh floor. The door opened and Osborn got out. So did the man in the gray suit. Osborn went one way, the man the other.

Walking down the hallway toward his room, Osborn breathed a little easier now. The initial shock of Jean Packard's death had worn off. What he needed was time to think about what to do next. Suppose Packard had told Kanarack about him. Given him his name and where he was staying? He'd murdered the detective, why wouldn't he try to murder him?

Suddenly Osborn was aware of someone walking behind him down the hallway. Glancing back, he saw it was the man in the gray suit. At the same time he remembered the man had pushed the button for the ninth floor, not the seventh. In front of him a man opened a door and set out a room service tray of dirty dishes. Looking up, he saw Osborn, then closed the door again and Osborn heard the chain lock slide closed.

Now he and the man were the only ones in the hallway. A danger alarm went off. Abruptly he stopped and turned.

"What do you want?" he said.

"A few minutes of your time." McVey's reply was quiet and unthreatening. "My name is McVey. I'm from Los Angeles, the same as you."

Osborn looked at him carefully. He was somewhere in his mid-sixties, about five feet ten and maybe a hundred and ninety pounds. His green eyes were surprisingly gentle and his brown hair was graying and beginning to thin on top. His suit was everyday, probably from The Broadway or Silverwoods. His pale blue shirt was a shiny polyester and the tie didn't match any of it. He looked more like someone's grandfather or what his own father might have looked like, had he lived. Osborn relaxed a little. "Do I know you?" he said.

"I'm a policeman," McVey said and showed him his LAPD shield.

Osborn's heart shot up in his throat. For the second time in a very few minutes he thought he might faint. Finally he heard himself say, "I don't understand. Is anything wrong?"

A middle-aged couple dressed for the evening came down the hallway. McVey stepped aside. The man smiled and nodded. McVey waited until they passed, then looked back at Osborn.

"Why don't we talk inside." McVey nodded toward the door to Osborn's room. "Or, if you'd rather, downstairs in the bar." McVey kept his manner low-key and easy. The bar was as good as the room if it made Osborn more comfortable. The doctor wouldn't bolt, not now anyway. Furthermore, McVey had already seen all there was to see in Osborn's room.

Osborn was anxious and he had to work not to show it. After all, he'd done nothing, not yet anyway. Even using Vera to get him the succinylcholine hadn't really been illegal. Bending the law a little, but not criminal. Besides, this McVey was from the LAPD—what jurisdiction could he have here? Just be cool, he thought. Be polite, see what he wants. Maybe it's about nothing.

"This is fine," Osborn said. Unlocking his door, Osborn ushered McVey in.

"Please sit down." Osborn closed the door behind them, putting his keys and the newspaper on a side table. "If you don't mind, I'll wash the city off my hands."

"I don't mind." McVey sat down on the edge of the bed and glanced around, while Osborn went into the bathroom. The room was the same as he'd left it earlier that afternoon when he'd shown his gold shield to a housekeeper and given her two hundred francs to let him in.

"Would you like a drink?" Osborn said, drying his hands.

"If you are."

"All I have is scotch."

"Fine."

Osborn came back in with a half-empty bottle of Johnnie Walker Black. Picking up two sanitary wrapped glasses from an enameled tray on top of a replica French writing table, he pulled the plastic off and poured them each a drink.

"No ice, either, I'm afraid," Osborn said.

"I'm not picky." McVey's eyes went to Osborn's running shoes. They were caked with the dried mud.

"Been out for a jog?"

"What do you mean?" Osborn said, handing McVey a glass.

McVey nodded at his feet. "Shoes are muddy."

"I—" Osborn hesitated, then quickly covered with a grin. "—was out for a walk. They're replanting the gardens in front of the Eiffel Tower. With the rain, you can't walk anywhere around there without stepping in mud."

McVey took a pull at his drink. It gave Osborn a moment to wonder if he'd picked up on the lie. It wasn't a lie really. The Eiffel Tower gardens were torn up, he'd remembered that from being out the day before. Best to get him off it quickly.

"So?" he said.

"So." McVey hesitated. "I was in the lobby when you went into the gift shop. I saw your reaction to the paper." He nodded at the newspaper Osborn had put on the side table.

Osborn took a drink of the scotch. He rarely drank. It was only after that first night when he had seen and pursued Kanarack, and then was picked up by the Paris police, that he'd called room service and ordered the scotch. Now, as he felt it go down, he was glad he had.

"That's why you're here . . ." Osborn locked eyes with McVey. Okay, they know. Be straight, unemotional. Find out what else they know.

"As you know, Mr. Packard worked for an international company. I was in Paris doing some unrelated work with the Paris police when this came in. Since you were one of Mr. Packard's last clients . . ." McVey smiled and took another sip of the scotch. "Anyway the Paris police asked me to come by and talk to you about it. American to American. See if you had any idea who might have done it. You realize I have no authority here. I'm just helping out."

"I understand that. But I don't think I can help you."

"Did Mr. Packard seem worried about anything?"

"If he was, he didn't mention it."

"Mind my asking why you hired him?"

"I didn't hire him. I hired Kolb International. He was the one they sent."

"That wasn't what I asked."

"If you don't mind, it's personal."

"Doctor Osborn, we're talking about a murdered man." McVey sounded as if he were addressing a jury.

Osborn set his glass down. He'd done nothing and felt

he was being accused. He didn't like it. "Look, Detective McVey. Jean Packard was working for me. He's dead and I'm sorry but I haven't the slightest idea who might have done it or why. And if that's the reason you're here, you've got the wrong guy!" Angrily, Osborn jammed his hands into his jacket pockets. When he did he felt the bag containing the succinylcholine and the packet of syringes Vera had given him. He'd meant to take it out earlier when he'd come back to change to go out to the river, but he'd forgotten. With the discovery, his demeanor changed.

"Look—I'm sorry, I didn't mean to snap like that. I guess the shock of finding out about him being killed like that . . . I'm a little on edge."

"Let me just ask if Mister Packard finished his job for you?"

Osborn wavered. What the hell was he going for? Do they know about Kanarack or not? If you say yes, then what? If you say no, you leave it open.

"Did he, Doctor Osborn?"

"Yes," Osborn said finally.

McVey looked at him a moment, then tilted his glass and finished the scotch. For a moment he held the empty glass in his hand as if he didn't know quite what to do with it. Then his eyes came back to Osborn.

"Know anyone named Peter Hossbach?"

"No."

"John Cordell?"

"No." Osborn was completely puzzled. He had no idea what McVey was talking about.

"Friedrich Rustow?" McVey crossed his legs. White, hairless calves showed between the top of his socks and the bottom of his pants legs.

"No," Osborn said again. "Are they suspects?"

"They're missing persons, Doctor Osborn."

"I never heard of any of them," Osborn said.

"Not one?"

"No."

Hossbach was German, Cordell, English, and Rustow, Belgian. They were three of the beheaded corpses. McVey tucked it away in his mental computer somewhere that Osborn hadn't flinched or even paused at the mention of any of them. A recognition factor of zero. Of course he could be an accomplished actor and lying. Doctors did all the time if they felt it was in the patient's best interest not to know something.

"Well, it's a big world and a lot of things cross in it," McVey said. "It's my job to find that thread where everything meets and try to sort it out."

Leaning over to the side table, McVey set his glass down beside Osborn's keys and stood up. There were two sets of keys. One was to Osborn's hotel room. The other set were automobile keys with the figurine of a medieval lion on the key chain. They were keys to a Peugeot.

"Thank you for your time, Doctor. Sorry to have bothered you."

"That's all right," Osborn said, trying hard not to show relief. This had been nothing but routine questioning on the part of the police. McVey was only helping the French cops, nothing more.

McVey was at the door and had a hand on the knob when he turned back. "You were in London on October third, isn't that right?" he said.

"What?" Osborn reacted with surprise.

"That was—" McVey took a small plastic card from his wallet and looked at it. "Last Monday."

"I don't know what you mean."

"You were in London?"

"Yes—"

"Why?"

"I—I was on my way home from a medical convention in Geneva." Osborn suddenly found himself stammering.

How did McVey know that? And what did it have to do with Jean Packard or missing persons?

"How long were you there?"

Osborn hesitated. Where the hell's this going? What's he after? "I don't understand what this has to do with anything," he said, trying not to sound defensive.

"It was just a question, Doctor. That's my business. Questions." McVey wasn't going to let go until he had an answer.

Finally Osborn relented. "A day and a half, about—"

"You stayed at the Connaught Hotel."

"Yes."

Osborn felt a trickle of sweat run down under his right armpit. Suddenly McVey wasn't looking like anybody's grandfather anymore.

"What did you do while you were there?"

Osborn felt his face redden with anger. He was being put into a corner he didn't understand and didn't like. Maybe they do know about Kanarack, he thought. Maybe this was some way to trap him into talking about it. But he wasn't going to. If McVey knew about Kanarack, it would be he who brought it up, not Osborn.

"Detective, what I did in London is my personal business. Let's leave it at that."

"Look, Paul," McVey said, quietly. "I'm not trying to pry into your private affairs. I've got some missing people. You're not the only person I'm talking to. All I'd like you to do is account for your time while you were in London."

"Maybe I should call a lawyer."

"If you think you need one, by all means. There's the telephone."

Osborn looked off. "I got in Saturday afternoon and went to a play Saturday night," he said, flatly. "I started feeling ill. I went back to my hotel room and stayed there until Monday morning."

"All Saturday night and all day Sunday."

"That's right."

"You never left your room."

"No."

"Room service?"

"Ever have a twenty-four-hour bug? I was full of chills and fever, diarrhea, alternating with antiperistalsis. That's vomiting, in English. Who would want to eat?"

"You were alone?"

"Yes." Osborn's reply was quick, definitive.

"And nobody else saw you?"

"Not that I know of."

McVey waited a moment, then asked softly, "Doctor Osborn, why are you lying to me?"

Tonight was Thursday evening. Before he'd left London for Paris, Wednesday afternoon, McVey had asked Commander Noble to check on Osborn's visit to the Connaught Hotel. At a little after seven Thursday morning, Noble had called. Osborn had signed in to the Connaught Saturday afternoon and checked out Monday morning. He'd registered as Doctor Paul Osborn of Los Angeles and gone to his room alone. A short while later a woman had joined him.

"I beg your pardon!" Osborn said, trying to cover dismay with anger.

"You weren't alone." McVey didn't give him the chance for a second denial. "Young woman. Dark hair. About twenty-five, twenty-six. Her name is Vera Monneray. You had sex with her during a cab ride from Leicester Square to the Connaught Hotel last Saturday night."

"Jesus Christ." Osborn was stunned. How the police worked, what they knew and how they knew it was unfathomable. Finally, he nodded.

"She why you came to Paris?"

"Yes."

"I suppose she was sick the entire time you were."

"Yes, she was . . ."

"Know her long?"

"I met her in Geneva at the end of last week. She came with me to London. Then went to Paris. She's a resident here."

"Resident?"

"A doctor. She's going to be a doctor."

Doctor? McVey stared at Osborn. Amazing what you find out when you just poke around. So much for Lebrun and his "off limits."

"Why didn't you mention her?"

"I told you it was personal—"

"Doctor, she's your alibi. She can verify how you spent your time in London—"

"I don't want her dragged into this."

"Why?"

Osborn felt the blood start to rise again. McVey was beginning to get personal with his accusations and, frankly, Osborn didn't like the intrusion into his private life. "Look. You said you have no authority here. I don't have to talk to you at all!"

"No, you don't. But I think you might want to," McVey said gently. "The Paris police have your passport. They can also charge you with aggravated assault if they want to. I'm doing them a favor. If they got the idea you were giving me a hard time about something, they might look a little differently at the idea of letting you go. Especially now, when your name has come up in conjunction with a murder."

"I told you I had nothing to do with that!"

"Maybe not," McVey said. "But you could sit around a French jail for a long time until they decided to agree."

Osborn suddenly felt as if he'd just been pulled out of a washing machine and was about to be shoved into the dryer. All he could do was back down. "Maybe, if you told me what you were really getting at, I could help," he said.

"A man was murdered in London the weekend you were there. I need you to verify what you were doing and when. And Ms. Monneray seems to be the only person who can do that. But obviously you're very reluctant to involve her—and just by doing that you *are* involving her. If you'd rather, I can have the Paris police pick her up and we can all have a chat down at headquarters."

Up until that moment Osborn had been doing everything he could to keep Vera out of this. But if McVey carried through on his threat, the media would find out. If they did, the whole thing—his link to Jean Packard, his and Vera's clandestine stay in London, Vera's own story and whom she was seeing—would become front-page entertainment. Politicians could do what they wanted with starlets and bimbos and the worst that could happen would be that they'd lose an election or an appointment, while their consorts would be featured on the covers of exploitation papers in every supermarket in the world, most probably in a bikini. But a woman on the verge of becoming a physician was something entirely different. The public didn't like the idea of its doctors being that human, so, if McVey pushed it, there was every chance Vera would not only lose her residency but her career as well. Blackmail or not, so far McVey had kept what he knew between himself and Osborn and he was offering to let it stay that way.

"It's—" Osborn started, then cleared his throat. "It's—" Suddenly he realized McVey had inadvertently opened a door. Not only for the Jean Packard matter, but for Osborn to find out how much the police knew.

"It's what?"

"The reason I hired a private investigator," Osborn

said. It was a deliberate lie but he had to take the chance. The police would have been through every piece of paper Jean Packard had in his home or office, but he knew Packard wrote almost nothing down. So they had to be looking for any lead they could find and they didn't care how they did it, even to sending an American cop to shake him down.

"She has a lover. She didn't want me to know. And I wouldn't have if I hadn't followed her to Paris. When she told me I got mad. I asked her who he was but she wouldn't tell me. So I decided to find out." As clever and tough as he was, if McVey bought his story, it meant the police didn't know a thing about Kanarack. And if they didn't know, there was no reason Osborn still couldn't go on with his plan.

"And Packard found out for you."

"Yes."

"You want to tell me?"

Osborn waited just long enough for McVey to get the idea it was painful for him to talk about it. Then he said, softly, "She's screwing the French prime minister."

McVey looked at Osborn for a moment. It was the right answer, the one he'd been looking for. If Osborn was holding something back, McVey didn't know what it was.

"I'll get over it. One day I'm sure I'll even laugh about it. But not now." Osborn's reply was reasonable, even sentimental. "That personal enough for you?"

24

MCVEY LEFT the hotel and crossed the street to his car with his gut telling him two things about Osborn: first, that he had nothing to do with the London murder, and second that he really cared about Vera Monneray, no matter whom she was sleeping with.

Closing the Opel's door, McVey put on his seat belt and started the engine. Turning on the wipers against what seemed an incessant rain, he made a U-turn and headed back in the direction of his hotel. Osborn hadn't reacted any differently than most people do when questioned by the police, especially when they're innocent. The emotional arc usually went from shock, to fear, to indignation and most often ended either in anger—sometimes with threats to sue the detective, sometimes the entire police department—or in a polite exchange where the cop explains his questioning was nothing personal, that he just had a job to do, apologizes for intruding and leaves. Which is what he'd done.

Osborn wasn't his man. Vera Monneray he might put in his book as a long shot, someone with medical training and along with it probably some surgical experience. In that respect she fit the profile and she had been in London when the last murder had taken place, but she and Osborn would be each other's alibi for what they'd done there. They might have been sick, as Osborn said, or they might have spent the entire time diddling each other, and if she'd gone out for an hour or two, no one at the hotel had seen her, and Osborn, because he thought he loved her, would cover for her even if she had. Moreover, he was sure if he ran her she'd almost certainly come up clean with no police record at all. Pushing it any further it would only serve to put Lebrun in a bad light and could end up embarrassing not only the entire department but probably the whole of France.

The rain came down harder and McVey worried that he knew no more about the headless slayings now than he did when he'd started more than three weeks ago. But unless you got a break fast, that was usually the way. It was the thing about homicide. The endless details, the hundreds of false leads that had to be followed, gone back over, followed again. The reports, the paperwork, the countless interviews that intruded on strangers' lives. Sometimes you got lucky; mostly you didn't. People got angry with you and you couldn't blame them. How many times had he been asked why he did it? Gave his life to this kind of ugly, infuriating and morbidly gruesome job? Usually he just shrugged and said that one day he woke up and realized that's what he did for a living. But inside he knew, and that's why he did it. He didn't know where it came from in him or how he got it. But he knew what it was. The sense that the murdered had rights, too. And so did their friends and the families who'd loved them. Murder was a thing you couldn't let somebody get away with. Especially if you felt that way and had the experience and the authority to do something about it.

Taking a wide lefthand turn, McVey found himself crossing a bridge over the Seine. It wasn't what he meant to do. Now he was all turned around with no idea where he was. The next thing he knew he was in a stream of traffic going past the Eiffel Tower. That's when one of those little things that always nagged him after an interview or interrogation started jabbing tiny pins in that certain corner of his conscience. The same kind of thing that had made him dial Vera Monneray's apartment that afternoon just to see who answered.

Moving into the left lane, he watched for the next side

street, took it and doubled back. He was moving along the far edge of a park where, between the trees, he could see the distant lighted ironwork mass that made up the base of the Eiffel Tower. Just ahead, a car pulled out from the curb and drove off. Slowly he passed the spot, then backed in and parked. Getting out, he pulled up his jacket against the rain, then rubbed his hands together to warm them. A moment later he was walking down a pathway that ran along the edge of the Parc du Champ de Mars, with the tower looming in the distance.

The park grounds were dark and it was hard to see. Overhanging trees lining the path gave some protection from the rainy weather, and he tried to stay under them as he walked. He could see his breath in the raw night air and he blew on his hands only to jam them finally into the pockets of his raincoat.

Gingerly dodging some sidewalk construction, he walked another fifty yards in the direction of the lighted area to where he could clearly see the tower reaching into the night sky. Suddenly his feet slid out from under him, and he nearly fell. Recovering, he walked on a little farther to where a street light shone on a park bench. The light from the tower spilled onto the grassy area where he'd just been. Most of it had been dug up, and was in the process of being replanted. Leaning against the bench with one hand, he lifted a foot and looked at his shoe. It was wet and covered with mud. The other was the same. Satisfied, he turned and started back for the car. It was why he had come. A simple follow-up to a simple answer to a simple question.

Osborn had told the truth about the mud.

25

MICHELE KANARACK had never seen her husband as distant and cold.

He was sitting in his underwear, a worn T-shirt and American jockey shorts, looking out the kitchen window. It was ten minutes after nine in the evening. At seven o'clock he'd come home from work, taken off his clothes and immediately put them in the washer. The first thing he'd reached for after that was wine, but he stopped abruptly after drinking only half a glass. After that he'd asked for his dinner, had eaten in silence, and said nothing since.

Michele looked at him without knowing what to say. He'd been fired, she was sure of it. How or why, she had no idea. The last thing he'd told her was that he was going to Rouen with Monsieur Lebec to look over a possible site for a new bakery. Now, little more than twenty-four hours later, here he was, sitting in his underwear and staring out at the night.

The night, that was a thing Michele had inherited from her father. Forty-one when his daughter had been born, he'd been a Parisian auto mechanic when the German army overran the city. A member of the underground, he spent three hours every evening after work on the roof of their apartment building clandestinely watching and recording Nazi military traffic on the street below.

The war had been over for seventeen years when he'd brought four-year-old Michele back to the apartment house and up onto the roof to show her what he'd been doing during the occupation. The traffic on the street below magically became German tanks, half-tracks and motorcycles. The pedestrians, Nazi soldiers with rifles and machine guns. That Michele hadn't understood the purpose behind his actions didn't matter. What did matter was that in taking her to that building and leading her up to the roof in the darkness to show her how and what he had done, he had shared a secret and dangerous past with her. He had included her in something very personal and very special and, in remembering him, that was what counted.

Looking to her husband now, she wished he could be like her father. If the news was bad, it was bad. They loved each other, they were married, they were expecting a child. The darkness outside only made his distance more painful to understand.

Across the room the clothes washer stopped, its cycle finished. Immediately Henri got up, opened the washer door and pulled out his work clothes. Looking at them, he cursed out loud, then crossed the room to pull open a closet door angrily. A moment later he was stuffing the still-wet laundry inside a plastic garbage bag and sealing it with a plastic tie.

"What are you doing?" Michele asked.

Abruptly, he looked up. "I want you to go away," he said. "To your sister's house in Marseilles. Take back your family name and tell everyone I've left you, that I'm a louse, and you have no idea where I've gone."

"What are you saying?" Michele was flabbergasted.

"Do what I tell you. I want you to leave now. Tonight."

"Henri, tell me what's wrong, please."

In answer, Kanarack threw down the garbage bag and went into the bedroom.

"Henri, please . . . Let me help. . . ." Suddenly she realized he meant it. She came into the room behind him scared half to death and stood in the doorway as he dug two battered suitcases from under the bed. He pushed them toward her.

"Take these," he said. "You can fit enough into them."

"No! I am your wife. What the hell is the matter? How can you say these things without explanation?"

Kanarack looked at her for a long moment. He wanted to say something but he didn't know how. Then, from outside, an automobile horn sounded once, then twice. Michele's eyes narrowed. Pushing past him, she went to the window. In the street below she could see Agnés Demblon's white Citroën, its motor running, its exhaust drifting upward in the night air.

Henri looked at her. "I love you," he said. "Now go to Marseilles. I will send money to you there."

Michele pushed back from him. "You never went to Rouen. You were with her!"

Kanarack said nothing.

"Get the hell out of here, you bastard. Go to your goddamn Agnes Demblon."

"It's you who has to go," he said.

"Why? She's moving in?"

"If that's what you want to hear. All right, yes, she's moving in."

"Then go to hell, for all time. Go to hell, you son of a bitch, and God damn you!"

26

"I SEE," François Christian said quietly and without emotion. A glass of cognac was in his hand; swirling it lightly, he looked off into the fire.

Vera said nothing. Leaving him was difficult enough,

she owed him a great deal and would not insult him, or them, by simply getting up and walking out as if she were a whore, because she wasn't.

It was a little before ten. They had just finished supper and were sitting in the large living room of a grand apartment on the rue Paul Valery between avenue Foch and avenue Victor Hugo. She knew François also kept a house in the country where his wife and three children lived. She also suspected he might have more than one apartment in the city, but she never asked. Any more than she'd asked if she were his only lover, which she suspected she wasn't.

Taking a sip of coffee she looked up at him. He still hadn't moved. His hair was dark, neatly trimmed, with a touch of gray at the temples. In his dark pin-stripe suit, crisp white cuffs protruding in tailored precision from the sleeves of his double-breasted jacket, he looked like the aristocrat he was. The wedding band on his left hand glinted in the firelight as he absently sipped at his drink while still staring into the flames. How many times had his hands caressed her? Touched her in a way only he had been able to touch her?

Her father, Alexandre Baptiste Monneray, had been a ranking career naval officer. In her early life, she, her mother and her younger brother had traveled the world following his variety of commands and naval postings. When she was sixteen her father retired to become an independent defense consultant and they settled permanently into a large home in the south of France.

It was here that François Christian, then an undersecretary in the Ministry of Defense, became, among others, a frequent guest. And it was here that their relationship began. It was François who talked to her at length about the arts, about life and about love. And, one very special afternoon, about the direction of her studies. When she told him medicine, he was astounded.

It was true, she'd argued. Not only did she *wish* to become a physician, she was determined to become one, if for nothing more than a defiant promise she'd made to her father at age six around a Sunday dinner table, when her parents had been discussing suitable careers for women. Out of the blue she'd announced she was going to be a doctor. Her father had asked her if she was serious and she'd said she was. She even remembered the slight smile he'd given to her mother when he accepted Vera's choice. The smile she'd taken as a challenge. Neither of her parents believed she could do it or would do it. Right then she determined to prove them wrong. And at that moment of resolve something had happened and a white light rose up around her and held there glowing. And though she knew no one else could see it, she felt warm and comforted and sensed a strength greater than anything she'd ever experienced. And she took it as an affirmation that her promise to her father was real and that her destiny was resolute.

And, that same afternoon, as she told her story to François Christian, the same glow appeared, and she told him it was there. Smiling as if he understood completely, he'd taken her hand in his and fully encouraged her to follow her dreams.

At age twenty she graduated from the University of Paris and was accepted immediately into the medical school at Montpellier, at which time her father relented and gave her his full blessing. A year later, after spending the Christmas holidays with her grandmother in Calais, Vera stopped in Paris to visit friends. For no reason, she suddenly had the idea to visit François Christian, whom she had not seen in nearly three years.

It was a lark, of course, with no purpose other than to say hello. But François was now leader of the French Democratic Party and a major political figure, and how to reach him through a battery of underlings she had no idea, except to go to his office and ask to be seen. To her surprise, she was shown in almost immediately.

The moment she entered the room and he rose from his desk to greet her, she'd sensed something extraordinary happening. He called for tea and they sat on a window seat overlooking the garden outside his office. He'd met her when she was sixteen; she was now almost twenty-two. In less than six years, a pert teenage girl had become a strikingly beautiful, extremely intelligent and wholly alluring young woman. If she did not believe it herself, his manner confirmed it and no matter what she did she could not take her eyes from him, nor he from her. That same evening he had brought her here to this apartment. They'd had dinner and then he'd undressed her on the couch by the fire where he now sat. Making love to him had been the most natural thing in the world. And continued to be, even as he became prime minister, for the next four years. Then Paul Osborn had come into her life, and in what seemed like only a matter of moments, everything changed.

"All right," he said softly, turning in his chair, his eyes, as they met hers, still holding the greatest love and respect for her. "I understand." With that he set the glass down and stood up. As he did, he looked back to her, as if to fix her image in his mind forever. For a long moment he just stood there. Then, finally, he turned and walked out.

27

OSBORN SAT on the edge of the bed and listened to Jake Berger complain about his watery eyes and runny nose and the ninety-degree heat that was pressure cooking Los Angeles into a first-degree smog alert. Berger was rattling on from his car phone somewhere between Beverly Hills and his opulent Century City offices; it didn't seem to matter that Osborn was six thousand miles away in Paris and might have problems of his own. He sounded more like a spoiled child than one of Los Angeles's top trial lawyers, the one who had turned Osborn onto Kolb International and Jean Packard in the first place.

"Jake, listen to me, please—" Osborn finally interrupted, then told him what had just taken place: the murder of Jean Packard, McVey's sudden visit, the personal questions. He left out the lie, the hiring of Jean Packard to uncover Vera's boyfriend, just as he'd dodged around the reason he needed a private investigator the first time he'd called Berger.

"You're sure it was McVey?" Berger asked.

"You know him?"

"Do I know McVey? What lawyer who ever defended a murder suspect in the city of Los Angeles doesn't know him? He's tough and thorough, with the tenacity of a pit bull. Once he gets into something, he doesn't let go until it's finished. That he's in Paris is no surprise—McVey's expertise has been sought by baffled homicide departments all over the globe for years. The question is: Why is he interested in Paul Osborn?"

"I don't know. He just showed up and started asking questions."

"Paul," Berger said directly. "McVey. He's not questioning you for the hell of it. I need a straight answer. What's going on?"

"I don't know," Osborn said. There was no hesitation in his voice. For a moment Berger was silent, then he warned Osborn not to talk to anyone else, and if McVey came back to have him call Berger in Los Angeles. In the meantime he'd try to get someone in Paris to find a way to get his passport back so that he could get the hell out of there.

"No," Osborn said abruptly. "Don't do anything. I just wanted to know about McVey, that's all. Thanks for your time."

Succinylcholine—Osborn studied the bottle under the bathroom light, then, abruptly putting it into his shaving kit alongside the sealed packet of syringes, closed the kit and tucked it away under several dress shirts in the suitcase he'd never unpacked.

Brushing his teeth, he swallowed two sleeping pills, doublelocked the door, then went to the bed and pulled back the covers. Sitting down, he realized how weary he was. Every muscle in his body ached from the tension.

There was no doubt McVey had unnerved him, and his call to Berger had been a cry for help. But then, as he spilled everything out in a rush, he'd suddenly realized his call had been made to the wrong person, the wrong professional, to someone eminently qualified to counsel law but not the soul. The truth of it was he'd been pleading for Berger to get him out of Paris and off the hook, just as earlier he'd tried to solicit Jean Packard to kill Kanarack. Instead of Berger, he should have called his psychologist in Santa Monica and asked for guidance in handling his own emotional crisis. But he couldn't do that without confessing homicidal intent, and if he did that, by law, the psychologist would have to inform the police. After that, the only person left he could talk to was Vera, but he couldn't without incriminating her.

In reality it made no difference whom he confided in because the ultimate decision was and only would be his. Either walk away from Kanarack or kill him.

McVey's showing up had tightened the screw. Crafty and experienced, he'd never once mentioned Kanarack, but how could Osborn be certain he didn't know? How could he be sure that if he followed his plan, the police wouldn't be watching?

Reaching over, Osborn clicked off the bedside lamp and lay back in the darkness. Outside, the rain drummed lightly on his window. The lights from avenue Kléber below illuminated the droplets running down the glass and magnified them on the ceiling overhead. Closing his eyes, he let his thoughts drift to Vera and their lovemaking that afternoon. He could see her naked above him, her head thrown back and her back arched so that her long hair touched his ankles. The only movement at all was the slow, sensuous, back-and-forth thrust of her pelvis as she rode the length of him. She seemed like a sculpture. The marrow of everything female. Girl, woman, mother. At once solid and liquid, infinitely strong, and yet fragile to the point of vanishing.

The truth was he loved her and cared for her in a way he'd never experienced. It made sense only if you came at it from far inside, filled with the want and hunger and sense of wonder that the ultimate love between two people can really be. And he knew beyond doubt that were they both to die that moment, that in the same instant they would be reunited in the vastness of space, and taking on whatever form or shape required, they would continue on intertwined, forever.

If that vision was romantic or childlike or even spiritual, it made no difference, because it was what Paul Osborn believed was true. And he knew that in her own way

Vera felt the same. She had proved it earlier that day when she had taken him to her apartment. And that in itself had clarified the next. And that was that if he and Vera were to go on, he could not allow the demon inside him to do what it had done to every other caring relationship he'd had since he was a boy. Destroy it. This time it was the demon that must be destroyed. Inexorably and forever. No matter how difficult, how dangerous or at what risk.

Finally, as the pills at last played their game and sleep began to overtake him, Paul Osborn's demon materialized before him. It was hunched over and menacing and wore a dusty coat. Though it was dark, he saw it raise its head. Its eyes were deep-set and staring, and its ears stuck out at sharp angles. The head was turned and he could not see the face clearly, yet he knew instinctively that the jaw was square and that a scar ran across the cheekbone and down toward the upper lip.

And there was no doubt. None at all.

The thing he saw was Henri Kanarack.

28

Click.

McVey knew it was 3:17 A.M. without looking because the last time he'd looked at the clock it was 3:11. Digital clocks were not supposed to make noise, but they did if you were listening. And McVey had been listening, and counting the clicks, while he thought.

He'd come back to his hotel, following his visit with

Osborn and his frolic in the rain in front of the Eiffel Tower, at ten minutes to eleven. The hotel's tiny restaurant was closed and room service wasn't available because there wasn't any. It was the kind of all-expense trip Interpol funded. A barely livable hotel, with faded carpets, a lumpy bed and food, if you could make it between six and nine in the morning and six and nine at night.

What was left was either to go back out in the rain to find a restaurant that was open, or to use the "honor bar," the tiny little refrigerated cabinet tucked between what served as a closet and the bathroom that flooded every time you used the shower.

McVey wasn't going back out in the rain, so it was the honor bar or nothing. Opening it with a tiny key attached to the ring on his room key, he found some cheese and crackers and a triangle of Swiss chocolate. Poking around, he also found a half bottle of a white wine that turned out to be a very nice Sancerre. Afterward, when he casually opened the desk drawer to check the honor bar price list, he found out why the Sancerre had been so agreeable. The half bottle cost 150 French francs, somewhere around thirty dollars U.S. A pittance to a connoisseur, a fortune to a cop.

By eleven thirty he'd stopped fuming and taken his clothes off and was about to step into the shower when the phone rang. Commander Noble of Scotland Yard was calling from his home in Chelsea.

"Hold on, McVey, will you?" Noble had said. "I've got Michaels, the Home Office pathologist, on the other line and I've got to figure out how to make this into a conference call without disconnecting everyone."

Wrapping a towel around him, McVey sat down at the Formica-topped desk opposite his bed.

"McVey? You still there?"

"Yes."

"Doctor Michaels?"

McVey heard the young medical examiner's voice join in. "Here," he said.

"All right, then. Doctor Michaels, tell our friend McVey what you've just told me."

"It's about the severed head."

"You've identified who it is?" McVey brightened.

"Not yet. Perhaps what Doctor Michaels has to say will help explain why the identification is being so troublesome," Noble said. "Go on, Doctor Michaels, please."

"Yes, of course." Michaels cleared his throat. "As you recall, Detective McVey, there was very little blood left in the severed head when found. In fact almost none. So it was very difficult to assess the clotting time in attempting to determine time of death. However, I thought that with a little more information I should be able to give you a reasonable time frame for when the chap was murdered. Well, it turns out, I couldn't."

"I don't understand," McVey said.

"After you left, I took the temperature of the head and selected some tissue samples, which I sent to the laboratory for analysis."

"And—?" McVey yawned. It was getting late and he was beginning to think more of sleep than murder.

"The head had been frozen. Frozen and then thawed out before it was left in the alley."

"You sure?"

"Yes, sir."

"I can't say I haven't seen it before," McVey said. "But usually you can tell right away because the inner brain tissues take a long time to thaw out. The inside of the head is colder than the layers you find as you work outward toward the skull."

"That wasn't the case. It was thawed completely."

"Finish what you have to say, Doctor Michaels," Noble pressed.

"When laboratory tissue samples revealed the head had been frozen, I was still bothered by the fact that the facial skin moved under pressure from my fingers as it would under normal conditions had not the head been frozen."

"What are you getting at?"

"I sent the entire head to a Doctor Stephen Richman, an expert in micropathology at the Royal College of Pathology, to see what he could make of the freezing. He called me as soon as he realized what had happened."

"What *did* happen?" McVey was getting impatient.

"Our friend has a metal plate in his skull. Undoubtedly the result of some sort of brain surgery done years ago. The brain tissue would have revealed nothing, but the metal did. The head had been frozen, not just solid, but to a degree approaching absolute zero."

"I'm a little slow this time of night, Doctor. You're over my head."

"Absolute zero is a degree of cold unreachable in the science of freezing. In essence, it's a hypothetical temperature characterized by the complete absence of heat. To even approach it requires extremely sophisticated laboratory techniques that employ either liquefied helium or magnetic cooling."

"How cold is this absolute zero?" McVey had never heard of it.

"In technical terms?"

"In whatever terms."

"Minus two hundred seventy-three point one five degrees Celsius or minus four hundred fifty-nine point six seven degrees Fahrenheit."

"Jesus Christ, that's almost five hundred degrees below zero!"

"Yes, quite."

"What happens then, assuming you did reach absolute zero?"

"I just looked it up, McVey," Noble interjected. "It means it's a point at which mutual linear motions of all the molecules of a substance would cease."

"Every atom of its structure would be absolutely motionless," Michaels added.

Click.

This time McVey did look at the clock. It was 3:18 A.M., Friday, October 7.

Neither Commander Noble nor Dr. Michaels had had any idea why someone would freeze a head to that degree and then discard it. Nor had McVey, either. There was a possibility it had come from one of those cryonic freezing organizations that accept the bodies of the recently departed and deep-freeze them in the hope that at some future time, when there is a cure for whatever ailment killed them, the bodies could be unfrozen, worked on, then brought back to life. To every scientist in the world it was a pipe dream, but people bought into it and legitimate companies provided the service.

There were two such companies in Great Britain. One in London, the other in Edinburgh, and Scotland Yard would follow up on them first thing in the morning. Maybe their John Doe hadn't been murdered, maybe his head had been severed after death and legitimately put away for some future time. Maybe it was his own investment. Maybe he'd put his life savings into the deep-freezing of his own head. People had done nuttier things.

McVey had gotten off the phone saying he was coming back to London tomorrow and requesting that the seven headless corpses be X-rayed to see if any of them had had surgery where metal might have been implanted into the skeleton. Replacement hip joints, screws that held broken bones in place—metal that could be analyzed, as the steel plate in John Doe's head had been. And if any of them did have metal, the cadavers were to be immediately forwarded to Dr. Richman at the Royal College to determine if they too had been deep-frozen.

Maybe this was the break they were looking for, the kind of left-field "incidental," usually right in front of an investigator's nose but that at first, second, third or even tenth look still remained wholly unseen; the kind that almost always turned the tide in difficult homicide cases; that is, if the cop doing the investigating persevered long enough to go over it that one last time.

Click.
3:19 A.M.
Getting out of his chair, McVey pulled back the covers and plopped down on the bed. It already *was* tomorrow. He could barely remember Thursday. They didn't pay him enough for these kind of hours. But then, they never paid any cop enough.

Maybe the frozen head would lead somewhere, probably it wouldn't, any more than the business with Osborn had led anywhere. Osborn was a nice guy, troubled and in love. What a thing, come on a business trip and fall for the prime minister's girlfriend.

McVey was about to turn out the light and get under the covers when he saw his muddy shoes drying under the table where he'd left them. With a sigh, he got out of bed, picked them up and carefully walked to the bathroom, where he put them on the floor.

Click.
3:24.
McVey slid under the sheets, rolled over and turned out the light, and then lay back against the pillow.

If Judy were still alive, she would have come on this trip. The only place they'd ever traveled together, besides the fishing trips to Big Bear, had been Hawaii. Two weeks in 1975. A European vacation they could never afford. Well, they would have afforded it this time. It wouldn't have been First Class, but who cared; Interpol would have paid for it.

Click.
3:26.

"Mud!" McVey suddenly said out loud and sat up. Turning on the light, he tossed back the sheets and went into the bathroom. Bending down, he picked up one of his shoes and looked at it. Then picked up the other and did the same. The mud that caked them was gray, almost black. The mud on Osborn's running shoes had been red.

29

MICHELE KANARACK looked up at the clock as the train pulled out of the Gare de Lyon for Marseilles. It was 6:54 in the morning. She'd brought no luggage, only a handbag. She'd taken a cab from their apartment fifteen minutes after she'd first seen Agnes Demblon's Citroën waiting outside. At the station she bought a second-class ticket to Marseilles, then found a bench and sat down. The wait would be almost nine hours, but she didn't care.

She wanted nothing from Henri, not even their child who'd been conceived in love less than eight weeks earlier. The suddenness of what had happened was overwhelming.

All the more so since it seemed to have sprung from nowhere.

Once outside the station, the train picked up speed and Paris became a blur. Twenty-four hours earlier her world had been warm and alive. Each day her pregnancy filled her with more joy than the day before, and that had been no different, and then Henri called to say he was going to Rouen with Monsieur Lebec to see about opening a new bakery there, perhaps, she even thought, with the promise of a managerial job. Then, with the wave of a hand, it was gone. All of it. She'd been deceived and lied to. Not only that, but she was a fool. She should have known the power that bitch Agnes Demblon carried over her husband. Maybe she had known it all along and refused to accept it. For that she had only herself to blame. What wife would let her husband be picked up and driven to work day after day by an unmarried woman, no matter how unattractive she might be? But how many times had Henri reassured her—"Agnes is just an old friend, my love, a spinster. What interest could I possibly have in her?"

"My love." She could still hear him say it, and it made her ill. The way she felt now she could kill them both without the slightest thought. Out the window the city faded to countryside. Another train roared past going toward Paris. Michele Kanarack would never go to Paris again. Henri and everything about him was done. Finished. Her sister would have to understand that and not try to talk her into going back.

What had he said? "Take back your family name."

That she would do. Just as soon as she could get a job and afford a lawyer. Sitting back, she closed her eyes and listened to the sound of the train as it quickened down the track toward the south of France. Today was October 7. In exactly one month and two days she and Henri would have been married for eight years.

* * *

In Paris, Henri Kanarack was curled up fetally, asleep in an overstuffed chair in Agnes Demblon's living room. At 4:45 he had driven Agnes to work and then returned to her apartment with the Citroën. His apartment at 175 avenue Verdier was empty. Anyone going there would find no one home, nor would they find any clue to where they had gone. The green plastic garbage bag containing his work clothes, underwear, shoes and socks had been tossed into the basement furnace and was vaporized in seconds. Every last thing he'd been wearing during the murder of Jean Packard had, by now, filtered down through the night air and lay scattered microscopically across the landscape of Montrouge.

Ten miles away, across the Seine, Agnes Demblon sat at her desk on the second floor of the bakery billing the accounts receivable that always went out on the seventh of the month. Already she had alerted Monsieur Lebec and his employees that Henri Kanarack had been called out of town on a family matter and probably would not return to work for at least a week. By 6:30 she had posted handwritten notes over the telephone at the small switchboard and at the front counter directing any inquiries about M. Kanarack promptly to her.

At almost the same time, McVey was carefully walking the Parc Champ de Mars in front of the Eiffel Tower. A drizzly morning light revealed the same overturned rectangular garden he'd left the night before. Farther down, he could see more pathways turned over for landscaping. Beyond them were more pathways, not yet turned over, that ran parallel to each other and crossed other pathways at about fifty-yard intervals. Walking the full length of the park on one side, he crossed over and came back down the other, studying the ground as he went. Nowhere did he see anything but the gray-black earth that again caked his shoes.

Stopping, he turned back to see if maybe he'd missed something. In doing so, he saw a groundskeeper coming toward him. The man spoke no English and McVey's French was unpardonable. Still, he tried.

"Red dirt. You understand? Red dirt. Any around here?" McVey said, pointing at the ground.

"Reddert?" the man replied.

"No. Red! The color red. R-E-D." McVey spelled it out.

"R-E-D," the man repeated, then looked at him as if he were crazy.

It was too early in the morning for this. He'd get Lebrun, bring him here to ask the questions. "*Pardon,*" he said with the best accent he could and was about to leave when he saw a red handkerchief sticking out of the man's back pocket. Pointing to it, he said, "Red."

Realizing, the man jerked it out and offered it to McVey.

"No. No." McVey waved him off. "The color."

"Ah!" The man brightened. "*La couleur!*"

"*La couleur!*" McVey repeated, triumphantly.

"*Rouge,*" the man said.

"*Rouge,*" McVey repeated, trying to roll the sound off his tongue like the Parisian. Then, bending over, he scooped a handful of the gray mud into his hand. "*Rouge?*" he asked.

"*La terrain?*"

McVey nodded. "*Rouge terrain?*" he said, sweeping his hand at the surrounding gardens.

The man stared at him, then swept his hand as McVey had. "*Rouge terrain.*"

"*Oui!*" McVey beamed.

"*Non,*" the man replied.

"No?"

"No!"

*   *   *

Back at his hotel, McVey called Lebrun and told him he was packing to go back to London and that he had the increasingly uncomfortable feeling Osborn might not be as kosher as he first thought, that it might pay to keep an eye on him until the next day when he was due to collect his passport and fly back to Los Angeles. "Oh yeah," he added. "He's got keys to a Peugeot."

Thirty minutes later, at 8:05, an unmarked police car pulled up to the curb across from Paul Osborn's hotel on avenue Kléber and parked. Inside, a plainclothes detective unhooked his seat belt and sat back to watch. If Osborn came out—leaving either by foot or waiting for his car to be brought around—the detective would see him. A phone call with an apology for ringing the wrong number had confirmed Osborn was still in his room. A check of rental-car companies had provided the year, color and license-plate number of Osborn's rented Peugeot.

At 8:10, another unmarked police car picked McVey up at his hotel to take him to the airport, courtesy of Inspector Lebrun and the First Paris Préfecture of Police.

Fifteen minutes later they were still in traffic. By now McVey knew enough of Paris to realize his driver wasn't taking the express route to the airport. He was right. In five minutes, they pulled into the garage at police headquarters.

At 8:45, still wearing the same rumpled gray suit that was unfortunately becoming his trademark, McVey sat across from Lebrun's desk studying an eight-by-ten photograph of a fingerprint. The print was a full finger, clear image enhancement, made from a smudge on the piece of broken glass the homicide tech crew had found in Jean Packard's apartment. The glass had been sent to the fingerprint lab at Interpol, Lyon, where a computer expert refined the smudge until it became a fully identifiable print. The print had then been scanned, enlarged, photographed and returned to Lebrun in Paris.

"You know Doctor Hugo Klass?" Lebrun said, lighting a cigarette and looking back at his empty computer screen.

"German fingerprint expert," McVey said, putting the photo back into a file folder and closing it. "Why?"

"You were going to ask about the accuracy of the enhancement, correct?"

McVey nodded.

"Klass now operates out of Interpol headquarters. He worked with the computer artist on the original smudge until they had a legible ridge pattern. After that Rudolf Halder at Interpol, Vienna, did a confirmation test with a new kind of forensic optical comparator he and Klass had developed together. A smart bomb couldn't be more precise."

Lebrun looked back to his computer screen. He was waiting for a reply to an identification request made to Central File/Criminal Records data center Interpol, Lyon. His initial request had come back "not on file," Europe. His second came back "not on file," North America. A third request was for "automatic retrieval" and sent the computer scanning "previous data."

McVey leaned over and picked up a cup of black coffee. No matter how hard he tried to be a contemporary cop and use the wide range of high-speed high-technologies available to him, he just couldn't get the old school out of his system. To him you did your legwork until you had your man and the evidence to back it up. Then you went after him *mano a mano* until he cracked. Still, he knew that sooner or later he'd better come around and make life a little easier on himself. Getting up, he walked around behind Lebrun and glanced at the screen.

As he did, a "retrieve" file came up from Interpol, Washington. Seven seconds later, the screen scrolled up the name MERRIMAN, ALBERT JOHN: wanted for murder, attempted murder, armed robbery, extortion—Florida, New Jersey, Rhode Island, Massachusetts.

"Nice guy," McVey said. Then the screen went blank, followed by a single scroll. DECEASED, NEW YORK CITY—DECEMBER 22, 1967.

"Deceased?" Lebrun said.

"Your hotshot computer's got a dead man murdering people in Paris. How you going to explain that to the media?" McVey deadpanned.

Lebrun took it as an affront. "Obviously Merriman faked his death and came up with a new identity."

McVey smiled again. "Either that or Klass and Halder aren't what they're cracked up to be."

"Do you dislike Europeans, McVey?" Lebrun was serious.

"Only when they talk in a language I don't understand." McVey walked off, looking up at the ceiling, then turned around and came back. "Suppose you, Klass and Halder are right and it is Merriman. Why would he come out of hiding after all these years to take out a private investigator?"

"Because something forced him out. Probably something this Jean Packard was working on."

The command—PHYSICAL DESCRIP–MUG SHOT–FINGERPRINTS–Y/N?—came up on Lebrun's screen.

Lebrun punched Y on his keyboard.

The screen went blank, then came back with a second command. FAX ONLY–Y/N–?

Again Lebrun punched the Y. Two minutes later a mug shot, physical description and fingerprints of Albert Merriman printed out. The mug shot was of Henri Kanarack almost thirty years younger.

Lebrun studied it, then handed it to McVey.

"Nobody I know," McVey said.

Flicking a cigarette ash off his sleeve, Lebrun picked up the phone and told whoever was on the other end to go back over Jean Packard's apartment and his office at Kolb International with a finer comb than they did the first time.

"I'd also suggest you have a police artist see if they can come up with a sketch of how Albert Merriman might look today." Picking up a battered brown leather bag that served as suitcase and portable homicide kit, McVey thanked Lebrun for the coffee then added, "You know where to reach me in London if our boy Osborn does anything he shouldn't before he leaves for L.A." With that he started for the door.

"McVey," Lebrun said as he reached it. "Albert Merriman was deceased in—New York."

McVey stopped, did a slow burn and turned back in time to see a grin creep over Lebrun's face.

"For the brotherhood, McVey. Make the call, *s'il vous plaît?*"

"For the brotherhood."

"*Oui.*"

30

LITTLE MORE than a stone's throw from the building on the rue de la Cité where McVey sat with Lebrun's phone trying to get through to the New York City Police Department regarding the late Albert Merriman, Vera Monneray walked along the Porte de la Tournelle, absently watching the traffic on the Seine.

It had been correct for her to end her relationship with François Christian. She knew the break had caused him pain, yet she had done it as kindly and respectfully as she knew how. She had not, she told herself, left one of the most esteemed members of the French government for an orthopedic surgeon from Los Angeles. The real truth was that neither she nor François could have continued on as they had and each continued to grow. And life without growth meant a withering and finally a dying out.

What she had done was no more than an act of personal survival, something François would, in time, have done to her when he finally resigned himself to the fact that his real love belonged to his wife and children.

Reaching the top of a long flight of stairs, she turned back and looked at Paris. She saw the sweep of the Seine and the grand arches of Notre Dame as if for the first time. The trees and rooftops and boulevard traffic were completely new to her, as was the romantic chatter of passersby. François Christian was a fine man and she was grateful she had had him in her life. Now, she was equally grateful it was over. Perhaps it was because, for the first time in as long as she could remember, she felt unencumbered and totally free.

Turning left, she started across the bridge to her apartment. Purposefully, she tried not to think of Paul Osborn, but she couldn't help it. Her thoughts kept coming back to him. She wanted to believe that he had helped free her. By giving her attention, even adoration, he'd renewed her belief in herself as an independent, intelligent and sexually attractive woman fully capable of making a life on her own. And that was what had given her the confidence and courage to make the break from François.

But that was only part of it, and not to admit it would be to lie to herself. Dr. Paul Osborn hurt, and she cared that he hurt. On one level she wanted to think that caring and concern were part of an instinctive female nurturing. It was what women did when they sensed pain in someone close to them. But it wasn't that simple and she knew it. What she wanted was to love him until he stopped hurting and after that to love him more.

"*Bonjour, mademoiselle,*" a round-faced, uniformed doorman said cheerily, holding open the filigreed iron outer door to her building.

"*Bonjour, Philippe.*" She smiled and went past him into the lobby, then quickly up the polished marble stairs to her apartment on the second floor.

Once inside, she closed the door and crossed the hallway into the formal dining room. On the table was a vase with two dozen long-stemmed red roses. She didn't have to open the card to know who'd sent them, but she did anyway.

"*Au revoir, François.*"

It was written in his own hand. François had said he understood and he had. The note and flowers meant they would always be friends. Vera held the card for a moment, then slid it back in its envelope and went into the living room. In one corner was a baby grand piano. Across from it, two large couches sat at right angles to one another, with a long ebony and leaded-glass coffee table in between. To her right was the entrance to the hallway and the two bedrooms and study that led off it. To the left was the dining room. Beyond that was a butler's pantry and the kitchen.

Outside, the low-hanging clouds obscured the city. The overcast and grayness made everything feel sad. For the first time the apartment seemed huge and ungainly, without warmth or comfort, a place for someone more formal and much older than she.

An aura of loneliness as bleak as the sky that sealed Paris swept over her and, without thinking, she wanted Paul there. She wanted to touch him and have him touch her, the same as they had yesterday. She wanted to be with him in the bedroom and in the shower and wherever else he wanted to take her. She wanted to feel him inside her and to make love to him over and over until they ached.

She wanted it as much for him as for herself. It was important he understand that she knew about the darkness. And even if she didn't know what it was, even if he couldn't tell her that it was all right for him to trust her. Because when the time was appropriate, he would tell her and together they would do something about it. But for now, what he had to know more than anything, was that she would be there for him, whenever and for as long as he needed.

31

THE 1961 movie *West Side Story* starring Natalie Wood was playing in its original English-language version at a small theater on the boulevard des Italiens. The film ran 151 minutes and its second show, starting at four, was the one that Paul Osborn would attend. When he was in college he'd taken two successive film history courses and had written a lengthy paper on translating stage musicals to the screen. *West Side Story* had been the centerpiece of his discussion and he still remembered it well enough to convince anyone he'd just seen it.

The theater on the boulevard des Italiens was halfway between his hotel and the bakery where Kanarack worked and had Métro stations within a five-minute walk in any of three directions.

Circling the name of the theater with his pen, Osborn closed his newspaper and got up from the small table where he'd been sitting. Crossing the hotel dining room to pay his breakfast bill, he glanced outside. It was still raining.

Entering the lobby, he looked around. Three hotel employees were behind the desk, and outside, two people huddled under the doorway overhang while a doorman summoned a cab. That was it, there was no one else.

Going to the elevator, he pressed the button and the door opened immediately. Getting in, he rode up alone. As he did, he weighed the situation with McVey carefully. He was sure it was Kanarack who had killed Jean Packard. The question was: Did the police know? Or, more pointedly, did they know it was Kanarack he had hired the private detective to find? As he had seen, what the police knew and how they knew it were beyond the reach of everyday people, himself included.

Playing a worst-case scenario—that the police knew nothing of Kanarack but suspected Osborn knew more about the private investigator's death than he'd let on— McVey or someone else would be watching the hotel and would follow him the moment he left. The problem was troublesome and he needed to find some way around it.

The elevator stopped and Osborn stepped into the hallway. A few moments later he let himself into his room and closed the door. It was 11:25 in the morning. Four hours before he would leave for the theater.

Tossing the newspaper on the bed, he went into the bathroom and brushed his teeth, then took a shower. It was while he was shaving he decided that the best way to solve his problem was to play the part he wanted the police to expect of him, the saddened lover spending his last day in Paris alone. And the sooner he started, the better the chance to shake anyone following him. And what more advantageous place to begin his lonely journey than the Louvre, with its multitudes of tourists and numerous exits?

Pulling on his raincoat, Osborn snapped off the light and turned for the door. As he did, he saw the darkened image of himself in the mirror and for the briefest instant everything turned inward. That the police might be watching only made what he was doing more difficult. Had Kanarack been caught and tried within a reasonable time, things would have been different. But he hadn't. Nearly thirty years later and a continent away, Kanarack's crime stood as a crime apart, with no law that either could, or would, administer punishment or justice. In the absence of law, all that was left was to make equity as one could. And Osborn hoped that whatever God there was would understand.

Deciding that being on foot gave him more options, Osborn left the rental Peugeot in the hotel garage and asked the doorman to call him a taxi. Five minutes later he was traveling down the Champs Elysées toward the Louvre. He thought he might have seen a dark car pull out from the curb and follow them as the cab had turned out of the hotel drive, but looking back he couldn't be sure.

Moments later the taxi pulled up in front of the Louvre. Paying the driver, Osborn stepped out into a light mist. As the cab pulled away, his immediate sense was to look around for the dark car. But if the police were watching, he dared not clue them in that he knew. Absently putting his hands in his pockets, he waited for traffic to pass, then crossed the rue de Rivoli and went into the museum.

Once inside, he took a solid twenty minutes studying

the works of Giotto, Raphael, Titian and Fra Angelico before leaving the gallery to find a men's room. Five minutes later, he joined a crowd of American tourists about to board a bus for Versailles and went with them out the main entrance. At the curb he left them, walked half a block and entered the Métro.

Within the hour he was back at his hotel, waiting for the Peugeot to be brought up from the garage. If the police had been following him, how could they imagine he was still not in the museum? Nevertheless he watched his mirror carefully as he drove off. To make sure, he turned down one street and, two blocks later, down another. As far as he could tell he was on his own.

Twenty minutes later he parked the Peugeot on a side street a block and a half from the movie theater, locked it and walked off. Taking the Métro back to the hotel, he waited until the attendant who had brought his car up from the garage left the front door to retrieve another car, then slipped inside and went up to his room.

As he came in, he looked at the clock on the bedside table. It was exactly 1:15 in the afternoon. Taking off his raincoat, he looked over at the phone. Earlier that morning he'd picked it up and started to dial the bakery to make certain nothing had gone awry and that Kanarack was at work as he should be. Then he had the thought that if something happened and things went wrong, the call could be traced back to his room. Immediately he'd hung up. Looking at the phone now, he felt the same urgency of wanting to know but decided against it.

Better to trust to the fates that had brought him this far and assume Kanarack would be spending his Friday as he had spent his Thursday and probably every other workday of the past years, quietly doing his job and keeping the lowest profile possible.

And now, Osborn took off the tan chinos and dark

Polo cardigan he had worn to the Louvre and changed into a nondescript pair of faded jeans, with an old sweater pulled over a plaid L.L. Bean flannel shirt. Even as he carefully tied his running shoes and put the dark blue watch cap bought at a surplus store that morning into the side pocket of his jacket, and turned, finally, to prepare the tools of the day, filling three hypodermic syringes with the succinylcholine—even as he did all that, with the clock ticking down to the moment he would leave for the movie theater on boulevard des Italiens, Henri Kanarack was already parking Agnes Demblon's white Citroën less than a half block from his hotel.

32

HAIR COMBED and neatly shaven, Henri Kanarack was dressed in the light blue overalls of an air-conditioning-company repairman. He had no trouble entering the service entrance nor of taking the maintenance elevator to the mechanical room floor. Jean Packard had given him Paul Osborn's name and the name of the hotel where he was staying. He had not had Osborn's room number or he would most certainly have given that up, too. Hotels did not give out room numbers of guests, especially five-star hotels like Osborn's on the avenue Kléber where the clientele was wealthy and international and carefully protected from outsiders who might have a political or personal ax to grind.

Picking up a toolbox from the mechanical room, Kanarack walked down a service corridor and took the fire stairs to the lobby. Pushing through the door, he stopped and looked around. The lobby was small, finished in dark wood and brass, and decorated mostly with antiques. To his left was the entrance to the bar and directly across from it, a small gift shop and a dining room. To the right were the elevators. Opposite them was the front desk, and behind it, a clerk in a dark suit was talking with an extraordinarily tall, black African businessman who was apparently checking in. For Kanarack to get Osborn's room number, he needed to get behind the front desk. Purposefully crossing the lobby, Kanarack approached the clerk and, when he looked up, immediately took the upper hand.

"Air-conditioning repair. Some problem with the electrical system. We're trying to locate the trouble," he said in French.

"I know nothing about it." The clerk was indignant. That haughty, superior attitude was something Kanarack had hated about Parisians from the day he got there, especially when it came from salaried workers who made little more than he did and barely made it from paycheck to paycheck.

"You want me to go, okay. The problem is not mine," Kanarack said with an animated shrug.

Instead of arguing, the clerk dismissed him with a tepid "Do what you have to do," and turned back to the African.

"Thanks," Kanarack said, and walked behind the desk to a position beside the clerk where he could examine a line of electrical switches directly above the master guest register. As he bent over to study them, he could feel the press of the .45 automatic tucked in the waistband under the bulky overalls. The short silencer fitted to the snout pushed against his upper thigh. A full clip in the magazine, a second clip was in his pocket.

"Pardon," he said, picking up the entire guest register and setting it to one side. At the same time the desk telephone rang and the clerk picked up. Quickly Kanarack ran down the register. Under the O's he found what he needed. Paul Osborn was in room 714. Quickly he set the register back in place, picked up his toolbox and walked from behind the desk.

"Thanks," he said again.

McVey stared out the window at the fog, tired and disgusted. The Charles de Gaulle Airport was socked in and all flights had been grounded. He wished he could tell if it was getting darker or lighter outside. If it was going to be socked in all day, he'd grab a nearby hotel room and go to bed. If it wasn't and there was the chance he'd get off, he'd do what everybody else had been doing for the last two hours—wait.

Before he'd left Lebrun's office, he'd put in a call to Benny Grossman at New York Police Department headquarters in Manhattan. Benny was only thirty-five but was as good a homicide detective as McVey had ever worked with. They'd jobbed together twice. Once when Benny had come to L.A. to retrieve an escaped killer from New York, and again when the NYPD asked McVey to come to New York to see if he could figure out something they couldn't. As it turned out, McVey couldn't get to the bottom of it either, but he and Benny had done the fumble work together and afterward had a few drinks and a few laughs. McVey had even gone to Benny's house in Queens for a Passover seder.

Benny had just come in when McVey called and had jumped on the line.

"Oy, McVey!" Benny said, which is what he always said when McVey called, then after some small talk got around to things with "So, boobalah, what can I do for you?" McVey had no idea if he was trying to sound like an old-time Hollywood agent or if he said that to everyone when they got down to business.

"Benny, sweetheart," McVey had quipped, thinking that if Benny was a frustrated agent why not play along, then explaining that he was not in Manhattan or L.A. but sitting in the headquarters of the Paris Préfecture of Police.

"Paris, like in France or Texas?" Benny asked.

"Like in France," McVey replied, and took the phone away from his ear at Benny's extended whistle. Afterward he got down to specifics. McVey needed to know what Benny could come up with on an Albert Merriman who had supposedly bought the farm in a gangland killing in New York in 1967. Since Benny was eight years old in 1967, he'd never heard of Albert Merriman, but he'd find out and call McVey back.

"Let me call you," McVey said, with no idea where he was going to be when Benny retrieved the information.

Four hours later McVey called back.

In the interval since they'd talked Benny had gone to the NYPD Records & Information archives and come up with a solid smattering of information on Albert Merriman. Merriman had been discharged from the U.S. Army in 1963 and very shortly afterward teamed up with an old friend, a convicted bank robber named Willie Leonard who'd just been released from Atlanta. Merriman and Leonard then went on a free-for-all and were wanted for bank robbery, murder, attempted murder and extortion in half-a-dozen states. They were also rumored to have made a few hits for organized crime families in New Jersey and New England.

On December 22, 1967, a body, later identified as Albert Merriman, was found shot to death and burned beyond recognition in a torched-out car in the Bronx.

"Mob job, looks like," Benny said.

"What happened to Willie Leonard?" McVey asked.

"Still wanted," Benny Grossman said.

"How was Merriman's body identified?"

"It's not on the sheet. Maybe you don't know, boobalah, but we don't keep extensive files on dead men. Can't afford the storage space."

"Any idea of who claimed the body?"

"That, I got. Hold on." McVey could hear a rustle of papers as Grossman looked through his notes. "Here it is. Looks like Merriman had no family. The body was claimed by a woman who's down on the sheet as a high-school friend. Agnes Demblon."

"Any address?"

"Nope."

McVey wrote Agnes Demblon's name on the back of his boarding pass envelope and put it in his jacket pocket.

"Any idea where Merriman's buried?"

"Nope again."

"Well, I'll bet you ten dollars to a Diet Coke if you locate the box you'll find it's Willie Leonard in there."

In the distance McVey heard his flight being called. Amazed, he thanked Benny and started to hang up.

"McVey!"

"Yeah."

"The Merriman file. Hasn't been touched in twenty-six years."

"So?"

"I'm the second guy to pull it in twenty-four hours."

"What?"

"A request came yesterday morning from Interpol, Washington. A uniform sergeant in R and I pulled the file and faxed them a copy."

McVey told Grossman Interpol was involved on the Paris end and had to assume that was the reason. Just then a final boarding call came for McVey's plane. Telling Grossman he had to run, he hung up.

A few minutes later, McVey buckled his seat belt and his Air Europe jet backed away from the gate. Glancing again at Agnes Demblon's name on the back of the boarding pass envelope, he let out a sigh and sat back, feeling the bump of the plane as it moved out onto the taxiway.

Glancing out the window, McVey could see a succession of rainclouds rolling across the French countryside. The wet made him think of the red mud on Osborn's shoes. Then they were up and in the clouds.

A flight attendant asked him if he wanted a newspaper and he took it but didn't open it. What caught his eye was the date. Friday, October 7. It was only this morning that Lebrun had been notified by Interpol, Lyon, that the fingerprint had even been made legible. And Lebrun himself had traced it to Albert Merriman while McVey stood there. Yet a request to the New York police for the Merriman file had come from Interpol, Washington, on Thursday. That meant that Interpol, Lyon, had sourced the print, uncovered Merriman and asked for data on him a full day earlier. Maybe that was Interpol procedure, but it seemed a little odd that Lyon would have a complete folder long before giving the investigating officer any information at all. But why did he think it made any difference anyway? Interpol's internal procedure was none of his business. Still, it was something that needed to be brought to light if for no other reason than to relieve his discomfort with it. But before bringing it up either to assignment director Cadoux at Interpol, Lyon, or cluing Lebrun, he'd better have his facts straight. He decided the simplest way was to backtrack from the time of day Thursday the Interpol, Washington, request had been made to the NYPD. For that he'd have to call Benny Grossman when he got to London.

Abruptly bright sunlight hit him in the face and he realized they'd cleared the cloud deck and were moving out over the English Channel. It was the first sun he'd seen in almost a week. He glanced at his watch.

It was 2:40 in the afternoon.

33

FIFTEEN MINUTES later, in Paris, Paul Osborn turned off the television in his hotel room and slipped the three succinylcholine-filled syringes into the righthand pocket of his jacket. He'd just pulled on the jacket and was turning for the door when the phone rang. He jumped, his heart suddenly racing. His reaction made him realize he was even more keyed up than he thought, and he didn't like it.

The phone continued to ring. He looked at his watch. It was 2:57. Who was trying to reach him? The police? No. He'd already called Detective Barras and Barras had assured him his passport would be waiting for him at the Air France counter when he checked in for his flight tomorrow afternoon. Barras had been pleasant, even to joking about the lousy weather, so it wasn't the police, unless they were toying with him or McVey had another question. And right now he had no interest in talking to McVey or anyone else.

Then the phone stopped. Whoever was calling had

hung up. Maybe it was a wrong number. Or Vera. Yes, Vera. He'd planned to call her later, when it was over, but not beforehand when she might hear something in his voice, or for some other reason insist on coming over.

He looked at his watch again. By now it was almost 3:05. *West Side Story* started at 4:00, so he needed to be there by 3:45 at the latest to make himself known to the ticket-taker. And he was going to walk, going out the hotel's side entrance, just in case anyone was watching. Besides, walking would help shake out the cobwebs and ease his nerves.

Turning out the light, he touched his pocket to double-check the syringes, then turned the knob and started to open the door. Suddenly it slammed backward in his face. The force knocked him sideways and into a corner area between the bathroom door and the bedroom. Before he could recover, a man in light blue overalls stepped in from the hallway and closed the door behind him. It was Henri Kanarack. A gun was in hand.

"Say one word and I'll shoot you right there," he said in English.

Osborn had been taken completely by surprise. This close, Kanarack was darker and more solidly built than he remembered. His eyes were fierce, and the gun, like an extension of the man, was pointed straight between his eyes. Osborn had no doubt at all that he'd do exactly as he threatened.

Turning the lock on the door behind him, Kanarack stepped forward. "Who sent you?" he said.

Osborn felt the dryness in his throat and tried to swallow. "Nobody," he said.

The next happened so quickly Osborn had almost no recollection of it. One minute he was standing there, then he was on the floor with his head jammed up against a wall and the barrel of Kanarack's gun pressed up under his nose.

"Who do you work for?" Kanarack said quietly.

"I'm a doctor. I don't work for anybody." Osborn's heart was thundering so wildly he was afraid he might literally have a coronary.

"Doctor?" Kanarack seemed surprised.

"Yes," Osborn said.

"Then what do you want with me?"

A trickle of sweat ran down the side of Osborn's face. The whole thing was a blur and he was having a lot of trouble with reality. Then he heard himself say what he never should have said. "I know who you are."

As he said it, Kanarack's eyes seemed to shift back in his head. The fierceness that was there before became ice, and his finger tightened around the trigger.

"You know what happened to the detective," Kanarack whispered, letting the barrel of the gun slide down until it rested on Osborn's lower lip. "It was on TV and in all the papers."

Osborn quivered uncontrollably. Thinking was hard enough, finding and forming words all but impossible. "Yes, I know," he managed, finally.

"Then you understand I'm not only good at what I do— once I start, I like it." The black dots that were Kanarack's eyes seemed to smile.

Osborn pulled away, his eyes darting around the room, looking for a way out. The window was the only thing. Seven floors up. Then the gun barrel was on his cheek and Kanarack was forcing him to look at him.

"You don't want the window," he said. "Too messy and much too quick. This is going to take a little time. Unless you want to tell me right away who you're working for and where they are. Then it can be over very fast."

"I'm not working for anybo—"

Suddenly the phone rang. Kanarack jumped at the

sound and Osborn was certain he was going to pull the trigger.

It rang three times more, then stopped. Kanarack looked back to Osborn. It was too dangerous here. Even now the front desk clerk might be asking someone about the problem with the air conditioning and learn there was none, that no one had called for a repairman. That would start them wondering and then looking. Maybe even calling security or the police.

"Listen very carefully," he said. "We're going out of here. The more you fight me, the harder it's going to be for you." Kanarack eased back and stood up, then motioned with the gun for Osborn to get up as well.

Osborn had little memory of what happened in the moments immediately following. There was a vague recollection of leaving the hotel room and walking close beside Kanarack to a fire stair, then the sound of their footsteps as they descended. Somewhere a door opened to an inner hallway that led past air-conditioning, heating and electrical units. A short time later, Kanarack opened a steel door and they were outside, climbing concrete steps. Rain was coming down and the air was fresh and crisp. At the top of the steps, they stopped.

Little by little Osborn's senses came back and he was aware they were standing in a narrow alley behind the hotel with Kanarack immediately to his left, his body pressed closely against Osborn's. Then Kanarack started them down the alley and Osborn could feel the hardness of the gun against his rib cage. As they walked, Osborn tried to collect himself, to think what to do next. He'd never been so afraid in his life.

34

A White Citroën was parked on the street at the end of the alley and Osborn heard Kanarack say something about it being their destination.

Then, unexpectedly, a large delivery truck pulled off the street and turned into the alley, coming toward them. If they stayed together as they were, there would be no room for the truck to get by without hitting them. That gave them two choices—separate, or step back against the alley wall and let the truck pass. The truck slowed and the driver gave a toot with his horn.

"Easy," Kanarack said, and pulled Osborn back against the alley wall. The driver shifted gears and the truck started forward again.

As they pressed against the wall, Osborn could feel the gun dig into his left side. That meant Kanarack had the automatic in his right hand and was holding Osborn's arm out of view of the driver with his left. Somehow Osborn managed to calculate that it would take the truck six to eight seconds to get past them. That same clarity of thought made him see an opportunity. The hypodermic syringes were in his right jacket pocket. If he could get one into his right hand while Kanarack was distracted by the passing truck, he'd have a weapon Kanarack wouldn't know about.

Carefully he turned his head to look at Kanarack. The gunman's full attention was on the truck that was almost upon them. Osborn waited, timing his move. Then, just as the truck reached them, he shifted his weight against the gun, as if to press farther back against the alley wall. As he did, he slipped his right hand into his jacket pocket, digging for a syringe. Then, as the truck passed, he took hold of one.

"Okay," Kanarack said. And they moved off toward the end of the alley where the Citroën was parked. As they went, Osborn eased the syringe from his pocket and held it tight against his side.

There were now maybe twenty yards between the two men and the car. Earlier, Osborn had put a rubber nosing over the tip of each syringe to protect the needle. Now his fingers worked feverishly to slide the rubber off without letting go of the entire works.

Suddenly they were at the end of the alley, with the Citroën less than ten feet away. Still the rubber tip hadn't come loose, and Osborn was certain Kanarack would see what he was doing.

"Where are you taking me?" he asked, trying to cover.

"Shut up," Kanarack breathed.

Now they were at the car. Kanarack looked up and down the street, then walked them to the driver's side and pulled open the door. As he did, the rubber tip came free and fell to the ground. Kanarack saw it bounce and glanced at it, puzzled. At the same instant, Osborn jerked hard to the right, wrenched his left arm free of the gun and drove the syringe through the overall material and deep into the flesh at the top of Kanarack's upper right buttock. He needed four full seconds to inject all of the succinylcholine. Kanarack gave him three before he tore loose and tried to bring the gun around. But, by then, Osborn had enough presence of mind to shove the open car door hard at him and Kanarack fell backward, hitting the pavement and dropping the gun.

In an instant he was on his feet, but it was too late; the gun was in Osborn's hand and he froze where he was. Then a taxi screeched around the corner, blasted its horn, swerved around them and sped off. After that there was silence and the two men stood facing each other in the street.

Kanarack's eyes were wide, not with fear but resolve. All the years of wondering if they would ever catch up to him were over. Out of necessity, he'd changed his life and become a different, simpler man. In his own way he was even kind, caring very much for a wife who was now to bear him a child. He'd always hoped that somehow he'd gotten away with it, but in the back of his mind he knew he hadn't. They were too good, too efficient, their network too broad.

Living every day without going crazy at a stranger's glance, a footfall behind him, a knock at the door had been more difficult than he could have imagined. The pain, too, in what he'd had to keep from Michele had kept him nearly at wit's end. He still had the touch, though, as he'd proven with Jean Packard. But this was the end and he knew it. Michele was gone. So was his life. Dying would be easy.

"Do it," he said in a whisper. "Do it now!"

"I don't have to." Osborn lowered the gun and put it in his pocket. By now nearly a full minute had passed since he'd injected the succinylcholine. Kanarack hadn't gotten a full dose, but he'd gotten enough and Osborn could see him beginning to wonder what was wrong. Why it was such a struggle just to breathe or even keep his balance.

"What's the matter with me?" A look of bewilderment settled over his face.

"You'll find out," Osborn said.

35

THE PARIS police had lost Osborn at the Louvre.

Lebrun had gone out on a limb as it was, and by two o'clock had either to create a story justifying new surveillance or pull his men off. As much as he wanted to help McVey, muddy shoes alone did not make a certified felon, especially if that person was an American physician who was leaving Paris the following afternoon and who, politely and forthrightly, had requested the return of his passport from one of his detectives so that he could do so.

Unable to justify the cost of Osborn's further surveillance to his superiors, Lebrun put his men onto some of the other things McVey had suggested, such as going back over Jean Packard's personal history from scratch. In the meantime, he'd had a police sketch artist work with the mug shot of Albert Merriman they received from Interpol, Washington, and now she was standing behind his desk, looking over his shoulder, as he studied her work.

"This is what you think he would look like twenty-six years later," Lebrun said rhetorically in French. Then looked up at her. She was twenty-five and had a chubby, twinkling smile.

"Yes."

Lebrun wasn't sure. "You should run this by the forensic anthropologist. He might give you a little clearer sense of how this man would age."

"I did, Inspector."

"And this is him?"

"Yes."

"Thanks," Lebrun said. The artist nodded and left. Lebrun looked at the sketch. Thinking a moment, he reached for the phone and called the police press liaison. If this was as close as they were going to get to what Merriman would look like now, why not run the sketch in the first editions of tomorrow's newspapers as McVey had run the sketch of the beheaded man's face in the British papers? There were almost nine million people in Paris, it would only take one of them to recognize Merriman and call the police.

At that same moment Albert Merriman was lying face up on the backseat of Agnes Demblon's Citroën, fighting with everything he had just to breathe.

Behind the wheel, Paul Osborn downshifted, braked hard, then accelerated past a silver Range Rover, clearing the traffic circling the Arc de Triomphe and turning down the avenue de Wagram. A short time later he made a right on the boulevard de Courcelles and headed for avenue de Clichy and the river road that would lead to the secluded park along the Seine.

It had taken him nearly three minutes to get the faltering, frightened Kanarack into the Citroën's backseat, find the keys and then start the car. Three minutes had been too much time. Osborn knew he would barely be under way when the effects of the succinylcholine would begin to wear off. Once they did, he'd have to deal with a fully aroused Kanarack who would have the advantage of being in the backseat behind him. His only recourse had been to give the Frenchman a second shot of the drug, and the effect of the two shots, one coming so quickly on top of the other, had put Kanarack out like a light. For a time Osborn feared it might have been too much, that Kanarack's lungs would cease to function and he'd suffocate. But then a hoarse cough had been followed by the sound of heavily labored breathing and he knew he was all right.

The problem was that now he had only one syringe left. If something went wrong with the car or if they were delayed in traffic, that syringe would be his last line of defense. After that he'd be on his own.

By now it was nearly 4:15 and the rain was coming down heavier. The windshield began to fog and Osborn fumbled for the defroster. Finding it, he clicked on the fan and reached up to clear the inside of the windshield with his hand. This was one day he was certain no one would be in the park. The weather, at least, was something he could be thankful for.

Glancing over his shoulder, he looked at Kanarack on the backseat. Every expansion and contraction of his lungs was a supreme effort. And Osborn could tell from the look in his eyes the horror he was going through, wondering, with each breath, if he'd have the strength for the next.

Ahead, a traffic light changed from yellow to red and Osborn stopped behind a black Ferrari. Once more he glanced over his shoulder at Kanarack. At this moment he had no idea how he felt. Incredibly, what should have felt a monumental triumph no longer did. In its place was a helpless human being, frightened beyond all measure, with absolutely no idea what was happening to him, battling with everything in him for no more than the air to keep him alive. That the creature was innately evil, had caused the deaths of two people and horribly and inexorably gnarled Paul Osborn's own life from childhood on, seemed, at this point, to have little meaning. It was enough to have gotten the beast this far. For Osborn to go through with the rest would make him the equal of Kanarack, and that was someone he was not. And if that was all, he might have stopped the car right there and simply walked away, thereby giving Kanarack back his life. But it wasn't all. The other thing had yet to be addressed.

The WHY of it. *Why* Kanarack had murdered his father!

Ahead of him, the light changed to green and traffic moved off. It was getting darker by the moment and motorists were switching on their yellow headlights. Directly ahead was avenue de Clichy. Reaching it, Osborn turned left and headed toward the river road.

Less than a half mile behind him, a new, dark green Ford pulled out in traffic and speeded up to pass. Turning onto avenue de Clichy, it changed quickly into the right lane and slowed, staying three cars behind Osborn's Citroën. The driver was a tall man with blue eyes and a pale complexion. Light blond eyebrows matched his hair and the hair on the backs of his hands. He was wearing a tan raincoat over a dull plaid sport coat, dark gray slacks and a gray turtleneck sweater. On the seat beside him was a small-brimmed hat, a hard-shell briefcase, and a street map of Paris that had been folded back. His name was Bernhard Oven and today was his forty-second birthday.

36

"CAN YOU hear me?" Osborn said, as he turned the Citroën northeast along the river road. The rain was coming down harder than before and the wipers beat a steady rhythm across the windshield. To his left, the Seine was just visible through the dark of the trees that lined the road. Little more than a mile ahead was the turnoff to the park.

"Can you hear me?" Osborn repeated, glancing first into the rearview mirror, then turning so that he could look into the backseat.

Kanarack lay staring at the car's ceiling, his breathing becoming more regular.

"Uh huh," he grunted.

Osborn looked back to the road ahead. "You asked me if I knew what happened to Jean Packard. I said yes. Maybe you'd like to know what happened to you. You were injected with a drug called succinylcholine. It paralyzes the skeletal muscles. I gave you just enough for you to understand what it does to the human body. I have another syringe filled with a much larger dose. Whether I inject you with it or not is up to you."

Kanarack's eyes focused on a button in the Citroën's ceiling upholstery. The act of doing it made him think about something other than the possibility of having to endure again what he had just gone through. To do it another time was impossible.

"My name is Paul Osborn. Tuesday, April 12, 1966, I was walking down a street in Boston, Massachusetts, with my father, George Osborn. I was ten years old. We were on our way to buy me a new baseball mitt when a man stepped out of a crowd with a knife and pushed it into my father's stomach. The man ran away. But my father fell down on the sidewalk and died. I'd like you to tell me why that man did what he did to my father."

"God!" Kanarack thought. "That's what this is about. It's not them at all! I could have taken care of it so damn simply. It could all be over."

"I'm waiting," the voice said from the front seat. Suddenly Kanarack felt the car slow. Outside he caught a glimpse of trees; the car turned and there was a jolt as they hit a pothole. Then they accelerated again and more trees flashed by. Another minute and they lurched to a stop and he heard Osborn shift gears. Immediately the Citroën backed up, then tilted sharply and continued downward. A few seconds more and it leveled off, then stopped.

Lack of motion was followed by a metallic sound as the emergency brake was pulled up. Then the driver's door opened and closed. Abruptly the door beside Kanarack's head jerked open and Osborn stood there, a hypodermic syringe in his hand.

"I asked you a question but I didn't get an answer," he said.

Kanarack's lungs were still burning. Even the slightest breath was agony.

"Let me help you understand." Osborn stood aside. Kanarack didn't move.

"I want you to look over *there!*" Suddenly Osborn grabbed Kanarack's hair and jerked his head hard to the left so that he could see over his shoulder. Osborn was trying to control his anger but it wasn't working very well. Slowly Kanarack shifted his gaze, straining to see into the growing darkness past Osborn. Then the river came into focus not ten yards away.

"If you think you just went through hell," Osborn said softly, "imagine what it will be like out there, with your arms and legs paralyzed. You'll stay afloat for what, maybe ten, fifteen seconds? Your lungs barely work anyway. What do you think will happen when you sink?"

Kanarack's mind flashed to Jean Packard. The private detective had been in possession of information he wanted and he had done whatever had been necessary to obtain it. Now someone was equally passionate about getting information from him. And he, like Jean Packard, had no alternative but to give it.

"I—was—a—contract—man." Kanarack's voice was no more than a raspy whisper.

For a moment Osborn wasn't certain he'd heard correctly. Either that, or Kanarack was fooling with him. Tightening his grip on Kanarack's hair, he jerked it back hard. Kanarack cried out. The effort made him suck in his lungs. Terrible pain shot through him and he cried out a second time.

"Let's try it again." Osborn's face was next to his

"I was paid to do it . . . Money!" Kanarack coughed. The expelled air seared like flame across his dry throat.

"Paid?" Osborn was shocked. That wasn't what he'd expected, nothing of the kind! He'd always seen his father's death as the random action of a crazed man. And lacking any other motive, so had the police. It was an act, they had said, done by a man who had hated his own father, or his mother, his brothers or his sisters. Done, he'd always believed, as an expression of unbearable anger and long pent-up fury, randomly and mindlessly unleashed. His father had merely been at the wrong place at the wrong time.

But no, Kanarack was telling him something altogether different. Something that made no sense. His father was a tool designer. A plain, quiet man who owed no one a penny, and had never raised his voice in anger in his life. Hardly the kind of man someone would pay to have killed. Suddenly it came to him that Kanarack was lying.

"Tell me the truth! You lying son of a bitch!" In a thundering rage Osborn dragged Kanarack from the car by the hair. Kanarack screamed in agony, the sound tearing against his throat and down into his lungs. A moment later they were knee-deep in the river. The syringe came up in Osborn's hand, then suddenly he pushed Kanarack under. Holding him there, he counted to ten, then pulled him up.

"Tell me the truth, God damn you!"

Kanarack, coughing and gagging, was aghast. Why didn't this man believe him? Kill him, for God's sake, but not like this!

"I am——" he rasped. "Your father—three others—too—in Wyoming—New Jersey—one in California. All for the same people. Then, afterward—they tried—to—kill me."

"What people? What the hell are you talking about?"

"You won't believe me——" Kanarack gagged, trying to spit out river water.

The current swirled around them and the rain came down in sheets, the growing darkness making it all but impossible to see. Osborn tightened his grip on Kanarack's collar and brought the syringe up directly in front of his eyes. "Try me," he said.

Kanarack shook his head.

"Tell me!" Osborn yelled, and dunked Kanarack again. Bringing him up, he tore open Kanarack's overalls and pressed the tip of the syringe against his bicep.

"Once more," Osborn whispered. "The truth."

"God! Don't!" Kanarack pleaded. "Please . . ."

Suddenly Osborn eased off. Whatever it was he saw in Kanarack's eyes told him Kanarack was telling the truth, that no man would lie in that situation.

"Give me a name," Osborn said. "Somebody who made the contact with you. Gave you the assignments."

"Scholl—Erwin Scholl. Erwin, with an E." Kanarack could see Scholl's face. A tall, athletic man in tennis clothes. Kanarack had been sent to an estate on Long Island in 1966, recommended for the job by a retired colonel in the United States Army. Scholl had been pleasant enough. It was a handshake deal. Each hit worth twenty-five thousand dollars in cash. Fifty percent down, report back to Scholl for the rest when finished. After the killings, he'd come back to collect his money and

Scholl had paid him the money due, had graciously thanked him and shown him out. Then, only moments later, on the way back into the city, Kanarack's car had been forced off the road by a limousine. Two men got out with automatic weapons. As they approached, Kanarack shot them both with a handgun and got away. After that, they tried three times in rapid succession to hit him: his apartment, a restaurant and on the street. On each occasion he'd eluded them but they always seemed to know where he was or would be, which meant it was only a matter of time before they got him. So with Agnes Demblon's help, he took things into his own hands. Killing his partner, he burned the body in his own car to make it look as if he'd been killed in a gangland execution. Then, he vanished.

"Erwin Scholl of *where*?" Osborn was holding Kanarack only inches above the rushing water. Demanding he verify what he had said.

"Long Island—big estate on Westhampton Beach," Kanarack said.

"Jesus Christ, you son of a bitch!" There were tears in Osborn's eyes. He was totally thrown off-balance. Kanarack had been no wild, demented man who had slain his father out of sheer malice. He'd been a professional killer, doing a job. Suddenly his murder had been depersonalized. Human emotions had had nothing to do with it. It had been nothing more than a business transaction.

And just as suddenly there it was again. The monstrous WHY? Then it came. It was a mistake. That was it. It had to have been. Osborn tightened his grip. "You're saying you got the wrong man, is that it? You took my father for someone else—"

Kanarack shook his head. "No. He was the one. The others too."

Osborn stared at him. It was crazy! Impossible! "Jesus Christ!" he screamed. "*Why*?"

Kanarack was looking up from the rush of water around him. His breathing was easier, the feeling in his arms and legs coming back. The needle was still in Osborn's hand. Maybe he still had a chance. Then Osborn suddenly looked off, as if something had startled him. Kanarack followed his gaze. A tall man in a raincoat and hat was coming down the ramp toward where they were. Something was in his hand. He raised it.

A split second later there was a sound like a dozen woodpeckers all hammering at once. Suddenly the water was boiling up all around them. Osborn felt something slap into his thigh and he fell backward. Still the water kept churning. He tried to raise up and saw the man in the hat wade out into the water, the thing in his hand still tap-tap-tapping.

Twisting away, Osborn dove down and swam off. Little noises, like pellets, slapped the water above. Under the water, what little light there was vanished and Osborn had no idea which direction he was going. Something bumped up against him, and seemed to hang there. Then the current caught him and whatever it was hanging with him and swept them away. Osborn's lungs were bursting for air, but the force of the current was sweeping him down toward the river bottom. Once again he felt the thing bump him and he realized he was entangled with it. Reaching across, he tried to free himself from it. It was bulky, like a grassy log, and seemed stuck to him. His lungs felt as if they were collapsing inward. He had to have air. Whatever it was he was entangled with, he had to ignore, and do nothing but fight his way to the surface. Giving an enormous kick, he swept his arms back and swam upward.

A moment later he broke free of the surface. Gasping, he gulped fresh air furiously into his lungs. At almost the same time he realized he was moving at considerable speed. Looking around, he could just make out the riverbank on the far shore. Turning back, he could see the headlights of cars moving along the river road behind him and he realized he was in midriver, being swept along by the Seine's swift current.

Whatever had been caught up with him had come loose when he broke the surface, or at least he thought it had, because he no longer felt it. He was riding free with the current when suddenly it bumped into him once more. Turning, he saw a dark object with a grassy clump at the end nearest him. He started to push it away. As he did a human hand came from beneath the surface and clenched onto his arm. Crying out in horror, he tried to wrench free. But the hand held him firmly in its grip. Then he saw that what he'd taken for grass wasn't grass at all, but human hair. In the distance he heard the rumble of thunder. Suddenly the rain came down in torrents. Reaching out, wildly trying to pry the fingers from his arm, the whole thing bobbed up, and rolled sideways at him. Screaming, he tried to shove it away. But it wouldn't go. Then lightning flashed and he found himself staring at a bloody eye socket hideously impaled with pieces of shattered teeth. On the other side was no eye at all, just a mangle of flesh where the face had been shot away. A moment later the thing lurched upward and gave a loud groan. Then the hand ever so gently let go of his arm, and what was left of Henri Kanarack floated off with the current.

As Henri Kanarack, or Albert Merriman, who he really was, had looked past Paul Osborn's shoulder and seen the tall man in the raincoat and hat coming down the ramp toward them, he thought there was something familiar about him, that he had seen him somewhere before. And then he remembered him as the man who had come into Le Bois the night after he'd killed Jean Packard. He recalled seeing him standing in the doorway and looking around, his eyes sweeping the terrace. Then remembered him turning toward the bar, where Kanarack was sitting, and their eyes making contact. He remembered being relieved the man was not Osborn, or the police. He remembered thinking the man was nobody, nobody at all.

He'd been wrong.

37

Friday, October 7.
New Mexico.

AT 1:55 in the afternoon, 8:55 in the evening, Paris time, Elton Lybarger sat in a lounge chair with a deck robe over him, watching the shadows cast by New Mexico's towering Sangre de Cristo mountains begin to inch across the valley floor a thousand feet below him. He was wearing Bass Weejuns, tan slacks and a royal blue sweater. A small yellow headset was connected to a Sony Walkman in his lap. He was fifty-six years old and listening to the collected speeches of Ronald Reagan.

Elton Lybarger had come to the exclusive Rancho de Piñon nursing home from San Francisco on May 3, seven months after suffering a massive stroke while on a business trip to the United States from his native Switzerland. The stroke had left him partially paralyzed and unable to speak. Now, nearly a year later, he could walk with aid of a cane and speak, if slowly, without slurring.

Six miles away, a silver Volvo turned out of the bright

high desert sunlight and into the deep shadows of the conifer-lined Paseo del Norte Road leading up from the valley to Rancho de Piñon. Behind the wheel was Joanna Marsh, a plain, somewhat overweight, thirty-two-year-old physical therapist who, for the last five months, had made the two-hour round trip from her Taos home five times a week. This would be her last visit to Elton Lybarger at Rancho de Piñon. Today they would drive to Santa Fe, where a chartered helicopter was waiting to take them to Albuquerque. Then, flying to Chicago, they would board American Airlines flight 38 for Zurich. Tonight, accompanied by Joanna Marsh, R.P.T., Elton Lybarger was going home.

Goodbyes were said, the car door closed and with a wave to the security guard at the entrance, Joanna maneuvered the Volvo through the gates of Rancho de Piñon and out onto Paseo del Norte Road.

Looking over, Joanna saw Lybarger staring out at the passing countryside smiling. For as long as she'd known him, she'd never seen him smile.

"Do you know where we're going, Mr. Lybarger?" she asked. Lybarger nodded.

"Where?" she teased him.

Lybarger didn't reply, just continued to stare out at the land as they descended the steep and twisting road that cut, knifelike, through the rich conifer forest.

"Come on, Mr. Lybarger. Where are we going?" Joanna wasn't sure if he'd heard her the first time, or if he'd heard and it hadn't sunk in. As well as he'd recovered from the stroke, there were still times when it seemed he didn't connect with what was being said to him.

Shifting his weight just a little, Lybarger sat forward and put out his hand against the dashboard to balance himself as the Volvo leaned through a series of turns. Still he didn't reply.

At the bottom of the canyon, Joanna turned onto New Mexico Highway 3 toward Taos. Adjusting the cruise control to sixty-five, she waved to a group of brightly clad bicycle racers.

"Friends of mine from Taos," she said with a smile, then glanced over to Lybarger, thinking maybe his silence was due to the emotion of his sudden freedom.

He was sitting forward, his weight against his seat belt, staring at her in a way that made it seem as if he'd suddenly come out of a long sleep and was totally bewildered.

"Are you all right?" she asked, suddenly flashing with the horror that maybe he was having another stroke and that she should turn around immediately and go back to the nursing home.

"Yes," he answered quietly.

Joanna judged him for a moment, then relaxed and smiled. "Why don't you sit back and rest, Mr. Lybarger. We have a long afternoon and night ahead of us."

Lybarger responded by sitting back, but then he turned and looked at her again. His puzzled expression remained.

"Is there something the matter, Mr. Lybarger?"

"Where is my family?" he asked.

"Where is my family?" Lybarger asked again.

"I'm sure they'll be there to meet you." Joanna lay back against her pillow in the first-class section and closed her eyes. They had been in the air less than three hours, and Lybarger had asked the same question, by her calculation, eleven times. She wasn't sure if it was a lingering effect of the stroke that kept him asking it over and over, or if he suddenly felt displaced at being away from Rancho de Piñon, and the family he was referring to were the staff he'd spent so much time with there, or if it was genuine concern that someone might not be waiting in Zurich to meet him when he arrived.

The truth was, in the entire time she had been treating him, not once, as far as she knew, had anyone besides his personal physician, an elderly Austrian doctor named Salettl who had made the trip from Salzburg to New Mexico six times, come to see him. So she had no idea whether or not he would have family waiting for him at Zurich airport when they got there. She could only assume he would. But other than Salettl, the only personal contact she'd had with anyone representing Lybarger's interests was when his attorney had called her at home to request she accompany Lybarger to Switzerland.

That, in itself, had been a complete surprise and had caught her totally off-guard. Joanna had rarely been outside New Mexico, let alone the United States, and the offer, first-class round-trip air fare and five thousand dollars, had been too generous to pass up. It would pay off the loan on the Volvo and, even though it was only for a short time, it would be an experience she would probably never otherwise have. But more than that, she'd been happy to do it. Joanna prided herself in taking special interest in all her patients, and Mr. Lybarger was no exception. When she started, he'd barely been able to stand, and all he'd wanted to do was listen to tapes on his Walkman or watch television. Now, though he still listened to his tapes and watched TV voraciously, he could easily walk a half mile with his cane, alone and unaided.

Coming out of her reverie, Joanna realized the cabin was dark and that most people were sleeping, even though a movie was playing on the screen in front of them. For the first time in a long time, Elton Lybarger was silent and she thought he might be sleeping as well. Then she realized he wasn't. The airline headset covered his ears and he was fully engrossed in the movie. Movies, television, audio tapes, trash to classics, sports to politics, opera to rock 'n' roll, Lybarger seemed to have an insatiable appetite either to learn or to be entertained, or both. What so intrigued him was beyond her. All she could imagine was that it was some kind of escape. From what, or to what, she had no idea.

Pulling the airline blanket up around him, Joanna settled back. Her one regret was that she'd had to put Henry, her ten-month-old Saint Bernard, in a kennel while she was away. Living alone, she had no one to take care of him, and asking friends to take in a hundred-pound bundle of ceaseless enthusiasm was beyond the name of decency. But, she would only be away for five days, and for five days, Henry could manage.

38

VERA HAD tried unsuccessfully to reach Paul Osborn since nearly three o'clock in the afternoon. She'd called four times without response. The fifth time, she called the hotel desk and asked if by some chance Mr. Osborn had checked out. He had not. Did anyone remember seeing him that day? The clerk put her through to the concierge desk, where she asked the same question. An assistant to the concierge volunteered that he'd last seen Mr. Osborn earlier that afternoon when he passed through the lobby to the elevators, presumably on his way to his room.

It was then a concern that Vera had been consciously keeping in the back of her mind became a distinct fear.

"I've rung his room several times since midafternoon with no response. Would you please send someone up to make certain he's all right?" she asked deliberately. She'd tried not to think about the succinylcholine, or Osborn's intended experiments with it, because she knew he was a very competent physician who understood precisely what he was doing and why. But anyone could make a mistake, and a drug like succinylcholine was nothing to fool with. An accidental overdose and a person would suffocate very quickly.

Hanging up, Vera looked at the clock. It was 6:45 in the evening.

Ten minutes later her phone rang. It was the hotel concierge calling back to report that Mr. Osborn was not in his room. There was a hesitancy in his voice and then he asked if she were a relative. Vera felt her pulse quicken.

"I'm a close friend. What's wrong?" she asked.

"There seems to . . . ," the concierge said haltingly. He was looking for the right word. ". . . have been some—'difficulty'—in Monsieur Osborn's room. Some of the furniture and furnishings have been abused."

"Abused? Difficulty? What are you talking about?"

"Mademoiselle, if I could please have your full name. The police have been called; they may want to question you."

Inspectors Barras and Maitrot of the First Paris Préfecture of Police had taken the call when hotel management reported that evidence of a physical disturbance had been discovered in the room of a hotel guest, an American doctor by the name of Paul Osborn. Neither knew what to make of it. The inside doorjamb to Osborn's room had been torn from the wall, apparently by someone breaking in from the hallway outside. The room itself was in wild disarray. The big double bed was shoved hard to one side, a table had been knocked over. A nearly empty bottle of Johnnie Walker Black was on the floor beside it, amazingly still intact. A bedside lamp hung precariously inches above the floor, having been knocked off the bed table but stopped short by its cord just before it hit the floor.

Osborn's clothes were still in the room, as were his toiletries and his briefcase containing his professional papers, traveler's checks, plane ticket and a hotel notepad with several telephone numbers written on it. On the floor under the television was a copy of today's newspaper open to the entertainment page with the name of a movie theater on the boulevard des Italiens circled in ink.

Barras sat down with the notepad and looked at the phone numbers. One he recognized immediately. It was his own at headquarters. Another was for Air France. Another for a car rental agency. There were four other numbers that had to be traced. The first was to Kolb International, the private investigation firm. The second was for an English-language movie theater on boulevard des Italiens, the same one that was circled in the newspaper. The third was for a private apartment on Île St.-Louis and listed as belonging to a V. Monneray, the same name and number provided by the hotel concierge. The last number was that of a small bakery in the section of Paris near the Gare du Nord.

"Know what this is?" Barras looked up. Maitrot had just come in from the bathroom and was holding a small prescription bottle between the thumb and forefinger of his left hand. Even though there was no evidence a felony had taken place in the room, the room belonged to Paul Osborn and there was enough disarray to evoke suspicion on the part of investigating officers. As a result, both men were wearing disposable surgical rubber gloves to avoid disturbing fingerprints or adding their own physical body presence to whatever was already there.

Taking the bottle from Maitrot, Barras looked at it carefully. "Succinylcholine chloride," he said, reading the label. Handing it back, he shook his head. "No idea. Local prescription, though. Check it out."

Just then a uniformed patrolman showed the hotel concierge into the room. Vera was with him.

"Messieurs. This is the young lady who placed the call."

Darkness and wet was all Paul Osborn knew. He was lying somewhere facedown in a spongy sand. Where he was or even what time it was, he had no idea. Somewhere nearby he heard the rush of water and was thankful he was no longer in it. Exhausted, he felt sleep begin to descend and with it came a darkness blacker than that around him and it came to him that it was death and if he didn't do something quickly he would die.

Picking his head up, he cried out for help. But there was only silence and the rushing water. Who would have heard him anyway in the pitch-black and in the middle of God knew where? But the fear of death and the effort of calling out had picked up his heart rate and sharpened his senses. For the first time he felt pain, a deep throbbing toward the back of his left thigh. Reaching down, he touched it lightly and felt the warm stick of blood.

"Damn," he cursed hoarsely.

Pulling himself up on his elbows, he tried to ascertain where he was. The ground beneath him was soft, moss on top of mushy sand. Putting out his left hand, he touched water. Shifting to his right, he was surprised to find something that felt like a fallen tree only inches from his face. Somehow he'd come ashore, either under his own power or pushed there by the current. His mind flashed to the horrid sight of Kanarack's mutilated body clinging to him in midriver, then being rushed off by the force of the water. As quickly he thought of the man on the embankment. The tall man in the hat who had obviously shot them both.

Suddenly it occurred to him that he might have somehow followed him and be waiting close by for daylight to finish what he had started. Osborn had no way of knowing how badly wounded he was, how much blood he'd lost or if he could even stand. But he had to try. He couldn't stay where he was even if the tall man was near, because if he did there was every chance he would bleed to death.

Inching forward, he reached for the fallen tree. Grasping it with one hand, he pulled himself toward it. As he did, searing pain stabbed through him and he cried out without thinking. Recovering, he lay still, his senses alert. If the tall man were near, Osborn's cry would bring him straight toward him. Holding his breath, he listened but heard only the moving river.

Unbuckling his belt, he pulled it from his waist, looped it around his left thigh above the wound, and buckled it. Then, finding a stick, he put it through the belt and twisted it several times until the strap tightened around his leg in a tourniquet. Nearly a minute passed before he could begin to feel the numbness. As it did, the pain eased a little. Holding the tourniquet tight with his left hand, Osborn pulled against the tree with his right. Struggling, he got his good leg under him and in a minute he was standing. Again, he listened. Again, he heard nothing but the rushing water.

Reaching out in the darkness, he found a dead branch the width of his wrist and broke it off. As he did, he felt a weight in his jacket pocket. Balancing himself against the tree, he reached in and felt his fingers close around the hard steel of the automatic he'd taken from Henri Kanarack. He'd forgotten about it and was amazed it hadn't come loose on his journey downriver. He had no idea if it would work or not. Still, just pointing it would give him advantage over most men. It might even give him a moment against the tall man. Picking up the tree branch, he used it as half crutch, half cane, and started off in the darkness, away from the sound of the river.

39

Saturday, October 8, 3:15 A.M.

AGNES DEMBLON sat in the living room of her apartment working on her second pack of Gitanes since midnight and staring at the telephone. She still wore the same wrinkled suit she'd worn at the office all day Friday. She hadn't eaten or even brushed her teeth. By now, Henri should have been back or at least called. Somehow she should have heard from him. But she hadn't. Something had gone wrong, she was sure. What, though? Even if the American had been a professional, Kanarack would have handled him with the same efficiency he had Jean Packard.

How many years had it been since he'd first pulled her hair and lifted up her skirt in front of everyone in the play yard of the Second Street School in Bridgeport, Connecticut. Agnes had been in the first grade and Henri Kanarack—no, Albert Merriman!—in the fourth grade when it had happened. He'd done it and laughed and then swaggered off with his friends to tease a fat boy and punch him and make him cry. That same afternoon Agnes got even. Following him home from school, she sneaked up behind him when he'd stopped to look at something. Stretching to her full height with both hands over her head, she brought a huge rock down on the top of his head. She remembered him hitting the pavement, with blood everywhere. She remembered actually thinking she'd killed him, until he suddenly reached out and tried to grab her ankle and she ran off. It had been the beginning of a relationship that had lasted more than forty years. How was it the same kind of people always sought each other out, even from the beginning.

Agnes stood up and rubbed out a Gitane in an overflowing ashtray. It was now 3:30 in the morning. Saturdays the bakery was open a half day. In less than two hours she would have to leave for work. Then she remembered Henri had her car. That meant taking the Métro, if it was open that early. She didn't know. It had been that long since she'd last done that.

Thinking she might have to call a taxi, she went into her room, took off her clothes and put on her robe. Then, setting her alarm for 4:45, she lay down on the bed. Pulling the top blanket over her, she turned out the light and lay back. If she could sleep, seventy-five minutes would be better than nothing.

Across the street, Bernhard Oven, the tall man, sat behind the wheel of a dark green Ford and looked at his watch. 3:37 A.M.

On the seat beside him was a small black rectangle that looked like the remote control to a television set. In the upper lefthand corner was a digital timer. Picking it up, he set the timer at three minutes, thirty-three seconds. Then, starting the Ford's engine, he pushed a small red button at the bottom right of the black rectangle. The timer activated and began counting down in tenths of seconds toward 0:0:00.

Glancing across at the darkened apartment building once more, Bernhard Oven put the car in gear and drove off.

3:32:16.

Strung across the cluttered floor in the basement of Agnes Demblon's apartment building were seven very small bundles of highly compact, incendiary plastic attached to a primary electronic fuse. At a little past 2:00 A.M., Oven had broken in through a cellar window. Working quickly, in less than five minutes he had placed the charges among stacks of old furniture and stored clothes and paid special attention to the thousand-gallon drum that held the building's heating oil. Afterward he slipped out the way he had come in and went back to his car. By 2:40 all the building's lights were out but one. At 3:35, Agnes Demblon turned hers out as well.

At 3:39 and thirty seconds the plastic charges went off.

40

AMERICAN AIRLINES Flight 38 from Chicago to Zurich touched down at Kloten Airport at 8:35 A.M., twenty minutes ahead of schedule. The airline had provided a wheelchair, but Elton Lybarger wanted to walk off the plane. He was going to see the family he hadn't seen in the year since he'd had his stroke and he wanted them to see a man rehabilitated, not a cripple who would be a burden to them.

Joanna collected their carry-on luggage and stood up behind Lybarger as the last of the passengers left the aircraft. Then, handing him his cane, she warned him to be careful of his footing and abruptly he stepped off.

Reaching the jetway, he ignored the flight attendant's smile and well-wish and firmly planted his cane on the far side of the aircraft door. Taking a determined breath, he stepped through it, entered the jetway and disappeared into it.

"He's a little anxious, but thank you anyway," Joanna said apologetically in passing as she moved to catch up with him.

Once inside the terminal, they waited in line to pass through Swiss Customs. When they had, Joanna found a cart and retrieved their luggage and they went down a corridor toward Immigration. Suddenly she wondered what they would do if there was no one there to meet them. She had no idea where Elton Lybarger lived or whom to call. Then they were out of Immigration and pushing through a glass door into the main terminal area. Abruptly a six-piece oompah band struck up a Swiss version of "For He's a Jolly Good Fellow," and twenty or more exceptionally well-dressed men and women applauded. Behind them, four men in chauffeur livery joined in the applause.

Lybarger stopped and stared. Joanna had no idea if he recognized them or not. Then a large woman in a fur coat and veil, carrying a huge bouquet of yellow roses, rushed forward and threw her arms around Lybarger, smothering him in kisses and saying, "Uncle. Oh, Uncle! How we've missed you! Welcome home."

As quickly the others moved in, surrounding Lybarger and leaving Joanna all but forgotten. The whole thing puzzled her. In five months of intensive physical therapy, Elton Lybarger had never once given her any indication of the wealth or position he seemed to have. Where had this entourage been the entire time? It didn't make sense. But then, it was none of her business.

"Miss Marsh?" An extremely good-looking man had left the crowd to approach her.

"My name is Von Holden. I am an employee of Mr. Lybarger's company. May I escort you to your hotel?"

Von Holden was in his thirties, trim and nearly six feet tall, with shoulders that looked like a swimmer's. He had light brown, close-cropped hair and wore an impeccably tailored, double-breasted navy pin-striped suit with a white shirt and dark crested tie.

Joanna smiled. "Thank you very much." Looking toward the crowd, she saw that someone had brought up a wheelchair and two of the chauffeurs were helping Lybarger into it. "I should say something to Mr. Lybarger."

"He'll understand, I'm sure," Von Holden said pleasantly. "Besides, you'll be joining him for dinner. Now, if you will—this way, please."

Taking Joanna's luggage, Von Holden led the way through a side door to a waiting elevator. Five minutes later they were in the backseat of a Mercedes limousine driving along highway N1B heading toward Zurich.

Joanna had never seen such green before. Trees and meadows everywhere were rich emerald. And beyond them, like ghosts on the horizon, were the Alps, even this early in the season capped with snow. Her New Mexico was a desert land that, despite high-rise cities and shopping malls, was still new and raw, and boiling with the restlessness of the frontier. Coyote, mountain lion and rattlesnake owned the land, and its deserts and canyons still housed men who chose to live alone. Its mountains and high meadows, lush with wildflowers at spring run-off, were, at this time of year, brown and dusty and dry as tinder.

Switzerland was entirely different. Joanna had seen it out the window as they'd flown in and could feel it all the more now as the limousine brought them into Zurich through the Old Town. Here was a place rich with the history of the Romans and Hapsburgs. A world of medieval alleys towered over by gray stone buildings of pre-Gothic architecture that had existed centuries before a single coal oil lamp shone in a New Mexico shanty.

In her mind Joanna had projected what it would be like when she got here. A small but compassionate and loving family waiting to greet Elton Lybarger. A hug goodbye from him, maybe even a kiss on the cheek. Then a pleasant room in a Holiday Inn–like place. And maybe a sightseeing tour of the city before her return trip the following day. The time would be short, but she'd do the best with it she could. And mustn't forget souvenirs! For her friends in Taos and for David, the speech therapist from Santa Fe she'd been seeing for two years but with whom she had never slept.

"You've never been to our country." Von Holden was looking at her, smiling.

"No, never."

"After you are checked into your hotel room, if you will permit me, I will show you some little of our country before dinner," Von Holden said, graciously. "Unless of course, you prefer not."

"No. Please. That would be terrific. I mean, I'd love to."

"Good."

The limousine turned left, down Bahnhofstrasse, and they passed block after block of elegant shops and exclusive cafés that increasingly broadcast an atmosphere of great and understated wealth. At the far end of Bahnhofstrasse glimmered a vast turquoise waterway—"The Zurichsee," Von Holden said—churning with lake steamers that left long ribbons of sunlit white foam in their wake.

Magic settled over Joanna like pixie dust. Switzerland,

she could tell everyone, was lush and genteel and permanent. Everything about it felt warm and hospitable and very, very safe. Besides, it reeked of money.

Abruptly she turned to Von Holden. "Do you have a first name?"

"Pascal."

"Pascal?" She'd never heard the name. "Is it Spanish or Italian?"

Shrugging, Von Holden grinned. "Both, either, neither," he said. "I was born in Argentina."

41

OSBORN STARED at the telephone and wondered if he had the strength to try it again. He'd already made three attempts without success. He doubted he could make three more.

Coming out of the woods at dawn he'd found himself in what he thought, in the early light, to be farmland. Nearby was a small shack that was locked but had a water connection outside. Turning the spigot, he drank deeply. Then, tearing back his trousers, he washed as much of the wound as he could. Most of the external bleeding had stopped and he'd been able to release the tourniquet without its starting again.

After that he must have passed out, because the next he knew two young men carrying golf clubs were looking down at him, asking him in French if he was all right. What he'd thought was farmland turned out to be a golf course.

Now he sat in the clubhouse, staring at the telephone on the wall. Vera was all he could think about. Where was she? In the shower? No, not for so long. At work? Maybe. He wasn't sure. He'd lost track of her schedule, the days she was on and off.

The manager of the clubhouse, a small, pencil-thin man named Levigne, had wanted to call the police, but Osborn had convinced him he'd only had an accident and that someone would come to pick him up. He was afraid of the tall man. But he was also afraid of the police. Most likely they'd already found Kanarack's car. It would have been impounded, listed as stolen or abandoned. But when his body floated up someplace downriver, they'd have gone over it with a toothbrush and magnifying glass. Osborn's fingerprints were all over it and they had his fingerprints. Barras himself had taken them that first night when they'd picked him up for attacking Kanarack in the café and then jumping the Métro turnstile in pursuit of him.

When had that been?

Osborn glanced at his watch. Today was Saturday. It had been Monday when he'd first seen Kanarack. Six days. That was all? After almost thirty years? And now Kanarack was dead. And after everything, his intricate plans, the police, Jean Packard . . . After everything, still he had no answer. His father's death was as much of a mystery now as it had been before.

There was a sound and he looked up. A heavy-set man was using the phone. Outside, golfers were moving toward the first tee. The early haze had become bright sun. The first day without overcast since he'd come to France. The golf course was near Vernon, twenty or more highway miles from Paris. The Seine, as it snaked back and forth through the countryside, had to have taken him at least twice that far. How long he'd been in the water, or how far he'd walked in the darkness, he didn't know.

On the table in front of him Osborn saw the dregs of the strong coffee the manager, Levigne, had brought him without charge. Fingering the cup, he picked it up and drained what was left, then set it back down. Just that, the effort of lifting a small cup and drinking, had tired him.

Across the room, the man hung up the phone and went outside. What if the tall man suddenly came in? He still had Kanarack's pistol in his jacket pocket. Did he have the strength to take it out, aim and fire? He'd practiced with a handgun for years and was good at it. Target ranges in Santa Monica and in the San Fernando and Conejo valleys. Why he'd done it, he didn't know. As an act of working out aggression? As a sport? As a defense against ever-increasing city crime? Or had it been something else? Something leading him toward a day when he would need it.

He looked back at the phone. Try. Once more. You have to!

By now his leg had stiffened and he was afraid movement would start the bleeding again. Further, the shock of his ordeal was wearing off and with it the protection of its natural anesthesia, causing the leg to throb with such ferocity he didn't know how much longer he could bear the pain without medication.

Putting his hands flat on the table, Osborn pushed himself up. The sudden movement made him lightheaded and for a moment he could do nothing but stand there and hold on, praying he wouldn't fall.

Several golfers just coming in saw him and stepped away. He could see one of them speak to Levigne, and gesture toward him. What did he expect, looking like he did? Glassy-eyed, barely able to stand, wearing torn, soggy clothes that stunk of the river, he looked like a derelict from hell.

But he couldn't worry about them. Couldn't think about them.

He looked back to the telephone. It was less than ten paces from where he stood but it might as well have been in California. Picking up the tree-branch cane that had brought him this far, he set it in front of him, putting his weight on it and moved forward. Right hand places the cane, right foot follows. Bring the left foot up. Right hand, right foot. Bring the left foot alongside. Stop. Deep breath.

The phone is a little closer now.

Ready? Again. Right hand, right foot. Left foot up. Though his focus was entirely on his movement and the goal toward which he was going, Osborn was acutely aware of people in the room watching him. Their faces blurred.

Then he heard a voice. His voice! It was talking to him. Clearly and succinctly.

"The bullet is lodged somewhere in the hamstring muscle. Not sure just where. But it has to come out."

Right hand, right foot. Left foot up. Right hand, right foot.

"Make a vertical incision along the middle of the back of the thigh from the lower fold of the nates." Suddenly he was back in medical school quoting from *Gray's Anatomy*. How could he remember it verbatim?

Right hand, right foot. Left foot. Stop and rest. Across the room, faces still watching. Right hand, right foot. Left foot up.

The telephone is right in front of you.

Exhausted, Osborn slowly reached for the receiver and took it off the hook.

"Paul, there is a bullet lodged in your hamstring muscle. It has to come out, now."

"I *know* dammit. I *know*. Take it out!"

* * *

"It *is* out. Just lie still."

"Do you know who I am?"

"Of course."

"What day is it?"

"I—" Osborn hesitated. "Saturday."

"You missed your plane." Vera pulled off her surgical gloves, then turned and walked out of the room.

Osborn relaxed and looked around. He was in her apartment and naked, lying facedown on the bed in her guest room. A moment later she came back. A hypodermic syringe was in her hand.

"What's that?" he asked.

"I might tell you it's succinylcholine," she said, sarcastically. "But that wouldn't be true." Walking behind him, she wiped a spot on his upper buttock with a piece of alcohol-soaked cotton, then slid the needle in and gave him the shot.

"It's an antibiotic. You probably ought to have a tetanus shot, too. God knows what was in that river besides Henri Kanarack."

"How do you know about that?" Suddenly everything that had happened flashed across his mind.

Vera reached down and gently pulled a blanket up over him. All the way up over his shoulders so that he was warm. Then she went over and sat down on the ottoman of a leather reading chair across from him.

"You passed out in the clubhouse of a golf course about forty kilometers from here. You came back long enough to give them my number. I borrowed a friend's car. The people at the golf course were very nice. They helped me get you in the car. All I had were a few tranquilizers. I gave you all of them."

"All?"

Vera smiled. "You talk a lot when you're fucked up.

Mostly about men. Henri Kañarack. Jean Packard. Your father."

In the distance they heard the singsong siren of an emergency vehicle and her smile faded.

"I've been to the police," she said.

"The police?"

"Last night. I was worried. They searched your hotel room and found the succinylcholine. They don't know what it is or what it was for."

"But you do—"

"Now I do, yes."

"I couldn't very well tell you, could I?"

Osborn's eyes were heavy, and he was beginning to drift off. "The police?" he said, weakly.

Getting up, Vera crossed the room and turned on a small lamp in the corner, then shut off the overhead light. "They don't know you're here. At least I don't think they do. When they find Kanarack's body and his car with your fingerprints in it they'll come here asking if I've seen you or heard from you."

"What are you going to tell them?"

Vera could see him trying to put everything together, trying to tell if he'd made a mistake calling her, if he could really trust her. But he was too weary. The lids came down over his eyes and he sank slowly back into the pillow.

Bending down, she brushed her lips over his forehead. "Nobody will know. I promise," she whispered.

Osborn didn't hear her. He was falling, tumbling. He was not whole. The truth had never been as stark or as fearfully ugly. He had made himself a doctor because he had wanted to take away hurt and pain, all the while knowing he could never take away his own. What people saw was the image of a doctor. To them, helpful and caring. They never saw the rest of his personality because it didn't exist. There was nothing there and never would be until the demons inside him were dead. What Henri Kanarack knew could have killed them, but it was not to be. Finding him had been a tease that made it worse than before. Suddenly his falling stopped and he opened his eyes. It was autumn in New Hampshire and he was in the woods with his father. They were laughing and skipping stones across a pond. The sky was blue, the leaves were bright and the air was crisp.

He was eight years old.

42

"OY, MCVEY!" Benny Grossman said, then as quickly asked if he could call him right back and hung up. It was Saturday morning in New York, midafternoon in London.

McVey, back in the pocket-size room in the hotel on Half Moon Street Interpol had so generously provided for him, swirled two fingers of Famous Grouse in a glass with no ice—because the hotel had none—and waited for Benny to call back.

He'd spent the morning in the company of Ian Noble, the young Home Office pathologist, Dr. Michaels, and Dr. Stephen Richman, the specialist in micropathology who'd discovered the extreme cold to which the severed head of their John Doe had been subjected.

After careful inventory taken at behest of Scotland Yard, neither of the two cryonic suspension companies licensed in Great Britain, Cryonetic Sepulture of Edinburgh or Cryo-Mastaba of Camberwell, London, reported a head—or entire body, for that matter—of a stored "guest" missing. So, unless someone was running an unlicensed cryonic suspension company or had a portable cryocapsule he was hauling around London with bodies or pieces of bodies frozen to more than minus four hundred degrees Fahrenheit, they had to rule out the possibility that Mr. John Doe's head had been voluntarily frozen.

By the time McVey, Noble, and Dr. Michaels had had breakfast and arrived at Richman's office/laboratory on Gower Mews, Richman had already examined the body of John Cordell, the headless corpse found in a small apartment across the playing field from Salisbury Cathedral. X rays of Cordell's body revealed two screws securing a hairline crack in his lower pelvis. Screws that probably would have been removed once the fissure had properly healed had the subject lived that long.

Metallurgical tests Richman had had done on the screws revealed microscopic cobweb-like fractures throughout, proving conclusively that Cordell's body had undergone the same extreme freezing—to temperatures nearing absolute zero—as had John Doe's head.

"Why?" McVey asked.

"That's certainly part of the question, isn't it?" Dr. Richman replied as he opened the door from the cramped laboratory where they had gathered to view the comparative slides of the failed screws taken from Cordell's body and the failed metal that had been the plate in John Doe's head, and led them down a narrow, yellow-green hallway toward his office.

Stephen Richman was in his early sixties, stout but fit with the kind of solidity that comes from hard physical labor in youth. "You'll excuse the mess," he said, opening the door to his office. "I wasn't prepared for a poker crowd."

His working area was little more than a closet, half the size of McVey's minuscule hotel room. Heaped helter-skelter among books, journals, correspondence, cardboard boxes and stacks of technical videos were dozens of vessels containing preserved organs from God knew how many species, some three or four to the jar. Somewhere among the clutter was a window and Richman's desk and his desk chair. Two other chairs were piled high with books and file folders, which he immediately cleared off for his visitors. McVey volunteered to stand, but Richman wouldn't hear of it and disappeared in search of a third chair. An exasperating fifteen minutes later, he reappeared, lugging a secretary's chair with one caster missing, which he'd located in a basement store-room.

"The question, Detective McVey," Richman said as they all finally sat down, picking up McVey's query asked nearly a half hour earlier as if he'd just now posed it—"is not so much 'why?' but 'how?'"

"What do you mean?" McVey said.

"He means we're talking about human tissues," Michaels said, flatly. "Experiments with temperatures approaching absolute zero have been conducted primarily with salts and some metals, like copper." Abruptly, Michaels realized he was overstepping courtesy. "Excuse me, Doctor Richman," he said apologetically. "I didn't mean to—"

"It's quite all right, Doctor." Richman smiled, then looked to McVey and Commander Noble. "What you have to realize is this all gets very muddied in scientific mumbo-jumbo. But the nut of it is the Third Law of Thermodynamics, which basically says science can never reach absolute zero because, among other things, it would then mean a state of perfect orderliness. Atomic orderliness."

Noble's face was blank. So was McVey's.

"Every atom consists of electrons orbiting around a nucleus, which is made of protons and neutrons. What happens as substances get colder is that the normal movement of these atoms and their parts becomes reduced, slowed, if you will. The colder the temperature, the slower their movements.

"Now, if we took an external magnet and focused it critically on these slowly moving atoms, we would create a magnetic field where we could manipulate the atoms and their parts, and make them do pretty much what we wanted. Theoretically if we could reach *absolute zero*, we could do more than pretty much, we could do *exactly* as we wanted because all activity would be stopped."

"That only gets us back to McVey's question," Noble said. "Why? Why freeze decapitated bodies and a head to that degree, assuming you could get them to absolute zero?"

"To join them," Richman said, wholly without emotion.

"Join them?" Noble was incredulous.

"It's the only reason I could begin to give."

Tugging at an ear, McVey turned away and looked out the window. Outside, the morning was bright and sunny. By contrast, Richman's office felt like the inside of a musty box. Swiveling back, McVey found himself nose to nose with the labeled brain of a Maltese cat suspended in some kind of liquid preservative inside a bell jar. He looked at Richman. "You're talking about atomic surgery, correct?"

Richman smiled. "Of sorts. Simply put, at absolute zero, under the application of a strong magnetic field all the atomic particles would be perfectly lined up, and under total control. If we could do that, we could perform atomic cryosurgery. Microsurgery beyond conception."

"Elaborate a little, if you would, please," Noble said.

Richman's eyes brightened and McVey could almost feel his pulse quicken. The whole idea of what he was discussing excited him tremendously. "What it means, Commander, assuming we could freeze people to that degree, operate on them and then thaw them out with no damage to the tissues, is that atoms could be connected. A chemical bond would be formed between them so that a given electron is shared between two different atoms. It would make a seamless connection. The *perfect seam*, if you will. It would be as if it had been created by nature. Like a tree that grew that way."

"Is somebody trying to do that?" McVey asked quietly.

"It's not possible," Michaels interjected.

McVey looked at him. "Why?"

"Because of the Heisenberg Principle. If I may, Doctor Richman." Richman nodded at the young pathologist, and Michaels turned to McVey. For some reason he needed the American to know that he knew his business, that he knew what he was talking about. It was important for what they were doing. And beyond that, it was his way of showing and, at the same time, demanding respect.

"It's a principle of quantum mechanics that says it's impossible to measure two properties of a quantum object—say an atom or a molecule—at the same time with infinite precision. You can do one or the other but not both. You might tell an atom's speed and direction but you could not, at the same time, say precisely where it was."

"Could you do it at absolute zero?" McVey was giving him his due.

"Of course. Because at absolute zero everything would be stopped."

"Detective McVey," Richman interjected. "It is possible to get temperatures to less than one-millionth of a degree above absolute zero. It has been done. The concept of absolute zero is just that, a concept. It cannot be reached. It's impossible."

"My question, Doctor, was not if it can or it can't. I asked if someone was trying to do it." There was a decided edge to McVey's voice. He'd had enough of theory and now wanted fact. And he was staring at Richman, waiting for an answer.

This was a side of the L.A. detective Noble had never seen and made him realize why McVey had the reputation he did.

"Detective McVey, so far we've shown that the freezing was done to one body and one head. X rays have shown metal in only two of the remaining six cadavers. When we have that metal analyzed, we might be able to arrive at a more conclusive judgment."

"What's your gut tell you, Doctor?"

"My gut is strictly off the record. Accepting such, I'd venture that what you have are failed attempts at a very sophisticated type of cryosurgery."

"The head of one person fused to the body of another."

Richman nodded.

Noble looked at McVey. "Someone is trying to make a modern-day Frankenstein?"

"Frankenstein was created from the bodies of the dead," Michaels said.

"Good Lord!" Noble said, standing and nearly knocking over a vessel containing the enlarged heart of a professional soccer player. Steadying the jar, he looked from Michaels to Richman. "These people were frozen alive?"

"It would appear so."

"Then why the evidence of cyanide poisoning in all the victims?" McVey asked.

Richman shrugged. "Partial poisoning? A part of the procedure? Who knows?"

Noble looked at McVey, then stood. "Thank you very much, Doctor Richman. We won't take more of your time."

"Just a second, Ian." McVey turned to Richman. "One other question, Doctor. The head of our John Doe was thawing from the deep freeze when it was discovered. Would it make any difference *when* it was frozen as to its appearance and pathological makeup when it thawed?"

"I'm not sure I follow you," Richman said.

McVey leaned forward. "We've had trouble learning John Doe's identity. Can't find out who he is. Suppose we've been looking in the wrong place, trying to find a man who's been missing for the last few days or weeks. What if it had been months, or even years? Would that be possible?"

"It's a hypothetical question—but I would have to say that if someone *had* found a means of freezing to absolute zero, then nothing molecular would have been disturbed. So when it thawed there would be no way to tell if the freezing had been done a week ago or hundred years ago or thousand, for that matter."

McVey looked to Noble. "I think maybe your missing-persons detectives better go back to work."

"I think you're right."

The telephone ringing at McVey's elbow brought him back and he snatched it up.

"Oy, McVey!"

"Hello, Benny, and cut that out will you? It's getting repetitive."

"Got it."

"Got what?"

"What you asked for. The Interpol, Washington, request for the Albert Merriman file was time-stamped by the sergeant who took it at eleven thirty-seven A.M., Thursday, six October."

"Benny, eleven thirty-seven A.M. Thursday in New York is four thirty-seven Thursday afternoon in Paris."

"So?"

"The request was for that file, nothing else—"

"Yeah—"

"It wasn't until about eight A.M., Paris time, *Friday*, that the inspector in charge of the case for the Paris P.D. got a photocopy of the *print*. Just a print. Nothing else. But fifteen hours *before* that, somebody at Interpol not only had the print, they had a name and a file to go with it."

"Sounds like you got interior trouble. A cover-up. Or private agenda. Or who knows—But if something goes wrong it's the investigating cop who's on the line because you can bet four ways from Sunday there won't be any record of who got the first transmission."

"Benny—"

"What, boobalah?"

"Thanks."

Interior trouble, cover-up, private agenda. McVey hated those words. Something was going on somewhere inside Interpol, and Lebrun was holding the bag without knowing it. He wouldn't like it, but he had to be told. The trouble was when McVey finally got through to him in Paris twenty minutes later, he didn't get that far.

"McVey, *mon ami*," Lebrun said, excitedly. "I was just about to call *you*. Things are suddenly very complex around here. Three hours ago Albert Merriman was found floating in the Seine. He looked like a big cheese chewed over with an automatic weapon. The car he'd been driving was discovered about ninety kilometers upstream, close to Paris. Your Doctor Osborn's prints were all over it."

43

WITHIN THE hour McVey was in a taxi, heading for Gatwick Airport. He'd left Noble and Scotland Yard scouring missing-person files for anyone who bore the description of their John Doe and who'd had head surgery requiring the implant of a steel plate and, at the same time, quietly checking every hospital and medical school in southern England for people or programs experimenting in radical surgery techniques. For a time he'd entertained the thought of requesting Interpol, Lyon, to have police departments do the same throughout Continental Europe. But because of the Lebrun/Albert Merriman file situation he decided to hold off. He wasn't sure what, if anything, was going on inside Interpol, but if something was, he didn't want something similar happening with his investigation. If McVey hated anything, it was having things going on behind his back. In his experience most of them were petty and backbiting, aggravating and time consuming but essentially harmless, but this one he wasn't so sure about. Better to hold off and see what Noble could turn up first, on the quiet.

It was now 5:30 P.M., Paris time. Air France Flight 003 had left Charles de Gaulle Airport for L.A. at five o'clock as scheduled. Doctor Paul Osborn should have been on it but he wasn't. He'd never shown up for the flight, which meant his passport was still in the hands of the Paris police.

Increasingly, McVey was distrusting his own judgment of the man. Osborn had lied about the mud on his shoes. What else had he lied about?

Outwardly and under questioning, he'd appeared to be,

and admitted being, exactly what McVey thought he was, a well-educated man approaching middle age head over heels in love with a younger woman. Scarcely anything significant in that. The difference now was that two men were violently dead and McVey's "well-educated man in love" was connected to both.

The killings of Albert Merriman and Jean Packard aside, something else was gnawing at McVey, and had been even before he'd spoken to Lebrun: Dr. Stephen Richman's off-the-record remark that the deep frozen, headless bodies might well be the result of failed attempts at a very advanced kind of cryosurgery attempting to join a severed head to a body not its own. And Dr. Paul Osborn was not only a surgeon, but an orthopedic surgeon, and expert in the human skeletal structure, someone who might very well know how these things could be done.

From the first McVey had believed he was looking for one man. Maybe he'd had him and let him go.

Osborn woke out of a dream and, for a moment, had no idea where he was. Then, with sudden clarity, Vera's face came into view. She was sitting on the bed next to him, wiping his forehead with a damp cloth. She wore black, wide-legged slacks and a loose sweater of the same color. The black of the cloth and soft light made her features seem almost fragile, like delicate porcelain.

"You were running a high fever; I think it's broken," she said gently. Her dark eyes held the same sparkle they had the first time they'd met, which Osborn, for some reason, calculated had been only nine days earlier.

"How long was I out?" he said, weakly.

"Not long. Maybe four hours."

He started to sit up, but sharp pain shot through the back of his thigh. Wincing, he lay back down.

"If you'd have let me take you to the hospital, you might be a little more comfortable."

Osborn stared at the ceiling. He didn't remember telling her not to go to a hospital, but he must have. Then he remembered he'd told her about Kanarack and his father and the detective, Jean Packard.

Getting up from the bed, Vera lay the wash cloth in the pan she'd been using to keep the cloth damp, and moved to a table under a small, clam-shaped window that had a dark curtain pulled across it.

Puzzled, Osborn looked around. To his right was the door to the room. To his left, another door was open to a small bathroom. Above him, the ceiling pitched sharply so that the side walls were much shorter than the end walls. This wasn't the room he'd been in before. He was somewhere else, in a room like an attic.

"You're at the top of the building in a chamber under the eaves. It was built by the Resistance in 1940. Almost no one knows it's here."

Lifting the cover from a tray on the table where she'd set the washbasin, Vera came back and set it down on the bed beside him. On it was a bowl with hot soup, a spoon and napkin.

"You need to eat," she said. Osborn only stared at her.

"The police came looking for you. So I had you moved up here."

"Had me?"

"Philippe, the doorman, is an old and trusted friend."

"They found Kanarack's body, didn't they?"

Vera nodded. "The car, too. I told you they'd come when that happened. They wanted to come up to the apartment but I said I was on my way out. I met them in the lobby."

Osborn let out a weak sigh and stared off.

Vera sat down on the bed beside him and picked up the spoon. "You want me to feed you?"

"That much I can manage." Osborn grinned weakly.

Taking the spoon, he dipped it into the soup and began to eat. It was a bouillon of some kind. The salt in it tasted good and he ate for several minutes without stopping. Finally, he laid the spoon aside, wiped his mouth with the napkin and rested.

"I'm in no shape to run from anybody."

"No, you're not."

"You're going to get in trouble helping me."

"Did you kill Henri Kanarack?"

"No."

"Then how can I get in trouble?" Vera got up and picked the tray from the bed. "I want you to rest. I'll come up later and change the bandages."

"It's not just the police."

"What do you mean?"

"How are you going to explain me to—*him*. Frenchy?"

Slinging the tray over one hip like a café waitress, Vera looked down at him. "*Frenchy*," she said, "is no longer in the picture."

"No?" Osborn was stunned.

"No—" A slight smile crept over her.

"When did that happen?"

"The day I met you." Vera's eyes never left him. "Now, go to sleep. In two hours I'll be back."

Vera closed the door and Osborn lay back. He was tired. As tired as he'd ever been in his life. He glanced at his watch. It was 7:35, Saturday night, October 8.

And outside, beyond the window curtain of his tiny cell, Paris was beginning to dance.

44

AT PRECISELY the same time, and some twenty-three miles out on the Autoroute A1, McVey's Air Europe Fokker 100 touched down at Charles de Gaulle Airport. Fifteen minutes later he was being driven back toward Paris by one of Lebrun's uniformed officers.

By this time he seemed to know every nook and turn in Charles de Gaulle Airport. He ought to; he'd barely been out of it twenty-four hours when he was back.

Nearing Paris, Lebrun's driver crossed the Seine and headed toward the Porte d'Orleans. In his broken English, he told McVey Lebrun was at a crime scene and wished McVey to meet him there.

The rain had started again by the time they pushed through a half block of fire equipment and rows of onlookers held back by uniformed gendarmes. Pulling up in front of a still-smoldering, burned-out shell of an apartment building, the driver got out and led McVey over a crisscross of high-pressure hoses and sweat-caked firemen still playing water on smoking hot spots.

The building was a total loss. The roof and the entire top floor were gone. Twisted steel fire escapes, arched and bowed by extreme heat into opposing courses, like unfinished elevated highway sections, dangled precariously from the upper floors, held there by brickwork that threatened to collapse at any moment. Between the floors, discernible through burned-out window casings, were the scorched and charred timbers that were once the walls and ceilings of individual apartments. And hanging over everything, despite the steadily falling rain, was the unmistakable stench of burned flesh.

Skirting a pile of debris, the driver took McVey to the

back of the building where Lebrun stood with Inspectors Barras and Maitrot in the glare of portable worklights, talking with a heavyset man in a fireman's jacket.

"Ah, McVey!" Lebrun said out loud as McVey stepped into the light. "You know Inspectors Barras and Maitrot. This is Captain Chevallier, assistant chief of the Port d'Orleans arson battalion."

"Captain Chevallier." McVey and the arson chief shook hands.

"This thing was set?" McVey said, glancing up again at the destruction.

"*Oui*," Chevallier said, finishing with a brief explanation in French.

"It burned very hot, and very quickly, set off by some kind of extremely sophisticated device, probably using a military-type incendiary," Lebrun translated. "No one had a chance. Twenty-two people. All dead."

For a long moment McVey said nothing. Finally he asked, "Any idea why?"

"Yes," Lebrun said definitively, not trying to hide his anger. "One of them owned the car Albert Merriman was driving when your friend Osborn found him."

"Lebrun," McVey said, quietly but directly. "First of all, Osborn's not my friend. Second, let me guess that the Merriman car was owned by a woman."

"That's a good guess," Barras said in English.

"Her name was Agnes Demblon."

Lebrun's eyebrows raised. "McVey. You truly amaze me."

"What do you have on Osborn?" McVey avoided the compliment.

"We found his rented Peugeot, parked on a Paris street more than a mile from his hotel. It had three parking tickets, so it hadn't been driven since early afternoon, yesterday."

"No sign of him since?"

"We have a citywide out for him, and provincial police are checking the countryside between where Merriman's body washed ashore and where his car was found."

Nearby, two burly firemen dragged the scorched remains of a child's crib through an open door and dropped it on the ground beside the burned-out shell of a box spring. McVey watched them, then turned back to Lebrun.

"The place you found Merriman's car, let's go there."

The yellow lights of Lebrun's white Ford cut through the darkness as the Parisian detective turned onto the road along the Seine leading toward the park where the police had found Agnes Demblon's Citroën.

"He called himself Henri Kanarack. He worked at a bakery near the Gare du Nord and had for about ten years. Agnes Demblon was the bookkeeper there," Lebrun said, lighting a cigarette from the lighter in the console. "Obviously they had a history together. What it was exactly we will have to imagine because he was married to a Frenchwoman named Michele Chalfour."

"You think she set the fire?"

"I won't rule it out until we question her. But if she was only a housewife, which it seems she was, I doubt she would have access to those kinds of incendiary materials."

Detectives Barras and Maitrot had been through Henri Kanarack's apartment on the avenue Verdier in Montrouge and had found nothing. The flat had been all but empty. A few of Michele Kanarack's clothes, a handful of catalogues advertising baby clothes, half-a-dozen unpaid bills, some food in the cupboards and refrigerator and that was it. The Kanaracks had evidently packed up and left in a hurry.

At this stage the only thing they knew for certain was that Henri Kanarack/Albert Merriman was in the morgue. Where Michele Kanarack was was totally up in the air. A check of hotels, hospitals, halfway houses, morgues and jails had come up blank. A trace of her maiden name, Chalfour, had done the same. She had no driver's license, no passport, not even a library card—under either name. Nor had there been a photograph of her in the apartment, or in Merriman/Kanarack's wallet. As a result, all they were left with was a name. Nonetheless, Lebrun had put out a wanted bulletin for her across France. Maybe local police would turn up something they couldn't.

"What killed Merriman?" McVey made a mental note of the landscape as they turned off the highway and onto the muddy road that encircled the park.

"Heckler & Koch MP-5K. Fully automatic. Probably with a muffler."

McVey winced. A Heckler & Koch MP-5K was a people-killer. A nine-millimeter light machine gun with a thirty-round magazine, it was a terrorist favorite and weapon of choice among serious drug merchants.

"You found it?"

Putting out his cigarette, Lebrun slowed to a crawl, navigating the Ford through and around a series of large rain puddles.

"No, that's from forensics and ballistics. We had a dive team working the river for most of the afternoon without success. There's a strong current that runs a long way here. It's what took Merriman's body so far, so quickly."

Lebrun slowed the car and stopped at the edge of the trees. "We walk from here," he said, pulling a heavy-duty flashlight from a clip just under the seat.

The rain had stopped and a moon was peeking out from behind passing clouds as the two detectives got out and started toward the cinder and dirt ramp that led down to the water. As they went, McVey looked back over his shoulder. In the distance he could just make out the lights of Saturday-night traffic moving along the road that hugged the Seine.

"Watch your footing, it's slippery here," Lebrun said as they reached the landing at the bottom of the ramp. Swinging the flashlight, he showed McVey what was left of the washed-out tracks Agnes Demblon's car had made when it was towed away.

"There was too much rain," Lebrun said. "Any footprints there might have been were washed away before we got here."

"May I?" McVey put out his hand, and Lebrun handed him the light. Swinging it out toward the water, he judged the speed of the current as it moved past just off the shoreline. Bringing the light back, he knelt down and studied the ground.

"What are you looking for?" Lebrun asked.

"This." McVey dug in a hand, came up with a scoop of it, shining the light on it just to make sure.

"Mud?"

McVey looked up. "No, *mon ami. Rouge terrain. Red mud.*"

45

COMPARED TO the boisterous reception at Kloten Airport, the dinner for Elton Lybarger was genteel and intimate, with guests taking up four large tables around a dance floor. More than an entry into an entirely new world, it was the setting Joanna found extraordinary, even incredible. In the private ballroom of a lake steamer leisurely exploring the shoreline of the Zurichsee, which the deep Alpine Lake Zurich overlooked, she felt as if she had become a character in some dazzlingly elegant, turn-of-the-century play.

Seated next to Pascal Von Holden, dashing and resplendent in a deep blue tuxedo and starched white, wing-tip shirt, Joanna was at a table for six. And although she smiled and made polite conversation with the other guests, paying attention as best she could, it was all but impossible for her to keep her eyes from the countryside they passed. It was the time just before sunset, and to the east, above a picturesque village with rambling villas built down to the water's edge, high wooded hills rose straight up to vanish into the magnificence of the Alps, the setting sun striking the snow on the uppermost peaks and turning them a golden rose.

"Sentimental, yes?" Von Holden smiled, looking at her.

"Sentimental? Yes, I suppose that's a good word. I would have said beautiful." Joanna's eyes held Von Holden's for the slightest moment, then she looked back to the others.

Next to her was a very attractive and obviously very successful young couple from Berlin, Konrad and Margarete Peiper. Konrad Peiper, from what she could gather, was president of a large German trading company and

Margarete, his wife, had something to do with show business. Just what, Joanna wasn't exactly sure, and it was difficult to ask her because most of her time was spent sitting back from the table talking on a cellular phone.

Seated across from her were Helmuth and Bertha Salettl, brother and sister. Both, Joanna guessed, were in their seventies, and had flown in that afternoon from their home in Austria.

Dr. Helmuth Salettl was Elton Lybarger's personal physician, and Joanna had met with him four of the six times he had visited Lybarger at Rancho de Piñon in New Mexico. The doctor, like his sister now, had been somber and austere, saying little and asking only a few pointed questions regarding Lybarger's general health and regimen. The fact was that although she dealt daily with the rich and famous who came to Rancho de Piñon to recuperate secretly from anything from drug or alcohol addiction to face-lifts, she had never encountered anyone like Salettl. His presence and entrenched arrogance frightened her. But she'd found as long as she answered his questions and acted professionally, everything would be all right because he would never be there for more than twenty-four hours.

Two tables away, Elton Lybarger sat talking with the plumpish woman who'd smothered him with kisses and called him "Uncle" at the airport. His earlier fears about his family seemed to have faded, and he looked relaxed and comfortable, smiling and acknowledging the well-wishes of the others, who, during the course of the evening, stopped by to take his hand and say a few personal words of encouragement.

Next to Lybarger was a heavy-set and plain-looking woman in her late thirties, who Joanna learned was Gertrude Biermann, an activist for the Greens, a radical environmental peace movement, who seemed to take great pleasure in interrupting Lybarger's conversations with others to engage him in talk herself. As the evening progressed, Joanna wished she wouldn't be so insistent, and even considered going to her and mentioning it, because she could see Mr. Lybarger was beginning to tire. Why he would have a dowdy political activist as a friend was something that plucked Joanna's interest. The idea seemed so incongruous with Lybarger and the rest there who seemed to represent some form or other of big business.

Holding court at the third table was Uta Baur, touted as "the most German of all German fashion designers," who, after first being feted at trade fairs in Munich and Düsseldorf in the early seventies, was now an international institution in Paris, Milan and New York. Pencil thin, and dressed all in black, she wore little if any makeup, and her hair, cut almost to the scalp, was white blond to the roots. Were it not for her animated gestures and the sparkle in her eyes as she talked to those at the table with her, Joanna might have taken her for a female version of the grim reaper. She was, as everyone there knew and Joanna later found out, seventy-four years old.

Standing back, near the entry door, were two men in tuxedos who had earlier been in the dress of chauffeurs at the airport. They were lean, short haired, and seemed to be constantly watching the room. Joanna was certain they were bodyguards of some kind and was about to ask Von Holden about them when a waiter in lederhosen asked if he might take away the remains of her supper.

Joanna nodded gratefully. The main course had been Berner Platte—sauerkraut garnished liberally with pork chops, boiled bacon, and beef, sausages, tongue and ham; at five foot four and twenty pounds overweight, Joanna had been carefully watching her diet. Especially of late, since she'd begun noticing most of her bicycle racing friends were just this side of emaciated and fitted nicely into spandex. Middle, top and bottom.

Privately, and discussed with her only true friend, her Saint Bernard, Henry, Joanna had begun watching crotches. Male crotches of the bike racers.

Joanna had grown up the only child of pious and simple parents in a small west Texas town. Her mother had been a librarian and almost forty-two when Joanna was born. Her father, a letter carrier, had been fifty. Both had assumed, the way only such parents can assume, that their only child would grow up to be like them— hardworking, grateful for what they had, average. And for a time Joanna had done just that, as a Girl Scout and member of the church choir, as an ordinary student getting by in school, and, following the lead of her best friend, applying to nursing school after twelfth-grade graduation. Yet plain and dutiful as she seemed and even viewed herself, inside Joanna was rebellious, even quirky.

She'd had her first sex when she was eighteen with the assistant pastor of the church. Horrified afterward, and certain she was pregnant, she fled to Colorado, telling everyone, friends, parents and assistant pastor included, that she'd been accepted to a nursing school affiliated with the University of Denver. Both were inaccurate—she had not been accepted to nursing school, nor was she pregnant. Still she'd stayed in Colorado, worked hard and become a licensed physical therapist. When her father became ill she moved back to Texas to help her mother care for him. And when both parents died, literally within weeks of each other, she'd immediately packed everything and gone to New Mexico.

On Saturday, October 1, one week before the homecoming dinner for Elton Lybarger, Joanna had turned thirty-two. She had not made love, nor been made love to, since that night with the west Texas assistant pastor.

A sudden round of applause followed two waiters across the room as they brought in a large cake overflowing with candles and set it in front of Elton Lybarger. As they did, Pascal Von Holden put his hand on Joanna's arm.

"Can you stay?" he asked.

Turning from the festivities at Lybarger's table, she looked at him. "What do you mean?"

Von Holden smiled, and the creases in his sunburned face turned white.

"I mean can you stay here, in Switzerland, to continue your work with Mr. Lybarger?"

Joanna ran a nervous hand through her freshly washed hair.

"Me, stay here?"

Von Holden nodded.

"For how long?"

"A week, perhaps two. Until Mr. Lybarger is physically comfortable at his home."

Joanna was completely taken aback. All evening she'd been looking at her watch, wondering when she would get back to her room to pack all the gifts and trinkets for her friends, which Von Holden had helped her purchase in their tour of Zurich that afternoon. When she would get to bed. What time she would have to get up to get to the airport for her flight home the following day.

"My d-dog," she stammered. The idea of staying in Switzerland had never occurred to her. The concept of spending any time outside her own self-made nest was all but overwhelming.

Von Holden smiled. "Your dog will be cared for while you are away, of course. And while you are here, you will have your own apartment on the grounds of Mr. Lybarger's estate."

Joanna didn't know what to think, how to respond or even react. There was a round of applause from Lybarger's table as he blew out the candles and again, seemingly from nowhere, the oompah band appeared and played "For He's a Jolly Good Fellow."

Coffee and after-dinner drinks were served along with squares of Swiss chocolate. The plump lady helped Lybarger cut his cake, and waiters brought pieces of it to each table.

Joanna drank the coffee and took a sip from what was very good cognac. The liquor warmed her and felt good.

"He will be uncomfortable and unsure without you, Joanna. You will stay, won't you?" Von Holden's smile was kindhearted and genuine. Moreover, the way he asked her to stay made it seem it was he, not Lybarger, who was encouraging her. She took another sip of the cognac and felt flushed.

"Yes, all right," she heard herself say. "If it's that important to Mr. Lybarger, I'll stay, of course."

In the background the oompah band struck up a Viennese waltz and the young German couple got up from their table to dance. Looking around, Joanna saw other people get up as well.

"Joanna?"

She turned and saw Von Holden standing behind her chair.

"May I?" he asked.

A broad smile unintentionally crossed her face. "Sure. Why not?" she said. She stood up and Von Holden drew back her chair. A moment later he led her past Elton Lybarger and out onto the floor among the others. And, to the outlandish strains of the oompah band, he took her in his arms and they danced.

46

"I ALWAYS tell the kids it won't hurt. Just a little jab under the skin," Osborn said, watching Vera draw .5ml of tetanus toxoid out of a vial and into a syringe. "They know I'm lying and I know I'm lying. I don't know why I tell them."

Vera smiled. "You tell them because it's your job." Withdrawing the needle, she broke it off, wrapped the syringe in tissue paper, did the same with the vial, then put them both in her jacket pocket. "The wound is clean and healing well. Tomorrow we'll start you on exercises."

"Then what? I can't stay here for the rest of my life," Osborn said, sullenly.

"You might want to." Vera plopped a folded newspaper down in front of him. It was the late edition of *Le Figaro*. "Page two," she said.

Opening the paper, Osborn saw two grainy photographs. One was of himself, a mug shot taken by the Paris police, the other was of uniformed police carrying a blanket-covered body up a steep river embankment. Linking both was a caption in French: "American doctor suspect in Albert Merriman murder."

All right, so they'd dusted the Citroën and found his prints on it. He knew it would happen. No need to be surprised or shocked. But—"Albert Merriman? Where did they get that?"

"It was Henri Kanarack's real name. He was an American. Did you know that?"

"I could have guessed. From the way he talked."

"He was a professional killer."

"That part he told me—" Suddenly Osborn saw Kanarack's face staring up at him from the rushing water, terrified that Osborn would give him another shot of the succinylcholine. At the same time he heard Kanarack's horror-stricken voice, as distinctly as if he were in the room with him now.

"I was *paid*—"

Again, Osborn felt the shock of disbelief—that his father's murder had been cold, detached business.

"Erwin Scholl—" he heard Kanarack say.

"*No!*" he shouted out loud.

Vera looked up sharply. Osborn's jaw was set and he was staring straight ahead, focused on nothing.

"Paul—"

Osborn rolled over and slid his legs over the side of the bed. Unsteadily, he pulled himself to his feet. Wavering, he stood there, his face white as stone, his eyes utterly vacant. Sweat stood out on his forehead and his chest heaved thunderously with every breath. Everything was catching up. He was on the edge of a breakdown and knew it, but there was nothing he could do about it.

"Paul." Vera came toward him. "It's all right. It's all right—"

His head snapped around to look at her and his eyes narrowed. She was crazy. Her reasoning came from the outside world where no one understood. "The hell it's all right!" His voice was thick with rage. But it was the tortured rage of a child. "You think I can do it, don't you? Well, I can't."

"Can't what—" Vera was very gentle.

"You know what I mean!"

"I don't. . . ."

"The hell you don't!"

"No—"

"You want me to say it?"

"Say what?"

"That. That . . ." He stammered. "That I can find

Erwin Scholl! Well, I can't. That's all! I can't! Not start all over again! So don't ask again. Is that clear?" Osborn was leaning over her, yelling at her. "Is that clear, Vera? Don't ask, because I won't! I won't, because I can't!"

Suddenly he glimpsed his pants hanging over the back of the chair by the window table and lunged for them. As he did, his bad leg gave way and he cried out. For a moment he glimpsed the ceiling. Then the floor hit him in the back. For a moment he just lay there. Then he heard someone sob and his vision blurred and he couldn't see. "I just want to go home. Please," he heard someone say. There was confusion because the voice was his own, only it was much younger, and it was choked with tears. Desperately he rolled his head, looking for Vera, but he saw nothing but unfocused gray light.

"Vera—Vera—" He cried out, suddenly terrified something had happened to his eyes. "Vera!"

Somewhere, somewhere near, he heard a thumping. It was a sound he didn't recognize. Then he felt a hand slide through his hair and he realized he was leaning against her breast and what he was hearing was the beat of her heart. In time he became aware of the rhythm of his own breathing. And he had the sense that she was on the floor with him, and had been for some time. That she was holding him and rocking him gently in her arms. Still his vision hadn't cleared and he didn't know why. It was then he realized he was crying.

"You're certain this is the man?"

"*Oui, monsieur.*"

"You, too?"

"*Oui.*"

Lebrun dropped the Paris police mug shots of Osborn on his desk and looked at McVey.

The detectives had left the park by the river and were

on their way back into the city when the call came in. McVey, listening to the French, had heard the names Osborn and Merriman but couldn't understand what was being said about them. When the transmission was finished, Lebrun signed off and translated.

"We ran Osborn's photo alongside the Merriman story in the paper. The manager of a golf clubhouse saw it and remembered an American that looked something like Osborn had come out of the river near his golf course this morning. He'd given him coffee and let him use the phone. He thought it might be the same man."

Now, with the identification of the photos, there was no question that it was indeed Osborn who had come out of the river.

Pierre Levigne, manager of the clubhouse, had been reluctantly dragged in by a friend. Levigne had not wanted to get involved, but his friend warned him that this was about murder and that he could get in a great deal of trouble if he didn't report it.

"Where is he now? What happened to him? Who did he call?" McVey asked, and Lebrun translated in French.

Levigne still didn't want to talk, but his friend pushed him. Finally he agreed, but on the condition the police keep his name out of the papers. "All I know is that a woman came to pick him up and he went off with her."

Two minutes later, thanked and praised for their keen sense of civic responsibility, Levigne and his friend left, escorted out by a uniformed officer. As the door closed behind them, McVey looked at Lebrun.

"Vera Monneray."

Lebrun shook his head. "Barras and Maitrot have already talked to her. She hadn't seen Osborn and never heard of Albert Merriman or his alter ego Henri Kanarack."

"Come on, Lebrun. What'd you think she was going to

say?" McVey said, cynically. "They get a look around her apartment?"

Lebrun paused, then said, matter-of-factly, "She was on her way out for the evening. They met her in the lobby of her building."

McVey groaned and looked at the ceiling. "Lebrun. Forgive me if I'm stepping all over your modus operandi, but you've got Osborn's picture in the paper and half of France shaking the walls to find him and you're telling me nobody bothered to check out his girlfriend's apartment!"

Lebrun answered by not answering. Instead he picked up the telephone and ordered a team of inspectors to search the area where Osborn came out of the river for the murder weapon. Then he hung up and deliberately lit a cigarette.

"Anybody happen to ask where she was going?" McVey was trying to control his temper.

Lebrun looked at him blankly.

"You said she was going out. Where the hell was she going?"

Lebrun took a deep breath and closed his eyes. This was a clash of cultures. Americans *were* boors! Further they had absolutely no sense of propriety!

"Let me put it this way for you, *mon ami*. You are in Paris and this is Saturday night. Mademoiselle Monneray may or may not have been on her way to rendezvous with the prime minister. Whichever it was, I suspect the investigating officers felt it more than somewhat indelicate to ask."

McVey took a deep breath of his own, then walked up to Lebrun's desk, leaned both hands on it and looked down at him. "*Mon ami*, I want you to know that I fully appreciate the situation."

McVey's rumpled suit jacket was open and Lebrun could see the butt of a .38 revolver, a safety strap over the hammer, resting in the holster on his hip. Where most of the world's police carried nine-millimeter automatics with a clip that held ten or fifteen shots, here was McVey with a six-shot Smith & Wesson. A six-shooter! Retirement age or not, McVey was—*mon Dieu!*—a *cowboy!*

"Lebrun, with all due respect to you and France, I *want* Osborn. I want to talk to him about Merriman. I want to talk to him about Jean Packard. And I want to talk to him about our headless friends. And if you say to me— 'McVey, you already did that and let him go'—I will say to you, 'Lebrun, I want to do it again!'"

"And with that in mind, chivalry and everything else considered, I'd say the most direct path to the son of a bitch is through Vera Monneray no matter who the hell she's fucking! *Comprenez-vous?*"

47

THIRTY MINUTES later, at eleven forty-five, the two detectives sat in Lebrun's unmarked Ford outside Vera Monneray's apartment building at 18 Quai de Bethune.

Quai de Bethune, even in traffic, is less than a five-minute drive from the headquarters of the Paris Préfecture of Police. At eleven thirty, they had entered the building and spoken with the doorman in the lobby. He had not seen Mademoiselle Monneray since she'd gone out earlier that evening. McVey asked if there was any way she could get back into the building without passing through the lobby. Yes, if she came in through the back entrance and walked up the service stairs. But that was highly unlikely.

"Mademoiselle Monneray does not use 'service stairs.'" It was basic as that.

"Ask him if he minds if I call up?" McVey said to Lebrun, as he picked up the house phone.

"I do not mind, monsieur," the doorman said crisply in English. "The number is two-four-five."

McVey dialed and waited. He let the phone ring ten times before he hung up and looked at Lebrun. "Not there or not answering. Shall we go up?"

"Give it a little time, eh?" Turning to the doorman, Lebrun gave him his card. "When she comes back, please ask her to call me. *Merci.*"

McVey looked at his watch. It was nearly five minutes to midnight. Across the street, the windows of Vera's apartment were dark. Lebrun glanced over at McVey.

"I can feel your American pulse wanting to go in there anyway," Lebrun said with a grin. "Up the back service stairs. A credit card slipped against the lock and you're in, like a cat burglar."

McVey took his eyes off Vera's window and turned to Lebrun. "What's your relationship to Interpol, Lyon?" he asked quietly. This was the first opportunity he'd had to bring up what he'd learned from Benny Grossman.

"The same assignment as yours," Lebrun said, smiling. "I am your man in Paris. Your French liaison to Interpol in the severed-head cases."

"The Merriman/Kanarack business is separate, right? Nothing to do with that."

Lebrun wasn't sure what McVey was getting at. "That's correct. Their help in that situation, as you know, was in providing the technical means to convert a smudge into a clear fingerprint."

"Lebrun, you asked me to call the New York Police Department. Finally I got some information."

"On Merriman?"

"In a way. Interpol, Lyon, through the National Central Bureau in Washington, requested the NYPD file on him more than fifteen hours before you were even informed they'd made a clear print."

"What?" Lebrun was shocked.

"That's what *I* said."

Lebrun shook his head. "Lyon would have no use for a file like that. Interpol is basically a transmitter of information between police agencies, not an investigative agency itself."

"I started kicking that around on the flight from London. Interpol requests, and gets, privileged information hours before the investigating officer is even informed there's a fingerprint that might eventually lead to the same information. That is, if the investigator knows what he is doing.

"Even if that sits a little raw, you have to say, okay, maybe it's internal procedure. Maybe they're checking to see if their communication system works. Maybe they want to know how good the investigator is. Maybe somebody's tinkering with a new computer program. Who knows? And if that's all there was, you say, fine, forget about it.

"But the trouble is, a day later you pull this same guy, someone who's supposed to have been dead for twenty-odd years, out of the Seine and he's all shot up with a Heckler & Koch automatic. A job which I sincerely doubt was the work of any angry housewife."

Lebrun was incredulous. "My friend, you are saying that someone at Interpol headquarters discovered Merriman was alive, learned where he was in Paris, and had him killed?"

"I'm saying fifteen hours before you knew about it,

somebody at Interpol got hold of that print. It led to a name and then a fast-forward trace. Maybe using the Interpol computer system, maybe something else. But when whatever system retrieved Albert Merriman and matched him with a guy named Henri Kanarack, alive and living in Paris, and gave that information out, what happened next happened awfully damn fast. Because Merriman was hit within hours of the positive I.D."

"But why kill a man who was already legally dead? And why the rush?"

"It's your country, Lebrun. You tell me." Instinctively McVey glanced up at Vera Monneray's window. It was still dark.

"Probably to keep him from talking when we got to him."

"That's what I'd guess."

"But after twenty years? What were they afraid of? That he had something on people in high places?"

"Lebrun." McVey paused. "Maybe I'm crazy, but let me throw it out anyway. All this just happened to take place now, in Paris. Maybe it was coincidence that it had something to do with a man we were already following, maybe not. But suppose this wasn't the first. Suppose whoever's involved has a master list of old foes gone underground and every time Lyon, as a kind of international clearing house for quirky law-enforcement problems, gets a new fingerprint, or nose hair, or some other kind of connecting reference, it automatically does a search and retrieve. And if a name comes up that's on that list, the word goes out. And it goes out worldwide, because that's how far Interpol reaches."

"You're suggesting an organization. One with a mole inside Interpol headquarters at Lyon."

"I said I might be crazy—"

"And you suspect Osborn is part of that organization, or is in the pay of it?"

McVey grinned. "Don't do that to me, Lebrun. I can theorize till I'm purple, but I don't make connections without evidence. And so far, there is none."

"But Osborn would be a good place to start."

"That's why we're here."

"Another," Lebrun smiled lightly, "would be to find who it was in Lyon that requested the Merriman file."

McVey's attention shifted as a car turned onto Quai de Bethune and came down the block toward them, its yellow lights cutting sharply through the rain that had begun to fall again.

The detectives sat back as a taxi slowed and stopped in front of number 18. A moment later the front door opened and the doorman came out carrying an umbrella. Then the passenger door opened and Vera got out. Ducking under the umbrella, she and the doorman went inside.

"Shall we go in?" Lebrun said to McVey, then answered his own question. "I think we shall." As he reached for the door, McVey put a hand on his arm.

"*Mon ami,* there's more than one Heckler & Koch in this world and more than one guy who knows how to use it. I'd be very careful how I went about my inquiry into Lyon."

"Albert Merriman was a criminal, in the dirt of a dirty business. You think they'd chance killing a policeman?"

"Why don't you take another peek at what's left of Albert Merriman. Count the entry and exit wounds and see how they're arranged. Then ask yourself the same question."

48

VERA WAS waiting for the elevator when McVey and Lebrun came in. She watched them cross the lobby toward her.

"You must be Inspector Lebrun," she said, looking at his cigarette. "Most Americans have quit smoking. The doorman gave me your card. What can I do for you?"

"*Oui, mademoiselle*," Lebrun said, then reached over and awkwardly put out his cigarette in a stone ashtray beside the elevator.

"*Parlez-vous anglais*?" McVey asked. It was late, well after midnight. Obviously Vera knew who they were and why they were there.

"Yes," she said, making eye contact with him.

Lebrun introduced McVey as an American policeman working with the Paris Préfecture of Police.

"How do you do?" Vera said.

"Doctor Paul Osborn. I think you know him." McVey was putting niceties aside.

"Yes."

"When was the last time you saw him?"

Vera glanced from McVey to Lebrun, then back to McVey. "Perhaps it would be better if we talked in my apartment."

The elevator was old and small and lined with polished copper. It felt like a tiny room in which every wall was a mirror. McVey watched as Vera leaned forward and pressed a button. The doors closed, there was a deep whir, the gears caught and the threesome rode up in silence. That Vera was poised and beautiful and had been unruffled in the lobby didn't impress him. After all, she was the mistress of France's most important minister. That in itself had to be an education in cool. But inviting them to her apartment showed moxie. She was letting them know she had nothing to hide, whether she did or not. That made one thing certain. If Paul Osborn had been there, he wouldn't be there now.

The elevator took them up one story. At the second floor, Vera pulled the door open herself, then led the way down the corridor toward her apartment.

It was now a quarter past midnight. At eleven thirty-five she had at last pulled the covers over a thoroughly spent Paul Osborn, turned on a small electric space heater to keep him warm, and left the room hidden under the eaves at the top of the building. A steep and narrow staircase inside a plumbing soffit led to a storage locker that opened into an alcove on the fourth floor.

Vera had just stepped out of the locker and was turning back to lock the storage closet when she thought of the police. If they had been there earlier, there was every chance they would come back, especially when they would have had no word of Osborn. They'd want to question her again, ask if she'd heard anything in the meantime, probe to see if maybe they'd missed something or if she was covering up.

The first time they'd come she'd told them she was on her way out. What if they were outside now, watching for her to come back? And what if they didn't see her come back and later found her asleep in her apartment? If that happened, the first thing they would do would be to search the building. Certainly the attic room was hidden, but not so well that some of the older police who had fathers and uncles in the Resistance against the Nazis wouldn't remember such hiding places and begin to look beyond the obvious.

Assuming she was right about the police, Vera took the service stairs to the street behind the building and telephoned the lobby from a public phone on the corner. Philippe not only confirmed her suspicions but read her Lebrun's card. Warning him to say nothing if the police came back, she'd crossed Quai des Celestins, turned down the rue de l'Hôtel de Ville and entered the Métro station at Pont Marie. Taking the line one stop to Sully Morland, she'd emerged from the station and hailed a cab back to her apartment on Quai de Bethune. The whole thing had taken less than thirty minutes.

"Come in, gentlemen, please," she said, opening the door and turning on the hallway light, then led the way into the living room.

McVey closed the door behind them and followed. To the left, in the semidarkness, he saw what looked like a formal dining room. Down the hall to the right was an open door to another room, and opposite it another open door. Everywhere he looked he saw antique furniture and oriental rugs. Even the runner in the long hallway was oriental.

The living room was nearly twice as long as it was wide. A large Art Deco poster framed in gold leaf—a Mucha, if McVey remembered his art history—covered most of the far end wall. And the one word that sang from it was "original." To one side, opposite a long white linen couch, was an old-fashioned armchair that had been completely redone. The curlicue design of its arms and legs was the same handpainted multicolor as the fabric and it looked, for all the world, like it could have been lifted straight from the set of *Alice in Wonderland*. But it wasn't a prop or a plaything, it was an objet d'art, another original.

Beyond that, with the exception of half-a-dozen carefully placed antiques and the rich oriental carpet, the room was purposefully spare. The wallpaper, a fibrous gold and silver brocade, was untarnished by the grime that in a city the size of Paris sooner or later tainted everything. The ceiling and woodwork were off-white and freshly painted. The entire room, and the rest of the apartment, he imagined, had the look of meticulous daily care.

Glancing out one of the two large windows that overlooked the Seine, he could see Lebrun's white Ford parked across the street. That meant that someone else, standing where he was, could have seen it too. Seen it pull up and the lights go out, but nobody get out. That is, until Ms. Monneray's cab pulled up and she went inside.

Vera turned on several lamps, then looked up to face her guests. "Could I offer you something to drink?" she said in French.

"I'd rather get to the point, if you don't mind, Ms. Monneray," McVey said.

"Of course," Vera said in English. "Please sit down."

Lebrun walked over and sat down on a white linen sofa, but McVey chose to stand.

"This is your apartment?" he asked.

"It belongs to my family."

"But you live here alone."

"Yes."

"You were with Paul Osborn today. You picked him up in a car about twenty miles from here, at a golf course near Vernon."

Vera was sitting in the Alice in Wonderland chair, and McVey was looking right at her. If the police knew that much, McVey knew she would be too smart to deny it.

"Yes," she said quietly.

Vera Monneray was twenty-six, beautiful, poised, and on her way to becoming a doctor. Why was she risking a hard-fought and important career by protecting Osborn? Unless something was going on McVey had no idea about, or unless she was truly in love.

"Earlier, when you were questioned by the police you denied having seen Doctor Osborn."

"Yes."

"Why?"

Vera looked from McVey to Lebrun, then back to McVey. "I'll be honest and tell you I was frightened, I didn't know what to do."

"He was here in the apartment, wasn't he?" McVey said.

"No," Vera said, coolly. "He wasn't." That was a lie it would be hard for them to catch. If she told the truth, they would want to know where he went from here and how he got there.

"Then you won't mind if we look around?" Lebrun said.

"Not at all." Everything in the guest room had been cleaned and put away. The sheets and bloody towels she'd used when she pulled the bullet from Osborn's leg had been folded and stored in the attic hiding place, the instruments sterilized and put back in her medical bag.

Lebrun got up and left the room. In the hallway he stopped to light his cigarette, then walked off.

"Why were you frightened?" McVey sat down in a straightbacked chair across from Vera.

"Doctor Osborn was hurt. He'd been in the river most of the night."

"He killed a man named Albert Merriman. Did you know that?"

"No, he didn't."

"Is that what he told you?"

"Detective, I told you he was hurt. It was not so much by the river, but because he'd been shot. By the same man who did kill Albert Merriman. He was hit in the back of the thigh."

"Is that so?" McVey said.

Vera stared at him a moment, then got up and went to a table near the doorway. As she did, Lebrun came back. Glancing at McVey, he shook his head. Pulling open a drawer, Vera took something from it, closed the drawer and came back.

"I took this out of him," she said, and laid the spent bullet she'd recovered from Osborn's thigh in McVey's hand.

McVey rolled it around in his palm and then held it up between his thumb and forefinger. "Soft point. Could be nine millimeter—" he said to Lebrun.

Lebrun said nothing, only nodded slightly. The nod was enough to tell McVey he agreed, that it could be the same kind of slug they'd taken out of Merriman.

McVey looked at Vera. "Where did you do the surgery?"

Say whatever comes into your head, she thought. Don't flinch. Make it simple. "By the side of the road, on the way back to Paris."

"Which road?"

"I don't remember. He was bleeding and almost delirious."

"Where is he now?"

"I don't know."

"Don't know that, either. . . . You seem to not know more than you know."

Vera looked at him but didn't back down. "I wanted to bring him here. More truthfully, I wanted him to go to a hospital. But he wouldn't. He was afraid whoever tried to kill him would come after him again if they knew he was alive. It would be easy enough in a hospital, and if he was here, he was afraid I might get hurt. That's why he insisted we do what we did. The wound wasn't deep. It was a relatively simple operation. As a doctor, he knew that. . . ."

"What did you use for water? You know, to keep everything clean?"

"Bottled water. I carry it with me in the car almost all the time. These days many people do. Even in America, I think."

McVey stared at her but said nothing. Lebrun did the same. They were waiting for her to continue.

"I left him at the Gare Montparnasse about four this afternoon. I shouldn't have, but he would have it no other way."

"Where was he going?" McVey asked.

Vera shook her head.

"You don't know that, either."

"I'm sorry. I told you he was concerned about me. He didn't want me involved any more than I already was."

"He could walk?"

"He had a cane, an old one that was in the car. It wasn't much, but it kept the pressure off his leg. He's healthy. That kind of wound will heal quickly."

Vera watched McVey get up and cross the room to look out the window.

"Where were you this evening? From the time you went out until now?" he said with his back to her, then turned to face her.

To this point, McVey had been direct, but for the most part he'd kept it friendly. But with this question his tone changed. It was hard, even ugly, and decidedly accusatory. It was something Vera had never encountered. This was no Hollywood movie cop, he was the real thing, and he scared the hell out of her.

McVey didn't have to look at Lebrun to know what his reaction would be. Horror.

And he was right. Lebrun *was* horrified. McVey was asking her point blank if she'd been having a clandestine rendezvous with François Christian. The trouble with his reaction was that Vera saw it too. It told her they knew about her relationship with François. It also told her they didn't know about the breakup.

"I'd rather not say," she said without expression. Then, crossing her legs, she looked at Lebrun. "Should I get an attorney?"

Lebrun was quick to answer. "No, mademoiselle. Not

now, not tonight." Standing, he looked at McVey. "Already it is Sunday morning. I think it is time we go."

McVey studied Lebrun a moment, then gave in to the Frenchman's deep sense of propriety. "Just let me finish a thought." He turned to Vera.

"Did Osborn know who shot him?"

"No."

"Did he tell you what he looked like?"

"Only that he was tall," Vera said politely. "Quite tall and slim."

"Had he seen him before?"

"I don't think so."

Lebrun nodded toward the door.

"One more question, Inspector," McVey said, still looking at Vera. "This Albert Merriman or Henri Kanarack as he called himself. Do you know why Doctor Osborn was so interested in him?"

Vera paused. What harm would it do to tell them? In fact, it might help if they understood the pressure Osborn had been under, make them realize he'd only been trying to question Kanarack, and had nothing at all to do with the shooting. On the other hand, the police had taken the succinylcholine from Osborn's hotel room. If she told them Kanarack had murdered Osborn's father, instead of being sympathetic, they would assume he'd been out for revenge. If they did and connected the drug, and then discovered what it was used for, they might go back over Kanarack's body and discover the puncture wounds.

Right now, Osborn was only a fugitive but if they had reason to go back and found the puncture wounds, they could, and probably would, charge him with attempted murder.

"No," she said, finally. "I really have no idea."

"What about the river?" McVey pressed.

"I don't know what you mean."

"Why were Osborn and Albert Merriman there?"

Lebrun was uncomfortable and Vera could have turned to him for help, but she didn't.

"As I said before, Detective McVey—I really have no idea."

Sixty seconds later Vera closed the door behind them and locked it. Walking back into the living room, she turned out the lights, then went to the window. Below, she saw them come out and cross to the white Ford parked across the street. They got in, the doors closed and they drove off. When they did, she let out a deep sigh. For the second time that evening she'd lied to the police.

49

JOANNA LAY in the dark, trembling. She'd never imagined sex could be like that. How she could feel, how she could still be feeling. Pascal Von Holden had been gone for nearly an hour, but the smell of him, his cologne, his perspiration, was still on her and she didn't want to lose it, ever. She tried to think back on how it happened. How one thing led to another.

The steamer was docking and the men in the tuxedos had gone to make sure the gangway was secure and that Elton Lybarger's limousine was waiting at the bottom of it. She and Pascal had finished dancing and she had gone to tell Mr. Lybarger the good news, that she was staying on to continue with his physical therapy.

When she'd reached him, he'd motioned for her to take him aside in his wheelchair. She'd looked to Von Holden waiting on the deck outside. She hadn't wanted to leave him, even for a moment, but he'd nodded and smiled and Joanna had wheeled Lybarger off. When they were safely away, Lybarger had suddenly reached out and taken her hand. He seemed tired and confused, even a little afraid. Looking at him, she'd smiled gently and told him she was staying on a little while longer to help him adjust to his new surroundings. It was then that he had drawn her close and asked her what he had asked before.

"Where is my family?" he said. "Where is my family?"

"They're here, Mr. Lybarger. They met you at the plane. They're here tonight, Mr. Lybarger, all around you. You're home, in Switzerland."

"No!" he said, emphatically, staring at her with angry eyes. "No! My family. Where are they?"

It was then the men in tuxedos had come back. It was time for Mr. Lybarger to be taken to his car. She'd told him to go with them and not to worry, that they would talk about it tomorrow.

Von Holden had put his arm around her and smiled reassuringly as they'd watched Lybarger being wheeled down the gangplank and gently helped into the limousine. She must be very tired, he said. Still on New Mexico time. "Yes, I am," she'd smiled, grateful for his caring.

"May I see you back to your hotel?"

"Yes. That would be nice. Thank you." She'd never met anyone as genuinely sincere or warm or kind.

After that she vaguely remembered the ride up from the lake and back through Zurich. Colored lights came to mind, and she remembered hearing Von Holden say something about sending a car for her in the morning to take her and her luggage to Lybarger's estate.

For some reason she recalled opening the door to her hotel room and Von Holden taking the key from her and closing the door behind them. He'd helped her off with her coat and hung it neatly in the closet. Then he'd turned and they'd come together in the darkness. His lips on hers. Gentle, and at the same time, forceful.

She remembered him undressing her and taking her breasts one after the other into his mouth, his lips encircling her nipples, making them grow harder than they ever had. Then, he'd lifted her up bodily and put her on the bed. Never taking his eyes from her, he'd undressed. Slowly, sensuously. His tie, then his jacket, his shoes, socks, then his shirt. The hair on his muscular chest was as light colored as that on his head. Her breasts ached and she could feel her own wetness as she watched him. She hadn't meant to, as if it were rude or something, but her eyes locked on his hands as they opened his belt and deliberately lowered the zipper on his fly.

Suddenly Joanna threw her head back in the dark and laughed. She was alone but she laughed loudly, raucously. If anyone in the room next to hers could hear, she didn't care. It was the old dirty joke the girls had told since junior high school, come true.

"Men come in three sizes," it went. "Small, medium and OH MY GOD!"

50

Paris, 3:30 A.M.
Same hotel, same room, same clock as the last time.
Click.
3:31.

* * *

IT WAS always three-thirty, give or take twenty minutes. McVey was exhausted but he couldn't sleep. Just to think hurt, but his mind had no "off" switch. It never had, not from the day he'd seen his first corpse lying in an alley with half its head shot away. The million details that could lead from victim to killer were what kept you wired and awake.

Lebrun had sent inspectors to the Gare Montparnasse to try to pick up Osborn's trail. But it was a wasted operation and he'd told that to Lebrun. Vera Monneray had lied about dropping him off at the train station. She'd taken him somewhere else and knew where he was.

He'd argued they should go back later that morning and tell her they'd like to continue the discussion at headquarters. A formal interrogation room worked wonders in getting people to tell the truth, whether they wanted to or not.

Lebrun said an emphatic "no!" Osborn might be a murder suspect, but the girlfriend of the prime minister of the Republique Française most certainly was not!

His sensibility factor strained to overload, McVey had slowly counted to ten and countered with another solution: a polygraph test. It might not make an untruthful suspect reveal all, but it was a good emotional setup for a second interview immediately following it. Especially if the polygraph examiner was exceptionally thorough and the suspect had been the slightest bit nervous, as most were.

But again Lebrun said no, and the best McVey had been able finally to waggle out of him was a thirty-six-hour surveillance. And even that had been a tooth pull because it was expensive and Lebrun had to go on the hook for three, two-man detective teams watching her movements around the clock for a day and a half.

Click.

This time McVey didn't bother with the clock. Shutting off the light, he lay back in the dark and stared at the vague shadows on the ceiling wondering if he really cared about any of it: Vera Monneray, Osborn, this "tall man," if he existed, who had supposedly killed Albert Merriman and wounded Osborn, or even the deep-frozen, headless bodies and the deep-frozen head some invisible, high-tech Dr. Frankenstein was trying to join. That that physician could possibly be Osborn was also incidental because, at this point, there was only one thing McVey knew for certain he did care about—sleep—and he wondered if he was ever going to get it.

Click.

Four hours later, McVey was behind the wheel of the beige Opel heading for the park by the river. Dawn had broken clear and he had to flip down the visor to keep the sun out of his eyes as he drove along the Seine looking for the park turnoff. If he'd slept at all, he didn't remember.

Five minutes later, he recognized the stand of trees that marked the entryway to the park. Pulling into it, he stopped. A grassy field was circumvented by a muddy road that ran around its periphery and was lined with trees, some of which were just beginning to turn color. Looking down, he saw the tire prints of a single vehicle that had entered the park and then left the same way.

He had to assume they belonged to Lebrun's Ford, because he and the French inspector had arrived after the rain had stopped; any new vehicle entering the park would have left a second set of tracks.

Accelerating slowly, McVey drove around the park to where the trees met the top of the ramp leading down to the water. Stopping, he got out. Directly in front of him two sets of washed-over footprints led down the ramp to the river. His and Lebrun's. Studying the ramp and the landing at the bottom, he imagined where Agnes Demblon's white Citroën would have been parked near the water's edge and tried to think why Osborn and Albert Merriman would have been there. Were they working together? Why drive the car to the landing? Was there something in it they were going to unload into the water? Drugs maybe? Or was it the car itself they had designs on? Trash it? Strip it for parts? But why? Osborn was a reasonably well-off doctor. None of it made sense.

Theorizing the red mud here was the same red mud he'd seen on Osborn's running shoes the night before the murder, McVey had to assume Osborn had been here the day before. Add to that the fact that three sets of fingerprints had been found in the car, Osborn's, Merriman's, and Agnes Demblon's, and McVey felt reasonably certain it was Osborn who had picked the river location and brought Merriman to it.

Lebrun had established that Agnes Demblon had worked at her job in the bakery the entire day on Friday and had still been there late in the afternoon, the time Merriman had been killed.

For the moment, and even before ballistics gave Lebrun a report on the bullet Vera Monneray said she had taken out of Osborn, McVey was willing to believe her story that a tall man had done the shooting. And unless he had worn gloves and had both Osborn and Merriman under his control, friendly or unfriendly, it was safe to assume he had not come to the park in the same car with them. And since the Citroën had been left at the scene, he would either have had to come in a separate car—or, if by the off chance he had ridden out with Osborn and Merriman, have had another car pick him up afterward. There was no public transportation this far out, nor would he have been likely to walk back to the city. It was possible, but very unlikely, that he'd hitched a ride. A man who used a

Heckler & Koch and had just shot two men was not the kind of man who stuck out his thumb, thereby providing a witness who could later identify him.

Now, if one followed the Interpol, Lyon, trail to New York Police Department records, it would make Merriman, not Osborn, the tall man's target. If that was so, did that mean there was a connection between Osborn and the tall man? If so, did the tall man, having killed Merriman, then double-cross Osborn and turn the gun on him? Or, had the tall man followed Merriman, perhaps from the bakery, to wherever he'd met Osborn, and then followed the two here?

Taking that theory further and assuming the fire that destroyed Agnes Demblon's apartment building was designed primarily to terminate her, it seemed reasonable to assume the tall man's orders were to take care not only of Merriman, but anyone else who might have intimately known him.

"His *wife*!" McVey suddenly said out loud.

Turning from the trail, he started back under the trees toward the Opel. He had no idea where the closest phone would be, and he cursed Interpol for giving him a car with no radio and no phone. Lebrun had to be alerted that Merriman's wife, wherever she was, was in serious danger.

Reaching the edge of the trees, McVey was almost to the car, when abruptly he stopped and turned around. The path he'd just taken, in a rush from the murder scene, was through the trees. Exactly what a gunman leaving a shooting might have done. The way McVey and Lebrun had walked to the ramp the night before had been around the trees, not through them. Lebrun's inspectors and tech crew had found nothing to indicate the presence of a third man the night of the killing. Hence they assumed Osborn had been the gunman. But had they searched up here, under the trees, this far back from the ramp?

This was a bright, sunny Sunday after nearly a week-long rain. McVey was in a quandary. If he left to warn Lebrun about Merriman's wife he ran the risk somebody, or a lot of people, with cabin fever would arrive at the park and inadvertently destroy evidence. Choosing, not too happily, to assume that since the French police had yet to find her, the tall man would have the same problem, McVey decided to steal the time he needed and stay where he was.

Turning back, he cautiously retraced his steps back toward the ramp, through the trees, the way he had come. The ground under the trees was a thick blanket of wet pine needles. Stepping on them, they sprang back like a carpet, which meant it would take something a great deal heavier than a man's step to leave any kind of impression on them.

Crossing to the ramp, McVey turned back. He'd found nothing. Walking a dozen yards east of where he was standing, he made the crossing again. Still, he found nothing.

Turning west, he moved to a spot halfway between his original crossing and the one he'd just made, and started across again. He hadn't gone a dozen paces before he saw it. A single flat toothpick, broken in half, nearly obscured by the pine needles. Taking out his handkerchief, he bent down and picked it up. Looking at it, he could see the split in it was a lighter color on the inside than on the outside, suggesting it had been broken in the recent past. Wrapping it in the handkerchief, McVey put it in his pocket and started back toward his car. This time he moved slowly, carefully studying the ground. He was almost to the edge of the trees when something caught his eye. Stopping, he squatted down.

The pine needles directly in front of him were a lighter shade than those surrounding them. In the rain they would have looked the same, but as they dried in the morning sun, they looked more as if they'd been scattered on purpose. Picking up a fallen twig, McVey brushed them lightly aside. At first he saw nothing and was disappointed. Then, continuing, he uncovered what looked like the impression of a tire track. Getting up and following it, he found a solid impression in the sandy soil just at the edge of a tree line. A car had been driven in under the trees and parked. Sometime later, the driver had backed up and seen his own tracks. Getting out, he'd gathered fresh pine needles and scattered them around, covering the tracks, but in doing so he'd neglected to note where he'd parked. Outside the tree line the tracks had washed away in the rain. But at the tree line, the overhang had protected the ground, leaving a small but distinct imprint in the soil. No more than four inches long and a half inch deep, it wasn't much. But for a police tech crew, it would be enough.

51

"SCHOLL!"

Osborn had just finished urinating and was flushing the toilet when the name jumped out at him. Turning awkwardly, and wincing in pain as he put weight on his injured leg, he reached out and picked up the cane Vera had left from where it hung on the edge of the sink. Shifting his weight, he started back into the room. Each step was an effort and he had to move slowly, but he realized the hurt was more from stiffness and muscle trauma than from the wound itself, and that meant it was healing.

The room, as he hobbled out of the cubicle that served as a toilet and started across it, seemed smaller than it had when he was lying down. With a blackout curtain drawn across the only window, it was not only dark but felt stuffy and confining and smelled of antiseptic. Stopping at the window, he set the cane aside and pulled back the curtain. Immediately the room flooded with the bright light of an early autumn day. Straining, he gritted his teeth against the tug of his leg, pulled open the small window and looked out. All he could see was the roofline of the building as it fell steeply away and, beyond it, the top of Notre Dame's towers glistening in the morning sun. What got him more than anything was the crispness of the morning air as it wafted across the Seine. It was sweet and refreshing and he breathed it in deeply.

Vera had come up sometime during the night and changed his bandages. She'd tried to tell him something but he'd been too groggy to understand, and had gone back to sleep. Later, when he awoke and his senses began to come back, he'd focused on the tall man and the police and what to do about them. But now it was Erwin Scholl who was in the front of his mind. The man Henri Kanarack swore, under the terror of the succinylcholine, was the person who'd hired him to murder his father. That had happened, he recalled, at almost the same moment the tall man had appeared out of the darkness and shot them both.

Erwin Scholl. From where? Kanarack had told him that, too.

Turning from the window, Osborn limped back to his bed, smoothed out the blanket a little, then turned around and eased himself down. The walk from his bed to the bathroom and back again had wearied him more than he liked. Now he sat there, on the edge of the bed, able to do little more than breathe in and out.

Who was Erwin Scholl? And why had he wanted his father dead?

Suddenly he shut his eyes. It was the same question he'd been asking for almost thirty years. The pain in his leg was nothing compared to what he felt in his soul. He remembered the feeling that had seared through his gut the moment Kanarack had told him he'd been paid to do it. In an instant the whole thing had gone from a lifetime of loneliness and pain and anger to something beyond comprehension. In stumbling upon Henri Kanarack, in finding where he lived and where he worked, he thought God had at last acknowledged him and that, at last, the suffering inside him would be ended. But it hadn't. It had only been handed off. Cruelly. Neatly. Like a football to another player in a game of keepaway. And he was the one they were keeping it from, as they had for so many years.

The river, at least, had carried him somewhere conclusive. Had that place been death it would have been preferable to the one to which he'd been returned; the one that allowed him no rest, that kept him forever enraged, that made it impossible for him to love or be loved without the awful fear he would destroy it. The monkey had not gone away at all. Only changed form. Henri Kanarack had become Erwin Scholl. This time with no face, just a name. What would it take to find him—another thirty years? And if he did have the courage and strength to do it and finally, after everything, found him, what then?

—another door leading somewhere else?

A sound on the far side of the wall snatched Osborn from his reverie. Someone was coming. Quickly he glanced around for a place to hide. There was none. Where was Kanarack's gun? What had Vera done with it? He looked back at the door. The knob was turning. The only weapon he had was the cane next to him. His hand closed around it and the door swung open.

Vera was dressed in white for work.

"Good morning," she said, entering. Once again she carried the tray, this time with hot coffee and croissants, and a plastic refrigerator box with fruit, cheese and a small loaf of bread. "How are you feeling?"

Osborn let out a sigh and set the cane on the bed. "Fine," he said. "Especially now that I know who was coming to visit."

Vera set the tray on the small table under the window and turned to look at him. "The police came back last night. An American policeman was with them, he seemed to know you quite well."

Osborn started. "McVey!" My God, he was still in Paris.

"You seem to know him too. . . ." Vera's smile was thin, almost dangerous, as if in some crazy way she liked all this.

"What did they want?" he said quickly.

"They found out I picked you up at the golf course. I admitted I'd taken a bullet out of you. They wanted to know where you were. I said I left you off at the railway station, that I didn't know where you were going and you didn't want me to know. I'm not sure they believed me."

"McVey will have you watched like a hawk, waiting for you to get in touch with me."

"I know. That's why I'm going back to work. I'm on for thirty-six hours. Hopefully, by the time I'm through, they'll be bored and assume I was telling the truth."

"What if they don't? What if they decided to search your apartment and then the building?" Osborn was suddenly frightened. He was in a corner with no way out. Never mind the condition of his leg; if he tried to get out and they were watching, they'd nab him before he'd gone a half block. If they decided to search the building, eventually they'd find their way up to where he was and he was done for anyway.

"There's nothing else we can do." Vera was strong, unruffled. Not only on his side and protecting him, but very much in control. "You have water in the bathroom and enough to eat until I get back. I want you to start exercising. Stretching and leg lifts if you can, otherwise make sure you walk back and forth across the room for as long as you can, every four hours. When we do leave, you're going to have to walk.

"And make certain you keep the window curtain pulled when it gets dark. The dormer is hidden in the roofline, but if someone's watching, the light would give you away in a moment. Here—"

Vera pressed a key into his hand.

"It's to my apartment—in case you have to get in touch with me. The telephone number is on a pad next to the phone. The stairs open into a closet on the floor below. Take the service stairway to the second floor." Vera hesitated and looked at him. "I don't have to tell you to be careful."

"And I don't have to tell you you can still walk away from this. Go to your grandmother's and deny you had any idea of what went on here."

"No," she said, and turned for the door.

"Vera."

She stopped and looked back. "What?"

"There was a gun. Where is it?"

Vera reacted, and Osborn could see she didn't like the sound of what he'd said.

"Vera—" He paused. "If the tall man finds me, what am I supposed to do?"

"How could he find you? He has no way to know about me. Who I am, or where I live."

"He didn't know about Merriman, either. But he's dead just the same."

She hesitated.

"Vera, please." Osborn was looking directly at her. The gun was to defend his life, not shoot policemen.

Finally, she nodded toward the table under the window. "It's in the drawer."

52

Marseilles.

MARIANNE CHALFOUR BOUGET reluctantly left eight o'clock Mass only ten minutes after it had begun, and only because her sister's weeping was causing other parishioners, most of whom she knew well, to turn and look. Michele Kanarack had been with her less than forty-eight hours and in the entire time had been unable to control her tears.

Marianne was three years older than her sister and had five children, the oldest of whom was fourteen. Her husband, Jean Luc, was a fisherman whose income varied with the season and who spent much of his time away from the family. But when he was home, as he was now, he wanted to be with his wife and children.

Especially with his wife.

Jean Luc had a voracious sexual appetite and was not ashamed of it. But it could be problematical, even embarrassing, when his urges overcame him and he suddenly swept his wife off her feet or out of her chair and carried her bodily into the bedroom of their tiny three-room apartment, where they made wild, and loud, love, for what seemed hours at a time.

Why Michele had suddenly come to live with them and for how long he couldn't understand. All married people had problems. But usually, with the help of a priest, they worked them out. Therefore, he was certain that Henri would show up at any moment, begging Michele to forgive him and go back to Paris.

But Michele, through her tears, was just as certain he would not. She had been there two nights, trying to sleep on the couch in their minuscule living room/kitchen, trampled by the children as they crowded around the small black-and-while television, fighting over programs. While in the other room, husband and wife made uproarious love to no one's attention but Michele's.

By Sunday morning Jean Luc had had enough of her tears and told Marianne so, directly and to the point in front of Michele. Take her to church and, before the eyes of God, make her stop crying! Or if not God, at least the monseigneur.

But it hadn't worked. And now as they left the church and walked out into the warm Mediterranean sunshine, turning onto the boulevard d'Athens toward Canebiere, Marianne took her sister's hand.

"Michele, you are not the only woman in the world whose husband has suddenly walked out. Nor are you the first pregnant one. Yes, you hurt and I understand. But life goes its merry way, so that is enough! We are here for you. Find a job and have your baby. Then find someone decent."

Michele looked at her sister, then at the ground. Marianne was right, of course. But it didn't help the hurt or the fear of being alone or the sense of emptiness. But thinking never took away tears. Only time did.

Having said what she had, Marianne stopped at a small

open-air market on the Quai des Belges to pick up a boiling chicken and some fresh vegetables for dinner. The market and the sidewalk, even at this hour, were crowded, and the sound of people and passing traffic kept the noise level high.

Marianne heard a strange little "pop" that seemed to rise above the other sounds. When she turned to ask Michele about it, she saw her sister leaning back against a counter packed high with melons, looking as if she'd been genuinely surprised by something. Then she saw a spot of bright red appear at the base of the white collar at Michele's throat and begin to spread. At the same time she felt a presence and looked up. A tall man stood in front of her and smiled. Then something came up in his hand and again she heard the "pop." As quickly, the tall man vanished and suddenly, it seemed as if the day was getting dark. She looked around her and saw faces. Then, curiously, everything faded.

53

BERNHARD OVEN could have flown back to Paris the same way he'd come to Marseilles, but a round-trip ticket bracketing the hours of a multiple murder was too easily traceable by the police. The Grande Vitesse TGV bullet train from Marseilles to Paris took four and three-quarter hours. Time for Oven to sit back in the first-class compartment and assess what had happened and what would come next.

Tracing Michele Kanarack to her sister's home in Marseilles had been a simple matter of following her to the station the morning she'd left Paris and observing what train she'd taken. Once he had a train and a destination, the Organization had done the rest. She'd been picked up as she got off the train and followed to her sister's home in the Le Panier neighborhood. After that, she'd been carefully watched and inventory taken of those she might confide in. That information in hand, Oven had taken an Air Inter flight from Paris to Marseilles and picked up a rental car at Provence Airport. Inside its spare tire casing was a Czechoslovakian CZ .22 automatic, supplemental ammunition and a silencer.

"Bonjour. Ah, le billet, oui."

Giving his ticket to the ticket collector, Oven exchanged the kind of meaningless pleasantries that would take place between a ticket collector and the successful businessman he appeared to be, then, sitting back, he watched the French countryside as the train moved rapidly north through the green of the Rhône Valley. Estimating, he judged they were traveling in the neighborhood of one hundred and eighty miles per hour.

It was just as well he'd taken care of the women where he had. If somehow they'd eluded him and gotten home, well, hysterical people were always cumbersome targets. And the sight of Marianne's husband and five children shot to death in their own apartment, no matter how neatly he'd done it, would most certainly have sent both women over the edge, bringing the neighbors and anyone else within earshot.

Of course the husband and children would be found, if they hadn't been already, and the reverberations would bring police and politicians scrambling out of the woodwork. But Oven had had no choice. The husband had been about to leave to join his cronies at the local café and that would have meant waiting until later in the day when everyone had gathered back at home. And that would have caused a delay he could not afford because he had even more pressing business in Paris; business in which the Organization, so far, had been unable to assist.

Antenna 2, the state-owned television network, had carried an interview with the manager of a golf clubhouse on the Seine near Vernon. A California doctor the police suspected in the murder of an expatriate American named Albert Merriman had crawled out of the river early Saturday morning and spent time recuperating in the manager's store before being picked up and driven off by a dark-haired Frenchwoman.

To date, everyone intimately involved with Albert Merriman Bernhard Oven had quickly and efficiently eliminated. But somehow, the American doctor, identified as a Paul Osborn, had survived. And now a woman was involved. Both had to be found and accounted for before the police got to them. Not so difficult, if time had not suddenly become the enemy. Today was Sunday, October 9. The agenda had to be cleared no later than Friday, October 14.

"Have you ever worked with Mr. Lybarger while he was in the nude, Ms. Marsh?"

"No, Doctor, of course not," Joanna said, surprised at the question. "There would be no reason."

Joanna liked Salettl no more in Zurich than she had in New Mexico. His shortness with her, his distant manner, were more than intimidating. He frightened her.

"Then you've never seen him undressed."

"No, sir."

"In his underwear, perhaps."

"Doctor Salettl, I'm not sure I understand what you're saying."

At 7:00 sharp that morning, Joanna had been wakened in her room by a call from Von Holden. Instead of the warm and affectionate lover of the night before, he'd been abrupt and to the point. A car would be by to pick up her and her things for transport to Mr. Lybarger's estate in forty-five minutes; he knew she would be ready. Puzzled by his distance, she said nothing more than yes, she would. Then, as an afterthought, had asked what she should do about her dog in the kennel in Taos.

"It has been taken care of," Von Holden had said, and with that hung up.

An hour later, still a little hung over from the combination of jet lag, dinner, drinks and marathon sex with Von Holden, Joanna sat in the backseat of Lybarger's Mercedes limousine as it turned off the main highway and stopped at a security gate. The driver pressed a button and the passenger window lowered enough for a uniformed guard to look inside. Satisfied, he waved them on, and the limousine moved up a long, tree-lined drive toward what Joanna would only later describe as a castle.

A middle-aged housekeeper with a pleasant smile had shown her to her quarters: a large bedroom with its own bath on the ground floor that looked out onto a sprawling lawn that ended at the edge of a thick forest.

Ten minutes later, she answered a knock at the door and was escorted by the same woman to Dr. Salettl's second-floor office in a separate building, where she was now.

"Judging by your ongoing reports, I see you have been as impressed as the rest of us with Mr. Lybarger's progress."

"Yes, sir." Joanna was determined not to be intimidated by Salettl's manner. "At the beginning, when I first started working with him, he hardly had any control over his voluntary motor functions. It was even hard for him to follow a clear train of thought. But each step of the way, he continually amazed me. He has an incredibly strong inner will."

"He is also physically robust."

"Yes, that too."

"Comfortable in a social atmosphere. Able to relax with people and converse intelligently with them."

"I—" Joanna wanted to say something about Lybarger's continual references to his family.

"You have reservations?"

Joanna hesitated. There was no point in bringing up something that had been wholly between Lybarger and her. Besides, each time he had made those references, he had either been tired or in the course of travel where his daily routine had been interrupted. "It's just that he tires easily. That's why I wanted the wheelchair for him last night on the boa—"

"The cane he uses." Salettl cut her off, made a note, then looked back at her. "Is it possible for him to stand and walk without it?"

"He's used to having it."

"Please answer the question. Can he walk without it?"

"Yes, but—"

"But, what?"

"Not very far and not very confidently."

"He dresses himself. Shaves himself. Uses the toilet without aid, does he not?"

"Yes." Joanna was beginning to wish she had declined Von Holden's offer and gone home today as planned.

"Can he pick up a pen, write his name clearly?"

"Pretty clearly." She forced a smile.

"What about his other functions?"

Joanna knotted her brow. "I don't know what you mean by other functions."

"Is he able to have an erection? Partake in sexual intercourse?"

"I—I—don't know," she stammered. She was embarrassed. She'd never been asked that kind of a question about one of her patients before. "I should think that's more of a medical question."

Salettl stared at her for a moment, then continued. "From your point of view, when would you say he will regain all of his physical abilities and be wholly functional, as if the stroke never occurred?"

"If—If we are talking about his basic motor functions. Standing, walking, talking, without tiring and that's all— the other things, as I said, are not my department—"

"Just motor functions. How much longer do you think it will take?"

"I—I'm not sure exactly."

"Estimate it, please."

"—I—really can't."

"That's not an answer." Salettl was glaring at her as if she were a misbehaved child instead of his patient's professional therapist.

"If—I work with him a lot and he responds like he has. I'd like to guess, maybe another month. . . . But you have to understand it's only a guess. It all depends on how he—"

"I'm going to give you a goal. By the end of the week, I want to see him walking without a cane."

"I don't know if that's possible."

Salettl touched a button at his sleeve and spoke into an intercom. "Miss Marsh is ready to work with Mr. Lybarger."

54

MCVEY STARED out Lebrun's office window. Five floors below he could see the Place du Parvis, the open plaza across from Notre Dame, crowded with tourists. At eleven thirty it was beginning to warm into an Indian summer day.

"Eight dead. Five of them children. Each shot once in the head with a .22. Nobody sees or hears a thing. Not the next-door neighbors, not the people in the market." Lebrun dropped the faxed report from the Marseilles police on his desk and reached for a chrome thermos on a table behind him.

"Professional with a silencer," McVey said, with no attempt to hide his anger. "Eight more on the tall man's list."

"If it was the tall man."

McVey looked up hard. "Merriman's widow? What do you think?"

"I think you are probably right, *mon ami,*" Lebrun said quietly.

McVey had returned to his hotel from the park by the river a little before eight and immediately called Lebrun at home. In response, Lebrun had put out a countrywide alert to local police agencies warning of the life threat to Michele Kanarack. The obvious problem, of course, was that she had yet to be found. And with little more than a description of her—given, finally, to Inspectors Maitrot and Barras by residents in her apartment building—Lebrun's alarm was a warning in the wind. Ghosts were very difficult to protect.

"My friend, how could we know? My men were out

there by the river a full day before you and found nothing to indicate a third man."

Lebrun was trying to help, but it didn't lift the bitterness or the feelings of guilt and helplessness that were churning McVey's stomach. Eight people were dead who might still be alive if somehow he and the French police had been just a little bit better at what they did. Michele Kanarack had been shot only a few moments after McVey had called Lebrun to alert him she was in danger. If he'd discovered the situation and made the call three hours earlier, or four, or five, would it have made any difference? Maybe yes, probably no. She was a needle who still would have been lost in the haystack.

"To protect and to serve" was the slogan lettered on the LAPD black-and-whites. Every day people laughed at it or scorned it or ignored it. "Serve?" Who knew what that meant. But protecting people was something else. If you cared, like McVey did. If they got hurt because you or your partner, or the department, wasn't up to the demands put on it, you hurt too. Real bad. Nobody knew it and you didn't talk about it. Except to yourself or maybe to the face in the bottom of a bottle when you tried to forget about it. It wasn't idealism— that went out the first time you saw somebody shot in the face. It was something else. Why you ended up, after how many years, doing what you did, and were still there. Michele Kanarack and her sister's family weren't a broken VCR that could be fixed. The people in Agnes Demblon's apartment building hadn't been a car that was a lemon and could be fought over at an auto dealership. They were people, the commodity policemen dealt in, for better or worse, every working day of their lives.

"That coffee?" McVey nodded toward the thermos in Lebrun's hand.

"Oui."

"I'll take it black," McVey said. "Just like the day."

By 9:30, Lebrun had had a tech crew at the park making a plaster cast of the tire track and sifting through the pine forest for anything McVey had missed.

At 10:45, McVey met Lebrun in his office and together they went to the lab to check on the tire imprint. They'd come in to find a technician working the hardening plaster with a portable hair dryer. Five minutes later, the cast was dry enough for an ink impression on paper.

Next came the collection of tire tread patterns provided the Paris police by tire manufacturers. Fifteen minutes later, they had it. The ink impression taken from the plaster cast made at the park clearly matched an Italian-manufactured Pirelli tire, size P205/70R14, and made to fit a wheel rim fourteen by five and a half inches. The following morning, Monday, a Pirelli factory expert would be called to examine the cast to see if further specifics could be determined.

On the way back to Lebrun's office, McVey asked about the toothpick.

"That will take longer," Lebrun said. "Maybe tomorrow, maybe the next day. Frankly, I doubt it will reveal much."

"Maybe we'll get lucky. Maybe when he was picking his teeth he nicked a gum and bled on it. Or maybe he has some kind of infection or other disease that would be carried in the salivary tract. Anything will be more than we have, Inspector."

"We have no way of knowing it was the tall man who used the toothpick. It could have been Merriman or Osborn or someone wholly anonymous." Lebrun opened the door to his office.

"You mean a possible witness," McVey said as they entered.

"No, I hadn't meant that at all. But it is a thought, McVey. A good one. Touché."

It was then the knock had come at the door and the uniformed officer had entered with the fax from the Marseilles Police.

McVey swallowed his coffee and walked across the room. On a bulletin board was posted a copy of *Le Figaro,* on it was a quarter-page picture of Levigne as he gave his story to the media. Clearly frustrated, McVey jabbed his finger at it.

"What gets me is this guy from the golf club is afraid we'd release his name to the media, then he goes ahead and does it himself. And what's that do but tell our friend that he's got an eyewitness out there who's still alive."

McVey turned away from the clipping, tugging at an ear. "All the king's horses, Lebrun. We don't find her, but *he* does." Turning back, he looked at the French detective directly.

"How did he know to go to Marseilles when nobody else did? And when he got there, how did he know where to find her?"

Lebrun pressed his fingertips together. "You're thinking the Interpol connection. Whoever it was in Lyon who requested the Merriman file from the New York police may have had similar means of tracking her down."

"Yeah, that's what I'm thinking."

Lebrun set his cup down, lit a cigarette and looked at his watch. "For your information, I'm taking the rest of the day off," he said quietly. "A short, one-man holiday. A trip by train to Lyon. Nobody knows where I'm going, not even my wife."

McVey frowned. "Pardon me if I don't understand. But you show up in Lyon and start asking questions, you think whoever did it is just going to raise his or her hand and say, 'It's me'? You might as well call a press conference first."

"Mon ami." Lebrun smiled. "I said I was going to

Lyon. I didn't say it was to Interpol headquarters. Actually, I've asked a very old friend to a very quiet supper."

"Go on," McVey said.

"As you know, Group D, to which your investigation of the headless bodies was assigned, is a subgroup under Interpol Division Two. Division Two is the police division revolving entirely around case tracking and analysis. Whoever made the request for the Merriman file will be a member of Division Two, quite possibly a high-ranking member.

"Division One, on the other hand, is general administration, which manages finances, staff, equipment procurement, custodial services and things like personnel, accounting, building maintenance and other everyday activities. One of those everyday activities is subgroup Security and is responsible for headquarters security. The individual in charge of this subgroup will have access to data records identifying the employee who requested the Merriman file."

Lebrun smiled, pleased with his plan. McVey stared at him.

"*Mon ami,* I don't mean to sound like a cynic, but what if that individual you're so nicely taking to supper turns out to be the one who made the request? Don't you realize you're the guy they were keeping the information from in the first place? So they'd have time to locate Merriman. You asked me before if I thought these guys would kill a cop. If you were uncertain before, look at the Marseilles report again."

"Ah, the man loves to warn via the bloody metaphor." Lebrun smiled and squashed out his cigarette. "My friend, I appreciate your concern. And were circumstances different, I would wholeheartedly agree with you that my approach was careless. However, I rather doubt the supervisor of interior security would harm his eldest brother."

55

A NEW, dark green Ford Sierra with Pirelli P205/70R14 tires and fourteen- by five-and-a-half inch wheels, drove slowly past the apartment building at 18 Quai de Bethune, turned the corner at the Pont de Sully and pulled in behind a white Jaguar convertible parked on the rue St.-Louis en l'Île. A moment later, the door opened and the tall man got out. It was a warm afternoon but he wore gloves just the same. Flesh-colored surgical gloves.

Bernhard Oven's train arrived at Gare de Lyon at twelve fifteen. From the station he'd taken a cab to Orly Airport, where he retrieved the green Ford. By 2:50 he was back in Paris and parked outside Vera Monneray's building.

At 3:07, he slipped the lock and stepped into her apartment, closing the door behind him. No one had seen him cross the street, or use the newly minted key that fit the security door to the service entrance. Once inside, he'd climbed the service stairs and entered the apartment through the rear hallway.

To most of France, the story first broadcast on Antenna 2 television and, soon after, repeated by every other media, about the mysterious, dark-haired woman who'd driven away the American murder suspect from the golf club after he had climbed out of the Seine, was a juicy, romantic intrigue. Just who she was and who the American might be were the subjects of reckless speculation—from a major French actress, film director and author, to an international tennis star, to an American rock singer, dressed in a black wig and speaking French; the doctor was whispered to be no doctor at all, the picture given the press a fake, but a famous Hollywood actor, currently in Paris promoting a film; darker stories vouched it was a veteran United States senator, his star diminished by still another tragedy.

Vera Monneray's identity and address, handprinted on a card, as well as the keys to the service door and her apartment, were in the glove box of Bernhard Oven's car when he'd picked it up at Orly. In the five plus hours since he'd left Marseilles, the Organization had proven itself meticulously efficient. As it had with Albert Merriman.

The ornamental clock on the table beside Vera Monneray's bed read eleven minutes past three in the afternoon.

Ms. Monneray, Oven knew, had gone to work that morning at seven o'clock and would not be through with her shift until seven the following night. That meant, factoring the possible unknown intrusion of a maid or handyman, he would not be disturbed as he searched her apartment. It also meant that if, by chance, the American was there, he would have him alone.

Five minutes later Oven knew the American was not there. The apartment was as empty as it was spotless. Letting himself out, carefully relocking the door, he retraced his steps down the service stairs, stopping at the landing where the service door opened onto the street. But instead of going out, he continued on down the stairs, descending into the basement.

Finding a light switch, he turned it on and looked around. What he saw was a long narrow hallway leading back under the building, with numerous doors and darkened storage areas off it. To his right, tucked back under a low ceiling of heavy timbers, were the trash receptacles for the building's tenants.

How innocently accommodating the upper-class Parisians, each apartment having its own refuse containers, and each painted with the apartment's number. A closer scan of the area quickly turned up the four trash bins allocated to Vera's apartment, only one of which was filled.

Removing the cover, Oven spread open a day-old newspaper and went through it piece by piece. Finding, in turn, four empty cans of Diet Coke, an empty plastic bottle of Gelave, hair conditioner, an empty container of Tic Tac mints, an empty box of Today contraceptive sponges, four empty bottles of Amstel light beer, a copy of *People* magazine, an empty and partially bent can of beef bouillon soup, a yellow plastic squeeze bottle of Joy dish soap and—Oven stopped, something rattled inside the bottle of Joy.

He was about to unscrew the cap when he heard a door above and someone start down the stairs. The footsteps stopped briefly at the landing where the service door opened to the street, then continued down. Turning out the light, Oven stepped into the shadows behind the low overhang of the stairs, at the same time lifting a .25-caliber Walther automatic from his waistband.

A moment later, a plump maid in a starched black-and-white uniform clumped down the steps carrying a bulging plastic trash bag. Snapping on the light, she lifted the lid to one of the rubbish cans, dropped the bag inside, then closed the lid and turned back for the stairs. It was then she saw the mess Oven had spread out on the newspaper. Muttering something in French, she walked over, scooped it up and plunked it into Vera's trash bin. Replacing the cover, she abruptly shut off the light and tromped back up the stairs.

Oven listened as her footsteps retreated. Satisfied she was gone, he slipped the Walther back into his waistband, then clicked on the light. Lifting the lid from the trash barrel, he took out the plastic soap bottle and unscrewed its cap, then turned it upside down and shook it. Whatever was inside rattled, but didn't fall out. Pulling a long, thin knife from his sleeve, he opened the blade and coaxed out a small bottle covered with soapy slime. Wiping it off, he held it up to the light. It was a medical vial from Wyeth Pharmaceutical Products; the label read, 5ML TETANUS TOXOID.

A hint of a smile crossed Oven's face. Vera Monneray was in her residency to become a doctor. Pharmaceuticals were available to her and she was qualified to give an injection. A wounded man coming out of a polluted river would very likely require a tetanus shot booster not only to prevent tetanus but diphtheria. And someone giving a shot would not be likely to do it elsewhere and then bring the empty vial back home to hide it in their kitchen soap bottle. No, the injection would have been given here, in Vera's apartment. And since the American was not in her apartment now, it meant he was somewhere close by, perhaps in another building, perhaps in this building itself.

Five and a half floors up from the basement where Bernhard Oven stood, Paul Osborn hunched over the small table under his window and stared out across the roofline, watching the afternoon shadows slide over Notre Dame's Gothic towers.

The hours he hadn't been sleeping, he'd been alternately pacing the tiny room for the exercise he knew he must have, or blankly staring out the window as he was now, trying to collect his thoughts.

There were certain obvious truths, he had concluded, there was no way around.

First: the police were still looking for him in connection with the death of Albert Merriman. Through Vera he knew they had found the remaining succinylcholine and taken it from his hotel room. If—when—they discovered its purpose, there was every chance they would reexamine—he still wanted to call him Kanarack—Merriman's body. If they did, they would find the puncture wounds. And if they hadn't already, McVey would make them. It wouldn't matter that he hadn't actually killed Merriman. They would still charge him with attempted homicide. And if they proved it, which they would, he'd not only spend God knew how many years in a French jail, he'd lose his medical license in the United States as well.

Second: he hadn't come out of the river unnoticed, and sooner or later the tall man, whoever he was, would learn he was still alive and come looking to kill him.

Third: even if he could somehow get out of Paris, the police still had his passport. So, for all intents, he was trapped in France because he could go to no other country without it, not even his own.

Fourth—and perhaps the cruelest and most painful of all, the thing he'd played over and over in his mind—was the clear and undeniable realization that the death of Albert Merriman had changed nothing. The demon haunting him had only become more complex and elusive. As if, after all his years of horror, such a thing were possible.

His insides screamed NO! in a hundred languages. Do not begin the pursuit again. Because this next door emblazoned with the name Erwin Scholl can only lead to what? Another door still! And by then, if you live that long, it can only open onto madness. Recognize instead, Paul Osborn, there will never be an answer. That this is your karma, to learn in this life that what you seek answers to, there may not be answers that are acceptable to you. It is only by understanding this that you will have peace and tranquility in the next life. Accept this truth and change.

But he knew that argument was nothing but avoidance and therefore not true. He could not change today any more than he had been able to change since he was ten. Kanarack/Merriman's death had been a terrible, emotional, blow. But what it had done was clarify and simplify the future. Before, he'd had only a face. Now he had a name. If this Erwin Scholl, if he found him, led to someone else, so be it. No matter the cost, he would go on and on until he knew the truth behind his father's death. Because if he did not, there would be no Vera, no life worth living. As there had been none since he was a boy. Peace and tranquility would come in this lifetime or not at all. *That* was his karma and his truth.

Outside, he could see the Notre Dame towers in full shadow. Soon the city lights would come on. It was time to pull the blackout curtain over his window and turn on his lamp. Having done that, he hobbled to his bed, and lay back. As he did, his resolve of the moment before faded and the pain flooded back, as raw as it had ever been.

"Why did this happen to my family—and to me?" he said out loud. He'd said it as a boy, as an adolescent, as a grown man and a successful surgeon. He'd said it a thousand times. Sometimes it came as a quiet thought, or part of a lucid conversation during a therapy session; other times, as emotion suddenly overwhelmed him, it had been thundered out loud wherever he stood, embarrassing ex-wives, friends and strangers.

Lifting the pillow, he brought out Kanarack's gun and hefted it in his hand. Tipping it toward him, he saw the hole where death came out. It looked easy. Even seductive. The simplest way of all. No more fear of the police, or of the tall man. Best of all, his pain would be instantly gone.

He wondered why he hadn't thought of it before.

56

FIFTEEN MINUTES later, at a quarter to six, Bernhard Oven rang the front bell to 18 Quai de Bethune and waited. He'd chosen to begin his search for the American with Vera Monneray's building, eliminating it first and then going on from there if necessary.

There was a click of the latch and Philippe, buttoning the top button of the tunic to his green uniform under his double chin, opened the door.

"*Bonsoir, monsieur,*" he said, apologizing for keeping the gentleman waiting.

"I have a delivery from the pharmacy at Sainte Anne hospital, sent by Doctor Monneray. She said to relay that it was urgent," Oven said in French.

"To whom?" Philippe was puzzled.

"To you, I suppose. The doorman at this address. That's all I know."

"The pharmacy, are you certain?"

"Do I look like a deliveryman? Monsieur, of course I'm certain. It's medicine, needed urgently. That's why I, the assistant manager, was sent all the way across town on a Sunday evening."

Philippe paused. The day before he had helped Vera bring Paul Osborn up the service stairs to her apartment from a car parked on the back street. Later in the day he'd helped her take him, heavily sedated after an operation, up to the hidden room under the eaves.

Osborn, he knew, had needed medical attention. Undoubtedly he still did, otherwise why would this delivery have come from the hospital pharmacy on a Sunday evening at Vera's request?

"Merci, monsieur," he said, and Oven handed him an official receipt book and a pen.

"Sign for it, please."

"Oui." Nodding, Philippe signed.

"Bonsoir," Oven said, then turned and walked away.

Closing the door, Philippe looked at the package, then quickly walked to the desk. Picking up the phone, he dialed Vera's private number at work.

Five minutes later, Bernhard Oven lifted the steel cover from the telephone panel in the basement of 18 Quai de Bethune, plugged a tiny earphone into a microrecorder connected to the front-desk phone line and hit "play." He heard the doorman's explanation of what had happened, followed by an alarmed female voice that had to be Mademoiselle Monneray's.

"Philippe!" she said. "I sent no package, no prescription. Open it, see what it is."

There was a rustling of paper followed by a grunt, then the doorman's voice once more.

"It's messy. . . . It—it looks like a medicine vial. Like doctors use when they give you a—"

Vera cut him off. "What does it say on the label?" Oven took note of the concern in her voice and smiled at it.

"It says . . . Excuse me, I have to get my glasses." There was a clunking sound as Philippe put down the phone. A moment later he came back on the line. "It says—'.5ml tetanus toxoid.' "

"Jesus Christ!" Vera gasped.

"What is it, mademoiselle?"

"Philippe, did you recognize the man? Was he one of the police?"

"No, mademoiselle."

"Was he tall?"

"Très"—Very.

"Put the vial in your own kitchen trash and do nothing.

I'm leaving the hospital now. I'll need your help when I get there."

"Oui, mademoiselle."

There was a distinctive click as Vera hung up, then the line went dead.

Calmly, Bernhard Oven unplugged the earphone from the microrecorder and unhooked the recorder from the phone line. A moment later he replaced the cover to the telephone console, turned out the light and retraced his steps up the service stairs.

It was 6:15 in the evening. All he had to do was wait.

Less than five miles away, McVey sat alone at a table at an outdoor café on the Place Victor Hugo. To his right, a young woman in jeans leaned on her elbows, staring off at nothing, an untouched glass of wine in front of her, a small dog dozing at her feet.

To his left, two elderly, very well dressed and obviously very rich matrons chattered in French over tea. They were cheery and animated and looked as if they'd been coming here every day at this hour for half a century.

Cradling a glass of Bordeaux, McVey found himself wishing that was the way he would go out. Not rich necessarily, but cheery and animated, and comfortable with the world around him.

Then a police car flew past with its emergency lights flashing, and he realized his last and final exit wasn't as much on his mind as was Osborn. He'd lied about the mud on his shoes because he'd been caught. He was a man in love, a tourist who had probably walked near the Eiffel Tower recently enough to know the gardens had been dug up and were muddy, and had been quick enough to make up a cover story for himself when asked about it. The trouble was, the mud there was gray-black, not red.

Where Osborn had been that Thursday afternoon—

barely four days ago—was at the riverbank by the park. The same place Merriman had been murdered and Osborn shot a day later.

What had Osborn planned that had gone sour? Was he going to kill Merriman himself, or had he set him up for the tall man? If the idea had been to kill him himself, where did the tall man tie in? If he had set him up for the tall man, how did it happen that Osborn became a victim as well? And why a guy like Osborn, a clean-cut, if somewhat fiery, orthopedic surgeon from California?

And then there was the drug the French police had found in Osborn's room. Succinylcholine.

A call to Dr. Richman at the Royal College of Pathology in London had established succinylcholine as a presurgery anesthetic, a synthetic curare used to relax the muscles. Richman had warned that outside professional hands it could be very dangerous. The drug completely relaxed the skeletal muscles, and could cause suffocation if improperly administered.

"Is it unusual for a surgeon to have that kind of a drug in his possession?" McVey had asked directly.

Richman's reply had been as forthcoming. "In his hotel room while he was ostensibly on vacation? I'd sure as hell say so!"

McVey had paused, thought a moment, then asked the million-dollar question, "Would you use it if you were going to sever a head?"

"Possibly. In conjunction with other anesthetics."

"What about the freezing? Would you use it for that?"

"McVey, you have to understand, this is a sport neither I nor the colleagues whom I've queried have ever encountered before. We don't have enough information about what was attempted or actually happened to even begin to suggest a procedure."

"Doctor, do me a favor," McVey had asked. "Get with Doctor Michaels and go over the corpses once more."

"Detective, if you're looking for succinylcholine, it breaks down in the body minutes after it's injected. You'd never find a trace of it."

"But you might find puncture wounds that would tell us they'd been injected with something, right?"

McVey could distinctly hear Richman agree with him and the sound of the phone as he hung up. Then all of a sudden it hit him. "Son of a bitch!" he said out loud. The little dog under the table jerked out of his sleep and started barking, while the two elderly ladies, who obviously understood enough English to be appalled, glared at him.

"Pardon," McVey said. Getting up, he left a twenty-franc note on the table. "You too," he said to the dog as he walked off.

Crossing Place Victor Hugo, McVey bought a token and entered the Métro. "Lebrun," he heard himself say, as if he were still in the inspector's office. "We never made a three-way association, did we?"

Looking at the Métro routes on a master scheduling board, McVey picked the route he thought would take him where he wanted to go and got on. His mind still focused on his imaginary meeting with Lebrun.

"We found Merriman because he left his print at the Jean Packard murder scene, right?"

"We knew Osborn hired Packard to find somebody. Osborn told me it was Vera Monneray's boyfriend and, at the time, it seemed reasonable. But what if he was lying about that, like he did about the mud on his shoes? What if it was Merriman he was trying to find? On our mothers' graves, how the hell could we miss that?"

Crowding onto a Métro car, McVey grabbed an overhead handrail and stood. Incensed as he was for not seeing the obvious sooner, he was still pumped up by the flow of thoughts.

"Osborn sees Merriman in the brasserie, maybe by

accident, and recognizes him. He tries to grab him, but the waiters wrestle him off and Merriman gets away. Osborn chases him into the Métro, where he gets picked up by Métro police and then turned over to you. He makes up a phony story that Merriman picked his pocket and your men say okay and let him go. Not unreasonable. Then Osborn contacts Kolb International, who assigns him Packard. Packard and Osborn put their heads together and a couple of days later Packard comes up with Merriman, hiding out as Henri Kanarack."

The train slowed in the tunnel, then entered a station, slowed more and stopped. McVey glanced at the station sign and stood back as half-a-dozen noisy teenagers got on. As quickly the doors closed, the train moved off again. The entire time McVey heard nothing but his own inner voice.

"I'd say it's a safe bet Merriman found out Packard was after him, and went after him instead, wanting to know what the hell was going on. And Packard, a tough-guy soldier of fortune, doesn't like being pushed around, especially in his own house. There's a big argument and it comes out in Merriman's favor. Or seems to have, until he leaves a fingerprint. Then this whole other business starts.

"After that it all begins to get a little fuzzy. But the key, if I'm right, is that it was Merriman who Osborn jumped in the café that first night. Your men determined it was Osborn who was the perpetrator, but nobody ever identified the victim. Unless Packard did, and that's how he got on Merriman's trail in the first place. But if it was Merriman Osborn attacked, and if we can find out why, it could very well make the circle back to the tall man."

The train slowed again. Again McVey looked for the name of the station as they came in. This was it! The place he was to change trains—Charles de Gaulle—Etoile.

Getting off, he pushed through a rush of passengers, went up a flight of stairs, passed a vendor selling sweet corn and rushed back down another flight of stairs. At the bottom, he made a right and followed the crowd into the station, pressing ahead, looking for the train that he wanted.

Twenty minutes later he walked out of the St.-Paul Métro station and onto the rue St.-Antoine. A half block down the street on his right was the Brasserie Stella.

It was 7:10, Sunday evening, October 9.

57

BERNHARD OVEN stood in the darkened bedroom window of Vera Monneray's apartment and watched the taxi pull up. A moment later, Vera got out and entered the building. Oven was about to step away when he saw a car turn the corner with its headlights out. Pressing back against the curtain, he watched a late-model Peugeot come down the street in darkness, then pull over and stop. Easing a palm-sized monocular from his jacket pocket, he put the glass on the car. Two men were in the front seat.

Police.

So they were doing it too, using Vera to find the American. They'd been watching her; when she left the hospital suddenly, they followed. He should have anticipated that.

Bringing the glass up again, he saw one of them pick up a radio microphone. Most likely they were calling in for instructions. Oven smiled; the police weren't the only ones aware of Mademoiselle Monneray's personal relationship with the prime minister. The Organization had been aware of it since François Christian had been appointed. And because of it, and the awkward political consequences that might follow if something went wrong, the likelihood the surveillance inspectors would be given a free hand to come in after her, no matter what they suspected, were almost nil. They would either remain where they were and continue the surveillance from outside or wait until superiors arrived. That delay was all the window Oven would need.

Quickly he left the bedroom and walked down the hall, stepping into the darkened kitchen just as the apartment door opened. Two people were talking and he saw a light go on in the living room. He couldn't make out what was being said, but was certain the voices belonged to Vera and the doorman.

Suddenly they were out of the living room and coming down the hall directly toward the kitchen. Moving around the center console, Oven stepped into a walk-in pantry, lifted the Walther automatic from his waistband and waited in the dark.

A moment later Vera came into the kitchen with the doorman at her heels and turned on the light. She was halfway across and heading for the rear service door when she stopped.

"What is it, mademoiselle?" the doorman said.

"I'm being a fool, Philippe," she said, coldly. "And the police are being clever. They found the vial and delivered it to you presupposing you would notify me and I'd do just what I did. They assume I know where Paul is, so they sent a tall inspector, hoping I would think it was the gunman and be frightened enough to lead them to Paul."

Philippe wasn't as certain. "How can you be sure? No one, not even Monsieur Osborn, has seen the tall man closely. If this man was a policeman, he's one I've never seen before."

"Have you seen every gendarme in Paris? I don't think so—"

"Mademoiselle, think the other way. What if, instead of a policeman, he was the one who shot Monsieur Osborn?"

Oven heard their footsteps retreat across the kitchen floor. The light was turned out and their voices diminished as they walked back down the hallway.

"Perhaps we should inform Monsieur Christian," Philippe said, as they reached the entrance to the living room.

"No," Vera said quietly. As yet, only Paul Osborn knew of her breakup with the prime minister. She hadn't decided how, or even if, to inform those who were privy to their relationship of the change in it. Besides, the last thing she wanted to do now was to expose François to something like this. François Christian was one of three would-be successors to the president and the in-fighting moving toward the next election had already become what insiders were describing as a "political bloodbath." A scandal now, especially one involving murder, would be ruinous and, lovers or not, she still cared for François far too deeply to risk destroying his career.

"Wait here." Leaving Philippe standing in the hallway, Vera went into the bedroom.

Philippe watched after her. His job was to serve Mademoiselle Monneray, and if necessary protect her. Not with his life, but with communication. At his desk in the lobby, he had the prime minister's private telephone number with instructions to call at any time, at any hour, if mademoiselle should be in difficulty.

"Philippe, come here," she called from the darkened bedroom.

When he entered he saw her standing at the curtain by the window.

"See for yourself."

Walking over, Philippe stood beside her and peered out. A Peugeot was parked across the street. Spill from a streetlamp was enough to illuminate the figures of two men sitting in the front seat.

"Go back down to the front desk," Vera said. "Do what you would normally do, as if nothing had happened. In a few minutes call a taxi for me. The destination will be the hospital. If the police should come in, tell them I came home feeling ill but shortly afterward felt better and decided to return to work."

"Of course, mademoiselle."

Oven watched from the dimness of the kitchen doorway as Philippe came out of the bedroom and turned down the hallway toward him. Immediately the Walther came up in his hand and he pressed back, out of sight. A moment later he heard the apartment door open, then close. After that came silence.

It meant one thing. The doorman had gone and Vera Monneray was alone in the apartment.

58

LOOKING UP from the dark of their Peugeot, Inspectors Barras and Maitrot could see the light in Vera's living room. Lebrun's instructions to all detail inspectors assigned to shadow her had been explicit. If she leaves the hospital follow her, then report in; don't tip your hand unless circumstances justify. "Justify" meant "unless she leads you to Osborn" or "to someone you suspect would lead you to him."

So far they had a writ and a warrant for Osborn's arrest but that was all they had. Tailing Vera had turned out to be nothing more than an exercise. She'd left her apartment early Sunday morning, arrived at the Centre Hospitalier Ste.-Anne at five minutes to seven and stayed there. Barras and Maitrot had taken over the shift at four and still nothing had happened.

Then at six-fifteen a taxi had driven up to the main entrance, Vera had rushed out and the cab pulled away. Barras and Maitrot radioed they were in pursuit and a second car pulled in after them as backup.

But the chase had only taken them back to her apartment and she'd gone inside. Leaving the police to sit on their pumped-up expectations and glance every so often at the brightly lit window, waiting for whatever, if anything, happened next.

Upstairs, Vera let go of the curtain and turned away from her bedroom window in the dark. The ornamental clock on her bedside table read 7:20. She'd been gone from the hospital for just over an hour, leaving on a slow night, she'd explained, because of intense menstrual cramps. In an emergency she could be back in no time.

If it had just been the Parisian police, things would have been different. It had been confirmed the night before in Lebrun's reaction to McVey's pressing queries. But McVey had no such delusions. She'd seen it in his eyes the first time she'd met him. And that made him extremely dangerous if he was against you. He might be American, but the Paris police, at least the inspectors assigned here, whether they realized it or not, were fully under his spell. What he wanted them to do, in one way or another, they would do. Which was why she believed the tall man who presented the vial to Philippe was a fake.

Part of a trick to frighten her into believing Osborn was in danger and thereby leading them to wherever he was hiding. And the police—she was certain the men in the car outside were police—proved she was right.

The phone rang next to her and she picked up.

"Oui? Merci, Philippe."

Her taxi was waiting downstairs.

Going into the bathroom, Vera opened a box of Tampax. Pulled a tampon from the paper and flushed it down the toilet. Then threw the wrapper into the wastebasket under the sink. If the police checked after she'd gone and later questioned her, at least she would have left evidence that her menstrual cycle was the reason she'd come home. Considering who she was, they wouldn't press it further than that.

Glancing in the mirror, she fluffed her hair and for a moment held there—Everything that had happened with Paul Osborn had seemed natural, even until now. The first time she'd seen him on the lectern in Geneva, a sense of change and fate had swept her. The first night she slept with him there was no more sense of cheating on François than if he'd been her brother. Before, she'd told herself she had not left François for Osborn. But it wasn't so, because she had. And because she had, what she was doing now was right. Osborn was in trouble and legality didn't matter.

Turning out the bathroom light, Vera crossed the bedroom in the dark, stopping to glance out the window once more. The police car was still there, and directly below was her taxi.

Picking up her purse, she went into the hallway and stopped. Shadows from the streetlight danced across the living room ceiling and into the hallway where she stood.

Something was wrong.

The light had been on in the living room. But it wasn't

now. She hadn't turned it off and neither had Philippe. Maybe the bulb had burned out. Yes. Of course. The bulb. Suddenly the thought flashed that she was wrong. That the men outside were not policemen. They were businessmen talking, or friends, or male lovers. Maybe the tall man had not been a policeman at all. Maybe her first instinct had been right. It was the killer who'd found the tetanus vial and delivered it to Philippe. It was he who wanted her to lead him to Osborn.

Oh, God! Her heart was pounding as if it were going to explode.

Where was he now? Somewhere in the building! Even here! In her apartment. How could she have been so stupid as to send Philippe away? The telephone! Pick it up and call Philippe. Quickly!

Turning, she reached out for the wall switch. Abruptly a strong hand clasped around her mouth and she was dragged back against a man's body. In the same instant she felt the sharp needle point of a blade press up under her chin.

"I really don't care to hurt you, but I will if you don't do exactly as I say. Do you understand?"

His voice was very calm and he spoke in French but with an accent that was either Dutch or German. Terrified, Vera tried to make herself think, but the thoughts wouldn't come.

"I asked you if you understood."

The knife point pressed further into her flesh and she nodded.

"Good," he said. "We are going to leave the apartment by the service stairway at the back of the kitchen." He was very collected and precise. "I am going to take my hand from your mouth. If you make a sound, I will cut your throat. Do you understand?"

Think! Vera. Think! If you go with him, he'll force you to take him to Paul. The taxi! The driver will be impatient! If you stall, Philippe will call again. If you don't answer, he will come up.

Suddenly there was a noise at the front door a dozen feet away. Vera felt him stiffen behind her, and the knife slid down and across her throat. At the same instant the door opened and Vera let out a cry against the hand over her mouth.

Osborn stood in the doorway. In one hand was the key to her apartment, in the other, Henri Kanarack's automatic. He was full in the light. Vera and the tall man were almost completely in the dark. It made no difference. They'd already seen each other.

The hint of a smile crossed Oven's lips. In a blink he shifted Vera to the side and the blade came up in his hand. In the same instant, Osborn raised the gun, screaming for Vera to hit the floor. As he did, Oven threw the knife at Paul's throat. Instinctively, Osborn flung up his left hand. The stiletto struck it full force, pinning it like a donkey tail to the open door.

Crying out, Osborn twisted around in pain. Shoving Vera aside, Oven dug for the Walther in his waistband. Vera's scream was lost in a stab of flame that was followed by a tremendous explosion. Oven fell sideways and Osborn, still pinned to the door, fired again. The big automatic thundered three times in rapid succession, turning the hallway into a howling storm of muzzle flashes punctuated by the deafening roar of gunshots.

On the floor, Vera caught a glimpse of Oven as he fled down the hallway and through the kitchen door. Then Osborn was tearing his hand from the door and hobbling past her after him.

"Stay here!" he screamed.

"Paul! Don't!"

Blood was running down Oven's face as he crashed through the pantry. Tipping over a rack of pots and pans, he flung open the service door and bolted down the stairs.

Seconds later, Osborn eased out into the dimly lit stairwell and listened. There was only silence. Craning his neck, he looked up the stairs behind him, then back down.

Nothing.

Where the hell is he? Osborn breathed. Be careful. Be very careful.

Then, from below, came the slightest creaking. Looking down, he thought he saw the door to the street just swing closed. Beyond it, on the far side of the landing, was gaping blackness where the stairs continued down, bending in a curl and vanishing into the basement below.

Swinging the automatic toward the door, Osborn took a guarded step down. Then another. Then another. A wooden stair moaned beneath his foot and he stopped short, his eyes probing the darkness beyond the door.

Did he go out? Or is he down there in the basement, waiting? Listening to me come down the stairs.

For some reason the thought came to him that his left hand felt cold and sticky. Looking down, he saw the tall man's knife still sticking in it. But there was nothing he could do. If he pulled it out, it would start bleeding again and he had nothing to stop it. His only choice was to ignore it.

One more step and he was on the landing opposite the door. Holding his breath, he cocked his head toward the basement. Still he heard nothing. His eyes went to the door to the street, then back to the darkness below it. He could feel the blood begin to pulsate around the knife in his hand. Soon the shock would wear off and the pain would begin. Shifting his weight, he took a step down. He had no idea how far the stairs went before they reached the cellar floor or what was down there. Stopping, he listened again, hoping he could hear the tall man breathe.

Suddenly the silence was broken by the scream of a car's engine and the shriek of tires on the street outside. In an instant Osborn had pushed off with his good leg and was at the door. Headlights raked his face as he came through it. Throwing up an arm, he fired blindly at a green blur as the car swept past. Then, tires squealing, it rounded the corner at the end of the block, flashed under a streetlight and was gone.

The automatic fell to his side and Osborn watched after it, not hearing the door as it slowly opened behind him. Suddenly he did. Terrified, he swung around, bringing the gun up to fire.

"Paul!" Vera was in the doorway.

Osborn saw her just in time. "Jesus God!"

Somewhere off came the singsong of sirens. Taking his arm, Vera pulled him back inside and closed the door.

"The police. They were waiting outside."

Osborn wavered, as if he were disoriented. Then she saw the knife sticking in his hand.

"Paul!" She started.

Above them a door opened. Footsteps followed. "Mademoiselle Monneray!" Barras' voice echoed down the staircase.

The reality of the police brought Osborn back. Tucking the gun under his arm, he reached down, grasped the hilt of the knife and pulled it out of his hand. A splattering of blood hit the floor.

"Mademoiselle!" Barras' voice was closer. By the sound of it, there was more than one man coming down the stairs.

Pulling a silk scarf from her neck, Vera wrapped it tightly around Osborn's hand. "Give me the gun," she said. "Then go to the basement and stay there." The footsteps were louder. The inspectors had reached the floor above and were starting down.

Osborn hesitated, then handed her the gun. He started to

say something, then their eyes met and for a moment he was afraid he would never see her again.

"Go on!" she whispered, and he turned and hobbled out of sight around the curve of darkened stairs, vanishing into the black of the basement below. A second and a half later, Barras and Maitrot reached the landing.

"Mademoiselle, are you all right?"

Henri Kanarack's gun in her hand, Vera turned to face them.

59

IT WAS 9:20 before McVey heard anything about it. His sojourn to the Brasserie Stella on rue St.-Antoine two hours earlier had started off as a flop, nearly became a fiasco, then ended with a jackpot.

Arriving at 7:15, he found the place packed. The waiters were running around like ants. The maître d', seemingly the only one who spoke even a hint of English, informed him the wait for a table was at least an hour, maybe more. When McVey had tried to explain he didn't want a table but only to speak to the manager, the maître d' had rolled his eyes, thrown up his hands saying that tonight even the manager couldn't get him a table, because the owner was giving a party and taking up the entire main room—and with that he'd rushed off.

So McVey simply stood there with Lebrun's police sketch of Albert Merriman in his pocket and tried to figure out another approach. He must have looked lonely or lost or both because the next thing he knew a short, slightly inebriated Frenchwoman in a bright red dress took him by the arm and led him to a table in the main room where the party was and began introducing him as her "American friend." While he was trying to extricate himself politely, somebody asked him in broken English where in the States he was from. And when he said, "Los Angeles," two more people started throwing questions about the Rams and the Raiders. Somebody else mentioned UCLA. Then an exceedingly thin young woman who looked and dressed like a fashion model slid between them. Smiling seductively, she asked him in French if he knew any of the Dodgers. The black man translated for her and stared, waiting for an answer. By now, all McVey wanted to do was get the hell out of there, but for some reason he said something like "I know Lasorda." Which was true because Dodger manager Tommy Lasorda had been involved in a number of police benefits and over the years they'd more or less become friends. At mention of Lasorda's name, another man turned around and in perfect English said, "I know him too."

The man was the owner of Brasserie Stella and within fifteen minutes two of the three waiters who had wrestled Osborn off Henri Kanarack the night of Osborn's attack were assembled in the manager's office looking at the sketch of Albert Merriman.

The first looked at it. "Oui," he said, then handed it to the second. The second studied it for a moment, then gave it back to McVey.

"L'homme." He nodded. The man.

Los Angeles.

"Robbery-Homicide, Hernandez," the voice had answered. Rita Hernandez was young and sexy. Too sexy for a cop. At twenty-five she had three kids, a husband in law school, and was the newest, and probably brightest, detective in the department.

"*Buenas tardes,* Rita."

"McVey! Where the hell are you?" Rita leaned back in her chair and grinned.

"I am the hell in Paris, France." McVey sat down on the bed in his hotel room and pulled off a shoe. Eight forty-five at night in Paris was 12:45 in the afternoon in L.A.

"Paris? You want me to come be with you? I'll leave my husband, my kids, everything. Pleeeeze, McVey!"

"You wouldn't like it here."

"Why not?"

"Not one decent tortilla, at least that I've found. Not like you make, anyway."

"The hell with tortillas. I'll take a brioche."

"Hernandez, I need a comprehensive sheet pulled on an orthopedic surgeon from Pacific Palisades. You got time?"

"Bring me back a brioche."

At 8:53 McVey hung up, used his key to open the "honor bar" and found what he was looking for, a half bottle of the Sancerre he'd had when he'd stayed in the room the last time. Whether he liked it or not, French wine was beginning to grow on him.

Opening the wine, he poured half a glass, took off his other shoe and put his feet up on the bed.

What were they looking for? What had Osborn wanted with Merriman so badly that after the initial attack and Merriman's escape he'd gone to the trouble and expense of hiring a private detective to find him?

It was possible that Merriman had somehow provoked Osborn in Paris. Maybe Osborn's story about Merriman's roughing him up in the airport and trying to take his wallet was true. But McVey doubted it, because Osborn's attack on Merriman in the brasserie had been too sudden and too violent. Hot-tempered as Osborn was, he was still a physician and smart enough to know you didn't assault people in public in foreign countries without risking all kinds of repercussions, especially if all the man had done was try and shake you down for your wallet.

So, unless Merriman had done something so outrageous as to provoke Osborn's anger earlier that same day, it seemed reasonable to look for something else. Which was what his gut told him. That whatever was between them had happened in the past.

But why would a doctor in L.A. have a tie to a professional killer who'd faked his own death and been out of sight for almost three decades, the last ten years of it hiding in France as Henri Kanarack? As far as Lebrun had been able to find out, Merriman, as Henri Kanarack, had been clean the entire time. That meant that whatever relationship existed between Osborn and Merriman had to have begun when Merriman was still in the States.

Getting up, McVey went to the writing table and pulled open his briefcase. Finding the notes he'd made from his conversations with Benny Grossman on Merriman, he ran his finger down the page until he found the date Merriman was supposed to have been killed in New York.

"Nineteen sixty-seven?" he said out loud. McVey took a swallow of the Sancerre, and poured a little more in his glass. Osborn was no more than forty, probably younger. If he knew Merriman in 1967 or before, he'd have to have been a kid.

Screwing up his face, McVey pondered the possibility Merriman could have been Osborn's father. A father who'd deserted the family and disappeared. As quickly, he discarded it; Merriman would have had to have been in his early teens to father someone as old as Osborn. No, it had to have been something else.

He was thinking about the drug Lebrun's men had found, the succinylcholine, and wondering what, if anything, that had to do with the Osborn/Merriman thing.

Thinking about it made him realize he hadn't heard back from Commander Noble. True, it had been hardly twenty-four hours since he'd left London, but twenty-four hours should have been ample time for the Special Branch's finest to uncover hospitals or medical schools in southern England experimenting with advanced techniques in radical surgery. The other obstacle, tracing back missing persons over years to find the one who matched the severed head with the metal plate in it, could take forever, and maybe they'd still come up with nothing.

And what about his request that Doctors Richman and Michaels go over the headless bodies for puncture wounds that might have been overlooked because of the various stages of decomposition of the bodies. Puncture wounds that might have been made by an injection of succinylcholine.

This was the kind of thing McVey disliked. He preferred working on his own, taking the time he needed to digest what was there and then acting accordingly. Still, he couldn't complain about the team around him. Noble and his staff along with the medical experts in London were doing precisely as he asked. Lebrun, in Paris, was too. Benny Grossman had been exceedingly helpful in New York, and now hopefully Rita Hernandez in L.A. would come up with a solid background sheet on Osborn that might give McVey some inkling of what might have gone before, something that might explain his tie to Merriman.

But that was the problem. Osborn and Merriman, the dead private investigator, Jean Packard, the tall man and his murderous exploits and the secretive goings-on involving Interpol, Lyon. That should have been one case.

The headless bodies found scattered over northern Europe, and the bodyless head found in London, all ultra-deep-frozen in some kind of bizarre medical experiment, should have been another.

Something told him they weren't, that somehow, in some way, the two wholly disparate situations were intertwined. And the coupling—though he had absolutely no evidence to back it up—had to be Osborn.

McVey didn't like it. The whole thing felt as if it was getting ahead of him.

"Open up the Osborn/Merriman thing, and you'll open up the other," he said out loud. As he did, he noticed the big toe on his left foot was beginning to push through his sock. Suddenly, and for the first time in years, he felt very much alone.

It was then the knock came at the door. Puzzled, McVey got up and went to the door. "Who is it?" he said, opening it to the chain lock. A uniformed policeman stood in the hallway.

"First Paris Préfecture of Police, Officer Sicot. There's been a shooting at Ms. Monneray's apartment."

60

MCVEY LOOKED at the .45 automatic Barras had so neatly laid on a linen napkin on Vera Monneray's dining room table. Taking a ballpoint pen from his jacket pocket, he stuck it in its snout and picked it up. It was a U.S.-made Colt, at least ten or fifteen years old.

Laying it back on the table and retrieving his pen,

McVey glanced around at the activity. Sunday night or not, the Paris police had managed to fill the place with tech experts.

Across the hall, in the living room, he could see Inspectors Barras and Maitrot talking with Vera Monneray. Standing to one side was a uniformed policewoman. Sitting on the Alice in Wonderland chair was the doorman whom everybody was suddenly calling Philippe.

Going into the hallway, McVey saw a wiry, bespectacled member of the tech crew scraping dried blood off the wall. Farther down, a balding photographer finished taking pictures, then a man who looked as if he could have been a professional wrestler moved in to delicately pry a spent bullet out of the splintered top of a cherry table.

Eventually, most of what was going on would provide a reasonably accurate picture of what had happened here. But for now, to McVey at least, the .45 on the dining room table was the thing.

A little palm-sized gun he could understand. A .25 or a .32 caliber. A Walther maybe, or an Italian Beretta. Or, more likely, a French-made Mab would be the arm of choice a ranking member of the French ministry might tuck away for his girlfriend to use in an emergency. But a U.S. Colt .45 automatic was a man's gun. Big and heavy, with a nasty recoil when it was fired. Right off, it didn't fit.

Moving past the photographer, who was now working the open door into the outer hall, McVey glanced into the living room. Barras had evidently just asked Vera Monneray something because she shook her head. Then she looked up and saw McVey watching her, and immediately turned back to Barras.

The first thing Barras told McVey when he'd arrived was that François Christian had been notified and had spoken with Vera on the telephone but that he would not be coming over. That was Barras' way of posturing. Letting McVey know there were bigger things at work here and that McVey best take a backseat to the proceedings, especially as far as Mademoiselle Monneray was concerned.

If Lebrun were here it might be different, but he wasn't. He'd left town late in the day on personal business—no one, not even his wife, seemed to know what it was or where he had gone—and was unreachable, even by electronic page. That's why McVey had been called. Obviously reluctantly, because Barras and Maitrot had been on the scene immediately after the shooting as part of the stakeout team, and it hadn't been until two hours later that Officer Sicot had been dispatched to McVey's hotel room.

McVey wasn't surprised. It was the same with police agencies everywhere. Cop or not, if you weren't one of theirs, you weren't one of theirs. You wanted to be on the inside, you had to be invited, and that took time. So, for the most part, you were treated cordially but you were on your own and sometimes the last guy on the wake-up call.

McVey walked back off down the hall and into the kitchen. A citywide alarm had been put out for a tall, blond man about six foot four, wearing gray slacks and a dark jacket, who spoke French with a Dutch or German accent. It wasn't much, but it was something. At least, unless Vera were making it up, which he doubted, it was proof the tall man existed.

Passing through the kitchen, he walked through an open door and into the service stairwell. Tech crews were working the stairs and the landing two floors down where a service door opened to the street. Taking stock as he went, McVey walked down the stairs to the landing and glanced out through the open door to where uniformed police were standing guard outside.

Vera had told Barras and Maitrot that she'd come home from the hospital after experiencing severe menstrual cramps. She'd come in, taken some special painkiller she kept at home, and had lain down. A short time later she began to feel better and decided to go back to work. She'd called Philippe for a taxi and when he told her it had arrived, she'd gone out into the hallway for her purse, wondering why it was darker than it should be, and realized the light in the living room had been turned out. That was when the man grabbed her.

Pulling free, she'd run into the dining room for the gun François Christian had put there for emergencies. Whirling, she pointed the gun and fired several shots—she didn't remember how many—at the tall man, who fled out the service door and down the back stairs to the street. She went down after him, thinking maybe she'd shot him, and that's where Barras and Maitrot had found her, by the door with the gun in her hand. She reported hearing a car drive away but did not see it.

McVey stepped outside into the glare of blue-white police worklights and saw the tech crew measuring rubber tire marks in the street, parallel to and almost directly across from the door he'd just exited.

Easing off the curb, he walked into the street and looked off in the direction the car had gone, then followed the line of the car's escape route until he was out of the spill of the worklights and in darkness. Another fifteen yards and he turned back. Squatting down, he studied the street. It was blacktop over cobblestone. Lifting his head, he brought his eyes level with the worklights farther down. Something glinted in the street five yards away. Standing, he walked over and picked it up. It was a sliver of shattered mirror, the kind of exterior mirrors that are on automobiles.

Slipping it carefully into the breast pocket of his jacket, he walked back toward the lights until he was exactly opposite the service door, then looked over his shoulder. Across the street, the windows of other apartments were ablaze with light, and the silhouettes of residents watching what was going on in the street.

Keeping in line with the service door, he crossed to the building on the far side of the street. The only illumination here was from a streetlight, a dozen paces away. Avoiding a freshly painted iron spike fence, McVey walked up to the building and studied its brick and stone surface as carefully as he could in the available light. He was looking for a fresh chip in the stone or brick, a spot where a bullet fired from across the street at a passing car might have hit. But he saw nothing and thought maybe he was wrong, that maybe the piece of mirror hadn't been shattered by a gunshot after all; maybe it had been lying in the street for some time.

The tech crew in the street had finished their measurements and were going back inside, and McVey was turning to join them when he noticed the top of one of the decorative iron spikes on the freshly painted fence was missing. Walking behind the fence, he hunched over and looked at the ground behind the missing spike. Then he saw it, lying in the shadow of a rainspout at the edge of the building. Moving over, he picked it up. The front half of the spike had been crushed and bent by some heavy impact. And where the object had struck it, the fresh black paint was shiny steel.

61

BERNHARD OVEN'S decision to retreat had been correct. The American's first shot, thrown off because of the knife in his hand, had seared a bloody path along the base of his jaw. He was lucky. Had it not been for the knife, Osborn probably would have shot him between the eyes. Had Oven had the Walther in his hand instead of a knife, he would have done the same to Osborn, and then killed the girl.

But he hadn't, nor had he chosen to stay and fight it out with the American because the police waiting outside would have, and no doubt did, come in very quickly at the sound of the gunshots. The last thing Oven wanted was to be pitted against an enraged man with a gun with the police coming in the front door behind him.

Even if he'd killed Osborn, there was every chance he would have been caught or wounded by the police. If that had happened, he might survive, at best, a day in jail before the Organization found a way to eliminate their problem. Which was another reason why his withdrawal had been timely and correct.

But his leaving had created another problem. For the first time, he had been clearly seen. By Osborn and by Vera Monneray, who would describe him to the police as quite tall, six foot four at least, with blond hair and blond eyebrows.

It was now almost 9:30, little more than two hours after the shooting. Getting up from the straight-backed chair where he'd been musing, Oven went into the bedroom of the two-room flat on the rue de l'Eglise, opened the closet door and took out a pair of freshly pressed blue jeans with a thirty-two-inch inseam. Laying them on the bed, he slipped out of his gray flannel slacks, hung them carefully on a hanger and put them in the closet.

Pulling on the blue jeans, he sat down on the edge of the bed and unhooked the Velcro straps that connected ten-inch-long leg and foot prosthetics to the stubs of his legs at the point where they had been amputated, halfway between the ankle and the knee.

Opening a hard plastic traveling case, he took out a second pair of prosthetics, identical to the others but six inches shorter. Fitting them to the nub of each leg, he reattached the Velcro straps, pulled on white athletic socks and then a pair of white, high-top Reeboks.

Standing, he placed the prosthetics box in a drawer and went into the bathroom. There, he put on a short, dark wig and darkened his eyebrows with mascara of the same color.

At 9:42, a light gauze dressing covering the bullet crease on his jaw, five-foot-ten-inch Bernhard Oven, with dark hair with dark eyebrows, left his flat on the rue de l'Eglise and walked a half block to the Jo Goldenberg restaurant at 7 rue Rosiers, where he took a table by the window, ordered a bottle of Israeli wine and the evening special, rolled grape leaves stuffed with ground beef and rice.

Paul Osborn lay huddled in the dark on top of the aging furnace in the basement of 18 Quai de Bethune, in a two-foot-square area that couldn't be seen from the floor, his head only inches from the dusty, spider-infested ceiling of ancient beams and mortar. He'd found the spot only moments before the first detectives had invaded the area and now, nearly three hours later, he was still there, having some while ago stopped counting the number of times scurrying rats had come up to sniff and stare with their hideous red, rodent eyes. If he could be thankful for anything it was that the night was warm and no one in the building had yet called up the heat, thereby turning on the furnace.

For the first two hours it seemed as if the police were in every corner of the basement. Uniformed police, police in plain clothes with I.D.s pinned to their jackets. Some left and came back. Talking vigorously in French, every once in a while laughing at some joke he didn't understand. He was lucky they hadn't brought dogs.

The bleeding in his hand seemed to have stopped, but it ached brutally, and he was cramped and thirsty and exceedingly tired. More than once he'd dozed off, only to be wakened again by police as they searched everywhere but where he was.

Now, for a long time it had been quiet, and he wondered if they were still there. They had to be, otherwise Vera would have come down looking for him. Then it occurred to him that she might not be able to. That the police might have posted guards to protect her in case the tall man came back. What then? How long should he stay there before he at least made some effort to get out?

Suddenly, he heard a door open above. Vera! He felt his heart jump and he raised himself up. Footsteps were coming down. He wanted to say something but he dared not. Then he heard whoever it was stop at the landing. It had to be Vera. Why would a policeman come down alone when the area had already been thoroughly covered? Maybe it was someone checking the service door to see if it has been secured. If so, they would go back up.

Abruptly there was a sharp creak as weight was put on a stair coming down to where he was. It was not a woman's step.

The tall man!

What if he had eluded the police just as Osborn had, and was still there? Or had found a way to come back? In a panic, Osborn looked around for a weapon. There was none.

The stairs creaked again and the footsteps descended further. Holding his breath and craning his neck, Osborn could just make out the bottommost stairs. Another step and a man's foot appeared, then a second, and he stepped into the basement.

McVey.

Lying back, Osborn pressed flush against the top of the furnace. He heard McVey's footfalls approach, then stop. Then move off again, going away from the furnace and deeper into the block-long, coffin-shaped cellar.

For several seconds, he heard nothing. Then there was a click and a light went on. A moment later there was a second click and more of the basement was illuminated. What little he could see he had seen before, when the French police had come through. The basement looked like a small warehouse. Old wooden coal bins, now jammed with tenants' furniture and private belongings, lined either wall and vanished into the darkness beyond the lights. Osborn thought that had he gotten that far, to the area where the lights ended, he could have hidden anywhere. Perhaps even found an exit at the far end.

Immediately there was a scattering sound overhead and something dropped onto his chest. It was a rat. Fat and warm. He could feel its claws press into the skin beneath his shirt as it moved across his chest and sniffed at Vera's scarf, sticky wet with drying blood, which bound his injured hand.

"Doctor Osborn!"

McVey's voice reverberated the length of the cellar. Osborn gave a start, and the rat dropped off and hit the floor. McVey heard it thud, then saw it disappear into the darkness under the stairs.

"I'm not crazy about rats. How do you feel about them? They bite when they get cornered, don't they?"

Inching up, Osborn could see McVey standing halfway between the furnace and the dark at the far end of the room. Piled to the ceiling on either side of him were dusty crates and ghostlike furniture, draped with protective cloths. The height of them made McVey seem almost miniature.

"With the exception of uniformed details at the front and rear of the building, the French police have left. Ms. Monneray has gone with them. To headquarters. They want her to see if she can pick the tall man out of photographs. If Paris is anything like L.A., she's going to be there a long time. There are a lot of books." McVey turned around and looked toward the furniture behind him.

"Let me tell you what I know, Doctor." Now he turned again and started walking slowly back toward him, his footsteps echoing lightly, his eyes searching, looking for any suggestion of movement.

"Ms. Monneray was lying when she told the French police *she* used the gun against the tall man. She's a highly educated, remarkably connected woman, who's also a physician in residence. Even if she managed to pull a gun as big as a forty-five automatic on an assailant, even if she shot at him, I rather doubt she'd chase after him down a dingy back stairway. Or follow him out into the street, still shooting as he drove away." McVey stopped where he was and looked back over his shoulder, then turned and continued on the way he had been going, moving slowly toward Osborn's hiding place, talking loud enough to be heard either in front or behind him.

"She says, by the way, that she heard a car drive off but that she didn't see it. If she didn't see it, how did she manage to shatter its rearview mirror with one shot and take the top off an iron fence post across the street with another?"

McVey would have known the French police had been all over the basement and found nothing. That meant he was taking a stab that Osborn was here. But it was only a stab, and he wasn't sure.

"There were fresh bloodstains on the hallway door upstairs. On the floor in the kitchen and on the landing by the service door that leads to the street. The Paris Préfecture of Police tech squad is pretty good. They determined in short order that there were two types of blood. Type O and type B. Ms. Monneray was not cut or bleeding. So I'm willing to bet that between you and the tall man one of you is O and the other B. How badly either of you is hurt, I guess we'll find out."

McVey was directly under Osborn now. Standing, looking around. For some reason Osborn smiled. If McVey had been wearing a hat like '40s L.A. homicide detectives, Osborn could have reached out and plucked it off his head. He pictured the expression on McVey's face if he did.

"By the way, Doctor, the Los Angeles Police Department is doing an in-depth profile on you. By the time I get back to my hotel, there'll be a fax waiting with preliminary stats. Somewhere on that sheet will be your blood type."

McVey waited and listened. Then he started back the way he had come, walking slowly, patiently, waiting for Osborn, if he was there, to make the mistake that would give him away.

"In case you're wondering, I don't know who the tall man is or what he's up to. But I think you should know he is directly responsible for a number of other deaths involving people who knew a man named Albert Merriman, or who you might have known as Henri Kanarack.

"Merriman's girlfriend, a woman named Agnes Demblon, burned up in a fire the tall man set at her apartment building. The fire also killed nineteen other adults and two children, none of whom probably ever heard of Albert Merriman.

"Then he went to Marseilles and found Merriman's wife, her sister, her sister's husband and their five kids. He shot them all in the head."

McVey stopped, reached up and turned out a bank of lights.

"It was you he was after, Doctor Osborn. Not Ms. Monneray. But of course, after tonight, now that she's seen him, he'll be concerned with her too."

There was a dull click as McVey turned out the second bank of lights. Then Osborn could hear him start back toward him in the dark.

"Frankly, Doctor Osborn, you're in a heckuva pickle. *I* want you. The Paris police want you. And the tall man wants you.

"If the police get you, you can bet the bank the tall man will find a way to take care of you in jail. And after he does, he'll go after Ms. Monneray. It won't happen right away, because for a while she'll be guarded. But somewhere on down the line, while she's shopping or maybe riding the Métro, or having her hair done or in the hospital cafeteria at three in the morning . . ."

McVey came closer. When he was directly beneath Osborn, he turned and looked back to the darkened basement.

"No one knows I'm here besides you and me. Maybe if we talked, I might be able to help. Think about it, huh?"

Then there was silence. Osborn knew McVey was listening for the slightest sound and held his breath. It was a good forty seconds before Osborn heard him turn back, cross to the stairs and start up, then he stopped again.

"I'm staying at an inexpensive hotel called the Vieux Paris on the rue Git le Coeur. The rooms are small but they've got a musty French charm. Leave word where to meet you. I won't bring anyone. It'll be just you and me. If you're nervous, don't use your own name. Just say Tommy Lasorda called. Give me a time and a place."

McVey climbed the remaining stairs and was gone. A moment later Osborn heard the service door to the street open, then close. After that, everything was silent.

62

THEIR NAMES were Eric and Edward, and Joanna had never seen such perfect men. At age twenty-four, they were seemingly flawless specimens of the human male. Both were five foot eleven and weighed exactly the same, one hundred and sixty-seven pounds.

She'd first seen them early in the afternoon when she'd been working with Elton Lybarger in the shallow end of the indoor pool in the building that housed the gymnasium on his estate. The pool was Olympic size, fifty meters long and twenty-five yards wide. Eric and Edward were doing butterfly stroke speed laps. Joanna had seen that before but usually only over short distances because the stroke itself was so demanding. At one end of the pool was an automatic lap meter that counted the number of laps whoever was in the pool was swimming.

When Joanna and Lybarger had come in, the boys had

already swum eight laps, or a half mile. By the time she and Lybarger were finished, they were still swimming butterfly, stroke for stroke, side by side. The lap meter read sixty-two, exactly two laps under four miles. Four miles of butterfly stroke nonstop? That was incredible, if not impossible. But there was no doubt, because she'd witnessed it.

An hour later, as a male attendant took Lybarger off for an exercise in diction therapy, Eric and Edward had come out of the pool house and were preparing for a run through the forest, when Von Holden introduced them to her.

"Mr. Lybarger's nephews," he said with a smile. "They were studying at East Germany's College for Physical Culture until it closed after unification. So they came home."

Both were extremely polite, had said, "Hello. Very pleased to meet you," and then they'd run off.

Joanna had wondered if they were training for the Olympics and Von Holden had smiled. "No. Not Olympics. Politics! Mr. Lybarger has encouraged them in that since their youth when their own father died. He thought then that Germany would one day reunite. And he was correct."

"Germany? I thought Mr. Lybarger was Swiss."

"German. He was born in the industrial town of Essen."

At precisely seven o'clock, family and guests sat down to dinner in the formal dining room of the Lybarger estate, which Joanna had learned was called "Anlegeplatz," embarkation point. Meaning that from there one might leave but would always return.

Joanna had come back to her room after an extended workout with Mr. Lybarger to find a formal dinner gown, picked out and fitted flawlessly, simply from a photograph of her, by the famous designer Uta Baur, to whom she'd been introduced briefly on the lake steamer the night before and who, it turned out, was a guest at Anlegeplatz. The dress was long, tight-fitting; and instead of compromising her ample figure, it complemented it by tightening and accenting. Designed to be worn without undergarments, thereby avoiding a line or bulge caused by tight elastic, it was deliberately risqué and elegantly erotic.

Black velvet, it closed several inches below the throat and had a woven, feathery pattern in gold that ran from the back of her neck across her bosom and down the other side, as if it were some kind of sleekly fitted boa. At the shoulders, a perfect nuance, hung the smallest golden tassels.

At first Joanna was reluctant. She had never expected to wear anything like it. But she had brought nothing at all dressy, and at Anlegeplatz, dinner was formal. So she had little choice but to put it on. When she did, she was transformed. It was magical. With makeup, and her hair in a French knot, she was no longer the cherubic, ordinary-looking physical therapist from New Mexico but a stylish and sexy international socialite, who carried herself with grace and panache.

The grand hall that was Anlegeplatz's dining room might have served as the set for some medieval costume drama. The twelve guests sat in hand-carved, high-backed chairs facing each other across a long, narrow dining table that could easily seat thirty, while half-a-dozen waiters saw to their every need. The room itself was two stories high and made entirely of stone. Flags with the crests of great families hung from the ceiling like battle standards, imparting the sense that this had been a place of kings and knights.

Elton Lybarger sat at the head of the table, with Uta Baur directly to his right, conversing with him in her animated style as if the two of them were the only creatures present. She was dressed entirely in black, which Joanna later learned was her trademark. Knee-length black boots, skintight black trousers, and black, single-breasted blazer, closed only by its button at the breast plate. The skin on her hands, face and neck was taut and iridescent, as if it had never been touched by sunlight. The cleavage of her smallish breasts, pushed upward by an underwire bra, was the same milk white, lined with surface veins of light blue, like tiny cracks in fine china. Under her extraordinarily short white hair the only accent was her plucked eyebrows. She wore no makeup or jewelry of any kind. She made a statement without it.

The dinner itself was long and leisurely and, despite the other guests—Dr. Salettl, the twins, Eric and Edward, and several people Joanna had been introduced to but didn't know—Joanna spent most of it talking with Von Holden about Switzerland, its history, its rail system and its geography. Von Holden seemed to be an expert, but he could have been talking about the dark side of the moon for all the difference it made. His cold, abrupt phone call that morning asking her to be ready to be picked up from her hotel had made her feel cheap and ugly, as if she'd been used the night before. But when he'd met her in the garden that afternoon, he'd been as warm and generous as he had been the night before and that behavior continued here at dinner. And as the evening wore on, and as much as she tried not to show it, the truth was, she was melting for his touch.

After dinner, Lybarger, Uta, Dr. Salettl and the other guests retired to the second-floor library for coffee and a dual piano recital by Eric and Edward.

Joanna and Von Holden, as employees, were not invited and excused for the evening.

"Doctor Salettl told me he expects Mr. Lybarger to be able to walk without a cane by this Friday," Joanna said as she watched Uta take Lybarger's arm and help him up the stairs.

"Will he?" Von Holden looked at her.

"I hope so, but it depends on Mr, Lybarger. I don't know what's so important about Friday. What difference would another few days make?"

"I want to show you something," Von Holden said, ignoring her question and leading her to a side door near the far end of the dining room. Entering a paneled hallway they walked to where a small door opened to a flight of stairs. Offering his hand, Von Holden led Joanna down a few stairs to another door, which in turn opened on a narrow passageway that led under the front drive and away from the house.

"Where are we going?" she asked quietly.

Von Holden said nothing and Joanna felt a quiver of excitement as they walked on. Pascal Von Holden was a man who could attract and have nearly any woman he wanted. He lived in a world of extremely rich and beautiful people, who were nearly royalty. Joanna was nothing but ordinary, a physical therapist with a southwestern twang. She'd had her foray with him last night and she knew she couldn't have been anything special. So why would he come back for more? If that's what he was doing.

At the far end of the corridor, steps led up. At the top was still another door, and Von Holden opened it. Standing aside, he ushered her in, then closed the door behind them.

Joanna stood open-mouthed, looking up. They were in a room taken up entirely by an enormous waterwheel driven by the flow of a deep and fast-running stream.

"The system provides independent electric power for the estate," Von Holden said. "Be careful, the floor is quite slippery."

Taking her arm, Von Holden led her across to another

door. Opening it, he reached inside and turned on the light. Inside was a room made of wood and stone, twenty feet square. In the middle was a pool of churning water, a cutout from the stream, with stone benches all around. Pointing to a wooden door, Von Holden said, "In there is a sauna. All very natural and good for the health."

Joanna could feel herself blush and at the same time feel the heat rise within her.

"I didn't bring anything to change into," she said.

Von Holden smiled. "Ah, but you see, that's the marvel of Uta's designs."

"I don't get it."

"The dress is form-fitting, and made to be worn without underclothing, is it not?"

Joanna blushed again. "Yes. But—"

"Form always follows function." Von Holden reached up, gently fingering one of the golden tassels at Joanna's shoulder. "This decorative tassel."

Joanna knew he was doing something, but she had no idea what. "What about it?"

"If one were to give it the slightest pull . . ."

Suddenly Joanna's dress undraped and slid as elegantly to the floor as a theatrical curtain.

"You see, ready for bath and sauna." Von Holden stood back and let his eyes run over her.

Joanna felt desire as she never had, more—if it was possible—than the night before. Never had the presence of a man felt so devastatingly erotic. At that moment she would have done anything he asked, and more.

"Would you like to undress me? Turnabout is fair play, isn't that how it goes?"

"Yes . . . ," Joanna heard herself whisper. "God, yes."

Then Von Holden touched her, and she came to him and undressed him and they made love in the pool and on the stone benches, and afterward in the sauna.

Love spent, they rested and touched and caressed, and

then Von Holden took her again, slowly and purposefully, in ways beyond her darkest imagination. Looking up, Joanna saw herself reflected in the mirrored ceiling and then again on the mirrored wall to her left, and those visions made her laugh in joy and disbelief. For the first time in her life she felt attractive and desired. And she savored it and Von Holden let her. The time was hers, for as long as she wanted.

In a dark-paneled study on the second floor of Anlegeplatz's main building, Uta Baur and Dr. Salettl sat patiently in armchairs and watched the exercise on three large-screen, high-definition television monitors receiving signals transmitted by remote cameras mounted behind the mirrored glass. Each camera had its own monitor, thereby providing full coverage of the action being recorded.

It's doubtful either was physically stirred by what they saw, not because they were both septuagenarians, but because the observance was wholly clinical.

Von Holden was merely an instrument in the study. It was Joanna who was the focus of their interest.

Finally, Uta's long fingers reached over and pressed a button. The monitors went dark and she stood up.

"*Ja,*" she said to Salettl. "*Ja,*" then walked out of the room.

63

By Osborn's watch it was 2:11 Monday morning, October 10.

Thirty minutes earlier he'd climbed the last stairs and taken the hidden elevator to the room under the eaves at 18 Quai de Bethune. Exhausted, he'd gone into the bathroom, opened the spigot and drunk deeply. After that he'd removed Vera's bloodsoaked scarf and cleaned the wound in his hand. The thing throbbed like hell and he had a lot of trouble opening his hand. But the pain was welcome because it suggested that as badly as he'd been cut, neither the nerves nor crucial tendons had been severely damaged. He'd taken the tall man's knife between the metacarpal bones just below the joint of the second and third fingers.

Because he could open the hand and close it, he was relatively certain no permanent damage had been done. Still, he would need an X ray to tell for sure. If a bone had been broken or splintered, he'd need surgery and then a cast. Left untreated, he ran the chance it would heal misformed, thus converting him to a one-handed surgeon and all but ending his career. That is, if there would be a career left to resurrect.

Finding the antiseptic salve Vera had used on his leg wound, he rubbed it into his hand, then covered it with a fresh bandage. After that he'd gone into the other room, eased down on the bed and awkwardly taken his shoes off with one hand.

He'd waited a full hour after McVey's exit before sliding off the furnace and climbing the darkened service stairs. He'd gone carefully, a step at a time, half expecting to be surprised and challenged by a man with a gun in uniform. But the moment hadn't come, so it was evident that whatever police were still on guard were outside.

McVey had been right. If the French police caught him and put him in jail, the tall man would find a way to kill him there. And then he would go after Vera. Osborn was caught, with McVey the third and final part of the triangle.

Loosening his shirt, Osborn shut out the light and lay back in the dark. His leg, though better, was beginning to stiffen from overexertion. The throbbing in his hand, he found, was less if he kept it elevated, and he arranged a pillow under it. As tired as he was, he should have fallen asleep immediately, but too many things were alive in his mind.

His abrupt intrusion on Vera and the tall man had been sheer coincidence. Certain she was at work and the apartment would be empty, he'd chanced coming down simply to use the telephone. He'd agonized for hours before finally coming to the conclusion that the most realistic thing he could do would be to call the American embassy, explain who he was and ask for help. In essence throwing himself on the mercy of the United States government. With luck, they would protect him from French jurisprudence and perhaps, in the best of all cases, consider the circumstances and exonerate him for what he had done. After all, it was not he who had killed Henri Kanarack. More important, it was an action that would put the focus entirely on him and remove Vera from the shadow of a scandal that could ruin her. His own private war had been going on for nearly thirty years. It was neither fair nor right that his personal demons bankrupt Vera's life no matter whatever else they might have between them. That was until he had opened the door and seen the tall man's knife at her throat. In that instant the simple clarity of his plan vanished and everything changed. Vera was in it whether either of them wanted it or not. If he went to the American envoy now, that would be the end, the same as if the police had him. At the very least he'd he held in protective custody while things were sorted out. And because of the publicity over Kanarack/Merriman's murder, the media would be all over it, thereby telling the tall man or his accomplices where he was. And when they got him, then they would go after Vera, as McVey had said.

Lying in his pigeonhole at the top of Paris, his hand throbbing above him in the dark, Osborn's thoughts turned to McVey and his offer to help. And the more he weighed one against the other, wondering if he could trust him, whether the overture was genuine or just a ruse to lure him out for the French police, the more he began to realize there was very little else.

At 6:45 A.M., McVey lay on his stomach in his pajama bottoms with one foot sticking out from under the covers, wanting to sleep but finding it impossible.

He'd played a hunch because it was all that was in his hand. Without Lebrun's presence, the French inspectors would not have permitted him to question Vera Monneray at any length. So he hadn't even tried. Even had Lebrun been there, he would have had trouble exacting the truth of what had happened because Ms. Monneray was smart enough to hide behind the respect of *l'amour*, or, more correctly, the prime minister of France.

Even if he'd been wrong and she had, out of fear or anger or outrage—he'd seen it before—chased after the tall man, blazing away with the gun as she'd said, her statement about not seeing the car killed her story. Because someone had most definitely gone out into the street and fired at it as it sped away.

If she'd admittedly done as she'd said, why would she lie about not seeing the car unless she'd arrived too late on the scene to be aware of what happened. Which, of course, meant someone else had shot at the car.

And since the tech crew had found two separate blood types, and since Vera herself had been uninjured, it meant at least three people had been in the apartment when the shooting took place. One of them had driven away and one of them was still in the apartment. That left one missing.

The first gunshot brought Barras and Maitrot to attention. The second and third had sent them running, with Barras radioing for backup. The tall man had gotten away in a fast car. Moments later, uniforms filled the area. Every apartment in the building and within a three-block radius had been checked, as had every alley, every rooftop, every parked car, and every passing barge on the Seine that a fugitive might have jumped onto from a bridge or a quai.

That meant one thing. The third person was still there. Somewhere. Because of the quickness of the police response and because gunfire had occurred just outside the service door, the most obvious place for that person to hide was the basement.

Yes, it had been thoroughly checked and secured. But it had been done without dogs. Experience had taught that desperate people can be exceedingly clever or sometimes just plain lucky. Which is why he had let the French police finish their job and then gone back.

At 6:50 he opened an eye, glanced at the clock and groaned. He'd been in bed for four and a half hours and was sure he hadn't slept two. One day he would get a solid eight. But when that day would come, he had no idea.

He knew people would give him until seven o'clock, then the calls would start. Lebrun, reporting he was on his way back from Lyon and setting a time to meet. Commander Noble and Dr. Richman calling from London.

Then there were two calls due from L.A. One from Detective Hernandez, whom he'd called when he got back to his room at two in the morning because there had been no fax waiting of the Osborn file he'd requested. Hernandez had not been in and no one else knew anything about it.

The other L.A. call would be from the plumber the neighbors had called when McVey's automatic sprinklers started going on and off at four-minute intervals around the clock. The plumber was calling back with an estimate of the cost to install an entirely new system to replace the old one McVey had put in himself twenty years earlier with a kit from Sears, the parts to which no longer existed.

Then there was one more call he was waiting for—rather *hoping* for, the one that had kept him tossing most of the night—the call from Osborn. Again he thought back to the basement. It was bigger than it looked and packed with a zillion cubbyholes. But maybe he'd been wrong, maybe he'd been talking in the dark.

6:52. Eight more minutes, McVey. Just close your eyes, try not to think about anything, let all the muscles and nerves and everything else relax.

And that's when the phone rang. Grunting, he rolled over and picked up.

"McVey."

"This is Inspector Barras. Sorry to bother you."

"It's all right. What is it?"

"Inspector Lebrun has been shot."

64

IT HAD happened in Lyon, at the Gare la Part Dieu shortly after six. Lebrun had just gotten out of a taxi and was entering the train station when a gunman on a motorcycle opened fire with an automatic weapon and then immediately fled the scene. Three others had been shot as well. Two were dead, the third seriously injured.

Lebrun had been hit in the throat and chest and had been taken to the Hospital la Part Dieu. Initial reports were that he was in critical condition but expected to live.

McVey had listened to the details, asked to be kept abreast of the situation and then gotten quickly off the phone. Immediately afterward he'd dialed Ian Noble in London.

Noble had just come in to the office and was having his first tea of the day when he found McVey on the line. Immediately he sensed McVey was being careful with what he said.

At this stage McVey had no idea whom he could trust and whom he couldn't. Unless the tall man had gone directly from Paris to Lyon after his escape from Vera Monneray's—which was very unlikely, because he'd know the police would throw an immediate dragnet out for him—it meant that whoever was behind what was going on not only had capable gunmen elsewhere, they were somehow monitoring everything the police did. With the exception of himself, no one knew Lebrun had gone to Lyon, yet he had been tracked there just the same, to the point that they knew precisely what train he was taking back to Paris.

Completely baffled, he had no idea who they were, what they were doing or why. But he had to suppose that if they'd taken out Lebrun when he got too close to their setup at Lyon, they would know he and the Paris detective had been working together on the Merriman situation and since he had not, as yet, been molested, the very least he could expect was a tap on his hotel phone. Accepting that, what he conveyed to Noble was what anyone listening would expect to hear. That Lebrun had been shot and was in Lyon at the Hospital la Part Dieu in grave condition. McVey was going to shower and shave, grab a quick breakfast roll and get to police headquarters as quickly as he could. When he had more news, he'd call back.

In London, Ian Noble had gently set the phone back in its cradle and pressed his fingertips together. McVey had just told him the situation, where Lebrun was, and that he was afraid his phone was tapped and would call him back from a public phone.

Ten minutes later, he picked up his private line.

"There's a mole of some kind in Interpol, Lyon," McVey said from a phone booth at a small café a block from his hotel. "It has to do with the Merriman killing. Lebrun went there to see what he could find out. Once they know he's still alive, they'll go after him again."

"I understand."

"Can you get him to London?"

"I'll do what I can. . . ."

"I assume that means 'yes,' " McVey said, hanging up.

Two hours and seventeen minutes later a British Royal Air Force medevac jet landed at Aerodrome Lyon-Bron. As it did, an ambulance carrying a British diplomat who'd suffered a heart attack raced out to the tarmac to meet it.

Fifteen minutes after that, Lebrun was airborne for England.

* * *

At five minutes past seven, a car pulled up in front of Vera Monneray's apartment building at 18 Quai de Bethune and Philippe, weary and ragged from a long, unsuccessful night of staring at photographs of known criminals, got out. Nodding to the four uniformed policemen standing guard at the front door, he entered the lobby.

"*Bonjour,* Maurice," he said to the night man behind the desk he was late to replace, and begged an extra hour to shave and get a little sleep.

Pushing through a door and into the service hallway, he went down a flight of steps to his modest basement apartment at the far end of the building. His key was out and he was almost to the door when he heard a noise behind him and someone call his name. Starting, he whirled around in fear, half expecting to see the tall man standing there with a gun aimed at his heart.

"Monsieur Osborn," he said in relief as Osborn stepped out from behind a door to a room that housed the building's electrical meters.

"You should not have left your room. There are police everywhere." Then he saw Osborn's hand, bandaged and held like a claw near his waist. "Monsieur——"

"Where's Vera? She's not in her apartment. Where is she?" Osborn looked as if he'd barely slept. But more than that, he looked frightened.

"Come inside, *s'il vous plaît.*"

Quickly Philippe unlocked the door and they entered his small flat.

"The police took her to work. She insisted. I was only going to the toilet and then up to see if you were there. Mademoiselle was equally concerned."

"I have to talk to her. Do you have a phone?"

"*Oui,* of course. But the police may be listening. They will trace the call back here."

Philippe was right, they would. "You call her, then. Tell

her that you are very concerned the tall man may find her. Tell her to ask the inspectors guarding her to take her to her grandmother's house in Calais. Don't let her argue. Tell her to stay there until . . ."

"Until when?"

"I don't know—" Osborn stared at him. "Until . . . it's safe."

65

"I'M GOING secure now." McVey punched a button and a light on the oversize "secure phone" in Lebrun's private office at police headquarters came on confirming the line was safe from wiretap. "Can you still hear me?"

"Yes," Noble said from a similar phone in the London Special Branch communications center. "Lebrun arrived about forty minutes ago, courtesy of the RAF. We've got him at Westminster Hospital under an assumed name. He's not in the best shape but the doctors seem to think he'll make it."

"Can he talk?"

"Not yet. But he can write or at least scrawl. He's given us two names. 'Klass' and 'Antoine'—Antoine has a question mark after it."

Klass was Dr. Hugo Klass, the German fingerprint expert working out of Interpol, Lyon.

"He's telling us it was Klass who requested the Merriman file from the New York Police Department," McVey said. "Antoine is Lebrun's brother, supervisor of internal security at Interpol headquarters," McVey said, wondering if the question mark after Antoine's name meant Lebrun was concerned about his brother's safety or that he might have been involved in the shooting.

"While we're at it, let me enlighten you about something else," Noble said. "We've got a name to go with our neatly severed head."

"Say what?" McVey was beginning to think the term *good luck* had been snatched from his vocabulary.

"Timothy Ashford, a housepainter from Clapham South, which you may or may not know is a working-class district in South London. He lived alone and worked as a day painter from job to job. His only relative is a sister living in Chicago but evidently they didn't have much to do with each other. He disappeared two years ago next month. It was his landlady who reported it. Came to the authorities when she hadn't seen him in several weeks and he was behind in his rent. She'd rented his flat but didn't know what to do with his belongings. He'd got his skull smashed by a billiard cue in a pub fight. It's our luck he also punched a bobby. Patching him up, they had to put a metal plate in his head; it was a matter of police record."

"That means you've got his fingerprints."

"You are absolutely correct, Detective McVey. We've got his fingerprints. Trouble is, all we've got of the rest of him now is his head."

There was a buzz and McVey heard Noble pick up the line to his office.

"Yes, Elizabeth," McVey heard him say. There was a pause and then he said, "Thank you," and came back on the line. "Cadoux is calling from Lyon."

"Is he on a secure phone?"

"No."

"Ian," McVey said quietly. "Before you pick up. Can you trust him? No reservations."

"Yes," Noble said.

"Ask him if he's at headquarters. If he is, find a way to tell him to leave the building and call your private line from a public phone. When you get him, plug me in, make it a three-way call."

Fifteen minutes later Noble's private line rang through, and Noble quickly picked up. "Yves, McVey is on the line from Paris. I'm putting him on with us now."

"Cadoux, it's McVey. Lebrun is in London, we got him out for his own safety."

"I presumed as much. Although I must tell you the hospital security people as well as the Lyon police are more than a little upset about how it was done. How is he?"

"He'll make it." McVey paused. "Cadoux, listen carefully. You have a mole at headquarters. His name is Doctor Hugo Klass."

"Klass?" Cadoux was taken aback. "He's one of our most brilliant scientists. The one who discovered the Albert Merriman fingerprint on the glass shard taken from the Jean Packard murder scene. Why would—?"

"We don't know." McVey could see Cadoux, his burly frame squeezed into a public phone booth somewhere in Lyon, twiddling his handlebar mustache, as understandably perplexed as they were. "But what we *do* know is that he requested the Merriman file from the NYPD, via Interpol, Washington, some fifteen hours *before* alerting Lebrun that he'd even come up with a print. Twenty-four hours later, Merriman was dead. And very soon after that so were his girlfriend in Paris, and his wife and her entire family in Marseilles. Somehow Klass must have learned Lebrun had come to Lyon and traced the file request. So he had him shut up."

"Now it starts to make sense."

"What does?" Noble asked.

"Lebrun's brother, Antoine, our supervisor of internal

security. He was found shot in the head this morning. It appears to have been suicide, but maybe not."

McVey cursed to himself. Lebrun was in bad enough shape himself without having to be told his brother was dead. "Cadoux, I doubt very much you're looking at a suicide. Something's going on that involved Merriman but reached a lot further. And whatever it is, whoever's behind it, is now killing cops."

"Yves, I think it's best you take Klass into custody as soon as possible," Noble said, directly.

"Excuse me, Ian. I don't think so." McVey was standing up, pacing behind Lebrun's desk. "Cadoux, find somebody you can trust. Maybe even from some other city. Klass doesn't suspect we're on to him. Get a wire on his private line at home and put a tail on him. See where he goes, who he talks to. Then work backward from Antoine's death. See if you can follow the line from the time he died until the time Sunday he met Lebrun. We don't know which side he was on. Finally, and very judiciously, find out who Klass got at Interpol, Washington, to make the Merriman file request to the New York police."

"I understand," Cadoux said.

"Captain—watch yourself," McVey warned.

"I shall. *Merci. Au revoir.*"

There was a click as Cadoux hung up.

"Who is this Doctor Klass?" Noble asked.

"Beyond who he appears? I don't know."

"I'm going to contact M16. Perhaps we can find out a little about Doctor Klass ourselves."

Noble clicked off and McVey stared at the wall, angered that he couldn't get some definitive grasp on what was going on. It was as if he'd suddenly become professionally impotent. Immediately there was a knock at the door and a uniformed policeman stuck his head in to tell him in English that the concierge from his hotel was on the phone. "Line two."

"Merci." The man left and McVey turned from the "secure phone" to lift the receiver on Lebrun's desk phone. "This is McVey."

"Dave Gifford, Hotel Vieux," a male voice said.

As he'd left his hotel earlier McVey had slipped the concierge, an expatriate American, a two-hundred-franc tip and asked to be informed of any calls or transmissions that came for him.

"I get a fax from L.A.?"

"No, sir."

What the hell was Hernandez doing with the Osborn information, hand-delivering it to Paris? Sitting down, McVey flipped open a notebook and picked up a pencil. He had two calls from Detective Barras, an hour apart. One from a plumber in Los Angeles confirming his automatic lawn sprinklers had been installed and were working. But wanted McVey to call back and let him know what days and length of watering time he wanted them set for.

"Jesus," McVey said under his breath.

Lastly there was a call the concierge felt was a crank. In fact the caller had rung back three times, wanting to speak to McVey personally. Each time he'd left no message, but each time he'd sounded a little more desperate.

He'd given his name as Tommy Lasorda.

66

JOANNA FELT as if she had been drugged and lived through a nightmare.

After her marathon sexual regatta with Von Holden in the mirrored pool room, Von Holden had invited her to come with him into Zurich. Her first reaction had been to smile and beg off. She was exhausted. She'd spent seven hours earlier that day with Mr. Lybarger, working him hard, and often against his will, to make him confident enough to walk without his cane. Trying to make Salettl's crazy Friday deadline. By 3:30 she'd seen he had done as much as he could do and had taken him to his quarters to rest. She'd expected he'd nap, have a light dinner in his room and probably go to bed very early. But, there he'd been, formally dressed at dinner, bright and alert and with enough reserve to listen to Uta Baur's never-ending chatter and then, afterward, walk to the second floor to attend the piano recital by Eric and Edward.

If Mr. Lybarger could do it, Von Holden teased, Joanna could certainly drive into Zurich for some infamous Swiss chocolat? Besides it was barely ten o'clock.

Their first stop had been at one of James Joyce's favorite restaurants on Ramistrasse, where they had chocolat and coffee. Then Von Holden had taken her to a crazy café on Munzplatz, just off the Bahnhofstrasse, to see the nightlife. After that they'd gone to the Champagne Bar at the Hotel Central Plaza and then to a pub on Pelikanstrasse. Finally they walked down to watch the moon over the Zurichsee.

"Want to see my apartment?" Von Holden smiled mischievously as he leaned on the railing and tossed a coin into the water for good luck.

"You're kidding!" Joanna thought she could never walk again.

"Not kidding at all." Von Holden reached out and touched her hair.

Joanna was amazed at her arousal. Even giggled out loud at it.

"What's funny?" Von Holden said.

"Nothing—"

"Come, then."

Joanna stared at him. "You are a bastard."

"Can't help it." He smiled.

They had cognac on his terrace overlooking the Old Town and he told her stories of his boyhood and growing up on a huge cattle ranch in Argentina. After that he'd taken her to his bed and they'd made love.

How many times has it been tonight? Joanna remembered thinking. Then remembered him standing over her, his penis still enormous, even in repose, and, smiling and embarrassed, asking her if she would very much mind if he tied her wrists and ankles to the bedposts. And then he'd stumbled around in a closet until he'd come out with the soft velvet straps he wanted to use. He didn't know why he wanted to, but always had. The thought of it excited him immensely. And when she'd looked and seen how immensely, she'd giggled and told him to go ahead if it would please him.

It was then, before he did it, that he'd told her he'd never had a woman do to him what Joanna did. And he'd dribbled cognac over her breasts and, like a Cheshire cat in heat, slowly licked them clean. In physical ecstasy, Joanna lay back as he bound her to the bedposts. By the time he lay down on the bed next to her, bright pinpoints of light were sparkling in the back of her eyes and she was beginning to feel a lightheadedness she'd never before experienced. Then she felt his weight on her, and the size of him as he slid so massively into her. And with each thrust, the pinpoints of light grew larger and brighter and behind them she saw incredible colored clouds floating in wild and grotesque formations. And somewhere, if there was a where, in the surreal kaleidoscope engulfing her—in the center of it, the center of her—she had the sensation that Von Holden had gone and that another man had taken his place. Struggling against her own dream, she tried to open her eyes to see if it was true. But that kind of consciousness wasn't possible and instead, she fell only deeper into the erotic whirl of light and color and the sensation of her own experience.

When she woke, it was already afternoon and she realized she was in her own bed at Anlegeplatz. Getting up, she saw her clothes from the night before, neatly folded on her dresser. Had she had a dream of dreams, or had it been something else?

It was a short time later, when she was showering, that she saw the scratch marks on her thighs. Looking in the mirror, she saw there were scratches on her buttocks as well, as if she had run naked through a field of thornbushes. Then she had the vaguest memory of running naked and horrified from Von Holden's apartment. Down the stairs and out the back door. And Von Holden had come after her and finally caught her in the rose garden behind his building.

Suddenly she didn't feel well at all. A wave of nausea swept over her. She was freezing cold and unbearably hot at the same time. Gagging, she flung open the toilet and threw up what was left of the chocolat and last night's dinner.

67

It Was 2:40 in the afternoon. Osborn had called McVey three times at his hotel, only to be told that Monsieur McVey was out, had left no time when he would be expected back, but would be checking in for messages. By the third call, Osborn was going through the roof, the built-up anxiety of what he had decided to do made all the worse by the fact that McVey was nowhere to be found. Rationally and emotionally he'd already put himself in the policeman's hands and, in doing so, had prepared himself for whatever that meant: a fellow American who would understand and help, or a quick ride to a French jail. He felt like a balloon stuck to a ceiling, trapped but free at the same time. All he wanted to do was be hauled down but there was no one to pull the string.

Standing alone, showered and freshly shaved, in Philippe's basement flat, he struggled with what to do next. Vera was on her way to her grandmother's in Calais, transported there by the police who had been guarding her. And even though Philippe had made the call, Osborn wanted to think she had realized it was he who was telling her, that Philippe was only his beard. He hoped she understood that he was asking her to go there not only for her own safety but because he loved her.

Earlier, Philippe had looked at him and told him to use his apartment to clean up. Laying out fresh towels, he'd unwrapped a new bar of soap and given him a razor to shave. Then, saying to help himself to whatever he found in the icebox, the doorman had done up his tie and gone back to work. From his position in the front lobby he would know what the police were up to. If something happened, he would telephone Osborn immediately.

Without doubt, Philippe had been an angel. But he was tired and Osborn had the sense he was one surprise away from coming unglued. Too much had happened in the last twenty-four hours to test not only his loyalty but his mental balance. Generous as Philippe was, he was, after all, and by his own choice, simply a doorman. And nobody, least of all himself, expected him to be daring forever. If Osborn went back up to his hiding place under the eaves there was no knowing how long he'd be safe. Especially if the tall man found a way to elude the police and came back looking for him.

Finally, he had realized there was only one choice. Picking up the phone, he rang Philippe at the front desk and asked if the police were still outside.

"Oui, monsieur. Two in front, two at the rear."

"Philippe—is there another way out of the building besides the front door or the service entrance?"

"Oui, monsieur. Right where you are. The kitchen door opens into a small hallway; at the end of it is a stairway up to the sidewalk. But why? Here you are safe and—"

"Merci, Philippe. Merci beaucoup," Osborn said, thanking him for everything. Hanging up, he made one more call. The Hotel Vieux. If McVey was picking up his messages, this would be one he would want. Osborn would give him a time and a place to meet.

7:00 P.M. The front terrace room of La Coupole, on the boulevard du Montparnasse. It was where he had last seen the private detective, Jean Packard, alive, and the one place in Paris he was familiar enough with to know it would be crowded at that hour. Thereby making it difficult for the tall man to risk taking a shot at him.

Five minutes later, he opened an outside door and climbed the short flights of stairs to the sidewalk. The afternoon was crisp and clear and barge traffic was passing on the Seine. Down the block he could see the police standing guard in front of the building. Turning, he walked off in the opposite direction.

At 5:20, Paul Osborn came out of Aux Trois Quartiers, a stylish department store on the boulevard de la Madeleine, and walked toward the Métro station a half block away. His hair was cut short and he was wearing a new, dark blue pin-stripe suit, with a white shirt and tie. Hardly the picture of a fugitive.

On the way there, he had stopped in the private office of Dr. Alain Cheysson on the rue de Bassano, near the Arc de Triomphe. Cheysson was a urologist two or three years younger than he with whom he'd shared a luncheon table in Geneva. They'd exchanged cards and promised to call one another when Osborn was in Paris or Cheysson in L.A. Osborn had forgotten about it entirely until he decided he'd better have someone look at his hand and tried to think how best to approach it.

"What happened?" Cheysson asked, once the assistant had taken X rays and Cheysson had come into the examining room to see Osborn.

"I'd rather not say," he said, trying to effect a smile.

"All right," Cheysson had replied with understanding, wrapping the hand with a fresh dressing. "It was a knife. Painful, perhaps, but as a surgeon you were very lucky."

"Yes, I know. . . ."

It was ten minutes to six when Osborn came up out of the Métro and started down boulevard du Montparnasse. La Coupole was less than three blocks away. That gave him more than an hour to play with. Time to observe, or try to observe, if the police were setting a trap. Stopping at a phone booth, he called McVey's hotel and was told that yes, Monsieur McVey had been given his message.

"Merci."

Hanging up, he pushed open the door and went back outside. It was nearing dark and the sidewalks were filled with the restless flow of people after work. Across the street and down a little way was La Coupole. Directly to his left was a small café with a window large enough for him to observe the comings and goings across the street.

Going inside, he picked a small table near the window that gave him a clear view, ordered a glass of white wine and sat back.

He had been lucky. The X rays on his hand had, as he'd thought, shown no serious damage and Cheysson, though a urologist and hardly an expert on hands, had assured him that he felt no permanent damage had been done. Grateful for Cheysson's help and understanding, he'd tried to pay for the visit, but Cheysson wouldn't hear of it.

"Mon ami," he'd said, tongue in cheek, "when I am wanted by the police in L.A. I know I will have a friend to treat me who will say nothing to anyone. Who will not even make a record of my visit. Eh?"

Cheysson had seen him immediately and treated him without question, all the while knowing Osborn was wanted by the police and jeopardizing himself by helping. Yet he had said nothing. In the end they'd hugged and the Frenchman had kissed him in the French way and wished him well. It was little enough he could do, he said, for a fellow doctor who had shared his lunch table in Geneva.

Suddenly Osborn put down his glass and sat forward. A police car had pulled up across the street. Immediately two uniformed gendarmes got out and went into La Coupole. A moment later they came back out, a well-dressed man in handcuffs between them. He was animated, belligerent and apparently drunk. Passersby watched as he was hustled into the backseat of the police car. One gendarme got in beside him, the other got behind the wheel. Then the car drove off in a singsong of sirens and flashing blue emergency lights.

That was how fast it could happen.

Lifting his glass, Osborn looked at his watch. It was 6:15.

68

AT 6:50 McVey's taxi crawled through traffic. Still, it was better than being in the Opel and trying to fight his way across Paris on his own.

Pulling out a tattered date book, he looked at the notes for that day, Monday, October 10. Most notably the last, *Osborn—La Coupole, boulv. Montparnasse, 7 p.m.* Scribbled above it was a memo regarding a message from Barras. The Pirelli tire representative had examined the tire casting made at the park by the river. The pattern of that tire was found on tires specially manufactured for a large auto dealer who had an ongoing contract with Pirelli to put their tires on his new cars. That tire was now standard equipment on two hundred new Ford Sierras, eighty-seven of which had been sold in the last six weeks. A list of the purchasers was being compiled and would be ready by Tuesday morning. Further, the glass shard of the auto mirror McVey had picked up in the street after the shooting at Vera Monneray's had been put through the police lab. It too had come from a Ford vehicle, though it was impossible to tell which make or model. Parking Control had been alerted and its officers directed to report any Ford or Ford Sierra with a broken exterior mirror.

The last notation on McVey's October 10 page was the lab report on the broken toothpick he had uncovered among the pine needles just before he'd found the tire track. The person who had held the toothpick in his/her mouth had been a "secretor"—a group-specific substance sixty percent of the population carry in the bloodstream that makes it possible to determine the blood group from other body fluids such as urine, semen and saliva. The blood group of the secretor in the woods was the same as the blood group found in the bloodstains on the floor in Vera Monneray's kitchen. Type O.

The taxi stopped in front of La Coupole at precisely seven minutes past seven. McVey paid the driver, got out and walked into the restaurant.

The large back room was being set up for the dinner crowd that had yet to arrive, and only a few tables were occupied. But the glassed-in terrace room facing the sidewalk in front was packed and noisy.

McVey stood in the doorway and looked around. A moment later, he squeezed past a group of businessmen, found a vacant table near the back and sat down. He was exactly as he wished to appear, one man, alone.

The Organization had tentacles reaching far beyond those who were members of it. Like most professional groups it subcontracted labor, often employing people who had no idea for whom they actually worked.

Colette and Sami were high-school girls from wealthy families who were into drugs, and consequently did whatever was necessary to feed their habit and at the same time keep their addiction hidden from their families. That put them on call at almost any hour, for any reason.

Monday's request was simple: Watch the lone exit at

the apartment building at 18 Quai de Bethune that the police were not watching, the entrance to the doorman's living quarters. If a good-looking man about thirty-five came out, report it and follow him.

Both girls had followed Osborn to Dr. Cheysson's office on rue de Bassano. Then Sami had trailed him to Aux Trois Quartiers on boulevard de la Madeleine, even flirted with him and asked him to help pick out a tie for her uncle while he was waiting for his suit to be tailored. After that, Colette had followed him into the Métro and stayed with him until he'd gone into the café across from La Coupole.

That was when Bernhard Oven took over, watching as Osborn left the café and crossed boulevard du Montparnasse to enter La Coupole at five minutes after seven.

At five foot ten and in dark hair, jeans, leather jacket and Reeboks, with a diamond stud in his left ear, Bernhard Oven was no longer a blond, tall man. He was, however, no less deadly. In his right jacket pocket, he carried the silenced Cz .22 automatic he'd used so successfully in Marseilles.

At 7:20, convinced that McVey had come by himself, Osborn got up from where he sat near the window, eased past several crowded tables and approached him, his bandaged hand held gingerly at his side.

McVey glanced at Osborn's bandaged hand, then indicated a chair next to him, and Osborn sat down.

"I said I'd be alone. I am," McVey said.

"You said you could help. What did you mean?" Osborn asked. His new suit and haircut meant nothing. McVey had known he'd been there all along.

McVey ignored him. "What's your blood type, Doctor?"

Osborn hesitated. "I thought you were going to find out."

"I want to hear it from you."

Just then a waiter in a white shirt and black pants stopped at the table. McVey shook his head.

"*Café,*" Osborn said, and the waiter walked off.

"Type B."

LAPD Detective Hernandez's preliminary report on Osborn had finally reached McVey by fax just before he'd left Lebrun's office. Among other stats it had included Osborn's blood type—type B. Which meant that not only had Osborn told the truth but that the tall man's blood was type O.

"Doctor Hugo Klass. Tell me about him," McVey said.

"I don't know a Doctor Hugo Klass," Osborn said, deliberately, still nervously wondering if there weren't plain-clothes detectives somewhere in the room waiting for McVey to give the signal.

"He knows you," McVey lied purposefully.

"Then I've forgotten. What kind of medicine does he practice?"

Either Osborn was very good, or very innocent. But then he'd lied about the mud on his shoes, so there was every possibility he was doing the same here. "He's a Ph.D. A friend of Timothy Ashford." McVey shifted gears in an effort to make Osborn stumble.

"Who?"

"Come on, Doctor. Timothy Ashford. A housepainter from South London. Good-looking man. Age twenty-four. You know who he is."

"I'm sorry, I don't."

"No?"

"No."

"Then I guess it wouldn't make any difference if I told you I had his head in a freezer in London."

A middle-aged woman in a lightly checked suit at the next table reacted sharply. McVey kept his eyes on Osborn. His statement had been offhand but loaded, designed to elicit the same kind of reaction from Osborn it had from the woman. But Osborn hadn't so much as blinked.

"Doctor, you lied to me before. You want me to help you. You've got to give me something I can use. A reason to trust you."

The waiter came with Osborn's coffee, set it on the table in front of him and then left. McVey watched him go. Several aisles away he stopped at the table of a dark-haired man wearing a leather jacket. The man had been sitting alone for ten minutes and so far had ordered nothing. He had a diamond stud in his left ear and a cigarette in his left hand. The waiter had stopped once before but he'd been waved off. This time the man glanced in McVey's direction, then said something to the waiter. The waiter nodded and walked away.

McVey looked back to Osborn. "What is it, Doctor, you feel uncomfortable talking here? Want to go somewhere else?"

Osborn didn't know what to do or think. McVey was asking him the same kind of questions he had the first time they'd met. He was obviously looking for something he thought Osborn was involved in, but he had no idea what it was. And that made it all the harder because every answer he gave seemed to be calculated avoidance, when, in fact, he was only telling the truth.

"McVey, believe me when I tell you I have no idea what you're talking about. If I did maybe I could help, but I don't."

McVey tugged at an ear and looked off. Then he looked back. "Maybe we should try a little different approach," he said, pausing. "How come you pumped Albert Merriman full of succ—een—ill—choline? I pronounce it right?"

Osborn didn't panic, his pulse didn't even jump. McVey

was too intelligent not to have found out, and he'd prepared himself for it. "Do the Paris police know?"

"Please answer the question."

"Albert Merriman—murdered my father."

"Your father?" That surprised McVey. It was something he should have considered, but hadn't, that Merriman had been an object of pursuit for revenge.

"Yes."

"You hire the tall man to kill him?"

"No. He just showed up."

"How long ago did Merriman kill your father?"

"When I was ten."

"Ten?"

"In Boston. On the street. I was there. I saw it happen. I never forgot his face. And I never saw him again, until a week ago, here in Paris."

In an instant McVey fit the pieces together. "You didn't tell the Paris police because you weren't finished with him. You hired Packard to find him. And when he did, you looked for a spot to do it and found the riverbank. Give him a shot or two of the drug. Get him in the water, he can't breathe or use his muscles, he floats off and drowns. Current is heavy there, the chemical dissipates quickly in the body and he's so bloated nobody thinks to look for puncture wounds. That was the idea."

"In a way."

"What way?"

"First, I wanted to find out why he had done what he did."

"Did you?" Suddenly McVey's eyes tracked off. The man in the leather jacket was no longer at the table where he had been. He was closer. Two tables away in a clear line to Osborn's immediate left. A cigarette was still in his left hand but his right was out of sight, under the table.

Osborn started to turn to see what McVey was looking

at when suddenly McVey was on his feet, stepping between Osborn and the man at the table.

"Get up and walk ahead of me. Out that door. Don't ask why. Just do it."

Osborn got up. As he did, he realized who McVey had been looking at. "McVey, that's him. The tall man!"

McVey whirled. Bernhard Oven was standing, the silenced Czechoslovakian Cz coming up in his hand. Somebody screamed.

Suddenly the air was shattered by two booming reports, one right on top of the other, followed almost immediately by a hailstorm breaking of glass.

Bernhard Oven didn't quite understand why the older American had hit him so hard in the chest. Or why he felt he had to do it twice. Then he realized he was flat on his back on the cement sidewalk outside, while his legs were still inside the restaurant, dangling across the sill of the window he had crashed through. Glass was everywhere. Then he heard people screaming, but he had no idea why. Puzzled, he looked up and saw the same American standing over him. A blue-steel .38 Smith & Wesson revolver was in his fist, its barrel pointed at his heart. Vaguely he shook his head. Then everything faded.

Osborn moved in and felt Oven's carotid artery. Around them was pandemonium. People were yelling. Screaming. Crying out in shock and horror. Some stood back watching. Others were shoving their way out, trying to get away, while still others moved closer, trying to see. Finally Osborn looked up to McVey.

"He's dead."

"You're sure it's the tall man."

"Yes."

McVey had two instantaneous thoughts. The first was that a new Ford Sierra with Pirelli tires and a broken mirror was parked somewhere nearby. The second was "He's no six foot four."

Kneeling down, McVey hiked a pant leg up over the dead man's sock line.

"Prosthetics," Osborn said.

"That's a brand-new one on me."

"You don't think he did it on purpose?"

"Had his legs amputated so he could alter his height?" McVey pulled a handkerchief from his back pocket, then reached down and tucked it around the Cz automatic still in Oven's hand. Pulling the gun free, he looked at it. Its handle was taped, its identifying marks filed off. Squirreled to its snout was a silencer. It was the workstation of a professional killer.

McVey looked up at Osborn. "Yeah," he said. "I think he did. I think he had his legs cut off on purpose."

69

McVEY STEPPED back from Oven's body and looked at Osborn. "Cover his face, huh?" Then he flashed his badge at a crowd of waiters gawking in horror and fascination a few feet away and told someone to call the police if somebody already hadn't and to get the spectators out of there.

Pulling a white tablecloth from a nearby table, Osborn covered Bernhard Oven's face while McVey went over the body for identification. Finding none, he reached into his jacket, ripped the stiff cardboard cover from his pocket notebook. Taking Oven's hand, he pressed the thumb into his bloodsoaked shirt, then pressed the bloody thumb against the cardboard, giving him a legible thumbprint.

"Let's get out of here," he said to Osborn.

Pushing quickly through the lingering onlookers, they crossed the dining room, went into the kitchen, and then out a back door and into an alley. As they came out, they heard the first singsong of sirens.

"This way," McVey said, not really certain where they were going. From the moment he'd first reacted, McVey's supposition had been that Oven had been about to shoot Osborn. But now as they stepped onto boulevard du Montparnasse walking toward boulevard Raspail, he realized the intended target could as easily have been himself. The tall man had killed Albert Merriman within hours after it was discovered he was still alive and living in Paris. Then, in quick order, Merriman's girlfriend, his wife and her family had been found and slaughtered. The last, in Marseilles, some four hundred and fifty miles to the south. But in a wink, the killer was back in Paris and in Vera Monneray's apartment looking for Osborn.

How had he found everyone in such rapid order? Merriman's wife, for instance, when every local police force in the country had been put on alert and still had been unable to find her? And Osborn—how had he so quickly discovered Vera Monneray was the "mystery woman" who'd picked Osborn up at the golf course after he'd come out of the Seine when the media was still in the speculation stage and the police were the only ones who knew for sure? And then, in almost the same breath, Lebrun and his brother had been attacked in Lyon. Though probably not by the tall man. Even he couldn't be in two places at once.

Clearly, what was happening was happening at an increasingly frantic pace. And, in turn, the deadly circle kept narrowing. That the tall man was suddenly out of the picture would probably make little difference. He couldn't have done what he had without the help of a complex, sophisticated and very well-connected organization. If they had infiltrated Interpol, why not the Paris Préfecture of Police?

A squad car flew by, then another. The city rocked with sirens.

"How did he know we were going to be there?" Osborn said, as they fought through the evening crowd made electric by what had happened.

"Keep going," McVey urged, and Osborn saw him glance back at the police cars sealing off boulevard du Montparnasse at either end of the block.

"You're worried about the police, aren't you?" Osborn said.

McVey said nothing.

Reaching the boulevard Raspail, they turned right and started up the street. In front of them was a Métro station. McVey thought briefly about taking it, then decided against it, and they kept on.

"Why would a policeman be afraid of the police?" Osborn demanded.

Suddenly a blue-black truck turned from a side street and jerked to a stop in the intersection just behind them. Its back door slammed open and a dozen Compagnie de Securité Republicaine antiterrorist police jumped out wearing flak jackets over paratroop jumpsuits and brandishing automatic weapons.

Swearing under his breath, McVey looked around. Two doors down was a small café. "In there," he said, taking Osborn by the arm and prodding him toward the door.

People were standing at the windows watching the action on the street and barely took notice as they entered. Finding a corner at the end of the bar, McVey turned Osborn into it and held up two fingers to the bartender.

"Vin blanc," he said.

Osborn leaned back. "You want to tell me what's going on?"

The bartender set two glasses in front of them and filled them with white wine.

"*Merci,*" McVey said, picking up a glass and handing it to Osborn. Taking a deep swallow, McVey turned his back to the room and looked at Osborn.

"I'll ask you your own question. How did he know we were going to be there? Answer. You were followed or I was. Or somebody was tapped into the message board at the Hôtel Vieux and figured I might not be meeting the real Tommy Lasorda for drinks.

"A friend of mine, a Parisian detective, was badly shot up this morning and his brother, also a cop, was murdered because he was trying to find out who, besides you, so suddenly got the line on Albert Merriman about a quarter of a century after the fact. The police may be involved, they may not, I don't know. What I do know is that something's going on that's making it dangerous as hell for anyone even remotely connected to Merriman. And right now, that's you and me, and the smartest thing we can do is get off the street."

"McVey—" Osborn was suddenly alarmed. "There's someone else who knows about Merriman."

"Vera Monneray." In the rush of everything, McVey had forgotten about her.

Dread swept over Osborn. "The French detectives who were guarding her here—I arranged to have them take her to her grandmother's in Calais."

70

"*YOU* ARRANGED?" McVey was incredulous.

Osborn didn't reply. Instead he set his glass on the bar and started down a dingy corridor past the toilets toward a pay phone in the rear of the café. He was almost there when McVey caught up with him.

"What're you gonna do, try and call her?"

"Yes." Osborn kept going. He hadn't thought it through, but he had to know she was all right.

"Osborn." McVey took him hard by the arm and pulled him around. "If she is there, she's probably okay, but the detectives with her will be monitoring the line. They'll let you talk while they trace the call. If the French police are involved, you and I won't get five feet out that door." McVey nodded toward the front. "And if she's not there, there's nothing you can do."

Osborn flared. "You don't understand, do you? I *have* to know."

"How?"

By now Osborn had an answer. "Philippe." Osborn would call him, have Philippe call Vera, then call Osborn back. They couldn't trace the second call.

"The doorman at her apartment?"

Osborn nodded.

"He helped you get out of the building, didn't he?"

"Yes."

"And maybe arranged the tail on you when you left?"

"No, he wouldn't. He's—"

"He's *what?* Somebody let the tall man know Vera was the mystery girl, and somebody told him where she lived. Why not him? Osborn, for now, your peace of mind is going to have to wait." McVey glared at him long enough to make his point, then looked past him for a way out the back.

A half hour later, paying cash and using an alias—saying their luggage had been lost at the train station—McVey checked them into connecting rooms on the fifth floor of the Hôtel St.-Jacques on the avenue St.-Jacques, a tourist hotel less than a mile from La Coupole and the boulevard du Montparnasse.

Obviously American and without luggage, McVey played upon the French disposition for amour. Entering the rooms, McVey gave the bellman an extra-large tip, telling him shyly but very sincerely to make certain they weren't disturbed.

"Oui, monsieur." The bellman gave Osborn a knowing smile, then closed the door behind him and left.

Immediately McVey checked out both rooms, the closets and bathrooms. Satisfied, he drew the window curtains, then turned to Osborn.

"I'm going down to the lobby and make a phone call. I don't want to make it from here because I want nothing traced to this room. When I get back, I want to go over everything you remember about Albert Merriman, from the moment he killed your father until the last second in the river."

Reaching into his jacket pocket, McVey took out Bernhard Oven's Cz automatic and put it in Osborn's hand. "I'd ask you if you knew how to use it, but I already know the answer." McVey's glare was enough, the edge in his voice only added to it. He turned for the door. "Nobody comes in but me. Not for any reason."

Easing open the door, McVey looked out, then stepped into a deserted hallway. The elevator was the same. At the lobby the doors opened and he got out. Except for a group of Japanese tourists coming in off a bus tour and following a leader carrying a little green and white flag, the area was all but deserted.

Crossing the lobby, McVey looked for a public phone and saw one near the gift shop. Using an AT&T credit card number billed to a post office box in Los Angeles, he dialed Noble's voice mail at Scotland Yard. A recording took his message.

Hanging up, he went into the gift shop, briefly looked at the selection of greeting cards, then bought a birthday number with a large yellow bunny on it. Back in the lobby, he took out the cardboard notebook cover with Bernhard Oven's dried bloody thumbprint and slipped it in with the card, addressing it to a "Billy Noble" care of a post address in London. Then he went to the front desk and asked the concierge to send it by overnight mail.

He'd just paid the concierge and was turning back for the lobby when two uniformed gendarmes came in from the street and stood looking around. To McVey's left were a number of tour brochures. Casually, he walked over to them. As he did, one of the policemen looked his way. McVey ignored him and thumbed through the brochures. Finally, he chose three and walked back across the lobby in full view of the police. Sitting down near the telephone, he started to look through them. Barge tours. Tours of Versailles. Tours of wine country. He counted to sixty, then looked up. The police were gone.

Four minutes later, Ian Noble called from a private residence where he and his wife were attending a formal dinner for a retiring British army general.

"Where are you?"

"Paris. The Hôtel St.-Jacques. Jack Briggs. San Diego. Wholesale jewelry," McVey said in monotone, giving him the location and the name he was registered under. A movement to his left caught his eye. Shifting his stance, he saw three men in business suits coming across the lobby toward him. One seemed to be looking directly at him, the other two were talking.

"You remember Mike, doncha?" he said with verve, opening his jacket, playing the extroverted American salesman, his hand inches from the .38 at his waist. "Yeah, I brought him along with me."

"You have Osborn."

"Sure do."

"Is he trouble?"

"Hell, no. Not yet anyway."

The men passed, going into the alcove toward the elevators. McVey waited until they entered and the door closed, then turned back to the phone and quickly ran down what had happened, adding that he had just put the tall man's thumbprint in the overnight mail.

"We'll run it straightaway," Noble said, then added he'd had words with the French chargé d'affaires, who had demanded to know what the hell the Brits thought they were doing shanghaiing a seriously wounded Parisian inspector from his hospital room in Lyon. Further, they wanted him back, posthaste. Noble had said he was appalled, that he'd never heard of such an incident and would look into it immediately. Then, changing subjects, he said they'd come up blank trying to find anyone in Britain experimenting in advanced cryosurgery. If such practice was going on, it was wholly out of sight.

McVey glanced around the lobby. He hated paranoia. It crippled a man and made him see things that weren't. But he had to face the reality that anyone, in uniform or not, could be working for this group, whoever or whatever they were. The tall man would have had no compunction about shooting him right there in the lobby and he had to assume his replacement would do the same. Or if not right then, at least report where he was. By lingering, he was pressing his luck on either account.

"McVey, are you there?"

He turned back to the phone. "What'd you find out about Klass?"

"M16 could find nothing but an exemplary record. Wife, two children. Born in Munich. Grew up in Frankfurt. Captain in the German Air Force. Recruited out of it by West German Intelligence, the Bundesnachrichtendienst, where he developed his skills and reputation as a fingerprint expert. After that, went to work for Interpol at Lyon headquarters."

"No. No good," McVey reacted. "They missed something. Go deeper. Look into people he associates with, outside his daily routine. Hold on—" McVey thought back, trying to remember Lebrun's office the day they had first received Merriman's fingerprint from Interpol, Lyon. Somebody else had been working with Klass—Hal, Hall, Hald—Halder!

"Halder—first name Rudolf. Interpol, Vienna. He worked with Klass on the Merriman print. Look, Ian, do you know Manny Remmer?"

"With the German Federal Police."

"He's an old friend, works out of headquarters in Bad Godesberg. Lives in an area called Rungsdorf. It's not too late. Get him at home. Tell him I said for you to call. Tell him you want anything he can find on both Klass and Halder. If it's there, he'll get it. Trust him."

"McVey—" There was concern in Noble's voice. "I think you've managed to open a rather large can of very disagreeable worms. And, frankly, I think you should get out of Paris damn quick."

"How? In a box or a limo?"

"Where can I reach you in ninety minutes?"

"You can't. I'll reach you."

It was past 9:30 before McVey knocked on the door to Osborn's room. Osborn opened the door to the chain and peered out.

"Hope you like chicken salad."

In one hand McVey balanced a tray with chicken salad in white plastic bowls with Stretch-Tight across the top, in the other he juggled a pot of coffee along with two cups, everything purchased from an irritable counter clerk at the hotel coffee shop as he was trying to close for the night.

By ten o'clock the coffee and chicken salad were gone and Osborn was pacing up and down, absently working the fingers of his injured hand, while McVey sat hunched over the bed, using it for a worktable, staring at what he'd written in his notebook.

"Merriman told you that an Erwin Scholl—Erwin spelled with an E—of Westhampton Beach, New York, paid him to kill your father and three other people sometime around 1966."

"That's right," Osborn said.

"Of the other three, one was in Wyoming, one in California, and one in New Jersey. He'd done the work and been paid. Then Scholl's people tried to kill him."

"Yes."

"That's all he said, just the names of states. No victims' names, no cities?"

"Just the states."

McVey got up and went into the bathroom. "Almost thirty years ago a Mr. Erwin Scholl hires Merriman to do some contract killing. Then Scholl orders him knocked off. The game of kill the killer. Make certain whatever's been taken care of is permanent, with no loose ends that might talk."

McVey tore the sanitary wrapper off a water glass, filled it, then came back into the room and sat down. "But Merriman outsmarted Scholl's people, faked his own death, and got away. And Scholl, assuming Merriman was dead, forgot about him. That was, until you came along and hired Jean Packard to find him." McVey took a drink of the water, stopping short of mentioning Dr. Klass and

Interpol, Lyon. There was only so much Osborn needed to know.

"You think Scholl is behind what's happened here in Paris?" Osborn asked.

"And Marseilles, and Lyon, thirty years later? I don't know who Mr. Scholl is yet. Maybe he's dead, or never was."

"Then who's doing this?"

McVey hunched over the bed, made another note in his dog-eared book, then looked at Osborn. "Doctor, when was the first time you saw the tall man?"

"At the river."

"Not before?"

"No."

"Think back. Earlier that day, the day before, the day before that."

"No."

"He shot you because you were with Merriman and he didn't want to leave a witness. That what you think?"

"What other reason would there be?"

"Well, for one, it could have been the other way around, that he was there to kill you and not Merriman."

"Why? How would he know me? And even if that were the case, why would he kill all of Merriman's family afterward?"

Osborn was right. Seemingly no one had known Merriman was alive until Klass discovered his fingerprint. Then the boom had been lowered. Most probably, as Lebrun had suggested, to keep him from talking, because they knew the police, once they had the print, would grab him in no time. Klass might have been able to delay release of the print, but he couldn't deny it existed because too many people at Interpol knew about it. So Merriman had to be shut up because of what he might say after he'd been caught. And since he'd been out of business for twenty-five-odd years, what he might have said would have been about what he had done when he *was* in business. Which would have been almost exactly the same time he was under the hire of Erwin Scholl. Which was why Merriman, along with anyone else he was close enough to have confided in, had been liquidated. To keep him, or them, from talking about what he had done while he was in Scholl's employ, or at the very least, from implicating Scholl in a murder-for-hire scheme. That meant they either didn't know who Osborn was or had missed the connection that he was heir to one of Merriman's victims and—

"Dammit!" McVey said under his breath. Why the hell hadn't he realized it before? The answer to what was happening lay not with Merriman or Osborn, but with the four people Merriman had killed thirty years earlier, Osborn's father among them!

McVey stood up in a surge of adrenaline. "What did your father do for a living?"

"His profession?"

"Yeah."

"He—thought things up," Osborn said.

"What the hell does that mean?"

"From what I remember, he worked in what was probably then a kind of high-tech think tank. He invented things, then built prototypes of what he invented. Mostly, I think, it had to do with the design of medical instruments."

"Do you remember the name of the company?"

"It was called Microtab. I remember the company name clearly because they sent a large floral wreath to my father's funeral. The name of the company was on the card but nobody from the company showed up," Osborn said vacantly.

McVey knew then the extent of Osborn's pain. He knew he could still see the funeral, as if it had happened yesterday. It had to have been the same when he saw Merriman in the brasserie.

"This Microtab was in Boston?"

"No, Waltham, it's a suburb."

Picking up his pen, McVey wrote: *Microtab—Waltham, Mass.—1966.*

"Any sense of how he worked? By himself? Or in groups, four or five guys hammering these things out?"

"Dad worked alone. Everybody did. Employees weren't allowed to talk about what they were working on, even with each other. I remember my mother discussing it with him once. She thought it was ridiculous he couldn't talk to the person in the next office. Later, I assumed it had to do with patents or something."

"Do you have any idea what he was working on when he was killed?"

Osborn grinned. "Yes. He'd just finished it and brought it home to show me. He was proud of what he did and liked to show me what he was working on. Although I'm sure he wasn't supposed to."

"What was it?"

"A scalpel."

"A scalpel?—as in surgery?" McVey could feel the hair begin to crawl up the back of his neck.

"Yes."

"Do you remember what it looked like? Why it was different from any other scalpel?"

"It was cast. Made of a special alloy that could withstand extreme variations in temperature and still remain surgically sharp. It was to be used in association with an electronic arm driven by computer."

Not only was the hair standing up on McVey's neck, it felt as if someone had poured ice cubes down his spine. "Somebody was going to do surgery at extreme temperatures. Using some kind of computer-driven gizmo that would hold your father's scalpel and do the actual work?"

"I don't know. You have to remember that in those days computers were gigantic, they took up whole rooms, so I don't know how practical it would have been even if it worked."

"The temperature business."

"What about it?"

"You said extreme temperatures. Would that be hot or cold or both?"

"I don't know. But experimental work had already begun with laser surgery, which is basically the turning of light energy into heat. So if they were experimenting with unexplored surgical concepts I would assume they would have been working in the opposite direction."

"Cold."

"Yes."

Suddenly the ice was gone and McVey could feel the rush of blood through his veins. *This* was the something that had kept pulling him back to Osborn. The connection between Osborn, Merriman and the headless bodies.

71

Berlin, Monday, October 10, 10:15 P.M.

"ES IST spät, Uta,"—It's late, Uta—Konrad Peiper said edgily.

"I apologize, Herr Peiper. But I'm sure you realize there's nothing I can do," Uta Baur said. "I'm certain they will be here at any minute." She glanced at Dr. Salettl, who didn't respond.

She and Salettl had flown in from Zurich earlier that evening on Elton Lybarger's corporate jet and driven directly here to make final preparations before the others arrived. In a normal situation she would have begun a half hour ago. Guests like those gathered here, in the private room on the top floor of Galerie Pamplemousse, a five-story gallery for *"neue Kunst,"* new art, on the Kurfürstendamm, were not the kind anyone kept waiting, especially this far into the evening. But the two men who were late were not men one insulted by leaving before they arrived, no matter who you were. Especially when you had come at their invitation.

Uta, dressed as always in black, got up and crossed the room to a side table upon which rested a large silver urn filled with fresh-ground Arabian coffee, plates of assorted canapés and sweets, and bottled waters, kept replenished by two exquisite young hostesses in tight jeans and cowboy boots.

"Refill the urn, please. The coffee is not fresh," she snapped at one of them. Immediately the girl did as she was told, pushing through the door and going into a service kitchen.

"I give them fifteen minutes, no more. I'm busy too, don't they realize?" Hans Dabritz set his stopwatch, put several canapés on a plate, and retreated to where he had been sitting.

Uta poured herself a glass of mineral water and looked around the room at her impatient guests. Their names read like a Who's Who of contemporary Germany. She could visualize the shorthand descriptions.

Diminutive, bearded, Hans Dabritz, fifty. Real estate developer and political powerbroker. Real estate activity includes massive apartment complexes in Kiel, Hamburg, Munich and Düsseldorf, industrial warehousing and high-rise, commercial office buildings in Berlin, Frankfurt, Essen, Bremen, Stuttgart and Bonn. Owns square blocks of downtown Bonn, Frankfurt, Berlin and Munich. Sits on the board of directors of Frankfurt's Deutsche Bank, Germany's largest bank. Contributions to local politicians extensive and ongoing; controls a majority of them. Joke often told that the biggest influence in Germany's lower house of parliament, the Bundestag, is in the hands of one of Germany's smallest men. In the cold and sober back halls of German politics, Dabritz is looked upon as the dominant puppeteer. Almost never fails to get what he wants.

Konrad Peiper, thirty-eight—who with his wife, Margarete, had been aboard the lake steamer in Zurich two nights earlier as part of the welcome home celebration for Elton Lybarger—president and chief executive officer of Goltz Development Group, GDG, the second largest trading company in Germany. Under his auspices, established Lewsen International, a de facto holding company in London. With Lewsen as a front, GDG put together a network of fifty small and medium-size German companies that became Lewsen International's main suppliers. Between 1981 and 1990 GDG, through the Lewsen front, secretly provided cash-rich Iraq key materials to wage chemical and biological warfare, upgrade ballistic missiles, and provide components for nuclear capability. That Iraq would lose most of what Lewsen had provided to Operation Desert Storm was of little consequence. Peiper had firmly established GDG as a world-class arms supplier.

Margarete Peiper, twenty-nine, Konrad's wife. Petite, ravishing, workaholic. By twenty, a music arranger, record producer and personal manager of three of Germany's top rock bands. By twenty-five, sole owner of the massive Cinderella, Germany's largest recording studio, two record labels and homes in Berlin, London and Los Angeles. Currently, chairman, principal owner and driving force behind A.E.A., Agency for the Electric Arts, a huge, worldwide, talent organization representing top writers, performers, directors and recording artists. Insiders say Margarete Peiper's guiding genius is that her psyche is permanently tuned to the "youth channel." Critics see her ability to stay on top of a vast and growing young contemporary audience as more frightening than extraordinary because what she does teeters so precariously between creative brilliance and outright manipulation of the will. A charge she has always denied. Hers, she maintains, is nothing more than a vigorous, lifelong commitment to people and to art.

Retired Air Force Major General Matthias Noll, sixty-two. Respected political lobbyist. Brilliant public speaker. Champion of the powerful German peace movement. Outspoken critic of rapid constitutional change. Held in high regard by a large population of aging Germans still ravaged by the guilt and shame of the Third Reich.

Henryk Steiner, forty-three. Number-one groundshaker in the new Germany's not so quietly rumbling labor unrest. Father of eleven. Stocky, immensely likable. Cut from the mold of Lech Walesa. Dynamic and extraordinarily popular political organizer. Holds the emotional and physical backing of several hundred thousand auto- and steelworkers struggling for economic survival within the new eastern German states. Imprisoned for eight months for leading three hundred truck drivers in a strike protesting dangerous and underrepaired highways, he was only two weeks out of jail before leading five hundred Potsdam police in a token four-hour work stoppage after red tape had left them unpaid for nearly a month.

Hilmar Grunel, fifty-seven, chief executive, HGS Beyer, Germany's largest magazine and newspaper publisher. Former ambassador to the United Nations and vociferous conservative, oversees daily operation and controls editorial content of eleven major publications, all of which take a strong and heady view from the right.

Rudolf Kaes, forty-eight. Monetary affairs specialist at the Institute for Economic Research at Heidelberg and key economic adviser to the Kohl government. Lone German representative on the board of the new European Economic Community's central bank. Vigorous advocate for a single European currency, acutely aware of how thoroughly the German mark already dominates Europe, and how a single currency based on it would only serve to enhance German economic might.

Gertrude Biermann (also a guest on the lake steamer in Zurich), thirty-nine. Single mother of two. A predominant force in the Greens, a radical leftist peace movement tracing its roots to the attempt to keep U.S. Pershing missiles out of West Germany in the early 1980s. Influence reaches deep into a German conscience disturbed by any attempt at all to align Germany with the military West.

There was a buzz and Uta saw Salettl pick up the telephone at his elbow. He listened, then hung up and glanced at Uta.

"*Ja,*" he said.

A moment later the door opened and Von Holden entered. Briefly he scanned the room, then stood aside.

"*Hier sind sie*"—Here they are—Uta said to the guests, at the same time glancing sharply at the hostesses, who immediately left through a side door.

A moment later, a strikingly handsome and exceedingly well-dressed man of seventy-five entered. "Dortmund is tied up in Bonn. We will go on without him," Erwin Scholl said in German to no one in particular, then sat down next to Steiner. Dortmund was Gustav Dortmund, chief of the Federal Bundesbank, Germany's central bank.

Von Holden closed the door and crossed to the table. Pouring a glass of mineral water, he handed it to Scholl, then stepped back to stand near the door.

Scholl was tall and slim, with close-cropped gray hair, a deep tan and startlingly blue eyes. Age and considerable fortune had done nothing but add character to an already chiseled face of broad forehead, aristocratic nose and deeply cleft chin. He possessed an old-style military bearing that commanded attention the moment he appeared.

"The presentation, please," he said quietly to Uta. A curious blend of studied shyness and complete arrogance, Erwin Scholl was the perfect *American* success story: a penniless German immigrant who had risen to become baron of a vast publishing empire, and, in turn, had taken on the mantle of philanthropist, fund-raiser, and intimate of U.S. presidents from Dwight Eisenhower to Bill Clinton. Like most of the others here, he depended on the masses for his wealth and influence but, out of choice and careful orchestration, was all but unknown to them.

"Bitte"—Please—Uta said into an intercom. Instantly the room darkened and a wall of abstract paintings in front of them broke into thirds and pulled back, revealing a flat, eight-by-twelve-foot high-definition television screen.

Immediately, a razor-sharp image appeared. It was a close-up of a soccer ball. Suddenly a foot flew into the frame and kicked it. As it did, the video camera zoomed back to reveal the manicured lawns at Anlegeplatz and Elton Lybarger's nephews, Eric and Edward, playfully kicking the soccer ball between them. Then the camera moved to the side to see Elton Lybarger standing with Joanna, watching them. Abruptly, one of the boys kicked the ball in Lybarger's direction and Lybarger gave it a healthy kick back toward his nephews. Then he looked at Joanna and smiled proudly. And Joanna smiled back, with the same sense of accomplishment.

Then the video cut and Lybarger was seen in his elegant library. Seated before a blazing fire, dressed casually in sweater and slacks, he was talking in detail to someone out of camera range about the axis Paris and Bonn had forged in making the new European Economic Community. Learned and articulate, the clear point he was making was that Britain's assumed role of "detached moral superiority" only served to keep Britain a malcontent in the equation. And that continuing to play that character would serve neither Britain nor the Economic Community well. His opinion was that there *must* be a Bonn–London rapprochement for the Community to be the major economic force it was created to be. His discourse ended lightly with a joke that was not a joke. "Of course, what I meant to say was that it should be a *Berlin*–London rapprochement. Because, as everyone knows, wise lawmakers, refusing to turn back the clock on German unity, have kept the pledge of the last forty years and promised to return the capital to Berlin by the year 2000. In doing so, they have made her once again the heart of Germany."

Then Lybarger's image faded and was replaced by something else. Perpendicular and slightly arched, it covered nearly the entire eight feet of the screen's height. For a moment nothing happened, then the thing turned, hesitated, moved determinedly forward. In that instant everyone recognized what it was. A fully engorged, erect penis.

Abruptly the angle shifted to the silhouette of another man standing in the darkness, watching. Then the angle shifted once more and what the audience saw was Joanna, unclothed and spread-eagled on a large poster bed, her hands and feet tied to the bedposts with lush strands of velvet. Her full breasts clung melon-like to either side of her chest, her legs were comfortably apart, and the dark V where they met undulated gently with the unconscious rhythm of her hips. Her lips were moist. Her eyes, open and glassy, were thrown back, perhaps in anticipation of some ecstasy to come. A portrait of pleasure and consent, she indicated nothing to suggest that any of this was against her will.

And then the man and penis were upon her and she took him wholly and willingly. A complex variety of camera angles recorded the authenticity of the act. The penis strokes were long and forceful, effective, yet unrushed, and Joanna reacted only with increasing pleasure.

A camera angle showed the other man as he stood back. It was Von Holden and he was completely nude. Arms folded over his chest, he watched indifferently.

Then the camera cut back to the bed, and a running time code, clocking the elapsed time from penal insertion to orgasm, appeared in the upper righthand corner of the screen.

At 4:12:04 Joanna visually experienced her first orgasm.

At 6:00:03, an electroencephalographic chart, tracking her brain waves, appeared in the upper middle of the screen. Between 6:15:43 and 6:55:03, she experienced seven separate excessive brain wave oscillations. At 6:57:23 an electroencephalographic chart appeared at the upper left of the screen, representing her male partner's brain waves. From then until 7:02:07, they were normal. In that time, Joanna had three more episodes of extreme brain wave activity. At 7:15:22, the male's brain activity increased threefold. As it did, the camera moved in on Joanna's face. Her eyes were thrown back in her head until only the whites showed and her mouth was open in a silent scream.

At 7:19:19, the male experienced total orgasm.

At 7:22:20, Von Holden stepped into camera range and escorted the male from the room. As they left, two cameras simultaneously focused on the man who had participated in the sex act with Joanna. Documenting without doubt that the man who had been in the bed was the same man who was now leaving the room. There was no question at all who it was, and that he had fully and thoroughly completed the act.

Elton Lybarger.

"Eindrucksvoll!"—Impressive!—Hans Dabritz said as the lights went up and the triangle of abstract paintings slid back into place over the video screen.

"But we're not going to be showing a video, are we, Herr Dabritz," Erwin Scholl said sharply. Abruptly his gaze shifted to Salettl.

"Will he be capable of our performance, Doctor?"

"I would like more time. But he is remarkable, as we have seen." In any other room in the world Salettl's remark would have drawn laughter, but not here. These were not humorous people. They had witnessed a clinical study upon which a decision was to be based. Nothing else.

"Doctor, I asked you if he will be ready to do what is required. Yes or no?" Scholl's rapier-like stare cut Salettl in two.

"Yes, he will be ready."

"No cane! No one to assist his walk!" Scholl goaded him.

"No. No cane. No one to assist his walk."

"Danke," Scholl said with contempt. Standing, he turned to Uta.

"I have no reservations." With that, Von Holden opened the door and he walked out.

72

AVOIDING THE elevator, Scholl walked down the four flights of gallery stairs with Von Holden at his side. At the street, Von Holden opened the door and they stepped into crisp night air.

A uniformed driver opened the door to a dark Mercedes. Scholl got in first and then Von Holden.

"Go down Savignyplatz," Scholl said as they moved off.

"Drive slowly," he said as the Mercedes turned onto a tree-lined square and drove at a crawl along a block of crowded restaurants and bars. Scholl leaned forward staring out, watching the people on the street, how they walked and talked to each other, studying their faces, their gestures. The intensity with which he was doing it made it seem as if it were all new, as if he were seeing it for the first time.

"Turn onto Kantstrasse." The driver swung onto a block of garish nightclubs and loud cafés.

"Pull over, please," Scholl said finally. Even though he was being polite, his manner was short and clipped, as if everything was a military order.

A half block down, the driver found a spot on the corner, pulled in and stopped. Sitting back, Scholl folded his hands under his chin and watched the squeeze of young Berliners trafficking relentlessly through the neon colors of their clamorous Pop Art world. From behind the tinted windows, he seemed a voyeur intent upon the pleasures of the world he was watching, but keeping his own distance from it.

Von Holden wondered what he was doing. He'd known something was troubling him the moment he'd picked him up at Tegel Airport and taken him to the gallery. He thought he knew what it was, but Scholl had said nothing and Von Holden thought that whatever it might have been had passed.

But there was no reading Scholl. He was an enigma hidden behind a mask of uncompromising arrogance. It was a temperament he seemed helpless or unwilling to do anything about because it had made him what he was. It was not unusual for him to work his staff eighteen hours a day for weeks and then either criticize them for not working harder or reward them with an expensive holiday halfway around the world. More than once he'd walked out of critical labor negotiations at the eleventh hour and disappeared, going alone to a museum or even a movie, and not returning for hours. And when he did return, he expected the problem to have been resolved in his favor. Usually it was, because both sides knew that he would fire his entire negotiating staff if it were not. If that happened, a new staff would be brought in and negotiations would be started from scratch, a process that would cost both Scholl and the opposition a fortune in new legal fees. The difference was that Scholl could afford it.

In both cases it was more than simply getting done what he wanted done, it was a control mechanism, the deliberate flaunting of a colossal ego. And Scholl not only knew it, he reveled in it.

Von Holden had been *Leiter der Sicherheit*—director of security—for Scholl's general European operations—two printing plants in Spain, four television stations, three in Germany, one in France, and GDG, Goltz Development Group, of Düsseldorf, of which Konrad Peiper was president—for eight years; personally hiring the security staffs and supervising their training. Von Holden's responsibility, however, did not end there. Scholl had other, darker and more far-ranging investments, and their safeguard fell under Von Holden's title as well.

The situation in Zurich, for example. The pleasuring of Joanna was a case of manipulation requiring skill and delicacy. Salettl believed Elton Lybarger wholly capable of complete recovery: emotionally, psychologically and physically. But early on, he had voiced concern that with no women in his life, when the time came to test Lybarger's reproductive capacity, a woman he was unfamiliar with could make him uncomfortable, to the point where he might possibly refuse to perform, or at least, be stilted in his performance.

A female who had been his physical therapist for an extended period and who had accompanied him all the way to Switzerland to look after him there would be someone he trusted and was comfortable with. He would know her touch, even her smell. And though he might never have looked upon her sexually, he would, at the time he was brought to have intercourse with her, be under the influence of a strong sexual stimulant. Fully aroused, yet not wholly aware of the circumstances, he would instinctively sense the familiar and in doing so relax and proceed.

Hence the choosing of Joanna. Far from home, with no immediate family, and not terribly attractive, she would be physically and emotionally vulnerable to a surrogate's seduction. A seduction whose sole purpose was to ready her for copulation with Elton Lybarger. The need for the surrogate had been Salettl's calculated judgment and he'd voiced it to Scholl, who had turned to his *Leiter der Sicherheit.* Von Holden's personal participation would not only guarantee Lybarger's security and privacy, it would further demonstrate Von Holden's allegiance to the Organization.

Across from the street, a digital neon clock over the entrance to a disco read 22:55. Five minutes to eleven. They had been there for thirty minutes and still Scholl sat in silence, absorbed in the young crowds filling the street.

"The masses," he said quietly. "The masses."

Von Holden wasn't sure if Scholl was talking to him or not. "I'm sorry, sir. I didn't hear what you said."

Scholl turned his head and his eyes found Von Holden's. "Herr Oven is dead. What happened to him?"

Von Holden had been right in the first place. Bernhard Oven's failure in Paris had been bothering Scholl all along, but it was only now that he'd chosen to discuss it.

"I would have to say he made an error in judgment," Von Holden said.

Abruptly Scholl leaned forward and told the driver to move on, then turned to Von Holden.

"We had no problems for a very long time, until Albert Merriman surfaced. That he and the factors surrounding him were eliminated as quickly and efficiently as they were only proved that our system continues to work as designed. Now Oven is killed. Always a risk in his profession, but troubling in its implication that the system might not be as efficient as we presumed."

"Herr Oven was working alone, operating on information provided him. The situation now is under control of the Paris sector," Von Holden said.

"Oven was trained by you, not the Paris sector!" Scholl snapped angrily. He was doing what he always did, making it personal. Bernhard Oven worked for Von Holden, therefore his failure was Von Holden's.

"You are aware I have given Uta Baur the go-ahead."

"Yes, sir."

"Then you realize the mechanisms for Friday night are, by now, already in place. Stopping them would be difficult and embarrassing." Scholl's stare penetrated Von Holden the same way it had Salettl. "I'm sure you understand."

"I understand. . . ."

Von Holden sat back. It would be a long night. He'd just been ordered to Paris.

73

A DAMP fog swirled around and it had started to mist. The yellow headlamps of the few cars still out cut an eerie swath as they moved up the boulevard St.-Jacques past the telephone kiosk.

"Oy, McVey!" Benny Grossman's voice cut through three thousand miles of underwater fiber-optic cable like bright sunshine. Twelve fifteen, Tuesday morning in Paris, was seven fifteen, Monday evening in New York, and Benny had just come back into the office to check messages after a very long day in court.

Down the hill, through the drizzle and the trees that separated the two-lane street, McVey could just see the hotel. He hadn't dared call from the room and didn't want to chance the lobby if the police came back.

"Benny, I know, I'm driving you crazy—"

"No way, McVey!" Benny laughed. Benny always laughed. "Just send my Christmas bonus in hundreds. So go ahead, drive me crazy."

Glancing out at the street, McVey felt the reassuring heft of the .38 under his jacket, then looked back to his notes.

"Benny. Nineteen sixty-six, Westhampton Beach. An Erwin Scholl—who is he? Is he still alive? If so, where is he? Also 1966—early, the spring, or even late fall of 'sixty-five, three unsolved murders, professional jobs. In the states of—"

McVey checked his notes again. "Wyoming, California, New Jersey."

"A snap, boobalah. And while I'm at it why don't I find out who the hell really killed Kennedy."

"Benny, if I didn't need it—" McVey looked out toward the hotel. Osborn was tucked in the room with the tall man's Cz, the same as the first time, and with the same orders not to answer the phone or open the door for anyone but him. This was the kind of business McVey heartily disliked, being in danger with no idea where it might come from or what it might look like. Most of his last years had been spent picking up the pieces and putting together evidence after drug dealers had concluded business transactions. Most of the time it was safe, because men who were dead usually didn't try to kill you.

"Benny"—McVey turned back to the phone—"the victims would have been working in some kind of high-tech field. Inventors, precision tool designers, scientists maybe, even a college professor. Somebody experimenting with extreme cold—three, four, five hundred degrees below zero cold. Or maybe, the reverse—somebody exploring heat. Who were they? What were they working on when killed? Now, last: Microtab Corporation. Waltham, Massachusetts, 1966. Are they still in business? If so, who runs the shop, who owns them? If not, what happened to them and who owned them in 1966?"

"McVey—what am I, Wall Street? The IRS? The Department of Missing Persons? Just punch this into a computer and out comes your answers?—When the hell you want it, New Year's 1995?"

"I'm going to call you in the morning."

"What?"

"Benny, it's very, very important. If you draw a blank, if you need help, call Fred Hanley at the FBI in L.A. Tell him it's for me, that I asked for the assistance." McVey paused. "One other thing. If you haven't heard from me by noon tomorrow, your time, call Ian Noble at Scotland Yard and give him everything you have."

"McVey—" Benny Grossman's voice lost its testy ebullience. "You in trouble?"

"Lots."

"Lots? What the hell's that mean?"

"Hey, Benny, I owe you—"

Osborn stood in the darkened window looking down at the street below. The fog was thick and the traffic almost nonexistent. No one passed on the sidewalks. People were home asleep, waiting for Tuesday. Then he saw a figure walk under a streetlamp and cross the boulevard toward the hotel. He thought it was McVey, but he couldn't be sure. Pulling the curtain back across the window, he sat down and clicked on a small bedside lamp, illuminating Bernhard Oven's .22 Cz. He felt like he'd been hiding for half a century, yet it had only been eight days since he'd first looked up and had seen Albert Merriman sitting across from him in the Brasserie Stella.

How many had died in eight days? Ten, twelve? More. If he'd never met Vera and come to Paris, each one of those people would still be alive. Was the guilt his? There was no answer because it was not a reasonable question. He had met Vera and he had come to Paris, and nothing could change what had happened since.

In the last hours, while McVey had been gone, he'd tried not to think of Vera. But in the moments when he did, when he couldn't help not think of her, he had to tell himself she was all right, that the inspectors who had taken her to her grandmother's in Calais were good, trustworthy cops, and not a corrupt tentacle of whatever the hell was going on.

Violence had struck him at an early age and its aftermath had been with him ever since. The nightmares after Merriman had been shot, the crippling emotional breakdown that had ended on the floor in the attic hideaway in Vera's arms had been little more than a desperate wrenching against an ungodly truth: that the death of Albert Merriman had settled nothing. The horrid, scar-faced killer he'd pursued from childhood had been simply replaced by a name and precious little else. In leaving Vera's building—in coming out of hiding, risking the tall man, the Paris police and the chance that McVey, once face to face, would arrest him on the spot—he was admitting that he could no longer go it alone. It wasn't mercy he'd come to McVey for, it was help.

A knock at the door startled him like a pistol shot. His chin came up and his head snapped around as if he'd been caught somewhere with his pants down. He stared at the door, uncertain if his mind was playing tricks.

The knock came again.

If it was McVey he'd say something or use his key. Osborn's fingers closed around the Cz just as the knob began to turn. The door pressed inward just enough to insure it was locked. As quickly the pressure ceased.

Crossing the room, he leaned back against the wall, just to the side of the door. He could feel the sweat build up in the grip of the gun. Whatever happened next was up to whoever was in the hallway.

"Sorry, honey. Ya got the wrong damn room," he heard McVey drawl loudly from outside the door. It was followed by a woman's voice flailing in French.

"Wrong room, honey. Believe me. Try upstairs—maybe you got the wrong floor!"

French spat back, angry and indignant.

Then there was the sound of the key in the lock. The door opened and McVey came in. He had a dark-haired girl by the arm and a rolled-up newspaper sticking out of his jacket pocket.

"You want to come in, come in," he said to the girl, then looked at Osborn.

"Lock it."

Osborn closed the door, locked it, then slid the chain lock across.

"Okay, honey, you're in. What now?" McVey said to the girl, who stood in the middle of the room with a hand on her hip. Her eyes went to Osborn. She was probably twenty, five foot two or three, and not the least bit frightened. She wore a tight silk blouse and a very short black skirt with net stockings and high heels.

"Fucky, fucky," she said in English, then smiled seductively, looking from Osborn to McVey.

"You want to screw the two of us. Is that it?"

"Sure, why not?" She smiled and her English got a lot better.

"Who sent you?"

"I am a bet."

"What kind of bet?"

"The night clerk said you were gay. The bellman said no."

McVey laughed. "And they sent you to find out."

"Oui." And pulled several hundred francs from the top of her bra to prove it.

"What the hell's going on?" Osborn said.

McVey smiled. "Aw hell, we was just funnin' with them, honey. The bellman's right." He looked at Osborn. "Want to fuck her first?"

Osborn jumped. "What?"

"Why not, she's already been paid." McVey smiled at her. "Take your clothes off. . . ."

"Sure." She was serious, and she was good at it. She looked them in the eyes the whole time. One and then the other and then back again, as if each piece as it came off was a special show for him alone. And slowly she took it all off.

Osborn watched open-mouthed. McVey wasn't actually going to do it? Just like that and with him standing there? He'd heard stories about what cops have done in certain situations, everybody had. But who believed it, let alone thought they'd be firsthand party to it?

McVey glanced at him. "I'll go first, huh?" He grinned. "Don't mind if we go into the bathroom, do you, Doctor?"

Osborn stared. "Be my guest."

McVey opened the bathroom door and the girl went in. McVey went in behind her and closed the door. A second later Osborn heard her give a sharp yelp and there was a hard bump against the door. Then the door opened and McVey came out fully clothed.

Osborn was dumbfounded.

"She came up here to get a look at us. She saw me in the hall, it was all she needed."

McVey tugged the newspaper from his jacket pocket and handed it to him, then went over to gather up the girl's clothes. Osborn unrolled it. He didn't even see which paper it was. Only the bold headline in French— HOLLYWOOD DETECTIVE SOUGHT IN LA COUPOLE SHOOTING! Beneath it, in smaller type, "Linked to American Doctor in Merriman Murder!" Once more Osborn saw the same Paris police mug shot of himself that had been printed earlier in *Le Figaro* and beside it a two- or three-year-old picture of a smiling McVey.

"They got that from the *L.A. Times Magazine.* An interview on the everyday life of a homicide investigator. They wanted gristle, they got boredom. But they ran it anyway." McVey put the clothes into a hotel dry cleaning bag and unlocked the door. Carefully he checked the hallway, then hung the bag outside.

"How did they know this? How could they even find out?" Osborn was incredulous.

McVey closed the door and relocked it. "They knew

who their man was and that he was tailing one of us. They knew I was working with Lebrun. All they had to do was send somebody down to the restaurant with a couple of photographs and ask, 'Are these the guys?' Not so hard. That's why the girl. They wanted to make sure they had the right Mutt and Jeff before they sent in the firepower. She probably hoped she could get a look, make up a story and walk away. But obviously she was prepared to do whatever she had to if it didn't work."

Osborn looked past McVey at the closed bathroom door. "What did you do to her?"

McVey shrugged. "I didn't think it was too good an idea to let her go back downstairs right away."

Handing McVey the paper, Osborn opened the bathroom door. The girl sat stark naked on the toilet, handcuffed to a water pipe on the wall beside it. A washcloth was stuck in her mouth and her eyes looked as if they were ready to pop from her head in fury. Without a word Osborn closed the door.

"She's a feisty one," McVey said, with the sliver of a grin. "Whoever finds her, she's going to make a big stink about her clothes before she lets anyone pick up a telephone. Hopefully that delay will add a few more seconds to our increasingly limited life span."

74

TEN SECONDS later, McVey, and then Osborn, stepped cautiously into the hallway and closed the door behind them. Both had guns in their hands but there was no need—the hallway was clear.

As far as they could tell, whoever had sent the girl was still waiting for her, probably downstairs. That meant whoever had sent her had only suspected who they might be, and wasn't sure. They were also giving her time. She was a professional and if she'd had to play sex with the suspects, she would. But McVey knew the time they would give her wouldn't be much.

The interior hallways on the fifth floor of Hôtel St.-Jacques were painted gray and had dark red carpeting. Fire stairs were at the end of each corridor, with a second set near the center of the building surrounding the elevator shafts. McVey chose the far stairs, farthest from the elevators. If something happened, he didn't want them caught in the middle.

It took them four and a half minutes to reach the basement, go through a service door and take a back alley to the street. Turning right, they walked off down the boulevard St.-Jacques through a thickening fog. It was 2:15 A.M., Tuesday, October 11.

At 2:42, Ian Noble's red bedside phone buzzed twice, then stopped, its signal light flashing. Careful not to disturb his wife, who suffered from painful arthritis and hardly slept, he slipped out of bed and pushed through the black walnut door that separated their bedroom from his private study. A moment later he picked up the extension.

"Yes."

"McVey."

"It's been a damn long ninety minutes. Where the hell are you?"

"On the streets of Paris."

"Osborn still with you?"

"We're like Siamese twins."

Touching a button under the overhang of his desk, Noble's desktop slid back, revealing an aerial map of Great Britain. A second press of the button brought up a coded menu. A third, and Noble had a detailed map of Paris and its surrounding environs.

"Can you get out of the city?"

"Where?"

Noble looked back to the map. "About twenty-five kilometers east on Autoroute N3 is a town called Meaux. Just before you get there is a small airport. Look for a civil aircraft, a Cessna, with the markings ST95 stenciled on the tail. Should be there, weather permitting, between eight and nine hundred hours. The pilot will wait until ten. If you miss it, look for it again, same time, the next day."

"*Gracias, amigo.*" McVey hung up and walked out to meet Osborn. They were in a corridor outside one of the entrances to a railroad station, the Gare de Lyon on the boulevard Diderot, just north of the Seine in the northwest quadrant of the city.

"Well?" Osborn said, expectantly.

"What do you think about sleep?" McVey said.

Fifteen minutes later, Osborn put his head back and surveyed their accommodations, a stone ledge tucked up under the Austerlitz Bridge over the Quai Henri IV, and in full view of the Seine.

"For a few hours we join the homeless." McVey pulled his collar up in the darkness and rolled over on his shoulder. Osborn should have settled in too, but he didn't. McVey raised up and saw him sitting against the granite, his legs out in front of him, staring at the water, as if he'd just been plunked down in hell and told to sit there for eternity.

"Doctor," McVey said quietly, "it beats the morgue."

Von Holden's Learjet touched down at a private landing strip some thirty kilometers north of Paris at 2:50 A.M. At 2:37, he'd been radioed that the targets had been identified by the Paris sector leaving the hotel St.-Jacques at approximately 2:10. They had not been seen since. Further information would be provided as it became available.

The Organization had eyes and ears on the streets, in police stations, union halls, hospitals, embassies and boardrooms of a dozen major cities across Europe, and a half-dozen more around the world. Through them Albert Merriman had been found, and Agnes Demblon and Merriman's wife and Vera Monneray. And through them Osborn and McVey would be found as well. The question was when.

By 3:10, Von Holden was in the backseat of a dark blue BMW on Autoroute N2 passing the Aubervilliers exit, moving into Paris. A commanding officer impatiently waiting to hear from his generals in the field.

To kill Bernhard Oven, this McVey, this American policeman, had to have been either very lucky or very good or both. To slip from their fingers just as he was discovered was the same. He didn't like it. The Paris sector was first rate, highly regarded and highly disciplined, and Bernhard Oven had always been one of the best.

And Von Holden would know. Though several years younger, he had been Oven's superior, both in the Soviet Army and, later, in the Stasi, the East German secret police, in the years before reunification and the Stasi's dissolution.

Von Holden's own career had begun early. At eighteen he'd left home in Argentina and gone to Moscow for his final years of schooling. Immediately afterward he'd started formal training under KGB direction in Leningrad. Fifteen months later, he was a company commander in the Soviet Army, assigned to the 4th Guards Tank Army protecting the Soviet embassy in Vienna. It was there he became an officer in the Spetsnaz special reconnaissance units trained in sabotage and terrorism. It was there too, he met Bernhard Oven, one of a half-dozen lieutenants under his command in the 4th Guards.

Two years later Von Holden was officially discharged from the Soviet Army and became assistant director for the East German Sports Administration assigned to oversee the training of elite East German athletes at the College for Physical Culture in Leipzig; among them had been Eric and Edward Kleist, the nephews of Elton Lybarger.

At Leipzig, Von Holden also became an "informal employee" of the Ministry for State Security, the Stasi. Drawing on his training as a Spetsnaz soldier, he schooled recruits in clandestine operations against East German citizens and developed "specialists" in the art of terrorism and assassination. It was at this point he requested Bernhard Oven from the 4th Guards Tank Army. Von Holden's appreciation of his talent did not go unrewarded. Within eighteen months, Oven was one of the Stasi's top men in the field and its best killer.

Von Holden remembered vividly the afternoon in Argentina when, as a boy of six, his entire career had been decided. He'd gone riding with his father's business partner, and on the ride the man had asked him what he planned to do when he grew up. Hardly an extraordinary question from a grown man to a boy. What was uncommon was his answer and what he'd done afterward.

"Work for you, of course!" Young Pascal had beamed, giving heels to his horse and racing off across the pampas. Leaving the man sitting alone astride his own horse, watching, as the tiny figure with sure hands and an already impertinent disposition coaxed his big horse up and off the ground, and in a flying leap cleared a high growth of vegetation to disappear from sight. In that instant Von Holden's future was cast. The man who'd asked the question, his riding partner, had been Erwin Scholl.

75

THE SMOOTH click of the wheels over the rails beneath was soothing, and Osborn sat back drowsing. If he'd slept at all during the two hours they'd spent huddled under Austerlitz Bridge, he didn't remember. All he knew was that he was very tired and felt grubby and unclean. Across from him, McVey leaned against the window, dozing lightly, and he marveled that McVey seemed to be able to sleep anywhere.

They'd climbed from their perch over the Seine at five o'clock and gone back to the station, where they'd discovered that trains for Meaux left from the Gare de l'Est, fifteen minutes by cab across Paris. With time pressing, they'd chanced a taxi ride across the city, hoping the randomly chosen taxi driver was no more than he appeared.

Reaching the station, they'd entered separately and through different doors, each man all too aware of the early editions jamming the front racks of every news kiosk inside, bold black headlines hawking the shooting at La Coupole with their photos printed starkly and graphically underneath.

Moments later, nervous hands had reached for tickets at

separate windows, but neither clerk had done more than exchange a ticket for money and serve the next customer in line.

Then they'd waited, apart, but within view of each other, for twenty minutes. Their only jolt came when five uniformed gendarmes had suddenly appeared leading four rough-looking, handcuffed and chained convicts toward a waiting train. It looked as if they were about to board the train to Meaux, but at the last minute they'd veered off and loaded their sullen cargo onto another.

At 6:25, they crossed the platform with a group of others and took separate seats in the same car of the train that left the Gare de l'Est at 6:30 and would arrive in Meaux at 7:10. Ample time for them to get from the station to the airfield by the time Noble's pilot touched down in his Cessna ST95.

The train had eight cars and was a local, part of the EuroCity line. Two dozen people, mostly early commuters, rode in the same Second Class compartment as theirs. The First Class section was empty and had been avoided. Two men alone were easily remembered and described even if they sat seats apart in an empty compartment. The same two men sitting alone among other travelers were less likely to be recalled.

Pulling back a sleeve, Osborn looked at his watch. Six fifty-nine. Eleven minutes until they reached the station at Meaux. Outside, he could see the sun rising on a gray day that made the French farmland seem softer and greener than it already was.

The contrast between it and the dry, sun-scorched brush of Southern California was disquieting. For no particular reason, it conjured up visions of who McVey was and the tall man and the death that surrounded them both. Death had no place here. This train ride, this green land, this birthing of a new day was something that should have been enshrouded in love and wonder. Suddenly Osborn was swept by an almost unbearable longing for Vera. He wanted to feel her. Touch her. Breathe in the scent of her. Closing his eyes, he could see the texture of her hair and the smoothness of her skin. And he smiled as he remembered the almost imperceptible fuzz of hair on her earlobes. Vera was what mattered. This was her land he was passing through. It was her morning. Her day.

From somewhere off came a heavy, muffled thud. The train shuddered, and Osborn was suddenly being thrown violently sideways toward a young priest who, seconds before, had been reading a paper. Then the car they were in was turning over and they both fell. It kept rolling, like some horrendous carnival ride. Glass crashing and the wrenching of steel meshed with human screams. He glimpsed the ceiling just as an aluminum crutch glanced hard off his head. A split second later Osborn was upside down with a body on top of him. Then glass exploded above him and he was awash in blood. The car spun again and the person on top of him slid down his chest. It was a woman, and she had no upper torso at all. Then there was horrible grating as steel screamed over steel. It was followed by a tremendous bang. Osborn rocketed backward and everything stopped.

Seconds, minutes afterward, Osborn opened his eyes. He could see a gray sky through trees with a bird circling above them. For a time he lay there doing nothing more than breathe. Finally, he tried to move. First his left leg, then his right. Then his arm, until he could see his still-bandaged left hand. He moved his right arm and hand. Miraculously, he had survived.

Easing up, he saw the massive twist of steel. What remained of a railroad car was lying on its side halfway down an embankment. It was then he realized he had been thrown from the train.

Farther up the embankment, he could see the other cars, some driven, accordion-like, into each other. Others were piled, almost piggyback, one on top of another. Bodies were everywhere. Some were moving; most were not. At the top of the hill, a group of young boys came into view, staring down at the wreckage and pointing.

Slowly Osborn began to understand what had happened. "McVey!" he heard himself say out loud.

"McVey!" he said again, struggling to his feet. Then he saw the first rescuers push past the boys and start down the hill.

The act of standing made him dizzy. Closing his eyes, he grabbed onto a tree for balance and took a deep breath. Reaching up, he felt the pulse at his neck. It was strong and regular. Then somebody, a fireman, he thought, spoke to him in French. "I'm all right," he said in English, and the man moved on.

Shrieks and cries of victims cleared his mind further, and he saw that everything around him was chaos. Rescue workers poured down the hillside. Climbed into cars. Began lifting people out through smashed windows, easing them out from beneath the wreckage. Blankets were tossed, in a rush, over the dead. The entire area became a frantic hill of activity.

And settling over everything—the shouts, the screams, the distant sirens, the cries for help—was the pungent, overwhelming, odor of hot brake fluid as it leaked from sheared lines.

The smell of it made Osborn cover his nose as he pushed through the tragedy around him.

"McVey!" he cried out again. "McVey! McVey!"

"Sabotage," he heard someone say in passing. Turning, he found himself looking into a rescue worker's face.

"American," he said. "An older man. Have you seen him?" The man stared back as if he didn't understand. Then a fireman came up and they ran back up the hill.

Stepping over broken glass, climbing over torn and ravaged steel, Osborn moved from one victim to another.

Watching the doctors work on the living, lifting the blankets to stare at the faces of the dead. McVey was nowhere among them.

Once, lifting the blanket to look at the face of a dead man, he saw the man's eyes flicker once, then close again. Reaching, he felt for a heartbeat and found it. Looking up, he saw a paramedic.

"Help!" he shouted. "This man is alive!"

The paramedic came with a rush and Osborn moved back. As he did, he began to feel cold and lightheaded. Shock, he knew, was beginning to set in. His first thought was to ask the paramedic where he could get a blanket and he started to, but suddenly had enough presence of mind to realize that if the train had been sabotaged, the act could well have been meant for McVey and himself. If he asked for a blanket, they would know he'd been a passenger. They would demand his name and he would be reported alive.

"No," he thought and backed away. "Best to get out of sight and stay there."

Looking around, he saw a thick stand of trees near the top of the grade not far from where he stood. The paramedic had his back to him and the other rescue workers were farther down the hill. It became a major physical effort for him to climb the few yards to the trees, and he was afraid it was taking too long and he would be seen. Finally he reached them and turned back. Still, no one looked his way. Satisfied, he melted into the thick undergrowth. And there, away from the hysteria, he lay down in the damp leaves and, using his arm for a pillow, closed his eyes. Almost immediately deep sleep overtook him.

76

WORD OF the Paris-Meaux train derailment reached Ian Noble less than an hour after it happened. First reports indicated sabotage. A second report confirmed that an explosive device had been set off directly under the engine.

That McVey and Osborn would be on the same route, at the same time, to rendezvous with Noble's pilot at the Meaux airstrip was too coincidental. And since the pilot had landed, waited the allotted time and then taken off with no sign of them, there was every reason to believe McVey and Osborn had been on the train.

Immediately, Noble put in a call to Captain Cadoux at his residence in Lyon and informed him what had happened. It was important he know what Cadoux had found out in his investigations into the German fingerprint expert, Hugo Klass, and the death of Lebrun's brother, Antoine. Noble was going under the assumption that McVey and Osborn had been on the train and that whatever organization Klass was working for, or Antoine might have been involved with, was responsible for the derailment. It was another demonstration of just how far their intelligence network reached. Never mind they had found Merriman, Agnes Demblon and the others, and knew who Vera Monneray was and where she lived—that they'd been able to pinpoint McVey's clandestine meeting with Osborn at La Coupole and then discover they were on the Paris-Meaux train was nothing short of astonishing.

Cadoux was speechless, and the situation made his own frustration all the worse. The tail he'd put on Klass had so far turned up nothing more sinister than the fact that he'd gone to work as usual on Monday. A tap on his phone had given up nothing. As for Antoine, he'd come directly home Sunday night after a late dinner with his brother, and gone directly to bed. For some reason he'd gotten up and gone to his study before dawn, which was not his habit. And it was there his wife found him at 7:30. He was on the floor beside his desk with his nine-millimeter Beretta on the carpet beside him. The gun had been fired once and there was a single gunshot wound in his right temple. An autopsy-ballistics report proved the bullet had come from the same weapon. The doors leading outside were locked, but the latch in a kitchen window was open. So it was possible someone had both come in and gone out that way, though there were no signs of it.

"Or just gone out," Noble said.

"Yes, we'd thought of that too," Cadoux said in his heavy French accent. "That Antoine had let someone in the front door and relocked it. At that hour he would have known whoever it was or he would not have let them in. Then they killed him and went out the window. Still, there were no signs of it, and the coroner has officially ruled it a suicide."

Noble was as baffled as he'd ever been. Everyone who knew Albert Merriman was either dead or a definitive target, and the man who had discovered him through a fingerprint seemed completely innocent.

"Cadoux. Interpol, Washington—who did Klass get there to request the Merriman file from the New York police?"

"He didn't."

"What?"

"Washington has no record of it."

"That's impossible. They were faxed there directly by New York."

"Old codes, my friend," Cadoux said. "In the past, top people at Interpol had private codes that gave them access to information no one else could get. That practice is no longer in effect. Still, there are those that remember them and can use them, and there is no way to trace it. The New York police may have faxed the material to Washington but it came straight to Lyon, somehow electronically bypassing Washington."

"Cadoux—" Noble hesitated. "I know McVey is against it, but I think we're running out of time. Have Klass quietly taken into custody and interrogate him. If you want, I'll come myself."

"I understand, my friend. And I agree. You will let me know the moment you get word on McVey. For better or worse, eh?"

"Yes, of course. For better or worse."

Hanging up, Noble thought a moment, then swiveled to a pipe tree behind his desk. Selecting a worn and yellowed Calabash, he filled it, then tamped the tobacco and lit it.

If McVey and Osborn had not been on the Paris-Meaux train and had simply missed connecting with his pilot at the Meaux airstrip, then they would be there when he touched down tomorrow. But twenty-four hours was too long to wait. He had told Cadoux he'd had to assume they had been on the train. And that was what he would go with now. If they were dead, that was one thing, but if they were alive, they had to be gotten out of there now, before the other side discovered the same thing.

A little after ten forty-five, almost four hours after the derailment, a tall, slim, very attractive reporter with press credentials from the newspaper *Le Mond* parked her car along the single-lane road with the other media vehicles, and joined the swarm of journalists already on the scene.

French Garde Nationale troops had joined Meaux police and firefighters in the rescue effort that, so far, counted thirteen dead, including the train's driver. Thirty-six more were hospitalized, twenty in serious condition, and fifteen more had been treated for minor abrasions and released. The rest were still buried in the wreckage, and grim estimates ranged from hours to days before the accounting would be complete.

"Is there a list of names and nationalities?" she said, entering a large media tent set up fifty feet back from the tracks. Pierre André, a graying medical adjutant in charge of victim identification for the Garde Nationale, glanced up from a worktable to the *Le Mond* press pass around her neck, then looked at her and smiled, perhaps his only smile of the day. Avril Rocard was indeed a handsome piece.

"Oui, madame—" Immediately he turned to a subordinate. "Lieutenant, a casualty accounting for madame, *s'il vous plaît.*"

Selecting a sheet from inside one of several manila folders in front of him, the officer stood smartly and handed it to her.

"Merci," she said.

"I must warn you, madame, that it is far from complete. Nor is it for publication until the next of kin have been informed," Pierre André said, this time without the smile.

"Of course."

Avril Rocard was a Parisian detective, assigned to the French government as a counterfeit specialist. But her presence here, playing a correspondent for *Le Mond,* was not at the request of the French government or of the Paris Préfecture of Police. She was here because of Cadoux. For a decade they had been lovers, and she was the one person in France he could trust as he could trust himself.

Walking off, she looked at the list. Most of the identified passengers had been French nationals. There were, however, two Germans, a Swiss, a South African, two Irish and an Australian. No Americans.

Leaving the scene, she went to her car, unlocked the

door and got in. Picking up the cellular phone, she dialed a number in Paris and waited while it rang through to Lyon.

"Oui?" Cadoux's voice was clear.

"So far nothing. No Americans at all on the list."

"What's it look like?"

"It looks like hell. What should I do?"

"Has anyone questioned your credentials?"

"No."

"Then stay there until all the victims have been accounted for—"

Avril Rocard clicked off the phone and slowly set the receiver back in its cradle. She was thirty-three years old. By now she should have had a home and a baby. She should have at least had a husband. What the hell was she doing this for?

77

IT WAS eight in the morning and Benny Grossman had just come home from work. He'd met Matt and David, his teenage sons, just as they were leaving for school. A quick "Hi, Dad, 'bye, Dad" and they were gone. And now his wife, Estelle, was leaving for her stylist's job at a Queens hair salon.

"Holy shit," she heard Benny say from the bedroom. He was in his jockey shorts, a beer in one hand and a sandwich in the other, standing in front of the television. He'd been in the precinct Records & Information Division all night working the phones and computers and enlisting the aid of some very experienced computer hackers to get into private databases, trying to fill McVey's request on the people killed in 1966.

"What's the matter?" Estelle said, coming into the room. "What's the holy shit about?"

"Shhh!" he said.

Estelle turned to see what he was looking at. CNN coverage of a train derailment outside Paris.

"That's terrible," she said, watching as firemen struggled to carry a blood-covered woman up an embankment on a stretcher. "But what's it got you in such an uproar about?"

"McVey's in Paris," he said, his eyes on the set.

"McVey's in Paris," Estelle said flatly. "So are a million other people. I wish *we* were in Paris."

Abruptly he turned to her. "Estelle, go to work, huh?"

"You know somethin' I don't?"

"Honey, Estelle. Go to work. Please—"

Estelle Grossman stared at her husband. When he talked like that, it was cop talk that told her it was none of her business.

"Get some sleep."

"Yeah."

Estelle watched him for a minute, shook her head, then left. Sometimes she thought her husband cared for his friends and family too much. If they asked, he'd do anything, no matter how much it knocked him out. But when he got tired, as he was now, his imagination worked as much overtime as he did.

"Commander Noble, this is Benny Grossman, NYPD."

Benny was still in his underwear, his notes spread out over the kitchen table. He'd called Noble because McVey had told him to, if he hadn't called. And he had a real, almost psychic, sense that McVey wasn't going to be calling, not today anyway.

In ten minutes he'd laid out what he'd uncovered:

—Alexander Thompson was an advanced computer programmer who had retired to Sheridan, Wyoming, from New York in 1962 for health reasons. While there, he was approached by a writer doing research for a science-fiction movie on computers to be made by a Hollywood studio. The writer's name was Harry Simpson, the studio was American Pictures. Alexander Thompson was given twenty-five thousand dollars and asked to design a program that would instruct a computer to operate a machine that would hold and accurately guide a scalpel during surgery, in effect replacing the surgeon. It was all theory, science fiction, futurism, of course. It just had to be something that would actually work, even on a primitive level. In January 1966, Thompson delivered his program. Three days later he was found shot to death on a country road. Investigators found there was no Harry Simpson in Hollywood, nor was there a company called American Pictures. Nor was there any trace of Alexander Thompson's computer program.

—David Brady designed precision tools for a small firm in Glendale, California. In 1964, controlling interest in the firm was bought by Alama Steel, Ltd. of Pittsburgh, Pennsylvania. Brady was put to work to design a mechanical arm that could be electronically driven, that would have the same range of motion as a human wrist and be capable of holding and controlling a scalpel with extreme precision during surgery. He had completed his working drawings and turned them in for review just forty-eight hours before he was found in the family swimming pool. Drowning was ruled out. Brady had an ice pick in his heart. Two weeks later, Alama Steel went out of business and the company closed down. Brady's drawings were never found. As far as Benny had been able to ascertain, Alama Steel never existed. Paycheck stubs were traced back to a company called Wentworth Products Ltd. of Ontario, Canada. Wentworth Products went out of business the same week Alama Steel did.

—Mary Rizzo York, Ph.D., was a physicist working for Standard Technologies, of Perth Amboy, New Jersey, a firm specializing in low-temperature science and under contract to T.L.T. International, of Manhattan, a company involved in the shipping of frozen meat from Australia and New Zealand to Britain and France. At some time during the summer of 1965, T.L.T. moved to diversify, and Mary York was asked to develop a working program that would allow shipment of liquefied natural gas in refrigerated supertankers. The idea was that cold liquefies gas, and since natural gas could not be sent across oceans by pipeline, it could be liquefied and sent by ship. To do that, Mary York began experiments with extreme cold, working first with liquid nitrogen, a gas that liquefies at minus 196 degrees centigrade or, approximately, minus 385 degrees Fahrenheit. After that she experimented with liquid hydrogen and later with liquefying helium, the last gas to liquefy as the temperature is reduced and becomes liquid at minus 269 degrees centigrade or minus 516 degrees Fahrenheit. At that temperature, liquid helium could be used to reduce other materials to the same temperature. Mary York was six months pregnant and working late in her lab when she vanished on February 16, 1966. Her lab had then been set on fire. Four days later, her strangled body washed ashore under the Steel Pier in Atlantic City. And whatever notes, formulas or plans she'd been working on either burned in the fire or were taken by whoever had killed her. Two months later, T.L.T. International went bankrupt after the company president committed suicide.

"Commander, two more things McVey wanted to know," Benny said. "Microtab Company in Waltham, Massachusetts. It went belly up in May of the same year. The second thing he wanted to know was—"

* * *

Ian Noble had recorded Benny Grossman's entire conversation. When they were through, he'd had a transcript made for his private files and took the tape and tape player to Lebrun's heavily guarded room at Westminster Hospital.

Closing the door, he sat down next to the bed and turned on the recorder. For the next fifteen minutes Lebrun, oxygen tubes still in his nose, listened in silence. Finally they heard Benny Grossman's New York accent finish—

"The second thing he wanted to know was what we had on a guy named Erwin Scholl who, in 1966, owned a big estate in Westhampton Beach on Long Island.

"Erwin Scholl *still* owns his estate there. Also one in Palm Beach and one in Palm Springs. He keeps a low profile but he's a real heavy hitter in the publishing business and is a mucho-bucks major art collector. He also plays golf with Bob Hope, Gerry Ford and once in a while with the president himself. Tell McVey he's got the wrong guy, this Scholl. He's very big. Very. An untouchable. And *that,* by the way, came from McVey's pal, Fred Hanley, with the FBI in L.A."

With that Noble shut down the machine. Benny had ended with a note of worry, bordering on deep concern for McVey, and Noble hadn't wanted Lebrun to hear it. As yet he hadn't been told of the train incident. He'd taken the news of his brother's death badly; there was no need for more.

"Ian," Lebrun whispered. "I know about the train. I might have been shot but I am not yet dead. I spoke with Cadoux myself, not twenty minutes ago."

"Playing the tough cop, are you?" Noble smiled. "Well, here's something you don't know. McVey shot the gunman who killed Merriman and tried to kill Osborn and the girl, Vera Monneray. He sent me the dead man's thumbprint. We ran it and came up blank. He was clean, no record. No I.D.

"For obvious reasons I couldn't use the services of Interpol for more extensive help. So I called on Military Intelligence, who kindly provided me with the following—" Noble took out a small notebook and flipped through the pages until he had what he wanted.

"Our shooter's name was Bernhard Oven. Address unknown. They did, however, manage to find an old telephone number: 0372-885-7373. Appropriately, it's the number of a butcher shop."

"Zero three seven two was the area code for East Berlin before unification," Lebrun said.

"Correct. And our friend, Bernhard Oven, was, up until it disbanded, a ranking member of the Stasi."

Lebrun put a hand to the tubes running in and out of his throat and whispered, hoarsely, "What in God's name are the East German secret police doing in France? Especially when they no longer exist."

"I hope and pray McVey will soon be around to tell us," Noble said soberly.

78

BY NIGHT, the mangled wreckage of the Paris-Meaux train was even more obscene than by day. Huge worklights illuminated the area as two giant cranes operating from flat cars on the tracks above struggled to remove the twisted, compressed cars from the side of the embankment.

Late in the afternoon a light mist had begun to fall, and

the damp chill woke Osborn from where he slept in the nearby growth of trees. Sitting up, he'd taken his pulse and found it normal. His muscles ached and his right shoulder was badly bruised but otherwise he was in surprisingly good condition. Getting to his feet, he moved through the trees to the edge of the thicket where he could watch the rescue operation and still remain hidden. There was no way to know if McVey had been found, dead or alive, and he dared not go out to inquire for risk of being discovered himself. All he could do was stay concealed and watch, hoping to see or overhear something. It was a terrible, helpless, feeling, but there was nothing else for him to do.

Hunkering down in the sodden leaves, he pulled his jacket around him and for the first time in a long time let his thoughts go to Vera. He let his mind drift back to when they first met in Geneva. And to her smile and the color of her hair and the absolute magic in her eyes when she looked at him. And in that she became everything that love was, or could be.

By nightfall Osborn had heard enough from passing rescue workers and national guardsmen to understand that it had indeed been a bomb that destroyed the train, and he became more certain than ever that he and McVey had been the targets. He was debating whether or not to go to the National Guard commander and reveal himself in hopes of finding McVey when a fireman working nearby for some reason removed his hat and coat, put them on a temporary police barricade and walked off. It was an invitation he couldn't let pass. Quickly he stepped out and snatched them up.

Putting the jacket on, he pulled the hat low and moved off through the wreckage, confident he looked official enough to keep from being challenged. Near a tent set up as a media command post, he waded past several reporters and a television crew and found a casualty list. Quickly scanning it, he found only one identified American, a teenage boy from Nebraska. That McVey wasn't on it meant he'd either walked away, as Osborn had, or was still buried under the hideous sculpture of tangled steel. Looking up, he saw a tall, slim, attractive woman with a press pass around her neck. She obviously had been staring and now she started toward him. Picking up a fire ax, he slung it over his shoulder and walked back into the work area. He looked back once to see if she was following him, but she wasn't. Setting the ax aside, he moved off into the darkness.

In the distance, he could see the lights of the town of Meaux. Population some forty-odd thousand, he remembered seeing written somewhere. Now and then a plane would take off or land from the small airport nearby. Which was where he would go at first light. He had no idea who McVey had called in London. And with no passport and little money, the best he could do was make his way to the airfield and hope the Cessna would return according to the original plan.

Abruptly, there was a loud shriek and tearing of steel as one of the cranes pulled a passenger car free of the wreckage, lifted it high in the air and swing it back over the top of the embankment and out of sight. A moment later a second crane swung into place, and workers climbed up to secure cables to the next car to be removed. Disheartened, Osborn turned away and went back to the dark of the trees at the top of the hill. Squatting down, he looked off.

How long had he known McVey? Five days, six at most since he first encountered him outside his hotel room in Paris. The memories flooded back. He'd been scared to death, with no idea what the detective was after or why he was even talking to him, but he'd been determined not to show it. Calmly fended off his questions, even lied about the mud on his shoes, all the while praying McVey wouldn't ask him to empty his pockets and then ask him to explain about the succinylcholine and the syringes. How could either one of them have known how quickly the web would spin, sending them both spiraling headlong into a complex, bloody weave of conspiracy and gunfire that had so abruptly ended here in this awful maze of twisted steel and horror. He wanted to believe that the night would pass without incident and that tomorrow morning he would find McVey on the Meaux airport tarmac waving him toward the waiting Cessna that would fly them to safety. But that was a wish, a dream, and he knew it. As time passed, a truer reality set in: in situations of mass destruction, the longer a person went unfound, the less the chances he would be discovered alive. McVey was out there, all right, maybe even within an arm's length of where he stood now, and eventually he would be found. All he could hope was that the end had come quickly and mercifully.

And with that hope came a sense of finality, as if McVey had already been found and pronounced dead. Someone he'd only just begun to know and would have wished to know better. The same way a boy, as he grows, might come to know his father. Suddenly Osborn realized there were tears in his eyes, and he wondered why that thought had come to him now. McVey as his father. It was a whimsical, curious thought that just hung there. And the longer it did, the more a feeling of enormous loss began to overtake him.

It was then, while he was trying to break the spell, he realized he'd been staring off for some time, looking down the hill, away from the rescue activity, his attention focused on something in a cluster of trees near the bottom of the embankment. In daylight, because of the thick foliage and the flat light of an overcast sky, it would have been easily missed. It was only now, in darkness, that the spill from the worklights above created the angular shadow that defined it.

Quickly, Osborn started down the steep of the hill. Slipping and sliding on the gravel, grabbing onto small trees for support, moving from one to the other, he worked his way toward it.

Reaching bottom, he saw the thing was a piece of railroad car, a section of passenger coach that had somehow been ripped intact from the train. It was sitting backward in the brush, the inner part facing out and directly up the hill. Moving closer, he saw it was a complete compartment and the door to it was jammed closed, creased by a massive dent. Then he saw what it was. The car's lavatory.

"Oh no!" he said out loud. But instead of horror in his voice, there was hilarity.

"Not possible." Moving closer, he started to laugh. "McVey?" he called as he reached it. "McVey, you in there?"

For a moment there was no reply. Then—

"—Osborn?" came the muffled, uncertain reply from within.

Fear. Relief. Absurdity. Whatever it was, the pin had been stuck in the balloon and Osborn burst into laughter. Roaring, he leaned against the compartment, banging on it with the flat of his hands, then pounding his thighs with his fists, wiping the tears from his cheeks.

"Osborn! What the hell are you doing? Open the damn door!"

"You all right?" Osborn yelled back.

"Just get me the hell out of here!"

As quickly as the laughter came, it vanished. Still in his fireman's jacket, Osborn rushed back up the hill. Moving purposefully past French troops patrolling with submachine guns, he went to the main salvage area. Under the glare of worklights, he found a short-handled iron crowbar. Slipping it under his jacket, he walked back the way he had come. At the top of the hill, he stopped and looked around. Certain no one was watching, he stepped over the side and went back down.

Five minutes later there was a loud snap and a creak of steel as the staved-in door popped off its hinges and McVey stepped out into fresh air. His hair and clothes were disheveled, he smelled like hell and had an ugly welt over one eye the size of a baseball. But, other than a silvery five o'clock shadow, he was amazingly sound.

Osborn grinned. "You wouldn't be that guy Livingston?"

McVey started to say something, then, through the darkness, he saw the giant salvage cranes working what was left of the destruction backlit farther up the hill. He didn't move, just stared.

"Jesus Christ—" he said.

Finally his eyes found Osborn. Who they were, why they were here, meant nothing. They were alive while others were not. Reaching out, they embraced strongly, and for the longest moment clung there. It was more than a spontaneous gesture of relief and camaraderie. It was a spiritual sharing of something only those who have stood in death's shadow, and been spared, could understand.

79

VON HOLDEN sat alone near the back of the Art Deco bar in the Hôtel Meaux sipping a Pernod and soda, listening to stories of the rail disaster from the noisy crowd of media types who'd spent the day covering it. The bar had become an end-of-the-day hangout for veteran reporters, and most were still connected via beeper or walkie-talkie to colleagues who'd remained on the scene. If anything new happened, they—and Von Holden—would know it in a millisecond.

Von Holden looked at his watch and then at the clock over the bar. His LeCoultre analog watch had kept precision time with a cesium atomic clock in Berlin for five years. A cesium atomic clock has an accuracy rate of plus or minus one second every three thousand years. Von Holden's watch read 9:17. The clock over the bar was one minute and eight seconds slow. Across the room, a girl with short blond hair and an even shorter skirt sat smoking and drinking wine with two men who appeared to be in their mid-twenties. One was thin and wore heavy rimmed glasses and looked like a graduate student. The other had a sturdier build and wore expensive slacks and a maroon cashmere sweater, accented by a mop of long curly hair. The way he tilted back on the legs of his chair, talking and gesturing with both hands, stopping now to light a fresh cigarette and toss the match in the direction of the ashtray on the table, gave him the casually spoiled look of a wealthy playboy on holiday. The girl's name was Odette. She was twenty-two and the explosives expert who had set the charges along the track. The thin man in the glasses and the playboy were international terrorists. All three worked out of the Paris sector and were there awaiting Von Holden's direction should either Osborn or McVey be discovered alive.

Von Holden felt they were lucky to be there at all. It had taken the Paris sector several hours to locate McVey and Osborn. But shortly after 6:00 A.M., a EuroCity ticket seller had spotted them at the Gare de l'Est and Von Holden had been alerted that they had tickets for the 6:30 train to Meaux. He had briefly debated trying to kill them in the station, then decided against it. There was too little time to mount a proper attack. And even if there had been, there was no guarantee of success and they would risk an onrush of antiterrorist police. It was better to do it differently.

At 6:20, ten minutes before the Paris-Meaux train left the Gare de l'Est, a lone motorcyclist rode out of Paris on Autoroute N3 to a rendezvous with Odette at a railroad grading two miles east of Meaux. He carried with him four packets of C4 plastic explosive.

Working together, they laid the explosive and set the charge just as the train reached the grading, then immediately disappeared into the countryside. Three minutes later, the full weight of the engine compressed the detonators, sending the entire train careening down the embankment at seventy miles an hour.

It might have been argued that they could have as easily moved one of the rails out of alignment, had the same effect, yet made the whole thing look like an accident.

Yes and no.

A train wreck, accidental or deliberate, did not ensure the death of those targeted. A moved rail could easily be overlooked in a preliminary investigation and a follow-up might or might not uncover it. A flagrant act of terrorism, however, could be laid to a hundred different causes. And a bomb, later thrown into a hospital ward packed with survivors, would only serve to validate the act.

Glancing at his watch once again, Von Holden got up

and left the room without so much as a glance at the threesome, then took the elevator to his room. Before leaving Paris, he'd secured enhanced photographs of the front-page newspaper photos of Osborn and McVey. By the time he reached Meaux, he'd studied them carefully and had a much stronger sense of whom he was dealing with.

Paul Osborn, he decided, was relatively harmless if it ever came to the point of dealing with him. They were about the same age and from his thin features, Osborn seemed to be in reasonable shape. But that ended the similarity. There was a look to a man who'd been trained in combat or even self-defense. Osborn had none of it. If anything, he looked "displaced."

McVey was different. That he was aging and maybe a little overweight meant nothing. Von Holden saw instantly what it was that had enabled him to kill Bernhard Oven. There was a sense about him ordinary men didn't have. What he had seen and done in his long career as a policeman was in his eyes, and Von Holden knew instinctively that once he got hold of you, figuratively or physically, he would never let you go. Spetsnaz training had taught him there was only one way to deal with a man like McVey. And that was to kill him the moment you saw him. If you didn't, you would regret it forever.

Entering his room, Von Holden locked the door behind him and sat down at a small table. Opening a briefcase, he took out a compact shortwave radio. Clicking it on, he punched in a code and waited. It would take eight seconds before he had a clear channel.

"Lugo," he signed on, identifying himself.

"Ecstasy," he said. Code name for the operation that had begun with Albert Merriman and was now focused on McVey and Osborn.

"E.B.D."—European Bloc Division—he followed.

Nichts."—Nothing.

Von Holden punched in his sign-off code and clicked off. He'd just informed the Organization's European Bloc Division that there was no confirmation on liquidation of the Ecstasy fugitives. Officially they were still "at large," and all operatives within the E.B.D. were to be alerted.

Putting the radio away, Von Holden shut out the light and looked out the window. He was tired and frustrated. By this time at least one of them should have been found. They had been seen boarding the train and it had made no stops. Either they were still under the wreckage or they had vanished like magicians.

Von Holden sat down on the bed and turned on the lamp, then picked up the phone and placed a call to Joanna in Zurich. He hadn't seen her since the night she'd run hysterical and naked from his apartment.

"Joanna, it's Pascal. Are you better?" For a moment there was silence. "Joanna?"

"—I haven't been feeling well," she said.

He could hear distance and anxiety in her voice. Something had happened to her that night, of course. But she would have no real memory of it because the drugs he'd given her beforehand had been too complex. Her reaction afterward had been akin to a bad LSD trip and that was what she was remembering.

"I was very concerned. I wanted to call sooner but it wasn't possible. . . . Frankly, you were acting a little crazy that night. Maybe too much cognac and jet lag don't mix. Maybe too much passion, too, do you think?" He laughed.

"No, Pascal. It wasn't that." She was angry. "I've had to work very hard with Mr. Lybarger. All of a sudden he has to be able to walk without a cane by this Friday. I don't know why, either. I don't know what happened the other night. I don't like working Mr. Lybarger so hard. It's not good for him. I don't like the way Doctor Salettl treats me or the way he bosses people around."

"Joanna, let me explain something. Please. I think Doctor Salettl is acting the way he is because he is nervous. This Friday, Mr. Lybarger has to make a speech to the major shareholders of his corporation. The wealth and direction of the entire company depends on whether or not they feel he is competent to resume his position as chairman once more. Salettl is on the spot because the supervision of Mr. Lybarger's recovery has been his responsibility. Do you understand?"

"Yes—No. I'm sorry, I didn't know. . . . But it's still no reason to—"

"Joanna, Mr. Lybarger's speech is to be given in Berlin. Friday morning, you and I, and Mr. Lybarger and Eric and Edward, will fly there on Mr. Lybarger's corporate jet."

"Berlin?" Joanna hadn't heard the rest, only Berlin. Von Holden could tell by her response that the idea upset her. He could feel that she had had enough and wanted to get back to her beloved New Mexico as quickly as possible.

"Joanna, I understand you must be tired. Maybe I have rushed you too much personally. I care for you, you know that. I'm afraid it is my nature to follow my feelings. Please, Joanna, bear up just a little longer. Friday will be here before you know it, and Saturday you can fly home, directly from Berlin if you like."

"Home? To Taos?" He could hear the rush of excitement.

"Does that make you happy?"

"Yes, it does." Designer clothes and castles aside, she was, she'd decided finally, just a plain country girl who liked the simplicity of her life in Taos. And that's where she wanted to go, more than anything.

"I can count on you then, seeing this through?" Von Holden's voice was warm and soothing.

"Yes, Pascal. You can count on me being there."

"Thank you, Joanna. I'm sorry for any discomfort, it wasn't meant that way. If you wish, I will look forward to one last night together in Berlin. Alone, perhaps to dance and say goodbye. Goodnight, Joanna."

"Goodnight, Pascal."

Von Holden could see her smile as she hung up. What he'd said had been enough.

80

CHIMES WOKE Benny Grossman from a sound sleep. It was 3:15 in the afternoon. Why the hell was the doorbell ringing? Estelle was still at work. Matt would be at Hebrew school, and David would be at football practice. He was in no mood for solicitations; let whoever it was knock on somebody else's door. He was starting to doze off when the chimes rang again.

"Christ," he said. Getting up, he looked out the window. No one was in the yard and the front door was out of sight directly beneath him.

"All right!" he said as the chimes sounded again. Pulling on a pair of sweatpants, he went down the stairs to the front door and looked out through the peephole. Two Hasidic rabbis stood there, one young and smooth shaven, the other old, with a long graying beard.

"Oh, my God," he thought. "What the hell's happened?"

Heart pounding, he yanked the door.

"Yes?" he said.

"Detective Grossman?" the older rabbi asked.

"Yeah. That's me." For all his years as a cop, for everything he'd seen, when it came to his own family, Benny was as fragile as a child. "What's wrong? What happened? Is it Estelle? Matt? Not David—"

"I'm afraid it's you, Detective," the older rabbi said.

Benny didn't have time to react. The younger rabbi lifted his hand and shot him between the eyes. Benny fell back inside like a stone. The young rabbi went in after him and shot him again, just to make sure.

At the same time, the older rabbi went through the house. Upstairs, on Benny's dresser, he found the notes Benny had used when he phoned Scotland Yard. Folding them carefully, the rabbi put them in his pocket and went back downstairs.

Next door, Mrs. Greenfield thought it odd to see two rabbis coming out of the Grossman house, closing the door behind them, especially in the middle of the afternoon.

"Is anything wrong?" she asked as they opened Benny's front gate and started past her down the sidewalk.

"Not at all. Shalom," the younger rabbi said pleasantly as they passed.

"Shalom," Mrs. Greenfield said, and watched as the younger rabbi opened a car door for the older man. Then, smiling at her once more, he got behind the wheel and, a moment later, drove off.

The six-seat Cessna dropped through a heavy cloud deck and settled down over the French farmland.

Pilot Clark Clarkson, a handsome, brown-haired former RAF bomber pilot with huge hands and a broad smile, held the small craft steady through the variable turbulence as they dropped even lower. Ian Noble was harnessed into the copilot's seat beside him, head pressed against the window looking toward the ground. Directly behind Clarkson, dressed in civilian clothes, was Major Geoffrey Avnel, a field surgeon and British Special Forces commando fluent in French. Neither British military intelligence nor Captain Cadoux's woman in the field, Avril Rocard, had been successful in obtaining any information on the fate of McVey or Paul Osborn. If they had been on the train, for all intents they had disappeared from it.

Noble was banking on the theory that one or both had been hurt and, fearing further attack from whoever had blown up the train, had crawled away from the wreckage. Both men knew the Cessna would come back for them today, which meant, if Noble was right, that they could be anywhere between the airfield and the wreckage site some two miles away. That possibility was the reason Major Avnel had come along.

Ahead of them was the town of Meaux, and to the right, its airfield. Clarkson radioed the tower and was given permission to land. Five minutes later, at 8:01 A.M., Cessna ST95 touched down.

Taxiing to a stop near the control tower, Noble and Major Avnel climbed out and went into the small building that served as a terminal.

In his mind Noble had no idea what he would face. The hazards of police work were drummed into every cop from his first day of duty. London was no different from Detroit or Tokyo, and the death of any cop killed in the line of duty was the death of any police officer in uniform because it could as easily have been him or her. It could happen to any one of them, on any day in any city on earth. If you were in one piece at the end of each day you were lucky. And that's how you took it, a day at a time. If you made it all the way through, you took your pension and retired and slipped into old age trying not to think of all the cops still out there, the ones who wouldn't be so fortunate. That was a policeman's life, what he or she did. Yet it was not McVey's. He was different, the kind of cop who would outlive everybody and still be on duty at ninety-five. That was a fact. It was how he was seen and what he believed himself, no matter how often he grumbled otherwise. The trouble was, Noble had a feeling. Tragedy was in the air. Maybe that was why he'd come along with Clarkson and brought Major Avnel, because he felt he owed it to McVey to be there.

There was a leadenness to his step as he approached the Immigration desk and flashed his Special Branch I.D. at the officer on duty. He felt it all the more as he and Avnel pushed grim-faced through the glass doors and into the terminal area itself.

Which was why the last thing he ever expected to see was McVey seated across from him, wearing a Mickey Mouse baseball cap and EuroDisney sweatshirt, reading the morning paper.

"Good God!" he exclaimed.

"Morning, Ian." McVey smiled. Standing up, he folded the paper under his arm and put out his hand.

Twenty feet away, Osborn, hair slicked back, still wearing the French firefighter's jacket, looked up from a copy of *Le Figaro* and watched Noble take McVey's hand, then saw Noble shake his head, step back and introduce a third man. As he did, McVey glanced in Osborn's direction and nodded. Then almost immediately, Noble, McVey and Major Avnel started back toward the door leading out to the tarmac.

Osborn joined them and they walked twenty yards to the Cessna. Clarkson fired up the engine and requested permission for takeoff. At 8:27, without incident, they were airborne.

81

As The Cessna climbed into the cloud cover over Meaux and disappeared from ground view, McVey explained how they'd escaped the train wreck, spent the night in the woods near the airstrip, then come into the terminal just before seven-thirty. Acting the tourist, he'd bought the hat and sweatshirt and a packet of toiletries, then gone into the men's room where Osborn waited, and changed in a stall. McVey shaved and got rid of his suit coat for the EuroDisney sweatshirt. Osborn had changed his appearance simply by slicking back his hair. With his stubble beard and fireman's coat he looked like an exhausted rescue worker come to meet someone arriving by plane. All they'd had to do then was wait.

Noble shook his head and smiled. "McVey, you are an amazing fellow. Amazing."

"Uh uh." McVey shook his head. "Just lucky."

"Same thing."

Noble gave McVey a few minutes to relax, then brought out a copy of the taped conversation with Benny Grossman. By the time they touched down two hours later, McVey had read it twice, digested it, and thrown it out for scrutiny and comment.

The facts they had were as follows:

Paul Osborn's father had designed and built a prototype scalpel capable of remaining razor-sharp even at the most exotic and improbable temperatures, most likely extreme cold. Category: HARDWARE.

The following, according to Benny Grossman were facts: Alexander Thompson, of Sheridan, Wyoming, designs a computer program that allows a computer to guide a machine built to hold and guide a scalpel during advanced microsurgery. Category: SOFTWARE.

David Brady, of Glendale, California, designs and builds an electronically driven mechanism with the range motion of a human wrist, capable of holding and controlling a scalpel during surgery. Category: HARDWARE.

Mary Rizzo York, of New Jersey, experiments with gasses that can bring temperatures down and cool surroundings to at least minus 516 degrees Fahrenheit. Category: RESEARCH & DEVELOPMENT.

All this happened during the period 1962 through 1966. Each scientist worked alone. As each project was completed, its inventor or scientist was terminated by Albert Merriman. By Merriman's admission to Paul Osborn, the person who hired him and paid him for his work was Erwin Scholl. Erwin Scholl, the immigrant capitalist who by then had acquired the means and the business acumen to fund, through dummy corporations, the experimental projects. This was the same Erwin Scholl, who, according to the FBI, is now, and has been for decades, an esteemed personal friend and confidant of a series of United States presidents, and is, therefore, all but untouchable.

Yet what did they have in the freezer in the basement of the London morgue but seven headless bodies and one bodyless head. Five of which were confirmed to have been frozen to a degree approaching absolute zero, a figure close enough to Marry Rizzo York's work to be of considerable significance.

Earlier McVey had asked eminent micropathologist Dr. Stephen Richman, "Assuming the state of absolute zero could somehow, someway, be reached, why freeze decapitated bodies and decapitated heads to that temperature?"

Richman's clear-cut answer: "To join them."

Had Erwin Scholl, nearly thirty years earlier, been bankrolling research into cryosurgery with the idea of joining deep-frozen heads to other, deep-frozen, bodies? If he had, what was so secret that he'd ordered his researchers killed?

Patents?

Possibly.

But as far as anyone knew—according to the investigation by the Metropolitan Police Special Branch throughout Great Britain and Noble's recently concluded telephone conversations with Dr. Edward L. Smith, president of the Cryonics Society of America, and Akito Sato, president of Cryonics Institute, Far East—no similar cryonic surgical experimentations were being done anywhere in the world.

Now, as twilight settled over London, Noble, McVey and Osborn faced each other in Noble's Scotland Yard office. McVey had discarded the Mickey Mouse ball cap but still wore the EuroDisney sweatshirt, and Osborn had traded Noble his French fireman's coat for a well-worn dark blue cardigan with a gold Metropolitan Police emblem stitched over the lefthand pocket.

A patent search by RDI International of London had turned up no known patents worldwide on hardware or software designed for the kind of advanced microsurgery they were talking about.

A combination Moody's/Dun & Bradstreet review of the corporate histories of the companies employing Albert Merriman's victims had been requested through the Serious Fraud Office but had not yet been completed.

There was a light tap at the door and Noble's forty-three-year-old, six-foot-tall, never-married secretary, Elizabeth Welles, entered. She carried a tray with cups and spoons, a small pitcher of milk, a silver dish holding cubes of sugar and a pot each of tea and coffee.

"Thank you, Elizabeth," Noble said.

"Of course, Commander." Drawing herself up to her full height, she glanced sidelong at Osborn and left.

"She thinks you're quite the handsome chap, Dr. Osborn. Very highly sexed she is too. Tea or coffee?"

Osborn grinned. "Tea, please."

McVey was staring out the window, absently watching a small man walk two large dogs down the street, and only vaguely aware of the brief comedy that had taken place behind him.

"Coffee, McVey?" he heard Noble ask.

Abruptly he turned and came back across the room. His eyes were sharp and there was temper in his walk.

"There've been times over the years where, at some point or other during an investigation, I've felt like a damned idiot because all of a sudden something hit me I should have seen from the start. But I'll tell you, Ian, this time we may have missed the boat altogether. You, me, Doctor Michaels, even Doctor Richman."

"What are you talking about?" Noble's hand held a lump of sugar just over the lip of his teacup.

"Life. Dammit." McVey glanced at Osborn to include him, then leaned on the desk in front of Noble. "Wouldn't you assume that if someone had been working all these years to perfect some way to marry a severed head to a body, the end goal of that would not just be the act itself but bringing the result back to life? To make this creature, this Frankenstein, live and breathe!"

"Yes, but why?" Noble let the sugar drop into his cup.

"No idea. But why else do it?" McVey turned back to Osborn. "Imagine the whole process medically. How would it go?"

"Simple. In theory, anyway." Osborn leaned against the back of a red leather chair. "Bring the frozen thing back to temperature. Back from nearly minus 560 degrees below zero to 98.6 degrees above zero. To do the operation, blood would have been drained off. As the thing thaws, blood is reintroduced. The difficult thing would be to get it to thaw uniformly."

"But it could be done?" Noble asked.

"I would say that if they'd been able to find a way to do the first, the second would have already been taken care of."

Immediately a sound emanated from the fax machine on the antique secretary behind Noble's desk. The light switched on, and a moment later it began printing out.

It was the Moody's/Dun & Bradstreet report requested from the Serious Fraud Office.

McVey and Osborn moved in behind Noble to watch as the information came in:

Microtab, Waltham, Massachusetts. Dissolved, July 1966. Owned by Wentworth Products, Ltd., Ontario, Canada. Board of directors: Earl Samules, Evan Hart, John Harris. All of Boston, Massachusetts. All deceased 1966.

Wentworth Products Ltd., Ontario, Canada. Dissolved, August 1966. Privately held company. Owned by James Tallmadge of Windsor, Ontario. Tallmadge deceased 1967.

Alama Steel, Ltd. of Pittsburgh, Pennsylvania. Dissolved, 1966. Subsidiary of Wentworth Products Ltd., Ontario, Canada. Board of directors: Earl Samules, Evan Hart, John Harris.

Standard Technologies, Perth Amboy, New Jersey. Subsidiary of T.L.T. International, 10 Park Avenue, New York, New York. Board of directors: Earl Samules, Evan Hart, John Harris.

T.L.T. International, wholly owned subsidiary of Omega Shipping Lines, 17 Hanover Square, Mayfair, London, U.K. Principal stockholder, Harald Erwin Scholl, 17 Hanover Square, Mayfair, London, U.K.

"There it is!" Noble said triumphantly at the printout of Scholl's name as the fax continued.

T.L.T. International dissolved 1967.

Omega Shipping Lines bought by Goltz Development Group, S.A., Düsseldorf, Germany, 1966. Goltz Development Group—GDG—partnership. General partners: Harald Erwin Scholl, 17 Hanover Square, London, U.K. Gustav Dortmund, Friedrichstadt, Düsseldorf, Germany. President—since 1978—Konrad Peiper, 52 Reichsstrasse, Charlottenburg, Berlin, Germany. (N.b. GDG acquired Lewsen International, Bayswater Road, London, U.K., a holding company, in 1981.)

END OF TRANSMISSION

Noble swiveled in his chair and looked up to McVey. "Well, our dear Mr. Scholl may not be quite as untouchable as your FBI seems to think. You know who Gustav Dortmund is—"

"Chief of Germany's central bank," McVey said.

"Right. And Lewsen International was a prominent supplier of steel, weapons parts and construction supervisors to Iraq during the eighties. I'll wager Messieurs Scholl, Dortmund and Peiper became very rich men in those years, if they weren't already."

"If I may." Osborn approached with a current issue of *People* magazine he'd picked from among several on Noble's sideboard. McVey watched perplexed as he set aside Noble's teacup and opened a double-page advertisement on the desk in front of him. It was a provocative ad for the latest recording of a young and very popular female rock singer. She was soaking wet and wore a skintight see-through dress and rode the back of a killer whale as it sprang dramatically out of the water.

Noble and McVey looked to Osborn blankly.

"Don't know, do you?" Osborn smiled.

"Know what?" McVey said.

"Your Konrad Peiper," Osborn said.

"What about him?" McVey had no idea what Osborn was getting at.

"His wife is Margareté Peiper, one of the most powerful women in show business. She runs a giant talent agency and manages and produces this young lady on the whale as well as probably a dozen more of the biggest young names in rock and video. And"—he paused—"she does it all from the penthouse office of her restored seventeenth-century mansion in Berlin."

"How in heaven do you know that?" Noble was astonished.

Osborn pulled the magazine back, folded it and tossed it back on Noble's sideboard. "Commander, I'm an orthopedic surgeon in Los Angeles. Probably half of my patients are kids under twenty who've been injured in athletics. I don't have all those trendy magazines in my waiting room for nothing."

"You *actually* read them?"

Osborn grinned. "You bet."

82

BECAUSE OF decreasing visibility, Clarkson had altered his flight plan and landed near Ramsgate on the English Channel, nearly a hundred miles southeast of his original destination. His chance maneuver had thrown Von Holden off.

An hour after the Cessna ST95 had flown out of Meaux, an airport custodian had found McVey's discarded suit coat at the bottom of the trash bin in the airport men's room. Within minutes the Paris sector had been alerted, and twenty minutes after that Von Holden had arrived to claim his uncle's misplaced jacket from lost and found. Smartly, McVey had torn the label out before getting rid of the coat. What he hadn't realized was the constant chafing over the butt of his .38 had worn the lining just enough to be noticeable, and Von Holden knew from experience that the only thing that chafed a jacket there was the handle of a gun.

Von Holden retreated to his hotel in Meaux while the Paris sector scanned flight plans of aircraft leaving Meaux between sunrise and the time the jacket had been found. By 9:30, he'd established a six-passenger Cessna with the marking ST95 had flown in from Bishop's Stortford, England that morning, landing at 8:01, and taken off for the same destination twenty-six minutes later, at 8:27. It wasn't a guarantee, but it was enough to alert the London sector. By three o'clock, operatives had located Cessna ST95 at Ramsgate field, and the London sector home office had traced its ownership to a small British agricultural company with headquarters in the western city of Bath. From there the trail had turned cold. The Cessna had been parked at Ramsgate field with the pilot leaving word he would return for the plane when the weather had cleared. After that he'd left, taking a bus for London in the company of another man. Neither had matched the descriptions of McVey and Osborn. That information was immediately forwarded to the Paris sector for transmission to "Lugo," who had returned to Berlin. By 6:15 that evening, London sector had copies of the enhanced newspaper photographs of both men and was on full alert to find them.

At 8:35, McVey sat alone in his undershirt on the edge of his bed in a refurbished eighteenth-century hotel in Knightsbridge. His shoes were off, and a glass of Famous Grouse scotch whisky rested on the telephone table, at his sleeve. Special Branch had checked him in as Howard Nichol of San Jose, California. Osborn, under the name Richard Green of Chicago, had been checked into the Forum Hotel not far away in Kensington, and Noble had gone home to his residence in Chelsea.

In his hand was a fax from Bill Woodward, chief of detectives at the LAPD, informing him of the murder of Benny Grossman. Initial and confidential NYPD investigations were centering on the probability the killing had been done by two men posing as Hasidic rabbis.

McVey tried to do what he knew Benny would do. Put his own feelings aside and think logically. Benny had been killed in his home approximately six hours after he'd called Ian Noble with the information McVey had requested. Never mind the other stuff. That Benny had spent his last entire night alive collecting the material because McVey had told him it was urgent. Or that he'd called Noble with it because he'd seen the satellite TV coverage of the Paris-Meaux train disaster and had a psychic jolt that McVey had been on the train, and that Noble would need whatever information he had as soon as he could get it to him.

The hard fact was that he'd called Noble from his home with his detailed list. What that meant was that not only did the group have operatives working in the States with very sophisticated information-retrieval technology accessed into classified police department computer systems, they also knew what information had been gathered, by whom and from where. If they could do that, they could get into telephone company logs and by now would know where Benny had called, and most likely whom, because Benny would have used Noble's private number.

And if they were set up to operate in France and the United States, they would almost assuredly be set up to operate here in England.

Taking a large swallow of scotch, McVey set the glass down, pulled on a fresh shirt and tie and took his only other suit from the closet. A few minutes later he slid his .38 into the holster at his hip, took another belt of scotch and left. There'd been no need to look in the mirror; he knew what he'd see.

Pushing through the hotel's polished brass front door, he walked the half block to the Knightsbridge Underground station. In twenty minutes he was in Noble's tastefully appointed house in Chelsea, waiting as Noble called New Scotland Yard on his direct line, ordering a car for his wife. Fifteen minutes later, they said their goodbyes and she was on her way under guard to her sister's home in Cambridge.

"Nothing she hasn't experienced one way or another before," Noble said after she'd gone. "The I.R.A., you know. Nasty business all the way around."

McVey nodded. He was worried about Osborn. Metropolitan detectives checking him into his hotel had warned him to stay in his room. McVey had tried calling him before he'd left his hotel to meet Noble but there'd been no answer. Now he tried again and got the same result.

"Nothing still?" Noble said.

McVey shook his head and hung up. The minute he did, Noble's red phone rang. The direct line from Yard headquarters.

Noble picked up. "Yes. Yes, he's here." He looked at McVey. "A Dale Washburn of Palm Springs has been trying to reach you."

"She on the line?"

Noble asked for a confirm and instead got a phone number where Washburn could be reached. Taking it down, he hung up and gave the slip of paper to McVey.

Walking into the hallway, McVey picked up Noble's house phone and dialed Palm Springs. "Try Osborn again, huh?" he said to Noble. It was a little after eleven in the evening, London time. Just after three in the afternoon in Palm Springs.

"This is Dale," a soft voice said.

"Hello, angel, it's McVey. What do you have?"

"Right now?"

"Right now."

"You want me to say it, just like that? There's a couple of other people here."

"Then they must be friends of yours. Tell me what you have."

"Two pair, lover. Aces over eights, the dead man's hand. There, you happy I gave it away?"

"Poker—"

"You got it, baby, I'm playing poker. Or I was until you called. Let me go into the other room." McVey heard her say something to someone else. A minute later she picked up the extension, and the other phone was hung up.

Dale Washburn stepped out of Raymond Chandler. She was thirty-five, a genuine platinum blonde, with a terrific body and a brain to match. She'd been an LAPD undercover cop for five years before her cover was blown during a screwed-up midnight drug raid in upscale Brentwood. With a bullet inoperably lodged in her lower back, she took a disability pension to Palm Springs, played cards with a few rich divorcés, male and female, and hung out a quiet shingle as a very private investigator. McVey had called her as soon as he'd checked into his Knightsbridge hotel. He wanted everything she could dig up about Mr. Harald Erwin Scholl in two hours.

"Nothing."

"Come on—*nothing* . . ." McVey heard the anger in his own voice. He wasn't handling Benny Grossman's murder as well as he thought.

"Nothing, baby. I'm sorry. Erwin Scholl's who he's supposed to be. A richer-than-hell publisher, art collector, and chum-chum with the ultras, as in presidents and prime ministers. In capital letters, my love. If there's more, it's dug deep in the sandbox where only the really big kids play. And little girls and boys like you and me aren't going to find it."

"What about a history—" McVey said.

"Poor immigrant comes here from Germany just before World War Two, works his keester off and the rest is what I already told you."

"Married?"

"Never, babe. Not as far as I could find out in a coupla hours. And if you're thinking gay, honey, the queens he plays with are the kind with emeralds and sable and armies. Ladies who have coronations and used to rule empires and probably still sit on jeweled heads."

"Angel, you're not giving me much."

"One fact I can give you, and you can do with it what you want—your man is in Berlin until Sunday. Big commemoration or something at a place called—wait'll I look at my notes—they're here somewhere—Yeah, here we go—the place, a palace or something called Charlottenburg."

"Charlottenburg Palace?" McVey looked to Noble.

"A museum in Berlin."

"Go back to your game, angel. I'll take you to dinner when I get back."

McVey, for you, anytime."

McVey clicked off. Noble was staring at him.

"Angel?" Noble grinned.

"Yeah, angel—" McVey said flatly. "What about Osborn?"

Noble's smile faded and he shook his head. "Nothing."

83

"VERA—"

"Oh God, Paul!"

Osborn could hear the relief and excitement in her voice. Despite everything, Vera hadn't been out of his mind for more than a moment. Somehow he'd had to get hold of her, talk to her, hear her tell him she was all right.

He couldn't use the phone in his room and knew it. So he'd gone down to the lobby. McVey wouldn't like it if he found out, but as far as he was concerned he had no other choice.

Once he reached the lobby, he'd found the phones near the entrance in use. Taking a chance, he'd gone to the desk and asked if there were others. A clerk had directed him to a corridor just off the bar where he'd found a bank of old-style private phone booths.

Entering, he closed the door and took out a small address book where he'd written the number of Vera's grandmother in Calais. For some reason the old burnished wood and the closed door seemed reassuring. He heard someone in the booth next to him finish a call, then hang up and leave. Looking out through the glass, he saw a young couple pass, going toward the elevators. After that the hallway was empty. Turning back, he picked up the phone, dialed the number and charged the call to his office credit card.

He heard the phone start to ring through on the other end. It rang for some time and he was about to hang up when the old woman surprised him and answered. Finally, the best he could garner was that Vera was not there and hadn't been. He felt his emotions begin to run away and he knew he'd go crazy if he didn't get a grip on them.

Then it crossed his mind that she was still at the hospital, that she'd never left. Using his credit card, he dialed her direct line. The number rang through and he heard her voice.

"Vera—" he said, his heart leaping at the sound of it. But she kept on talking and in French and he realized it was her voice mail. Then he heard a click and a recorded voice tell him to dial "O." A moment later a woman answered. *"Parlez-vous anglais?"* he asked. Yes, the woman spoke a little English. Vera, she said, had been called away two days earlier on a family emergency; it was not known when she would return. Would he like to speak with another doctor? "No. No, thank you," he said, and hung up. For a long moment he stared at the wall. There was only one place left. Maybe, for some reason, she'd gone back to her apartment.

For the third time he used his credit card, this time wondering if he shouldn't go to another phone, one outside the building. Before he could hang up, the number rang through and on just the second ring a man answered.

"Monneray residence, *bonsoir.*"

It was Philippe picking up the call from the switchboard. Osborn was silent. Why was Philippe monitoring Vera's calls without giving them a chance to ring long enough for her to pick them up herself? Maybe McVey had been right and it had been Philippe who'd alerted this "group" to who Vera was and where she lived, then later helped him escape from under the noses of the police, but not until he'd notified the tall man.

"Monneray residence," Philippe said again. This time his voice was hollow, as if he were suddenly suspect of the call. Osborn waited a half beat, then decided to take the chance.

"Philippe, it's Doctor Osborn."

Philippe's reaction was anything but cautious. He was

excited, delighted to hear from him. He made it sound as if he'd been worrying himself to death about him.

"Oh, monsieur. The shooting at La Coupole. It was all over the television. Two Americans, they said. You are all right? Where are you?"

Uh uh, Osborn told himself. Don't tell him.

"Where is Vera, Philippe? Have you heard from her?"

"Oui, oui!" Vera had telephoned earlier in the day and left a number. It was to be given only to him if he called, and to no one else.

A noise outside the phone booth made Osborn look around. A small black woman in a hotel uniform was vacuuming the hallway. She was old, and her hair twisted up under a bright blue scarf made her look Haitian. The hum of the vacuum grew louder as she worked closer.

"The number, Philippe," he said, turning his back to the hallway.

Fumbling a pen from his pocket, Osborn looked for something to write on. There was nothing, so he wrote the number on the palm of his hand, then repeated it just to make sure.

"Merci, Philippe." Without giving the doorman a chance for another question, he hung up.

Against the sound of the old woman's vacuum, Osborn picked up the phone, again debated moving to another telephone, then said the hell with it, dialed the number written on his hand and waited for it to ring through.

"Oui?" He started as a man's voice came on, tough and forceful.

"Mademoiselle Monneray, please," Osborn said.

Then he heard Vera say something in French and add the name Jean Claude. The first line clicked off and he heard Vera say his name.

"Jesus, Vera—" he breathed. "What the hell is going on?—Where are you?" Of all the women he'd ever known, none affected him as Vera did. Mentally, emotionally, physically—and what had been built up inside him came gushing out pell-mell, like an adolescent, without thought or judgment.

"I call your grandmother's worried to death about you and her English is worse than my French and the best I can understand is she hasn't heard from you. I start thinking about the Paris inspectors. That they're mixed up in this and I sent you to them. . . . Vera, where the hell are you? Tell me you're okay—"

"I am okay, Paul, but—" She hesitated. "I can't tell you where I am." Vera glanced around the small, cheery, yellow-and-white bedroom with a single window that looked out on a long floodlit driveway. Beyond it were trees and then darkness. Opening the door she saw a stocky man in a black sweater with a pistol at his waist monitoring the call on a wireless recorder. An assault rifle leaned against the wall next to him. Looking up, he saw her staring at him, her hand covering the phone.

"Jean Claude, please . . . ," she said in French. He wavered for a moment, then turned off the machine.

"Who are you talking to? Those aren't the police. Who was the man that answered?" Osborn snapped suddenly. He could feel the jealousy surge through him like an ugly wave. Outside the phone booth, the solid hum of vacuum seemed louder than ever. Turning angrily, he saw the old woman staring in at him. When their eyes met, she abruptly lowered her head and moved off, the whir of the vacuum vanishing with her.

"Dammit, Vera!" Osborn turned back to the phone. He was angry and hurt and confused. "What the hell is going on?"

Vera said nothing.

"Why can't you tell me where you are?" he said again.

"Because—"

"Why?"

Osborn glanced out through the glass. The hallway was

empty now. Then, brutally and with a rush, he realized. "You're with him! You're with Frenchy, aren't you?"

She could hear the hard rasp of his anger and she hated him for it. Like that, he was telling her he didn't trust her. "No, I am not. And don't call him that!" she snapped.

"Dammit, Vera. Don't lie to me. Not now. If he's there, just tell me!"

"Paul! Stop it! Or I'll tell you to go to hell and that will be the end of our relationship."

Suddenly he realized he wasn't listening, not even thinking, but instead doing what he'd always done, since the day of his father's murder, reacting to his own numbing fear of losing love. Rage, anger and jealousy—that was how he fended off hurt, protected himself. Yet, at the same time, he was forcing away those who might have loved him and reducing any feelings left to little more than sadness and pity. Then, blaming them, he would slink away, as he always had, to the dark corner of his own exile, ravaged and raw, alienated from everything human on earth.

Like an addict suddenly aware, he realized that if he was ever going to stop his own destruction, it had to be now, at this moment. And difficult as it was, the only way to do it was to damn the outcome and find the courage to trust her.

Digging deep inside, he brought the receiver back.

"I'm sorry . . . ," he said.

Vera ran a hand through her hair and sat down at a small wooden desk. On it was a clay sculpture of a donkey that had obviously been crafted by a child. It was awkward and primitive but wholly pure. Picking it up, she looked at it, then held it comfortingly against her breast.

"I was afraid of the police, Paul. I didn't know what to do. In desperation I called François. Do you know how hard that was for me after I'd left him? He brought me here, to a place in the country, and then went back to

Paris. He left three Secret Service agents to protect me. No one is to know where I am, that's why I can't tell you. In case someone is listening. . . ."

Abruptly Osborn's veil lifted, jealousy was gone, replaced by the deep concern that had been there before. "Are you safe, Vera?"

"Yes."

"I think we should get off the line," he said. "Let me call you again tomorrow."

"Paul, are you in Paris?"

"No. Why—?"

"It would be dangerous if you were."

"The tall man is dead. McVey killed him."

"I know. What you don't know is that he was a member of the Stasi, the old East German secret police. They can say they're disbanded but I don't believe it's true."

"You found that out from François."

"Yes."

"Why would the Stasi have wanted to kill Albert Merriman?"

"Paul, listen to me, please." There was urgency in her voice. But she was also frightened and confused. "François is resigning. It will be made public in the morning. He's doing it because he's being pressured from inside his own party. It has to do with the new economic community, the new European politics."

"What do you mean?" Osborn didn't understand.

"François thinks they are all being subjugated by Germany and that Germany will end up controlling the purse strings of all of Europe. He doesn't like it and thinks France is becoming too involved for its own good."

"You're telling me he's being forced out."

"Yes—very reluctantly, but with no choice. It's become very ugly."

"Vera, is François afraid for his life if he doesn't resign?"

"He never spoke to me about it. . . ."

Osborn had hit a nerve. Maybe they hadn't discussed it, but she'd thought about it. And probably couldn't stop thinking about it. François Christian had sequestered her someplace in the country with three Secret Servicemen guarding her. Did that mean the fact that the tall man had been a Stasi agent somehow interconnected with what was going on in French politics? And that François was worried Vera might be in danger because of it, that they would do something to her as a warning to him? Or was she hidden away and protected because of her connection to Osborn and now McVey, and what had happened to Lebrun and his brother in Lyon?

"Vera—if they're listening, I don't give a damn," he said. "I want you to think carefully. From what François said, is there a connection between Albert Merriman and me and the situation with François?"

"I don't know. . . ." Vera looked at the tiny, sculpted donkey still in her hand, then gently set it back on the table. "I remember my grandmother telling me what it was like in France during the war. When the Nazis came and stayed," she said quietly. "Every moment was filled with fear. People were taken away with no explanation and they never came back. People were spying on each other, sometimes in the same families, and reporting what they saw to the authorities. And men with guns were everywhere. Paul—" She hesitated, and he could hear how afraid she really was. "I feel that same shadow now—"

Suddenly Osborn heard a noise behind him. He wheeled around. McVey was outside the phone booth. So was Noble. McVey jerked the door open.

"Hang up," he said. "Now!"

84

OSBORN WAS hustled through the bar and out an exit onto the street. He'd tried to sign off with Vera, but McVey had reached in and cut off the phone with his hand.

"The girl, wasn't it? Vera Monneray," McVey said, pulling open the door to an unmarked Rover at the curb.

"Yes," Osborn said. McVey had pushed into his private world and he didn't like it.

"She with the Paris police?"

"No. The Secret Service."

Doors slammed, and Noble's driver pulled into traffic. Five minutes later they were rounding Piccadilly Circus and turning on Haymarket for Trafalgar Square.

"Unlisted number?" McVey said flatly, staring at the numbers Osborn had scrawled on his hand.

"What are you getting at?" Osborn said defensively, tucking his hands up under his armpits.

McVey stared at him. "I hope you didn't kill her."

Noble turned from his seat next to the driver. "Did you inquire about the telephone you were using or did you find it yourself?"

Osborn turned from McVey. "What difference does it make?"

"Did you inquire about the telephone or did you find it yourself?"

"The phones in the lobby were being used. I asked if there were any others."

"And someone told you."

"Obviously."

"Anybody see you place the call? See what booth you went into?" McVey let Noble continue.

"No," Osborn said quickly, then suddenly remembered.

"A hotel employee, an old black woman. She was vacuuming the hallway."

"Not hard to trace a call from a public telephone," Noble said. "Especially if you know which phone it is. Listed or unlisted, fifty pounds in the right hands will get you the number, the town, the street address and most likely what's being served for dinner. All in the bat of an eyelash."

Osborn sat for a long time in silence and watched as nighttime London flashed by. He didn't like it, but Noble was right. He'd been foolish, stupid. But this wasn't his world. Where every thought had to have a forethought, and everyone was under suspicion no matter who they were.

Finally he looked to McVey. "Who's doing this? Who are they?"

McVey shook his head.

"Did you know the man you shot was a member of the Stasi," Osborn said.

"She tell you that?"

"Yes."

"She's right."

Osborn was incredulous. "You knew?"

McVey didn't reply. Neither did Noble.

"Let me tell you something you probably *don't* know. The French prime minister has resigned his office. It'll be announced in the morning. He was forced out by people in his own party because of his opposition to France's part in the new European community. He thinks the Germans have too much power, they disagree."

"Nothing new in that." Noble shrugged and turned to say something to the driver.

"It's new if he thinks they'd kill him if he didn't. Or kill Vera as a point to him and his family."

McVey and Noble exchanged glances.

"Is that what you think or what she said?" McVey asked.

Osborn glared at him. "She's scared, all right? For a lot of reasons."

"You didn't help her any. Next time when I tell you to do something, you do it!" McVey turned to look out the window. After that, silence fell over the car, and there was only the hum of the tires against the road. Occasionally lights from oncoming traffic illuminated the men inside, but for the most part they sat in darkness.

Osborn leaned back. In his life he thought he'd never been so tired. Every limb ached. His lungs, as they lifted and fell with each breath, felt as if they were lead. Sleep. He couldn't remember the last time he'd done that. Absently he ran his hand along the roughness of his jaw and supposed that somewhere along the way he'd forgotten to shave. Looking at McVey, he saw the same weariness in him. Deep circles hung under his eyes and gray-white stubble showed on his chin. His clothes, fresh as they were, looked as if he might have been sleeping in them for a week. And Noble, sitting in front, looked no better.

The Rover slowed and turned into a narrow side street and a block later swung into an underground garage. Suddenly it occurred to Osborn to ask where they were going.

"Berlin." McVey beat him to it.

"Berlin?"

Two uniformed policemen approached the car as it stopped and opened the doors.

"Right this way if you would, gentlemen." The uniforms led the way down a corridor and then out a door leading onto the tarmac. They were at the far corner of a commercial airport. In the distance a twin-engine plane sat waiting, its interior lights on, a portable stairway leading up to an open door in the fuselage.

"The reason you're coming along," McVey said as they walked toward it, "is to give a deposition before a German judge. I want you to tell him what Albert Merriman said to you just before he was shot."

"You're talking about Scholl."

McVey nodded.

Osborn could feel his pulse jump. "He's in Berlin."

"Yes."

Ahead of them, Noble went up the steps and into the plane.

"My deposition is to help get a warrant for his arrest."

"I want to talk to him." McVey started up the stairs.

Osborn was euphoric. It was why he'd gambled meeting with McVey in the first place. To take him the next step, to help him get to Scholl.

"I want to be there when you do."

"That's what I assumed." McVey disappeared inside the plane.

85

"YOU SEE, no sign of struggle and no evidence of foul play. The perimeter fences are monitored by video and have been checked by foot patrol with dogs. There is no evidence that security has been compromised." Georg Springer, the slim, balding, head of security for Anlegeplatz, crossed Elton Lybarger's huge bedroom glancing at his slept-in but now empty bed, listening to an armed security officer. It was 3:25, Thursday morning.

Springer had been wakened just after three and informed that Lybarger was missing from his room. Immediately he'd contacted central security, whose cameras monitored the main gate, the twenty miles of perimeter fencing and the only other ingresses, the guarded service entrance near the garage and a maintenance facility a half mile up a winding road to the rear. In the preceding four hours, no one had passed in or out.

Springer gave Lybarger's room one last glance, then started for the door. "He could have become ill and wandered off in search of help, or he could be in some state of sleep where he doesn't know where he is. How many personnel are on duty?"

"Seventeen."

"Get them all. Search the grounds carefully, including every room and bedroom. I don't care if people are sleeping or not. I'll waken Salettl."

Elton Lybarger sat in a straight-backed chair watching Joanna. In five minutes she hadn't moved. If it weren't for the minor heave of her breasts under her nightgown, he would have taken the chance and called for help for fear she was ill.

It had been less than an hour since he'd found the video. Unable to sleep, he'd gone into his library for something to read. Lately, sleep had not been easy. And the little he'd had had been fitful, filled with strange dreams where he wandered alone among an array of people and places he thought were familiar but had no real fix on. And the times through which he passed were as distinctly different as the people, varying from prewar Europe to incidents as recent as that morning.

In his library he'd thumbed through several magazines and newspapers. Still sleepless, he'd wandered out onto the grounds. A light was on in the bungalow kept by his nephews Eric and Edward. Going to the door, he'd knocked. When no one answered he let himself in.

The luxurious main room, dwarfed by a massive stone fireplace and filled with expensive furniture, state of the art audio and video equipment, and shelf upon shelf of athletic trophies, was empty. The doors to the rear bedrooms were closed.

Assuming his nephews were asleep, Lybarger was turning to go when he saw a large envelope lying on a shelf near the door, probably left there for a messenger. On it was written "Uncle Lybarger." Thinking it was for him, he opened it and found a video cassette inside. Curious, he'd taken it and gone back to his study where he put it into his video deck, turned on his TV and sat back to watch whatever it was the boys had been about to send him.

What he saw was a tape of himself kicking a soccer ball with Eric and Edward, a political talk he had given that had been carefully coached by his speech therapist, a drama professor at the University of Zurich. And then—shockingly—a sequence showing himself and Joanna in bed, with all kinds of numbers running on the screen, and Von Holden standing by, naked as the moment he was born.

Joanna was his friend and companion. She was like his sister, even his daughter. What he'd seen had horrified him. How could it be? How had this happened? He had no memory of it whatsoever. Something, he knew, was terribly wrong.

The question was: Did Joanna know about it? Was this some kind of sick game she was playing with Von Holden? Filled with shock and anger, he'd gone immediately to her room. Waking her from a deep sleep, he'd loudly and indignantly demanded she look at the tape immediately.

Confused and more than a little upset by his manner and his presence in her bedroom, she'd done as he asked. And now, as the tape unspooled, she was as unnerved as he. Her terrifying dream of a few nights earlier had been no nightmare at all, but instead a vivid remembrance of what had actually taken place.

When it was done, Joanna shut off the machine and turned to face Lybarger. He was pale and trembling, as drained as she.

"You didn't know, did you? You had no idea that had happened?" she said.

"Nor you—"

"No, Mr. Lybarger. I most certainly did not."

Suddenly there was a sharp rap at her door. It opened immediately and Frieda Vossler, a square-jawed, twenty-five-year-old member of Anlegeplatz's security force entered.

Salettl and security chief Springer came into Joanna's room several minutes later to find an indignant Lybarger hammering the video into the palm of his hand and screaming at guard Vossler, demanding to know the meaning of such an outrage.

Calmly Salettl had taken away the video and asked Lybarger to relax, warning him that what he was doing could bring on a second stroke. Leaving Joanna in the company of the security force, Salettl had seen Lybarger back to his room, taken his blood pressure and put him to bed, giving him a strong sedative laced with a mild psychedelic drug. Lybarger would sleep for some time and the sleep would be filled with surreal and fanciful dreams. Dreams, Salettl trusted, Lybarger would confuse with the incident of the video and his visit to Joanna's room.

Joanna, on the other hand, had been less cooperative, and when Salettl returned to her room, he considered firing her on the spot and sending her back to America on the first flight available. But he realized her absence might be even more disruptive. Lybarger was used to her, trusted her for his physical well-being. She had brought him this far, even to the point of getting him to walk confidently without aid of a cane, and there was no way to tell what he would do if she were no longer there. No, Salettl had decided, firing her was out of the question. It was vitally important she accompany Lybarger to Berlin and stay with him until he left to give his speech. Politely he had prevailed upon her, for Lybarger's sake, to return to bed. That an explanation of what she had seen would be given her in the morning.

Frightened, angry and emotionally drained, Joanna had had the presence of mind not to press it.

"Just tell me," she'd said. "Who knew about it besides Pascal? Who took the damn pictures?"

"I don't know, Joanna. I certainly haven't viewed it so I'm not certain what *it* even is. That's why I ask you to wait until morning when I can give you a conclusive answer."

"All right," she'd said, then waited for them to leave before closing the door behind them and locking it.

Outside, Salettl had immediately posted security agent Frieda Vossler at her door with instructions that no one was to enter or exit without his permission.

Five minutes later he sat down at his office desk. It was already Thursday morning. In less than thirty-six hours, Lybarger would be in Berlin about to be presented at Charlottenburg Palace. After everything, and so close to the hour, that something could go wrong in Anlegeplatz was a circumstance none of them had even considered. Picking up the phone, he dialed Uta Baur in Berlin. Expecting to wake her, he was transferred to her office.

"*Guten Morgen,*" her voice was crisp and alert. At 4:00 A.M., she was already at work for the day.

"I think you should know . . . there has been some confusion here at Anlegeplatz."

86

BY OSBORN'S watch it was nearly 2:30 in the morning, Thursday, October 13.

Next to him, in the dark, he could see Clarkson scanning the red and green lighted instrument panel of the Beechcraft Baron as he held it at a steady 200 knots. Behind them, McVey and Noble dozed fitfully, looking more like weary grandfathers than veteran homicide detectives. Below, the North Sea shimmered in the light of a waning half-moon, its strong tide running full against the Netherlands coast.

A short while later they banked to the right and entered Dutch air space. Then they were crossing over the dark mirror that was the Ijsselmeer, and soon afterward flying east over lush farmland toward the German border.

Osborn tried to picture Vera holed up in a house in the French countryside. It would be a farmhouse with a long drive up to it so that the armed men guarding her could see anyone coming well before they got there. Or maybe not. Maybe it was a modern two-story home on the rail line of a small town that trains passed by a dozen times a day. A nondescript house like thousands of others throughout France, ordinary and plain looking, with a five-year-old car parked out front. The last place a Stasi agent would ever guess housed his target.

Osborn must have dozed off himself because the next thing he saw was the faint glow of dawn on the horizon and Clarkson was dropping the Beechcraft through a light deck of clouds. Directly beneath, he said, was the river Elbe, dark and smooth, like a welcoming beacon that stretched as far in front of them as either of them could see.

Descending farther, they followed its southern bank for another twenty miles until the lights of the rural city of Havelberg shone in the distance.

McVey and Noble were awake now, watching as Clarkson dipped the left wing and banked sharply. Coming around, he cut the throttle and made a low, nearly silent, pass over the shadowy landscape. As he did, a signal light on the ground blinked twice then went out.

"Take us in," Noble said.

Clarkson nodded and brought the Baron's nose up. Giving the twin 300-horsepower engines a burst of power, he executed a steep righthand roll, then eased off the throttle and dropped back down. There was a bump as the landing gear came down, then Clarkson leveled off and came in just above the treetops. As he did, a row of blue lights came on, defining a grass landing strip in front of them. A minute later the wheels touched, the nose came over and the front wheel settled down. Immediately the landing lights went out and there was a deafening roar as Clarkson gave the propellers full reverse thrust. Several hundred feet later, the Baron rolled to a stop.

"McVey!"

A thick German accent was followed by a heavy laugh as McVey stepped out onto the dewy wet grass of the Elbe meadow some sixty miles northwest of Berlin and was instantly swept up in a giant bear hug by a huge man in a black leather jacket and blue jeans.

Lieutenant Manfred Remmer of the Bundeskriminalamt, the German Federal Police, stood six foot four and weighed two hundred and thirty-five pounds. Emotional and outspoken, ten years younger and he could have played linebacker for any team in the NFL. He was still that solid, that coordinated. Married and the father of four daughters, he was thirty-seven and had known McVey since he'd been sent to the LAPD as a young detective twelve years earlier in an international police exchange program.

Assigned to a three-week stint in Robbery-Homicide, two days later Manny Remmer had become McVey's partner-in-training. In those three weeks, trainee Manfred Remmer was present at six court dates, nine autopsies, seven arrests, and twenty-two questioning and interrogation sessions. He worked six days a week, fifteen hours a day, seven of those without pay, sleeping on a cot in McVey's study instead of the hotel room provided, in case something happened that needed their immediate and undivided attention. In the sixteen-odd days he and McVey were together, they arrested five hard-core drug dealers with outstanding murder warrants and tracked down, apprehended and obtained a full confession from a man responsible for killing eight young women. Today, that man, Richard Homer, sits on San Quentin's death row, having exhausted a decade of appeals, waiting for execution.

"I am glad to see you, McVey. Happy to see you well and joyful to hear you were coming," Remmer said as he fishtailed a silver unmarked Mercedes off the meadowland and onto a dirt road. "Because I turned up a little information on your friends inside Interpol, Herren Klass and Halder. Not easy to get. Better to tell you in person than on the telephone—He's okay, yes?" Remmer threw a glance over his shoulder at Osborn sitting in back with Noble.

"He's okay, yes," McVey said, with a wink at Osborn. There was no longer need to keep him in the dark about what else was going on.

"Herr Hugo Klass was born in Munich in 1937. After the war he went with his mother to Mexico City. Later they moved to Brazil. Rio de Janeiro, later São Paulo." Remmer banged the Mercedes hard through a drainage ditch and accelerated onto a paved road. Ahead of them the sky was brightening, and with it came just a hint of the baroque Havelberg skyline.

"In 1958, he came back to Germany and joined the German Air Force and then the Bundesnachrichtendienst, West German Intelligence, where he developed a reputation as a fingerprint expert. Then he—"

Noble leaned over the front seat. "Went to work for Interpol at headquarters. Precisely what we got from MI6."

"Very good." Remmer smiled. "Now tell us the rest."

"What rest? That's all there is to tell."

"No background information? No family history?"

Noble sat back. "Sorry, that's all I have," he said dryly.

"Don't keep us guessing." McVey put on his sunglasses as the rising sun filled the horizon.

In the distance, Osborn saw a gray Mercedes sedan pull out of a side road and turn onto the highway in the same direction they were going. It was moving slower than they were, but when they caught up to it, accelerated to speed and Remmer stayed directly behind it. A moment later he was aware the same kind of car had pulled in behind them and was holding there. Turning, he could see two men in the front seat. Then, for the first time, he noticed the submachine gun in a holder on the door at Remmer's left elbow. The men in the cars in front and behind were obviously federal police. Remmer was taking no chances.

"Klass is not his birth name. It's Haussmann. During the war his father, Erich Haussmann, was a member of the Schutzstaffel, the SS. Identification number 337795. He was also a member of the Sicherheitsdienst, the SD. The security service of the Nazi party." Remmer followed the lead Mercedes south onto the Uberregionale Fernverkehrsstrasse, the interregional through-route highway, and all three cars picked up speed.

"Two months before the war ended, Herr Haussmann vanished. Frau Bertha Haussmann then took her maiden name, Klass. Frau Haussmann was not a wealthy woman when she and her son left Germany for Mexico City in

1946. Yet she lived in a villa there with a cook and a maid and took them with her when she went to Brazil."

"You think she was supported by expatriate Nazis after the war?" McVey asked.

"Maybe, but who's to prove it? She was killed in a 1966 automobile accident outside Rio. I can tell you, however, Erich Haussmann visited her and her son on more than two dozen occasions while she lived in Brazil."

"You said the old man vanished *before* the war ended." Noble leaned forward again.

"And headed straight for South America, along with the father and older brother of Herr Rudolf Halder, your man in charge of Interpol, Vienna. The man who helped Klass so deftly reconstruct Albert Merriman's fingerprint from the piece of glass found in the Paris apartment of the dead private investigator, Jean Packard." Remmer took a pack of cigarettes from the dashboard, shook one out and lit it.

"Halder's real name was Otto," he said, exhaling. "His father and older brother were both in the SS and the SD, the same as Klass' father. Halder and Klass are the same age, fifty-five. Their formative years were spent not just in Nazi Germany, but in the households of Nazi fanatics. Their teen years were spent in South America, where they were educated, overseen and funded by expatriate Nazis."

Noble looked at McVey. "You don't think we're looking at a neo-Nazi conspiracy—"

"Interesting idea, you add it all up. The killing of Merriman by a Stasi agent the day after he's discovered alive by a man strategically positioned in a place where worldwide police inquiries come and go a hundred times a day. The hunting down of Merriman's girlfriend and the killing of his wife and family in Marseilles. The shooting of Lebrun and his brother when they started looking into what Klass was doing in Lyon, pulling the Merriman file from the NYPD by using old Interpol codes most people don't even know exist. Blowing up the train Osborn and I were on. The gunning down of Benny Grossman in his house in Queens after he collects and passes information to Noble about people Erwin Scholl allegedly had killed thirty years ago.

"You're right, Ian. Put it all together and it sounds like the work of an espionage unit, a KGB kind of operation." McVey turned to Remmer.

"What do you think, Manny? Does the Klass-Halder connection turn this into some kind of neo-Nazi thing?"

"What the hell do you mean, neo-Nazi?" Remmer snapped. "Head-busting, sieg-heiling, skinheads with potatoes in their pockets filled with nails? Assholes who beat up immigrants and burn them out of their camps and are TV news every night?" Remmer looked from McVey to Noble behind him and then to Osborn. He was angry.

"Merriman, Lebrun, the Paris-Meaux train, Benny Grossman, who, when I called him for where to stay when I took the kids to New York, said, 'Stay at my house!' You say KGB like I think we should be saying not neo-Nazi but neo-Nazi working with old Nazi! A continuum of the thing that murdered six fucking million Jews and destroyed Europe. Neo-Nazis are the nipple on the tit, they're bullshit. For the moment, a nuisance. Nothing. It's underneath where the sickness still lives, lying behind the blinking faces of bank clerks and cocktail waitresses without them even knowing it, like a seed waiting for the right time, the right mixture of elements to give it rebirth. You spend the time I have on the streets and in the back halls of Germany and you know it. Nobody will ever say it, but it's there, like the wind." Remmer glared at McVey, then stamped out his cigarette and looked back to the road in front of him.

"Manny," McVey said quietly. "I hear you talking your private war. Guilt and shame and everything else thrown at you by another generation. What happened was their doing, not yours, but you bought the ticket anyway. Maybe you had to. And I'm not arguing with you about what you're saying. But, Manny, emotion is not fact."

"You're asking if I have firsthand information. The answer is no, I don't."

"What about the Bundeskriminalamt or Bundesnach christ and dice—or however the hell you pronounce the name for German Intelligence."

Remmer looked back. "Has hard evidence been found of an organized pro-Nazi movement large enough to have influence?"

"Has it?"

"Same answer. No. At least not that I or my superiors are aware of, because such things are discussed all the time between police agencies. It is government policy to remain *je wachsam.* That means ever alert, ever vigilant."

McVey studied him for a moment. "But personally, you say what? The mood is ripe—"

Remmer hesitated, then nodded. "It will never be spoken of. When it comes, you will never hear the word *Nazi.* But they will have the power just the same. I give it two, three years, five on the outside."

On that pronouncement, the men in the car fell silent, and Osborn thought of what Vera had said about the resignation of François Christian and the new Europe. Her grandmother's haunted memories of the Nazi occupation of France: people taken away for no reason and never seen again, neighbor spying on neighbor, family on family, and everywhere, men with guns. "I feel that same shadow now—" The sound of her voice was as clear as if she were there beside him, and the fear in it chilled him.

The cars slowed as they reached the outskirts of a small town and started through it. Looking out, Osborn saw the early sun reaching across rooftops. Saw autumn leaves carpeting the village in bright red and gold. Schoolchildren waited on street corners, and an elderly couple walked along the sidewalk, the old woman leaning on a cane, her free arm tucked proudly into that of her husband. A traffic cop stood near an intersection arguing with a truck driver, and everywhere shopkeepers were setting out their goods.

It was hard to tell how big the town was. Two or three thousand maybe, if you counted the side streets and neighborhoods you couldn't see but knew were there. How many more like it were waking throughout Germany this morning? Hundreds, thousands? Towns, villages, small cities; each with its people going about their daily lives somewhere on the arc from birth to death. Was it possible that any of them still secretly yearned for the sight of goose-stepping storm troopers in tight shirts and swastika armbands, or hungered for the sound of their polished jackboots ringing off every door and window in the Fatherland?

How could they? The terrible era was a half century past. The moral right and wrong of it were worn and everyday themes. Collective guilt and shame still weighed on generations born decades after it was over. The Third Reich and what it stood for was dead. Maybe the rest of the world wanted always to remember, but Germany, Osborn was certain as he looked around, wanted to forget. Remmer had to be wrong.

"I have another name for you," Remmer said, breaking the silence. "The man who was instrumental in securing permanent positions for Klass and Halder within Interpol. Its current assignment director, a former officer in the Paris Préfecture of Police. I think you know him."

"Cadoux? No. It can't be! I've known him for years!" Noble was shocked.

"Yes, that's right." Remmer leaned back from the wheel and lit another cigarette. "Cadoux."

87

AT 6:45 A.M., Erwin Scholl stood at the window in the office of his top-floor suite in the Grand Hotel Berlin watching the morning sun come up over the city. A gray Angora cat was in his arms and he stroked it absently.

Behind him Von Holden was on the phone to Salettl in Anlegeplatz. Through the closed door to the outer office, he could hear his secretaries fielding a battery of international calls, none of which he was taking.

Outside, on the balcony, Viktor Shevchenko smoked a cigarette and looked out over what had been East Berlin, waiting for instructions. Shevchenko was thirty-two, with the tough, wiry build of a street brawler. He, like Bernhard Oven, had been recruited from the Soviet Army and brought into the Stasi as an enforcer by Von Holden. Then, with reunification, he had moved over and joined the Organization as chief of the Berlin sector.

"Nein!" Von Holden said sharply, and Scholl turned around.

"No. Not necessary!" he said in German and shook his head.

Scholl turned back to the window, still stroking the cat. He'd heard the only words he'd needed at the beginning of Von Holden's conversation: Elton Lybarger was resting comfortably and would arrive in Berlin tomorrow as scheduled.

In thirty-six hours, one hundred of Germany's most influential citizens would have come from across the country and gather at Charlottenburg Palace to see him. At a little after nine, the doors to the private dining room would be opened, the room would hush and Lybarger would make his grand entrance. Resplendent in formal dress, no cane at his side, he would walk alone down the beribboned center aisle, wholly aloof from those who watched him. At room's end, he would climb the half dozen stairs to the podium, and there, to a thunderous ovation, he would turn like a monarch to face them. Finally, he would raise his arms for silence and then would deliver the most important and magnificent address of his life.

Hearing Von Holden sign off, Scholl came out of his reverie. Dropping the cat on an overstuffed chair, he sat down at his desk.

"Mr. Lybarger found the video by accident and showed it to Joanna," Von Holden said. "This morning he has little or no memory of it. She, however, is still causing some trouble. Salettl will take care of it."

"He wanted you to do it, to come there to smooth it over. That was the argument?"

"Yes, but it is not necessary."

"Pascal, Dr. Salettl is correct. If the girl continues to be disturbed, it will carry over to Lybarger, which is something quite unacceptable. Salettl may assuage her but hardly to the extent you can. It's the difference between thinking and feeling. Consider how much more difficult it is to change an emotion than a thought. Even if he changes her mind, she can simply change it back again and cause the kind of disruption we cannot have. But if she's soothed and stroked, she will end up purring and content like the cat who now sleeps peacefully on the chair."

"That may be so, Mr. Scholl, but right now my place is here in Berlin." Von Holden looked at Scholl squarely. "You were concerned our system might not be as efficient as we thought. Well, it is and it isn't. London sector has found the wounded French policeman, Lebrun, at Westminster Hospital in London. He's protected around the clock by the London police. London sector working with Paris traced a phone call made in London by the American, Osborn, to a farmhouse outside Nancy. Vera Monneray is there, under the guard of the French Secret Service." Scholl sat motionless, listening, his hands clasped on the desk in front of him.

"Osborn and McVey have been joined by a Special Branch commander of the Metropolitan Police," Von Holden continued. "His name is Noble. They came into Havelberg by private aircraft just before dawn and were picked up and driven off by a Bundeskriminalamt inspector named Remmer. They were escorted by two unmarked Bundeskriminalamt police cars. We have to assume they are coming here, to Berlin."

Von Holden stood up and crossed to a sideboard where he filled a glass with mineral water. "Not the best of news but timely and factual just the same. The problem with it is that they have managed to get this far. That's where our system is no longer working. Bernhard Oven should have shot them both in Paris. Instead, it was the American policeman who shot him. They should have been killed in the train explosion or by the Paris sector operatives who were with me in Meaux waiting for the list of survivors to make our move. It didn't happen. Now they are coming here a day and a half before Mr. Lybarger is to be presented."

Von Holden drained the glass and set it back on the sideboard. "It is a problem I cannot resolve if I am in Zurich."

Scholl leaned back and studied Von Holden. As he did, the cat slid out of the chair where it had been sleeping, and with a feathery leap, jumped into his lap.

"If you leave now, Pascal, you will be back by evening."

Von Holden stared at him as if he were crazy. "Mr. Scholl, these men are dangerous. Isn't that clear?"

"Do you know why they are coming to Berlin, Pascal? I can tell you why in two words: Albert Merriman. He told them about me." Scholl effected a smile—the idea seemed to flatter him.

"When I first came to Palm Springs in the summer of 1946, I met a man who was then ninety. As a youth in the 1870s, he had been an Indian fighter. One of the many things he told me was that the Indian fighters always killed the young Indian boys whenever they found them. Because, he said, they knew that if they didn't, one day the boys would grow up to be men."

"Mr. Scholl, what's the point of this?"

"The point, Pascal, is that I should have remembered that story when I first hired Albert Merriman." Scholl's long fingers stroked through the cat's silky coat like delicate razors. "A short while ago I went back through my personal files. One of the people Herr Merriman took care of for me was a man who designed medical instruments. His name was Osborn. I have to believe it is his son who is with the policemen coming to Berlin."

Pushing back from his desk, with the cat cradled in one arm, Scholl got up and walked to the door that opened onto the balcony. As he reached for the handle, Viktor Shevchenko opened it from the outside.

"Leave us," Scholl said, stepping past him and into the sunshine.

To the outside world Erwin Scholl was an elegant, self-made man, alive with charisma. His own persona all but impenetrable, he had an almost mystical ability to see what motivated others. To presidents and statesmen, it was a gift beyond value because it provided critical insight into the most guarded ambitions of their adversaries. But to those he chose not to charm, he was cold and arrogant, choosing to manipulate through intimidation and fear. And the handful of people close to him—Von Holden among them—he made servile to the darkest side of his nature.

Scholl looked over his shoulder to see that Von Holden had come out onto the balcony and was standing behind him, and for a moment let his gaze fall to the traffic on Friedrichstrasse, eight stories below. He wondered why he valued young men and at the same time distrusted them. Perhaps it was the reason he could never show himself to them sexually. In fewer years than he cared to count, he would be eighty, and his sexual desire was as strong as ever. Yet, the fact was, he had never in his life had unclothed sex with anyone, man or woman. His partner would disrobe, of course, but for him to do so would be unthinkable because it would involve a degree of trust and vulnerability it was utterly impossible for him to express. It was a truth that he had never been totally naked with another human being since he was a child. And the one child who had seen him that way he later bludgeoned to death with a hammer and hid the body in a cave, and that had been at the age of six.

"They are not coming to Berlin because of Mr. Lybarger, or because they have some idea of what is going on at Charlottenburg. They are coming here because of me. If the police had any real evidence of my involvement with Merriman, they would have already acted. What they have at best is something told, most probably to Osborn, by a man who is now dead. As a result, theirs will be the probing action of policemen. Strategic, calculated but predictable, easily countered by attorneys, and, in one way or another, disposed of.

"Osborn, I agree, is different. He is coming because of his father. He has no allegiance to the police, and I would assume he has merely used them, hoping somehow to get to me. Once he is here, he will take chances. And that, I'm afraid, is a passion and recklessness that could unsettle things." Scholl turned to face him, and in the bright sunlight Von Holden could see the deep lines of age time had etched into his face.

"They are coming here heavily protected. Find them, watch them. At some point they will try to get in touch with me, to arrange a time and place where we can talk. That will be our opportunity to isolate them. And then you and Viktor will do as is appropriate. In the meantime, you will go to Zurich."

Von Holden looked off, then back. "Mr. Scholl. You are underestimating these men."

Until now Scholl had been quiet and matter-of-fact. Gently stroking the cat in his arms, he'd simply laid out a plan of action. But suddenly his face reddened. "You think I like it that these men, as you call them, are still alive or that Lybarger's woman therapist is causing trouble? All of it, Pascal, all of it is your responsibility!" The cat rose in alarm in Scholl's arms but he held it firm, stroking it almost mechanically.

"And after these failures you talk back to me. Did *you* find out why these men were coming to Berlin? Did *you* understand what they were after and come to me with a plan about what to do about it?"

Scholl held Von Holden in his stare. The prized son, who could do no wrong, suddenly had. It was more than disappointment, it was a betrayal of faith, and Von Holden knew it. Scholl had had to fight Dortmund, Salettl and Uta Baur to make him director of security for the entire Organization and bring him into the inner circle. It had taken months, and he'd finally done it by convincing them that they were the last of the hierarchy still living. They were old, he told them, and had made no provisions for the future. The greatest empires in history had been lost almost overnight because there had been no clear plan for succession of power. In due course, others would take their place at the head of the Organization. The Peipers, perhaps, or Hans Dabritz, Henryk Steiner, even Gertrude Biermann. But that time was not yet here, and until it was the Organization needed to be protected from within. Scholl had known Von Holden as a boy. He had the background and the training and had long proven his ability and loyalty. They needed to trust him, to make him the man in charge of security, if for nothing else than the future safety of everything they had worked to attain.

"I am sorry, sir, to have disappointed you," Von Holden said in a whisper.

"Pascal." Scholl softened. "You know that you are the closest thing to a son I have," he said quietly. The cat relaxed in his arms, and Scholl began to stroke it again. "But today I cannot afford to talk to you like a son. You are *Leiter der Sicherheit*, and wholly answerable for the security of the entire operation."

Suddenly Scholl's hand closed on the scruff of the cat's neck. With an abrupt wrench, he lifted the animal free of the arm that had been cradling it and held it out over the side of the balcony and the traffic eighty feet below. The animal shrieked, struggling wildly. Screaming, it rolled up in a ball, clawing at Scholl's arm and hand, desperately trying to find a way to cling to it.

"You must never question my orders, Pascal."

Suddenly the cat's right forepaw shot out, raking a jagged, bloody path across the back of Scholl's hand.

"Never. Is that clear?" Scholl ignored the cat. Having torn flesh, it struck again and again until Scholl's arm and wrist ran with blood. But Scholl's eyes remained on Von Holden's. There was no pain because nothing else existed. Not the cat. Not the traffic below. Only Von Holden. He was demanding total allegiance. Not just for now but for as long as he lived.

"Yes, sir. It is clear," Von Holden breathed.

Scholl stared for a moment longer. "Thank you, Pascal," he said quietly. With that he opened his hand and the cat, screaming in terror, dropped out of sight like a stone. Then Scholl brought his hand in from over the balcony railing, palm held upward, the blood running in a half circle around his wrist before disappearing into the stark white of his shirt sleeve.

"Pascal," he said, "when the time comes, be most respectful of the young doctor. Kill him first."

Von Holden's eyes went to the hand in front of him and then back to Scholl. "Yes, sir . . . ," he breathed again.

Then, as if following a dark and ancient ritual, Scholl lowered his hand and Von Holden sunk to his knees and took the hand in his. Bringing it to his mouth, he began to lick the blood from it. First the fingers. Then slowly working his way to the palm and then farther up, to the wrist itself. He did it deliberately and with his eyes open, knowing that Scholl stood above him, watching trans-fixed. And he continued that way, his tongue and lips suckling the wounds over and over until finally and at length Scholl gave a profound shudder and drew back.

Von Holden stood slowly and for a moment stared, then quickly turned and went back inside, leaving Scholl in private to recover from the fulfillment of his desire.

88

London, 7:45 A.M.

MILLIE WHITEHEAD, Lebrun's extraordinarily large bo-somed, and therefore his favorite, nurse, had just finished giving him a sponge bath and was fluffing the pillows under his head when Cadoux walked in in full uniform.

"Much easier to get through airports this way," he said of his uniform, with a broad smile.

Lebrun raised a hand to take his old friend's. Oxygen was still being fed through tubes to his nose and the way they hung down over his mouth made talking difficult.

"Of course I didn't come to see you, I came to see a lady,"

Cadoux bantered, smiling at Nurse Whitehead. Blushing, she giggled, winked at Lebrun, and then left the room.

Pulling up a chair, Cadoux sat down next to Lebrun. "How are you my friend? How are they treating you?"

For the next dozen or so minutes Cadoux carried on about old times; recalling their days growing up, best friends in the same neighborhood, the girls they'd known, the women they'd finally married, the children they'd had with them, laughed out loud at the vivid memory of running away to enlist in the Foreign Legion then being rejected and escorted abruptly back home by two real legionnaires because they were only fourteen. Cadoux's smile was broad and he laughed often in a genuine attempt to cheer his wounded comrade.

All the while they talked, the index finger of Lebrun's right hand rested on the stainless steel trigger of a .25 caliber automatic, concealed beneath his bedclothes and pointed at Cadoux's chest. The coded warning from McVey had been absolutely clear. Never mind that Cadoux was an old and cherished friend; there was every indication he was a major conspirator working with the "group," as they were now calling it. Most likely, it was he who controlled the covert operations within Interpol, Lyon, and he who had ordered the execution of Lebrun's brother and the attempted murder of Lebrun himself at the Lyon railway station.

If McVey was right, Cadoux had come visiting for one reason: to finish the job on Lebrun himself.

But the more he talked, the more convivial he became, and Lebrun began to wonder if McVey could have been wrong or his information incorrect. Further, how would he dare attempt it when there were armed police standing twenty-four-hour guard just a few feet away on the other side of the door, and the door itself open?

"My friend," Cadoux said, standing. "Forgive me but I must have a cigarette and I know I can't do that in here."

Gathering his cap, he started toward the door. "I'll go down to the lounge and come back in a few moments."

Cadoux left and Lebrun relaxed. McVey had to have been wrong. A moment later, one of the Metropolitan policemen outside his room entered.

"Everything all right, sir?"

"Yes, thank you."

"Chap here to change your bed." The policeman stood aside as a large man in the dress of a hospital orderly came in with fresh linens.

"Good day, sir," the man said with a Cockney accent, setting the linens down on a chair next to the bed. The policeman went back into the hallway.

"We'll have a little privacy, eh, sir?" he said and, taking two steps, closed the door.

Lebrun's danger alarm went off. "Why are you closing the door?" he cried out in French. The man turned and smiled. Then suddenly reached across and jerked the tubes from Lebrun's nose. A split second later, a pillow was shoved over his face and the man's full weight came down on it.

Lebrun struggled frantically, his right hand digging for the automatic. But the large man's weight, combined with his own weakness, made it a battle out of Lebrun's favor. Finally his hand closed around the gun and he fought to bring it up so he could fire into the man's belly. Abruptly the man's weight shifted and the gun barrel caught in the sheets. Lebrun grunted, feverishly trying to jerk the pistol free. His lungs screamed for air but there was none. And in that single moment he realized he was going to die, as quickly everything faded to gray, then to an even darker gray that was almost black but wasn't. He thought he felt someone take the gun from his hand, but he couldn't be certain. Then he heard a muffled pop and saw the brightest light he'd ever seen.

It would have been impossible for Lebrun to see the orderly tug back the sheets, rip the automatic from his hand and put it to his ear beneath the pillow. In the same way, it would have been as impossible for him to see the bloody rush of his brains and pieces of his skull splatter off the wall next to his bed and cling to the white-painted plaster like so much flecked crimson Jell-O.

Five seconds later, the door opened. Startled, the orderly swung the gun toward it. Cadoux, entering, put up a hand and calmly closed the door behind him. Easing off, the orderly lowered the gun and nodded in the direction of Lebrun. As he did, he glimpsed the revolver as it cleared Cadoux's service holster.

"What's that?" he yelled. His cry was drowned out by a thundering explosion.

The Metropolitan police running in from the hallway heard two more shots and found Cadoux standing over the dead man. Lebrun's .25 automatic still in the orderly's hand. "This man just shot Inspector Lebrun," he said.

89

Brandenburg, Germany.

"THIS CHARLOTTENBURG Palace, where Scholl's attending this shindig. What is it?" McVey was leaning forward from the backseat as Remmer followed the lead car down a boulevard of magnificent autumn yellow trees and past the burgher houses of the fifteenth-century town of Brandenburg, heading east in bright sunshine toward Berlin.

"What is it?" Remmer glanced up at McVey in the mirror. "A treasure of baroque art. A museum, a mausoleum, a house of a thousand riches particularly dear to the German heart. The summer residence of almost every Prussian king from Friedrich the First to Friedrich Wilhelm the Fourth. If the chancellor lived there now, it would be like the White House and all the great museums of America rolled into one."

Osborn looked off. The morning sun was working its way higher, lifting a cluster of lakes from dark purple to a brilliant blue. The consummation of all that had happened in the last ten days—so quickly, so brutally, and after so many years—was numbing. The idea of what would unfold in Berlin was even more so. In one way he felt as if he'd been swept up in a surging tide over which he had no control. Yet, at the same time, he had the singular and calming sense that he'd been brought to this point because some unknown hand had guided him, and that whatever lay ahead, however obscure or dangerous or horrifying, would be there for a reason, and that instead of fighting it, he should trust in it. He wondered if that were true for the others. McVey and Noble and Remmer were disparate men, from different worlds, with more than thirty years spread across their ages. Had their lives and his been driven together by the same force he now felt? How could it, when barely a week before he'd never met any of them? Yet what other explanation was there?

Letting his mind drift, Osborn turned his gaze back to the passing countryside, a rolling, gently forested, pastoral land, forever dotted with lakes. Abruptly, and for the briefest moment, his view was blurred by a large stand of conifers. As quickly they vanished and in the distance he saw sunlight touch the highest spires of a fifteenth-century cathedral. And the perception came that he was right, that they were all here—McVey, Noble, Remmer and himself—because of some greater design, that they were part of a destiny beyond their knowing.

Nancy, France.

THE MORNING sun peeked up over the hills, lighting the brown-and-white farmhouse like a Van Gogh.

Outside, Secret Service agents Alain Cotrell and Jean Claude Dumas relaxed on the front porch, with Dumas cradling a mug of coffee in one hand and a nine-millimeter carbine in the other. A quarter mile down the long driveway, at the halfway point between the highway and the farmhouse, agent Jacques Montant, a French Famas assault rifle slung over his shoulder, leaned against a tree, watching a parade of ants march in and out of a hole at its base.

Inside, Vera sat at an antique vanity near the front bedroom window, five handwritten pages of a long love letter to Paul Osborn already done. In them, she was trying to make some sense of all that was happening and had happened since they'd met, and at the same time using them as a diversion against the abrupt ending to his phone call the night before.

At first she'd thought it had been a problem with the telephone system and that he would call back. But he hadn't, and as the hours stretched on she knew something had happened. What that might be, she refused to consider. Stoically, she'd spent the rest of the evening and most of the night reading over two medical journals she'd brought with her almost as an afterthought when she'd so hurriedly left Paris. Anxiety and fear were impossible companions, and this, she'd been afraid, might be a journey filled with them.

By daybreak, when she'd still had no word, she'd decided to talk to Paul. To say things on paper, she would say if he were there with her and they had time alone. As if none of this had happened and they were everyday people, finding each other under everyday circumstances. It was all, of course, to keep from being overwhelmed by her own imagination.

Laying down her pen, she stopped to read what she'd written and suddenly burst out laughing. What was intended to have come from the heart was, instead, a rambling, long-winded, pseudo-intellectual treatise on the meaning of life. She'd meant to write a love letter, but what she'd put down was more like a writing sample for a position as an English teacher at a private girls' school. Still smiling, she tore the pages in quarters and threw them in the wastebasket. It was then she saw the car turn off the highway and start up the long drive toward the house.

As it approached, she could see it was a black Peugeot with blue emergency lights mounted on the roof. As it reached the halfway point, she saw agent Montand step into the roadway with his hands raised, motioning the car to stop. When it did, Montand walked to the driver's window. A moment later he spoke into his radio, waited for a reply, then nodded and the car proceeded on.

As it neared the house, Alain Cotrell walked out to meet it, and like Montand, motioned the driver to stop. Jean Claude Dumas came up behind him, sliding the carbine from his shoulder.

"Oui, madame," Alain said, as the driver's window rolled down and a very attractive woman with dark hair looked out.

"My name is Avril Rocard," she said in French, flashing a picture I.D., "from the First Préfecture of Paris Police. I am here for Mademoiselle Monneray, to bring her to Paris at the request of Detective McVey. She'll know who I mean." She produced an official order on French government stationery. "By order of Captain Cadoux of Interpol. And at the behest of the prime minister, François Christian."

Agent Cotrell took the paper, looked at it, then handed it back. As he did, Jean Claude Dumas walked to the far side of the car and looked in. Other than the woman, it was empty.

"One moment," Cotrell said. Stepping back, he took his own radio from his jacket and walked off. As he did, Dumas came back to the driver's side.

Glancing in her mirror, Avril saw agent Montand behind her, a hundred feet back down the driveway.

A moment later Cotrell abruptly put away his radio and turned back, approaching the car. His entire body language had changed, and Avril could see his hand moving out of sight behind his jacket.

"Is it all right if I open my purse for a cigarette?" Avril said, looking at Dumas.

"Oui," Dumas nodded, then watched as Avril's right hand went to her purse for the cigarette. It was her left hand that took him by surprise. There were two quick pops and he fell backward into Cotrell. For an instant, Cotrell was off balance and all he could see was the Beretta in Avril's hand. It jumped once. And Cotrell grabbed for his neck. Her second shot, the one between the eyes, killed him.

Montand was running toward her, the Famas assault rifle coming up to fire, when she leveled the Beretta. Her first shot hit him in the leg, punching him down and sending the Famas clattering out of reach across the driveway. He was on the ground, gritting his teeth in pain and straining for it, when she walked up. Looking down at him, she raised the pistol slowly. Gave him a moment to think about it, then shot him. Once just under the left eye. Once in the heart.

Then, straightening her jacket, she turned and started for the farmhouse.

90

VERA HAD seen everything from the bedroom window. Immediately, she'd reached for the telephone but could get only a dial tone. Nothing she could do would clear the line or ring through to an operator.

Earlier, when François had first brought her there, she'd asked him for a pistol to protect herself in case something went wrong. Nothing could go wrong, he'd told her. The men guarding her were the finest in the French Secret Service. She'd argued that too much had already happened, that whoever these people were, they had a very definitive way of *making* things go wrong. François' answer was that that was why she was here, two hundred miles from Paris, sequestered out of harm's way and guarded by his best and most loyal men. And that had ended the discussion.

And now his best and most loyal men lay sprawled in the driveway and the woman who had killed them was almost in the house.

Avril Rocard reached the edge of the driveway and walked over a small expanse of lawn and stepped onto the front porch. So far the Organization's intelligence had been valid. Three men had been guarding the house. It was possible, she'd been warned, that a fourth agent might have somehow been missed and could be waiting inside. It was also possible the second agent had broadcast an alert on his radio before she'd killed him. Assuming that was true, it meant the rest, fourth agent or not, had to be done swiftly.

Snapping a fresh clip into the Beretta, she stepped to the side of the front door, turned the knob with her left hand and pushed gently. The oak door swung partway open. Inside, it was silent. The only sound came from behind her, where the songbirds had started vocalizing once more, following their abrupt silence at the first gunfire.

"Vera," she said sharply. "My name is Avril Rocard. I am a police officer. The telephones are out. François Christian sent me to get you. The men protecting you were criminals who had infiltrated the Secret Service."

Silence.

"Is someone with you, Vera? Is that why you can't speak out?"

Slowly, Avril pushed the door open enough for her to step inside. To her left was a long bench with a blank wall behind it. In front of her, through the door frame, was the living room. Beyond it, the hallway continued into shadow and then out of sight.

"Vera?" she said again.

Still there was no answer.

Vera stood alone, just inside the hallway entrance. She'd started to go out the back door, but realized it opened to a wide lawn that ran down to a duck pond. If she went out there, she'd be nothing but a target.

"Vera." Avril's voice came again and she could hear the wide plank floorboards creak beneath her feet.

"Don't be afraid, Vera. I'm here to help you. If someone has you, don't move. Don't struggle. Just stay where you are. I'll come to you."

Vera took a deep breath and held it. A small window was to her right and she glanced out, hoping someone would be coming up the driveway. Agents sent to relieve the dead guards, a postman, anything.

"Vera." Avril's voice was closer now. She was coming toward her. Vera looked down. She was a doctor, trained to save lives. She had no training in taking them. Still, she wouldn't die, not here, if she could do anything at all to prevent it. Between her hands was a length of dark blue drapery cord, pulled from the bedroom curtains.

"If you're alone and hiding, please come out, Vera. François is waiting for word of your safety."

Vera cocked an ear. Avril's voice was retreating. Perhaps she'd gone into the living room. Letting out her breath, she relaxed. As she did, the small window to her right suddenly shattered.

Avril was right there! There was a sharp report, and the wood fragments exploded everywhere. Vera screamed as splinters riddled her neck and face. Then Avril's hand was inside the window frame, her gun looking for the final shot. Blindly, Vera's two hands shot forward, encircling Avril's gun hand with the dark blue cord. At the same time she jerked them tight, and pulled backward with all her strength. Caught off guard, Avril's head shot face-first through the broken glass. There was a dull thud as the Beretta dropped at Vera's feet.

Face cut and bleeding from the shattered glass, Avril struggled wildly to pull free. But her struggle only strengthened Vera's resolve. Tugging backward on the cord, she extended Avril's arm to its full length. Now, with Avril's body pressed up against the outside of the house, Vera heaved backward with both hands. There was a pop, and Avril screamed as her shoulder dislocated. Then Vera let go, and slowly Avril slid back out the window and slumped on the ground below, crying in agony.

"Who are you?" Vera said, as she approached from outside. Avril's Beretta was in her hand and she had it pointed directly at the long-legged figure in the dark skirt slumped on the ground, her dislocated arm twisted awkwardly under her.

"Answer me. Who are you? Who do you work for?"

Avril said nothing. Very carefully Vera moved forward. The woman on the ground was a professional. In the last five minutes she had seen her shoot three men to death and try to kill her.

"Put your good hand out and roll over where I can see both your hands," she commanded.

Avril didn't move. Then Vera saw a crimson ooze of blood where her breast and shoulder touched the ground. Reaching out, she kicked at Avril's foot. Nothing happened.

Trembling, she moved closer, the gun pointed, ready to fire. Bending down carefully, she took hold of Avril's shoulder and rolled her over on her back. Blood ran down from beneath her chin and onto her blouse. Her left fist was closed. Easing down on one knee, Vera opened it. When she did, she cried out, and moved back. In it was a single-edged razor blade. In the time it had taken Vera to pick up Avril's gun and come out of the house, Avril Rocard had cut her own throat.

91

Berlin, 11 A.M.

A BLONDE waitress in a Bavarian costume smiled briefly at Osborn, then set a steaming pot of coffee on the table and left. They had come into Berlin on the autobahn and driven directly to a small diner on Waisenstrasse that billed itself as one of Berlin's oldest restaurants. The owner, Gerd Epplemann, a slight, balding man in a starched white apron, took them directly downstairs to a private dining room where Diedrich Honig waited.

Honig had dark, wavy hair and a neatly trimmed beard flecked with gray. He was nearly as tall as Remmer but his slim build, and the way his arms hung out from jacket sleeves that were too short, made him look taller. That, and his manner of standing, slightly hunched over, head bent from the neck, made him look startlingly like a German Abraham Lincoln.

"I want you to consider the risk. Herr McVey, Herr Noble," Honig said, as he crossed the room, pacing, his eyes locked on the men he was addressing.

"Erwin Scholl is one of the most influential men in the West. If you approach him, you will be opening a nest far beyond what you consider to be the realm of your experience. You risk horrid embarrassment. To yourselves and to your police departments. To the point where you would either be fired or forced to resign. And it would not end there because once you are out of the protection of your organizations, you will be sued by a sea of attorneys for violation of laws you may never have heard of, and in ways you will not begin to fathom. They will break you down to nothing. They'll find a way to take your homes, your cars, everything. And when it's done, if you have pensions left, you will be lucky. Such is the power of a man like that."

That said, Honig sat down at the long table and poured himself a cup of the strong black coffee the Bavarian waitress had left. The now retired superintendent of the Berlin police was a man courted by the very wealthy and the very powerful at the highest levels of German industry. The latter stages of the cold war had not lessened the deadly resolve of international terrorism. As a result, personal security for one's self and family had increasingly become de rigueur for the European corporate officer. In Berlin, protection of the fiscal barons had fallen to Honig. So, if anyone was in position to know how the rich and powerful protected themselves in clinches, especially in Berlin, it was Diedrich Honig.

"With all respect, Herr Honig," McVey bristled, "I've been threatened before and so far I've survived. You can say the same for Inspectors Noble and Remmer. So let's forget that and get on to why we're here. Murders. A series of them that may have begun thirty or more years ago and are still going on today. One of them happened in New York, sometime within the last twenty-four hours. The victim was a little Jewish guy named Benny Grossman. He was also a cop and a very good friend of mine." McVey's voice was heavy with anger. "We've been working this for some time, but it's only in the last day or so we've started to get some idea of a source. And each time we go around, the more Erwin Scholl's name comes up. Murder for hire, Herr Honig. A long-term, even capital offense almost anywhere in the world."

Directly overhead came the sound of laughter, followed by the creaking of floorboards as a number of people came in for lunch. At the same time, the pungent smell of sauerkraut wafted through the air.

"I want to talk to Scholl," McVey said.

Honig was hesitant. "I don't know if that's possible, Detective. You are an American. In Germany you have no authority. And unless you have hard evidence of a crime committed here, I—"

McVey ignored his reticence. "It goes this way. An arrest warrant in Inspector Remmer's name, directing Scholl to hand himself over to the German Federal Police to be held for extradition to the United States. The charge is suspicion of murder for hire. The American consulate will be informed."

"A warrant like that will mean nothing to a man like Scholl," Honig said quietly. "His lawyers will eat it for lunch."

"I know," McVey said. "But I want it anyway."

Honig crossed his hands on the table in front of him and shrugged. "Gentlemen, the most I can tell you is that I will do what I can."

McVey leaned in. "If you can't arrange it, say so now and I'll find somebody who can. It needs to be done today."

92

VON HOLDEN had left Scholl's suite at the Grand Hotel Berlin at 7:50. At 10:20 his private jet banked for the final approach to Kloten Airport in Zurich.

At 10:52 his limousine pulled into Anlegeplatz and by 11:00 Von Holden was knocking gently on Joanna's bedroom door. Joanna had to be coaxed and stroked and whatever else was necessary to put her back into her earlier frame of mind, where she was both cooperative and eager to care for Elton Lybarger. Which was why Von Holden carried the jet-black Saint Bernard puppy he'd ordered to have ready upon his arrival.

"Joanna," he said, after his first knock went unanswered. "It's Pascal. I know you're upset. I have to talk with you."

"I have nothing to say to you or anyone else!" she snapped through the closed door.

"Please—"

"No! Dammit! Now, go away!"

Reaching down, Von Holden put his hand on the knob and turned it.

"She's locked the door," security guard Frieda Vossler said toughly.

Von Holden turned to look at her. Severe and authoritarian, she was square-jawed and heavily built. She needed to relax and smile and make herself more feminine, if that were possible, before any man would look at her with more than contempt.

"You may leave," Von Holden said.

"I was ordered to—"

"You may leave." Von Holden glared at her.

"Yes, Herr Von Holden." Frieda Vossler clicked her

walkie-talkie onto her belt, glanced sharply at him, then walked off. Von Holden stared after her. If she were a man and in the Spetsnaz, he would have killed her for that single glance alone. Then the puppy whimpered and squirmed in his arms and he turned back to the door.

"Joanna," he said, gently. "I have a gift for you. Actually it's for Henry."

"What about Henry?" Suddenly the door flung open, and Joanna stood there, barefoot, in jeans and sweatshirt. The thought someone might have harmed her dog, still back in the kennel in Taos, terrified her. Then she saw the puppy.

Five minutes later, Von Holden had kissed the tears from Joanna's eyes and had her on the floor playing with the five-week-old Saint Bernard. The video she had seen of the explicit sexual escapade involving her, he'd explained, was a cruel study vigorously protested by himself but insisted upon by Lybarger's board of directors after they'd seriously questioned the man's ability to resume control of his fifty-billion-dollar multinational corporation. Afraid of a second stroke or heart attack, their insurance underwriters wanted unequivocal proof of his strength and physical stamina under the most vigorous of everyday conditions. Usual tests were not sufficient, and the underwriters had asked their chief physician, in concert with Salettl, to design one.

And Salettl, knowing Lybarger had no wife or love interest at present and realizing how deeply he cared for and trusted Joanna, knew that she was the only one he would be comfortable with. Fearing either or both would reject the proposal if asked, Salettl ordered them both secretly sedated. The experiment was done, recorded and the results passed on to the board of directors. The lone videotape had since been destroyed. No one else had been there, the cameras had been operated by remote control.

"Joanna, to them, it was business and nothing else. I tried to fight against it to the point of being asked to leave the company if I protested further. That I could not do, for Mr. Lybarger's sake. Or yours. Because I knew that at least I would be there and not some stranger. I'm sorry . . . ," he said gently as tears welled up in her eyes. "One more day, please, Joanna. For Mr. Lybarger. Just the trip to Berlin, and then you will be on your way home."

Von Holden got down on the floor beside her and rubbed the puppy's belly as it rolled over on its back. "If you want to go now, I will understand and put a car for the airport at your disposal. We can hire a temporary therapist and make do with Mr. Lybarger tomorrow as best we can."

Joanna stared at Von Holden, wavering as to what to do; angry and outraged at what had been so ruthlessly done to her, she was confused as well because she realized Elton Lybarger had been as much the victim as she and that she still deeply cared for his well-being.

Von Holden put out his hand, and the black fur ball struggled up on its feet and licked his fingers. In reaction, Von Holden rubbed its head and tousled its ears, smiling the same warm, loving smile that had melted her heart the first day she'd seen him. In that moment Joanna decided that everything he'd told her was true and that under the circumstances his request was not all that unreasonable.

"I'll go with you to Berlin," she said with a sad, shy smile.

Leaning forward, Von Holden brushed his lips against her forehead and thanked her for her understanding.

"Joanna, I must return to Berlin today for last-minute preparations. I apologize, but I have no other choice. You will come tomorrow, with Mr. Lybarger and the others?"

Joanna hesitated, and for a moment he thought she was going to change her mind, then she relented. "I'll see you there, won't I?"

"Of course." Von Holden grinned.

Joanna felt herself smile. And for the first time since she'd seen the video, she relaxed. Roughing the puppy's ears playfully one more time, Von Holden stood, then took Joanna's hand and helped her up. As he did, he slid an envelope from his pocket and laid it on the desk beside her.

"A corporate way of helping ease your embarrassment and soothe your wounds. Not very personal I'm afraid, but decidedly useful. See you in Berlin," he whispered and left.

Joanna stared at the envelope while the puppy whimpered at her feet. Finally, she picked it up and opened it. When she saw what was inside, she gasped. A cashier's check was made out in her name for five hundred thousand dollars.

93

REMMER TURNED the Mercedes off Hardenbergstrasse into the underground garage of a glass-and-concrete municipal building at number 15. One of the gray unmarked federal police escort cars followed them in and backed into a space across from theirs. Osborn could see the faces of the detectives as he got out and walked with the others toward the elevators. They were younger than he expected, probably not even thirty. For some reason that surprised him and he flashed on a whole vanguard of people younger than he was coming up behind him as professionals. It didn't make him feel old as much as it put things out of balance. Policemen had always been older than he was and he was always in the front line of young men coming up, the others were still kids in school. But suddenly they weren't anymore. Why he thought about it now he didn't know except that maybe he was trying to keep from thinking about where they were going and what could conceivably happen when they got here.

They'd stayed in the private room in the restaurant for more than two hours eating lunch and drinking coffee and waiting. Then Honig had sent word that criminal court judge Otto Gravenitz would see them in his chambers at three.

On the way over, McVey had counseled him on what to say in his deposition. Merriman's words immediately before his death were all that were important and Osborn was to give only the bare essentials of what had happened. In other words, he was to make no mention of the hired private detective, Jean Packard. No mention of the syringes. No mention of the drug Osborn had administered. What McVey was doing was finding a way to ease Osborn's unstated but undoubtedly very real fear of going into a situation where he might be forced to incriminate himself into a charge of attempted murder.

McVey's gesture was intended to be generous and Osborn was supposed to appreciate it and he did, except that he knew it had a second edge. McVey's concern wasn't that Osborn might put himself on the spot, it was that he didn't want a complication jeopardizing his chance for a murder-for-hire writ against Scholl. That meant the hearing had to be kept simple and pointed at Scholl, both for the judge and for Honig, whose opinion obviously carried a great deal of weight. If Osborn went too far with what he said, they'd get into a whole different matter, one that could shift the focus from Scholl to Osborn and seriously endanger the main argument.

"What do you think?" McVey said to Remmer as the elevator doors slid closed. "They know we're here?"

Remmer shrugged. "All I can tell you is that we were not followed from the plane to Berlin. Nor from the restaurant to here. But who knows what eyes we don't see. Safer to assume they know, I think, yes?"

Noble glanced at McVey. Remmer was right: safer to be

on guard than not. Even if the "group" didn't know they were here, they had to believe they soon would. They'd seen too much of the way they worked already.

At the sixth floor, the elevator stopped and they walked out into a reception area where they were ushered into a private office and asked to wait.

"Do you know this judge? Gravenitz? That his name?" McVey looked around at what was obviously a civil servant's office. The plain steel desk and chair that went with it would fit into any public building in L.A. So would the inexpensive bookcase and the cheap prints on the wall.

Remmer nodded. "Not well, but yes."

"What can we expect?"

"Depends what Honig told him. Unquestionably it was enough for him to agree to see us. But don't think because Honig set it up or Gravenitz agreed to see us right away it's guaranteed. Gravenitz will take convincing."

McVey glanced at his watch and sat down on a corner of the desk, then looked at Osborn.

"I'm okay." Osborn walked over and leaned against the wall by the window. McVey hadn't forgotten his assault on Merriman and wouldn't. That was something else he didn't want to think about, not now. Still, it hung there because he knew at some point it would become an issue.

The door opened and Diedrich Honig came in. Judge Gravenitz, he apologized, had been delayed but would see them momentarily. Then he looked at Noble and told him a message had come for him to call his London office immediately.

"A break, maybe?" Noble went to the desk and picked up the phone. In thirty seconds he had his office. Twenty seconds after that he was transferred to the chief homicide superintendent of the London police.

"Oh God, no," he said a moment later. "How did it happen? He had a twenty-four-hour guard."

"Lebrun," McVey breathed.

"Well where in God's name is he now?" Noble said irritably. "Find him and when you get him, hold him in isolation. When you have any information at all, relay it through Inspector Remmer's office in Bad Godesberg." Hanging up, Noble turned to McVey with the details of Lebrun's murder and the fact that Cadoux had disappeared in the confusion immediately following his shooting of the orderly.

"I don't have to bet whether the orderly's dead," McVey said through clenched teeth.

"No, you don't."

Running a hand through his hair, McVey walked across the room. When he turned back he was looking directly at Honig. "You ever lose one of your friends in the line of duty, Herr Honig?"

"You don't do this game without it . . . ," Honig said quietly.

"Then how much longer do we have to wait for Judge Gravenitz?" It wasn't a question, it was a demand.

94

GRANDIOSE, SHORT and red faced, with a shock of silver white hair, district Kriminal Richter Otto Gravenitz gestured toward a grouping of leather and Burmese teak chairs and bade them in German to sit down. Standing until they were seated, he crossed in front of them and sat down behind a massive rococo desk, the soles of his shoes barely reaching down to the oriental carpet beneath them. In contrast to the Spartan decor of the rest of the building, Gravenitz's office was a rich oasis of taste, antiques and wealth. It was also a well-calculated display of power and position.

Turning to the others, Honig explained in English that because of Scholl's prominence and the severity of the charge against him, Judge Gravenitz had chosen to conduct the deposition himself, without the presence of a state prosecutor.

"Fine," McVey said. "Let's get on with it."

Leaning forward, Gravenitz turned on a tape recorder and, at three twenty-five, they got to business.

In a brief opening statement, translated into German by Remmer, McVey explained who Osborn was, how he chanced to see his father's murderer in a Paris café and how, in the absence of police and the fear he would lose sight of him, he had followed him to a park along the Seine. There he gathered the courage to approach and question him, only to have Merriman shot to death moments later by an assailant they believed also to have been in the hire of Erwin Scholl.

Finished, McVey looked at Osborn measuredly, then gave him the floor and sat down. Remmer translated as Gravenitz swore Osborn in, then Osborn began his testimony. In it, he restated what McVey had said and then simply told the truth.

Sitting back, Gravenitz studied Osborn and at the same time listened to the translation. When Osborn finished, he glanced at Honig, then back to Osborn. "You are certain Merriman was your father's murderer? Certain after nearly thirty years?"

"Yes, sir," Osborn said.

"You must have hated him."

McVey shot Osborn a warning glance. Be careful, it said. He's probing.

"You would too," Osborn said without flinching.

"Do you know why Erwin Scholl would have wanted your father to be killed?"

"No, sir," Osborn replied quietly and McVey breathed a sigh of relief. Osborn was doing well. "You have to remember I was a little boy. But I saw the man's face and I never forgot it. And I never saw it again until that night in Paris. I don't know how much more I can tell you."

Gravenitz waited, then looked to McVey.

"Are you certain, beyond doubt, that the Erwin Scholl who is now here in Berlin is the same man who hired Albert Merriman?"

McVey stood up. "Yes, sir."

"Why do you believe the individual who shot Herr Merriman was also employed by Herr Scholl?"

"Because Scholl's men had tried to kill him before and because Merriman had been in hiding for a long time. They finally tracked him down."

"And you are certain, beyond doubt, Scholl was behind it."

This was the kind of thing McVey had tried to avoid, but Gravenitz, like respected judges everywhere, had a second sense, the same kind parents had, and it carried the same warning: Lie and you're dead. "Can I prove it? No, sir. Not yet."

"I see . . . ," Gravenitz said.

Scholl was an international figure, huge and important, and Gravenitz was teetering. A thinking judge would no more casually sign an arrest warrant for Erwin Scholl than he would for the chancellor of the country, and McVey knew it. And Osborn's deposition, strong as it was, bottom line, was in reality hearsay and nothing more. Something had to be done to push Gravenitz over or they would have to go to Scholl without a writ and that was the last thing he wanted to do. Remmer must have sensed it too because suddenly he was standing up, pushing back his chair.

"Your Honor," he said in German. "As I understand it, one of the primary reasons you agreed to see us on such short notice was because two police officers working on the case were shot. One could have been coincidental, but two—"

"Yes, that was a strong consideration," Gravenitz said.

"Then you would know one was a New York detective, killed right in his own home. The second, a highly respected member of the Paris police, was seriously wounded at the main rail station in Lyon, then taken to London and put in a hospital under a false name and a twenty-four-hour police guard." Remmer paused, then continued. "A short time ago he was shot to death in that very same hospital room."

"I'm sorry—" Gravenitz said, genuinely.

Remmer accepted his sentiment, then went on. "We have every reason to believe the man responsible was working for Scholl's organization. We need to interrogate Herr Scholl personally, Your Honor, not talk to his lawyers. Without a writ we will never be able to do that."

Gravenitz put his palms together and sat back, then looked to McVey, who was staring right at him, waiting for his decision. Expressionless, he leaned forward and made a note on a legal pad in front of him. Then, running a hand through his silvery mane and glancing at Honig, his eyes found Remmer.

"Okay," he said in English. "Okay."

95

McVEY WAITED with Noble and Osborn until Gravenitz signed the *Haftbefehl,* the arrest warrant for Erwin Scholl, and presented it to Remmer. Then, thanking Gravenitz and shaking hands with Honig, the four left the judicial chambers and took Gravenitz's private elevator to the garage.

They were walking on eggshells and knew it, Osborn included. For all intents, the court order now resting in McVey's pocket, as Honig had suggested, was all but useless. Presented to Scholl in your everyday knock and notice—"Good evening, sir, we are the police and have a warrant for your arrest and this is why"—Scholl might be carted off to jail like John Doe, but within the hour would come a battery of attorneys who would do all the talking, and in the end Scholl would walk out, most likely never having said a word.

In the weeks that followed, a volume of depositions would be filed by Scholl and a number of extremely distinguished others vouching for Scholl's character and swearing his total noninvolvement, denying he'd ever known, had business with or had reason to have business with Osborn's father or any of the deceased; denying he'd ever heard of, let alone known and had dealings with, a man called Albert Merriman; avowing he'd been elsewhere and not at his Long Island estate during the dates mentioned; denying he'd ever heard of, let alone had dealings with, a former Stasi agent named Bernhard Oven; avowing he'd been in the United States and nowhere near Paris at the time of Merriman's murder. And those sworn testimonies, backed by the prominence of those who had given them, would in effect, warrant Scholl's complete innocence. Adding to that the fact there was no real evidence, the charges would be promptly dismissed.

And then, perhaps a year or more later, with Scholl's name and person fully distanced and the episode all but forgotten, would come the cold, detached retribution Honig had warned about. And McVey, Noble, Remmer and Osborn would see their careers and then their lives crumble into nothing. Friends, co-workers and people they'd never heard of would come forward with accusations of theft, corruption, sexual depravity, malpractice and worse. Their families would be held up to ridicule and their once-proud names would be splashed across media headlines for as long as it took to ruin them. Compared to them, Humpty-Dumpty would be a great granite edifice, chiseled eternally whole alongside the other grand survivors atop the cliffs at Mount Rushmore.

With a squeal of tires Remmer wheeled out of the garage and onto Hardenbergstrasse with a federal police escort car right behind.

Five minutes later, he pulled into a garage on a street across from the twenty-two-story glass-and-steel Europa-Center. *"Auf Wiedersehen. Danke,"* he said into his radio.

"Auf bald." See you later. The escort car accelerated off in traffic.

"I assume you feel we're safe," Noble said, as Remmer pulled into a spot away from the entrance.

"Sure we're safe." Getting out, Remmer lifted the submachine gun from its door holder and locked it in the trunk. Then, lighting a cigarette, he led them down a ramp, through a steel utility door and along a corridor filled with electrical and plumbing conduit that ran directly under the street above and connected to the Europa-Center complex on the far side.

"Do we know where Scholl is?" McVey's voice echoed in the long chamber.

"The Grand Hotel Berlin. On Friedrichstrasse, across the Tiergarten. From here, a long walk for an aging gentleman like yourself." Remmer grinned at McVey, then pushed through a fire door at the end of the corridor. Stabbing out his cigarette in an ashtray, he stopped at a service elevator and pressed the button. The door opened almost immediately and the four entered. Remmer punched the sixth-floor button, the doors closed and they started up. It was only then that Osborn realized Remmer had been carrying a gun at his side the entire time.

Looking at the three as they stood there silently in the pale light of the elevator, he felt wholly out of place, as if he were a fifth for bridge or the best man at an ex-wife's wedding. These were veteran policemen, professionals, whose lives were intertwined in that world like so much muscle and bone. The warrant in McVey's pocket had come from one of the state's most prestigious criminal judges and the man they were going up against was very nearly a world figure who would have an army of his own. McVey had told him the reason he was coming with them to Berlin was to give a deposition, and he had. And now there was no need for him. Was he so naïve as to believe McVey was actually going to go the next step and honor what he'd said and let him come along when he confronted Scholl? Suddenly a knot tightened in his stomach. McVey didn't give a damn about Osborn's personal war. His agenda was his and nobody else's.

"What is it?" McVey caught him staring at him.

"Just thinking," Osborn said quietly.

"Don't overdo it." McVey didn't smile.

The elevator slowed and then stopped. The door opened and Remmer stepped out first. Satisfied, he led them down a carpeted hallway. They were in a hotel. The Hotel Palace. Osborn saw a brochure on a table as they passed.

Then Remmer stopped and knocked on the door to room 6132. The door opened and a stocky, tough-looking detective ushered them into a large suite that had two good-sized bedrooms connected by a narrow hallway. The windows in both rooms angled out toward the green of the Tiergarten park, with the window in the first room looking at an angle toward rooms in what appeared to be a newer wing.

Remmer slipped the gun inside his jacket and turned to talk to the detective who had let them in. McVey went into the hallway and looked into the second bedroom. Then came back. Noble wasn't particularly fond of the proximity of the new wing, which had any number of rooms that could see, albeit on a slant, into theirs, and said so. McVey agreed.

The stocky detective threw up his hands and told them with a heavy accent they'd been lucky to get rooms at all, let alone a suite. Berlin was alive with trade shows and conventions. Even the federal police didn't have a lot of pull when rooms had been overbooked three months in advance.

"Manfred, in that case, we're overjoyed," McVey said. Remmer nodded, then said something in German to the detective and the man left. Remmer locked the door behind him.

"You and I'll camp out here," McVey said to Remmer. "Noble and Osborn can have the other room." Crossing to the window, he fingered the feather-light material of the draw shade and looked down at the traffic on the Kurfürstendamm below. "Phones secured?" His gaze lifted to the dark expanse that was the Tiergarten across the street.

"Two lines." Remmer lit a cigarette and took off his leather jacket, revealing a muscular upper body and an old-fashioned leather shoulder holster that cradled what Osborn now saw was a very large automatic.

McVey pulled off his own jacket and looked at Noble. "Check on the situation with Lebrun, huh? See if they've found who the shooter was. How he got in. What the word is on Cadoux. See if anybody knows where he went, where he is now. We need to determine if he was there by chance or on purpose." Hanging up his jacket, he looked at Osborn. "Make yourself at home. We're gonna be here for a while." Then he went into the bathroom and washed his hands and face. When he came out he was drying his hands on a towel and talking to Remmer.

"This Charlottenburg deal tomorrow night. Let's find out what it is and who's going to be there. I trust your people in Bad Godesberg can do that for us."

Osborn left them, went into the second bedroom and looked around. He was working like hell to control the paranoia growing inside him. Twin beds with olive-and-blue bedspreads. Small table between the beds. Two small chests of drawers. A TV. A window looking out. Its own bathroom. He knew McVey's mind was tracking the whole, a field officer with a slim ace up his sleeve maneuvering a small combat unit against a king's army and searching every way possible to gain advantage against it. Osborn wasn't even in his thoughts. He'd been purposely roomed with Noble so McVey wouldn't find himself in a position where they would be alone and Osborn might ask questions. Because then McVey would be in the awkward situation of having to explain why Osborn would not be going along when they went to meet Scholl. That was smart. String him along. Save it to the last minute. Just go out the door saying, "Sorry, this is police business." Then leave him in the custody of the federal police waiting outside in the hallway.

96

"PRIVATE DINNER. Black tie. One hundred guests. Invitation only." Remmer was sitting in his shirt sleeves at a small table, a coffee cup in one hand, a cigarette in the other. In the last hour a half-dozen calls had gone back and forth between Remmer and operatives at the Intelligence Division at Bundeskriminalamt—BKA—Headquarters in Bad Godesberg as they tried to work a profile of the affair at Charlottenburg Palace.

Osborn sat in the room with them, his sleeves rolled up, watching McVey pace up and down in his stockinged feet.

He'd decided the best thing would be to use McVey as McVey had used him. Quietly, unassumingly. Try to find some way to take advantage of his situation without giving the police any sense of what he was thinking. The Hotel Palace, he'd learned, was part of the giant Europa-Center complex of shops and casinos smack in the heart of Berlin. The Tiergarten, directly across from them, was like Central Park in New York, huge and sprawling, with roads cutting through it and pathways everywhere. From what he'd been able to conclude from a variety of conversations between the policemen themselves and a battery of phone conversations with others, besides the plainclothes BKA detectives stationed in the hallway outside their room, others were downstairs working two-man shifts watching the lobby, two more were posted on the roof and backup radio-car units were on standby alert. A security check had been done on the guests occupying the six rooms in the wing across with sight lines into theirs. Four were occupied by Japanese tourists from Osaka, the other two by businessmen attending a computer trade show. One was from Munich, the other from Disney World in Orlando. All were who they said they were. What it meant was they were about as safe as they could be even if the "group" had discovered where they were and tried to do something about it. The problem was, it also meant Osborn's chances of doing anything other than what McVey wanted were all but nil.

"A Swiss corporation called the Berghaus Group is giving it." Remmer was reading from notes he'd scratched on a yellow legal pad. To his left, Noble was talking animatedly on the telephone, a pad like Remmer's at his elbow.

"The occasion is a welcoming celebration for an—" Remmer looked at his notes again. "Elton Karl Lybarger. An industrialist from Zurich who had a severe stroke a year ago in San Francisco and has now fully recovered."

"Who the hell is Elton Lybarger?" McVey asked.

Remmer shrugged. "Never heard of him. Or this Berghaus Group either. Intelligence Division is working on it, also on providing us with the guest list."

Noble hung up and turned around. "Cadoux sent a coded message to my office saying he fled the hospital because he was afraid the police on guard had let Lebrun's killer in. That they were part of the 'group' and would get him next. He said he would be in contact when he could."

"When did he send it and from where?" McVey asked.

"It came in little more than an hour ago. It was faxed from Gatwick Airport."

Held up by fog, Von Holden's jet touched down at Tempelhof Airport at 6:35, three hours later than planned. At 7:30, he got out of a taxi on Spandauerdamm and crossed the street to Charlottenburg Palace, now dark and closed for the evening. He was tempted to go around and in through a side door to personally check out the final security preparations. But Viktor Shevchenko had done it twice today already and reported to him en route. And Viktor Shevchenko he would trust with his life.

Instead, he stood there looking in through the iron gates, visualizing what would be taking place in less than twenty-four hours. He could see it and hear it. And the thought that they were on the eve of it thrilled him almost to the point of tears. Finally, he let it go and began to walk.

As of five o'clock that afternoon, Berlin sector had established that McVey, Osborn and the others had arrived in the city and were headquartered at the Hotel Palace where they were under the protection of the federal police. It was exactly as Scholl had predicted, and he was no doubt right as well when he'd said they had come to Berlin to see him. Lybarger was not on their agenda, nor was the ceremony at Charlottenburg.

Find them, watch them, Scholl had said. At some point they will try and get in touch, to arrange a time and place where we can meet. That will be our opportunity to isolate them. And then you and Viktor will do as is appropriate.

Yes, Von Holden thought, as he walked on—we shall do as is appropriate. As quickly and resourcefully as possible.

Still, Von Holden was uncomfortable. He knew Scholl was underestimating them, McVey in particular. They were smart and experienced and they had also been very lucky. It was not a good combination, and it meant whatever plan he came up with would have to be exceptionally resourceful, one in which experience and luck would play as little a hand as possible. His real preference was to take the initiative and get it done quickly, before they had the chance to implement their own plans. But getting to four men, at least three of whom would be armed, guarded by police in a hotel that was part of a complex as huge as the Europa-Center, was all but impossible. It would require significant overt action. It would be too bloody, too loud and nothing would be guaranteed. Besides, if something went wrong and anyone were caught, it chanced compromising the entire Organization at the worst possible time.

So, unless they made an unthinkable mistake and somehow left themselves open, he would stay with Scholl's orders and wait for them to make the first move. From his own experience he knew there was little question that whatever countermeasure he devised would be successful as long as he was there to command the operation personally. He also knew his energy was better spent on the logistics of a working plan than worrying about his adversaries. But they were a troubling presence and he was uncomfortable almost to the point of requesting Scholl postpone the celebration at Charlottenburg until they had been taken care of. But that was not possible. Scholl had said so from the beginning.

Turning a corner, he walked a half block, then went up the steps to a quiet apartment building at number 37 Sophie-Charlottenstrasse and pressed the bell.

"Ja?" a voice challenged through the intercom.

"Von Holden," he said. There was a sharp buzz as the door lock released and he climbed the flight of stairs to the large second-floor apartment that had been taken over as security headquarters for the Lybarger party. A uniformed guard opened the door and he walked down a hallway past a bank of desks where several secretaries were still working.

"Guten Abend." Good evening, he said quietly and opened the door to a small but serviceable office. The problem was, his thought train continued, the longer they stayed in the hotel without contacting Scholl, the less time he had to formulate a plan of action and the more time they would have to work out a blueprint of their own. But that was something he had already begun to turn in his favor. Time went both ways, and the longer they were there, the longer he had to set the forces in motion that would tell him how much they knew and what they were plotting.

97

"GUSTAV DORTMUND, Hans Dabritz, Rudolf Kaes, Hilmar Grunel—" Remmer put down the faxed description sheet and looked across to where McVey sat reading the same five-page copy of the Charlottenburg guest list. "Herr Lybarger has some very wealthy and influential friends."

"And some not so wealthy, but just as influential," Noble said, studying his own copy of the list. "Gertrude Biermann, Matthias Noll, Henryk Steiner."

"Politically, far left to far right. Normally they wouldn't be caught in the same room together." Remmer shook out a cigarette, lit it, then leaned over and poured himself a glass of mineral water from a bottle on the table.

Osborn leaned against the wall, watching. He'd not been given a copy of the guest list nor had he asked for one. In the last hours, as more information came in and the detectives increased their concentration on it, he'd been almost wholly ignored. Its effect was to alienate him further and intensify the feeling he'd had earlier: that when they left to meet Scholl, he would not be going.

"Naturalized or not, Scholl seems to be the only American. Am I right?" McVey asked, looking at Remmer.

"Everyone else identified is German," Remmer said. There were seventeen names on the guest list Bad Godesberg had so far been unable to trace. But with the exception of Scholl, all of those who had been identified were highly respected, if politically disparate, German citizens.

Looking at the list again, Remmer exhaled a cloud of cigarette smoke that McVey waved off as it passed him.

"Manfred, you mind? Why don't you just up and quit, huh?" Remmer glared and started to reply but McVey held up a hand. "I'm gonna die, I know. But I don't want you to be the one who takes me out."

"Sorry," Remmer said flatly, and stamped the butt into an ashtray.

Increasingly irritable snippets of conversation, underscored by long periods of silence, evidenced the collective frustrations of three markedly tired men trying to piece together what was going on. Beside the fact that the Charlottenburg celebration was being held in a palace instead of a hotel ballroom, on the surface it seemed to be no more than that, the kind of thing done hundreds of times a year by groups all over the world. But the surface was only the surface, and the interest was in what lay beneath. Among them they had more than a hundred years of experience as professional policemen. It gave them an instinct for things others wouldn't have. They had come to Berlin because of Erwin Scholl and, as far as they could tell, Erwin Scholl had come to Berlin because of Elton Lybarger. The question was—Why?

The "why?" became even more intriguing when one realized that, of all the illustrious people invited to the affair in his honor, Lybarger was the least illustrious and least known of any of them.

Bad Godesberg's search of records showed him born Elton Karl Lybarger in Essen, Germany, in 1933, the only child of an impoverished stonemason. Graduated public school in 1951, he'd vanished into the mainstream of postwar Germany. Then, thirty-odd years later, in 1983, he'd suddenly reemerged as a multimillionaire, living in a castle-like estate called Anlegeplatz twenty minutes outside Zurich, surrounded by servants, and controlling considerable shares of any number of first-rate Western European corporations.

The question was—How?

Early income tax filings from 1956 until 1980 showed his occupation as "bookkeeper," and gave addresses that were drab, lower-class apartment complexes in Hannover, Düsseldorf, Hamburg and Berlin, and then, finally, in 1983, Zurich. And in every year until 1983 his income had barely reached the mean wage. Then, with the 1983 filing, his income soared. By 1989, the year of his stroke, his taxable income was in the stratosphere, more than forty-seven million dollars.

And there was nothing, anywhere, to explain it. People were successful, yes. Sometimes almost overnight. But how did anyone, after years of work as an itinerant bookkeeper, living in a world a foot up from poverty, suddenly emerge as a man of opulent wealth and influence?

Even now, he remained a mystery. He sat on the boards of no European corporations, universities, hospitals or charities. He held membership in no private clubs, had no registered political affiliation. He had no driver's license or record of marriage. There wasn't so much as a credit card issued in his name. So who was he? And why were one hundred of Germany's richest and most influential citizens arriving from all parts of the country to applaud his health?

Remmer's reasoned guess was that in all those years, Lybarger had been secretly dealing in the drug world, moving from city to city, amassing a fortune in cash and laundering it into Swiss banks, where in 1983 he had enough to suddenly go legitimate.

McVey shook his head. There was something that struck both him and Noble the moment they had seen the guest list. Something they hadn't shared with Remmer. Two of the names on it—Gustav Dortmund and Konrad Peiper—were principals, along with Scholl, in GDG—Goltz Development Group, the company that had acquired Standard Technologies of Perth Amboy, New Jersey. The firm that in 1966 had employed Mary Rizzo York to experiment with super-subzero cooling gasses. The same Mary Rizzo York, Ph.D., Erwin Scholl had allegedly hired Albert Merriman to murder in that same year.

It was true that takeover had happened at a time when only Scholl and Dortmund were involved with GDG. Konrad Peiper hadn't come aboard until 1978. But since then, as its president, he had forged GDG to the forefront, however illegally, as a world-class arms supplier. The obvious was that both before Peiper and afterward, Goltz Development was hardly a wholesome, straightforward operation.

When McVey asked Remmer what he knew of Dortmund, the German detective joked and said that aside from his relatively minor position as head of the Bundesbank, the central bank of Germany, Dortmund was already one of the pedigreed super-rich. Like the Rothchilds, his family had been one of the great European banking families for more than two centuries.

"So, like Scholl, he's beyond reproach," McVey said.

"It would take one hell of a scandal to bring him down, if that's what you mean."

"What about Konrad Peiper?"

"Him, I know almost nothing about. He's rich and has an extraordinarily beautiful wife who has a great deal of money and influence of her own. But all one really needs to know about Konrad Peiper is that his paternal grand-uncle, Friedrich, was supplier of arms to half the planet in both world wars. Today that same company does very well making coffeepots and dishwashers."

McVey looked at Noble, who merely shook his head. The thing was as mystifying now as when they started. The Charlottenburg affair had attracted a gathering that included Scholl, the chief of the Bundesbank, the head of an international munitions trade and a guest list of German citizens who were the Who's Who of the ultra-rich and powerful and the truly politically connected; many of whom, under other circumstances, would be philosophically and maybe even physically at each other's throats. Yet here they all were, coming arm in arm to an ornate museum built by Prussian kings, to celebrate the return to wellness of a man with a history so shadowy you could put a hand through it.

And then there was the Albert Merriman situation and the swath of horror that had followed it, including the sabotaging of the Paris-Méaux train and the murders of Lebrun in England, his brother in Lyon and the gunning down of Benny Grossman in New York. Not to mention the hidden Nazi past of Hugo Klass, the respected fingerprint expert at Interpol, Lyon, and Rudolf Halder, the man in charge of Interpol, Vienna.

"The first one taken out was Osborn's father, in April 1966, just after he designed a very special kind of scalpel." McVey padded a few feet across the carpet and sat down on the window ledge. "The latest was Lebrun, sometime this morning," he said, bitterly. "Shortly after he connected Hugo Klass to the killing of Merri-man .... And from first to last, one link through it all, the straight line, from then until now is—"

"Erwin Scholl," Noble finished for him.

"And now we're back to square one with the same questions. "*Why* For what reason? What the hell is going on?" Most of McVey's career had been spent on the circular route, asking the same question hundreds of times. That's what you did in homicide, unless you just happened to walk in and find somebody holding a smoking gun. And almost always the route ended with a detail overlooked until then, one that was suddenly as clear as if it had been a huge rock sitting there the whole time with the word *CLUE* spray-painted on it in red.

But not this one. This was a circle with a beginning but no end. It was round and kept going. The more information they garnered, the bigger the circle got and that was all.

"The headless bodies," Noble said.

McVey threw up his hands. "All right, why not? Let's work that angle."

"What angle? What are you talking about—?" Remmer looked from Noble to McVey and back again.

Remmer's Bundeskriminalamt, like all police agencies in the countries where the decapitated bodies had been found, received copies of McVey's status reports to Interpol. Purposely, McVey had not informed Interpol about the bodies' ultra-deep-freezing or the projections about the experiments that lay behind the freezing. So naturally Remmer was in the dark; he didn't know enough. Under the circumstances, now seemed an extraordinarily good time to tell him.

98

GERD LANG was a good-looking, curly-headed, computer software designer from Munich, in Berlin for a three-day computer arts show. He was staying in room 7056 in the new Casino wing of the Hotel Palace. Thirty-two and coming off a painful divorce, it was only natural that, when an attractive twenty-four-year-old blonde with an engaging smile struck up a conversation with him on the showroom floor, and began asking him questions about what he did and how he did it, and how she could develop skills in that direction, he would invite her to discuss it over a drink and perhaps dinner. It was an unfortunate decision because, after several drinks and very little dinner, and feeling emotionally cheered after a very long depression over his divorce, he was hardly in a state to be fully prepared for what would happen when she accepted his invitation for an after-dinner drink in his room.

His first thoughts, as they'd sat on the couch touching and exploring each other in the dark, had been that she was simply reaching out to stroke his neck. Then her fingers had tightened and she'd smiled as if she were teasing and asked him if he liked it. When he started to reply, they'd locked in a vise grip. His immediate reaction had been to reach up and jerk her hands away. But he couldn't—she was incredibly strong and she smiled as she watched his attempt, as if it were some sort of game. Gerd Lang struggled to throw her off, to tear out of her iron grasp, but nothing worked. His face turned red and then deep purple. And his last living thought, crazy and perverse as it was, was that the whole time she never stopped smiling.

Afterward, she carried his body into the bathroom, put him in the tub and pulled the curtain. Coming back into the living room, she took a pair of day/night field binoculars from her handbag and trained them on the lighted window of room 6132 at an angle across and one floor below. Adjusting the focus, she could see a translucent curtain had been pulled across it and what appeared to be a man with white hair standing just inside it. Switching to night vision, she swung the glasses up toward the roof. In the greenish glow of the night scope she could see a man standing just back from the edge, an automatic rifle slung over his shoulder.

"Police," she breathed and swung the glasses back toward the window.

Osborn sat on the edge of a small table, listening as McVey gave Remmer a basic primer on cryonic physics, then told him the rest: about what appeared to be an attempt at joining a severed head to a different body through a process of atomic surgery that was performed at temperatures at or near absolute zero. It was a narrative that, as Osborn now heard it, bordered perilously on science fiction. Except it wasn't, because someone was either doing it, or trying to do it. And Remmer, standing with one foot on a straight-backed chair, the blue steel automatic dangling from his shoulder holster, hung, fascinated, on McVey's every word.

Suddenly it all faded as Osborn was hit by the stark and overwhelming thought that McVey might not be able to pull it off. That as good as he was, maybe this time he was in over his head and that Scholl would get the upper hand as Honig had suggested. What then?

The question was no question at all because Osborn knew the answer. Every inch he had gained, as close as he had finally come, it would all blow up in his face. And with it would go every ounce of hope he ever had in his life. Because from that moment on no one from the outside world would ever get that close to Erwin Scholl again.

"Excuse me," he said abruptly. Getting to his feet, he

brushed past Remmer and went into the room he was sharing with Noble and stood there in the dark. He could hear their voices filtering in from the other room. They were talking as they had before. It made no difference if he was there or not. And tomorrow it would be the same when, warrant in hand, they would walk out the door to visit Scholl, leaving him behind in the hotel room, with only a BKA detective for company.

For no reason the room suddenly felt unbearably close and claustrophobic. Going into the bathroom, he switched on the light and looked for a glass. Seeing none, he cupped his hand and bent over and drank from the faucet. Then he held his wet hand to the back of his neck and felt its coolness. In the mirror he saw Noble enter the room, pick something off the dresser, then glance in at him before going back to the others.

Reaching to shut off the water, his eyes were drawn to his own image. The color was gone from his face and sweat had beaded up on his forehead and upper lip. He held out his hand and it was trembling. As he stood there, he became aware of the thing stirring inside him again and at almost the same time heard the sound of his own voice. It was so clear that for a moment he thought he'd actually spoken out loud.

"Scholl is here in Berlin, in a hotel across the park."

Suddenly his entire body shuddered and he was certain he was going to faint. Then the feeling passed, and as it did one thing became unequivocally clear. This was something McVey was not going to steal from him, not after everything. Scholl was too close. Whatever it took, however he had to circumvent the men in the other room, he could not and would not live another twenty-four hours without knowing why his father had been murdered.

99

THE VIGNETTE of three men talking in a hotel room could be interesting or dull, especially when seen from a darkened room at an angle across from them and photographed in close-up by a motor drive camera using a telephoto lens.

The camera was abruptly discarded in favor of binoculars as a fourth man emerged from a back room, pulling on a suit coat. One of the initial three got up and went to him. There was a brief conversation, then one of the others picked up the telephone. A moment later he hung up and the first man started for the door. He was almost to it when he turned and said something to the man who had gone to him. The man hesitated, then he turned and went out of sight. When he came back he gave the first man something. Then the man opened the door and left.

Putting aside the binoculars, the attractive blonde with the dead software designer working toward rigor mortis in the elegant marble bathroom only feet away picked up a two-way radio. "Natalia," she said.

"Lugo," came the reply.

"Osborn just left."

Osborn was certain McVey would never have given him the automatic, or even let him out of the room, if he'd known what he meant to do. He'd simply said that he had nothing to contribute to the police business, that he was feeling a little woozy and claustrophobic, and wanted to go for a walk to clear his head.

It was then five minutes to ten, and McVey, overly tired and with a great deal on his mind, had considered, then finally agreed. Asking Remmer to have one of the BKA detectives go with him, he'd warned him not to leave the complex and to be back by eleven.

Osborn hadn't protested, just nodded and started for the door. It was then he'd turned and asked McVey for the pistol. It was a calculated move on Osborn's part, but he knew McVey would have to seriously evaluate what had happened and realize, police protection or not, all Osborn was asking for was a little extra insurance. Still, it had been a long, uncomfortable moment before McVey relented and gave him Bernhard Oven's Cz automatic.

Osborn hadn't gone a dozen paces toward the elevator when he was met by BKA Inspector Johannes Schneider. Schneider was about thirty and tall, with a flat hump across the bridge of his nose that suggested it had been broken more than once.

"You want to get some air," he said breezily in accented English. "Let's got for it."

Earlier, when they'd first settled in, Osborn had found a brochure that described the Europa-Center as a complex with more than a hundred shops, restaurants, cabarets and a casino. It was complete with diagrams marking venue locations and building entrances and exits.

Osborn smiled. "Have you ever been to Las Vegas, Inspector Schneider?" he asked.

"No, I haven't."

"I like to gamble a little," Osborn said. "How is the casino here?"

"Spielbank Casino? Excellent and expensive." Schneider grinned.

"Let's go for it." Osborn grinned back.

Taking the elevator down, they stopped at the hotel's front desk while Osborn changed his remaining French francs into Deutschmarks, then he let Schneider lead the way to the casino.

Fifteen minutes later, Osborn asked the policeman to

take over his hand at the baccarat table while he made a quick trip to the men's room. Schneider saw him ask a security guard for directions and walk off.

Osborn crossed the casino floor and turned a corner, made sure Schneider hadn't followed, then walked out. Stopping at a newsstand in the lobby, he bought a tourist map of the city, put it in his pocket and went out a side door, taking a left on Nurnbergerstrasse.

Across the street, Viktor Shevchenko saw him come out. Dressed in jeans and a dark sweater, he was standing on the sidewalk just out of the glare of a brightly lit Greek restaurant listening to heavy metal through the headset of what appeared to be a Sony Walkman. Lifting his hand as if to stifle a cough, he spoke into it.

"Viktor."

Lugo." Von Holden's voice crackled through Viktor's headset.

"Osborn just came out alone. He's crossing Budapester-strasse toward the Tiergarten."

Dodging traffic, Osborn crossed Budapesterstrasse to the far sidewalk and glanced back toward the Europa-Center. If Schneider was following, he couldn't see him. Stepping back from the glare of the streetlights, he started off in the direction of the Berlin Zoo, then, sensing he was going in the wrong direction, turned back the way he had come. The pavement was covered with leaves made slick by a light drizzle and the air was cold enough for him to see his breath. Looking back, he saw a man in a raincoat and hat slowly walking a dog that wanted to sniff at every tree and lamppost. There was still no sign of Schneider. Picking up his pace, he walked a good two hundred yards farther before stopping under the lighted overhang of a parking structure, and opened the map.

It took several minutes before he found what he was

looking for. Friedrichstrasse was on the far side of the Brandenburg Gate. By his estimate it was a ten-minute cab ride or a half hour walk through the Tiergarten. A taxi they could trace. Walking was better. Besides, it would give him time to think.

"Viktor?"

"Lugo," Von Holden's voice said.

"I have him. He's walking east. Going into the Tiergarten."

Von Holden was still in his office in the apartment on Sophie-Charlottenstrasse. He was on his feet talking into his two-way radio, unable to believe his good luck.

"Still alone?"

"Yes." Viktor's voice was crystal clear through the radio's tiny speaker.

"The fool."

"Instructions?"

"Follow him. I will be there in five minutes."

100

NOBLE HUNG up and looked at McVey. "Still nothing from Cadoux. Nor is there an answer at his confidential number in Lyon."

Disturbed and frustrated, McVey looked to Remmer, who was on his third cup of black coffee in the last forty minutes. They'd been over the guest list twenty times and, despite the handful of names Bad Godesberg still had been unable to trace, had found nothing more than they had the first time they went over it. Maybe somewhere among those missing people they'd find a key, maybe they wouldn't. It was McVey's sense they should be concentrating on what they had as opposed to what they didn't, and he asked Remmer to see if they could get a more comprehensive breakdown on the guests that had already been identified. Maybe it wasn't who the people were or what they did, maybe, like Klass and Halder, it had to do with their families or their backgrounds, something more than was immediately apparent.

Perhaps they hadn't had enough to go on to begin with, to make the process work and uncover the big rock with the red *CLUE* on it they were after. Then again, maybe there was nothing here at all. It could be that Scholl was in Berlin legitimately and the whole Lybarger thing was nothing more than what it appeared: an innocent testimonial to a man who had been ill. But McVey wasn't going to let it go until he knew for sure. And while they were waiting for more from Bad Godesberg, they went around again, this time coming back to Cadoux.

"Let's take the Klass/Halder situation and point it at Cadoux." McVey was sitting in a chair with his feet up on one of the twin beds. "Could he have had a father, brother, cousin, whatever—who might have been Nazis or Nazi sympathizers during the war?"

"Did you ever hear of Ajax?" Remmer asked.

Noble looked up. "Ajax was a network of French police who worked with the Resistance during the Occupation. After the war they discovered only five percent of its members actually resisted. Most of them were smuggling for the Vichy government."

"Cadoux's uncle was a judicial cop. A member of Ajax in Nice. After the war he was relieved of duty following a purge of Nazi collaborators," Remmer said.

"What about his father, was he in Ajax too?"

"Cadoux's father died the year after he was born."

"You're saying his uncle raised him," McVey said, then sneezed.

"Correct."

McVey stared off, then got up and walked across the room. "Is that what this is all about, Manny? Nazis? Is Scholl a Nazi? Is Lybarger?" Coming back, he picked the guest list from the bed. "Are all these wealthy, educated, prominent people—a new breed of German Nazi?"

Just then the light on the fax machine went on. There was a whirring sound and the paper rolled out. Remmer picked it off the machine and read it.

"There is no birth record for an Elton Lybarger in Essen in 1933 or bracketing years. They are checking further." Remmer read on, then looked up. "Lybarger's castle in Zurich."

"What about it?"

"It's owned by Erwin Scholl."

Osborn had no idea what he was going to do when he got to the Grand Hotel Berlin. The thing with Albert Merriman in Paris had been different. He'd had time to plan, to think out a course of action while Jean Packard tracked Merriman down. The obvious question now, as he walked a lighted pathway that cut through the dark lawns and trees of Tiergarten, was threefold—how to get Scholl alone, how to make him talk, what to do afterward.

Imagining what a man in Scholl's position must be like, it was safe to assume he would have an entourage of assistants and hangers-on, and at least one bodyguard, maybe more. That meant getting him alone would be extremely difficult, if not impossible.

That aside, assuming he did get him alone, what would make Scholl reveal what he wanted revealed? Say what he wanted him to say? Scholl, as Diedrich Honig had professed, with or without lawyers, would deny that he ever heard of Albert Merriman, Osborn's father or any of the others. Succinylcholine might work, as it had on Merriman, but he had no allies in Berlin to help him get it. For an instant his mind went to Vera. How she was, where she was. Why any of this had to be. As quickly he put it away. He had to keep his concentration on Scholl. Nothing else.

They could see him ahead of them, maybe two hundred yards. He was still alone, walking on a path that, in a few moments, would take him to the edge of the park near Brandenburg Gate.

"How do you want to do it?" Viktor asked.

"I want to look him in the eyes," Von Holden said.

Osborn glanced at his watch: 10:35.

Would Schneider still be hunting for him or would he have already reported him missing to Remmer? If he had, McVey would have alerted the Berlin police and he would have to be on the lookout for them as well. He had no passport and McVey might well let them throw him in jail just to keep him out of the way.

Abruptly the thought came that maybe that wasn't so. And with it the notion that he could have been wrong about the other thing, too. He was as tired as the rest of them. Maybe his worry that McVey would leave him behind when they went after Scholl was just that. He'd sought out McVey's help in the first place and come this far with him. Why was he turning his back on him now and trying to do everything alone? It was all coming in a rush. His emotions running away with him as they had for almost thirty years. He was too close to the end to let them ruin everything now. Didn't he understand that? He'd wanted to be strong and take his responsibility, his love for his father, into his own hands and end it. But this wasn't the way, he didn't have the tools or the experience to do it alone, not with somebody like Scholl. He'd realized that in Paris. Why didn't he now?

Suddenly he felt disoriented and terribly confused. What had been so decisive and purposeful such a short time before now seemed filmy, even vague, as if it were in a distant past. He had to stop his mind from working. For even a little while, he had to not think.

Looking around, he tried to settle on the reality of where he was. It was still cold but the drizzle had ended. The park was deserted and dark and filled with trees. Only the lighted pathways and tall buildings in the distance assured him he was in the city and not the deep woods. Looking back, he saw that he had just crossed a place where five pathways came together in a kind of hub. Which had he come down? Which was he on now?

A few feet away was a park bench, and he walked over to it and sat down. He would give himself a few moments for his mind to clear and then decide what to do next. The cold air felt clean and good, and he breathed it in deeply. Absently, he put his hands in his jacket pockets to warm them. When he did, his right hand touched the automatic. It was like an object stuffed away long ago and forgotten. Just then, something made him look up.

A man was approaching. His collar turned up, he walked slightly hunched to the side, as if he had some sort of physical impairment. As he got closer, Osborn realized that he was taller than he looked, trim, with broad shoulders and close-cropped hair. He was only a few feet from him when he lifted his head and their eyes met.

"Guten Abend," Von Holden said.

Osborn nodded slightly, then turned away to avoid further contact, his hand sliding into his jacket pocket, gripping the automatic. The man was barely ten paces past him when he stopped and turned back. The move was unnerving, and Osborn reacted immediately. Jerking the pistol from his jacket, he pointed it directly at the man's chest.

"Go a-way!" he said, enunciating the English.

Von Holden stared at him for a moment, then let his eyes fall to the gun. Osborn was agitated and nervous but his hand was steady, his finger resting easily on the trigger. The gun was a Czech Cz. Small caliber but very accurate at close range. Von Holden smiled. The gun was Bernhard Oven's.

"What's funny?" Osborn snapped. As he did, he saw the man glance past him over his shoulder. Immediately Osborn stepped backward, keeping the gun where it was. Turning his head slightly, he looked to his right. A second man stood in the shadow of a tree, not fifteen feet away.

"Tell him to walk over next to you." Osborn's eyes came back to Von Holden.

Von Holden said nothing.

"Sprechen Sie Englisch?" Osborn said.

Still Von Holden was silent.

"Sprechen Sie Englisch?" Osborn said again, this time more forcefully.

Von Holden nodded ever so slightly.

"Then tell him to walk over to you." Osborn held back the hammer with his thumb, the gun's trigger pulled. If they rushed him, all he had to do was let his thumb slip sideways and the weapon would fire point-blank. "Tell him now!"

Von Holden waited a moment longer, then called out in German: "Do as he says."

At Von Holden's command, Viktor stepped from under the tree and slowly crossed over the grass to where Von Holden stood.

Osborn stared at them for a moment in silence, then backed slowly away, the gun still pointed at Von Holden's chest. He continued walking backward for another twenty yards. Then, passing under a tree, he turned and ran. Crossing a lighted pathway, he bounded up a short flight of steps and ran across the grass through still more trees. Looking back, he saw them come after him. Dark figures silhouetted for only an instant against the night sky as they came on the run through the stand of trees where he had just been.

Ahead, he could see bright lights and traffic. He looked back again. The trees blended into darkness. He had to assume they were still coming, but there was no way to tell. Heart pounding, feet slipping on the wet grass beneath him, he ran on. Finally he felt pavement and saw he'd reached the edge of the park. Streetlights and a steady flow of traffic were directly in front of him. Without stopping, he ran into the street. Horns blared. He dodged one car and then another. There was a shriek of tires, then a tremendous bang as a taxi swerved to avoid him and slammed into a parked car. A split second later, another car plowed into the taxi, a piece of its bumper scything off into the darkness.

Osborn didn't look back. His lungs on fire, he ducked behind a row of parked cars and ran low for a half block, then cut down a side street. There was an intersection in front of him and a brightly lit street. Breathless, he turned the corner and pushed quickly down a sidewalk filled with pedestrians.

Shoving the gun into his belt, he covered it with his jacket and kept on, trying to gather his wits. Passing a Burger King, he turned and looked behind him. Nothing. Maybe they hadn't come after him after all. Maybe it had been his imagination. He kept walking, moving with the crowd.

Several preposterously dressed teenagers passed him in the opposite direction and a dark-haired girl smiled at him. Why had he pulled the gun? All the man had done was turn around. For all he knew the second man might not even have been with him, just someone out for a walk. But the stranger's unnatural stance, the way he had turned back so measuredly after saying good evening, made Osborn believe he was going to be attacked. That was why he had done what he had. Of course it was. Better safe than set upon.

A clock in a window read 10:52.

Until this moment he'd totally forgotten McVey. In eight minutes he was due back to the hotel, and he had no idea where he was. What now? Call him? Make up a story, say you were—turning a corner, he saw the Europa-Center directly in front of him. Below it the lighted sign of the Hotel Palace hung over its motor entrance.

At six minutes to eleven, Osborn stepped into an elevator and pushed the button for the sixth floor. The doors closed and the elevator started up. He was alone and safe.

Trying to forget the men in the park, he glanced around the elevator. The wall next to him was a mirror, and he brushed back his hair and straightened his jacket. On the wall opposite was a tourism poster of Berlin with photographs of must-see attractions. Centermost was an exposure of Charlottenburg Palace. Suddenly he remembered what Remmer had said earlier. "The occasion is a welcoming celebration for an Elton Karl Lybarger. An industrialist from Zurich who had a severe stroke a year ago in San Francisco and has now fully recovered."

"Damn," he swore under his breath. "Damn."

He should have realized it before.

101

AT 10:58 exactly, Osborn knocked on the door to room 6132. A moment later McVey opened it. Five men stood behind him and they all stared in silence. Noble, Remmer, Detective Johannes Schneider and two uniformed members of the Berlin Police.

"Well, Cinderella," McVey said flatly.

"I got separated from Detective Schneider. I looked for him all over the place. What was I supposed to do?" Ignoring McVey's glare, Osborn crossed the room and picked up the telephone. There was a silence and then it rang through. "Doctor Mandel please," he said.

Remmer shrugged and thanked the Berlin cops and McVey shook hands with Schneider, then Remmer saw the three men out and closed the door.

"I'll call back, thank you." Osborn hung up and looked to McVey. "Tell me if I'm wrong," he said with an energy McVey hadn't seen since they'd left England, "but from everything I've been party to, arrest warrant or not, the chances of getting enough evidence to bring Scholl to trial, let alone get a conviction, are close to nil. He's too powerful, too connected, too far above the law. Right?"

"You have the floor, Doctor."

"Then let's look at it another way and ask why somebody like Scholl would come halfway around the world to honor a man who seems to hardly exist while at the same time apparently directing a wave of killings that snowballs as this thing at Charlottenburg gets closer."

Osborn glanced quickly at the others, then back to McVey. "Lybarger. I bet he's the key to this. And if we find out about him, I bet we find out a lot more about Erwin Scholl."

"You think you can turn up something the German federal police can't, help yourself," McVey said.

"I hope I am, McVey." Osborn nodded toward the phone. He was pumped up. Going it alone, he now knew, was impossible, but they weren't going to keep him out of the game either.

"That call was to Doctor Herb Mandel. He's not only the best vascular surgeon I know, he's chief of staff at San Francisco General Hospital. If it's true Lybarger had a stroke, he would have a *medical history*. And it would have begun in San Francisco.

Von Holden was angry. He should have shot Osborn on the approach, as he sat on the park bench. But he'd wanted to make sure he was the right man. Viktor and Natalia were both trustworthy, but they were only going by Osborn's photo. The problem was not so much that he might have killed the wrong man as it was in thinking he'd killed the right man when he hadn't. Which was why he'd come as close to Osborn as he had, even to the point of wishing him a good evening. Then Osborn had surprised him with the gun. It was something he should have been prepared for because it went hand-in-hand with Scholl's assessment that Osborn was emotionally charged and therefore highly unpredictable.

Even so, he should have been able to kill him. His glance at Viktor had been deliberate, designed to make Osborn turn and follow it. That instant would have been all he needed. But instead, Osborn had stepped backward to take in both men and at the same time kept the Cz pointed at Von Holden. The fact that he'd eased back the hammer with the trigger pulled meant that if he was shot, his thumb would slip off the hammer, discharging the gun directly at Von Holden. And Von Holden had been much too close to risk being hit.

It was true that as Osborn fled, and they ran after him

through the park, he'd had the opportunity for one clear shot. And if the American had stopped for so much as a millisecond instead of running full into traffic on Tiergartenstrasse, he would have had it. But he hadn't, and the two cars that crashed together immediately afterward had taken away his line of fire as well as any second opportunity.

Climbing the last steps to the apartment on Sophie-Charlottenstrasse, Von Holden was troubled not so much by his failure—because such things happened. What bothered him was an uneasiness in general. Osborn's isolation had been a gift and he, of all people, should have been able to carry through. But he hadn't. It seemed to be a pattern. Bernhard Oven should have eliminated him in Paris. He hadn't. Bombing the Paris-Meaux train should have resulted in the deaths of both Osborn and McVey, either in the crash itself or by the assassination team he'd assembled to kill them if they'd survived. But they were still alive. It wasn't luck as much as something else. And to Von Holden personally, it was something far more foreboding.

"Vorahnung."

It was a word that had haunted him since youth. It meant premonition and for him carried with it the portent of an untimely and terrible death. It was a feeling he had no control over. Something that seemed to exist on its own all around him. Strangely, the more he worked for Scholl, the more he began to realize that he too was under the same spell, and that his road, and the road of those who followed him, was ultimately doomed to catastrophe. Though certainly there was no proof, or even hint of it, because everything Scholl touched went the way he guided it, and had for years. Yet, the feeling remained.

There were times the sensation would ebb. Often for days, even months. But then it would come back. And with it would come terrible dreams, where great surreal curtains the translucent red and green of the Aurora Borealis and rising thousands of feet high would undulate up and down in the vortex of his mind like gigantic pistons. The terror came in their sheer size, and that he was helpless to do anything to control their existence.

And when he woke from these "things"—as he called them—he would be in a cold sweat and shivering with horror and he would force himself to stay awake the rest of the night for fear that if he slept, they would come again. He often wondered if he were ill with some chemical imbalance or even a brain tumor but knew that couldn't be because of the long periods of good health in between.

And then they'd vanished. Simply vanished. For almost five years he had been free of them and he was certain he was cured. In fact, in the last years he'd given them almost no thought whatsoever. That was until last night, when he'd learned McVey and the others had left London by private plane. There was no need to guess their destination, he already knew. And he'd gone to bed, afraid to sleep, knowing in his soul the "things" would come back. And they did. And they'd been more terrifying than ever.

Entering the apartment, Von Holden nodded to the guard and turned down a long hallway. When he reached the bank of secretaries' desks, a tallish, plump-faced woman with dyed red hair looked up from a computer check she was running of Charlottenburg's electronic security system.

"He is here," she said in German.

"*Danke*." Von Holden opened the door to his office and a familiar face smiled at him.

Cadoux.

102

IT WAS just after two in the morning. Three hours and a dozen phone calls after they'd begun, Osborn and McVey, working with Dr. Herb Mandel in San Francisco and Special Agent Fred Hanley of the Los Angeles office of the FBI, had put together a serviceable history of what had happened to Elton Lybarger while he was in the United States.

There was no record that any San Francisco area hospital had ever treated Lybarger as a stroke patient. But, in September of 1992, an E. Lybarger had been brought by private ambulance to the exclusive Palo Colorado Hospital in Carmel, California. He'd stayed there until March of 1993, when he had been transferred to Rancho de Piñon, an exclusive nursing home just outside Taos, New Mexico. Then, barely a week ago, he'd flown home to Zurich accompanied by his American physical therapist, a woman named Joanna Marsh.

The hospital in Carmel had provided facilities but no staff. Lybarger's own doctor and one nurse had accompanied him in the ambulance. A day later, four other medical attendants had joined them. The nurse and medical attendants carried Swiss passports. The doctor was Austrian. His name was Helmuth Salettl.

By 3:15 A.M., Bad Godesberg had faxed Remmer four copies of Dr. Helmuth Salettl's professional credentials and personal history, and Remmer handed them around, this time including Osborn.

Salettl was a seventy-nine-year-old bachelor who lived with his sister in Salzburg, Austria. Born in 1914, he had been a young surgeon in Berlin University at the outbreak of the war. Later an SS Group leader, Hitler made him commissioner for public health; then, in the final days of the war, had him arrested for trying to send secret documents to the Americans and sentenced him to be executed. Imprisoned in a villa outside Berlin awaiting execution, he was, at the last moment, moved to another villa in northern Germany where he was rescued by American troops. Interrogated by Allied officers at Camp Oberursel near Frankfurt, he was taken to Nuremberg, where he was tried and acquitted of "having prepared and carried out aggressive warfare." After that, he returned to Austria, where he practiced internal medicine until the age of seventy. Then he retired, treating only a few select patients. One of whom was Elton Lybarger.

"There it is again—" McVey finished reading and dropped the papers on the edge of the bed.

"The Nazi connection," Remmer said.

McVey looked to Osborn. "Why would a doctor spend seven months in a hospital sixty-five hundred miles from home overseeing the recovery of one stroke patient? That make any sense to you?"

"Not unless it was an extremely severe stroke and Lybarger was highly eccentric or neurotic, or his family was, and they were willing to pay through the nose for that kind of care."

"Doctor," McVey said emphatically. "Lybarger has no family. Remember? And if he was sick enough to need a physician at his side for seven months, he would have been in no shape to have set it up himself, at least not in the beginning."

"Somebody did. Somebody had to send Salettl and his medical crew to the U.S. and pay for it," Noble added.

"Scholl," Remmer said.

"Why not?" McVey ran a hand through his hair. "He owns Lybarger's Swiss estate. Why shouldn't we expect he'd run his other affairs as well? Especially where his health was concerned."

Noble wearily lifted a cup of tea from a room service tray at his elbow. "All of which brings up back to *why?*"

McVey eased down on the edge of the bed and for the umpteenth time picked up the five-page, single-spaced fax of the background dossiers on the Charlottenburg guests sent from Bad Godesberg. There was nothing in any of them to suggest they were anything other than successful German citizens. For a moment his thoughts went to the few names they had *not* been able to identify. Yes, he thought, the answer could be among them, but the odds were heavily against it. His gut still told him the answer was in front of them, somewhere in the information they already had.

"Manfred," he said, looking at Remmer. "We turn around, we poke, we look, we discuss, we get highly confidential information on private citizens through one of the world's most effective police agencies, and what happens? We keep coming up empty. We can't even open the door.

"But we know there's something there. Maybe it has something to do with what's going on tomorrow night, maybe it doesn't. But yes or no, sometime tomorrow, writ in hand, we're going to put our big fat fannies on the line, corner Scholl and ask him some questions. We're going to get one shot at it before the lawyers take over. And if we don't make him sweat enough to roll over right then and confess, or at least bend him enough so that he gives us something we can use to keep coming after him, if we don't know more at the end than we do at the beginning—"

"McVey," Remmer said carefully, "why are you calling me Manfred when you always call me Manny?"

"Because you're German and I'm singling you out. If this Lybarger thing should turn out to be a gathering of some kind of Nazi-like political force—what would they be about? Another shot at exterminating Jews?" McVey's voice became softer, yet more passionate. It wasn't that he expected an answer so much as an explanation. "Funding a military machine to blow through Europe and Russia with designs on the rest of us? A replay of what happened before? Why would anybody want that? Tell me, Manfred, because I don't know."

"I—" Remmer clenched a fist. "—don't know either...."

"You don't."

"No."

"I think you do."

The room was deathly silent. There were four men in it and not one moved. They barely breathed. Then Osborn thought he saw Remmer take a step backward.

"Come on, Manfred ...," McVey said lightly. But it wasn't intended lightly. He'd hit a nerve and he'd meant to, and it had caught Remmer off guard.

"It's unfair, Manfred, I know," McVey said quietly. "But I'm asking anyway. Because it just might help."

"McVey, I can't—"

"Yes you can."

Remmer glanced around the room. "Weltanschauung," he said in a voice just above a whisper. "Hitler's view of life. That it was an eternal struggle where only the strongest survived and the strongest of the strong ruled. To him, the Germans had once been the strongest of the strong. Therefore destined to rule. But that strength had become weakened over the generations because the true Germans race mixed with others far less superior. Hitler believed that throughout history the mixing of bloodlines was the sole cause of the dying out of old cultures. That was why Germany lost the first war, because the Aryan had already given up the purity of his blood. To Hitler, the Germans were the highest species on earth and could again become what they once were—but only through exceedingly careful breeding."

The hotel room had become a theater with an audience of three, and Remmer the sole actor on the stage. He stood with his shoulders thrown back. His eyes glistened and sweat stood out on his forehead. His voice had risen from a whisper to an oratory so concise it seemed, for the moment, to have been learned. Or, more rightly, learned, and then consciously forgotten.

"At the beginning of the Nazi movement, there were eighty-some million Germans; within a hundred years he envisioned two hundred and fifty million, maybe more. For that, Germany would need *Lebensraum*—living space, a lot of it, enough to assure the nation room for total freedom of existence on its own terms. But living space and the soil beneath it, Hitler said, exist only for the people who possess the force to take them. By this, he meant that the new Reich must again set itself along the road of the Teutonic knights. Obtain by the German sword sod for the German plow, and bread for the German stomach."

"So they set themselves back on the straight and narrow by wiping out six million Jews to keep them from sleeping around?" McVey sounded like an old country lawyer, as if somehow he'd missed something and didn't get it. He played it light because he knew Remmer would push back, defending what had happened. Defending his guilt.

"You have to understand what was going on. This was after a shattering defeat in World War One: the Treaty of Versailles had taken away our dignity, there was huge inflation, mass unemployment. Who was going to challenge a leader who was giving us back our pride and self-respect?— He enamored us and we became swept up in it, lost in it. Look at the old films, the photographs. Look at the faces of the people. They loved their Führer. They loved his words and the fire behind them. And because of that, it was totally forgotten that they were the words of an uneducated, demented man—" Remmer's expression went blank and he stopped, as if he'd suddenly forgotten his train of thought.

"*Why?*" McVey hissed like an offstage prompter. "We've had the history lesson, Manfred. Now tell us the truth. *Why* did you get swept up in Hitler's words? *Why* did you get lost in the ideas of and passion of an uneducated, demented man? You're blaming it all on one guy."

Remmer's eyes darted around the room. He'd gone as far as he could, or would.

"The Nazis were more than Hitler, Manfred." McVey was no longer the old country lawyer who didn't get it, he was a voice piercing Remmer's subconscious, demanding he dig deeper. "Powerful as he was, it wasn't just him—"

Remmer was staring at the floor. Slowly he raised his head, and when he did his eyes were filled with horror. "Like a religion, we believe the myths. They are primitive, tribal, inbred . . . and they lie just beneath the surface waiting for the moment in history when a charismatic leader will rise up to give them life. . . . Hitler was the last of them, and to this day we would follow him anywhere. . . . It is the old culture, McVey—of Prussia and long before. Teutonic knights riding out of the mists. Full in armor. Swords thrust high in iron-covered fists. Thundering hooves shaking the ground, trampling everything in their path. Conquerors. Rulers. Our land. Our destiny. We *are* superior. The master race. Pure-blooded German. Blond hair, blue eyes and all."

Remmer fixed McVey with a stare. Then, turning away, shook out a cigarette, lit it and crossed the room to sit down on a couch by himself. It was as far away as he could get from the others. Hunching forward, he pulled an ashtray toward him and looked at the floor. The cigarette between his nicotine-stained fingers remained untouched. The smoke from it wisped toward the ceiling.

103

OSBORN LAY in the dim light of daybreak listening to Noble's heavy breathing as it rose from the bed across from him. McVey and Remmer were asleep in the other room. They'd turned out the lights at 3:30, it was now a quarter to six. He doubted he'd slept two hours.

Since they'd been in Berlin, he'd felt McVey's growing frustration, even despair, as they'd tried to tear away the layers protecting Erwin Scholl. It was the reason McVey had put Remmer on the spot, trying, however brutally, to uncover some essential none of them had been able to grasp. And he had—it wasn't Teutonic knights riding out of the mist Remmer had been talking about. It was *arrogance*. The idea that they or anyone could dub themselves the "master race" and then set out to destroy everyone else in order to prove it. The word fit Scholl like a condom, the conceit of a man who could manipulate and murder and at the same time tout himself as father confessor to kings and presidents. It was an attitude they would have to deal with when they met Scholl face-to-face. Yet that's all it was, an angle, an edge up. It wasn't concrete.

Lybarger was. And Osborn was certain he remained central to everything. Yet there seemed to be nothing more they could uncover about him than the little they already had. The only thing of promise was that Dr. Salettl was on the Charlottenburg guest list, but so far the BKA had been unable to find him anywhere. Austria, Germany, or Switzerland. If he was coming, where was he?

Somehow, some way, there had to be more. But what? And where to find it?

* * *

McVey was awake, making notes, as Osborn came through the door.

"We keep assuming Lybarger has no family. But how do we know for certain?" McVey said forcefully.

"I'm an Austrian physician in Carmel, California, working with a gravely ill Swiss patient for seven months. Little by little he's getting better. A level of trust is developing. If he had a wife, child, brother—"

"He'd want them to know how he was," McVey filled in.

"Yes. And if he was a stroke victim like Lybarger, he would have trouble with his speech and probably his handwriting. Communicating would be a problem, so he'd ask me to do it for him. And I would. Not a letter, but a call. At least once a month, probably more."

Remmer, awake now, sat up. "Telephone company records."

Little more than an hour later, a fax came in from FBI Special Agent Fred Hanley in Los Angeles.

Page after page of telephone calls initiated from Salettl's private line at the Palo Colorado Hospital in Carmel, California. Seven hundred and thirty-six calls in all. Hanley had circled in red the more than fifteen separate numbers around the world made to Erwin Scholl, most of the rest were either local, or to Austria or Zurich. Interspersed among them, however, were twenty-five calls made to country code 49—Germany. The city code was 30—Berlin.

McVey put down the pages and turned to Osborn. "You're on a roll, Doctor." He glanced at Remmer. "It's your town, what do we do?"

"Same as L.A. We look her up."

7:45 A.M.

"This Karolin Henniger," McVey said, as Remmer pulled the Mercedes up in front of the expensive antique gallery on Kantstrasse. "I don't think we can assume she's a direct connection to Lybarger. She could be a relative of *Salettl's,* a friend, even a lover."

"I guess we'll find out, won't we?" McVey opened the door and got out. The plan was his and McVey let him run with it. He was an American doctor trying to locate a Dr. Salettl for a colleague in California. Remmer was a German friend, along to translate if Karolin Henniger did not speak English. Whatever she said, they'd take it from there.

McVey and Noble watched from the Mercedes as they went into the building. Across the street, backup BKA detectives kept surveillance from a light green BMW.

Earlier, as Remmer had run down Karolin Henniger's name and address, McVey had called an old friend in Los Angeles, Cardinal Charles O'Connel. Scholl, McVey knew, was Catholic and a major fund-raiser for both the New York and Los Angeles archdioceses and therefore would know O'Connel well. This was the one area where Scholl was like any other Catholic. If a cardinal made a personal request, it was granted, graciously and without question. McVey was in Berlin, he'd told O'Connel, and asked if the cardinal could arrange a late-afternoon meeting between himself and Scholl, who was also in Berlin. It was important. O'Connel did not ask why, only said he would do what he could and get back.

"It's important to understand," Remmer said, as he and Osborn climbed up the narrow stairs to the apartments on the gallery's top floor, "this woman has committed no crime and is under no obligation to answer questions. If she doesn't want to talk, she doesn't have to."

"Fine." Legal restrictions were something Osborn didn't want to think about. They were running out of time; getting some kind of a step up on Scholl was all that mattered.

Apartments 1 and 2 were immediately right and left at the top of the stairs. Apartment 3, at the end of a short hallway, was Karolin Henniger's.

Osborn reached the door first. Glancing at Remmer, he knocked. For a moment there was silence, then they heard footsteps, the dead bolt was thrown and the door opened to the chain lock. An attractive woman in a business suit looked out at them. She had short salt-and-pepper hair and was probably in her mid-forties.

"Karolin Henniger?" Osborn asked politely.

She looked at Osborn, then past him to Remmer. "*Ja*—" she said.

"Do you speak English?"

"Yes." She glanced at Remmer again. "Who are you? What do you want?"

"My name is Osborn. I'm a doctor from the United States. We're trying to locate someone you might know—a Doctor Helmuth Salettl."

Suddenly the woman went white. "I know no one by that name," she said. "No one, I'm sorry. *Auf Wiedersehen!*"

Stepping back, she shut the door. They heard the dead bolt fall and she shouted someone's name.

Osborn pounded on the door. "Please, we need your help!"

From inside, they heard her talking, her voice trailing away. Then came the distant thud of a door slam.

"She's going out the back." Osborn turned for the stairs.

Remmer put out a hand, restraining him. "Doctor, I warned you. She's within her rights, there's nothing we can do."

"Maybe *you* can't!" Osborn pushed past him.

McVey and Noble were in an exchange about the likelihood that Salettl himself might be the surgeon responsible for the headless bodies when Osborn came out the front door on the run.

"Come on!" he yelled, then cut a corner and disappeared down an alley.

Osborn was going at full speed when he saw them.

Karolin Henniger had unlocked the door to a beige Volkswagen van and was hurrying a young boy inside.

"Wait!" he yelled. "Wait! Please!"

Osborn reached the car just as she fired the engine.

"Please, I have to talk to you!" he begged. There was a screech of tires and the car accelerated forward. "Don't!" Osborn was running alongside. "I won't harm you—"

It was too late. Osborn saw McVey and Noble jump back as the car reached the end of the alley. Then it fishtailed onto the street and was gone.

"We took a chance, it didn't work. Sometimes it doesn't," McVey said, minutes later, as they got into the Mercedes and Remmer drove off.

Osborn looked at Remmer in the mirror; he was angry. "You saw her face when I mentioned Salettl. She knows, dammit. About Salettl and, I bet, Lybarger."

"Maybe she does, Doctor," McVey said quietly. "But she's not Albert Merriman, and you can't try to kill her to find out.

104

SUNLIGHT SUDDENLY streamed in through porthole windows as the sixteen-seat corporate jet broke the cloud deck and banked northeast for the ninety-minute flight to Berlin.

Joanna sat back and for a moment closed her eyes at the release. Switzerland, as beautiful as it was, was behind her. By this time tomorrow she would be at Tegel Airport in Berlin waiting for her flight to Los Angeles.

Across from her, Elton Lybarger dozed peacefully. If he had any concern about the events to take place later in the day, none showed. Dr. Salettl, looking pale and tired, sat in a swivel chair facing him, making notes in a black leather notebook in his lap. Occasionally he glanced up to converse in German with Uta Baur, who had flown in from a showing in Milan to accompany them to Berlin. In the seats directly behind her, Lybarger's nephews, Eric and Edward, played a silent and dramatically rapid game of chess.

Salettl's presence troubled Joanna as it always did and she purposefully let her thoughts go to "Kelso," the name she had given the black Saint Bernard puppy Von Holden had given her. Kelso had been fed and walked and kissed goodbye. Tomorrow he would be sent on a direct flight from Zurich to Los Angeles, where he would be held for the few hours before Joanna arrived to meet him. Then they would fly to Albuquerque. A three-hour drive after that, and they would be home in Taos.

Joanna's first thoughts immediately after she'd seen the video had been to get a lawyer and sue them. But then she'd thought—to what end? A lawsuit would only hurt Mr. Lybarger and could even have serious physical repercussions, especially if it dragged on. And she wouldn't do that because she cared a great deal for him and besides, he'd been as innocent as she. And later as horrified. All she'd wanted to do was leave Switzerland as quickly as possible and pretend it had never happened. Then Von Holden had come with the puppy and with his deep apology and finally he'd presented her with a check for an enormous amount of money. The company had apologized, so had Von Holden. What else could she really expect?

Still, she wondered if, in accepting Lybarger's corporate check, she'd done the right thing. She also had second thoughts about having told Ellie Barrs, head nurse at Rancho de Piñon, that she wouldn't be coming back to work right away, "if at all," she'd added. Maybe she shouldn't have done that. But all that money. My God, half a million dollars! The thing she'd do was find an investment counselor and put it all away, then live off the interest. Well, maybe she would buy a few things, but not much. Prudent investment, that was the smart thing.

Suddenly a red light on a telephone mounted in a console directly in front of her began to blink. Uncertain of what it meant, she did nothing.

"The call is for you." Eric leaned around her seat from behind.

"Thank you," she said and picked up the phone.

"Good morning. How are you?" Von Holden sounded light and cheery.

"I'm fine, Pascal." She smiled.

"How is Mr. Lybarger?"

"He's very well. He's taking a nap now."

"You should be landing in one hour. A car will be waiting for you."

"You won't be meeting us?"

"Joanna, you flatter me by the disappointment in your voice but I'm sorry, I won't be seeing you until later in the day. I'm afraid I have last-minute arrangements. I only wanted to make sure all was well."

Joanna smiled at the warmth in Von Holden's voice. "All is well. Don't worry about anything."

Von Holden hung up the cellular phone in a module next to the gearshift, then slowing, turned the steel gray BMW right onto Friedrichstrasse. Directly ahead a delivery truck pulled up sharply and he had to jam the brakes heavily to avoid hitting it. Cursing, he swung around it, absently passing a hand over a rectangular plastic case on the seat beside him to make sure it was still there and hadn't been thrown off the seat by the force of his quick stop. A red neon digital clock in the window of a jewelry building read 10:39.

In the last hours things had changed dramatically. Perhaps for the better. Berlin sector had tapped the two supposedly "secure" telephone lines in Room 6132 at the Hotel Palace using a prototype microwave receiver located in a building across the street. Calls to and from the room had been recorded and delivered to the apartment on Sophie-Charlottenstrasse, where they were transcribed and given to Von Holden. The equipment had not been set up until nearly eleven o'clock the night before and so they had missed most of the early transmissions. But what they had recorded afterward was enough for Von Holden to request an immediate meeting with Scholl.

Passing the Hotel Metropole, Von Holden crossed Unter den Linden and pulled up sharply in front of the Grand Hotel. Clutching the plastic case, he got out and went inside, taking an elevator directly to Scholl's suite.

A male secretary announced him and then showed him in. Scholl was on the phone at his desk when Von Holden entered. Across from him was a man he disliked immensely and hadn't seen in some time, Scholl's American attorney, H. Louis Goetz.

"Mr. Goetz."

"Von Holden."

Slick and crude, Goetz was fifty, too fit and too studied. He looked as if he spent half the day getting to look like he looked. Nails manicured and polished, deeply tanned and dressed in a blue pinstripe Armani suit, his dark, blow-dried hair showed just the toniest touch of white at the temples, as if it had been bleached that way on purpose. He carried an air of having just flown in from a tennis match in Palm Springs. Or a funeral in Palm Beach. There were rumors he was connected to the mob, but all Von Holden knew for certain was that at the moment he was a key figure in helping Scholl and Margarete Peiper buy into a top Hollywood talent agency where the Organization could more effectively influence the recording, movie and television industries. And, not so coincidentally, the audiences they served. Cold was a lacking description of Goetz's demeanor. Ice, with a mouth, was more like it.

Von Holden waited for Scholl to hang up, then set the plastic case in front of him and opened it. Inside was a small playback machine and the tapes of the conversations the Berlin sector had recorded.

"They have the complete guest list and a detailed dossier on Lybarger. They know about Salettl. Furthermore, McVey has arranged to have the cardinal of Los Angeles call you sometime this morning to request you meet with him at Charlottenburg this evening, one hour prior to when the guests will arrive. He knows you will be distracted and is counting on that for purposes of interrogation."

Ignoring the others, Scholl took the transcripts and studied them. When he finished, he handed them to Goetz, then pulled on the headset and listened to the tapes, fast-forwarding through them just enough to pick up excerpts. Finally, he clicked off the machine and removed the headset.

"All they have done, Pascal, is precisely what I anticipated. Using their resources and predictable pathways to gather information about my business here in Berlin and then arranging a way to meet with me. That they know about Mr. Lybarger and Doctor Salettl, that they have the guest list even, is meaningless. However, now that we know for certain they are coming, we shall do what we want."

Goetz looked up from the transcripts. He didn't like what he was reading or hearing. "Erwin, you're not gonna whack 'em? Three detectives and a doctor?"

"Something like that, Mr. Goetz. Why, is it a problem?"

"Problem? For Chrissakes, Bad Godesberg has the guest list. You knock these guys off, you get the whole goddamn federal police involved, what the fuck is that? You want them to start sticking their fucking noses up everybody's asshole?"

Von Holden said nothing. How Americans loved the ugly vernacular, no matter who they were.

"Mr. Goetz," Scholl said quietly. "Tell me how the federal police will become involved. What would they have to report? A middle-aged man recovered from a grave illness gives a mildly rousing, but in essence boring, speech to a hundred sleepy well-wishers at Charlottenburg and then everyone goes home. Germany is a free country for its citizens to do in and believe as they please."

"But you still got three dead cops and a dead doctor who put them onto this in the first place. What're they fuckin' gonna do about that, let it ride?"

"Mr. Goetz. The gentlemen in question, like you and Von Holden and myself, are in a major European city filled with any number of ambitious and nefarious people. Before the day's end Detective McVey and his friends will find themselves in a situation wholly untraceable to the Organization. And when the authorities begin to put it together they will be quite surprised to find that these seemingly outstanding citizens have quite sordid, interconnected pasts, filled with dark and private secrets they successfully kept hidden from families and co-workers. In essence, not the kind of men who should be point accusing fingers at figures like myself or one hundred of Germany's most respected friends and citizens, unless, of course, it were to be for private gain, for instance through blackmail or extortion. Am I not right, Pascal?"

Von Holden nodded. "Of course." The isolation and execution of McVey and Osborn and Noble and Remmer was his responsibility; the rest Scholl would take care of through sector operatives in Los Angeles, Frankfurt and London.

"There, you see, Mr. Goetz. We have nothing at all to concern ourselves with. Nothing at all. So, unless you think I have overlooked something worth further discussion, I would prefer to return to the subject of our agency acquisition."

Scholl's telephone buzzed and he picked it up. Listening, he looked to Goetz and smiled. "By all means," he said. "I am always available for Cardinal O'Connel."

105

OSBORN STOOD under the shower trying to calm down. It was just after 9:00 A.M., Friday, October 14, eleven hours before the ceremony at Charlottenburg was scheduled to begin.

Karolin Henniger was a way in and they couldn't use it. Remmer had checked again when they'd returned to the hotel. Karolin Henniger was a German citizen and single mother of an eleven-year-old boy. She had spent the late 1970s and most of the eighties in Austria, then returned to Berlin in the summer of 1989. She voted, paid her taxes, and had no criminal record of any kind. Remmer had been right; there was nothing they could do.

Yet she *knew*. And Osborn *knew* she knew.

Suddenly the bathroom door banged open.

"Osborn!" McVey barked. "Get out here. Now!"

Thirty seconds later, naked and dripping, a towel around his waist, Osborn stood staring at the television McVey had on in the front room. It was a live news special from Paris showing extremely somber proceedings in the French parliament, one speaker after another getting up to make a brief statement before sitting back down.

Over it was urgent narrative in German and then someone was being interviewed on screen in French and McVey heard the name François Christian.

"His resignation," Osborn said.

"No," McVey said. "They found his body. They're saying he committed suicide."

"Jesus Christ," Osborn breathed. "Oh, Jesus Christ."

Remmer was on one phone to Bad Godesberg, Noble on the other to London. Both wanted more details. McVey pushed a button on the remote and they got an English-language simulcast.

"The prime minister's body was found hanging from a tree in the woods outside Paris by an early-morning jogger," a female voice said over a long shot of wooded area cordoned off by French police.

"Christian reportedly had been despondent for days. Pressure for a United States of Europe had turned France against the French and he was a minority voice outspokenly against it. Because of his insistence, he had lost the confidence of the ministry. Sources inside the government say he had been forced to resign and that announcement was to have come as early as this morning. However, reports attributed to his wife say that at the last minute he had chosen to rescind his resignation and had called for a meeting today with party leaders." The narrator paused, then went on, over a matching video. "French flags fly at half mast and the president of France has declared a national day of mourning."

Osborn knew McVey was talking to him, but he didn't hear any of it. He could only think of Vera. Wonder if she knew yet and, if she did, how she'd found out. Or if she didn't know, where and how she would find out. And how she would be afterward. The notion flashed of how remarkable it was for him to be so concerned over the fate of her former lover. But that was how much he loved her. Her anguish was his anguish. Her pain, his. He wanted to be with her, hold her, share it with her. Be there for her. Whatever McVey was saying, he didn't care.

"Shut up for a minute and listen to me, would you please!" Osborn suddenly lashed out. "Vera Monneray— François Christian took her to wherever she was when I called her from London. It's somewhere in the French countryside. She may not have heard. I want to call her. And I want you to tell me if it's safe to do that."

"She's not there." Noble had just put down the phone and was looking at him.

"What do you mean?" Anxiety shot through Osborn. "How would you even—?" He stopped short. It was a foolish question. He was over his head with these people. So was Vera.

"It came in on the wire to Bad Godesberg," McVey said quietly. "She was in a farmhouse outside Nancy. The three French Secret Service officers guarding her were found shot to death on the premises. A policewoman named Avril Rocard from the First Préfecture of Police in Paris was also there. From what they can tell, she cut her own throat. Why, or what she was doing there, nobody knows. Except that your Ms. Monneray took her car and later left it at the Strasbourg railroad station when she bought a ticket to Berlin. So, unless she got off somewhere along the way, I think we'd better assume she's here now."

Osborn's face was beet red. He was incredulous. He no longer cared what they knew or how they knew it. That they could think what they were thinking was crazy. "She's not there and you suppose she's one of them? Just like that! Part of the group? What proof do you have? Go ahead. Tell me. I want to know."

"Osborn, I know how you feel, I'm only passing on information." McVey was calm, almost sympathetic.

"Yeah? Well you can go to hell!"

"McVey—" Remmer turned from the phone. "An Avril

Rocard checked into the Hotel Kempinski Berlin a little after seven this morning."

The room was empty when they came in. Remmer was first, the automatic in his hand, then came McVey, Noble and finally Osborn. Outside in the hallway, two BKA detectives guarded the door.

Moving quickly, Remmer went into the adjacent bedroom and then checked the bathroom. Both were empty. Coming back, he notified McVey, then went in and worked his way out from the bathroom. Pulling on surgical gloves, Noble went into the bedroom. McVey did the same and went over the living room. It was richly furnished with a view looking over the Kurfürstendamm below. Vacuum cleaner marks were still in the carpet, indicating the suite had been recently cleaned. A room-service breakfast tray was on a coffee table in front of the sofa. On it were a small glass of orange juice, several slices of untouched toast, a silver coffee thermos and a coffee cup, half filled with cold, black coffee. On the table beside the tray, a newspaper was face up, the headline of François Christian's suicide stark and brutal in large type.

"She take it black?"

"What?" Osborn stood in a daze. It was inconceivable Vera could be here in Berlin. It was even more inconceivable that she could be involved with the group.

"Vera Monneray," McVey said. "She take her coffee black?"

Osborn stammered, "I don't know. Yes. Maybe. I'm not sure."

There was the sound of a beeper in the other room. A moment later Remmer came in wearing surgical gloves like the others, and picked up the telephone. Dialing, he waited, then said something in German. Taking a small notebook from his pocket, he wrote something in pencil. "*Danke*," he said and hung up.

"Cardinal O'Connel called back," he said to McVey. "Scholl's expecting your call. This number." He tore off the sheet and handed it to him. "Maybe we won't need the warrant after all."

"Yes, and maybe we will."

Remmer went back into the other room, and McVey began working the front room again. Paying close attention to the couch and the carpet directly beneath it, where whoever was drinking the coffee and looking at the newspaper would have been sitting.

"This Avril Rocard." Osborn was working to be civil, logical, to make some sense of what was so overwhelming to him. "You say she's with the Paris police. Have they positively identified her body? Maybe it was someone else. Maybe Avril Rocard *is* here, maybe it's not Vera at all."

"Gentlemen—" Noble stood in the door to the bedroom. "Would you come in, please."

Osborn stood back and watched with the others as Noble slid open the door to the bedroom closet. Inside were two sets of day clothes, a black velvet evening dress, and a silver mink stole. Leading them to a low bureau, Noble sat down, pulled open the top drawer and lifted out several pairs of lace underwear with matching bras, five unopened packets of Armani pantyhose, and a see-through silvery silk nightgown. The drawer beneath revealed two purses, one a black formal clutch to go with the evening dress. The other was a brown leather over-the-shoulder bag.

Taking out the black clutch, Noble opened it. Inside were two jewelry cases and a velvet drawstring bag. The first jewelry case held an opera-length diamond necklace, the second matching earrings. In the drawstring bag was a small, silver-plated, .25-caliber automatic. Putting them back the way he found them, Noble hefted the over-the-shoulder purse. Inside, held together by a rubber band, was a packet of unpaid bills addressed to Avril Rocard, 17 rue

St.-Gilles, Paris, 75003. A Paris Préfecture of Police I.D. and a small, black nylon sport bag. Opening it, Noble laid out Avril Rocard's passport, a clear Ziploc bag containing a packet of German Deutschmarks, an unused first-class Air France ticket from Paris to Berlin, and an envelope with a reservation confirmation from the Hotel Kempinski, dated for arrival on Friday, October 14, and checking out on Saturday, the fifteenth. Looking up at the faces surrounding him, Noble reached into the purse once more and came out with an elaborately engraved envelope, already opened. From it, he took out an engraved invitation to the dinner for Elton Lybarger at Charlottenburg Palace.

Instinctively, McVey reached inside his jacket for the guest list.

"No need. I've already checked, an A. Rocard is there, a half-dozen names ahead of Doctor Salettl, one of the guests we had no information on," Noble said, getting up. "One more thing . . ."

Crossing to a bedside table he picked up an object wrapped in a dark silk scarf. "It was tucked under the mattress." Unwrapping the scarf, he pulled out a long, dog-eared leather wallet. As he did, he saw Osborn react. "You know what it is, Doctor Osborn—"

"Yes—" Osborn said. "I know what it is. . . ."

He'd seen it before. In Geneva. In London. And in Paris. It was Vera Monneray's passport case.

106

OSBORN WAS not the only distraught man in Berlin.

Waiting for Von Holden in his office at the Sophie-Charlottenstrasse apartment, Cadoux was an anxious wreck. He'd spent two very troubled hours complaining to anyone who would listen—about German coffee, about why he couldn't get a French-language newspaper, about nothing at all; every bit of it disguising his growing concern over Avril Rocard. It had been nearly twenty-four hours since she should have completed her assignment at the farmhouse outside Nancy and reported back to him, yet he had had no word.

Four times he'd called her apartment in Paris and four times there'd been no answer. After a sleepless night, he'd telephoned Air France to see if she had checked in for her early flight from Paris to Berlin. When that proved negative, he started to fall apart. Trained terrorist, murderer and professional policeman; from his position within Interpol, the man assigned to coordinate security for Erwin Scholl anywhere he traveled in the world—and had for more than thirty years—inside, Cadoux was a prisoner of the heart. Avril Rocard was his life.

He finally risked a phone trace and made contact with an operative inside the French Secret Service who confirmed three Secret Service agents and a woman had been found dead at the Nancy farmhouse, but more detail was not available. Literally frantic, Cadoux tried the one last, and in retrospect, perhaps his most obvious, option. He telephoned the Hotel Kempinski.

To his enormous relief, Avril Rocard had checked in at 7:15 that morning, arriving by a cab from Bahnhof Zoo, Berlin's main railway station. Hanging up, Cadoux reached for a cigarette. Blowing out the smoke, he smiled, he beamed, he pounded on the desk with his fist. Then, thirty seconds later, at 10:59 exactly, and with Von Holden still in his meeting with Scholl, Cadoux picked up the phone and placed a call to Avril Rocard's room at the Hotel Kempinski. As luck would have it, the line was busy.

McVey was using it to call Scholl. The first part of their conversation had been formal and polite. They discussed their mutual friendship with Cardinal O'Connel, the Berlin weather compared to Southern California, and the irony of being in the city at the same time. Then they got around to the reason for McVey's call.

"It's something I'd rather discuss in person, Mr. Scholl. I wouldn't want it to be misinterpreted."

"I don't think I understand."

"Let's just say, it's personal."

"Detective, my calendar for the day is full. Isn't this something that could wait until my return to Los Angeles?"

"I'm afraid not."

"How much time do you think it will require?"

"Half hour, forty minutes."

"I see—"

"I do know you're busy, and I appreciate your cooperation, Mr. Scholl. I understand you'll be at the Charlottenburg Palace for a reception this evening. Why don't we meet there beforehand? How is about sev—"

"I will meet you promptly at five o'clock at number 72 Hauptstrasse, in the Friedenau district. It's a private residence. I'm sure you will be able to find it. Good morning, Detective."

There was a click on the other end as Scholl hung up and looked at Louis Goetz and then to Von Holden, as both hung up extensions.

"That was what you wanted?"

"That was what I wanted," Von Holden said.

107

EVEN THOUGH the call Cadoux had placed to Avril Rocard at the Hotel Kempinski had never rung through, the front desk, on orders from the BKA, had kept the caller on hold long enough for the federal police to trace the call.

Because of it, Osborn was once again in the company of Inspector Johannes Schneider. Only this time there was a second BKA inspector along. Littbarski, a beefy, balding, single father of two. The three were crammed into a tiny wooden booth in a crowded Kneipe, a tavern a half block away, drinking coffee and waiting as McVey, Noble and Remmer climbed the stairs to the apartment on Sophie-Charlottenstrasse.

A middle-aged woman with dyed red hair and wearing a small telephone headset, looking as if she'd come to the door from a switchboard, opened the door and Remmer, flashing a BKA I.D., introduced himself in German. Within the last hour someone had placed a call to Hotel Kempinski Berlin and they wanted to know who it was.

"I couldn't tell you," she said in German.

"Let's find someone who can."

The woman was hesitant. Everyone had gone to lunch, she said. Remmer told her they'd wait. And if she had a problem with that, they'd get a search warrant and come back. Suddenly the woman raised her head, as if she were listening to something distant. Then she looked back and smiled.

"I'm sorry," she said. "It's just that we are very busy. This is the welcoming headquarters for a private party tonight at Schloss Charlottenburg. Many prominent people are coming and we are trying to coordinate everything. Several are staying at the Hotel Kempinski. It was probably I who called earlier. To make certain our guests had arrived and that everything was all right."

"Which guest were you checking on?"

"I—I told you. There are several."

"Name them."

"I have to check my book."

"Check it."

She nodded and asked them to wait. Remmer said it would be better if they came in. Again the woman raised her head and looked off. "All right," she said finally, and led them down a narrow hallway to a small desk in an alcove. Sitting down next to a multiline phone, she moved a small vase holding a wilting yellow rose and opened a three-ring binder. Turning a page marked Kempinski, she brusquely shoved it under Remmer's nose for him to read for himself. Six of the guest names were on the Kempinski list, including Avril Rocard.

Letting Remmer handle the woman, McVey and Noble stepped back and looked around. To their left was another hallway. Halfway down and at the end were doors. Both were closed. Across was the apartment's living room, where two women and a man sat at what looked like rented desks. One typed on a computer, the other two were working telephones. McVey stuck his hands in his pockets and tried to look bored.

"Somebody's talking to her through that headset," he said quietly, as if he were talking about the weather or the stock market. Noble glanced back at her in time to see her nod past Remmer toward the man in the living room working the telephones. Remmer followed her gaze, then walked over and showed him his I.D. They talked for several minutes and then Remmer came back to McVey and Noble.

"According to them, he was the one who called Avril Rocard's room. Neither of them know where either Salettl or Lybarger are staying. The woman thinks they'll go directly to Charlottenburg from the airport."

"What time are they due to land?" Noble asked.

"She doesn't know. Their job seems to be to take care of the guests and that's all."

"Who else is here, in the other rooms?"

"She says there are just the four of them."

"Can we go back there?" McVey nodded toward the hallway.

"Not without cause."

McVey looked down at his shoes. "What about a search warrant?"

Remmer smiled cautiously. "On what grounds?"

McVey looked up. "Let's get out of here."

Von Holden watched on closed-circuit television as the detectives descended the stairs and went out. He'd returned from his meeting with Scholl barely ten minutes earlier to find Cadoux seated in his office, still trying to get through to Avril Rocard at the Hotel Kempinski. Seeing him, Cadoux had slammed the phone down, outraged. At first her line had been busy! Now there was no answer at all! Angered, Von Holden had told him forget it, he was not in Berlin on vacation. It was then the police had arrived. Instantly Von Holden knew how and why, and that he'd had to act quickly, delaying them at the front door while he replaced one of the female secretaries in the front room with the male security guard.

Now, as he watched the door close behind the policemen and saw McVey turn back to study the building's exterior, he turned angrily to Cadoux, his sharp features illuminated by the bank of black-and-white security monitors.

"You were a fool to call her room from a telephone here." His voice had the warmth of a steel rod.

"I am sorry, Herr Von Holden." Cadoux was apologetic but refused to relinquish his soul to a man fifteen years his junior. The rest of the world, Von Holden included, could go to hell when it came to Avril Rocard.

Von Holden looked up at him. "Forget it. By this time tomorrow, it will have made little difference." A moment before he had been ready to tell him Avril Rocard was dead. To throw it in his face coldly, in simple conversation, and enjoy the pleasure of his anguish. There was something else he could tell him too. Avril Rocard had not only been beautiful and an excellent marksman, she'd also been an internal spy inside the Paris sector and as such, not only Von Holden's confidante but his lover as well. It was why she had been invited to Berlin. As added security for Lybarger inside Charlottenburg once the celebration had begun; and later, for Von Holden's own pleasure. All of that could be told to Cadoux to amplify his pain, but none of it would be, at least not now. Cadoux had been brought to Berlin for another reason entirely, one that would require his full and undivided attention, and because of that, Von Holden would say nothing.

Osborn was trying not to think of Vera, where she was and what she might be doing, the idea that she, of anyone, might be involved with the group was impossible, but why else was she here playing someone called Avril Rocard? His entire being felt raw and unnerved, and he heard himself talking to Schneider and Littbarski, attempting to explain the elements of American football over the din of the tavern, crowded, it seemed, with every tourist in Berlin.

At first, the prattle through Schneider's hand radio had seemed to be simply a routine police broadcast in German. The volume was up and heads in nearby booths turned at the staccato intrusion. Immediately Schneider reached over to turn the volume down. As he did, Vera's name came through, and Osborn's heart jumped in his throat.

"What the hell is it?" he said, grabbing Schneider's wrist. At the move Littbarski stiffened.

"*Sich schonen.*" Take it easy, he said to Osborn.

Osborn released his grip and Littbarski relaxed.

"What about her?" Schneider could see the tenseness in Osborn's neck muscles.

"Two federal policewomen apprehended Ms. Monneray as she was coming out of the Church of Mary Queen of Martyrs," Schneider said in his heavily accented English.

Church? Why would Vera be in church? Osborn's mind raced. He never remembered her mentioning church or religious beliefs or anything like it. "Where are they taking her?"

Schneider shook his head. "Don't know."

"That's a lie. You do know."

Again Littbarski tensed.

Schneider picked up the radio and started to get up. "My orders are that if anything happened, I am to take you back to the hotel."

Unmindful of Littbarski, Osborn put out a hand to stop him. "Schneider, I don't know what's going on. I want to believe this is a mistake but I can't know anything until I see her. Talk to her. I don't want McVey getting her alone first. Dammit, Schneider. I'm asking you, please—help me."

Schneider looked at him. "I can see it in your eyes. You are crazy about her. That's the right saying in American—crazy about her?"

"Yes, that's the right saying. And I am crazy about her. . . . Take me to wherever they're taking her—" If Osborn wasn't begging he was close to it.

"You ran out on me before."

"Not this time, Schneider. Not this time."

108

VON HOLDEN watched the city in a blur, alternatively slowing, accelerating, then stopping the BMW completely in heavy midday traffic, only to move on again a few moments later. He was driving on automatic pilot, his mind torn by outrage and absurdity. Three of the four men he had sworn to kill, one of them McVey himself, had walked into his offices and bullied his help as if he were some kind of street front merchant. Worse, he had been helpless, unable to do anything but let them in and then watch from behind closed doors for fear that failure to do so would bring a full-scale invasion by the federal police.

The madness of it was that it had been set off by Cadoux's emotional appetite for a woman who hadn't the slightest interest in him beyond what information he could unknowingly pass on about the loyalty of the operatives inside Interpol. It was then, in his anger at Cadoux's stupidity, the final pieces of his strategy came together.

72 Hauptstrasse, 12:15 P.M.

Joanna saw the BMW turn in from the street, stop briefly at the guardhouse, then pass through the gate and swing around the circular drive to stop in front of the residence. From where she stood in the upstairs bedroom window it was difficult to see directly below, but she was sure she caught a glimpse of Von Holden as he got out and started for the house.

Going quickly to the mirror, she ran a brush through her hair and touched up the expensive, wet-look lipstick Uta Baur had given her. For reasons she couldn't explain or begin to understand, and despite all that had happened to her, she felt more sexually aroused than she ever had in her life. As if some insatiable hunger or thirst had suddenly and uncontrollably swept over her so powerfully that it could only be satisfied by the act itself.

Opening the door, she stepped into the hallway and saw Von Holden in the downstairs foyer conferring with Eric and Edward. A moment later he stepped off and disappeared from view. Her instinct was to fly down the stairs after him, but she couldn't with Lybarger's nephews still there.

Trying to shake the feeling free, she crossed the hall and knocked gently on a closed door. Immediately it was opened by a white-haired, pale, pig-faced man in a tuxedo. His skin had so little pigmentation she thought he might be albino.

"I—I'm Mr. Lybarger's . . ." The man's appearance and almost superior way he looked at her made her nervous.

"I know who you are," he said in a throaty voice.

"I would like to see Mr. Lybarger," she said, and was shown in without hesitation.

Elton Lybarger was sitting in a chair by the window reading from a dog-eared sheaf of papers typed with very large print. It was the speech he would give tonight, and in the last few days he'd done almost nothing but go over it.

"I wanted to make sure you were comfortable and that everything was all right, Mr. Lybarger," she said. It was then she noticed another man, also in a tuxedo, standing back near a window that looked out onto a large backyard. Why Mr. Lybarger needed two bodyguards in his room, in a house as elegant and genteel as this, and with a guardhouse and a gate out front, she had no idea.

"Thank you, Joanna. Everything is fine," he said without looking up.

"Then, I will see you a little later." She smiled caringly.

Lybarger nodded absently and continued reading. Smiling pleasantly at the pig-faced bodyguard, Joanna turned and left.

* * *

Von Holden was alone in a dark paneled study when she came in and closed the door quietly behind her. He was sitting in a chair with his back to her, talking in German on the telephone. The room was dark compared to the bright sunshine in the yard outside. The grass was a vibrant green that caught and displayed like a quilt the brilliant yellow and red leaves that flitted down from a massive copper beech in the far corner of the yard. To the left of the tree she could see a large five-car garage and beyond it an iron gate that appeared to lead to a service drive in the rear of the estate.

Suddenly Von Holden hung up and swiveled around in his chair. "You shouldn't come in when I'm on the telephone, Joanna."

"I wanted to see you."

"Now you see me."

"Yes," she said, smiling. She thought he looked more tired than she'd ever seen him. "Did you have lunch?"

"I don't remember."

"Breakfast?"

"I don't know."

"You're tired. You even need to shave. Come up to my room. Shower, rest a little."

"I can't, Joanna."

"Why?"

"Because, I have things to do." Suddenly he stood. "Don't mother me, I don't like it."

"I don't want to mother you—I want to—make love to you." She smiled and wet her lips. "Come upstairs, now. Please, Pascal. We may never be able to be alone ever again."

"You sound like a schoolgirl."

"I'm not . . . and you know it. . . ." She moved closer, so that she was standing directly in front of him. Her hand slid down over his crotch. "Let's do it right here. Right now." Everything about her, the purr of her voice, the movement of her body as she drew herself closer to him, was totally sexual. "I'm wet," she whispered.

Abruptly Von Holden reached down, took her hand away. "No," he said. "Now, leave. I will see you tonight."

"—Pascal. I—love you. . . ."

Von Holden stared at her.

"You should know that by now—"

Suddenly the pupils in his eyes receded to tiny dots and the eyes themselves seemed to press back into his skull. Joanna's breath caught and she pulled back. Never, ever, had she seen anyone filled with anger or as dangerous as Von Holden was now.

"Get out," he hissed.

With a cry, she turned, bumped into a chair, then pushed around it and ran from the room, the door left open behind her. He could hear her heels on the stone foyer and the sound as she ran up the stairs. He was about to cross to the door to close it when Salettl came in.

"You are angry," Salettl said.

Von Holden turned his back and stared out the window. He had called Scholl from the car with the final plan. Scholl had listened and agreed. Then, as quickly, he'd taken Von Holden out of it. It was too dangerous, he'd said. Von Holden was too well known as Scholl's director of European security, and Scholl could not afford to chance the possibility that something would go wrong, with Von Holden killed or captured and the connection made back to him. The police were too close. No, Von Holden would plan it, but Viktor Shevchenko would execute it. That evening Von Holden would be seen publicly escorting Mr. Lybarger to Charlottenburg. And, afterward, he would quietly leave "to do the other," as Scholl had put it. Those had been the orders and he'd hung up.

"You know, *Herr Leiter der Sicherheit*," Salettl said

softly. "On this day, of all days, your personal safety is beyond value."

"Yes, I know." Von Holden turned to face him. Obviously Salettl knew what had taken place between Scholl and Von Holden because it was the "other" he was referring to. Immediately following the celebration at Charlottenburg, there was to be a second ceremony for a very privileged few of the guests. Secret and unannounced, it was to take place in the mausoleum, the temple-like building on the palace grounds that housed the tombs of the Prussian kings. Von Holden was to deliver the highly sensitive material to be presented there, and the access codes necessary to retrieve it had been programmed for him, and him alone, and could not be changed.

That he had been selected was in recognition of the high regard in which he was held and the power he had been given. Angry as he'd been, Scholl had been right, as had Salettl. For more than one reason, today of all days, his personal safety was beyond value. He had to realize he was no longer the Spetsnaz soldier that was still in his blood. He was no longer a Bernhard Oven or Viktor Shevchenko. He was *Leiter der Sicherheit*. Chief of security was no longer a job description but a mandate for the future. As the man who would one day oversee the succession of power for the entire Organization, it made him, for all intents, "keeper of the flame." And if he hadn't fully understood it before, he should now, today, more than ever.

109

THE INTERROGATION room in the basement of the building on Kaiser Friedrichstrasse was stark white. Floor, ceiling and walls. The same decor as the half-dozen six-by-eight-foot cells that adjoined it. Few people, even those who worked in the building which housed the collection bureau for the municipal public works department, knew the facility existed. But fully one-third of the six-thousand square-foot subbasement was occupied by a special investigations unit of the BKA. Built immediately following the massacre at the 1972 Olympic games in Munich, its primary use was to interrogate captured terrorists and terrorist informants. It had in the past served as a temporary holding area for members of the Baader-Meinhof group, the Red Army Faction, the Popular Front for the Liberation of Palestine, and suspects from the bombing of Pan Am flight 103. Besides its stark whiteness, its other distinguishing characteristic was that the lights were never turned off. The effect, in concert, was that within thirty-six hours, prisoners became wholly disoriented, with things usually going downhill from there.

Vera sat alone in the prime interrogation room on a white bench made of a PVC-like plastic molded to the floor. There was no table, no chairs. Only the bench. She had been photographed and fingerprinted. She wore dully gray pull-on slippers and a lighter gray, almost white, nylon jumpsuit with the words GEFANGER, *Bundesrepublik Deutschland*—PRISONER, *Federal Republic of Germany*—stenciled in Day-Glo orange on the back. She looked shocked and worn, but was still lucid when the door opened and Osborn entered. For a moment, a short, block-shaped policewoman stood in the doorway behind them. Then almost immediately she stepped back and closed the door.

"My God——" Osborn whispered. "Are you all right?"

Vera's mouth was open; she was trying to say something but couldn't. Tears burst forth instead, and then they were in each other's arms and both were crying. Somewhere between the sobs and frightened caresses he heard her say, "François dead"——"WhyamIhere?"——"Everyone killed at farmhouse"——"What—haveIdone?"——"Came—to—Berlin—only—place—left—to—go—to—find—you."

"Vera. Shhh. It's all right, honey." He held her tight against him. Protectively, like a child. "It's okay. It's going to be okay. . . ." Brushing back her hair, he kissed her tears and wiped her cheeks with his hands.

"They even took my handkerchief," he said, trying to smile. He had no belt, and they'd taken the laces from his shoes. Then they were holding each other again. Pressed together, arms around each other.

"Don't let go," she said. "Don't ever . . ."

"Vera—tell me what happened. . . ." She took his hand, and held it tight and they sat down on the bench. Brushing away tears, she closed her eyes and thought back. All the way to yesterday.

She could see the farmhouse outside Nancy and the bodies of the three slain Secret Service agents lying where they had fallen. Not far away, Avril Rocard stared unseeingly, blood slowly oozing from her throat.

The phones had been dead when she'd gone back inside. Unable to find the keys to the Secret Service Ford, she'd taken Avril Rocard's black police Peugeot and driven into the city, where she'd used a public telephone and tried to reach François in Paris. But the phones in both his office and his private number at home had been busy. No doubt, she thought, because news of his resignation had just been released. Still in shock from the killings, she'd gotten back into the Peugeot and driven to a park on the edge of the city.

There, sitting in the car, trying to work through a blur of fear and emotions, trying to think what to do next, she'd seen Avril's purse on the floor on the passenger side. Opening it, she'd found Avril's police I.D. and her passport case. Inside the case, tucked behind the passport, was a first-class Air France ticket from Paris to Berlin and an envelope with a reservation confirmation from the Hotel Kempinski. There was also an elaborate engraved invitation in German to a formal dinner to be held at the Charlottenburg Palace at 8 P.M. Friday October 14, in honor of a man named Elton Lybarger. Among the sponsors was the name Erwin Scholl. The same man who hired Albert Merriman to kill Osborn's father.

Her only thought was that if Scholl was in Berlin, perhaps Paul Osborn might have found out and gone there too. It wasn't much to go on, but it was all she had. She looked enough like Avril Rocard that unless someone knew her personally, she could pass for her even though she was several years younger. That had been Thursday, the Charlottenburg thing was Friday. From Nancy the fastest way to Berlin was by train from Strasbourg, and so that was where she went.

Twice on the road from Nancy to Strasbourg she'd stopped to call François. The first time, the lines were tied up. The second time, at a highway rest stop, she got through to his office. By then it was nearly four in the afternoon and François had not been seen or heard from since he'd left his home at seven that morning. The media had not yet been informed that he was missing, but the Secret Service and police were on full alert and the president had ordered François' wife and children to be taken to an unknown destination and kept there under armed guard.

She remembered hanging up and feeling only numbness. Nothing existed. There was no François Christian. No Dr. Paul Osborn of Los Angeles. Nor was there a Vera Monneray who could go back to her apartment and her life in Paris and carry on as if nothing had ever happened. Four people were dead at a farmhouse behind her and the only men she had ever known and cared about, loved as completely and deeply as she had, were gone, vanished, like steam into the air. It was then a sense came over her that what was happening was only a prelude to what was to come. And once again she felt the awful and shadowed echo of her grandmother's past, and the horror and unending fear that went with it. The only answer seemed to lie in Berlin, as it had in her grandmother's day. Only now it had become a great deal more personal. Whatever had happened to François was part of it, but Osborn was too because he was on the same path as well.

She'd checked into Avril's room and found Avril's clothes already there. Then room service brought her breakfast. On the tray had been the newspaper and the word of François' suicide. Feeling faint at first, she knew she needed to get outside and into the air to recover, to think, to plan what to do when and if someone contacted her. Or what to do if they did not, and if she should simply go to Charlottenburg that night alone. So, hiding her passport under the mattress for fear someone would discover who she really was, she'd gone out.

It was while she was walking she'd come upon the Church of Mary Queen of Martyrs. Ironically it was a religious memorial, dedicated to the martyrs for the freedom of belief and conscience from 1933 to 1945. It was like an omen beckoning her, and she thought that inside she might find some kind of answer to what was happening. What she'd found instead were the German police waiting when she came out.

Detective Schneider had lied when he'd told Osborn that if anything happened he was to take him back to the hotel. The truth was that if Vera Monneray was found, Osborn was to be taken directly to where she was being held.

McVey wanted Osborn and Ms. Monneray to think they were alone, thereby giving McVey the chance to garner whatever candid information such a meeting would reveal. The idea was to make it seem the concept had been Osborn's; and with Schneider's help it worked; Osborn had played right into it.

Suddenly the door to the interrogation room was pulled open. Osborn swung around and saw McVey coming through the doorway. "Get him out of here, now!" McVey said angrily, and abruptly two uniformed federal policemen were jerking Osborn to his feet and hustling him out. "Vera!" he cried out, trying to look back. "Vera!" His second cry was followed by the booming slam of a heavy steel door. Then he was walked quickly down a narrow hallway and up a short flight of stairs. A door was opened and he was taken into another white room. The policemen went out, and the door was closed and locked.

Ten minutes later McVey came in. His face was red and he was breathing heavily, as if he'd just climbed a long flight of stairs.

"What'd you get on the tape? Anything of interest?" Osborn said icily the moment the door opened. "Convenient for me to get there first, wasn't it! Maybe she'd tell me what she wouldn't tell you or the German police and the mikes would pick everything up. But it didn't work, did it? All you got was the truth from a terrified woman."

"How do you know it was the truth?"

"Because I do, dammit!"

"Did she ever mention Captain Cadoux of Interpol—ever talk about him, say his name?"

"No. Never."

McVey glared at him, then softened. "Okay. Let's believe her. Both of us."

"Then let her go."

"Osborn. You are here because of me. And by that I

mean not dead on the floor of some Paris bistro with a Stasi shooter's bullet between your eyes."

"McVey, that has nothing to do with this and you know it! The same as you have no reason to hold her. You know that too!"

McVey never took his eyes from Osborn's. "You want to know the *why* about your father."

"What happened to my father has got nothing to do with Vera."

"How do you know? How do you know for sure?" McVey wasn't being cruel, he was probing. "You said you met her in Geneva. Did you find her or did she find you?"

"I—It doesn't make any—"

"Answer me."

"—She . . . found me. . . ."

"She was François Christian's mistress. And on the day of this thing with Lybarger, he's suddenly dead and she shows up in Berlin with an invitation to the ball."

Osborn was angry. Angry and confused. What was McVey trying to do? That Vera might be part of the "group" was crazy. It wasn't possible. He believed what she had just told him. They loved each other too much for him not to! Her love meant too much. Turning away, he looked up at the ceiling. Above him, hanging out of reach from anyone standing on the floor, was a bank of bright lights. Glaring, hundred-and-fifty-watt bulbs that would never be turned off.

"Maybe she is innocent, Doctor," McVey said. "But it's out of your hands and in those of the German police."

Behind them the door opened and Remmer came in. "We have video of the house on Hauptstrasse. Noble is waiting."

McVey looked back to Osborn. "I want you to see this," he said directly.

"Why?"

"It's the house where we're to meet Scholl. By *we*, Doctor, I mean you and me."

110

JOANNA'S SUITCASE was on the bed and the last of her things were going into it when Von Holden came in.

"Joanna, I apologize. Forgive me. . . ."

Ignoring him, she went to the closet and took out the Uta Baur original she was to wear this evening. Coming back, she laid it out on the bed and began to fold it. Von Holden stood quietly for a moment, then came up behind her and put his hand on her shoulder. When he did, she froze.

"This is a very tense time for me, Joanna. . . . For you as well, and for Mr. Lybarger. Please forgive me for acting the way I did downstairs. . . ."

Joanna remained as she was, her eyes focused on the glare of the distant window.

"I have to tell you the truth, Joanna. . . . In my entire life, no one has ever told me they loved me. You—frightened me. . . ."

He felt the breath go out of her. "*I* frightened *you?*"

"Yes. . . ."

Ever so slowly she turned. The horrid, hate-filled eyes that had terrified her barely an hour before were now soft and vulnerable.

"Don't do this to me. . . ."

"Joanna, I don't know if I am capable of love. . . ."

"Don't . . ." Joanna felt her eyes brim and a tear begin to steal down her cheek.

"It's true. I don't—"

Abruptly she pressed her fingers against his lips to stop him. "You are—" she said.

Slowly he put his hands around her waist and she came into his arms. And then he kissed her gently and she returned it and felt him grow hard against her. Emotion crept over her body, taking away reason. Whatever fearful thing she had seen in him before was gone. Unremembered in the sense that it had never existed.

From a single fly-over at five hundred feet, the helicopter view of the house at 72 Hauptstrasse showed a nineteenth-century villa, a three-story main building with a five-car garage to the rear. A semicircular driveway was entered past a guardhouse, through wrought-iron gates from the street. The driveway to the garage was to the right of the house, while to the left was a red clay tennis court. The entire premises were surrounded by a high stone wall, grown over with deciduous ivy.

"There's a gate at the back beside the garage. It looks like it opens to a service alley," Noble said as he watched the fly-over on the large Sony screen.

"It does, and it's operable," Remmer said.

The four—Noble, Remmer, McVey and Osborn—were sitting in theater-like seats in a video room one floor up from cell level. Osborn was leaning back, his chin resting on his hand. A floor below, Vera was being interrogated. His imagination flailed at what they might be doing to her. On the other hand—his mind raced—what if, after everything, McVey had been right and she was working with the "group"? What had she learned from François Christian that she might have passed to them? If so, how did he, Osborn, fit in? What did she want with him? Maybe that he had been involved with Merriman had been an accident, a sheer coincidence. She couldn't have known about that in Geneva because he hadn't seen Merriman until he followed her to Paris.

"This was taken from a laundry truck while the driver made a delivery to the house across the street," Remmer said, as broadcast-quality color video rolled on the screen. "We only have short pieces shot from different vehicles. That's the reason there's only one fly-over take. We don't want to create suspicion they are under surveillance."

Now the hidden camera pushed in toward the house. A Mercedes limousine was parked in the driveway and a gardener was at work on the lawn. Nothing else seemed to be happening. The camera held, then started to pull back.

"What's that?" McVey said abruptly. "A movement in the upstairs window, second from the right."

Remmer stopped the machine, backed it up. Then played it forward again in slow motion.

"Someone's standing in the window," Noble said.

Again Remmer replayed it. This time in extreme slow motion and using a special zoom lens on the playback to move in on the window. "It's a woman. Can't see much of her."

"Get it enhanced, will you?" Noble said.

"Right." Touching the intercom and asking for a technician, Remmer took out the cassette, put it aside and inserted another. Basically it was the same shot of the house but from a slightly different angle. A small movement in the upstairs window suggested McVey was right, that someone was standing there looking out. Suddenly a gray BMW pulled in off the street and stopped at the guardhouse. A moment later the gate opened and the car drove in. Pulling up at the main entrance, a tall man got out and went inside.

"Any idea who he is?" McVey asked. Remmer shook his head.

"This will be unmitigated joy," Noble said flatly as he

opened an alphabetized file of photographs. So far, Bad Godesberg had sent them photos of sixty-three of the one hundred invited guests. Most were driver's license Polaroids, but others were copies of publicity, corporate or news photographs. "I'll take A through F, the rest of you can fight over what remains of the alphabet."

"Let's put him on the zoom." Remmer punched rewind, then hit the slow-mo play button. This time the car entered in slow motion and Remmer moved in on it with the zoom. As it reached the front of the house, the car stopped and the man got out—

"Jesus Christ—" Osborn said.

McVey's head came around like a bullwhip. "You know that guy?" Remmer backed up the tape and froze the picture as Von Holden was just stepping out of the car.

"He followed me into the park." Osborn pulled away from the screen to look directly at McVey.

"What park? What the hell are you talking abou—"

"The night I went out. I ditched Schneider on purpose." Osborn was pumped up. His lie had come back on him but he didn't care. "I was walking through the Tiergarten, on my way to Scholl's hotel. Suddenly I realized I didn't know what the hell I was doing. That I might blow the whole thing. I was turning back when this guy—that guy there"— he looked back at Von Holden on the screen— "is coming up behind me. I had the gun in my pocket. I freaked, I guess. I pulled it on him. He had a friend, hiding in the bushes—I told them to leave me alone. Then I ran like hell."

"You sure it's him?"

"Yes."

"That means they're watching the hotel," Remmer said.

Noble looked at Remmer. "Could we see him walk into the house? At normal speed, please."

Remmer hit "play," and Von Holden's image unfroze. Closing the door to the BMW, he crossed the driveway and moved quickly up a short flight of steps, someone opened the front door and he entered.

Noble sat back. "Once more, please." Remmer repeated the action, stopping the tape once Von Holden had gone inside.

"One hundred to one he was trained as a Spetsnaz soldier," Noble said. "A saboteur and terrorist, schooled in special reconnaissance units of the old Soviet army. It takes a bit of experience to recognize it. They may not even know they do it, but their training effects a certain walk, a kind of bearing and balance that make them look as if they were on a circus wire." Noble turned to Osborn. "If he *was* following you, you are incredibly lucky to be sitting here telling us about it." Noble looked to McVey and Remmer.

"If Lybarger is staying in the house, it's possible our friend here is a security operative, possibly even the man in charge."

"Either that or he's securing it for Scholl," Remmer said.

"Or doing something else entirely." McVey sat staring at the screen, intent on the frozen image of Von Holden.

"Setting us up?" Noble said.

"Don't know." McVey shook his head uncertainly, then looked to Remmer. "Let's get an enhancement on him too, see if we can find out who he is. Maybe we can take the circle down one more notch."

A line lit up and the phone buzzed at Remmer's elbow. "*Ja,*" he said, picking up.

It was fifteen minutes past two when they got there. Berlin police had already cordoned off the block. Homicide investigators stood aside as Remmer led the way through the shop and into the back room of the antique store on Kantstrasse.

Karolin Henniger lay on the floor wrapped in a sheet.

Her eleven-year-old son, Johann, was next to her. He, too, was covered by a sheet.

Remmer knelt and pulled back the covering.

"Oh God—" Osborn breathed.

McVey eased the sheet from the boy. "Yeah," he said, looking up at Osborn. "Oh God . . ."

Both mother and son had a single gunshot wound to the head.

111

NINETY MINUTES later, at 3:55 P.M., Osborn stood at the window in a large room at the ancient Hotel Meineke staring out at the city. Like all of them, he was trying to separate the horror of what they'd just seen from what they had to do at the present. Their focus had to be on Scholl, nothing else. Still, it was impossible to shake the thoughts.

Who was Karolin Henniger really, that someone would do that to her and her child? Did the perpetrator think that she had told the police something that morning? If so, what did she know she might have confided? And then there was the other question, the one he could see in McVey's eyes: If they had never gone to see her, would Karolin Henniger and her son still be alive? That burden had to be his and he knew it, more dead because of him. He had to forget about it.

Going into the bathroom he washed his hands and face. They'd moved the entire operation to the Meineke following the discovery of a body in a seventh-floor bathroom of the Casino wing of the Hotel Palace, a room that had an almost perfect view into theirs in the main building. A special tech team was being flown in from Bad Godesberg to go over the room for evidence.

The reason they'd come to the Meineke was that it was only one building, and the only way up or down was via a creaky elevator that serviced the entire hotel. A stranger or even a friend would have a great deal of trouble getting past the BKA detectives in the lobby, or the team of Schneider and Littbarski detailed near the elevator lading two doors down. That protection left McVey and the others free to consider a severe complication.

Cadoux.

He'd suddenly reappeared, seemingly from nowhere, leaving a message for Noble through his office at New Scotland Yard that, guess of guesses, he was in Berlin. He'd emphasized he was in trouble, and said it was extremely important he speak to Noble or McVey as soon as possible and that he would call back within the hour.

McVey didn't know what to think. He saw Osborn eye him as he dumped a handful of mixed nuts onto his palm from a plastic bag. "I know. Too much fat, too much salt. I'm gonna eat 'em anyway." Carefully picking out a Brazil nut, he held it up, studied it, then popped it in his mouth. "If Cadoux's telling the truth and the group's onto him, he *is* in trouble," he said, chewing. "If he's lying, he's probably working for them. And if he is, he knows we're in Berlin. His job will be to try and sucker us out to where they can—"

A knock at the door cut McVey off in midsentence. Getting up, Remmer slid the automatic from his shoulder holster and went to the door. "*Ja.*"

"Schneider ."

Remmer opened the door and Schneider stepped in, followed by a handsome brunette in her early forties. She was taller than Schneider and wider. Pale lipstick emphasized a mouth that was turned up at the corners in a perpetual smile. Tucked under her arm was a large manila envelope.

"This is Lieutenant Kirsch," Schneider said, adding that she was a member of the BKA computer-enhancement team. Nodding at Remmer, she looked to the others and spoke in English. "I am happy to report the identity of the man driving the BMW. His name is Pascal Von Holden and he is director of security for Erwin Scholl's European business operations. We are running a profile on him now." Opening the envelope, she took out two 8 x10 black-and-white glossy photographs from the enhanced video taken of the house at 72 Hauptstrasse. The first was of Von Holden as he got out of the car. It was grainy but clear enough to make out his features. The second was grainy as well and less exact. Still, it was enough to define a youngish, dark-haired woman, standing by the window looking out.

"The woman was a little more difficult, but a positive I.D. came back from the FBI just as I was leaving to bring you the photographs," Lieutenant Kirsch said. "She is American. A licensed physical therapist. Her name is Joanna Marsh. Her residence is Taos, New Mexico."

"Elementary police work, eh McVey?" Noble raised an eyebrow in admiration.

"Luck," McVey smiled. The BKA had sent a fax of both computer-enhanced photos to the police departments in Berlin and Zurich, and, at his request, the photo of the woman to Fred Hanley at the L.A. office of the FBI. It was a long shot, but he'd had a hunch that if Lybarger was in Berlin and staying at the house in Hauptstrasse, there was a very good chance his physical therapist would be there as well. And now, with her identification confirmed, the reversal of the same ought to hold true. To wit: if she was there, so was Lybarger.

"*Danke,*" Remmer said, and Lieutenant Kirsch and Schneider left together.

There was a dull banging as the building's heat came on. McVey stared at first at one photo, then the other, memorizing them, then handed them to Noble and walked over to the window. He tried to imagine himself in Joanna Marsh's position. What was she thinking as she stood staring out from that window? How much does she know about what's going on? And what could or would she tell them if they could get to her?

Lybarger, he agreed with Osborn, was the key. What was ironic, as well as maddening, was that although they now had a clear photo of Lybarger's therapist, computer-enhanced from a videotape and identified literally in a matter of minutes by an organization halfway around the world, the only photograph Bad Godesberg had been able to rouse of Lybarger himself was a four-year-old black-and-white passport picture. And that was it. Nothing else. Not even a snapshot of him. Which was crazy. A man as important, or as seemingly important, as Lybarger should have had his picture published at least once. Somewhere. Some magazine, some newspaper, or, at the very least, some kind of investment journal. But as far as anyone could tell, he hadn't. It was as if the harder they looked, the fainter he became. Fingerprints would have been a gift from all that was holy, if for nothing else than to run them and, in all likelihood the way things were going, discount them. Clearly, Elton Lybarger had to be the most secretive, most protected man in the civilized world.

McVey looked at his watch: 4:27.

Barely thirty minutes before they were to meet Scholl. The one prayer they'd had, or hoped to have anyway, was Salettl, who McVey had desperately wanted to interview before they encountered Scholl. Maybe Karolin Henniger could have helped reach him. Who knew? But Salettl, of anyone, might have given them some insight into Lybarger, the man. Not to mention the possibility that Salettl himself was involved in the murders of the headless men. But unless things changed dramatically in a very short time, such an interview wasn't to be, and they would have to go with what they had, which was excruciatingly little.

Suddenly, the thought came to get Joanna Marsh on the telephone and try to pump her for as much as he could before she either hung up or someone did it for her. It was worth a try. At this point anything was, and he was about to ask Remmer to get the phone number of the house on Hauptstrasse when line two on the pair of secured room phones rang. Remmer glanced at McVey and picked up.

"Cadoux. Patched through from Noble's office in London," he said.

Motioning Noble to the extension, McVey took the phone from Remmer, covering the mouthpiece with his hand. "Get a trace on it." Remmer nodded and went into the bedroom, where he punched up the other line.

"Cadoux, this is McVey. Noble is on the extension. Where are you?"

"A public phone inside a small grocery in the north part of the city." Cadoux wasn't comfortable with English and spoke haltingly. He sounded tired and frightened and was talking not to be overheard, just above a whisper. "Klass and Halder are the moles inside Interpol. They arranged for the murders of Albert Merriman and Lebrun and that of his brother in Lyon."

"Cadoux, who are they working for?" McVey was pressing him right from the beginning to reveal which side he was on.

"I— I can't tell you."

"What the hell does that mean? Do you know or don't you?"

"McVey, please understand what I'm doing—this is very difficult for me—"

"All right. Take it easy. . . ."

"They—Klass and Halder—forced me to participate in the killing of Lebrun because of an old connection to my family. They brought me to Berlin because they know you are here. They wanted to use me to set you up. I cooperated with them once but it's no good and I told them so . . . I won't do it again. . . ."

"Cadoux." McVey was suddenly sympathetic. "Do they know where you are?"

"Perhaps, but I think not. At least for the moment. They have informants everywhere. It's how they knew where to find Lebrun in London. Listen to me, please." Cadoux's voice became more urgent. "I know you have a meeting scheduled with Erwin Scholl before the reception at Charlottenburg Palace tonight. I must see you before you confront him. I have information you need. It has to do with a man named Lybarger and his connection to the headless bodies."

McVey and Noble exchanged surprised glances.

"Cadoux, tell me what it is—"

"It's unsafe for me to remain here longer."

"Cadoux, this is Noble. Was a Doctor Salettl involved in removing the heads?"

"I'm staying at the Hotel Borggreve. Number 17 Borggrevestrasse. Room 412, top floor in the back. I have to hang up now. I'll expect you."

Noble let the phone settle back into the cradle and looked to McVey. "Do we have a sudden light at the end of the tunnel or is it an oncoming train."

"No idea," McVey said. "At least part of what he's told us is the truth."

Remmer came in from the bedroom. "His call came from a food shop near Schonholz subway station. Inspectors are on the way."

McVey put his hands on his hips and looked off. "Okay, he was telling the truth about that, too."

"You're worried it's a setup," Remmer said.

"Yeah, I'm worried it's a setup. But that's balanced against another worry. The same one I've had all along. That other than Osborn's testimony, our case against Scholl doesn't exist."

"What you're saying is Cadoux might be able to fill in a lot of blanks," Noble said quietly. "And trouble or not, you think we ought to meet him."

McVey waited a long moment. "I don't think we have any choice."

112

4:57 P.M.

THE THIN red glow of a setting sun sat on the horizon as a silver Audi sedan turned out of traffic on Hauptstrasse and pulled up to the front gate of the house at number 72. The driver rolled down his window as a security guard came out of the stone guardhouse, and flashed a BKA I.D.

"My name is Schneider. I have a message for Herr Scholl," he said in German. Immediately, two other security guards, one with a German shepherd on a leash, appeared out of the enveloping darkness. Schneider was asked to step out of the car and it was thoroughly searched. Five minutes later he drove through the gate and up to the main entry.

The front door opened and he was ushered inside. A pale, pig-faced man in a tuxedo met him in the foyer. "I have a message for Herr Scholl."

"You can tell me."

"My orders are to speak to Herr Scholl ."

They went into a small paneled room where he was frisked.

"Not armed," he said as another man, also in a tuxedo,

entered. He was tall and good-looking, and Schneider knew instantly he'd met Von Holden.

"Please, sit down," he said, then left through a side door. He was younger and more fit than his photograph allowed. Close to Osborn's age, Schneider thought.

Ten minutes or more passed with Schneider seated and the pig-faced man standing, watching him, before the same door opened and Scholl entered, followed by Von Holden.

"I am Erwin Scholl."

"My name is Schneider of the Bundeskriminalamt," Schneider said, getting up. "Detective McVey has unfortunately been delayed. He has asked me to apologize and to see if another time can be arranged."

"I'm sorry," Scholl said. "I am leaving for Buenos Aires this evening."

"That's too bad." Schneider paused, using the time to try to get a sense of the man.

"I had very little time as it was. Mr. McVey knew that."

"I understand. Well, again his apologies." Bowing slightly, Schneider nodded to Von Holden, then turned on his heel and left. Moments later, the gate opened and he drove off. He'd been asked to keep a sharp eye for Lybarger or the woman in the photograph. All he'd been allowed to see was the foyer and the small paneled room. Scholl had addressed him with complete indifference. Von Holden had been cordial, nothing more. Scholl had been there at the appointed time as promised, and there had been nothing to indicate he planned otherwise. That meant there was every chance they had no idea what Cadoux was up to and lessened the probability of a setup. For that, Schneider breathed a sigh of relief.

Scholl himself had seemed little more than a well-preserved old man used to subservience and getting what he wanted. The curious thing—and it was curious—was not so much the zigzag of deep scratches healing on Scholl's left hand and wrist, but the prominent way he held the hand up, as if he were displaying it and at the same time saying: Any other man would find pain in this and look for sympathy; I, instead, have found pleasure, which is something you could never understand.

113

THEY WERE riding in two cars. Noble with Remmer in the Mercedes. Osborn at the wheel of a black Ford, with McVey in the passenger seat beside him. Unmarked BKA backup cars, one with veteran inspectors Kellermann and Seidenberg, and one with Littbarski and a boyish-looking detective named Holt, were already outside the hotel. Kellermann/Seidenberg in the back alley, Littbarski/Holt across the street in front. Kellermann and Seidenberg had checked out the small grocery near the Schonholz subway entrance where Cadoux had made his call. The proprietor vaguely remembered a man of Cadoux's description using the telephone and seemed to think he'd been there only a short time and had been alone.

In front of them Remmer pulled to the curb and shut out the lights. "Keep going to the corner. When you find a spot pull in," McVey said to Osborn.

The Hotel Borggreve was a small residential hotel on a particularly dark section of street northeast of the Tiergarten. Four stories tall, maybe sixty feet wide, it linked two taller apartment buildings. From the front, it looked old and poorly kept. Room 412, Cadoux had told them. Top floor in the back.

Osborn turned the corner at the end of the block and parked behind a white Alfa Romeo. Unbuttoning his suit coat, McVey slid out the .38 and flipped open the chamber to make sure it was loaded. "I don't like being lied to," he said. McVey had said nothing of Osborn's confession since he'd identified Von Holden during the screening of the Hauptstrasse house video. He was saying it now because he wanted to remind Osborn who was in control of the situation.

"It wasn't your father who was murdered," Osborn said, looking at him. There was no apology, no backing away. He was still angry at the way McVey had used him to try to get Vera to make a mistake and say something he could catch her on. And he was still angry as hell at the way she'd been treated by the police. The whole thing with Vera—the emotional rush of seeing her, of holding her—had played against his doubt of who or what she might really be, had slammed him once more with the emotional roller coaster his life had been. Seeing her like that had simplified things for him because it focused his priorities. He had to have an answer from Scholl before he could even begin to consider what Vera meant or who she was. That's why there was no apology to McVey, nor would there be. At this point they were equals or nothing.

"It's going to be a long night, Doctor, with a lot on the line. Don't start getting big for your britches." Holstering the revolver, McVey picked a two-way radio off the seat and clicked it on.

"Remmer?"

"I'm here, McVey." Remmer's voice came back sharply through the tiny speaker.

"Everybody on line?"

"*Ja.*"

"Tell them we don't know what this is, so everybody take it easy."

They heard Remmer relay the message in German, then

McVey clicked open the glove compartment. Reaching in, he took out the Cz automatic Osborn had carried with him in the park and handed it to him. "Keep the lights out and the doors locked." Fixing him with a stare, McVey pushed the door open and stepped out. Cold air wafted in, then the door slammed and he was gone. Looking in the rearview mirror, Osborn could see him reach the corner and open his suit coat. Then he turned the corner and the street was empty.

The rear of the Hotel Borggreve faced a narrow alley lined with trees. On the far side, a row of apartment buildings ran the entire block. Whatever happened in the alley and the back of the Hotel Borggreve belonged to Inspectors Kellermann and Seidenberg. Kellermann was standing in the shadows beside a dumpster, binoculars trained on the window of the room second from the left on the top floor. From what he could tell, a lamp was on in the room, but that was all he could tell. Then he heard Littbarski's voice through the earphone of his two-way radio.

"Kellermann, we're going inside. Anything?"

"*Nein.*" He spoke softly into the tiny microphone on his lapel. Across the alley he could see Seidenberg's bulky form silhouetted against an oak tree. He was holding a shotgun and watching the hotel's back door.

"Nothing here, either," Seidenberg said.

Salettl stood in a large bedroom on the second floor of the house on Hauptstrasse watching as Edward and Eric playfully helped each other knot the bow ties at the throats of their formal shirts. If they weren't twin brothers, he thought, they might well be youthful homosexual lovers.

"How do you feel?" he asked.

"Well," Eric said, turning quickly and very nearly coming to attention.

"And I, the same," Edward echoed.

Salettl stood a moment longer, then left.

Downstairs, he crossed an ornate, oak-paneled hallway and entered an equally ornate den where Scholl, resplendent in white tie, stood in front of a crackling fire, a snifter of cognac in his hand. Uta Baur, in one of her all-black creations, sat in a chair beside him, smoking a Turkish cigarette held in a cigarette holder.

"Von Holden is with Mr. Lybarger," Salettl said.

"I know," Scholl said.

"It was unfortunate that the policeman involved the cardinal—"

"Nothing should concern you but Eric and Edward and Mr. Lybarger." Scholl smiled coldly. "This night is ours, good doctor. *All* of ours." Suddenly he looked off. "Not just the living, but those now dead who had the vision and courage and the dedication to begin it. Tonight is for them. For them, we will experience and savor and touch the future." Scholl's eyes came back to Salettl. "And nothing, good Doctor," he said quietly, "will take that from us."

114

I WOULD like the key to room 412, please," Remmer said in German to a gray-haired woman behind the desk. She wore thick glasses and had a brownish shawl pulled up over her shoulders.

"That room is taken," she said indignantly, then looked up to McVey, who stood behind him to the left of the elevator. "What is your name?"

"Why should I answer that question? Who the hell do you think you are?"

"BKA," Remmer said, flashing his I.D.

"My name is Anna Schubart," she said quickly. "What do you want?"

McVey and Noble stood halfway between the front door and a stairway covered by a worn burgundy carpet. The lobby itself was small, painted the color of dark mustard. A wood-framed velvet couch sat at an angle to the desk, while behind it, two faded and unmatched overstuffed chairs faced a fireplace where a small fire was burning. An elderly man dozed in one of them, an open newspaper across his lap.

"The stairway goes all the way to the top floor?"

"Yes."

"That and the elevator are the only ways in and out?"

"Yes."

"The old man sleeping, is he a guest?"

"He's my father. What's going on?"

"You keep quarters here?"

"Back there." Anna Schubart tossed her head, indicating a closed door behind the desk.

"Take your father and go inside. I'll tell you when to come out."

The woman's face turned red and she was about to tell him to go to hell, when the front door opened and Littbarski and Holt came in. Littbarski carried a shotgun. An Uzi submachine gun dangled at Holt's side.

That was enough for Anna Schubart's pride. Reaching to a wall box behind her, she took out the key to room 412 and gave it to Remmer. Then, walking quickly to the old man, she shook him awake. "*Komm, Vater,*" she said. Helping him up, she walked him, blinking and staring, around the desk and into the back room. With a sharp glance back at the police, she closed the door.

"Tell Holt to stay here," McVey said to Remmer. "You

and Littbarski take the stairs. The old men'll take the elevator. We'll wait for you at the top."

Crossing to the elevator, McVey punched the button and the door opened immediately and he and Noble stepped inside. The door slid closed, and Remmer and Littbarski went up the stairs.

Outside, in the back alley, Kellermann thought he saw a light brighten in the room next to Cadoux's, but even with the binoculars it was hard to tell. Whatever it was, it seemed too insignificant to report.

The elevator banged to a stop on the top floor and the door opened. Thirty-eight in hand, McVey looked out. The hallway was dimly lit and empty. Putting the elevator on "lock," he stepped out. Noble followed, carrying a matte black .44 Magnum automatic.

They'd gone about twenty feet when McVey pulled up and nodded to a closed door across from them.

Room 412.

Suddenly a shadow ran up the ceiling at the far end of the hallway, and both men pressed back against the wall. Then Remmer turned the corner, gun in hand. Littbarski was at his heels. Stepping out, McVey pointed at the 412 doorway and the men came toward it from either end of the hallway. McVey and Noble from the left, Remmer and Littbarski from the right.

As they came together, McVey motioned Littbarski into the center of the hallway so he could take up a position that would give him a clear shotgun blast at the door.

Shifting the .38 to his left hand, McVey stood to the side of the door, then eased the key into the lock and turned it.

Click.

The dead bolt slid back and they listened.

Silence.

Bracing himself, Littbarski aimed the shotgun directly at the center of the door. A trickle of sweat ran down the side of Remmer's face as he pressed back tight against the wall on the far side of the door. Noble, two hands on the Magnum military style, stood at the ready, a foot behind McVey on the near side.

Taking a breath, McVey reached out and grasped the doorknob. Twisting it, he shoved gently. The door opened several inches and stopped. Inside they could just make out part of a dimly lit rococo floor lamp and the corner of a couch. A radio, at low volume, played a Strauss waltz.

"Cadoux," McVey called out loud.

Nothing. Only the sound of the waltz.

"Cadoux," he said again.

Still nothing.

Glancing at Remmer, McVey gave the door a hard shove and it swung open far enough for them to see Cadoux sitting on the couch facing them. He was wearing a dark corduroy sport coat over a blue shirt, and a narrow tie was knotted loosely at his throat. A crimson stain had spread over most of what was visible of the shirt, and the tie had three holes in it, one right over the other.

Straightening, McVey looked up and down the hallway. The doors to the five other rooms were closed and no light showed beneath them. The only sound came from the radio in Cadoux's room. Bringing the .38 up, McVey stepped into the doorway and eased the door all the way open with the toe of his shoe. What they saw was a double bed with a cheap nightstand next to it. Beyond it was a partially open door to the darkened bathroom. McVey looked over his shoulder at Littbárski, who tightened his grip on the shotgun and nodded. Then McVey looked to Remmer on the far side of the doorway, then to Noble at his left shoulder.

"Cadoux is dead. Shot," Remmer said in German into the microphone at his collar.

In the lobby, Holt moved back, covering the front door with the Uzi. In the back alley, Seidenberg blinked his eyes to clear them and pulled deeper into the shadows behind the oak tree, covering both the rear door and the alley. Kellermann refocused his binoculars on the window.

"We're going into the room." Remmer's voice came through all the radios again. The men tensed as if they had a sudden and universal premonition something was going to happen.

Littbarski stood his ground in the hallway as McVey led the way into the room. Abruptly it lit up brighter than the sun.

"Look out!" he screamed.

There was a thundering explosion. Littbarski was blown off his feet and the entire window of room 412 erupted outward into the alley, casing and all. Immediately, a huge rolling fireball roared skyward pulling with it a trail of heavy black smoke.

At the same instant, the door of the hotel clerk's living quarters was jerked open and Anna stepped into the lobby.

"What was that?" she snapped at Holt in German.

"Get back inside!" he yelled, looking up as dust and plaster rained down from the ceiling. Then it occurred to him she was no longer wearing the thick glasses. He looked back too late. A .45 caliber assault pistol was in her hand, a silencer squirreled to the barrel.

PTTT. PTTT. PTTT.

The gun bucked in her hand and Holt stumbled backward. He tried to get the Uzi up, but couldn't. His lower jaw and the left side of his face were gone.

McVey was flat on his back on the floor. Fire was everywhere. He heard somebody screaming, but he didn't know who it was. Through the flame, he saw Cadoux above him. He was smiling and had a gun in his hand. Rolling over, McVey raised up and fired twice. Then he realized the only thing left of Cadoux was his upper torso, the gun in the hand was part of something else but it was something he couldn't see.

"Ian!" he cried out, trying to get up. The heat was unbearable. "Remmer!"

Somewhere off, over the roar of the flames, he thought he heard a burst of automatic weapons fire followed abruptly by the heavy boom of Littbarski's shotgun. Pushing himself off the floor, he tried to visualize where he was and where the door was. Someone was groaning and coughing nearby. Putting up an arm against the heat and flame, he moved toward the sound. A heartbeat later he saw Remmer, gagging and coughing in the smoke, on one knee trying to get up. Moving to him, he threw an arm under his elbow and lifted.

"Manny! Get up! It's okay!"

Grunting in pain, Remmer stood, and McVey started them off through the smoke, in the direction he thought the door ought to be. Then they were out of the room and into the hall. Littbarski was on the floor, blood oozing from a close pattern of bullet holes in his chest. Partway down the hall was what was left of a young woman. A machine pistol was on the floor nearby. Littbarski's shotgun had decapitated her.

"Christ!" McVey swore. Looking up, he saw the flames had broken out into the hallway and were climbing up the walls. Remmer had slumped back to one knee and was grimacing in pain. His left forearm was bent backward, his wrist dangling at an unnatural angle.

"Where the hell is Ian?" McVey started back into the room. "Ian! Ian!"

"McVey." Remmer was using the wall to help him stand. "We've got to get the hell out of here!"

"IAN!" McVey cried out again into thick smoke and roaring inferno inside the room.

Then Remmer had McVey by the arm and was tugging

him down the hallway. "Come one, McVey. Jesus Christ! Leave him! *He* would!"

McVey's eyes locked on Remmer's. He was right. The dead were dead and the hell with them. Then there was a sound at their feet and Noble crawled through the doorway. His hair was on fire, so were his clothes.

Two shots from a Steyr-Mannlicher telescopic rifle, fired from a rooftop across the alley, had taken down Kellermann and Seidenberg. And now Viktor Shevchenko, having discarded the Steyr-Mannlicher for a Kalashnikov automatic rifle, was rushing up the stairs to the lobby to help Natalia and Anna take care of any unfinished business. The trouble was there was one person he hadn't counted on, and neither had Anna—Osborn, who'd come running at the sound of the explosion, Bernhard Oven's Cz in his hand.

His first encounter had been with an old man who had been right outside the car just as he'd opened the door. The startled moment between them had given Osborn the split second he needed to see the automatic in the old man's hand and to shove the Cz into his stomach and fire. Then he'd run the half block to the hotel and raced into the lobby at full speed at the moment Anna put a just-to-make-sure shot into Holt. Seeing him, Anna swung the gun, firing in a fan pattern toward him. With no other choice, Osborn had simply stood his ground and squeezed the trigger. His first shot hit her in the throat. His second grazed her skull, spinning her around and throwing her face-first onto the chair above Holt's body.

Ears still ringing from the blast of the gunshots, Osborn had the sense he'd better turn around. As he did, Viktor came through the door swinging the Kalashnikov from his waist. He saw Osborn but wasn't quick enough, and Osborn pumped three shots into his chest before he crossed the threshold. For a second Viktor just stood there, totally surprised that it was Osborn who had shot him, and that anything at all could happen that fast. Then the look faded to disbelief and he stumbled backward, tried to catch himself on the handrail, then fell headfirst down the stairs.

With the acrid smell of gunsmoke still hanging in the air, Osborn looked down at Viktor, then stepped back inside and looked around. Everything seemed strangely off-angle, as if he'd walked into the middle of a bizarre and bloody sculpture. Holt lay on his side near the fireplace where he had fallen. Anna, his killer, was facedown, half kneeling on the chair next to him. Her skirt, obscenely hiked up over her rump, exposed a tight-fitting half stocking, and above it, a white fleshy thigh. A soft breeze washing in through the front door worked at cleansing everything, but couldn't. In the space of no time, Osborn had killed three people, one of them a woman. He tried to make sense of it but couldn't. Finally, in the distance, he heard sirens.

Then, real time lurched back.

A grinding sound to his right was followed by a heavy thud. Swinging around, he saw the elevator door start to open. Heart racing, he stepped back, wondering in the same instant if he had any ammunition left. Abruptly a figure started out.

"HALT!" he yelled, trying desperately to think of the German, his finger closing on the trigger, the ugly snout of the Cz coming up to fire.

"OSBORN! JESUS CHRIST, DON'T SHOOT!" McVey's voice rang out at him. They staggered forward out of the elevator, retching and coughing, trying to suck in fresh air. McVey and Remmer, bloody, tattered and reeking of smoke, with Noble, painfully burned and semiconscious, somehow propped between them.

Osborn rushed to them. Seeing Noble up close, he grimaced. "Get him down in a chair. Easy!"

McVey's eyes were bright red from the smoke and they

came up to Osborn and hung on him. "Pull the alarm," he said carefully, as if making absolutely certain he was understood. "The whole top floor is burning."

115

6:50 P.M.

"I AM comfortable tonight," Elton Lybarger said, smiling easily, looking from Von Holden to Joanna beside him. Theirs was the middle car in a train of three armor-plated black Mercedes-Benz limousines traveling bumper to bumper across Berlin. Scholl and Uta Baur rode in the lead car; in the last were Salettl and the twins, Eric and Edward. "I am relaxed and feel confident. My thanks go to both of you."

"It's why we are here, sir. To make you feel at ease," Von Holden said as the limousines turned onto Lietzenburgerstrasse and sped off in the direction of Charlottenburg Palace.

Brushing a piece of lint from the arm of his tuxedo, Von Holden picked up the phone from the backseat console and dialed a number. Joanna smiled. If he'd been less distracted he might fully have appreciated the way she looked because she'd done it for him. Her makeup flawless, her hair was parted on the left, then teased up and dampened so that it fell in a natural cascade over the right side of her face, setting off the stunningly seductive Uta Baur creation she wore—a floor-length white-and-emerald gown, closed at the throat but then open again nearly to the sternum in a teasingly erotic display of her breasts. With a short black mink coat thrown over her shoulders, she looked, on her last night among European aristocracy, as if she were part of it.

Von Holden smiled thinly back at her while the phone continued to ring on the other end. Abruptly a recorded voice interceded in German. "Please call back, the vehicle is unattended."

Von Holden let the phone slip through his fingers and he hung up slowly, trying not to show his frustration. Once again came the feeling that he should have argued more forcefully with Scholl, that his place was with the operation at the Hotel Borggreve, not delivering Lybarger to Charlottenburg. But he hadn't, and there was nothing on earth he could do about it now.

At three that afternoon, he had forged the final details of his plan with the Stasi-trained operatives who would execute it—Cadoux, Natalia, and Viktor Shevchenko. Joining them had been Anna Schubart and Wilhelm Podl, explosives specialists and Libyan-trained terrorists, who had arrived by train from Poland.

Meeting in a dingy back room of a motorcycle repair shop near the Ostbahnhof, one of East Berlin's two main train stations, Von Holden had used photographs and drawings of Hotel Borggreve, one of several buildings owned by a nonexistent company fronting the Berlin sector, to carefully blueprint the tactics and timing of what he wanted done. His planning had been so detailed as to include how Anna and Wilhelm, playing the role of her aging father, would dress, the type and number of weapons that would be used, and the size of the charge and the manner of detonation of the Semtex explosive.

McVey and the others had been handed a situation they could not afford to turn down. What gave Von Holden the only edge he would need was what Scholl had pointed out and what he had known from the beginning: that, capable as McVey and the others had proven, they were still police-men. They would think as policemen and prepare as police-men, cautiously but predictably. Von Holden understood this because many of his own operatives had been recruited from the ranks of the police and he had found, early on, how completely unequipped they were in the terrorist mind-set, and how thoroughly retrained they had to be.

Understanding this, the process itself was simple. Cadoux, having reached them by telephone and given them enough truthful information to incriminate himself, would then promise them the intelligence they needed to pursue Scholl. Telling them he was afraid for his life at the hands of the men he had double-crossed, he would give them an address where they could find him, and then hang up.

When they came, he would start to give them the infor-mation they needed, then excuse himself to go to the john. Not wholly trusting him, one of the men would accompany him. And he wouldn't protest. As soon as they'd left the room, Natalia would trigger the plastic explosive by re-mote control. Cadoux would shoot the man with him and Natalia would take out any policemen waiting in the hall-way outside. Viktor, Anna and Wilhelm Podl would handle the traffic in the lobby and outside the building. Overall it was exceedingly simple. They were leading their victims into a small box and then exterminating them.

At 3:45 exactly, the meeting broke up. The others went to the hotel and Von Holden drove Cadoux to the grocery nearby to make the call. Once done, they went directly to the hotel, ran over the plan one more time and planted the explosives. Then, telling the others he wanted to talk with Cadoux privately, he closed the door to room 412.

What he'd wanted to do was make Cadoux feel impor-tant, that there were no hard feelings from his earlier mis-take, because he knew how much Avril Rocard meant to him. Wishing him well, he'd started to go, then turned back realizing he had forgotten to provide Cadoux with a weapon. Opening his briefcase, he took out a nine-millimeter automatic pistol, an Austrian made Glock 18. The Glock 18 could be switched to fully automatic fire and was fitted with a magazine that carried thirty-three rounds, and Cadoux had brightened at the sight of it. "Good choice," Von Holden remembered him saying.

"One other thing," Von Holden had said before handing him the gun. "Mademoiselle Rocard is dead. She was killed at the farmhouse near Nancy."

"What?" Cadoux roared in disbelief.

"Unfortunate. Especially from my point of view."

"Your point of view?" Cadoux was ash white.

"She was in Berlin at my invitation. We were lovers, or didn't you know? She enjoyed a good fuck, not the impossible thing she tolerated from you."

Cadoux came at him in a rush. Screaming with rage. Von Holden did nothing until Cadoux reached him, then he simply lifted the Glock and squeezed off three quick rounds. Cadoux's body had muffled the report, the slugs barely making a sound. After that he'd put him on the couch in a sitting position and left.

In the distance, Von Holden could see the brightly lit facade of Charlottenburg as they approached. Picking up the phone once more, he punched in the number and waited as it rang. Again he got the same answer. The vehicle was unattended. Hanging up, he stared off. His instructions had been rigidly clear. Immediately following the detonation of the Semtex and what should have been the simple mop-up operation afterward, the four were to leave the hotel and drive off in a blue Fiat delivery truck parked diagonally across the street. They were to go south away from the area, until Von Holden contacted them by car phone for a report. Afterward, they were to leave the truck on Borussiastrasse near Tempelhof Airport, and go off alone and in different directions. By ten o'clock, they were to have been out of the country.

"Is something wrong, Pascal?" Joanna asked.

"No, nothing," Von Holden smiled at her.

Joanna smiled back. Then they were swinging through the iron gates, over the pavement stone of Charlottenburg's entryway, and around the equestrian statue of the Great Elector, Friedrich Wilhelm I. In front of them Von Holden could see Scholl's limousine, and Scholl and Uta Baur getting out. Next, his driver was pulling up. The limousine stopped. The door was opened and a heavyset security guard in a tuxedo extended his hand to Joanna.

Three minutes later they were being shown into the Historical Apartments, the rich, ornate, private living quarters of Friedrich the First and his wife, Sophie-Charlotte. Scholl, suddenly acting like an excited theatrical producer, had Lybarger, Eric and Edward in a corner and was trying to locate a still photographer to take pictures.

Taking Joanna aside, Von Holden asked her to make certain Lybarger was taken to a room where he could rest until he was called.

"Something is wrong, isn't it?"

"Not at all. I'll be back," he said quickly. Then, avoiding Scholl, he left by a side door and pushed his way through a corridor filled with serving personnel. Moving toward the main reception area, he turned into an alcove and tried to raise the Hotel Borggreve by radio. There was no reply.

Snapping off the radio, he nodded to a security agent and went out through the main entrance where the others were beginning to arrive. He saw the exceedingly short, bearded Hans Dabritz step out of a limousine and extend his hand to a tall, exquisitely thin, black fashion model, thirty years his junior. Keeping in the shadows, he walked toward the street. Crossing the driveway, he glimpsed Konrad and Margarete Peiper in the backseat of a limousine as it passed him. Behind them was a solid line of limousines waiting to turn in through the main gate. If Von Holden called for his, it would be at least ten minutes before it arrived. And right now ten minutes was far too long to stand passively by waiting for a limousine. Across the street, he saw activist Gertrude Biermann get out of a taxi and cross determinedly toward him, her thick ankles all too visible beneath the loden green of her military overcoat. As she reached the main entrance, her plain, militant appearance caused a rush of security personnel. And she reacted in kind, baring her temper as well as her invitation. Across, the taxi she had arrived in was still by the curbside, waiting to pull out in traffic. Quickly Von Holden moved to it, opened the rear door and got in.

"Where do you want to go?" the taxi driver asked, staring over his shoulder at the river of oncoming headlights then abruptly accelerating off with a squeal of tires.

That afternoon after he'd made love to Joanna in her room at the house on Hauptstrasse, Von Holden had immediately fallen asleep. And even though it had been only for a few minutes, it had been long enough for the dream to come back. Overwhelmed by the horror, he'd awakened with a shout, soaked in sweat. Joanna had tried to comfort him but he'd pushed her aside and drenched himself in the rush of an ice-cold shower. The water and press of time revived him quickly and he blamed the whole episode on exhaustion. But it was a lie. The dream had been real. The "Vorahnung," the premonition, had come back. It had been there again the moment he put his hand on the limousine telephone and felt the jolt of fear that there would be no answer when he dialed. That even before he called, he knew something had gone dreadfully wrong.

"I asked you where you wanted to go?" the driver said again. "Or should I drive around in circles while you make up your mind?"

Von Holden's eyes went to the driver's reflection in the

mirror. He was young, twenty-two at most. Blond, smiling and chewing gum. How was he to know there was only one place his passenger could go?"

"The Hotel Borggreve," Von Holden said.

116

LESS THAN ten minutes later the taxi turned onto Borggrevestrasse and immediately stopped. The street was blocked off by a police barricade with fire trucks, ambulances and police cars. In the distance, Von Holden could see flames reaching into the night sky. It was exactly what he should have seen if everything had gone as planned. But with no communication with the operatives, there was no way to know for certain what had happened.

Suddenly Von Holden's heart began to palpitate violently and he broke into a cold sweat. The palpitations increased. It felt as if someone were tying a knot inside his chest. Terrified, struggling to breathe, he put his hands out beside him for fear he would black out and fall over. Somewhere he thought he heard the taxi driver ask him where he wanted to go now, because the police were kicking everyone out of the area. Reaching up, he clawed at his collar, his fingers fumbling with his tie. Finally he tore it free and lay back, gasping for air.

"What's the matter?" the driver turned around in his seat to look at him over his shoulder.

Just then an emergency vehicle pulled up beside them, its flashing lights skip-jacking like knives through his ocular nerves. Crying out, he threw up a hand and turned away trying to find darkness.

Then they came.

The monstrous candy-colored ribbons of green and red undulating up and down in perfect rhythm. Huge, demonic pistons shoving through the very center of his being. Von Holden's eyes rolled back and his tongue caught in his throat as if to strangle him. Never had the dream come while he was awake. And never in so horrible a way.

Certain he would die if he didn't get out of the cab, he lunged for the door. Flinging it open, he dragged himself across the seat and stepped out into the night air.

"Hey! Where are you going?" the driver yelled over the seat. "What the hell do you think this is, free service?" The smiling, gum-chewing kid was suddenly an angry capitalist. It was then Von Holden realized the driver was a woman. With her hair tucked up under a cap and loose-fitting jacket, he hadn't noticed at first.

Breathing deeply, Von Holden stared back. "Do you know Behrenstrasse?" he said.

"Yes."

"Take me to number 45."

Lights of oncoming traffic illuminated the men in the car. Schneider was driving with Remmer beside him. McVey and Osborn were in the back. McVey's lower right cheek and most of his lower lip had been burned raw and had been covered with salve to protect them. The hair on Remmer's head had been singed back to the scalp and his left hand had been broken in a number of places when part of the ceiling had come crashing down a split second after the explosion. Osborn had taken over for the paramedic at the scene and bandaged it tightly when Remmer insisted that as long as he could walk, the night was not yet over. To a man they remembered Noble as he was being put into the ambulance. Burned over two-thirds of his body, fluid drip-dripping into his system from an IV held over his head, he should have been at the edge of death and out cold. Instead, he'd opened his eyes and looked up at them and in a hoarse voice, through an oxygen mask, managed—"Plastic explosive. Stupid bastards, aren't we—" Then his voice grew strong and rose in anger. "Get them," he said, and his eyes glistened. "Get them and break them."

Remmer held on as Schneider wheeled the Audi through a sharp turn, then looked back at McVey. "We won't surprise Scholl, you know. Security will let him know the moment we arrive."

McVey was staring off and didn't respond. Noble had been right. They were stupid bastards, the way they'd blundered into the trap. But they'd been anxious and they'd had the pressure of time, of getting to Cadoux before the group did. In retrospect, it was a situation where they should have gone in with marines, not policemen— or at least called in a Berlin P.D. swat team. But they hadn't and of the four of them, it was Noble who had paid for it the worst of all. The slain German cops angered him too. But there was nothing any of them could do about that now. The only consolation, if there was one, was that four of the group's people had gone down too. Hopefully, identification of the bodies would open new doors.

Remmer pressed. "Not only will security inform Scholl, they won't want to let us inside. Our warrant is only for Scholl. Their position will be that it's not for the premises. We can't serve a warrant if we can't get to him."

McVey looked up. "Tell them that if they attempt to delay us, we will have the fire minister close the building. That doesn't work, use your imagination. You're a cop, they're only security." Abruptly he turned to Osborn and leaned in close. His facial burns were ugly and painful but his eyes were alive and intent, and he spoke quickly and with determination. "Scholl may deny it or excuse it out of hand, but he'll know who you are and that this whole thing got started because of your business with Albert Merriman in Paris. He will assume Merriman told you about him and that you told me. What he won't know, or at least I *think* he won't know, is how much we've put together about the rest. Even if his security people alert him, he'll still be surprised to see us because he'll think we're dead. He's also arrogant enough to be upset that we're interrupting his party. Which is something I'm counting on. For reasons we're not entirely sure of, this is a very big deal for him and he's going to want to get rid of us fast as he can and get back to his guests. But we're not going to let him. Which is going to make him even madder. And then we're going to make him madder still."

Osborn looked at him uncertainly. "I don't follow."

"We're going to tell him everything we know. About your father's murder. The scalpel he invented and the occupations and murders of the other people killed the same year he was. And at some point we're going to throw in a few things we don't know but are going to act like we do. The idea is to put so much pressure on him that he breaks. Squeeze him so hard that he rolls over and cops out. Confesses to murder for hire." McVey suddenly looked at Remmer. "How many backup units did you request?"

"Six. With six more holding—waiting for our instructions. We have uniforms behind that if there is a reason for mass arrest."

"McVey," Osborn said. "You said we were going to tell him what we don't know. What do you mean?"

"Suppose, for Herr Scholl's benefit, we tell him we've been searching high and low for a profile of his guest of honor, Herr Lybarger, and have come up with nothing. We're curious and would like to meet him. For a lot of reasons he'll refuse. And to that we say, okay, since you won't let us meet him we have to assume the reason we've come up with nothing is that the poor guy is dead and has been for a long time."

"Dead?" Remmer said from the front.

"Yeah. Dead."

"Then who's playing Lybarger and why?"

"I didn't say it wasn't Lybarger. I simply said the reason we don't know anything about him is that he's dead. At least most of him is—"

Osborn felt ice creep down his spine. "You think he's a successful experiment. That it's Lybarger's head on someone else's body. Done by atomic surgery at absolute zero."

"I don't know if I think it but it's not a bad theory, is it? Lying or not, it was Cadoux who made the connection for us when he said he had information connecting Scholl to Lybarger, and Lybarger to the headless corpses. Why else the mystery surrounding Lybarger's stroke and his isolation with Doctor Salettl at the hospital in Carmel and his long recuperation at the nursing home in New Mexico? Richman, the micropathologist, said if the operation were done and successful, it would be seamless, undetectable, like a limb grown on a tree. Even his physical therapist, the American girl, wouldn't know. Wouldn't in her wildest imagination have any idea."

"McVey, I think you've been in Hollywood too long." Remmer lit a cigarette and held it between tightly bandaged fingers. "Why don't you try selling that to the movies."

"I bet that's what Scholl says, but I think we ought to take a shot at proving it or disproving it anyway."

"How?"

"Lybarger's fingerprints."

Remmer stared at him. "McVey, this is no theory. You actually believe it."

"I don't disbelieve it, Manfred. I'm too old. I can believe anything."

"Even if we get Lybarger's prints, which won't be the easiest thing on earth, what good are they? If your Frankenstein theory is right and his own body from the shoulders down is dead and buried God knows where, we would have nothing to compare them to anyway."

"Manfred, if you were going to have your head joined to another body wouldn't you pick a much *younger* body?"

"This is a bizarre side of you I have never seen." Remmer smiled.

"Pretend it's not bizarre. Pretend it's done all the time."

"Well—If I was—Yes, sure, a younger body. With my experience, think of all the young, beautiful girls I could get." Remmer grinned.

"Good. Now let me tell you we've got the once deep-frozen head of a man in his early twenties sitting in a morgue in London. His name is Timothy Ashford of Clapham South. He was once in a fight with a couple of bobbies, so the London P.D. has his prints in their Records Bureau."

Remmer's smile faded. "You actually think this Timothy Ashford's fingerprints could belong to Lybarger?"

McVey raised a hand and touched the salve covering his burns. Wincing, he took his hand away and looked at the black flecks of his own charred skin in clear salve.

"These people have gone to a lot of trouble to keep anyone from finding out what's going on, and a lot of people are dead because of it. Yes, I'm guessing, Manfred. But Scholl's not going to know that, is he?"

117

THE SPRAWLING works of the German Romantic artists Runge, Overbeck, and Caspar David Friedrich—whose brooding landscapes portrayed humans as insignificant against the overwhelming enormity of nature—covered the walls of Charlottenburg's Gallery of Romantic Art, while a string quartet alternating with a concert pianist played a selection of Beethoven sonatas and concertos, to provide an apt mood and setting for the gathering of the powerful guests come to honor Elton Lybarger. Intermingling loudly, they argued politics, the economy and Germany's future, while formally dressed waiters danced among them with cornucopian trays brimming with drink and hors d'oeuvres.

Salettl stood alone near the gallery entrance watching the whirlwind. From what he could tell, nearly everyone invited had come, and he smiled at the turnout. Crossing the room, he saw Uta Baur with Konrad Peiper. And Scholl, along with German newspaper magnate Hilmar Grunel and Margarete Peiper, stood listening to his American attorney, Louis Goetz, hold court in English. Four words Goetz threw out in a matter of seconds told the direction of his take. Hollywood. Talent agencies. Kikes.

Then Gustav Dortmund entered with his wife, a staid, white-haired woman in a dark green evening dress whose plainness was offset by a dazzling show of diamonds. Almost immediately Scholl went over to Dortmund and the two went off to a corner to talk.

Summoning a waiter, Salettl lifted a glass of champagne, then looked at his watch. It was 7:52. At 8:05 the guests would be ushered up the grand stairway to the Golden Gallery, where dinner would be served. At 9:00 exactly, he would excuse himself and go to the mausoleum to check on Von Holden's preparations for the privileged proceedings that would take place there following Lybarger's speech. By 9:10, he would have made his way to Lybarger's quarters, where Lybarger, in the company of Joanna and Eric and Edward, would be in the final stages of his preparation.

Taking Joanna aside, he would tell her her assignment was complete and dismiss her, ordering a driver to take her immediately from the palace. That meant that once she had gone, and with the exception of carefully screened security and service personnel. the entire building would now be free of outsiders. At 9:15, Lybarger would make his entrance into the Golden Gallery. His speech would be over at 9:30, and by 9:45 everything would be done.

Behrenstrasse was a street of town homes lined with stately and ancient trees. A middle-aged couple out for a stroll after dinner passed under a streetlight and walked on as Von Holden's taxi pulled up in front of number 45.

Telling the driver to wait, he got out, pushed through an iron gate and went quickly up the steps of the four-story building. Pressing the bell, he stood back and looked up. The clear sky of earlier had turned to a low overcast and the weather service called for drizzle and fog later in the evening. It was a bad sign. Fog kept planes grounded, and Scholl was due to fly out for his estate in Argentina immediately after the final ceremony at Charlottenburg. Of all nights, this was not the one for fog.

There was a sharp sound and abruptly the door opened, and a bone-thin man of sixty or so squinted out at him.

"*Guten Abend,*" he said, recognizing Von Holden and standing aside to let him enter.

"Yes, good evening, Herr Frazen."

Two women and a man, all Frazen's age, looked up from a card table as Von Holden passed the sitting room and disappeared down the hallway. The women giggled girlishly, agreeing what a dashing figure Von Holden cut in a tuxedo. The men told them to shut up. How Von Holden was dressed or what he was doing there at that time of night was none of their business.

At the far end of the hallway, Von Holden unlocked a door and entered a small paneled study. Impatiently closing the door, he relocked it and went to a grandfather clock in the corner behind a heavy desk. Opening the clock, he took out its winding key and inserted it into a nearly invisible hole in a panel to its left. A quarter twist, and the panel slid back, exposing a highly polished, stainless-steel door with a digital panel inlaid in its upper right corner. As if he were using an automatic teller machine, Von Holden punched in a code. Immediately the door slid back exposing a small elevator. Von Holden stepped in, the door closed and the carved panel slid back into place.

For a full three minutes the elevator descended, then it stopped and Von Holden stepped into a large, rectangular room four hundred feet below the surface of Behrenstrasse. The room was completely bare. Its floor, ceiling and walls were constructed of the same material, five-foot-square panels of ten-inch-thick black marble.

At the far end of the room was a luminous steel panel that looked little more than an expensive metallic abstract. Von Holden's footsteps echoed as he approached it. Reaching it, he stopped and stood directly in front. "Lugo," he said. Then he gave his ten-digit identification number, followed with "Bertha," his mother's name.

Immediately, a panel to his left pulled back and he entered a long, diffusely lit corridor. This, like the outer room, was also walled with marble. The only difference was that the polished black of the former here was a bluish white, making the effect almost ethereal.

The passage was nearly seventy yards long, without a break for doors, other corridors, or cosmetic decoration. At the far end was another elevator. Reaching it, he gave the same verbal identification, but this time he added a secondary number: 86672.

Five hundred feet down, the elevator stopped. "Lugo," he said again, and the door slid open and he entered "*der Garten*," the Garden, a place only a dozen living people knew existed. With every visit, he felt as if he had stepped onto the set of some fantastic futuristic movie. Even the hackneyed entryway through the private house, with its hidden door and sliding panel, seemed out of some period theatrical melodrama.

But, exaggerated as it was, it was no movie set. Designed in 1939, its original construction was completed in the years 1942–1944 when anti-Nazi intelligence operatives were infiltrating the highest levels of the German Army General Staff, and Allied bombers were striking ever deeper into the heart of the Third Reich.

The existence of *der Garten,* with its simple, innocuous name, was so secret that at the beginning of construction a side tunnel was cut into a nearby subway line, the line closed off for repairs, and the excavated dirt dug out for the elevator shafts, corridors and rooms pushed into the subway line and trucked off by ore cars using the subway tracks. Equipment, workers and supplies were brought in the same way.

And although the project had taken four hundred men, working around the clock, twenty-one months to complete, no one, not the reidents on Behrenstrasse above, nor the rest of Berlin, had had any idea what was happening beneath their feet. As a final precaution, the four hundred who built it—architects, engineers, laborers—were gassed and buried under a thousand cubic yards of concrete at the base of the second elevator shaft while drinking champagne and celebrating its completion. Relatives who questioned their disappearance were told they had become casualties of Allied bombings. Those who persisted in their inquiries were shot. Later, and over the years, as electronic and structural upgrades were done, the small number of select designers, engineers and craftsmen carefully screened and then employed met similar fates, albeit on a much more singular and clandestine scale. An automobile accident, a freak electrocution, an accidental poisoning, a hunting blunder. Things tragic but understandable.

So, except for the select handful at the highest level of

Nazi power who knew, the immense piece of work that was *der Garten* simply did not exist. And now, nearly a half century later, save for Scholl and Von Holden and the remaining few others at the top of the Organization, it still didn't.

A door slid open in front of Von Holden and he entered a long spherical corridor inlaid with thousands of white ceramic tiles. It was now 8:10. Whatever had happened at the Hotel Borggreve, he had to put it out of his mind. Other than what he had seen, he had no information; therefore it was impossible for him to do anything other than to follow instructions as ordered.

At the halfway point in the corridor, he stopped and faced a door made of red ceramic tiles fused to titanium. Running his fingers over a Braille-like square, he punched in a five-number code and waited until a light above the square glowed green. When it did, he punched in three more numbers. The green light went out and the door raised up from the floor. Ducking his head, he entered, and the door lowered behind him.

It was a long moment before his eyes became accustomed to the near translucent blue-silver hue that filled the room. Even then, there was no feeling of depth or even space. It was as if he had entered a place with no existence at all. A figment of a dream.

Directly in front of him was the vague outline of a wall. Beyond it lay Sector F, *der Garten's* innermost room. Small and square, it was protected from above and below and on all four sides by walls of fifteen-inch-thick titanium steel, reinforced by ten feet of concrete that had been laminated every eighteen inches by partitions of a jelly-like substance designed to keep the inner room stable even if subjected to the direct hit of a hydrogen bomb or the rumbling of a ten-point-zero earthquake.

"Lugo," Von Holden said out loud, waiting as his voiceprint was digitally compressed and matched to the digitally compressed original in the archives. A moment later, a panel on the wall next to him slid back and an illuminated translucent glass screen appeared. "Zehn—Sieben—Sieben—Neun—Null—Null—Neun—Null—Vier" (Ten—Seven—Seven—Nine—Zero—Zero—Nine—Zero—Four), he enunciated carefully. Three seconds later black letters materialized on the screen.

LETZTE MITTEILUNG/LEITER DER SICHERHEIT

FREITAG/VIERZEHN/OKTOBER

(Final Memorandum/Director of Security

Friday/Fourteen/October)

Then the letters disappeared. Leaning forward, Von Holden pressed both hands firmly on the glass, then stood back. Immediately the glass went dark and the panel slid closed. Ten seconds elapsed while his fingerprints were scanned. Seven seconds later a matrix of dark blue dots appeared on the floor, moving toward the center of the room until they formed an exact two-foot by two-foot square.

"Lugo," he said again. The square faded and a platform rose out of the floor in its place. On it, cased inside a transparent housing, was a gray metallic-looking box made of a composite of fibers, including carbon, liquid-crystal polymers, and Kevlar. It measured twenty-six inches high by two feet square. It was what he had come for, and what would be presented to the select few at the ceremony in the Charlottenburg Mausoleum minutes after Elton Lybarger had finished speaking.

From the beginning, it had been code-named *Übermorgen,* "the day after tomorrow." Both a vision and a dream, it was now, and had been, the focus of everything, the thing that would carry the Organization into the next century and beyond. And once it left *der Garten,* Von Holden would protect it with his life.

118

GRETA STASSEL was the twenty-year-old cabdriver Von Holden had left waiting outside number 45 Behrenstrasse. She'd seen him look at her posted driver's papers and wondered if he'd remembered her name. She doubted it. He'd seemed troubled, but he was also very sexy and she was thinking how she might help him with whatever was bothering him, when the streetlights flickered and then went out.

She started as a figure suddenly appeared out of the darkness and tapped on her window. Then she realized who it was and that he was telling her through the glass that he had something to put in the trunk. Taking the keys from the ignition, she got out and walked to the back of the cab. Yes, he was sexy and very handsome and he seemed calm, so maybe he wasn't troubled after all.

"Where is it?" She smiled, unlocking the trunk.

For a moment Von Holden lost himself, thinking he'd never seen such a beautiful smile. Then Greta saw the square white plastic carrying case sitting on the curb. The red glow of the taxi's taillights highlighted the words stenciled on its top and sides: FRAGILE—MEDICAL INSTRUMENTS.

"I'm sorry, that's not it—" Von Holden said as she moved to pick it up.

Turning back, she looked puzzled but smiled anyway. "I thought you had something you wanted put in the trunk—"

"I do—"

She was still smiling when the slug from the nine-millimeter Glock penetrated her skull at the very top of her nose. Von Holden caught her just as her knees began to buckle. Picking her up, he rolled her into the trunk in a fetal position. Closing the lid, he took the keys, put the case in the front seat next to him, then started the engine and drove off. A half block later he turned onto the brightly lit Friedrichstrasse. Finding the driver's log, he tore off the top page, folded it with one hand and put it in his pocket. The clock on the dash read 8:30.

At 8:35, Von Holden was passing through the dark expanse of the Tiergarten on Strasse 17 Juni, five minutes away from Charlottenburg. He gave no thought to the body of the cabdriver in the trunk. Killing her meant nothing. It had simply been a necessary means to an end.

"*Übermorgen*," the pinnacle of everything, sat gently swaying in the white case on the seat beside him. Its presence lightened his heart and gave him courage. Even though twice more he had radioed for his operatives and still had no response, things were changing for the better. News broadcasts from radio correspondents on the scene at the Hotel Borggreve were reporting at least three members of the German federal police killed in a shootout, explosion and fire. Two unidentified bodies had been removed, burned beyond recognition. Two other bodies had been found but had not yet been identified. A factional terrorist organization had called police claiming responsibility. Von Holden relaxed and sat back, breathing deeply at the turn of fortune. Perhaps his anxiety had been unfounded, perhaps all had gone as planned.

A mile away, parked limousines lined Spandauer Damm in front of Charlottenburg, their drivers collected in groups, smoking and talking, collars turned up and caps pulled down against the rawness of the thickening fog.

On the sidewalk directly across the street, Walter van Dis, a seventeen-year-old Dutch guitar player in a black leather jacket and hair to his waist, stood with a crowd of spectators watching the palace. Nothing was happening but they were watching anyway, entertained by the spectacle of a luxury that would never be theirs unless the world changed dramatically.

The dull staccato of car doors slamming caught his attention and he changed position a little to see what was going on. Four men had just gotten out of a car and were crossing the street, heading toward Charlottenburg's front gate. Immediately, he stepped back into the shadows, at the same time lifting a hand to his mouth.

"Walter," he said into a tiny microphone.

A moment later Von Holden's radio beeped. Eagerly he switched on, expecting to hear the voice of one of his Hotel Borggreve operatives. Instead, he came in on anxious chatter between Walter and several of the palace's security people demanding details. What men was he talking about? Was he sure of the number? What did they look like? What direction were they coming from?

"This is Lugo!" he said sharply. "Clear the line for Walter."

"Walter."

"What have you got?"

"Four men. Just got out of a car and are approaching the front gate. By description one looks like the American, Osborn. Another might be McVey ."

Von Holden swore under his breath. "Hold them at the gate! Under no circumstances are they to be let inside!"

Abruptly he heard a man identify himself as Inspector Remmer of the BKA and say that he had police business inside the palace. Then he heard the familiar voice of Pappen, his security chief, defy him. This was a private affair, with private security. The police had no business there. Remmer said that he had a warrant for the arrest of Erwin Scholl. Pappen said he never heard of an Erwin Scholl, and unless Remmer had a warrant to enter the property, he would not be allowed inside.

McVey and Osborn followed Remmer and Schneider across the cobblestone courtyard toward the palace entrance. When even the threat of the fire marshal's closing the building didn't dissuade them. Remmer had radioed for three backup units. Lights flashing, they'd arrived within seconds and taken the chief of security and his lieutenant into custody for interfering with a police operation.

Racing through traffic, Von Holden pulled up in the snarl created by Remmer's action just as Pappen and his second in command were wrestled into a police car and driven away. Getting out of the cab, he stood beside it and watched the remainder of his central gate security force step aside as the intruders reached the front door and entered the building.

Scholl would be furious, but he'd brought it on himself. Von Holden knew at the time he should have argued longer and harder, but he hadn't, and it made the truth all that more bitter.

There was no doubt in his mind, none whatsoever, that had he been at the Hotel Borggreve, neither Osborn nor McVey would now be at Charlottenburg.

119

WEARING A big Hollywood smile, Louis Goetz came down the grand stairway toward the men waiting at the bottom.

"Detective McVey," he said, immediately picking McVey out and extending his hand. "I'm Louis Goetz, Mr. Scholl's attorney. Why don't we go someplace we can talk."

Goetz led the way through a maze of hallways and into a large paneled gallery and closed the door. The room had a polished gray-white marble floor and was coupled at either end by enormous fireplaces of the same material. A side wall groaned with the weight of heavy tapestries and opposite, French doors opened to a lighted formal garden that faded quickly into the darkness beyond. Over the door they had entered hung a 1712 portrait of Sophie-Charlotte herself, the corpulent, double-chinned queen of Prussia.

"Sit down, gentlemen," Goetz gestured toward a gathering of high-backed chairs placed around a long, ornate table. "Geez, Detective, that's a mess. What happened?" he said, looking at McVey's facial burns.

"I was kind of sloppy about watching what was cooking," McVey said with a straight face and eased into one of the chairs. "Doctor suspects I'll live."

Osborn sat down across from McVey, and Remmer pulled up a chair beside him. Schneider stood back near the door. They didn't want this looking like an invasion of detectives.

"Mr. Scholl had set time aside to see you earlier. I'm afraid he's tied up for the rest of the evening. Right afterward he leaves for South America." Goetz sat down at the head of the table.

"Mr. Goetz, we'd just like to see him for a few minutes before he leaves," McVey said.

"That won't be possible tonight, Detective. Maybe when he gets back to L.A."

"When's that?"

"March of next year." Goetz smiled as if he'd just given a punch line, then held up a hand. "Hey, it's true. I'm not trying to be a wise-ass."

"Then I guess we better see him now." McVey was dead serious and Goetz knew it.

Goetz sat back sharply. "You know who Erwin Scholl is? You know who he's entertaining up there?" He glanced at the ceiling. "What the hell do you think, he's gonna get up in the middle of everything and come down here to talk to you?"

From upstairs came the sound of an orchestra playing a Strauss waltz. It reminded McVey of the radio inside the room where they found Cadoux. He looked to Remmer.

"I'm afraid Mr. Scholl will have to change his plans," Remmer said, dropping the *Haftbefehl,* the arrest warrant, on the table in front of Goetz. "He comes down and he talks to Detective McVey, or he goes to jail. Right now."

"What the hell is this, for Chrissake? Who the fuck do you think you're dealing with?" Goetz was outraged. Picking up the warrant, he glanced at it, then threw it back on the table in disgust. It was written totally in German.

"With a little cooperation maybe we can save your client a great deal of embarrassment. Maybe even keep him on his schedule." McVey shifted in his chair. The painkiller Osborn had given him was beginning to wear off, but he didn't want more for fear it would make him groggy and he'd lose his edge. "Why don't you just ask him to step down here for a few minutes."

"Why don't you just tell me what the fuck this is all about?"

"I'd just as soon discuss that with Mr. Scholl. Of course you have every right to be present. Or—we can all go with Detective Remmer here and have our conversation in much less historical surroundings."

Goetz smiled. Here was a civil servant, totally out of his league and not even in his own country, trying to play hardball with one of the world's top power brokers. The problem was the warrant. It was something none of them had anticipated, chiefly because not one of them would have believed McVey capable of convincing a German judge to issue one. Scholl's German lawyers would handle it as soon as they'd been notified. But that would take a little time, and McVey wasn't about to give it. There were two ways to deal with it. Tell McVey to go fuck himself or play the mensch and ask Scholl to come down and spread a little confectionery sugar around and hope everything would ease over long enough to get the Kraut lawyers here.

"I'll see what I can do," he said. Getting up, he glanced briefly at Schneider standing by the door and left.

McVey looked at Remmer. "This might be a good time to see what you can do about finding Lybarger.

Von Holden turned the taxi onto a darkened residential street a dozen blocks from Charlottenburg. Finding a space, he parked and shut off the lights. The neighborhood was quiet. In the fog and damp people were inside. Opening the door, he got out and looked around. He saw no one. Reaching back inside, he pulled out the white plastic case, attached a nylon carrying strap to clips at the top, and hefted it over his shoulder. Tossing the keys back in the taxi, he locked it and walked off.

Ten minutes later he was in sight of Charlottenburg. Crossing a footbridge over the Spree River at Tegeler Weg, he approached a service gate at the back of the palace grounds. Beyond it, he could see the building's lights looming through the damp and realized how much heavier the fog had become in the last hour. By now the airports would be closed and unless the weather changed, no planes would fly until morning.

A guard stationed at the service gate let him in and he walked down a path lined with chestnut trees. Crossing another bridge, he followed the path under an avenue of pines to an intersection where he turned left and approached the mausoleum.

"It's nine o'clock. Where have you been?" Salettl's voice shot out at him from the darkness and then he appeared on the pathway directly in front of Von Holden. Pencil-thin and wrapped in a dark cloak, his skull alone stood out in the blackness.

"The police are here. They have a warrant for Scholl's arrest." Salettl came closer. As he neared, Von Holden could see the pupils in his eyes were little more than dots and every part of him seemed wired, as if he were pumped full of amphetamine.

"Yes, I know," Von Holden said.

Salettl's eyes darted to the white case thrown over Von Holden's shoulder. "You treat it as if it were some kind of picnic box."

"I apologize. There was no other way."

"For now the ceremony here at the mausoleum is postponed."

"By whose order?"

"Dortmund."

"Then I will return to *der Garten*."

"Your orders are to wait in the Royal Apartments until further notice."

Thick fog swirled around the rhododendrons on the path where they stood. Further down, the mausoleum loomed against the trees shrouding it like the vortex of a Gothic nightmare, and Von Holden felt himself being drawn toward it as if pulled by some unseen hand. Then they came again, the colossal red and green curtains of the aurora, slowly undulating, threatening to absorb the core of his entire being.

"What is it?" Salettl snapped.

"I—"

"Are you ill?" Salettl snapped again.

Fighting it to break it, Von Holden shook his head. Then he took a deep breath of cold air. The aurora vanished and everything cleared.

"No," he said, sharply.

"Then go to the Royal Apartments as you have been told."

120

8:57 P.M.

JOANNA WAS brushing the lint off Elton Lybarger's midnight blue tailcoat and thinking of her puppy, now somewhere over the Atlantic on his way back to the holding kennel at Los Angeles Airport where he would be kept until she picked him up. Abruptly there was a sharp knock at the door and Eric and Edward came in followed by Remmer and Schneider. Behind them were Lybarger's tuxedoed bodyguards and two men with armbands that identified them as security.

"Uncle," Eric said protectively. "These men asked to see you for a moment, they are police."

"*Guten Abend.*" Lybarger smiled. He was in the process of taking a small group of vitamin pills. One by one, he put them in his mouth, and washed them down with small sips from a water glass.

"Herr Lybarger," Remmer said. "Excuse the intrusion." Smiling, polite and offhand, he studied Lybarger quickly and carefully. Little more than one hundred and fifty pounds and five feet seven, he stood erect and looked physically fit. He wore a white stiff-bosomed shirt fastened at the wrists with French cuffs and at the throat by a white bow tie. For all the world, he appeared as he looked, a man in his early to mid-fifties in good health and dressed to speak to an important audience.

Finishing with the pills, Lybarger turned. "Please, Joanna." He held out his arms and Joanna helped him on with his jacket.

Remmer immediately recognized Joanna as the woman identified by the FBI as Lybarger's physical therapist,

Joanna Marsh of Taos, New Mexico. He had hoped to find the other man videotaped, the suspected Spetsnaz soldier Noble had I.D.'d getting out of the BMW, but he wasn't among the men in the room.

"What is the meaning of this?" Eric asked. "My uncle is about to give an important speech."

Remmer turned and moved into the center of the room, purposefully drawing the attention of Eric and Edward and the bodyguards. As he did, Schneider eased back, glanced around the room, then walked into the bathroom. A moment later he came out.

"We were informed there might be some problem with Mr. Lybarger's personal safety," Remmer said.

"What problem?" Eric demanded.

Remmer smiled and relaxed. "I can see there is none. Sorry to bother you, gentlemen. *Guten Abend.*" Turning, he looked at Joanna and wondered how much she knew, how involved she might be. "Goodnight," he said courteously, then he and Schneider left.

121

9:00 P.M.

McVEY AND Scholl faced each other in silence. The warmth of the room had turned the salve on McVey's face to an oily liquid, making his facial burns appear even more grotesque than they were.

A moment before, Louis Goetz had advised Scholl not to say another word until his criminal lawyers arrived and

McVey had countered by suggesting that while Scholl had every right to do so, the fact that he was not cooperating with a police investigation would not look good when it came time for a judge to make a decision whether or not to grant him bail. Never mind, he'd added measuredly, the not-so-coincidental ramifications once the media got wind that a man as distinguished as Erwin Scholl had been arrested for suspicion of murder for hire, and was being held for extradition to the U.S.

"What kind of crap are you throwing around?" Goetz steamed. "You've got no authority here whatsoever. The fact that Mr. Scholl has left his guests to meet you is evidence of cooperation enough."

"If we relax a little, we might finish up and go home," McVey said, addressing Scholl quietly and ignoring Goetz. "This whole thing is as distasteful to me as it is to you. Besides, my face is killing me, and I know you want to get back to your guests."

Scholl had left the dais more out of his own curiosity than the threat of McVey's warrant. Stopping briefly to inform Dortmund of what was happening and, thereby, sending Dortmund immediately in search of a phone and a battery of top German criminal lawyers, he'd left the Golden Gallery by a side door and started down the stairs, when an agitated Salettl came out after him, asked where he was going and how he dared leave their guests at a time like this. Then it had been ten minutes to nine, a full twenty-five minutes before Lybarger would make his entrance.

"I have a brief rendezvous with a policeman, one who obviously leads an exceptionally charmed life." He'd smiled, arrogantly. "There is ample time for it, my good Doctor, ample time."

Tanned and resplendent in his hand-tailored tuxedo, Scholl had been exceedingly polite when he'd come in, and all the more so when McVey had introduced him to Osborn. He'd listened attentively and done his best to be forthright with his answers—though he'd seemed genuinely puzzled at the questions—even after McVey had advised him of his rights as an American citizen.

"Let's go over it again," McVey had said. "Doctor Osborn's father was murdered in Boston on April 12, 1966, by a man named Albert Merriman. Albert Merriman was a professional killer who, a week ago in Paris, was found by Doctor Osborn, and confessed to the murder. In doing so, he said that you had hired him to do it. Your reply was that you never knew or heard of Albert Merriman."

Scholl sat expressionless. "Correct."

"If you didn't know Merriman, did you know a George Osborn?"

"No."

"Then why would you hire someone to kill a man you didn't even know?"

"McVey, that's a bullshit question and you know it." Goetz didn't like it at all that Scholl was giving McVey his head and allowing the questioning to go on.

"Detective McVey," Scholl said calmly, without so much as a glance at Goetz, "I never hired anyone to commit murder. The idea is quite outrageous."

"Where is this Albert Merriman? I'd like to meet him," Goetz demanded.

"That's one of our problems, Mr. Goetz. He's dead."

"Then there's nothing more we have to talk about. Your arrest warrant is as full of crap as you. Hearsay from a dead man?" Goetz stood. "Mr. Scholl, we're finished here."

"Goetz, the problem is—Albert Merriman was murdered."

"Big deal."

"It is a big deal. The man who killed him was a gun for hire too. Also employed by Mr. Scholl. His name was Bernhard Oven." McVey looked to Scholl. "A member of the East German secret police before he went to work for you."

"I've never heard of a Bernhard Oven, Detective,"

Scholl said evenly. A clock on the mantel over McVey's shoulder read 9:14. In one minute the doors would be opened and Lybarger would enter the Golden Gallery. To his surprise, Scholl was finding himself intrigued. McVey's knowledge was remarkable.

"Tell me about Elton Lybarger," McVey surprised him, suddenly shifting gears.

"He's a friend."

"I'd like to meet him."

"I'm afraid that's not possible. He's been ill."

"But he's well enough to give a speech."

"Yes, he is. . . ."

"I don't understand. He's too ill to talk to one man, but not a hundred."

"He's under a physician's care."

"You mean Doctor Salettl. . . ."

Goetz looked at Scholl. How long was he going to allow this to go on? What the hell was he doing?

"That is correct." Scholl adjusted the left sleeve of his jacket with his right hand, making a deliberate display of the still-healing abrasions. He smiled. "It's ironic that we should both have painful physical wounds at the same time, Detective. Mine came from playing with a cat. Yours, obviously, from playing with fire. We both should know better, don't you think?"

"I wasn't playing, Mr. Scholl. Somebody tried to kill me."

"You are fortunate."

"A few of my friends weren't."

"I'm sorry." Scholl glanced at Osborn, then looked back to McVey. McVey was, without doubt, the most thoroughly dangerous man he'd ever met. Dangerous because he cared about nothing but the truth, and to that end, he was capable of anything.

122

9:15 P.M.

THE ROOM was hushed. Every eye in it followed Elton Lybarger as he walked alone down the beribboned center aisle of Georg Wenzeslaus von Knobelsdorff's grand rococo creation, the green-marbled, gold-gilded, mesmerizing Golden Gallery. One foot place sturdily before the other. No longer reliant on cane or nurse. Smashingly resplendent in dress, he was aloof, practiced, self-assured. A symbolic monarch of the future passing in exhibition for those who had helped bring him here.

A wave of adoration rose in the chests of Eric and Edward as they sat on the dais and watched him make his way toward the podium. Beside them, Frau Dortmund wept openly, unable to control the emotion that washed over her. Then, in a gesture that swept the room, Uta Baur stood and began to applaud. Across the room, Matthias Noll followed. Then Gertrude Biermann. Hilmar Grunel. Henryk Steiner and Konrad Peiper. Margarete Peiper stood to join her husband. Next came Hans Dabritz. And then Gustav Dortmund. And then the rest of the one hundred were on their feet making the tribute unanimous. Lybarger's eyes swept left to right, smiling, acknowledging, as the thunder of their applause shook the room, rising in force as each step brought him closer to the podium in front of them. The pinnacle of achievement was at hand and the ovation for it deafened.

Salettl looked at his watch.

9:19.

That Scholl was not yet back was inexcusable. Looking up, he saw Lybarger reach the podium steps and begin to mount them. As he gained the top and looked out, the acclaim soared, rising in a crescendo that pounded the walls and shook the ceiling. This was the prelude to *"Übermorgen."* The beginning of "The Day After Tomorrow."

Outside, Remmer and Schneider crossed the stone pavement of Charlottenburg's courtyard. They walked quickly, saying nothing. Ahead of them, a black Mercedes turned in at the gate and was waved through. Stepping aside, they saw the driver stop at the entryway and go inside. Remmer's first thought was that Scholl was leaving and he hesitated, but then nothing happened. The Mercedes stayed where it was. It could be there for an hour, he thought. Pulling his radio from his jacket, Remmer spoke into it. Then they moved on. Passing the gate, Remmer made deliberate eye contact with the security guards on duty. Both men looked away, and he and Schneider passed unchallenged. As quickly, a dark blue BMW squealed out of traffic and slid to a stop at the curb beside them. The two got in and the car drove off.

If Remmer or Schneider or either of the two BKA detectives in the BMW with them had looked back, they would have seen the palace's main door open and the driver of the black Mercedes emerge, accompanied not by Scholl or any of the prestigious guests but by Joanna.

Helping her into the rear seat, the driver closed the door and got behind the wheel. Pulling on his seat belt, he started the engine and drove off, circling the courtyard and then turning left on Spandauer Damm, the opposite direction from the way Remmer's BMW had gone. A moment later the driver saw a silver Volkswagen sedan pull from the curb, make a quick U-turn across traffic, and settle into the lane behind him. So he was being followed. He smiled. He was merely taking her to a hotel. There was no law against that.

Alone in the backseat, Joanna pulled her coat around her and tried not to cry. She didn't know what had happened, only that Salettl, at the last moment, had sent her away without even giving her a chance to say goodbye to Elton Lybarger. The doctor had entered Lybarger's room and taken her aside only moments after the police left.

"Your relationship with Mr. Lybarger has ended," Salettl had commanded. He seemed nervous and very jittery. Then in an abrupt turn of character, he became almost kindly. "It's best for both of you if you think no more about it." Then he handed her a tiny package that had been wrapped as a gift. "This is for you," he said. "Promise me you won't open it until you get home."

Shocked and confused by his abruptness, she vaguely remembered agreeing and thanking him, then absently putting his present in her purse. Her mind had been on Lybarger. They had been together for a long time, and shared a great deal, not all of it entirely pleasant. The least Salettl could have let her do was to wish him well and say goodbye. Gift or not, what he had done had been curt, even rude. But what came next was even worse.

"—I know you expected to spend this last evening with Von Holden," Salettl said. "Don't act as if it's a surprise that I know. Unfortunately, Von Holden will be occupied with duties for Mr. Scholl and will be leaving with him for South America immediately after the dinner."

"I won't see him?" She suddenly felt heartsick.

"No."

She didn't understand. She was to have spent the night at a Berlin hotel, then fly out to Los Angeles in the morning. Von Holden had said nothing about leaving with Scholl. He was to have come to her after the ceremony at Charlottenburg. The night was to have been theirs together.

"Your things have been packed. A car is waiting downstairs for you. Goodbye, Miss Marsh."

And that had been that. A security guard had taken her downstairs. And then she was in the car and gone. Turning to look back, she could just see the palace. Barely visible in the thick fog, it slowly faded from sight. It was as if it, and everything she had done leading up to it, Von Holden included, had been a dream. A dream that, like Charlottenburg, simply vanished.

"Hubschrauber," helicopter, Remmer said, cradling the radio against his broken hand. The BMW sped past the Charlottenburg Hospital complex and then, a half mile later, turned abruptly into the dark expanse of Ruhwald Park. Two-thirds of the way across it, the BKA detective at the wheel turned out the yellow fog lamps, then abruptly pulled over and stopped. Almost immediately the bright spotlight of a police helicopter illuminated the ground fifty feet away, and with a deafening roar settled down onto the grass. The pilot cut his engine and Schneider got out of the car and ran toward the machine. Ducking under the rotor blades, he opened the door and climbed inside. There was a roar of engine, followed by a storm of blowing grass and dust as the helicopter lifted off. Clearing the tree line, it spun a hundred and eighty degrees to the left and vanished into the night.

From his seat next to the pilot, Schneider could just make out the fog lamps of the BMW as it circled out of the field and turned left toward Charlottenburg Palace. Leaning back, he tightened his shoulder harness, then unbuttoned his coat and lifted out the handkerchief-covered prize he was taking to the fingerprint laboratory at Bad Godesberg: the water glass Elton Lybarger had used to swallow his vitamin pills.

123

"SEVERAL DAYS before Doctor Osborn's father was murdered"—McVey had taken a small, dog-eared notebook from his jacket, and was half looking at it as he talked to Scholl—"he designed a scalpel. A very special kind of scalpel. Designed and made for his employer, a small company outside Boston. It was a company you owned, Mr. Scholl."

"I never owned a company that manufactured scalpels."

"I don't know if they manufactured scalpels, I only know one was made."

McVey had known from the moment Goetz went upstairs to advise him what had happened, that Scholl would leave his guests and come down to meet him. His ego would make him. How could he pass up the chance to meet the man who had just survived a deadly ambush and still had the hubris to invade his private arena? But the curiosity would be fleeting, and as soon as he had seen enough he would leave. That is, unless McVey could take that same curiosity and run with it. That was the trick, working the curiosity, because the next level was emotion and he had a gut sense that Scholl was a lot more emotional than he let on to anyone. Once people started reacting emotionally, they were apt to say anything.

"The company was called Microtab and based in Waltham, Massachusetts. At the time, it was controlled by a privately held company called Wentworth Products Limited, of Ontario, Canada. The man who owned it was"—McVey squinted at his handwriting—"Mr. James Tallmadge of Windsor, Ontario. Tallmadge and the board of directors of Microtab—Earl Samules, Evan Hart and a John Harris, all of Boston—died within a half-dozen months of each other. The Microtab people in 1966. Tallmadge in 1967."

"I never heard of a company called Microtab, Mr. McVey," Scholl said. "Now, I think I've given you enough time. Mr. Goetz will entertain you while I return to my guests. Within the hour the proper attorneys will be here to answer your warrant."

Scholl pushed back his chair and stood, and McVey could see Goetz sigh with relief.

"Tallmadge and the others were involved with two other of your companies." McVey kept on as if Scholl had never spoken. "Alama Steel, Limited of Pittsburgh, Pennsylvania, and Standard Technologies of Perth Amboy, New Jersey. Standard Technologies, by the way, was a subsidiary of a company called T.L.T. International of New York, which was dissolved in 1967."

Scholl stared in amazement. "What is the purpose of this recitation?" he said coldly.

"I'm simply giving you the opportunity to explain."

"Just what is it you wish me to explain?"

"Your connection to all these companies and the fact that—"

"I have no connection to these companies."

"You don't?"

"Absolutely not." Scholl's retort was crisp and edged with anger.

Good, McVey thought. Get mad. "Tell me about Omega Shipping Lines—"

Goetz stood up. It was time to stop it. "I'm afraid that's all, Detective. Mr. Scholl, your guests are waiting."

"I was asking Mr. Scholl about Omega Shipping Lines." McVey's eyes were locked on Scholl. "I thought you had no connection to these companies. Isn't that what you told me?"

"I said no more questions, McVey," Goetz said.

"I'm sorry, Mr. Goetz, I'm trying to help your client stay

out of jail. But I can't get a straight answer from him. A moment ago he told me he had no connection to Microtab, Alama Steel, Standard Technologies or T.L.T. International. T.L.T. International controlled those companies and is, itself, controlled by Omega Shipping Lines. Mr. Scholl happens to be the principal stockholder of Omega Shipping Lines. I'm sure you see what I'm getting at. It's got to be one way or the other. Mr. Scholl, you either were involved in these companies or you weren't. Which is it?"

"Omega Shipping Lines no longer exists," Scholl replied flatly. Clearly he had underestimated McVey. His persistence as well as his resilience. It was his fault he hadn't given Von Holden his head in killing him. But that was a situation that would be rectified soon enough. "I've given you all the consideration you asked for and a great deal more. Good evening, Detective."

McVey stood up and took two photographs from his jacket pocket. "Mr. Goetz, would you mind asking your client to look at these?"

Osborn watched Goetz take the photos and study them.

"Who are these people?" Goetz said.

"That's what I'd like Mr. Scholl to tell me."

Osborn watched Goetz look to Scholl, then hand him the pictures. Scholl glared at McVey, then glanced at the photos in his hand. When he did, he started, but quickly covered it.

"I have no idea," he said, directly.

"No?"

"No."

"Their names are Karolin and Johann Henniger." McVey paused. "They were murdered sometime today."

This time Scholl showed no emotion at all. "I told you, I have no idea who they are."

Handing the photos to Goetz, Scholl turned and started for the door. Osborn looked to McVey. Once he was through it, it would be the last they would see of him for a long time, if ever.

"I appreciate your taking the time to talk to us," McVey said quickly. "I also know you appreciate the fact that Doctor Osborn has never been able to close the emotional door on his father's killing. I promised him a question. It's simple. Off the record."

Scholl turned back. "You carry impudence beyond good manners."

Goetz pulled open the door and Scholl was almost through it when Osborn spoke.

"Why did you have Elton Lybarger's head surgically attached to another man's body?"

Scholl froze where he was. So did Goetz. Then slowly, Scholl turned back. He looked—exposed. As if suddenly his clothes had been torn from him and he'd been sexually violated. For the briefest instant he seemed ready to crack. Instead, what seemed to be a self-willed mask descended over his face, from top to bottom. Exposure gave way to contempt and contempt to rage. And then, quickly, icily, terrifyingly, he brought it back to where he could control it. "I suggest you both turn to writing books of fiction."

"It's not fiction," Osborn said.

Suddenly a door at the far end of the room opened and Salettl entered.

"Where is Von Holden?" Scholl commanded as Salettl approached.

Salettl's shoes echoed on the marble floor as he walked toward them. "Von Holden is upstairs, waiting in the Royal Apartments." The jumpiness, the deep intensity of earlier, was gone. In its place was a manner that was almost calm.

"Get him and bring him here now."

Salettl smiled. "I'm afraid that's out of the question. The Royal Apartments and the Golden Gallery are no longer accessible."

"What are you talking about?"

McVey and Osborn exchanged glances. Something was

going on but they had no idea what. Scholl didn't like it either.

"I asked you a question."

"It would have been more fitting if you had been upstairs." Salettl had crossed the room and was within a few feet of Scholl and Goetz.

"Get Von Holden!" Scholl snapped at Goetz.

Goetz nodded and was shifting his weight toward the door when there was a sharp report. Goetz jumped as if he'd been slapped. Grabbing at his neck, he pulled his hand away and looked at it. It was covered with blood. Wide-eyed, he looked at Salettl. Then his gaze ran down to his hand. A small automatic was clutched in it.

"You shot me, you fuck!" Goetz screamed at him. Then he shuddered and slumped back against the door.

"DROP THE GUN, NOW!" McVey's .38 was in his right hand, he was using his left to ease Osborn out of the line of fire.

Salettl looked to McVey. "Of course." Turned to Scholl, he smiled. "These Americans nearly ruined everything."

"DROP IT, NOW!"

Scholl stared in utter contempt. "Vida?"

Salettl smiled again. "She's been living in Berlin for nearly four years."

"How dare you?" Scholl drew himself up. He was furious. Superior. Totally insolent. "How dare you take it upon yourself to—"

Salettl's first shot caught Scholl just over his bow tie. The second tore into his chest at the top of his heart, exploding his aorta and showering Salettl with blood. For a moment Scholl tottered on his feet, his eyes rocked with disbelief, then he simply collapsed as if his legs had been kicked out from under him.

"DROP IT! OR I'LL SHOOT YOU RIGHT THERE!" McVey bellowed, his finger closing on the trigger.

"McVey—DON'T!" he heard Osborn shout behind

him. Then Salettl's gun hand dropped to his side, and McVey's finger eased off the trigger.

Salettl turned to face them. He was ghostly white and looked as if he'd been splattered with red paint. That he was wearing a tuxedo made it all the worse because it gave him the appearance of a grotesque, gruesome clown.

"You should not have interfered." Salettl's voice was resonant with anger.

"Open your fingers and let the gun fall to the floor!" McVey kept inching forward with no reservations about shooting the man dead if he had to. Osborn had yelled for fear McVey would fire and kill maybe the only remaining person who knew what was going on. In that he was right. But Salettl had just shot two men; McVey wouldn't give him the chance at two more.

Salettl stared at them, the automatic still held loosely at his side.

"Let the gun fall to the floor," McVey said again.

"Karolin Henniger's real name was Vida," Salettl said. "Scholl ordered her and the boy killed some time ago. I secretly brought them here, to Berlin, and changed their identities. She called me as soon as she ran from you. She thought you were the Organization. That they had found her." Salettl paused. The next was barely a whisper. "The Organization knew where you went. Because of that they would have discovered her very quickly. And afterward, they would have come to me. And that would have sabotaged everything."

"You killed them," McVey said.

"Yes."

Osborn took a step forward, his eyes glistened with emotion. "You said everything would have been sabotaged. *What* was it? What did you mean?"

Salettl didn't reply.

"Karolin, Vida, whatever her name was. She was Lybarger's wife," Osborn pressed. "The boy was his son."

Salettl hesitated. "She was also my daughter."

"Oh, Jesus." Osborn glanced at McVey. They both felt the same horror.

"Mr. Lybarger's physical therapist will be on the morning plane to Los Angeles," Salettl said abruptly, and wholly out of context, almost as if he were inviting them to join her.

Osborn stared at him. "Who the hell *are* you people? You murdered my father, your own daughter and grandchild and God knows how many others." Osborn's voice raged with anger. *"Why? For what?* To protect Lybarger? Scholl? This 'Organization'?—*WHY?"*

"You gentlemen should have left Germany to the Germans," Salettl said quietly. "You survived one fire this evening. You will not survive the next if you do not leave the building immediately." He tried to force a smile. It didn't work, and his eyes found Osborn. "This should be the hard part, Doctor. It isn't."

In the blink of an eye he raised the automatic to his mouth and pulled the trigger.

124

"PRIVATE ENTERPRISE," Lybarger said into the microphone, his voice stabbing to the farthest corners of the gold and green-marbled rococo fantasy of the Golden Gallery, "cannot be maintained in the age of democracy. It is conceivable only if the people have a sound idea of authority and personality."

Pausing, he stood with both hands on the podium,

studying the faces in front of him. His speech, although changed somewhat, was not original, and most there knew it. The original had been given to a similar group of business leaders on February 20, 1933. The speaker allying himself with moneyed institutions that wintery night had been Germany's newly entrusted chancellor, Adolf Hitler.

On the dais, Uta Baur leaned forward, her strong chin resting on her hands, wholly enraptured by the wonder of what she was witnessing, the agony, doubt, the secret labor of fifty years standing alone, speaking triumphantly before her. Beside her, Gustav Dortmund, chief of the Bundesbank, sat ramrod straight, emotionless, an observer, nothing more. Yet inside, he could feel his bowels churning with the excitement of what was at hand.

Farther down on the dais, Eric and Edward, fists clenched, neck muscles pressing against the starch of their tight collars, hunched forward like matched mannequins, hanging on Lybarger's every word. Theirs was a different exaltation. Who Lybarger was, within days, one of them would become. Which one was a decision yet to be made. And as the moment wound closer, as it did now with every word, every sentence, the anticipation of that moment when the choice would be made became almost unbearable.

HYDROGEN CYANIDE: an extremely poisonous, mobile volatile liquid or gas that has the odor of bitter almonds; a blood agent that interferes with oxygen in the blood tissues, literally taking the oxygen out of the blood and, in essence, suffocating the victim.

"All worldly goods we possess we owe to the struggle of the chosen, the pure German people!" Lybarger's words echoed off the hallowed walls of the Golden Gallery and into the hearts and minds of the people who sat within them.

"We must not forget that all the benefits of culture must

be introduced with an iron fist! And in that we will restore our power, military and otherwise, to the highest levels— There will be no retreat!"

As Lybarger finished, the entire room came to its feet in a thundering ovation that made the one at his entrance seem like well-mannered applause. Then, perhaps because of his proximity to the rear of the room and the doors leading out of it, he was the first to hear what the others could not.

"Listen!" he said over the microphone, holding up both hands for silence.

"Listen! Please!"

It was a moment before anyone knew what he was talking about. Did he have more to say? What did he mean? Then they understood. He wasn't asking them to be quiet. He was telling them something was happening.

A series of muted whirrings was followed by a half-dozen heavy mechanical thuds, and the room shook as if someone had pulled down weighted blinds around the outside of it. Then it stopped and everything was silent.

Uta Baur was the first to get up. Moving behind Eric and Edward on the dais, she passed Dortmund and walked down the short staircase to an exit door in the corner of the room. Throwing it open, she suddenly stepped back, her hand clamped over her mouth. Frau Dortmund screamed. Where the open doorway should have been was a huge metal door, closed tight and locked solidly in place.

Dortmund came quickly down the stairs. "*Was ist es?*" What is this?

Moving to the door, he shoved at it. Nothing happened. A wave of uneasiness crossed the room.

Getting up quickly, Eric pushed past the anxious, jeweled Frau Dortmund. Climbing the podium, he took the microphone from Lybarger.

"Be calm. A security door has come down by accident. Walk to the main door and file out in orderly fashion."

But the main door to the Golden Gallery was sealed the same way. As was every other door in the room.

"*Was geht hier vor?*"—What's going on here?—Hans Dabritz yelled.

Major General Matthias Noll pushed back his chair and went to the closest door. Using his shoulder he tried to force it outward but he had no more luck than Dortmund had a moment earlier. Henryk Steiner added his stocky shoulder. Together he and Noll rammed the door. Two others joined them, but the door didn't budge.

Then came the faintest scent of burnt almonds. People looked at each other and sniffed. What was it? Where was it coming from?

"*Ach, mein Gott!*" Konrad Peiper shrieked, as a tiny mist of amethyst-blue crystals suddenly rained down on his table from an air conditioning vent in the ceiling. "Cyanide gas!"

The odor became stronger as more of the crystals found their marks, vats within the ventilation pathwork containing distilled water and acid that would dissolve the crystals into deadly cyanide gas.

Suddenly people were crowding back from the ventilation openings. Pressed against the walls, each other, even the closed and locked steel doors, they stared up in silent disbelief at the grated vents so tastefully and carefully concealed in the gilded rococo ornamentation and green marbled walls of the grand eighteenth-century structure.

They were waiting to die. But not one of them believed it. How could it be? How could so many of Germany's most influential and celebrated citizens, bejeweled and bedecked in clothing the worth of which would feed half the world for a year, and protected by a virtual army of security personnel, be helplessly trapped in a room in one of the most historic buildings in the nation, waiting for enough cyanide gas to collect to kill them all?

Outrageous. Impossible. A joke.

"*Es ist ein Streich!*"—It's a prank!—Hans Dabritz laughed. "*Ein Streich!*"

Others laughed too. Edward moved to his chair on the dais and picked up his glass.

"*Zu Elton Lybarger!*" he cried. "*Zu Elton Lybarger!*"

"*Zu Elton Lybarger!*" Uta Baur lifted her glass.

Elton Lybarger stood at the podium and watched Konrad and Margarete Peiper, Gertrude Biermann, Rudolf Kaes, Henryk Steiner and Gustav Dortmund move back to their tables and raise their glasses.

"*Zu Elton Lybarger!*" The Golden Gallery shook with salutation.

Then it began.

Uta Baur's head suddenly snapped back, then fell forward, her biceps and upper back trembling violently. Across the room Margarete Peiper did the same. Falling to the floor, she shrieked, writhing in agony, her muscles and nerves reacting in violent spasms, as if she were being jolted with fifty thousand volts of electricity, or thousands of insects had suddenly been released under her skin and were madly devouring one another in a frenzied race to survive.

Suddenly, and en masse, those who could stampeded toward the main door. Clawing and mauling each other, they tore at the massive steel door and the ornate wood framing around it. Gasping for air. Screaming for help and mercy. They dug fingers, nails, even gold watches into the unforgiving metal, hoping somehow to loosen it. The pounding of fists, shoe heels, even each other, reverberated over and over against it until all were finally overcome by the same writhing and horrid convulsions.

Of them all, Elton Lybarger was the last to die, and he did so sitting in a chair in the center of the room staring at the death massing around him. He understood, as they all did, finally, that this was a payback. They had let it happen because they didn't believe it could. And when ultimately they did, it was too late. The same as it had been at the extermination camps.

"Treblinka. Chelmno. Sobibór," Lybarger said, as the gas began to invade him. "Belzeč, Maidanek—" Suddenly there was a twitch of his hands and he inhaled deeply. Then his head snapped back and his eyes rolled into it. "Auschwitz, Birkenau . . . ," he whispered. "Auschwitz, Birkenau . . ."

125

REMMER HAD no idea what to expect as he and the two BKA detectives who had seen Schneider to the helicopter turned into the Charlottenburg courtyard and got out of the BMW. Immediately they were approached by uniformed security guards.

"We're back," Remmer said, flashing his I.D., and pushing past them toward the main entrance. The only hard information he had was that neither McVey nor Osborn had come out of the palace. With any luck, he thought as he reached the door, McVey and Scholl are still downstairs having at each other. Either that or McVey is surrounded by a herd of criminal lawyers demanding his scalp, in which case he will be in prodigious need of help.

It was then that the first incendiary device went off. Remmer, the two detectives, and the security guards were thrown to the ground as a fusillade of mortar and stone rained down around them. Immediately a dozen more firebombs detonated. One after the other. Rapid-fire, like a string of high-explosive firecrackers, they circled the palace's entire upper perimeter on the side housing the Golden Gallery. Bursting inward, the charges ignited a furnace of gas jets embedded in the gilded molding along the room's floors and ceiling and in the apartments immediately adjacent.

McVey pulled back against the door, forcing Goetz's body aside, giving them enough room to get out. The explosions had toppled books from shelves, shattered priceless eighteenth-century porcelain and cracked one of the marble fireplaces. With a final tug, McVey forced the door open. A blast of heat hit him, and he saw the hallway ouside and the stairway beyond it wholly engulfed in flame. Slamming the door, he turned in time to see a wall of fire race down the outside of the building, sealing off any chance they might have to escape into the garden through the French doors. Then he saw Osborn, on his hands and knees, blindly tearing through Scholl's pockets like some madman rifling a corpse for whatever plunder he could find.

"What the hell are you doing? We've got to get out of here!"

Osborn ignored him. Leaving Scholl, he began the same with Salettl, tearing through his jacket, his shirt, his pants. It was as if the fire raging around them didn't exist.

"Osborn! They're dead! Leave them, for Chrissake!" McVey was on top of him, wrestling him to his feet. The dead men's blood smeared Osborn's hands and face. He was staring crazily, almost as if he were the one who had done it. He was demanding an answer to his father's death from the only men left who could give it. That they were dead was secondary. They were the end of the line and there was no other place to go.

Suddenly there was a rocking blast overheard as a gas conduit exploded with the heat. Instantaneously the ceiling ignited in a rolling fireball that went from one end of the room to the other in a millisecond. A second later the firestorm started by roaring gas knocked them off their feet, sucking everything in the room toward its center to feed it. Osborn vanished from sight and McVey grabbed onto a leg of the conference table, burying his head in the crook of his arm. For the second time that night he found himself surrounded by fire, this one a holocaust a thousand times more furious than the first.

"Osborn! OSBORN!" he screamed.

The heat was unbearable. His facial skin, so badly burned in the first fire, was now being literally fried against his skull. What little air there was seemed to be coming from the interior of a furnace. Any breath at all seared the lungs raw.

"Osborn!" McVey cried out again. The thundering of the flames was like roaring surf. There was no way anyone could be heard. Then he caught the odor of burnt almonds. "Cyanide!" he said out loud.

He saw something move in front of him. "OSBORN! IT'S CYANIDE GAS! OSBORN! CAN YOU HEAR ME?" But it wasn't Osborn. It was his wife, Judy. She was sitting on the front porch of their cabin above Big Bear Lake. The peaks, purple behind her, were touched with snow at the crest. The grass was long and golden and the air around her was punctuated with tiny insects. It was clean and pure and she was smiling. "Judy?" he heard himself say. Suddenly someone else's face dropped into his, as close as you could get. He didn't recognize it. The eyes were red and the hair was singed and the face was like blackened Creole fish.

"Give me your hand!" the face yelled.

McVey was still watching Judy.

"Goddammit!" the face screamed. "Give me your hand!"

Then McVey drew himself away and reached out. He felt a hand, then heard breaking glass. Suddenly he was up and half on his feet. The face had an arm under him and they were climbing out through shattered French doors. Then he saw thick fog and cold air filled his lungs!

"Breathe! Breathe deep! Come on! Breathe, you son of a bitch! Keep on breathing!" He couldn't see him but he was sure Osborn was yelling at him. He knew it was Osborn. It had to be. It was his voice.

126

JOANNA LOOKED out from her hotel room. Berlin was obscured, enclosed in an ever-thickening shroud of fog. She wondered if her plane would be able to take off in the morning. Going into the bathroom, she brushed her teeth and then swallowed two sleeping pills.

Why Dr. Salettl had so abruptly and rudely changed her plans, she had no idea. Why Von Holden had said nothing of leaving with Mr. Scholl immediately after the ceremony troubled her deeply, and she wondered even if it were true.

Who was Salettl anyway? What power did he have that he could control the comings and goings of someone like Von Holden, or even Scholl for that matter? Why he had even bothered to give her a present was beyond her. She meant no more to him than a mosquito clinging to a screen, to be suddenly snapped free or crushed at will. He was cruel and manipulative, and she was certain the dreadfully dark sexual incident with Elton Lybarger could be traced directly to him. But it didn't mater. Von Holden was the one, he had made everything else that happened seem merely a dream.

She went to bed thinking of him. She saw his face and

felt his touch, and knew that for the rest of her life she would never love anyone else.

Von Holden's entire being bordered on complete exhaustion. Never, through all his training with the Spetsnaz, the KGB and the Stasi, had he experienced such mental and physical weariness. They could take his Spetsnaz evaluation—that he "performs constantly, under the highest stress, with calm and clear judgment"—and send *it* back for "evaluation."

Immediately following his encounter with Salettl outside the mausoleum, he had gone to the apartments within the Golden Gallery complex to wait for Scholl as ordered.

But the moment he'd closed the door he'd felt the stab of the *Vorahnung*—the premonition. It wasn't a full-blown attack, but he could feel its clock counting off the seconds like a time bomb and after five minutes he'd left. Salettl was old, so was Scholl, so were Dortmund and Uta Baur. Power and wealth and time had made them despotic. Even Scholl, for all his seeming concern that McVey and Osborn could destroy everything, did not really believe it. The concept of true danger had long since vanished. The idea that they could somehow fail was absurd. Even the arrival of McVey and BKA inspectors with an arrest warrant did not faze them.

The ceremony at the mausoleum had not been canceled, only postponed. And would go on as planned as soon as the lawyers had intervened and the police had left the premises. The final arrogance of it was that the ceremony not only involved the presentation of the Organization's most closely guarded secret, it centered around murder. Step two of "*Übermorgen*"—the ritualistic assassination of Elton Lybarger. The prelude to what "*Übermorgen*" was truly about.

Let them play the insolent fools if they could do no better, but Von Holden was different, he was *Leiter der*

Sicherheit, the last guardian of the Organization's security. He had taken the vow to protect it from enemies within and without, at whatever cost. Scholl had prevented him from leading the attack at the Hotel Borggreve, and Salettl had relayed Dortmund's order to wait in the Royal Apartments in the Golden Gallery complex for his next command. Waiting there, alone, with the dark throb of the *Vorahnung* ticking inside him, hearing the roar of applause as Lybarger entered the Golden Gallery in the room next to him, he made the decision that at that moment the enemies from within were as dangerous as those from without. And that because of it, the next command would not be theirs, but his. Taking a back staircase, he'd gone out a side door, ordered a car from the security force and driven the white Audi directly back to the house at 45 Behrenstrasse, intending to return the box to the deep safety of *der Garten.* It wasn't possible. The street was filled with fire equipment. And the house itself was fully engulfed in flame.

Sitting there, in the darkness halfway down the street, the unimaginable before him, he'd felt the horror begin to rise once more. It began as transparent waves undulating slowly like spots before his eyes, then came the red of the Aurora and with it the unearthly green.

Fighting it off, he picked up the radio. Damn them and what they were doing, but someone of them had to be informed. Scholl, Salettl, Dortmund or even Uta Baur. But even as the radio was in his hand, the call had come through from the palace. "Lugo!" His radio had crackled with the desperate voice of Egon Frisch, Charlottenburg's acting security chief—*"Lugo!"*

For a moment he'd hesitated, then finally replied. "Lugo."

"All hell has broken loose! The Golden Gallery is locked and on fire! All entrances and exits are sealed!"

"Sealed? How?"

"By security doors, latched into place. There is no electricity, no way to move them!"

Leaving Behrenstrasse, Von Holden had driven like a madman through Berlin. How could this be? There had been no sign, no indication. The security doors had been installed in every room in the palace two years before in case of fire and to prevent vandalism, a full eighteen months before the date or even the location for celebration had been chosen. Automated computer security checks scanned the Behrenstrasse house twenty-four hours a day, and had done the same for the last week at Charlottenburg. Late that afternoon Von Holden had personally inspected the systems within the Golden Gallery, and in the Galerie der Romantik where the cocktail reception had been held. Nothing was out of place. Everything had checked.

Nearing the palace, he'd found the entire area sealed off. The crossing at Caprivi Bridge was as close as he could get, and he'd had to do that on foot. Even from there, a quarter of a mile away, he could see the flames rampaging into the sky. By morning the entire palace would be reduced to ashes. It was a national tragedy of profound proportion, and headlines, he knew, would liken it to the Reichstag fire of 1933. Whether they would find reason later to liken it to what happened in German immediately afterward, he had no idea. What he did know was that had he obeyed Salettl's order and stayed, he and the priceless box he had retrieved from *der Garten* would have been in the center of the conflagration he now watched. Neither would have survived.

It was then, while he stood on Caprivi Bridge, watching Charlottenburg burn, Von Holden unilaterally put Sector 5, the *"Entscheidendes Verfahren"*—the Conclusive Procedure —into operation. Planned in 1942 as the last and final measure in the face of impossible odds, it had been refined and rehearsed by those in charge for half a century. Each member of the Organization's highest circle had been taught the procedure, had practiced it two dozen times, could do it in his sleep. Purposely designed to be operational for one man acting alone and under extreme pressure, the route and modes of transportation were left open to ingenuity at the time of execution. Its charm was its simplicity and its mobility, and because of that it worked. And had, time and again, even against top Organization operatives acting as enemy agents attempting to stop it.

The decision made, Von Holden returned to the Audi and drove off through a horde of rubberneckers rushing to get a view of the fire. That both fires, Charlottenburg and Behrenstrasse, were obviously the work of saboteurs, meant it was essential he get out of Germany as quickly as possible. Whoever was responsible—the BKA, German Intelligence, the CIA, the Mossad, French or British Military Intelligence—would be watching every exit point for anyone in the Organization who might have escaped the terror. The heavy fog that had concerned him earlier prohibited escape by air, even by private jet. Using the Audi was an alternative, but the drive was long and there could be roadblocks or mechanical failure. A bus, if stopped, left no room for escape. That left the train. A man could lose himself in a crowded station and then take a private sleeping compartment. The borders were not checked as closely as they once had been and besides, if there was a problem, a pulled emergency cord could stop a train anywhere along the line and a passenger could slip away in the confusion. Still, a man alone buying overnight passage in a sleeping compartment could be remembered. And if he was remembered, he could be traced and then captured. Yet there was no other way, and Von Holden knew it. What he needed was a complication.

127

By Now seventeen engine companies had converged on the horror of Charlottenburg and more were coming from outlying districts. Spectators by the thousands strained to see from distant parameters, held there by several hundred helmeted Berlin police. Despite the heavy fog, media, police and fire helicopters fought for airspace directly over the conflagration.

The fire brigade's Second Engine Company *Feuerwehrmanns* had worked their way to the rear, cutting through temporary security fences and trampling formal gardens, trying to concentrate hoses on the furiously burning upper floors, when Osborn came screaming for help out of the dark.

He'd left McVey where he'd dragged him, flat on his back in the grass, as far away from the terrible heat as he could get. The policeman had been unconscious and laboring to breathe and Osborn had torn open his jacket and shirt, tearing away anything that might restrict the flow of air. But he'd been helpless to do anything about violent spasms in McVey's neck muscles and upper arms. He needed an antidote for the cyanide, and he needed it fast. Across the Spree he could see spectators, and, gagging and nauseated, poisoned himself by the gas but to a lesser degree, he'd run to the river's edge yelling and waving his arms. But it was only a moment before he'd realized a new enemy. Distance and darkness. No one could see or hear him. Turning back, he saw McVey writhing in the grass, and beyond him, the raging inferno. McVey was going to die and there was nothing he could do about it but watch. It was then the firemen had come.

"Cyanide gas!" he yelled, coughing and choking, into

the face of the young, bull-like fireman who rushed with him through a rain of burning embers and swirling fog. He knew American fire companies carried cyanide antidote kits because burning plastics give off cyanide gas; he prayed the Germans were as high-tech.

"We need cyanide antidote! Amyl nitrite! Do you understand? Amyl nitrite! It's an antidote for the gas!"

"Ich verstehe nicht Englisch"—I don't understand English—the fireman said, agonizing with the American.

"A doctor! A doctor! Please!" Osborn pleaded, enunciating as carefully as he could. Praying the man would understand.

Then the fireman nodded. *"Arzt! Ja!"* A doctor, yes! *"Ich brauche schnell einen Arzt!* Cyanide gas!" He spoke quickly and authoritatively into the radio microphone on the collar of his jacket, asking for medical help immediately.

"Amyl nitrite!" Osborn said, then, turning away, bent over and vomited in the grass.

Remmer rode with them in the ambulance as the drug began to take effect. The German paramedic who had administered it and two other paramedics were with them as well. An oxygen mask covered McVey's nose and mouth. His breathing was returning to normal. Osborn lay beside him, an IV in his arm like McVey, staring up at Remmer, listening to the staccato crackle of his police radio that overrode the singsong of the ambulance siren. It was all in German, but somehow Osborn understood. Charlottenburg and nearly everyone in it had perished in the fire. Only he and McVey and a few of the help and security guards had escaped. The Golden Gallery was still sealed by the metal doors, now a molten, twisted mass. It would be hours, even days, before rescuers with gas masks could go inside.

Lying back, he tried to push away the vision of McVey in the grass. That, as a grown man, he had acquired the skills of a doctor meant nothing. He'd been helpless to do anything but watch—finally to run, screaming, for help. It was the same precious little he'd been able to do for his own father as he lay in the gutter of the Boston street so many years before.

He felt the shudder of an uncontrolled sob as he realized that the enigma of his father's death was ended, entombed in the fiery rubble of Charlottenburg. The most he'd been able to gain from all that had happened was that his father, and any number of others, had been victims of a complex and macabre conspiracy involving a secret, elitist Nazi group's experiment in low-temperature atomic surgery. One that, if McVey's theory about Elton Lybarger was true, had apparently been successful. But for the *why* of it, he still had no answer. Perhaps what he had learned was already too much. He thought of Karolin Henniger and her son, running from him in the alley. How many more had died because of his own personal quest? Most had been totally innocent. In that, the guilt was his. The nightmare of his existence had been extended unfairly to others. Lives that should never have crossed, tragically had.

Whatever God that had deserted him when he was ten, deserted him still. Even to Vera, who, for a single few days, had been a light he'd never dreamed of. What had this God done about her but brand her a conspirator, tear her away and cast her in prison.

Suddenly he visualized her under the terrible glare of the ever-present lights. Where was she at this moment? What were they doing to her? How was she managing against them? He wanted to reach out and touch her, comfort her, tell her that eventually everything would be all right. Then the thought came that even if he could tell her, she would pull back, recoiling from his touch, no longer trusting him. Had everything that had happened destroyed that too?

"Osborn . . ." Suddenly McVey's voice rasped out through the oxygen mask. Looking over, Osborn could see Remmer's face lit by the interior lights of the ambulance. He was watching McVey. He wanted him to live, to be well again.

"Osborn's here, McVey. He's all right," Remmer said.

Pulling off his own oxygen mask, Osborn moved to take McVey's hand and saw the detective staring up at him. "We'll be to the hospital soon," Osborn said, trying to reassure him.

McVey coughed, his chest heaved painfully and he closed his eyes.

Remmer looked to the German doctor.

"He'll be okay," Osborn said, still holding McVey's hand. "Just let him rest."

"The hell with that. Listen to me." Abruptly McVey's grip tightened on Osborn's hand and his eyes opened. "Salettl—" McVey paused, breathed deeply, then went on. "—said—Lybarger's physical therapist—the girl—would be on—"

"The morning plane to L.A.!" Osborn finished for him, his words coming in a rush. "Jesus Christ, he said it for a reason! She's got to be alive. And here, in Berlin!"

"Yes—"

128

THE PRIVATE room on the sixth floor of Universitäts Klinik Berlin was dark. McVey had been checked into the room and then taken to the burn unit, Remmer had gone to have his broken wrist X-rayed and set, and Osborn had been left alone. Dirty and exhausted, hair and eyebrows singed so short he thought he could have passed for Yul Brynner or a marine grunt, he'd been examined, bathed and put to bed. They'd wanted to give him a sedative but he'd refused.

Berlin police scouring the city for Joanna Marsh, Osborn should have simply drifted off, but he didn't. Maybe he was overtired, maybe a minor case of cyanide poisoning had a side effect that nobody knew about and worked like an adrenaline rush that kept you pumped up. Whatever it was, Osborn was wide awake. He could see his clothes along with McVey's rumpled suit hanging in the closet. Past them, through the open door, he could see the central nurses' station. A tall blonde was on duty, talking on the phone and at the same time making an entry into a computer workstation in front of her. Now a doctor came in making late-night rounds, and Osborn saw her look up and wink as the doctor stopped to scrutinize some paperwork. How long had it been since he'd made hospital rounds? Had he ever? It seemed he'd been in Europe for eons. A doctor in love had, in quick turn, become a pursuer, a victim, a fugitive and, finally, a pursuer again with policemen from three countries as allies. And in that he had shot to death three terrorist gunmen, one of whom had been a woman. His life and practice in California existed only in vague memory. There, but not. In a way it mirrored his life. There, but not. It had all happened because he had never been able to put to rest the death of his father. And after everything, it was still not done. That was what was keeping him awake. He'd tried to find the answer on the bodies of Scholl and Salettl. There was none. And it had seemed to be journey's end until McVey had remembered what Salettl had said. He may or may not have been telling them to find Joanna Marsh. She might have some kind of answer, she might be completely innocent. But she was a piece still hanging, as Scholl had been after the death of Albert Merriman. So the journey was not yet done. But with McVey down and out for who knew how long, the question became—How to continue?

129

BAERBEL BRACHER, her small dog tugging at his leash, stood talking to homicide inspectors from Polizeipräsidium, Berlin's central police station. Baerbel Bracher was eighty-seven and it was 12:35 in the morning. Her dog, Heinz, was sixteen and had bladder problems. She walked him as often as four times a night. Sometimes five or more on a bad night. Tonight had been a bad night; she'd been out for the sixth time when she'd seen the police cars and then the policemen and teenagers gathered around the parked taxi.

"Yes, I saw him. He was young and handsome and wearing a tuxedo." She stopped as the coroner's van arrived and the coroner and white-coated assistants got out and approached the cab. "At the time I thought it strange a good-looking man in a tuxedo should be getting out of a taxi, throwing the keys inside and walking away." She watched them bring over a gurney and body bag, then open the trunk and lift out the body of the young taxi driver, put her in the bag and then zip it closed over her head.

"But then, it's none of my business, is it? He had a big white case over his shoulder, too. Something else I thought strange, a young man in a tuxedo, lugging an awkward-looking box like that. But anything can happen these days. I don't think about anything anymore. I have no opinions."

The tuxedo was the thing that connected him to Charlottenburg, and by 1:00 A.M. Baerbel Bracher was at police headquarters looking at photographs. Because of the Charlottenburg connection, the BKA was notified. Immediately, Bad Godesberg contacted Remmer.

"Mix in the still picture of Scholl's director of security

made from the videotape taken outside the house on Hauptstrasse," he said from his hospital room. "Don't make a point of it. Just put it in with the others."

Twenty minutes later, Bad Godesberg called back with an affirmative. That meant a member of what Dr. Salettl had called the "Organization" had escaped the Charlottenburg fire and was at large. Instantly an all-points bulletin was issued, and Remmer requested an international arrest warrant for a murder suspect known as Pascal Von Holden, an Argentine national carrying a Swiss passport.

Within the hour a judge in Bad Godesberg issued the warrant. Moments later, Von Holden's photograph was electronically circulated to all police agencies in Europe, the United Kingdom and North and South America. The circulation was a code "Red"—arrest and detain. Subheading: should be considered armed and extremely dangerous.

"How do you feel?" It was after two when Remmer came into Osborn's room.

"I'm all right." Osborn had drifted off but woke as Remmer came in. "How's your wrist?"

Remmer held up his left arm. "Temporary cast."

"McVey?"

"Sleeping."

Remmer came closer, and Osborn could see the intensity in his eyes.

"You've found Lybarger's nurse!"

"No."

"What, then?"

"Noble's Spetsnaz soldier, the same man you encountered in the Tiergarten, escaped the fire."

Osborn started. Another thread still dangling. "Von Holden?"

"A man matching his description was seen boarding the 10:48 train to Frankfurt. We're not certain it's him, but

I'm going there anyway. It's too foggy to fly. There are no trains. I'm going to drive."

"I'm going with you."

Remmer grinned. "I know."

Ten minutes later, a dark gray Mercedes left Berlin on the autobahn. The car was a six-liter V-8 police model. Its top speed was classified, but it was rumored to be nearly two hundred miles per hour on a straightaway.

"I have to know if you get carsick," Remmer looked at Osborn purposefully.

"Why?"

"The Berlin train gets in at four minutes past seven. It's now a little after two. A fast driver on the autobahn can make Berlin to Frankfurt in five and half hours. I'm a fast driver. I'm also a cop."

"What's the record?"

"There is no record."

Osborn smiled. "Make one."

130

VON HOLDEN sat back in the dark and listened to the sound of the train as it skipped over the rails beneath him. A small town flashed by in the darkness, then shortly after, another. Little by little the disaster of Berlin was being left behind, letting him more fully concentrate on what lay ahead. Glancing across, he saw her staring at him from the bunk.

"Please go to sleep," he said.

"Yes . . . ," Vera said, then rolled over and tried to do as she'd been told.

It had been after ten when they'd come for her. Taking her from her cell, they'd led her to another room and told her to get dressed, giving her back the clothes she'd been wearing when she was arrested. Then they'd taken her up in an elevator and out to a car where this man waited. He was a *Hauptkommissar*, a chief inspector, of the federal police; she was being released in his custody and was to do exactly as he said. His name, he told her, was Von Holden.

Moments later they were handcuffed together, crossing a platform and boarding a train at Bahnhof Zoo.

"Where are you taking me?" she'd asked guardedly as he closed the door to a private compartment and locked it.

For a moment he'd said nothing, only slipped a large case from his shoulder and set it on the floor. Then he'd leaned forward and removed the handcuffs.

"To Paul Osborn," he'd said.

Paul Osborn. The words rocked her.

"He's been taken to Switzerland."

"Is he all right?" Her mind raced. Switzerland! Why? My God, what's happened?

"I have no information. Only orders," Von Holden had said, then he had shown her to the bunk and taken a chair opposite. Shortly afterward the train left the station and within moments Von Holden had turned off the light.

"Goodnight," he'd said.

"Where in Switzerland?"

"Goodnight."

Von Holden smiled in the dark. Vera's reaction had been spontaneous, grave concern followed almost instantly by hope. As frightened and exhausted as she had to be, her main focus remained on Osborn. It meant she would be no trouble as long as she believed she was being taken to him. That she was ostensibly in the custody of a BKA *Hauptkommissar* was double insurance.

Von Holden had been notified of her arrest by Berlin sector operatives inside the prison earlier that day. At the time the information had been incidental, but in the turn of things it had become highly significant. Within a half hour of his directive, Berlin sector had arranged for her release. In that time Von Holden had changed clothes, secured the box inside a special black nylon case that could either be carried over the shoulder or worn like a knapsack, and been provided with BKA identification.

By arresting Vera, McVey had ironically and unwittingly provided Von Holden the complication he needed. He was no longer one man traveling alone, but one sharing a private first-class compartment with an extremely handsome woman. More important, she served another, more exacting, purpose: she gave him a hostage of prime importance to the police.

Von Holden looked at his watch. In little more than five hours they would be in Frankfurt. He would give himself four hours' sleep, then decide what to do.

131

VON HOLDEN woke precisely at six. Across from him, Vera still slept. Getting up, he went into the small bathroom and closed the door.

Washing his face, he shaved with the toiletries provided. As he did, his thoughts went to Charlottenburg. And the more he considered what had happened, the more he believed the betrayal had to have come from someone, maybe several, within the Organization. Thinking back, he remembered Salettl's ghastly appearance outside the mausoleum. How nervous he'd been when he'd told Von Holden the police were there with a warrant for Scholl. How deliberate he'd seemed when he'd ordered him to take the box and wait in the Royal Apartments, thereby putting him in a situation where he would have died had he not seized the initiative and left.

Yet the idea that Salettl could have been the one seemed absurd. The doctor had been with *"Übermorgen"* since its inception in the late 1930s. He had overseen every medical aspect of it, supervised the surgical beheadings and the experimental operations. Why, at the height of everything he'd devoted himself to for more than half a century, would he suddenly turn and destroy it all? It made no sense. Still, who else had as much access as he, not just to Charlottenburg, but to the deepest inner workings of *"Übermorgen"*?

The sound of the train's whistle brought Von Holden out of his reverie. In forty minutes they would arrive in Frankfurt. He'd already decided to avoid the airports and rely on the train as far as it would take him—which was, with any luck, the rest of the way. At 7:46 there was an Inter City Express that would get them to Bern, Switzerland, at twelve minutes after noon. From there it would be an hour and a half to Interlaken and then the last changes to the cogwheel trains of the Bernese-Oberland Railway for the breathtaking climb into the Alps and then the final ascent to the top on the Jungfrau Railway.

132

FOR ALL intents, Remmer had not slept for twenty-one hours, and the day before that he'd barely slept three, which was why he'd had trouble reacting to the line of highway flares on the rain-slicked autobahn just north of Bad Hersfeld. Osborn was the first to cry out, and Remmer's automatic-pilot reaction on the brakes slowed the big Mercedes from one hundred and eighty to less than a hundred in seconds.

Osborn's knuckles turned white against the leather seats as the Mercedes' rear end broke loose and the car spun wildly through a three-hundred-and-sixty-degree skid, giving him his first glimpse of the catastrophe in front of them. At least two trailer trucks and maybe a half-dozen cars were spewed over the highway. The Mercedes was spinning at eighty miles an hour and was no more than fifty yards from the first overturned truck. Osborn, bracing himself for the impact, glanced at Remmer. Remmer sat motionless, with both hands on the wheel as if he were riding directly into an abyss and were powerless to do anything about it. Osborn was about to lurch for the wheel, tear it out of his hands and try to steer past the truck from the passenger side, when the nose came around. As it did, Remmer's right foot touched the accelerator. Instantly the tires grabbed and the Mercedes snapped out of its spin and shot forward. Then Remmer backed off the gas, tapped the brakes, and the car rocketed past the wrecked truck with inches to spare. With another touch of brakes and turn of wheel, Remmer avoided an overturned Volvo. Then they hit the soft gravel on the shoulder; the Mercedes went up on two wheels, teetered, then settled back down and came to a stop.

* * *

The train was moving at a crawl as it crisscrossed the rail lines coming into the Hauptbahnhof, the main rail station at Frankfurt. Von Holden stood to the side of the window looking out as they entered the station. He was alert, as if he might be expecting something.

Vera sat on the bunk watching him. She'd spent the night half sleeping, half awake, her thoughts whirling. Why was Paul in Switzerland? Why were the police bringing her to him? Was he hurt, even dying—?

She felt the train slow even more, then it stopped. A sharp hiss of air brakes was followed by the sound of the rail car doors being opened.

"When we go out, we will change to another train," Von Holden said directly. "I remind you that you are still in custody of the federal police."

"You're taking me to Paul—do you think I'm going to run away?"

Suddenly there was a sharp knock at the door.

"Police. Open the door, please!"

Police? Vera looked at Von Holden.

Ignoring her, he went to the window and looked out. People moved up and down the platform, but he saw no other police, at least not in uniform.

The knock came again. "Police. Open the door immediately!"

"A mistake, they must be looking for someone else." Von Holden turned back.

Crossing the compartment, he opened the door just enough to peer out. "*Ja?*" he said, pulling on a pair of glasses, as if to see them better.

Two men in civilian clothes stood there, one a little taller than the other. Behind them was a uniformed policeman, a submachine gun in his hands. The first two were obviously detectives.

"Step out of the compartment, please," the taller one said.

"BKA," Von Holden said, opening the door wider, letting them see Vera.

"Step out of the compartment!" the taller man said again. They'd been sent after a fugitive named Von Holden. This man might be him, but it might not. They had only a photograph and in it the man did not wear glasses. Besides, the BKA? What was that business? And who was the woman?

"Of course." Von Holden stepped into the passageway. The short detective was staring in at Vera. The uniform was staring at him. Von Holden smiled at him.

"Who is she?" the taller man asked.

"Prisoner in transit. A terrorist suspect."

"Transit to where?"

"Bad Godesberg. BKA headquarters."

"Where is the female officer? The policewoman?"

Vera looked at Von Holden. What were they talking about?

"There is none," Von Holden said calmly. "There was no time. It has to do with Charlottenburg."

"Identification."

Von Holden saw the uniform glance out the window as an attractive woman passed by. They were relaxing, beginning to believe him.

"Of course." Reaching into his lapel pocket with his right hand, he lifted out a thin wallet and handed it to the shorter detective.

Von Holden looked at Vera. "Are you all right, Miss Monneray?"

"I don't understand what's going on."

"Nor do I."

Von Holden turned back and there were two quick sounds like someone spitting. The uniform's eyes suddenly went wide and his knees buckled. At the same time the squat muzzle of a silencer came up against the shorter detective's forehead. There was another pop and he jolted backward, the rear of his skull shot away. Von Holden twisted sideways as the taller detective's nine-millimeter Beretta cleared his jacket. His silenced, palm-sized .38 automatic caught him twice, once above and once below the breast bone. For an instant the man's face twinged with anger, then he fell back and slid to the floor.

A moment later Von Holden and Vera were coming down out of the train and walking across the platform, mixing with the crowd from the train moving toward the interior of the station. Von Holden had the nylon case over his left shoulder; his right hand grasped Vera's arm tightly. She was white with horror.

"Listen to me." Von Holden was looking ahead, as if engaged in no more than casual conversation. "Those people were not police."

Vera walked on, trying to regain her composure.

"Forget that it happened," he said. "Erase the image from your mind."

Now they were inside the station. Von Holden looked around for police but saw none. A clock over a newspaper kiosk read 7:25. Looking up, he scanned the overhead schedule of trains. When he saw what he wanted, he directed Vera into a fast-food kiosk and ordered coffee. "Drink it, please," he said. When she hesitated, he smiled encouragingly. "Please."

Vera picked up the cup. Her hands were shaking. She realized how frightened she still was. Taking a sip, she felt the coffee's warmth run down inside her. She sensed that Von Holden had turned away; when he came back he was holding a newspaper.

"I said those people were not police." He leaned close, talking so as not to be overheard. "Inside Germany there is a new kind of Nazi movement that has come together since unification, underground at the moment but determined to become a major power once again. Last night one hundred of Germany's most powerful and influential democratic Germans gathered at Charlottenburg Palace in Berlin. They were there to be enlightened about what was going on in their country and to pledge their support in fighting it."

Glancing at the clock over the kiosk, Von Holden opened the newspaper. On the cover was a dramatic photo of Charlottenburg engulfed in flame. The headline, in German, read *"Charlottenburg Brent!"*—Charlottenburg Burns!

"It was fire-bombed. Everyone there was killed. This new Nazi movement was responsible."

"You have a reason for telling me." Vera knew he was keeping something back.

In the distance, Von Holden saw a half-dozen uniformed police running toward the train they had just left. Again he glanced at the clock: 7:33.

"Walk with me, please."

Taking her arm, Von Holden moved off toward a waiting train.

"Paul Osborn discovered the men he was with were not who they seemed."

"McVey?" Vera didn't believe it.

"For one, yes."

"No, never. He's an American, like Paul."

"Is there some coincidence that the French policeman McVey was working with in Paris was shot and killed in a London hospital at almost the same hour yesterday that the body of the prime minister was found?"

"Oh God—" Vera could see Lebrun standing with McVey in her apartment. It was the horror of the German occupation of France all over again. Pick a thousand faces and trust not one. It was the essence of what François Christian had been fighting against in France. What he feared most—French sentiment slipping under the influence of Germany. While Germany itself, torn by strife and civil unrest, sleepwalked into the hands of fascists.

"It's the reality of what we're dealing with," Von Holden pressed. "Organized, highly trained neo-Nazi terrorists operating in Europe and the Americas. Osborn found out and came to us. We took him out of Germany for his own safety. The same is true for you."

"Me?" Vera stared at him in disbelief.

"I am not the one they were after just now, it was you. They know of your involvement with François Christian. They will assume you know things whether you do or not."

All too clearly Vera saw Avril Rocard approaching the farmhouse outside Nancy, the dead French Secret Service agents sprawled on the ground behind her.

"How did *you* know about François?" she asked painfully.

"Osborn told us. That's why we got you out of jail, before McVey and his friends could extend their influence further."

Now they were turning down a platform, walking in a crowd alongside a waiting train. Von Holden was looking for car numbers. A loudspeaker announced the arrival of one train, the departure of another. How had the police known he was on the train? He scanned the faces and body movements of the people around them. Attack could come from anywhere. In the distance came the blare of sirens. Then he saw the car he was looking for.

At 7:46, the Inter City Express pulled out of the Hauptbahnhof. Vera settled uncertainly into a crushed red velvet seat in a first-class compartment next to Von Holden. As the train accelerated, she leaned back and turned to look out the window. That McVey could have been other than what he seemed was impossible. Yet Lebrun was dead and so was François Christian. And Von Holden knew too much about all of it not to be believed. And now a hundred more had died in the Charlottenburg fire, to say nothing of the men Von Holden had killed in the railroad station. At another time, under other circumstances, she might have thought more clearly. But too much had happened, too quickly and too brutally.

Most terrifying of all, it had been done beneath the specter of a rising German political movement far too horrendous to contemplate.

133

FOR AN hour, the idea of anything but the immediate carnage disappeared as Osborn, first with Remmer's help, then with the aid of the first arriving paramedics, worked emergency triage on the bloody tarmac of the autobahn. All his skills as a surgeon, everything he'd learned from the first day of medical school, he had to draw on. He had no instruments, no medicine, no anesthesia.

The blade of a truck driver's Swiss Army knife held over a match for sterilization served as a scalpel for a tracheotomy that opened the windpipe of a seventy-year-old nun.

Leaving her, Osborn moved to a middle-aged woman. Her teenage son was near hysteria, screaming that her leg had been horribly cut and that she was bleeding to death. Only the leg wasn't cut, it had been severed. Tearing off his belt, he used it as a tourniquet to stop the bleeding, but then had to call on her son to hold it tight. Remmer was yelling for him to help pull a young woman from under a small car that was so crushed it looked as if no one could have survived. They were down flat on the tarmac, Osborn easing her out, Remmer talking to her in German, using his legs to lift a pile of tangled steel. Then they had her out and it was only at that moment that they saw she had a baby in her arms. The baby was dead. When she realized it, she simply got up and walked away. Moments later, the driver of a smashed Volkswagen bus, cradling a broken arm himself, ran after her as he realized she was walking back past the rows of stopped cars and into oncoming traffic. Police cars, ambulances and fire equipment were still arriving, and a medevac helicopter was on its way from Frankfurt, when Remmer held the skeletal body of a young man in the last stages of AIDS in his arms while Osborn maneuvered to relocate his badly dislocated shoulder. The man never said a word, never cried out though the pain must have been excruciating. Finally he lay back and mouthed "Danke."

After that, emergency workers took over. It had been daybreak when they'd started; it was light now. The carnage around them looked like a war zone. They were walking back toward the Mercedes in the soft shoulder off the pavement as the medevac helicopter set down in a roaring churn of dust. Rescue workers ran toward it carrying a litter, a paramedic running alongside holding an IV bottle overhead.

Osborn looked at Remmer. "I think we missed the train," he said quietly.

"Ja." Remmer's hand was on the Mercedes' door when its radio crackled. A brief staccato of code numbers was followed by Remmer's name. Immediately, Remmer picked up the microphone and replied. Rapid-fire German followed. Remmer listened, then gave a terse answer and clicked off. "Von Holden shot three policemen at the Frankfurt railway station. All three are dead. Von Holden escaped." Remmer finished the sentence but continued to stare at Osborn.

The look made Osborn uncomfortable. "You're not telling me something. What is it?"

"There was a woman with him."

"So—"

"Vera Monneray was released from jail at 10:37 last night," Remmer said over the squeal of tires as they sped from the accident scene. "The administrator responsible for her release was found dead less than an hour ago in the backseat of a car parked near the Berlin railway station."

"You're not trying to tell me Vera was the woman with Von Holden." Osborn could feel the anger and resentment rise within him.

"I'm not making a judgment, merely giving you a fact. In the light of things it was important that you know."

Osborn stared at him. "She was released but nobody knows what happened after that."

Remmer shook his head.

"Remmer—what the hell is going on?"

"I wish I could tell you."

Three people had seen a man and a woman leaving the Berlin-Frankfurt train shortly after it had reached the Hauptbahnhof. They had crossed the platform and disappeared into the station. All three had loud and differing opinions as to where they might have gone. However, the one thing they all agreed upon was that the man was the one in the police photographs and that he had been carrying some kind of case over his shoulder.

From the testimony of the three, and the evidence at hand, grimfaced Frankfurt homicide inspectors pieced together the chain of events. The deceased policemen had met the Berlin train when it arrived at 7:04. And had been killed very shortly afterward, perhaps within five or six minutes, by shots fired from someone inside the compartment occupied by the man called Von Holden. Their bodies had been discovered at approximately 7:18 by an Italian businessman leaving the next compartment. He had heard people talking in the corridor but had heard no gunshots, suggesting strongly the killer's weapon had been equipped with a silencer. By 7:25, the first police had arrived on scene. By 7:45 the station was cordoned off. For the next three hours no train, person, bus or taxi was allowed to leave until thoroughly searched.

The radio call had come into Remmer at 7:34. At 8:10, he and Osborn entered the station.

Immediately Remmer went over details with the Frankfurt detectives and then personally questioned the three witnesses. Osborn listened carefully, trying to understand what was being said. But for a word here and there, couldn't. The main concern, Remmer had pointed out as soon as the radio call had come in, was logistics. As he saw it, Frankfurt was a major transport hub and not a final destination, meaning Von Holden had been on his way elsewhere. The airport was only six miles from the railroad station and was serviced by direct subway. But it was obvious he had been surprised by the detectives or he would have gotten off the train at one of the earlier stops. So, having killed them, the pressure was on. That made it unlikely he would attempt to get on a plane, especially at Frankfurt. That gave him two choices. Escape into the city itself and lie low for a period of time, or get out of the city by means other than air. If he attempted to get out, there were three alternatives: train, bus or car. Unless he hijacked a car or had one waiting, that choice was unlikely because he couldn't get a rental car without drawing attention to himself simply by the rental process itself. That narrowed the alternatives to bus or train. A problem for the police, because two hundred European cities have bus links with Frankfurt. And even though every bus had been searched, it was possible that somehow they could have slipped through. It was the same with trains. Searching of them had only begun once the station was cordoned off at 7:45. In the thirty minutes from 7:15 to 7:45, roughly the time between when the murders had taken place and the station was cordoned off, sixteen trains had left Frankfurt. Bus tickets had to be secured before boarding, and no ticket agents of bus lines at Hauptbahnhof had sold tickets to anyone resembling Von Holden. Train tickets, however, could be, and often were, purchased on the train after it had left the station. Nothing would be left to chance—Frankfurt police would drag the city to find if he was holed up there, the airport would be watched for days—buses and trains would continue to be searched. Still, it was Remmer's gut feeling that Von Holden had taken one of the sixteen trains that had left before the station was cordoned off.

"What did they say she looked like?" Osborn pushed through the witnesses and up to Remmer. He was incensed and anxious at the same time.

"The descriptions of the woman varied," Remmer said quietly. "It might have been Ms. Monneray, it might not."

"Here! This man saw them!" A uniformed cop was pushing through the crowd with a thin black man wearing an apron.

Remmer turned as they came up.

"You saw them?"

"Yes, sir." The man insisted on looking at the floor.

"He served the woman coffee about seven-thirty," the policeman said, standing tight against the black man and towering over him by nearly a foot.

"Why didn't you speak up at once" Remmer asked.

"He's Mozambique. He's been beaten up by skinheads before. He's afraid of anyone white."

"Look," Remmer said gently. "Nobody's going to hurt you. Just tell what you saw."

The black man raised his eyes, looked at Remmer, then

looked back to his feet. "The man order kaffee for woman," he said in broken German. "She very pretty, very scared. Hands shake, hardly drink kaffee. He go away, then come back with newspaper. Show her paper. Then they go off—"

"Where, which way did they go?"

"There, to train."

"*Which* train?" Remmer gestured to a maze of waiting trains.

"There, or there. Not sure." The black man nodded in the direction of one track and another beside it and shrugged. "Didn't look much after they go."

"What did she look like?" Osborn was suddenly face to face with the black man; he'd held back long enough.

"Take it easy, Doctor," Remmer said.

"Ask him what color hair she had," Osborn pressed. "Ask him!"

Remmer translated into German.

The black man smiled faintly and touched his own hair. "*Schwarz.*"

"Jesus God—" Osborn knew what it meant. Black. Like Vera's.

"Let's go," Remmer said to Osborn, then turned and pushed through a crowd of police and onlookers. A moment later they slammed into the stationmaster's office, with Remmer glancing at the clock as they came in. It was 8:47.

"What trains left tracks C 3 and C 4 between seven-twenty and seven-forty-five?" he demanded of the surprised stationmaster. Behind him was a wall map of Europe, lit with a myriad of little dots and showing every rail line on the continent. "*Mach schnell!*" Remmer snorted. Hurry up!

"C 3—Geneva. Inter City Express. Arrives fourteen-six with a change in Basel. C 4. Strasbourg. Inter City. Arrives ten thirty-seven with a change at Offenburg." The numbers rolled out of him like information stored in a computer.

Remmer bristled. "Switzerland or France. Either way they're out of the country. What time do the trains reach Basel and Offenburg?"

Within minutes Remmer had taken over the stationmaster's inner office and alerted the police in the German town of Offenburg, the Swiss cities of Basel and Geneva, and the French city of Strasbourg. Every passenger getting off the trains at Offenburg and Basel would be guided through a single exit gate, while at the same time teams of plainclothes inspectors would board the trains for the final leg of the journeys to Geneva and Strasbourg. If Von Holden and the woman with him tried to get off at either midway point, they would be surrounded and captured at the exit gate. If they chose to stay on the train, they would be singled out, then overpowered and taken into custody.

"What happens to—" Osborn said as Remmer hung up, "—her?"

"She will be taken into custody. The same as Von Holden." Remmer knew what Osborn meant. Police officers had been asked to bring in a cop killer. If the fugitives were on either train, and he was certain they were, their chances of escaping a second time were nonexistent. And if they put up any resistance at all, they would be shot.

"What do we do?" Osborn was staring at him. "You go to one place and I go to the other?"

"Doctor—" Remmer paused, and Osborn suddenly felt as if the rug was about to be jerked out from under him. "I know you want to be there, how important it is to you. But I can't take a chance that you won't get caught in the middle."

"Remmer, I'll take the chance. Don't worry about it."

"I'm not talking about you, Doctor. You've got a lot on your mind and you could fuck things up royally. A nineteen-year-old cabdriver and three policemen were murdered in cold blood. The method suggests Noble was right, that this Von Holden, maybe the woman too, whoever she is, is a Spetsnaz soldier. That means he or they were trained by the Soviet Army and maybe after that by GRU, which is about six steps above your most efficient former KGB agent. That puts them into the elite of the best schooled and deadliest killers in the world with a mind-set you could not begin to comprehend. Taking them will not be easy. I won't risk losing another cop for you or anybody else. Go back to Berlin, Doctor. I promise I will let you question them both at the proper time." With that, Remmer pushed back from the stationmaster's desk and started for the door.

"Remmer." Osborn took him by the arm and pulled him around. "You're not getting rid of me like that. Not now. McVey wouldn't—"

"McVey wouldn't?" Remmer cut him off with a laugh, then took Osborn's hand from his sleeve. "McVey brought you along for *his* purposes, Doctor Osborn. And for his purposes only. Don't ever think he didn't. Now do as I say, yes? Go back to Berlin. Take a room at our old campground, the Hotel Palace. I will contact you there."

Opening the door, Remmer brushed past the stationmaster and went back into the station. Osborn followed, but not closely. In the distance he could see Remmer with the gathering of Frankfurt police, then saw him step aside to talk briefly with the three witnesses and the black counterman. And then they dispersed. All of them. Faceless people filled the place where they'd been, and it was as if it had all never happened. And like that, Osborn found himself alone in the Frankfurt railroad station. He could have been a tourist passing through with nothing more on his mind than that day's schedule. Except that he wasn't.

Von Holden and the woman with him—it was *not* Vera, Osborn decided, it was someone else, maybe someone with black hair who resembled her, but it was not Vera—were on their way to either France or Switzerland. And then where?

What was worse? That Remmer's dragnet failed and they got away, or that it didn't? No matter what Lybarger's nurse knew or didn't know, assuming they would find her, it was Von Holden who was the last of the Organization, the last direct connection to his father's death. If the police closed in, Von Holden would fight. And in doing so, he would be killed. And that would be the end of everything.

Go back to Berlin, Remmer told him. Go there and wait. He'd already waited thirty years. He wasn't going to do it again.

Suddenly Osborn realized he'd been walking across the station the whole time and was nearly to a door leading to the street. Then something caught his eye and he saw the black counterman walking quickly in his direction. He was looking over his shoulder, as if someone might be following him, and at the same time tearing off his white work apron. Reaching the door, he gave a final glance back, then, tossing the apron into a trash receptacle, pushed through to the street. For a moment Osborn wondered what was going on. Then it hit.

"The son of a bitch was lying!"

134

BRIGHT, HAZY sunlight hit Osborn like a wall, and for a moment he was blinded by it. Shading his eyes, he tried to find the man in the traffic in front of the station but couldn't. Then he saw him dart across the street and turn a corner. Osborn went after him.

Turning the same corner, he saw him halfway down the

block on the far side of the street, walking quickly along a maze of curio shops and storefront cafés. Osborn crossed to the same side of the street and picked up his pace. Suddenly it was Paris again and instead of a black man it was Albert Merriman, or Henri Kanarack, as he'd called himself. Kanarack had fled into the subway system and vanished. It had taken three days to find him again. Can't let that happen this time, Osborn thought. In three days Von Holden and whoever's with him will be on the far side of the earth.

Osborn started to run. At the same time the man looked back and saw him. He started to run himself. Twenty paces later, he cut into an alley.

Knocking a bag of groceries from a middle-aged woman in glasses, Osborn turned into the same alley, ignoring her angry shouts. Down the block, the man vaulted a fence. Osborn did the same. On the far side was a courtyard and the back door to a restaurant. The door was just swinging closed as Osborn hit the ground.

A moment later he was inside. A short hallway, a pantry, then a small kitchen. Three kitchen workers looked up as he came in. The only other door led directly into the restaurant. Osborn slammed through it and into a businessmen's breakfast. The speaker stopped and stared. Osborn turned on his heel and went back into the kitchen.

"A black man came in here. Where the hell is he?" Osborn snapped. The kitchen workers looked at each other.

"What do you want?" the fat, sweaty chef in a smeared apron asked in German. Taking a step toward Osborn, he picked up a meat cleaver.

Osborn glanced to his right, back down the hallway he'd come in.

"Sorry—" he said to the chef and started for the back door. Halfway down the hallway he suddenly stopped and shoved on the pantry door. It banged open and he stepped inside. The pantry was empty. He turned to go out, then suddenly lunged sideways. The black man tried to scramble out from behind a stack of flour bags but Osborn had him by the collar. Jerking him around hard, he pulled him face to face.

The black man turned away and threw up a hand to protect himself. "Don't hurt!" he yelled in English.

"You speak English?" Osborn said, his eyes boring in on his captive.

"Little—Don't hurt."

"The man and the woman in the station. What train did they take?"

"Two track." He shrugged and tried to smile. "Don't know. Don't see!"

Osborn flared. "You lied to the police. Don't lie to me! Or I'll call them and you'll go to prison. Understand?"

The man stared, then finally nodded. "Odder man he say, he get skinheads if I tell. They beat me. My family."

"He *threatened* you? He didn't pay you?"

The man shook his head violently. "No, no pay. Say skinheads. Come hurt. Again."

"No skinheads will come," Osborn said quietly, then relaxed his grip and reached into his pocket. The man cried out and tried to scramble away but Osborn grabbed him again. "I'm not going to hurt you." Osborn held up a fifty Deutschmark bill. "What train did they take? What destination?"

The man stared at the money, then looked at Osborn.

"No hurt. Pay," Osborn said.

The man's lower lip quivered and Osborn could see he was still afraid.

"Please, it's very important. To *my* family. Do you understand?"

Slowly the man's eyes came up to Osborn's.

"Bern."

Osborn released his grip.

135

MCVEY LAY on his back and stared at the ceiling. Remmer was gone. Osborn was gone. And nobody had told him a thing. It was five minutes to ten in the morning and all he had in his hospital room was the newspaper and Berlin television. A gauze bandage covered a good third of his face and he was still sick to his stomach from cyanide poisoning, but other than that he was fine. Except that he didn't know anything and nobody would tell him anything.

Suddenly he wondered where his things were. He could see his suit hanging in the closet and his shoes on the floor beneath it. Across the room was a small chest of drawers next to a chair for visitors. His briefcase with his case notes and passport and suitcase should still be in the hotel where he'd left them. But where the hell was his wallet and I.D.s? Where the hell was his gun?

Throwing back the covers, he slid his legs over the side of the bed and stood up. He felt a little shaky and stood still for a moment to make sure he had his balance.

Three uneven steps later, he'd crossed to the chest of drawers. In the top drawer were his boxer shorts, his undershirt and socks. In the next were his house keys, his comb, his glasses and his wallet. But no gun. Maybe they'd locked it up, or maybe Remmer had it. Closing the drawer, he started back for the bed, then stopped. Something wasn't right. Turning back, he jerked open the second drawer, took out his wallet and opened it. His badge and his letter of introduction from Interpol were gone.

"Osborn!" he said out loud. "Goddammit!"

No Remmer. No McVey. No police. Osborn sat back as Swissair flight 533 taxied out onto the tarmac and waited for takeoff clearance. He'd done what he could picture McVey doing, called Swissair and asked for the chief of security. When he got him, he explained that he was a Los Angeles homicide detective working in conjunction with Interpol. He was in hot pursuit of a prime suspect in the fire-bombing of Charlottenburg Palace. The man had arrived in Frankfurt by train from Berlin and escaped again, murdering three Frankfurt policemen in the process, and was on his way to Switzerland. It was urgent he be on the ten-ten flight to Zurich. Was there any way he could be helped through check-in?

At three minutes past ten, Osborn was met at the Swissair gate at Frankfurt International Airport by the captain of flight 533. Osborn identified himself as Detective William McVey, Los Angeles Police Department. He'd presented his .38 revolver, his badge and his letter of introduction from Interpol, and that was it—everything else, his LAPD I.D. and his passport had been left in his hotel in the rush out of Berlin. The one other thing he did have was the photo of the suspect, a man called Von Holden. The captain studied the photo and looked over the Interpol letter, then he looked up at the man calling himself a Los Angeles police officer. Detective McVey was definitely American and the bags under his eyes and stubble beard said he'd definitely been up for a long time. It was now ten-six, four minutes before they were scheduled to pull back from the gate.

"Detective—" The captain was staring him straight in the eye.

"Yes sir." What's he thinking? That I'm lying? That maybe I'm the fugitive and somehow got hold of McVey's badge and gun? If he accuses you, deny it. Hold your ground. You're in the right here no matter what and you don't have time to argue about it.

"Guns make me nervous—"

"Me, too."

"Then if you don't mind, I'll keep it in the cockpit until we land."

And that had been it. The captain went on board, Osborn paid for his ticket in Deutschmarks, then took a seat in coach class just behind the bulkhead. Closing his eyes, he waited for the whine of engines and the thrust back into his seat that would tell him he'd made it, that the captain wouldn't reconsider or that McVey had found his things missing and alerted the police. Suddenly the engines revved and the thrust came. Thirty seconds later they were airborne.

Osborn watched the German countryside fade as they climbed into a thin cloud deck. Then they were up and in bright sunshine with the sky deep blue against the white of the cloud tops.

"Sir?" Osborn looked up. A stewardess was smiling at him. "Our flight is not full. The captain has invited you to the first-class cabin."

"Thank you very much." Osborn smiled gratefully and got up. The flight was short, just over an hour, but in first class he could sit back and maybe sleep for forty minutes or so. And in first-class lavatories they might provide a razor and shaving cream. It would be a chance to freshen up.

The captain must have been a fan of either law enforcement or L.A. cops because, besides the star treatment, he also gave Osborn something else and of infinitely greater value when they landed, an introduction to Swiss airport police—personally vouching for who he was and why he was there without passport, and stressing the essence of time in his pursuit of the suspected perpetrator of the Charlottenburg holocaust. This was followed immediately by a hasty police chaperon through Swiss immigration and a hearty good-luck wish.

Outside, the captain returned the gun and asked where he was going and if he could drop him along the way.

"Thank you, no," Osborn said, greatly relieved but purposefully not revealing his destination.

"Be well, then."

Osborn smiled and took his hand. "If you're ever in Los Angeles, look me up. I'll buy you a drink."

"I will."

It was then 11:20, Saturday morning, October 15. By 11:35, Osborn was on the EuroCity express out of Zurich. At 12:45 it would arrive in Bern, thirty-four minutes after Von Holden's train had arrived from Frankfurt. By now Remmer would have scoured the Strasbourg and Geneva trains and come up empty. And with egg on his face. He'd have to turn somewhere, but where?

Then the thought came to Osborn that if the black man had lied to Remmer, why couldn't he have done the same to him? Was he coming into Bern thinking he'd cut the odds of catching Von Holden from nothing to little more than thirty minutes or would he end up the same way Remmer had, with nothing? Nothing at all—again.

136

IN FORTY-FIVE minutes Osborn would be in Bern, and he needed to think about what he was going to do when he got there. He could have shortened the distance between himself and Von Holden mightily, but still there was a thirty-four-minute overlay. Von Holden knew where he was going; Osborn didn't. What he had to do was put himself in

Von Holden's place. Where and what had he come from, where was he going and why?

Bern, he'd learned in Frankfurt when he was trying to find the fastest way to get there, had a small airport that was serviced from London, Paris, Nice, Venice and Lugano. But flights were infrequent. Daily, not hourly. And a small airport could easily be watched. Von Holden would think about that. On the plus side were civil aircraft. He could have a plane waiting.

There was a roar as a train passed in the opposite direction. Then it was gone and in its place was green farmland and behind it steep hills covered with thick forest. For a moment Osborn was lost in the beauty of the land, the clarity of blue sky against radiant green, sunlight that seemed to dance off every leaf. A small town passed, and then the train rounded a sweeping bend and on a distant hill Osborn saw the dominating silhouette of a huge medieval castle. He knew he wanted to come back here.

Suddenly he found comfort in his conviction that it was not Vera but some other woman who was with Von Holden. Vera, he was certain, had been released from jail legitimately and was, at this moment, on her way back to Paris. Thinking of her that way, picturing her safely back in her apartment, living the life she had before all this happened, a longing fell over him that was painful and beautiful at the same time. It was for them and a life together. Against the Swiss countryside he saw children and heard laughter and saw Vera's face and felt the touch of her cheek against his. He saw them smiling and holding hands and—

"*Fahrkarte, bitte.*" Osborn looked up. A young ticket collector was standing beside him, a black leather ticket case slung from his shoulder.

"I'm sorry. I don't— "

The ticket collector smiled. "Your ticket, please."

"Yes." Osborn reached in his jacket and gave the ticket collector his ticket. Then he had a thought. "Excuse, me.

I'm meeting a man in Bern. He's coming in on the train from Frankfurt that's due in at twelve twelve. He—ah, doesn't know I'm coming, it's going to be a—surprise."

"Do you know where in Bern he will be staying?"

"No, I—" That was it right there. Von Holden couldn't have planned Bern as a final destination either; his main thought would have been to get out of the country as quickly as possible following the shootings. If that was so, the idea that he might have a plane waiting was wrong.

"I think he's taking another train. Maybe to—" Where would he go? Not back to Germany. Not to an eastern country; there would be too much disruption there. "France maybe. Or Italy. He's a—salesman."

The ticket collector stared at him. "Just what is it you are asking me?"

"I—" Osborn grinned sheepishly. The ticket collector had helped clarify his thinking, but he was right, what did Osborn expect him to do? "I guess I was just trying to figure my next step if I missed him. You know, if he's already gone and not there, waiting for another train."

"My best suggestion is that you take a Eurail schedule and look over the trains that have left Bern between twelve twelve when he gets there and twelve forty-four, when you do. May I also suggest you have him paged once you get to the station."

"Paged?"

"Yes, sir." With that the ticket collector nodded, handed Osborn a train schedule and moved on.

Osborn looked off—"Paged."

Von Holden waited outside a pastry shop within the depths of the Bern rail station. Vera had gone into the women's room directly across from him. She was exhausted and had said little on the entire trip but he knew she'd been thinking of Osborn. And because of that, because she was certain he was taking her to him, he had no doubt she would return to him as she had promised.

The first hour of the trip from Frankfurt to Bern had been his greatest concern. If the black counterman had been less intimidated than he'd seemed when Von Holden had taken him aside and threatened him that skinheads would show up at his door if he didn't do exactly as he was told, and instead revealed to the police what train he was really on— they would have stopped the train in no time with a battery of police. That hadn't happened. Nor had he seen any more than the usual station security when they'd reached Bern.

At seven minutes to one, Vera came out of the women's room and went with him while he purchased two multiday passes on the Eurail system. They were good for travel anywhere on the continent. It would give them flexibility of movement, he told her. What he didn't tell her was that he could suddenly put them on any train at all without her knowing where it was going.

"*Achtung! Herr Von Holden, Telefon anruf, bitte. Herr Von Holden, Telefon, bitte.*" Von Holden started. He was being paged over the public address system. What was going on? Who could possibly know he was there?

"*Achtung! Herr Von Holden, Telefon anruf, bitte.*"

Osborn stood at a bank of phones, his back against the wall. From there he could see most of the station. The ticket windows, shops, restaurants, the foreign money exchange. If Von Holden was in the station at all—which was a long shot, since from the time Von Holden had arrived until now, at least thirteen trains had left Bern, six for cities within Switzerland, one for Amsterdam and the rest for Italy—but if he was there and moved to answer a courtesy telephone, there was every chance Osborn would see him. The other possibility was that he could be waiting for a train on one of the upstairs platforms. Osborn had counted at least eight tracks as they'd come in from Zurich.

"I'm sorry, sir. Mr. Von Holden does not answer," the operator said in English.

"Would you please try once more, it's very important."

The page came again and Von Holden took Vera by the arm and moved her quickly away from the ticket windows and into the corridor leading to the tracks.

"Who is it? Who's calling you?"

"I don't know." Von Holden looked over his shoulder. He saw no one he recognized. They turned a corner and started up the stairs toward the tracks. Then they were at the top of the stairs and onto the platform. At the far end of the station a train was waiting.

Osborn hung up and headed for the tracks. If Von Holden had been in the station he hadn't answered the page, nor had Osborn seen him in the crowds going toward the tracks. If he was there, the only thing left was that he was already on the platform, either on a train or waiting to board one.

Now Osborn was in the corridor leading to the trains. Stairs went up to his left and right, and he had to choose between at least four platforms. He went for the third, knowing it would put him on a platform somewhere toward the middle of the station.

His heart was pounding as he reached the top of the stairs. He expected to see the station filled with people, as it had been when he'd arrived. To his amazement it was all but deserted. Then he saw a train at the far end of the station, two tracks away. A man and a woman were walking rapidly toward it. He could see neither clearly, but he could tell that the man had a pack of some kind thrown over his shoulder. Osborn ran down the platform he was on. He didn't dare jump the track because he was afraid that if it had a third rail he would be electrocuted. Now, the couple were almost to the train; both had their backs to him. Osborn was running as fast as he could and very nearly coming abreast of them. He saw them reach the train and the man help the woman on, then the man turned back and looked across. As he did, Osborn slid to a stop. For the briefest moment they stared at each other, then the man pulled himself up and disappeared inside the train. A moment later the train gave a lurch and started forward. Then it picked up speed and pulled out of the station.

Osborn stood frozen where he was. The face that had stared back at him from the train was the face that had stared back at him that night in the Tiergarten. The same face that glared out of the video enhancement taken at the house on Hauptstrasse. It was Von Holden.

The woman he'd only glimpsed for a second as she boarded the train. But in that instant his world and everything in it was destroyed. There was no question who it had been. No question at all.

Vera.

137

"PASCAL," SCHOLL had said, "be most respectful of the young doctor. Kill him first."

"Yes . . . ," Von Holden had answered.

But he hadn't done it. For whatever myriad of reasons he hadn't done it. But reasons made no difference when they were excuses. Osborn was alive and had followed him to Bern. How he had accomplished that was beyond comprehension. But it was a fact. It was also a fact that he would be on the next train behind them.

* * *

"Interlaken," a railway supervisor on the platform had told Osborn when he asked the destination of the train that had just left the station. Trains to Interlaken left every half hour.

"*Danke,*" Osborn said.

He went downstairs and into the main station in a daze. He wanted to believe Vera was Von Holden's prisoner and being held against her will. But it wasn't like that and he knew it, not the way they were walking together toward the train. So what he wanted to believe made no difference. The truth was there and McVey had been right about it. Vera was part of the Organization and wherever Von Holden was going, she was going too. Osborn had been a fool to believe her, to fall in love.

Reaching the ticket window, he started to buy a ticket to Interlaken when he had the thought that maybe it was only a stop along the way. They might change trains, once, twice, even more. He couldn't stop to buy a ticket each time. So instead of one ticket, he used a credit card and bought a pass for five days. It was now 1:15, a quarter of an hour before the next train for Interlaken.

Crossing to a restaurant, Osborn ordered a cup of coffee and sat down. He needed to think. Almost immediately he realized he had no idea where Interlaken was. If he knew that, he might have some idea of where Von Holden was going. Getting up, he went to a newsstand next door and bought a map and guidebook of Switzerland. In the distance he heard a train announced in German. He understood only one word, but it was all he needed: "Interlaken."

"How much farther is it, this place we're going?" Vera said over the clicking of the wheels as the train glided slowly into the small city of Thun. She'd been half dozing, half staring off into space, and now she was sitting up and questioning him directly. Outside, the huge tower of Thun Castle passed like a hovering stone giant still caught in the twelfth century.

Von Holden was watching for signs of police as they approached the station. If Osborn had alerted the authorities, Thun would be the first logical place to stop the train and search it. He had to be prepared if they did. Vera, he was certain, had not seen Osborn or she would not be acting the way she was. But this was the reason he'd brought her. A card to play that his pursuers wouldn't have.

Within seconds they were abreast of the station. If the train was going to stop, it would have to be now. As quickly, they were out of the station and the train picked up speed. Von Holden breathed a sigh of relief and a moment later they were back in the countryside and moving along the shores of Lake Thun.

"I asked how much longer it would be until—"

Von Holden's eyes found hers. "I am not permitted to tell you our destination. It is against orders."

Abruptly he got up and walked down the aisle to the lavatory. The train was nearly empty. The early trains would have been busy. Saturday excursions into the mountains began in the morning so that people would have the entire day to explore the stirring Alpine landscape. At Interlaken they would change trains, walking from one end of the station to the other. There would be enough time between trains to provide Von Holden with a distinct opportunity.

Boarding the waiting train with Vera, he would make an excuse—he had to make a phone call or something—then, leaving her on the train, he would get off and go back into the station and wait to kill Osborn when he arrived.

138

THE ROUTE out of Bern took Osborn across a bridge over the steel green of the river Aare with the magnificent Gothic cathedral, Münster, sitting high above the city behind it. Then the train leaned into a curve and increased its speed and the vision of Münster faded into a rattle of more tracks and warehouses, then passing trees and abruptly into farmland.

Sitting back, Osborn let his hand slide inside his jacket and he felt the solid butt of McVey's .38, where it rested tucked in his waistband. He knew McVey would have found it missing by now, along with his badge and identification papers. It wouldn't take him long to figure out what happened, or who had them. McVey's anger wasn't important now. It lived somewhere else, in a different world.

From his study of the map of Switzerland, Osborn had seen that Interlaken was south and east of Bern. Von Holden was going deeper into the country, not out of it. What was in Interlaken or beyond it?

Through a rush of trees Osborn could see sunlight gleam off a river or lake, then his thoughts went to the black rucksack Von Holden had slung over his shoulder as he boarded the train. There had been something inside it, bulky, and boxlike, and he remembered his conversation with Remmer as they'd left Berlin. The old woman who had seen Von Holden leave the taxi cab said he carried a white case, slung from a strap over his shoulder. The witnesses at the station in Frankfurt had described it too. That meant he'd taken it from the taxi cab in Berlin and carried it onto the Berlin-Frankfurt train and then carried it off the train in Frankfurt.

"If I had just killed three policemen and was trying to

get the hell out of there, would I worry about a box?" Osborn thought. "I would if it was that important."

Whatever it was, it was now in the black rucksack and still in Von Holden's possession. But that didn't help in trying to understand where he was going or what he was going to do when he got there.

Then he realized that the whole time he'd been thinking, he'd been absently scanning the pages of the Swiss guidebook he'd bought in Bern. He realized it because something in it had caught his eye. It wasn't a picture. It was a word.

Berghaus.

He read the entire piece. "From the trainside of the Jungfraujoch station—the highest in Europe—a rocky corridor used to lead to the Berghaus, Europe's highest hotel and restaurant. This burned down in 1972, but it has been replaced by the fine Inn-Above-the-Clouds restaurant and cafeteria."

"Berghaus." This time he said it out loud and it chilled him. Berghaus had been the name of the group sponsoring the celebration for Elton Lybarger at Charlottenburg.

Quickly he opened the map of Switzerland and ran his finger over it. Jungfraujoch was near the summit of the Jungfrau, one of the highest peaks in the Alps, sister mountain to Monch and Eiger. Looking back to his guide book he found it was served by Europe's highest railroad, the Jungfrau Railway. Suddenly he felt the hair stand up on the back of his neck. The starting point for the trip to the Jungfrau was Interlaken.

139

McVey Wanted Remmer and he got him. Finally. At 1:45 in the afternoon.

"Where the hell is Osborn?"

Remmer was in Strasbourg and there was static on the line. "I don't know," his voice crackled through.

"Remmer!—The son of a bitch has my badge, my Interpol letter and my gun! Now where the hell is he?"

The static got louder, then suddenly there was a loud crackle, three bars of Beethoven, and a dial tone. Burning, McVey hung up.

"Goddammit!"

Sunlight cut across the platform at a sharp angle as the Bern train came slowly into Interlaken station. Steel screeched on steel and the train stopped. A ticket collector came down the steps of the first car, followed by three girls in parochial school uniforms. A half-dozen nondescript people came down from the second car, crossed the platform and went into the station. Then twenty or so American railroad enthusiasts noisily exited the third car and moved off in a group. After that everything was still, with the train left sitting there against the distant Alps like an abandoned toy.

Then, on the far side of it, away from the station, a foot touched down on the gravel alongside the track. For a moment it hesitated, then a second foot came down and Osborn turned and walked quickly along the length of the train to the end of it. Easing carefully around the last car, he looked out. The station platform was empty. So were the tracks in front of it. Once again he felt for the pistol in his waistband. There was no doubt Von Holden had recognized him on the platform in Bern. Nor would Von Holden have any doubt that Osborn would be on the next train. In retrospect he wished he had never taken the ticket collector's advice and had Von Holden paged in Bern. Its only effect had been to tell him he had been followed. And did he think the man would have been so foolish as to answer a page in the first place? It had been a mistake, the same as running toward the Interlaken train on the platform, letting himself be recognized. Another mistake like that could cost him his life.

In the distance he heard a train whistle. Then the train for Jungfraujoch was announced over the P.A. system. If he missed it, it would be thirty minutes before the next train. That would put him an hour behind Von Holden. Twice the time he was behind him now. That was unless Von Holden was here, somewhere, waiting for him.

Again came the announcement for Jungfraujoch. If he were going to make the train, he would have to cross from where he was and walk the length of the station to reach it. Von Holden would know that too. If he was still here, lying in wait, Osborn's only ally would be that it was the middle of the afternoon, broad daylight in a small public railway station. It would take a daring move on Von Holden's part to try something so bold and expect to get away with it. But then, wasn't that exactly what had happened to his father?

Scanning the station again, Osborn stepped from behind the train, crossed the platform and walked toward the far end of the station. He moved quickly, his jacket open, his hand near the gun. All his senses were alert. A movement in a shadow, a footstep behind him, someone appearing suddenly from a doorway. He flashed back to Paris and the tall man dead on the Montparnasse sidewalk outside La Coupole, with McVey lifting his pant leg to reveal his artificial limbs that could let him be tall or short or somewhere in between at will. Was Von Holden filled with the same tricks? Or had he others, even more bizarre and ingenious?

Osborn stayed out in the open where he could be seen by everyone. He passed an old man walking slowly, using a cane. Osborn wondered if he'd live that long.

An old man with a cane!

Osborn whirled, his hand under his jacket, ready to jerk out the revolver and fire. But the old man was just an old man and kept going. Again the announcement train whistle, and Osborn turned back toward it. Ahead he could see the American railroad enthusiasts. They were going for the Jungfraujoch train too. If he could catch up, he could blend in with them.

"Achtung! Achtung! Doktor Osborn. Telefon, bitte!" The public address page echoed through the station. Osborn stopped in his tracks. Von Holden not only knew he was there, he knew his name.

"Doctor Osborn of the United States, telephone, please!"

Osborn looked around for a telephone. He saw them at the edge of the building. A double phone booth, side by side. Both were empty. His first inclination was to ask someone where the paging operator was located, but he didn't have time. Through the open door he could see the last of the Americans boarding the train. What was Von Holden doing? Was he positioned somewhere outside with a high-powered rifle targeted on the telephones? Was some kind of high-tech explosive device connected to the phones and set to go off automatically on pickup, or be detonated by remote control like the blast at the Hotel Borggreve?

A final announcement for the Jungfraujoch train was followed immediately by the announcement of an incoming train. Then came another page for him. Outside, conductors were hurrying the last of the passengers onto the Jungfraujoch train.

Think! Think! Osborn said to himself. You know nothing about Jungfraujoch station or what Von Holden plans to do when he gets there. If this is a trick, and you miss the train, he'll be a full hour ahead of you. Enough time to get away completely now that he knows you're this close. But if he's still here and watching and you get on the train, all he has to do is wait for it to leave and he's home free. Takes the next train out and it's the last you ever hear of him. Maybe he was never going to Jungfraujoch in the first place. On the other hand, what if he was? Jungfraujoch is the last stop on the line. If he is going there, because of the Berghaus thing, think *why!* What's his objective? If he's carted whatever he's got in his rucksack all the way from Berlin to Interlaken—especially after escaping the fire at Charlottenburg and killing the Frankfurt policemen—whatever it is must be very important, maybe even crucial to the Organization. If so, he may be delivering it to someone at Jungfraujoch, someone even more powerful than Scholl. If that's the case, what would be more important, the mission or the lone man trying to stop it? If he kills me here, he's set. But if something goes wrong and he misses, or he's captured, then whatever he's doing ends here.

"Attention, Doctor Osborn. Telephone, please!"

No! Don't fall for it! He's having you paged but it's a trick! He's already on the train ahead of this one! Suddenly Osborn moved. In two steps he was out the door and running for the train. A moment later he reached out, grasped the rear handrail and swung on board. Almost immediately the train started off. Behind him, the colorful hotels and chalets of Interlaken, their planter boxes of geraniums still in bright bloom, slowly slid from view. Then he felt the train begin to climb and he saw the rich reds and yellows of autumn leaves and beyond, as the grade became steeper, the deep blue expanse of Lake Thun.

140

COMRADE SENIOR Lieutenant they'd called him in the Spetsnaz. Who and what was Von Holden now? Still *Leiter der Sicherheit*, head of security, or a last, lone soldier on the most critical assignment of his life? Both, he thought. Both.

Beside him, Vera stared out at passing countryside, content, he guessed, simply to pass the time. Von Holden shifted in his seat and looked out. Moments before they had changed trains at Grindelwald, and now he heard the grind of the cogs as they took hold of the center rail and the train pushed steeply upward through a forest of lush alpine meadows dappled with wildflowers and grazing dairy cattle.

In another twenty minutes they'd reach Kleine Scheidegg where the meadows would abruptly end against the base of the Alps. There they would change once more, this time to the brown-and-cream-colored train of the Jungfrau Railway that would take them up into the marrow of the Alps, past the stops of Eigerwand and Eismeer, and finally into Jungfraujoch station. To Von Holden's left was the Eiger, and beyond it the snow-covered summit of the Monch. Beyond them, not yet in view, but as familiar as the lines in his hand, was the Jungfrau. Its summit at thirteen and a half thousand feet was nearly half a mile higher than rail's end at Jungfraujoch station. Looking back, he studied the Eiger's harrowing north face, a sheer limestone cliff rising fifty-four hundred feet straight from the Eiger meadows to the top, and thought of the fifty or more true professionals who had died trying to climb it. It was a risk, like anything else. You prepared, you did your best, and then something unforeseen happened and you fell. Death, all around you, simply closed in.

Thun had been the first logical place the police would have intercepted the train. That they hadn't left only Interlaken. But there had been no police there either, and that meant however Osborn had managed to catch up, he'd done it alone. How many trains per day passed through Interlaken, Von Holden didn't know. What he did know was that a train for Lucerne had left ten minutes after his train had arrived from Bern. Lucerne was a major connecting point for destinations as disparate as Amsterdam, Belgium, Austria, Luxembourg and Italy. Jungfraujoch was a side trek, an interlude for tourists, Alpine hikers or serious mountaineers. Von Holden was a man on the run from the law and would hardly be expected to take a leisurely afternoon's excursion into the mountains, especially where the destination was a dead end. No, he would be trying to put as much distance between himself and his pursuers as possible. And if, in doing that, he could cross the border into a different country, so much the better.

Von Holden had abandoned the idea of killing Osborn at Interlaken as too risky. Instead, he'd turned Osborn's trick against him and had him paged, with the intention of both throwing him off and frightening him. Muddle whatever cunning and instinct that had brought him this far and in the process send him scurrying, none too coherently, after the only thing left. Logic. After arriving from Bern, there were only two ways out of Interlaken, the train up into the mountains or the narrow-gauge train to Lucerne. And a train for Lucerne, Osborn would learn, had left Interlaken only minutes after Von Holden had arrived from Bern. Von Holden would have no choice but to be on it. Accepting that, Osborn would rush onto the next train after it in pursuit of a shadow.

Osborn jumped from the train at Grindelwald station and quickly crossed to the waiting cars of the train that would connect with one at Kleine Scheidegg and take him the final leg to Jungfraujoch. This time there was no hesitation. He was certain Von Holden would be on the train ahead of him, not lying in wait here. Von Holden was arrogant enough to think he'd thrown him off at Interlaken and believe he was either still there, frightened and wondering what to do, or, better yet, had done the most obvious and followed the train Von Holden should have been on to Lucerne.

Jungfraujoch station, he'd learned in a brief conversation with one of the American railroad buffs on board, consisted of a tiny post office and souvenir shop, a tourist exhibit called the Ice Palace with ice sculptures literally cut into glacier walls on which the station was built, a small, automated weather station, and the Inn-Above-the-Clouds restaurant. Most of these were on different levels and served by elevators. Other than that there was nothing but the mountain and the desolate expanse of the great Aletsch glacier that lay before it. If Von Holden was meeting someone to transfer the contents of the rucksack, it would be within the confines of the station. Who that would be, or where it might take place, he had no idea. But there was nothing he could do until he got there.

With a sharp grate of engine cogs, the train leaned into a curve, and for the first time Osborn saw the full expanse of the mountains above him, their peaks stark white against the late afternoon sky. Closest was the Eiger, and even at this distance he could see wind-driven snow devils dance just below its summit.

"We're going straight up there, once we get past Kleine Scheidegg, darlin'." A smiling bleached blonde, one of the American railroaders, was talking to him, referring to the summit he was looking at. It wasn't hard to see she'd had a face-lift, nor, as she patted his knee with a ringless left hand, that she was single and making a point of it. "Right up into the wall of Eiger and a tunnel inside where you can look out and see this whole valley all the way back to Interlaken."

Osborn smiled and thanked her for the information, then looked at her blankly until she took her hand away. It wasn't that aggressive women bothered him, it was that he was thinking about something else. Wishing that besides McVey's .38, he had at least one vial of the muscle-relaxing succinylcholine he'd prepared in Paris for his attack on Albert Merriman.

141

VON HOLDEN, too, was watching the mountains, looking for a wisp of cloud or undue snow-devil activity that would indicate the wind was picking up and weather might be approaching. But he saw none and for a change it was a good sign. It would make things easier later on if there was a problem and he had to go out on the mountain.

Vera sat across, looking at him. He was somewhere else, lost in thought. Increasingly, something about him was troubling her. But it was vague and she couldn't put her finger on it. Yes, he was a policeman. Yes, he was taking her to Paul Osborn. It had to be true because she'd been released from jail in his custody and he knew things that were unknowable if he was not who he said he was. Still, something wasn't right and she wished she knew what it was. Glancing up, she saw his nylon rucksack riding in the luggage rack overhead. He'd been carrying it with him since Berlin and she'd never really thought about it until now—what it was, what was inside.

"Evidence," Von Holden said quietly.

The train was climbing steeply now, with rock formations, rushing mountain streams and waterfalls dropping away sharply at either side.

"Documents and other things exposing the core of the neo-Nazi movement. Names, places, financial data."

The car in which they rode had a half-dozen other passengers as did the car in front of them. The cog engine on the tiny, two-car train pushed from behind. Vera was becoming aggressive, and Von Holden didn't like it. The trauma caused by her ordeal in Berlin and capped by the killings in Frankfurt was wearing off. She was becoming aware, beginning to examine her situation, to probe, maybe even doubt. It meant he had to stay a step ahead, offer something of himself to keep her trust.

"I think it's safe to tell your our destination is Jungfraujoch station." He smiled. "They call it the Top of Europe. You can send a card from the highest post office on the continent."

"That's where Paul is."

"Yes, as well as a guarded repository for the documents."

"What happens when we get there?"

"That's not for me to say. My orders were to safely deliver you and the documents. After that"—he smiled again—"I will go home, hopefully."

Suddenly the train plunged into a tunnel and the only light was from the electric lamps inside the train.

"Twenty minutes more," Von Holden said. Vera relaxed and leaned back against the seat. For the moment she's satisfied, he thought. Once they reached Jungfraujoch station they would leave the train with the other passengers, then go immediately to the weather station. After that, what Vera thought or did would make no difference, because once inside they would vanish into its depths and no one on earth could find them.

Abruptly the train slowed and they came into Eiger-wand, a small railway station carved into the rocky tunnel inside the north face of the Eiger. The train pulled effortlessly onto a siding and stopped, leaving the main rail free so that another train could pass on the way down. The driver opened the doors and invited everyone out to enjoy the view and take photographs.

"Come." Von Holden smiled and stood up. "For the time being we're tourists like everyone else. We should relax and enjoy it."

Leaving the train, they crossed the platform with the other passengers and walked into one of several short tunnels where enormous windows had been cut into the face of the mountain. From there they could see for miles back across the sunlit valley floor toward Kleine Scheidegg and Grindelwald and Interlaken, the way they had come. Von Holden had seen it two dozen times and each time it was more impressive than the last, as if seeing the world from the mountain's point of view. Behind them the driver sounded his whistle and the other passengers started back for the train.

It was then Von Holden saw the train behind them approaching Kleine Scheidegg. Suddenly his breath caught and he felt his heart begin to palpitate. There was a pulsing behind his eyes and curtains of red and green started to come.

"Are you all right?" Vera asked.

For a brief moment Von Holden wavered, then he exhaled sharply, pulling himself out of it.

"Yes, thank you. . . ." He took her arm and they started back. "The altitude, perhaps." It was a lie. His attack had not been because of the altitude, or weariness or anything else. It had been real. The "Vorahnung." And it meant only one thing.

Osborn was on that train.

142

OSBORN FELT the press of gravity as the train began to move out of Kleine Scheidegg and start up the long grade toward the face of the Eiger. The bleached-blonde divorcée—her name was Connie and she was a divorcée, twice in fact—kept trying to talk to him. Finally he excused himself and went into the front car. He needed to think. In little more than forty minutes they would reach Jungfraujoch. He had to know what he was going to do, right from the moment the train came into the station and he stepped off. Once again he felt the heft of McVey's .38 in his waistband. For some reason it made him think about avalanches. More than once a gunshot had set off a thundering avalanche. Mountain teams and ski areas used recoilless rifles to start them on purpose, to clear them away before opening the snow areas to the public. But it was barely mid-October and the weather was clear. An avalanche should be the last thing on his mind.

But it wasn't.

His subconscious was working toward something. What was it? This was early October, but Von Holden was purposely going into snow country. Jungfraujoch was at an altitude of more than eleven thousand feet and built on top of or within a glacier. Inside were tourist sideshows, rooms carved out of the glacial ice.

Ice.

Cold. Deep cold. A glacier was as cold as you got in nature. Especially if you could get deep inside it. Men and animals had been found in it, perfectly preserved for centuries. Was it possible Jungfraujoch was the place where the experimental surgeries had been done? Was Jungfraujoch, seemingly a tourist attraction, really a cover for a secret medical facility deep within the glacier itself?

The grinding of the engine cogs and the click, click of the wheels over the rails became more pronounced.

Suddenly Osborn was pushing back into the other car.

"Connie," he said, sliding onto the seat next to her. "You've been to Jungfraujoch before."

"Sure have, darlin'."

"Is there any place that's off limits to tourists?"

"What you got in mind, darlin'?" Connie smiled and teasingly ran her fake ruby red nails along the top of his thigh.

Osborn was sure she was a riot after a couple of martinis, but that was something he never wanted to find out.

"Look, Connie. I'm just trying to get some information. Nothing—with a big N—else. Okay. Now, please be a good kid and try and remember."

"I like you."

"I know."

"Well, lemme think."

Osborn watched as she got up and stood looking out the window. It wasn't easy, the car was climbing the face of the Eiger and tilted at almost a forty-degree angle. Abruptly everything went dark as they entered a tunnel.

Five minutes later Osborn and Connie were looking out of the cutouts in the Eiger wall at Eigerwand station. Connie had her arm through his and was holding tight.

"I don't like to admit it, but I do get dizzy."

Osborn looked at his watch. Von Holden should be there now, or almost there anyway. Maybe he had been wrong about the medical facility. Maybe Von Holden was simply meeting someone there as he'd thought earlier. If that were the case, Von Holden could give him whatever he was carrying in the rucksack and take the next train down. The whole thing could be done in a matter of minutes.

"There's a weather station."

"What?" Connie was speaking to him and at the same time they were being called back to the train.

"A weather station, you know, some kind of observatory."

Now they were crossing the platform toward the train. As they did, a train was coming down from Jungfraujoch, passing their train on the siding, slowly winding its way by on the lone track.

"Darlin', you listenin' to me or am I just talkin' to entertain myself?"

"Yes, I hear you." Osborn was straining to see inside the passing train. It was going slowly enough for him to see faces. He recognized none.

Then they were back in the train and sitting down and the train was moving into the tunnel and upward. Picking up speed.

"I'm sorry. You said something about—"

"A weather station. Did you or did you not ask if there was a place where the public couldn't go. Well, there's a weather station there. Upstairs, I think. Must be run by the government or something. 'Course there's the kitchen."

"What kitchen?"

"For the restaurant. Why do you want to know this anyway?"

"Research. I'm—writing a—book."

"Darlin'—" Connie put her hand on his thigh again and leaned so close her lips were brushing his ear. "I know you're not writin' a book," she whispered. "Because if you were you'd wait to find out what you're askin' till we get there and you could see for yourself. I also"—she blew a knot of hot air into his ear— "know you've got a gun stickin' in your belt. What're you gonna do with it, shoot somebody?" Connie sat back and smiled. "Darlin', will you promise me one thing? Yell first. I'd like to get the fuck out of the way."

143

EISMEER WAS the last station before Jungfraujoch, and like Eigerwand the train stopped while the passengers got out to take pictures and ooh and aah from the cutouts in the rock. But the view from Eismeer was different from Eigerwand and everything else they had passed. Instead of rolling meadows and lakes and deep green forests bathed in lazy autumn sunshine, here was a white, frozen landscape. Vast rivers of snow and glacial ice ran from view or stopped hard against jagged rock cliffs. In the distance, driven snow on a topmost peak was blushed rose red by a dying sun, while overhead hung a thin and endless sky broken only by the smallest wisps of cloud. In the morning, or at midday, it might have looked different. But now, in the last hour before dark, it seemed cold and ominous: a vast and foreign place where man did not belong. The feeling seemed a natural warning: that if, by some accident or design, he were to wander out there, away from people, away from the trains, he should understand that this place was not his. He would be on his own. And God would not protect him.

The whistle sounded for reboarding and the passengers turned back toward the train. Osborn looked at his watch. It was ten minutes to five. It would be just five when they arrived in Jungfraujoch and the last train down left at six. By then it would be pitch dark. At most he would have an hour to find Von Holden and Vera and do his business with them. And, if he lived, to catch the last train down.

Osborn was the last to board. Immediately the door closed behind him, there was a lurch and he felt the cog gears catch on the rail beneath him. Leaning back, he took a deep breath, and then absently glanced around the car.

Connie was sitting near the rear, talking to her railroaders, not so much as looking at him. That was good, he thought, one less thing to deal with. Then, strangely and quite surprisingly, he found himself wishing for her company. He thought that maybe, if he sat down, with an open seat next to him, she might get up and join him. Walking back toward the railroaders, he found a vacant double seat and sat down facing her. If she saw him she didn't acknowledge it, just kept on talking. He watched her gesture with her hands and wondered why she wore those long fake red nails. Or bleached her hair that awful blond. It was then he realized he was frightened to death. Remmer had clearly warned him to stay away from Von Holden. Noble had told him that after his encounter with him in the Tiergarten he was extremely lucky to still be alive. The man was a thoroughly schooled assassin who, in the last twenty or so hours, had sharpened his skills by murdering a nineteen-year-old-woman cabdriver and three German policemen. He knew who Osborn was and that he was following him. And having come this far, would Von Holden be so simple to think he was now blithely chugging his way toward Lucerne? Not likely. Since Von Holden had been on neither train coming down, it meant he was still at Jungfraujoch. And at Jungfraujoch there was no place *but* Jungfraujoch.

In less than five minutes, he thought, he was going to be delivered straight into a hell of his own creation. A stream of unfinished business spewed through him like an uncontrolled printout. Patients—house—car payments—life insurance—who arranges to get my body home? Who gets my things? After the last divorce I never made another will. He almost laughed. It was a comedy. Life's loose ends. He had come to Europe to give a speech. He had fallen in love. And after that it was straight downhill. *"La descente infernale,"* he could hear Vera say in French. The ride to hell.

Vera—he was hearing her as he remembered her, not as who she was. Time and again she had come forward in his thoughts, time and again he'd forced her out. What was

was and the way it stood. When the time came and he finally faced her, that's when he would deal with the reality of it, but for now it was Von Holden who had to stay centered in his mind—

He felt the train slow. A sign passed by the window. Jungfraujoch.

"Jesus Christ," he whispered. Instinctively his hand touched the butt of the revolver. At least he still had that.

"Think of your father!" he told himself. "Hear the sound of Merriman's knife hit him in the stomach! See the look on his face! See his eyes come to you, asking you what happened. See his knees buckle as he collapses on the sidewalk. Somebody screams! He's scared. He knows he's going to die. See his hand reach up to you. For you to take, to help him through it. See that, Paul Osborn. See that and do not fear what is ahead."

There was a shriek of brakes, then a bump, and the train slowed more. There were two tracks and light at the far end, and they were almost there. The station was inside the tunnel like Eigerwand and Eismeer, Connie had told him. Only here the tracks did not continue through, they stopped at the end. The only way out was the way they were coming in. Back through the tunnel.

144

"A FIRE in the weather station, sir. It happened last night. No one was hurt but the station is beyond repair," a railroad worker had said of the pile of charred debris stacked against the side of the tunnel.

Fire! Last night. The same as Charlottenburg. The same as *der Garten*. Von Holden had been increasingly apprehensive as they'd neared the Jungfraujoch station and he was fearful the attacks would come again. The source of his concern, he'd thought, was not so much Osborn as Vera. For the last part of the trip she'd been quiet, almost detached, and his sense had been that she'd caught on and was trying to make up her mind what to do. He'd countered that quickly by moving her out of the train and toward the elevator the moment they'd arrived. They were no more than three minutes from the weather station, four at most. Once there, everything would be all right because very shortly afterward she would be dead. It was then he'd seen the debris and been told of the fire. The destruction of the weather station was something he'd never considered.

"That's where Paul was, up there—"

"Yes," Von Holden said. They were outside in the growing twilight, climbing a long series of steps toward the burned-out shell of what had been the weather station. Behind them was the brightly lit massive cement and steel structure that housed the restaurant and Ice Palace. On their right, falling away beneath them, was the ten-mile-long Aletsch glacier, a frozen, twisted, now darkening sea of ice and snow. Above them rose the nearly fourteen-thousand-foot Jungfrau peak, its snowy crest blood red with the setting sun.

"Why are there no rescue workers? No firemen? No heavy equipment?" Vera was angry, afraid, incredulous, and Von Holden was grateful for it. It told him that no matter what else she might have been thinking, her main concern was still Osborn. That, in itself, would keep her off guard if he couldn't reach the inner passageways he hoped had survived the fire and they had to go back outside.

"There is no rescue attempt because no one knows they are here. The weather station is automated. No one goes there except an occasional technician. Our levels are belowground. Emergency generators automatically seal each floor in case of fire."

Then they were at the top and Von Holden tore aside a heavy sheet of plywood covering the entrance and they pushed past a frame of charred timbers. Inside it was dark, heavy with the acrid smell of smoke and molten steel. The fire had been extremely hot. Hotter than any fire started by accident. A melted steel door in the back of an instrument closet attested to it. Finding a crowbar left by the demolition crew, Von Holden tried to pry it open but it was impossible.

"Salettl, you bastard," he said under his breath. In disgust he threw the bar aside. There was no need even to attempt to open it; he knew what he would find inside. A ceramic-lined, six-foot-high titanium tunnel, melted into an impassable mass.

"Come on," he said, "there is another entrance." If the lower levels had been sealed off from the fire as they should have been, everything would still be all right.

Leading the way outside, Von Holden let Vera go down the steps ahead of him. As she did, the last rays of the sun touched her hair, bathing her in soft vermilion. For the briefest moment Von Holden wondered what it would be like to be an ordinary man. And in that he thought of Joanna, and the truth of what he had said to her in Berlin, that he didn't know if he was capable of love and she had replied, "You are——" It was a thought out of time and it led to another: that however simple and plain she was, at heart she was truly beautiful, perhaps the most beautiful woman he'd ever known and he was astonished to think that maybe she was right, that he was capable of love and the love he held was for her.

Then his eyes were drawn to a large clock on the wall at the bottom of the steps. Its minute hand stood straight up. It was exactly five o'clock. At the same moment came the announcement of an arriving train. As quickly his dream vanished and something else stood in its place.

Osborn.

145

OSBORN STOOD back from the door, letting the other passengers go out first. Absently, he wiped perspiration from his upper lip. If he was trembling, he didn't notice.

"Good luck, darlin'." Connie touched his arm on the way out and then she was gone, following the last of the railroaders toward an open elevator at the far end of the tracks. Osborn looked around. The car was empty and he was alone. Lifting out the .38, he flipped open the chamber. Six shots. McVey had left it fully loaded.

Closing the chamber, he stuck the gun in his waistband and he let his jacket slide across it. Then, taking a deep breath, he stepped sharply from the train. Immediately he felt the cold. It was the kind of mountain cold you felt on ski trips when you stepped from a heated gondola and out into the half-open barn where the gondolas stopped.

He was surprised to see a second train in the station and he had to think that since the last train left at six, the second train must be for the help who would go down later, after they'd closed up.

Crossing the platform, Osborn joined several British tourists and took the same elevator Connie and the railroaders had taken. The car went one stop and the door opened, revealing a large room with a cafeteria and souvenir shop.

The Brits stepped out and Osborn went with them.

Dropping back, he stopped at the souvenir shop and absently looked over an assortment of Jungfraujoch T-shirts, postcards and candy while at the same time trying to study the faces of the people crowding the cafeteria farther down the room. Almost immediately a short, chubby boy of maybe ten walked up with his parents. The family was American and both the father and boy wore identical Chicago Bulls jackets. In that one single instant Osborn felt more alone than at any time in his life. He wasn't quite sure why—was it that he had so distanced himself from the rest of the world that death, if it came at Von Holden's hands or even Vera's, would go wholly unnoticed, that no one would care that he had ever been? Or had the vision of the boy and his father only magnified the bitterness of what had been taken from him? Or was it that other thing, the thing that had eluded him his entire life, a family of his own?

Pulling himself from the depths of his own emotion, Osborn studied the room once more. If Von Holden or Vera were there, he didn't see them. Leaving the souvenir area, he crossed to the elevator. Almost immediately the door opened and an elderly couple walked out. Scanning the room a last time, Osborn went into the elevator and pressed the button for the next floor. The door closed and he started upward. Several seconds later the elevator stopped, the door slid open, and he looked out at a world of blue ice. This was the Ice Palace, a long semicircular tunnel cut into glacial ice and filled with caverns holding ice sculptures. Ahead of him, he could see the last of the railroaders, Connie among them, as they walked along enchanted by the sculptures—of people, of animals, of a full-size car, a replica of a bar, complemented with chairs and tables and an old-fashioned whiskey barrel.

Osborn hesitated, then stepped out and started down the corridor, trying to blend in, to look like anybody else. As he walked, he searched the faces of tourists coming toward him. Maybe he'd made a mistake not staying with the railroaders. Reaching out, he ran his fingers delicately along the side of the corridor, as if he doubted it was ice and might instead be some manufactured product. But it was ice. The same as on the ceiling and floor. The surrounding of ice intensified the thought that this place could have been the site of the experimental surgeries done at extreme cold.

But where? Jungfraujoch was small. Surgeries, especially surgeries as delicate as these would be, required space. Equipment rooms, prep room and surgery rooms, intensive-care post-op rooms. Rooms to house the staff. How could it be done here?

The only place out of bounds, Connie had told him, was the weather station. Fifteen feet away a Swiss guide stood by as teenagers posed for a photograph in the ice tunnel. Crossing to her, Osborn asked directions to the weather station. It was upstairs, she said. Near the restaurant and the outside terrace. But it was closed because of a fire.

"Fire?"

"Yes, sir."

"When did it happen?"

"Last night, sir."

Last night. The same as Charlottenburg.

"Thank you." Osborn continued on. Unless it was some great coincidence, what happened there, happened here. Meaning whatever had been destroyed there had been destroyed here, too. But Von Holden wouldn't have known that or he wouldn't have come, unless it was to meet someone. Suddenly something made Osborn look up. Vera and Von Holden stood at the end of the corridor bathed in the eerie blue light created by the ice. They looked at him a half second more, then abruptly turned down the corridor and vanished.

Osborn's heart felt as if it was trying to pound through his ears. Gathering himself, he turned to the guide.

"Down there," he pointed to where the two had stood. "Where does that lead?"

"Outside to the ski school and the dogsled area. But of course they are closed now for the day."

"Thank you." Osborn's voice was barely a whisper. His feet were like stone, as if they had frozen to the ice beneath them. His hand slid into his jacket and took hold of the .38. The ice walls glistened cobalt blue and he could see his breath. Grasping the hand rail he moved cautiously ahead until he reached the turn in the tunnel where Von Holden and Vera had vanished.

The corridor ahead was empty, and at the end was a door. A sign for the ski school pointed toward it. There was another for dogsled rides.

You want me to follow you, don't you? Osborn's mind raced. That's the idea. Through that door. Outside. Away from other people. Go out there. You do that, he's got you. You won't come in again. Von Holden will take what's left of you and throw you over the side someplace. Into some deep crevasse. They won't find you till spring. They may never find you.

"What are you doing? Where are you taking me?" Vera and Von Holden entered a small, claustrophobic room of ice in a passageway off the main corridor. He had held her arm going down the passage and stopped her the moment they'd seen Osborn. Purposely he waited until he felt her about to call out, then he'd pulled her around and they'd gone quickly back, turning into a side tunnel and then into the room.

"The fire was set. They are here, waiting for us. For you, for the documents I have."

"Paul—"

"Perhaps he is one of them as well."

"No. Never! He escaped somehow—"

"Did he?"

"He had to have—" Suddenly Vera flashed on the men posing as Frankfurt police moments before Von Holden shot them. "Where is the female officer? The police-woman?" they had asked.

"There is none," Von Holden answered. "There was no time."

It hadn't been another fugitive that concerned them, it had been *procedure!* A male detective would not transport a female prisoner alone in a closed compartment without the accompaniment of a policewoman!

"We have to find out about Osborn, or neither of us will leave here alive." Von Holden's breath hung in the air and he smiled gently as he came toward her. The nylon ruck-sack was over his left shoulder, his right hand at his waist. His manner was easy, relaxed, the same as it had been when he faced the men on the train. The same as Avril Rocard's had been when she gunned down the French Se-cret Service agents at the Nancy farmhouse.

In that instant Vera understood—the thing that had trou-bled her since they'd left Interlaken, the thing she'd been too emotionally overwhelmed and exhausted to grasp be-forehand, the thing that had been there all along. Yes, Von Holden had had all the right answers, but it was for a different reason. The men on the train *had* been police. It was not they who were Nazi killers, it was *Von Holden.*

146

OSBORN WALKED quickly back the way he had come. Now he saw the railroaders loading into the elevator at the far end of the Ice Palace. Walking even faster, he caught up with them just as the door was closing. Stopping it with his hand, he squeezed in among them.

"Sorry . . . ," he lied, smiling.

The door closed and the elevator rose. What to do now? Osborn could feel the pump of blood through his carotid arteries. The *thud! thud! thud!* of it felt like a jackhammer. Abruptly the elevator stopped and the door opened out into a large self-service restaurant. Osborn had to step out first. Then he held back and tried to stay with the crowd. Outside it was almost dark. Through a bank of windows he could just make out the peaks at the far end of the sloping Aletsch glacier. Beyond them, in the eerie twilight, he could see weather clouds moving in.

"What're you doin' now?" Connie was walking beside him. Osborn looked at her and then started as a sudden gust of wind rattled across the windows.

"Doing?" Osborn's eyes nervously swept the room as they followed the others toward the food service line. "I thought maybe I'd have a—cup of coffee."

"What's the matter?"

"Nothing. Why would anything be the matter?"

"You in trouble or something? The police after you?"

"No."

"You sure?"

"Yes. I'm sure."

"Then why're you so nervous? You're skitty as a newborn colt."

Now they were at the food counter. Osborn looked back

at the room. Some of the railroaders were already sitting down, pulling up chairs between two tables nearby. The family he'd seen at the souvenir shop was at another table, with the father pointing off toward the restrooms and the young boy in the Chicago Bulls jacket heading toward it. Two young men sat at a table near the door, smoking cigarettes and chatting earnestly.

"Sit over here with me and drink this." They were already through the cashier and Connie was leading him to a table away from the railroaders.

"What is it?" Osborn looked at the glass Connie had set in front of him.

"Coffee with cognac. Now be a good guy and drink it."

Osborn looked at her, then picked up the cup and drank. What to do? He thought. They're here, in the building or outside it. I didn't go after them. Which means they'll come after me.

"Are you Doctor Osborn?"

Osborn looked up. The boy in the Chicago Bulls jacket was right there.

"Yes."

"A man said to tell you he's waiting outside."

"*Who* is?" Connie's bleached eyebrows furrowed together.

"By the dogsled run."

"Clifford, what are you doin'? I thought you were goin' to the lavatory." The boy's father was taking him by the hand. "Sorry," he said to Osborn. "What're you doin' bothering those folks, huh?" he said to his son as they walked off.

Osborn saw his father on the sidewalk. Primal fear in his eyes. Terrified. His hand reaching up for his son to ease him into death. Suddenly he got up. Without looking at Connie, he stepped around the table and started for the door.

147

VON HOLDEN waited in the snow, back from the empty runs where they kept the sled dogs during the day. The box in the black backpack rested nearby. In his hands he cradled a nine-millimeter Skorpion automatic pistol mounted with a flame and sound suppressor. It was light and maneuverable and had a thirty-two-round magazine. Osborn, he was certain, would be armed, as he had been the night in the Tiergarten. There was no way to know how well trained he was, but it made little difference because this time Von Holden would give him no opportunity.

Fifty feet away, between himself and the ski school door, Vera stood in the darkness. She was handcuffed to a safety railing that followed the icy path toward the dog runs. She could cry, scream, anything. Out here in the dark, with the restaurant closing up for the night, the only one who would hear her was Osborn when he came out. Fifty feet was close enough for her to be heard and seen by Osborn but far enough away form the building for anyone who might be inside looking out. Von Holden's purpose was to get them both away and into the darkness past the dog runs where the killing would be best. That was why he'd left Vera where he had. She was serving the purpose he had planned for her from the beginning. Except that now, instead of a hostage, she had become bait.

Forty yards beyond her the ski school door at the end of the Ice Palace tunnel opened, light spilled out, and a lone figure emerged from it. A thick stand of heavy icicles by the door glistened in the darkness. then the door closed and the figure stood silhouetted against the snow. A moment later it moved forward.

Vera watched Osborn come; he was walking in a snow-mobile track that was used for the dogsled rides and looking straight ahead. She knew he was vulnerable in the darkness because his eyes would take time to adjust to the dim light. Glancing back she saw Von Holden shoulder the pack and slide backward over a small crest and out of sight. He had brought her out of the Ice Palace through an air shaft, then handcuffed her without a word and walked off. Whatever he was planning had been carefully thought out, and whatever it was, Osborn was walking right into the middle of it.

"Paul!" Vera's cry resonated across the darkness. "He's out here waiting. Go back! Telephone the police!"

Osborn stopped and looked in her direction.

"Go back, Paul! He'll kill you!"

Vera saw Osborn hesitate, then abruptly move sideways and disappear from sight. Immediately she looked to where Von Holden had gone but saw nothing. It was then she realized it had begun to snow. For a moment there was nothing but silence and she saw her own breath in the cold. Suddenly she felt the press of steel against her temple.

"Don't move. Don't even breathe." Osborn was right there, McVey's .38 at her head, his eyes searching the darkness beyond her. Suddenly he looked at her. "Where is he?" he hissed. His stare was fierce, unforgiving.

"Paul—?" she cried out. What was he doing?

"I said where *is* he?"

OH-GOD-NO! Suddenly she realized. He believed she was one of them. Part of the Organization. "Paul," she pleaded, "Von Holden took me from jail in his custody. He said he was a German federal policeman, that he was bringing me to you."

Osborn eased the weapon back. Again he looked away, probing in the darkness. Suddenly his right foot shot out and there was a crack life a rifle shot. The wooden handrail split in two and Vera was freed from her tether, her hands still cuffed together in front of her.

"Walk," he said, shoving her forward toward the dog run, keeping her tightly between him and Von Holden's line of fire.

"Don't, Paul, please—"

Osborn ignored her. Ahead was the closed ski school and beyond it the wood and wire runs where they kept the sled dogs during the day. Then, just past them, a faint blue light shown through the falling snow like an hallucination. Osborn pulled her back, glancing over his shoulder behind them. There was nothing. He turned back.

"That light. What is it?"

"It's—" Vera hesitated. " . . . an air shaft. A tunnel. How we came out from the Ice Palace."

"Is that where he is?"

Osborn twisted her around to face him. "Is that where he is? Yes or no."

He didn't see her; he saw only someone he was certain had betrayed him. He was afraid and desperate but he was going on nonetheless.

"I don't know." Vera was terrified. If Von Holden was there and they went inside after him, there were any number of twists and turns where he could wait in ambush.

Osborn glanced quickly around, then moved her forward again toward the circle of light spilling from the shaft. The only sound was the mutter of the wind and the crunch of their feet on the snow. Seconds passed and they were at the dog runs and almost to the light.

"He's not in the tunnel at all, is he, Vera?" Osborn swept the darkness, trying to see through the snow. "But out in the dark, waiting until you lead me into the light, like a duck in a shooting gallery. You wouldn't even be at risk. He's a marksman, a trained Spetsnaz soldier."

How could he not understand what had happened to her, not believe she was telling the truth?

"Dammit, Paul! Listen to me—" Vera was starting to turn around, to look at him. Suddenly she stopped. There were tracks in the snow in front of them. In the bluish glow of the light, Osborn saw them too. Footprints dusted over by fresh snow, leading from where they were directly toward the tunnel. Von Holden had stood where they were only moments before.

Abruptly Osborn jerked her aside, roughing her into the shadows against the wood and wire of the dog runs. Then he looked back, studying the tracks.

She could see him trying to decide what to do next. He was exhausted. Very nearly at the end of his rope. Von Holden was on his mind and nothing else. He was making mistakes and didn't realize it. And if he went on as he was, in a short while Von Holden would kill them both.

"Paul, look at me!" suddenly she screamed at him, her voice rocked with emotion. "*Look at me.*"

For a long moment he stayed motionless, the snow falling silently around him. Then slowly, reluctantly, he turned to her. Despite the cold he was soaked with sweat.

"Listen to me, please," she said. "It doesn't matter how you've come to the conclusions you have. The truth is I've nothing to do with Von Holden or the Organization and never have. This is the moment when you must believe me, you *have* to believe me and trust me. Believe and trust that what we have together is *real* and transcends anything else—anything . . . " Her voice trailed off.

Osborn stared at her. She'd hit a chord deep within him, a nerve he no longer thought was there. If he chose no, that was one thing. Simple and done with. To choose yes was to trust beyond anything he knew or had ever known. To cast himself, his father, everything, aside. Make it all irrelevant. To say, after everything—I do trust you and my love for you—and if in doing that I die, then I die.

It would have to be total trust. Total.

Vera was looking at him. Waiting. Behind her, through

the falling snow, were the lights of the restaurant. It was all on him. What he chose.

Ever so slowly he raised his hand and touched her cheek.

"It's all right," he said, finally. "It's all right."

148

VON HOLDEN came up on his elbows and inched forward. Where were they? They'd come right up to the edge of the light and then disappeared from view. It should have been simple. He'd tested Osborn by showing himself and Vera in the Ice Palace tunnel. If Osborn had followed them he would have dragged him into the side tunnel where he'd taken Vera and killed him there. But he hadn't. Which was why he'd used Vera now. She'd been a drawing card, nothing more. He knew Osborn had seen them board the train together in Bern. The last time he'd seen her she'd been arrested by the German police in Berlin. What could he think but that she and Von Holden were co-conspirators, fleeing the disaster at Charlottenburg. Filled with rage and betrayal, Osborn would find a way to free her and no matter her argument otherwise would make her take him to Von Holden, either as a hostage or bargaining chip.

A gust of wind twisted a snow devil across the snow in front of him. Wind. He didn't like it. Any more than he liked the snow. Looking up, he saw a line of clouds advancing from the west. And it was getting colder. He should have killed them sooner, as soon as they'd started toward the ski school, but taking out two people and getting rid of their bodies that close to the main building was risky, especially when it might jeopardize his main objective. The air tunnel was eighty yards away from it, in the dark and snow, distant enough to be safe for the killing. And Osborn, upset and unbalanced, would follow his footprints straight toward it. The two shots a split second apart wouldn't make a sound. Then Von Holden would take their bodies to the back of the dog runs where the cliffs fell sharply away and toss them over into the black nothing of the abyss. Osborn first, and then—

"Von Holden!" Osborn's voice echoed out of the darkness. "Vera's gone back to telephone the police. I thought you might like to know that."

Von Holden started, then scrambled backward and slid behind a rock outcropping. Whatever had happened had abruptly turned against him. Even if the police were called, it would be an hour or more before they got there. He would have to forget everything else and move on.

Directly in front of him, like some ghostly sentinel, the Jungfrau rose up more than two thousand feet. A hundred yards to his right and down maybe forty feet, a rocky path led around the face of the cliff on which Jungfraujoch was built. Three-quarters of the way down that, hidden by a rock formation, was a secondary air shaft that had been opened in 1944 when the impenetrable system of tunnels and elevators had been constructed below the weather station inside the glacier. If he could reach that before the police came, he could hide. For a week, two weeks. Longer, if need be.

149

OSBORN HUNCHED a few feet to the side of the dog run and listened. But all he heard was the soft coo of the wind as little by little it increased in intensity. Before he'd gone out with McVey in Berlin he'd changed to a pair of black high-top Reeboks. Other than that he was still dressed in the shirt and business suit he'd been wearing since he got there. Not much at eleven thousand feet in the dark and snow, with the wind picking up.

In one incredible instant Osborn's anger and distrust of Vera had vanished. It was what she'd said and what he'd seen in her eyes when she'd said it. The challenge to him of who he really was and what he really believed.

In that moment doubt disappeared and he remembered pulling her back away from the dog run and down into the snow on the far side of the cages, holding her against him, both crying, sharing the realization of what had happened, and of what he had almost let happen. Then he'd sent her back.

For a moment she'd been stunned. They'd both go back. Von Holden wouldn't come after them in there, not with the bright lights and other people around.

"What if he does?" Osborn had said. And he was right. Von Holden was capable of anything.

"There is a blonde woman, an American," he told her; "she'll be waiting to take the train down. Her name is Connie. She's a good person. Take the train with her to Kleine Scheidegg and call the Swiss police from there. Have them get in touch with a Detective Remmer of the German Federal Police at Bad Godesberg."

He remembered her staring at him for a long time. He wasn't staying behind only to protect her. It was why he'd come after Von Holden in the first place, why he'd done what he had to Albert Merriman in Paris, why he'd gone to Berlin with McVey. It was for himself and for his father, and there was no going back until it was finished. It was then she'd pressed her lips to his and turned to go.

As she did, he pulled her back. His eyes were alive. He was already shifting gears. Preparing for the next. Asking her deliberately if she knew what was inside the case Von Holden had carried from Berlin.

"He said they were documents exposing the neo-Nazi conspirators. But I'm sure it's not true."

Osborn watched her move back through the shadows and toward the safety of the main building. Seconds passed and there was a shaft of light as the door opened and she went inside, then there was darkness, as it closed behind her. Instantly his thoughts went to what Von Holden really carried in the rucksack. Without a doubt they *were* documents, but they would hardly be a listing of prominent neo-Nazis, instead they would be about the cryosurgery. Reports, discourses on how it was done. The procedures for freezing and thawing, software instructions for the computers, design schematics for the instruments, perhaps even his father's scalpel. They would be one of a kind, which was why he was guarding them so carefully. For whatever evil the process had been conceived, to the world of medicine the procedure was fantastic, and no matter what happened it was imperative the notes be protected.

Suddenly Osborn realized he had been drifting; Von Holden could easily be coming up behind him. He looked around quickly but saw nothing. Then, checking the .38's firing action, making sure it hadn't frozen in the cold, he slid the gun in his waistband and glanced back toward the main building. By now Vera should have reached it and be inside looking for Connie.

Moving up, he eased along the edge of the dog run until

he saw the light of the tunnel. The footprints, he was certain, had been a trick to draw him into the light. Von Holden had crossed toward the tunnel but would not have gone back to it, it was too confining and he could be trapped, especially if someone came through from the other side.

To Osborn's right the Jungfrau itself rose almost straight up. To his left the land dipped down and seemed to level off a little. Blowing on his hands to warm them, he moved off in that direction. Assuming he was right, it was the only logical way Von Holden would have gone.

Übermorgen, and the box that housed it inside his backpack, remained Von Holden's fundamental concern. As it should have for the last survivor of the Organization's hierarchy. Sector 5, *"Entscheidend Verfahren,"* the Conclusive Procedure, had been intended for this kind of emergency. That it had become more difficult than anticipated was the reason he had been chosen in the first place and why he had survived. Perhaps, he thought optimistically, the worst might be over. There was every chance that the lower elevators had not been destroyed in the fire because the air shaft above them would have worked as a chimney, an exhaust for the heat, thus sparing the mechanical workings below.

The thought of still reaching the elevators, and the sense that he was executing his duty as a soldier, lifted him as he worked his way along the rock shale path against the face of the cliff. The falling snow, the increasing wind and cold, would hinder Osborn as much as himself. Probably more so because Osborn would not have his training in mountain survival. The advantage would extend his window of escape. His chance to get to the air shaft and inside with all traces covered by the snow.

That left only Osborn and himself, and time.

150

THE TRAIL cut away sharply to the left and Osborn followed it. He was looking for Von Holden's tracks in the snow but he'd seen nothing so far and the snow wasn't falling fast enough to cover them. Perplexed and fearful that he might be going the wrong way, he came to the top of a rise and stopped. Looking back, he could see only a swirl of snow and darkness. Dropping down to one knee, he looked over the side. Below him a narrow trail snaked downward along the edge of a cliff, but there seemed no way to get to it. There was no way to know if it was the trail Von Holden would use, anyway. It could be one of dozens.

Osborn stood and was about to turn back when he saw them. Fresh tracks, tight against the side of the cliff. Someone had passed that way and not long before. They'd gone down close against the inside edge of the trail that cut along the face of a sheer cliff. Whoever it had been must have found the way down several hundred yards or more up the trail. But trying to find where that was could take hours and by then the tracks would be covered.

Moving to one side, Osborn thought it might be possible to drop over the side and slide. It wasn't far. Twenty feet at most. Still, it was dangerous. Everything here was tundra. Just rock and ice and snow. No trees, roots or branches, nothing to grab on to. With no way of knowing what was on the far side, if he got going too fast and was unable to stop, he could sail headlong over the side and into a gaping chasm and drop thousands of feet like a stone.

Osborn was willing to chance it anyway, when he saw

a sharp outcropping of stone that fell away directly to the trail below. It was covered with a massive buildup of icicles caused by a constant melting and refreezing of glacier ice. They looked sturdy enough to use for handholds. Venturing out on the rock, he dropped down, eased to the edge and slid over the side. The trail here was no more than fifteen feet below him. If the icicles held, he would be down in no time. Reaching out, he took hold of an icicle three or four inches in diameter and tested it. It held his weight easily and he swung around, starting down. Feeling for a foothold, he got a toe in and started to pull his upper hand free to grab the icicle below it. But his hand wouldn't move. The warmth of his skin had bonded it to the ice. He was stuck, his right hand above his head, his left foot extended to a toehold far below him. His only choice was to jerk his hand free. Which meant tearing the skin from it. But there was no alternative. If he clung much longer, he would freeze to death right there.

Taking a deep breath, Osborn counted to three and tugged. There was a searing pain and his hand came free. But the motion cost him his toehold and he rocketed off, sliding on his back. A second later he hit sheer ice and picked up speed. Desperately, he used his hands, his feet, elbows anything to slow the rate of his descent, but it didn't work. He went faster and faster. Suddenly he saw darkness open up below him and he knew he was going over the side.

In a last desperate attempt he grabbed out at the only rock he saw with his left hand. His hand slid off, but the crook of his arm caught around it and he stopped, his feet only inches from the edge.

He could feel his entire body shudder and begin to tremble. Lying back, he dug a heel into the snow. Then another. Wind came in a gust, and the snow blew savagely. Closing his eyes, Osborn prayed that he had not come this far, these many years, to freeze to death above a wild and godless glacier. It would make his life useless. And he refused to have his life be useless!

Beside him was a solid crack in the stone face of the rock wall. Easing up on his side, he swung one foot over the other and kicked a toehold in the snow. Then, rolling over on his stomach, he grasped the crack with both hands and pulled himself up. A little bit more and he got a knee into the crack, and then a foot. Finally he could stand.

Von Holden was above him. Maybe thirty yards directly up the cliff face, standing back against the edge. He'd been on the trail when Osborn slid past him. If he'd been five feet closer, Osborn would have taken him over the side with him.

Looking down, he could just see the American clinging to the stone facing above a two-thousand-foot drop. If he was going to climb back up, he would have to do it over an impossible incline of ice and rock made even more treacherous by the wind and falling snow. Von Holden, at this point, was less than three hundred yards of steep, twisting trail from the opening of the air shaft. It would be treacherous going, but even in the snow it could be made in no more than ten or fifteen minutes. And Osborn could not possibly climb—if he could climb at all—from where he was to the spot where Von Holden stood, in those minutes, let alone get down to where Von Holden was going. Once inside the air shaft, Von Holden would vanish.

Yes, the police would come but unless they stayed around for a week or more until he reemerged, which was highly doubtful, they would assume Vera had summoned them there to cover Von Holden's escape elsewhere. Either that or they'd believe he'd plunged into a crevasse or disappeared into one of the hundreds of bottomless holes in the Aletsch glacier. One way or another they would leave, taking Vera with them as an accessory to the murder of the Frankfurt police.

As for Osborn, even if he did somehow manage to survive the night where he was, his story would be no better than hers. He'd chased a man out onto the mountain. And then what? Where was he? How would Osborn answer that? Of course it would be better if he were dead. To that end Von Holden could venture to the edge and risk a shot at him in the darkness. But that would be no good all around. The footing was bad enough as it was and if he slipped or fired and missed, none of it was worth it. And if he hit Osborn—killed or wounded him, even if he fell— they would know Von Holden had been there, thus corroborating Vera's story. And a further hunt would be on. No. Better to let him stay where he was and trust he would either fall or freeze to death. That was the correct thinking. The reason Scholl had made him *Leiter der Sicherheit*.

151

OSBORN'S FACE and shoulders were flat against rock. The toes of his Reeboks dug in tight to what seemed little more than a two-inch ledge in the stone. Beneath him was cold, empty darkness. He had no idea how far he would fall if he slipped, except that a large stone above had somehow come loose and bounced past him. He'd listened but he never heard it land. Looking up, he tried to see the trail, but an icy overhang blocked his view. The crack he was standing on ran horizontally across the face of the rock wall that he clung to. He could go either left or right but not up, and after moving several feet in both directions he found the ledge to the right opened up more easily. The ledge widened and there were jagged pieces of rock overhead he could use as handholds. Despite the cold, his right hand, where the skin had pulled off as he'd torn free of the icicle, felt like someone was pressing a hot iron against it. And it made closing his fingers over the rock handholds excruciating. But in a way it was good because if focused his attention. Made him think only of the pain and how best to grasp onto a knot of rock without losing his grip. Hand right. Grab on. Foot right, slide, find footing, test it. Weight shift. Balance. Left hand, left foot the same.

Now he was at the edge of the cliff face, where it bent inward toward a kind of steep ravine. A chute, they called it in skiing. A couloir. But with the snow and wind it was impossible to tell if the crack kept running or simply stopped. If the crack stopped there on the edge, he doubted he could go back and reverse the moves he'd made to get here. Osborn stopped and put a hand to his mouth and blew on it. Then did the same with the other. His watch had somehow worked its way up inside his sleeve and would be impossible to get out without severely testing his balance so he had no idea how long he'd been out there. What he did know was that it was many hours until daylight and if he stopped moving, he'd die of hypothermia within minutes. Suddenly there was a break in the clouds and for the briefest instant the moon came out. To his immediate right and down ten or twelve feet was a wide ledge that led back toward the mountain. It looked icy and slick but wide enough for him to walk on. Then he saw something else. A narrow trail winding downward toward the glacier. And on it, a man with a backpack.

As quickly as the moon appeared it vanished and the wind picked up. Blowing snow stung Osborn's face like shards of shattered glass fired from a high-pressure hose, and he had to turn his head back into the mountain. The ledge is there, he thought. It's wide enough to hold you. Whatever force has brought you this far has given you another chance. Trust it.

Inching to the edge, Osborn put out a foot. There was nothing but air. Trust it, Paul. Trust what you saw. With that, Osborn pushed off into darkness.

152

FOR NO reason Von Holden was thinking of Scholl and why he'd had the terrible, even murderous, fear of being seen unclothed. There had been rumors—that Scholl had no penis, that it had been severed in some kind of accident during his youth. That he was a true hermaphrodite and had female uterus and breasts as well as a penis, and therefore thought of himself as a freak—

It was Von Holden's contention that Scholl refused to be seen unclothed because he had a revulsion of any human warmth and that included the human body. The mind and the power of the mind were all that mattered, therefore physical and emotional needs disgusted him even though they remained as much a part of him as of anyone else. Abruptly Von Holden's reverie passed and he became aware of the trail in front of him and the glacier stretching out for miles to his left.

Looking up, he saw the moon hovering between clouds. Then he saw a shadow move on the cliff above him. Osborn was climbing along the face of the rock! Directly beneath him was a wide ledge. If he saw that and reached it, it would be only moments before he found Von Holden's tracks in the fresh snow.

Then clouds passed in front of the moon and it became dark again. Looking up, he thought he saw Osborn let go and drop to the ledge. He still had fifty or more yards to the air shaft entrance and Osborn, as close as he was, could easily follow his trail. Enough, Von Holden thought. Kill him now and you can take his body into the shaft. No one will ever find it.

Osborn's fall to the ledge had knocked the wind out of him and it took him a long moment to get his senses back. When he did, he came up on one knee and looked down toward where he'd last seen Von Holden. He could just make out the trial along the cliff face but Von Holden was gone. Standing, he was suddenly afraid he'd lost McVey's gun. But no, it was still there in his waistband. Taking it out, he opened the chamber and turned it so that the hammer and firing pin sat on a live round. Then, with one hand against the rock wall, the gun in the other, he started forward along the ledge.

Von Holden slid the pack from his shoulders and moved into a position where he could clearly see the trail coming down behind him. Then he pulled up the nine-millimeter automatic pistol, eased back and waited.

As Osborn reached the main trail, the ledge suddenly narrowed. As it did, the moon slid out from behind the clouds once more. It was as if someone had put a spotlight on him. Instinctively he dropped to the ground just as a quick burst from some kind of automatic weapon exploded the rock wall where he had been standing. Pieces of rock and ice showered him. Then the moon went away and darkness and silence rushed in with the wind. He had no idea where the shots had come from. Nor had he heard the gun. Which meant Von Holden's weapon probably had both a silencer and flame suppressor. If Von Holden was above him, or working toward that position, Osborn was wide open. Easing forward on his stomach, he reached the edge and peered over the side. Five feet below him was a rock outcropping. It wasn't much but it was better protection than he had. Using the darkness for cover, he suddenly stood up, ran, and dove. As he did, he felt something hard slap against his shoulder. If flung him sideways and backward. At the same time he heard a tremendous boom. Then he felt the snow hit him hard in the back, and for an instant everything went black. When he opened his eyes all he could see was the top of the cliff. He smelled gunpowder and realized that his own gun must have gone off. Putting out a hand, he was starting to ease himself up when a shadow stepped into his circle of vision.

It was Von Holden. The rucksack was on his back and an odd-looking pistol was in his hand.

"In the Spetsnaz we were taught to smile at the executioner," Von Holden said quietly. "It will make you immortal."

Suddenly Osborn realized he was going to die. And everything that had brought him this far would all end, now, within a matter of seconds. The sad, tragic thing was that there was absolutely nothing he could do about it. Yet he was still alive and there was the chance Von Holden would give him something before he shot him.

"Why was my father murdered?" he said. "For the scalpel he invented? For the surgery on Elton Lybarger?— Tell me. Please."

Von Holden smiled arrogantly. *"Für Übermorgen,"* he said triumphantly. "For the day after tomorrow!"

Suddenly Von Holden looked up as a thundering roar spilled out of the darkness above them. It was like an enormous wind that groaned and screamed as if the earth were literally being torn from itself. The roar became deafening and there was a spray of rock and shale. Then the front wall of the avalanche hit, and both he and Osborn were hurled backward, tossed like dolls over the trail's edge. Down they plunged, head over heels, into a narrow and very steep couloir. Once, in midair, as he was turning, Osborn caught sight of Von Holden, his expression unnerved and disbelieving, frozen in some untold horror. Then he was gone. Swept away in a bellowing tide of ice and snow and debris.

153

VON HOLDEN emerged first, thrown free onto a nearly flat plate of rock and loose stone. Staggering up, he looked around. Above was the avalanche trail and the narrow chute down which he'd fallen. Rivulets of ice and snow still rolled down it in the aftermath. Turning, he saw the glacier, where it should have been. But nothing else looked familiar. Where he was, in relation to the trail he had been on, he had no idea. Looking up, he hoped to see the moon reemerge from behind the clouds but instead he saw the sky. No longer gray and overcast, it was crystal clear. But there was no moon or stars. In its place, reaching far into the heavens, were the red and green of the Aurora. The massive, overpowering ribbon-candy curtains of his nightmare.

Crying out, he turned and ran. Desperately looking for the trail that would lead to the entrance to the shaft. But nothing was as it should have been. He had never been in this place before. Terrified, he ran on, only to be confronted by a wall of stone, and he realized he had entered a cul-de-sac, with rock cliffs reaching hundreds of feet straight up into the red-green sky.

Breathless, heart pounding, he turned back. The red and green grew brighter and the towering curtains began to descend toward him. At the same time beginning to slowly undulate up and down, like the huge monolithic pistons of his dreams.

The curtains came closer, undulating obscenely, bathing him in the colors of their glow. Threatening to settle like a shroud around him.

"No!" he shouted, as if to break the spell and make them go away. His voice echoing off the rock masses and out across the glacier. But the spell did not break and instead they came closer, pulsating steadily, as if they were some living organism that owned the heavens. Abruptly they became translucent, like the hideous tentacles of jellyfish, and suddenly descended further as if to smother him. In silent terror, he turned and ran back the way he had come.

Once again he was in the cul-de-sac and face-to-face with headwalls of stone. Turning back, he watched in dread as the tentacles came toward him. Translucent, glowing, undulating. Lowering. Were they here to warn of his imminent death? Or this time, was it death itself? He shrunk back. What did they want? He merely was a soldier following orders. A soldier doing his duty.

Then that same sense rose in him and the fear left. He was a Spetsnaz soldier! He was *Leiter der Sicherheit!* He would not allow death to take him with his purpose not yet done! *"Nein!"* he shouted out loud.

"Ich bin der Leiter der Sicherheit!" I am chief of security! Tearing the pack from his shoulders, he undid the straps and took the box from inside. Cradling it in his arms, he took a step forward.

"*Das ist meine Pflicht!*" This is my duty! he said, offering the box up in both hands.

"*Das ist meine Seele!*" This is my soul!

Abruptly the Aurora vanished and Von Holden stood trembling in the moonlight, the box still in his arms. A moment passed before he could hear his own breathing. A moment more, and he felt his pulse return to normal. Finally, he started forward out of the cul-de-sac. Then he was out and on the edge of the mountain overlooking the glacier. Below him he saw the clear trail to the air shaft. Immediately he started down it, the box still clutched in his arms.

By now the storm had passed and the moon and stars were stark in the sky. The clarity of the moonlight and the angle from which it came gave the snowy landscape a raw timelessness that made it at once past and future, and Von Holden had the sense that he had demanded and been given passage through a world that existed only on some far-removed plane.

"*Das ist meine Pflicht!*" he said again, looking up at the stars. Duty above all! Above Earth. Above God. Beyond time.

Within minutes he'd reached the split of rock that concealed the opening to the air shaft. The rock itself jutted out over the edge of the cliff and he had to step out and around it to enter. As he did, he saw Osborn sprawled on a snow-covered shelf thirty yards downhill from where he stood, his left leg turned under him at an odd angle. Von Holden knew it was broken. But he wasn't dead. His eyes were open and he was watching him.

"Don't take another chance with him," he thought. "Shoot him now."

There was a puff of snow from Von Holden's boot as he stepped closer to the edge and looked down. His movement had put him in deep shadow, with the full light of the moon on the Jungfrau above him. But even in the darkness Osborn could see him shift the weight of the box and cradle it in his left arm. Then he saw a secondary movement and the pistol come up in his right hand. Osborn no longer had McVey's gun—it had been lost in the rush of the avalanche that had saved his life. He'd been given one chance. he wouldn't get another unless he did something himself.

Grimacing in agony as his fractured leg twisted beneath him, Osborn dug in with his elbows and kicked out with his other leg. Unbearable pain shot the length of his body as he inched backward, squirming like a broken animal over the ice and rock, trying wildly to drag himself across the shelf and out of the line of fire. Suddenly he felt his head dip backward and he realized he had come to the edge. Cold air rushed up from below and he looked over his shoulder and saw nothing but a vast dark hole in the glacier beneath him. Slowly he looked back. He could feel Von Holden smile as his finger closed around the pistol's trigger.

Then Von Holden's eyes flashed in the moonlight. His gun bucked in his hand and he jerked sideways, his shots spraying off into space. Von Holden kept shooting and his entire body jumped with the rattle of the gun until it was empty. Then his hand went limp and dropped to his side and the gun fell away. For a moment he just stood there, his eyes wide, the box still cradled in his left arm. Then, ever so slowly, he lost his balance and pitched forward, his body plunging downward, sailing over Osborn, free-falling in the clear night air toward the gaping darkness below.

154

OSBORN REMEMBERED hearing dogs and then saw faces.

A local doctor and Swiss paramedics. Mountain rescuers who carried him in a litter up through the snow in the darkness. Vera. Inside the station. Her face white and taut with fear. Uniformed policemen on the train as he went down. They were talking but he didn't remember hearing them. Connie. Sitting beside him, smiling reassuringly. And Vera again, holding his hand.

Then drugs or pain or exhaustion must have taken over because he went out.

Later he thought there was something about a hospital in Grindelwald. And an argument of some kind as to who he was. He could have sworn Remmer came into the room and after him, McVey in his rumpled suit. With McVey pulling up a chair next to the bed and sitting down, watching him.

Then he saw Von Holden back on the mountain. Saw him teeter on the edge. Saw him fall. For the briefest instant he had the impression that someone was standing on the ledge directly behind him. He remembered trying to think who it could be and realized it was Vera. She held an enormous icicle and it was covered with blood. But then that vision faded to one infinitely clearer. Von Holden was alive and falling toward him, the box still clutched in his arms. He was falling not at normal speed but in some sort of distorted slow motion and in an arc that would send him over the edge and down into the fathomless darkness thousands of feet below. Then he was gone, and all that was left was what had been said before, just as the avalanche struck.

"Why was my father murdered?" Osborn had asked.

"Für Übermorgen," Von Holden had answered. "For the day after tomorrow!"

155

Berlin, Monday, October 17.

VERA SAT alone in the back of a taxi as it turned off Clay Allee onto Messelstrasse and into the heart of Dahlem, one of Berlin's handsomest districts. A cold rain was falling for the second day and people were already complaining about it. That morning the concierge at the Hotel Kempinski had personally delivered a single red rose. With it had come a sealed envelope with a hastily scrawled note asking her to take it to Osborn when she visited him at the small, exclusive hospital in Dahlem. The note had been signed "McVey."

Because of road construction, the route to Dahlem backtracked and she found herself being driven past the destruction that had been Charlottenburg. Workmen were out in the heavy rain, gutting the structure. Bulldozers steamrolled over the formal gardens clearing the ruins, pushing them into great piles of charred rubble that were then machine-loaded into dump trucks and driven away. The tragedy had made headlines worldwide and flags flew at half mast across the city. A state funeral had been planned for the victims. Two former presidents of the United States were to attend as was the president of France and the prime minister of England.

"It burned before. In 1746," the cabdriver told her, his

voice strong and filled with pride. "It was rebuilt then. It will be rebuilt again."

Vera closed her eyes as the taxi turned on Kaiser Friedrichstrasse for Dahlem. She'd come down with him from the mountain and had stayed with him as long as they'd let her. Then she'd been given an escort to Zurich and told Osborn would be taken to a hospital in Berlin. And that's where she'd gone. It had all happened in too little time. Images and feelings collided, beautiful, painful, horrifying. Love and death rode hand in hand. And too closely. It seemed, almost, as if she'd lived through a war.

Through most of it had been the overriding presence of McVey. In one way, he was a kind and earnest grandfather who cared for the human rights and dignity of everyone. But in another, he was his own sort of Patton. Selfish and ruthless, relentless, even cruel. Driven by pursuit of truth. At any cost whatsoever.

The taxi let her off under an overhang and she entered the hospital. The lobby was small and warm and she was startled to see a uniformed policeman. He watched her carefully until she announced herself at the desk. Then he immediately rang for the elevator and smiled at her as she entered.

Another policeman stood outside the second-floor elevator and a plainclothes inspector was outside the door to Osborn's room. Both men seemed to know who she was, the last even greeting her by name.

"Is he in danger?" she asked, concerned at the presence of the police.

"It is simply a precaution."

"I understand." Vera turned to the door. Beyond it was a man she barely knew, yet loved as if centuries had passed between them. The brief time they'd spent together had been like no other. He'd touched her on a level no one else ever had. Perhaps it was because when they'd looked at each other the first time, they'd also looked down the road. And what they'd seen, they'd seen together, as if there would never be a time when they would part. And then out on the mountain, under the most cruel of situations, he'd confirmed it. For both of them.

At least that was what she thought. Suddenly she was afraid that everything she felt was hers alone. That she'd misread it all and that whatever they'd had between them had been fleeting and one-sided, and that on the other side of the door she'd find not the Paul Osborn she knew but a stranger.

"Why don't you go in?" The inspector smiled and opened the door.

He lay in bed, his left leg beneath a sprawling web of pulleys and ropes and counterweights. He was wearing his L.A. Kings T-shirt, bright red jockey shorts and nothing else, and when she saw him all her fears vanished and she started to laugh.

"What's so damn funny?" he demanded.

"Don't know . . ." She giggled. "I don't know at all. . . . It just is . . ."

And then the inspector closed the door and she crossed the room and came into his arms. And everything that had been—on the Jungfrau, in Paris, in London and in Geneva came rushing back. Outside, it was raining and Berlin was complaining. But to them, it made no difference at all.

156

Los Angeles.

PAUL OSBORN sat on the grass and stone patio of his Pacific Palisades home and stared out at the horseshoe of lights that was Santa Monica Bay. It was seventy-five degrees and ten o'clock at night a week before Christmas.

What had happened on the Jungfrau was too tangled and complex to try to make sense of. The last moments were especially disturbing because he couldn't say for certain exactly what had happened, or how much of what he thought had happened had really taken place at all.

As a physician, he understood that he had suffered significant physical and emotional trauma. Not just in the last weeks but across the arc of his entire life from childhood to adult, though certainly he could point to the closing days in Germany and Switzerland as the most tumultuous of all. But it had been there on the Jungfrau that the line between reality and hallucination finally ceased to exist. Night and snow had melded with fear and exhaustion. The horror of the avalanche, the certainty of imminent death at the hands of Von Holden, and the excruciating pain of his broken leg rubbed whatever cognizance there still was out of existence. What was real, what was a dream, was all but impossible to tell. And now that he was home, broken but alive and mending, did it make any difference anyway?

Taking a sip of iced tea, Osborn looked back out at the bay. In Paris it was seven in the morning. In an hour Vera would be on the train to Calais to meet her grandmother. Together they would take the Hoverspeed to Dover and from there the train to London. And at eleven the next morning they would fly out of Heathrow Airport on British Airways for Los Angeles. Vera had been to the United States once, with François Christian. Her grandmother had never been. What the old Frenchwoman would think of Christmas in Los Angeles he had no idea but there was no doubt she'd make her sentiments known. About tinsel and sunshine and about him, as well.

That Vera was coming was excitement enough. That she was bringing her grandmother gave it legitimacy. If she was going to stay and become a physician in the U.S., it meant, in essence, she would have to satisfy the strict requirements of the Educational Commission for Foreign Medical Graduates. For some things she might have to return to school, for others there would be a strict and tedious internship. It would be a grueling and difficult commitment in time and energy, one that she did not have to make because for all intents she was already a doctor in France. The trouble was he'd asked her to marry him. To come to California to live happily ever after.

Her answer to his proposal, given in his hospital room with a smile, was that—she'd "see." Those were her words.

"I'll see. . . . "

See what? he'd asked. If she wanted to marry him? Live in the U.S.? In California?—But all he could get out of her was the same "I'll see. . . ." Then she'd kissed him and left Berlin for Paris.

The package Vera had brought him from McVey had been his passport, retrieved from the First Paris Préfecture of Police. With it had been a note, written in French and signed by Parisian detectives Barras and Maitrot, wishing him good luck and sincerely hoping that in the future he would do everything in his power to stay out of France. Then, a week to the day after he'd been brought down off the Jungfrau and flown to Berlin, two days after Vera had left for Paris, he'd been released from the hospital.

Remmer, in from Bad Godesberg, had driven him to the airport and brought him up to date. Noble, he learned, had been airlifted back to London and was in a burn rehabilitation center. It would be months and a number of skin graft operations before he could return to a normal life, if that would be possible at all. Remmer himself, broken wrist and all, was back at work full-time, assigned to the investigation of the events leading up to the Charlottenburg fire and the shootout at the Hotel Borggreve. Joanna Marsh, Lybarger's American therapist, had been found at a Berlin hotel. Questioned extensively and released, she'd been escorted back to the U.S. by McVey. What had happened to her after that Remmer didn't know. He assumed she'd gone home.

"Remmer—" Osborn remembered asking carefully as memories of the last night on the Jungfrau came back. "Do you know where she called the Swiss police from? Which station. Kleine Scheidegg or Jungfraujoch?"

Remmer turned from the wheel to look at him. "You're talking about Vera Monneray."

"Yes."

"It wasn't she who called the Swiss police."

"What do you mean?" Osborn was startled.

"The call was made by another American. A woman. She was a tourist. . . . Connie something, I think. . . ."

"Connie?"

"That's right."

"You're saying Vera knew where I was out there? That she told them where to find me?"

"The dogs found you," Remmer wrinkled his brow. "Why would you think it was Ms. Monneray?"

"She was at Jungfraujoch station when they brought me in . . . ," Osborn said, uncertainly.

"So were a number of other people."

Osborn looked off. Dogs. All right, let it go at that. Let his image of Vera standing on the trail just after Von

Holden fell, an enormous bloody icicle in her hands, remain only that, an illusion. Part of his hallucinatory dreams. Nothing else.

"You're really asking if she's innocent. You want to believe she is, but you're still not sure."

Osborn looked back. "I am sure."

"Well, you're right. We found the printing equipment used to make Von Holden's false BKA I.D. It was in the apartment of the mole the Organization had working as a supervisor in the jail, the one who released her in Von Holden's custody. She did believe he was taking her to you. He knew too much for her to expect otherwise until just before the end."

Osborn didn't need the confirmation. If he hadn't believed it on the mountain, he certainly had by the time Vera left Berlin for Paris.

"What about Joanna Marsh?" he asked. "Did she give any indication why Salettl sent us after her?"

Remmer was silent for a long moment, then shook his head. "Maybe one day we will find out, yes?" There was something about Remmer's manner that suggested he knew more than he was telling. And he had to remember that no matter how much they'd been through together, Remmer was still police. Look what they had done to Vera even when they knew, probably within a few hours, maybe even right away, that she'd had nothing to do with the Organization and that she was not Avril Rocard. It was a frightening power to have because it was so easy to misuse.

"What about McVey?" Osborn said.

"I told you. He escorted Ms. Marsh back home."

"He sent me my passport."

"You couldn't leave Germany without it." Remmer smiled.

"He never talked to me. Even when he came to the hospital in Grindelwald, he never said a word."

"Bern."

"What?"

"You were brought to the hospital in Bern."

Osborn' expression went blank. "You're sure?"

"Yes. We were with the Bern police when the call came in they'd found you up on the mountain."

"You were in *Bern?* How—?"

"McVey had your track." Remmer smiled. "You bought a Eurail pass in Bern. You paid for it with a credit card. McVey had an eye on all your accounts, just in case. When you used it it told him where you were and what time you'd been there."

Osborn was astonished. "That can't be legal."

"You took his gun, his personal papers, his badge." Remmer hardened. "You were not authorized to impersonate a police officer."

"Where would Von Holden be now if I didn't?" Osborn pushed back. Remmer said nothing. "What happens now?"

"It's not for me to say. It's not my case. It's McVey's."

157

"IT'S NOT my case. It's McVey's." A day hadn't passed that Remmer's words didn't ring in Osborn's ears. What was the penalty for doing what he had done? Not only had he taken a police officer's gun and identification, he'd used them to cross an international border. He could be tried in L.A. and then extradited to Germany or Switzerland to face charges there. Maybe even France if Interpol wanted to get involved. Or maybe, God forbid, those would be secondary charges, incidentals. The real one would be the attempted murder of Albert Merriman. Hiding in Paris or not, Merriman had still been an American citizen. Those were things McVey would not forget.

By now it was almost Christmas and Osborn hadn't heard so much as a word from him. Yet every time he saw a police car he jumped. He was driving himself crazy with guilt and fear, and he didn't know what to do about it. He could call a lawyer and prepare a defense but that could make it worse if McVey felt he'd been through enough and decided to let it go at that. Purposely he stopped thinking about it and concentrated on his patients. Three nights a week he spent in physical therapy working his broken leg back to normal. It would be a month before he could get rid of the crutches and two more before he could walk without a limp. But he could live with it, thank you, considering what the alternative might have been.

And daily, time itself was beginning to heal the deeper things. A great deal of the mystery of his father's death had been answered, though the real why and purpose still drifted. Von Holden's answer—"*Für Übermorgen,* for the day after tomorrow"—if, in truth, that part of Osborn's experience on the Jungfrau had been real and not an hallucination—seemed a meaningless abstract that told him nothing.

For his own sanity, for his future, for Vera, he had to put it, and Merriman and Von Holden and Scholl, in the past. Just as he had to let go of the tragic memory of his father, which, little by little, he was finding himself able to do.

Then, at five minutes to noon, on the day before Vera and her grandmother were to arrive, McVey called.

"I want to show you something. Can you come down?"

"Where—?"

"Headquarters. Parker Center." McVey was matter-of-fact, as if they talked like this every day.

"—When?"

"An hour."

Jesus Christ, what does he want? Sweat stood out on Osborn's forehead. "I'll be there," he said. When he hung up, his hand was shaking.

The drive from Santa Monica to downtown took twenty-five minutes. It was hot and smoggy and the city skyline was nonexistent. That Osborn was scared to death didn't help it any.

McVey met him as he came through the door. They said hello without shaking hands, then went up in an elevator with half a dozen others. Osborn leaned on his crutches and looked at the floor. McVey had said nothing more than that he wanted to show him something.

"How's the leg?" McVey said as the elevator doors opened and he led the way down a hallway. The burn on his face was healing well and he seemed rested. He even had a little color, as if he might have been playing some golf.

"Getting there. . . . You look good." Osborn was trying to sound easy, friendly.

"I'm all right for an old guy." McVey glanced at him without smiling, then led him through a ganglia of corridors peopled with faces that looked at once tired and confused and angry.

At the end of a hallway, McVey pushed through a door and into a room cut in half by a wire cage. Inside were two uniformed cops and shelf upon shelf of sealed evidence bags. McVey signed a sheet and was given a bag that held what looked like a video cassette. Then they crossed the corridor and went into an empty squad room. McVey closed the door and they were alone.

Osborn had no idea what McVey was doing, but whatever it was, he'd had enough. He wanted it out in the open and now.

"Why am I here?"

McVey walked over and closed the venetian blinds. "You see the TV this morning? Vietnamese family, out in the valley."

"Yeah, sort of . . . ," Osborn said, vacantly. He'd seen something as he was shaving. An entire Vietnamese family in an upscale neighborhood in the San Fernando Valley had been found murdered. Parents, grandparents, children.

"It's my case. I'm on my way to autopsy so let's do this fast." McVey opened the plastic bag and took out the video cassette. "There are only two copies in existence. This is the original. The other is with Remmer in Bad Godesberg. The FBI wants this one yesterday. I told them they could have it tomorrow. It's why Salettl sent us after Joanna Marsh. He'd given her a present. It was a key to a box hidden inside a dog cage. A puppy Von Holden had given her in Switzerland and she'd had shipped to L.A. Inside the box was another key. To a safe deposit box in a Beverly Hills bank. The cassette was in the box."

McVey popped the cassette into a VCR under the TV set.

"I don't get it." Osborn was completely thrown off.

"You will. But there are a couple of things you ought to know first. You said that when Von Holden fell off the Jungfrau and disappeared over the side you never saw him land."

"It was pitch-black."

"Well, he fell, or we think he fell, into what's called a dark ice crevasse. A deep hole in the glacier. A Swiss mountain team went down as far as they could but found no sign of him. That means he's either still down there somewhere and will be for the next two thousand years or—he's not. By that I mean we can't say for certain he's dead.

"The second thing has to do with Lybarger's fingerprints. Or the fingerprints of the man calling himself Lybarger. The man both Remmer and Schneider saw and talked to a half hour before Charlottenburg went up in smoke." McVey coughed, and when he did, he winced a little. His burn still bothered him. "BKA fingerprint experts matched Lybarger's prints with those of Timothy Ashford, the decapitated housepainter from London."

"Jesus God." The hairs stood straight out from Osborn's neck. "You were right. . . ."

"Yeah," McVey nodded. "The trouble is Lybarger is now like everybody else who was in that room. Ashes. So all we have is an assumption that the head of one man was successfully joined to the body of another and that the creature lived. And walked and thought and talked as if he were as real as you and I. And with no visible scars as far as either Remmer or Schneider could tell. Or Joanna Marsh, either, for that matter. She told us that in a deposition yesterday morning. As his physical therapist, she spent a great deal of time with him and saw nothing that would indicate surgery of any kind had been done."

"The symptoms of a man recovering from a stroke," Osborn mused, "were caused not by a stroke at all, but by recovery from a phenomenal surgical procedure." He looked up at McVey. "Is that what the tape is about?"

"What the tape is about is between you and me and the fencepost. If anybody says anything at all, it will come from Washington or Bad Godesberg." McVey picked up a remote and handed it to Osborn. "This time, Doctor, nobody does anything on his own. Personal reasons or anything else. I hope you understand that because there are *other* things we can come back to. I'm sure you know what I mean."

For a moment the two men stood facing each other in silence. Then McVey abruptly opened the door and walked out. Osborn watched him cross an outer office and push through a wooden gate. Then he was gone. Like that, he'd taken him off the hook and let him go.

158

OSBORN SAT for a long moment in silence, then raised the remote, pointed it toward the VCR in the cart under the TV and hit "play." There was a click and a whirring sound, then the television screen flickered and an image appeared. The scene was a formal study with a straight-backed leather chair prominent in the foreground. A large desk was to the left with a wall of books to the right. A window, only partially visible behind the desk, provided most of the light. Several seconds passed and then Salettl walked in. He was wearing a dark blue suit and had his back to the camera. When he reached the chair, he turned and sat down.

"Please excuse this primitive introduction," he said. "But I am alone and am operating the video camera myself." Crossing his legs, he sat back and became more formal. "My name is Helmuth Salettl. I am a physician. My home is Salzburg, Austria, but I am, by birth, German. My age, as of this taping, is seventy-nine. When you view this, I will no longer be living." Pausing, Salettl's gaze into the camera sharpened. Seemingly to underscore the seriousness of what he had to say. The idea of his own death seemed to have no effect on him.

"What follows is a confession. To murder. To fanaticism. To invention. I hope you will excuse my English.

"In 1939 I was a young surgeon at Berlin University.

Optimistic and perhaps arrogant, I was approached by a representative of the Reich chancellor and asked to become a member of an advisory council on advanced surgical practices. Later, as a member of the Nazi party and a group leader in the Schutzstaffel, the SS, I was promoted to the office of commissioner for public health. Some of this you may be aware of because it is public record. More detailed information can be found in the Federal Archives at Koblenz."

Salettl paused and reached for a glass of water. Taking a sip, he put the glass down and turned back to the camera.

"In 1946, I was put on trial at Nuremberg, charged with the crime of having prepared and carried out aggressive warfare. I was acquitted of those charges and soon after located to Austria, where I practiced internal medicine until my retirement at age seventy. Or, so it appeared. In truth, I continued to be a minister of the Reich, even though it had officially ceased to exist.

"In 1938, under the direction of Martin Bormann, Hitler's secretary, and later deputy *Führer*, a man who believed as Hitler believed that God will only help a nation that does not give up, set about doing just that—preserving the Third Reich. To that end he both created a program and a means to carry it out.

"It began with a costly, elaborate, and highly detailed socioeconomic and political projection of the future. Commissioning a wide range of experts who were told little or nothing about what they were working on or toward, Bormann was able, within two years, to make a highly speculative, yet, in hindsight, remarkably accurate forecast of the world situation from 1940 until the year 2000.

"Without going into detail, I will say, simply, that the work predicted the defeat of the Reich by the Allied armies, followed by the partition of Germany. The rise of the superpowers, the United States of America and the Soviet Union, and the inevitable 'Cold War' and arms race that ensued. The development of Japan as an economic might, powered by a worldwide demand for superior automobiles and advanced technology. Included in this were four extremely important elements that would take place over nearly five decades: the ascent from the ashes of war of a West Germany that would become an industrial and economic bulwark with perhaps the most solid economy in the Western Hemisphere; a realized necessity of economic cooperation between the European states; the reunification of Germany, and lastly, that the arms race would bankrupt the Soviet Union and cause not only it, but the entire Soviet Bloc built in its wake, to crumble. In those studied assumptions, vastly oversimplified here, the seeds for the secret preservation of the Third Reich were sown.

"A clandestine organization—that always remained unnamed and is peopled by members in countries all over the world—was formed by a handful of wealthy and powerful German businesspersons, patriots and expatriates alike, who were resolutely dedicated to the Nazi cause but who had never been exposed. Over the years the Organization grew, its members carefully screened.

"The movement was to emerge slowly at first, as a small trickle within the German political right. Nationalism was its key word. The terms *Reich, Aryan, Nazi* were never used. It was to be done quietly and with careful calculation, driven by enormous wealth and popular influence across the broadest spectrum of German society, from left to right, from the elderly to the vibrant youth, from the successful businessperson to the intellectual to the displaced, to the uneducated and the unemployed. Then, as Germany reunited, the beat would become louder, a little more distinct, exploiting the confusion of reunification, the haves of the West against the have-nots of the former Communist East. A growing atmosphere of mistrust and anger would be fueled by a vast wave of immigrants pouring into Germany from the shattered remnants of the Soviet Bloc.

"And Germany was not all. For years we had been working covertly with singular, sympathetic movements inside the established governments of the European community. From France were to come the first rumblings. Others, similarly seeded, were to follow at our instruction.

"To show what we, as leaders, were capable of—done at first as a uniting point for ourselves, and then later, at the right moment when we chose to reveal it, for the rest of the world—we began on a highly ambitious technological program of our own.

"Constructed during the war was an experimental medical facility hidden deep beneath the city of Berlin. Structurally safe from Allied bombers, it was called The Garden. It was there, at *der Garten*, we would develop our fountainhead. The program was given a top-secret code name, '*Übermorgen*,' 'the day after tomorrow,' symbol of the day the Reich would reemerge as a terrifying and dominant world power. This time our strength would be economic, the military would be used merely as a police force."

Suddenly Osborn stopped the tape. His heart was pounding. He felt lightheaded, as if he were in a swoon and about to faint. Consciously he started breathing deeply, then got up and walked across the room. Turning back, he looked at the TV as if it had been playing a trick on him. But all he saw was a gray-white screen and the red glow of the VCR's ready light.

"*Übermorgen!*" The day after tomorrow!

Salettl's words hung like acid smoke in the quick of his mind. It wasn't possible! It couldn't be! He had to have heard incorrectly. Salettl must have said something else. Going back, he sat down and picked up the remote. Pointing it at the VCR, his thumb found "rewind." The machine whirred. Immediately he hit "stop." Then, taking a breath, hit "play."

"—*der Garten*, we would develop our fountainhead." Salettl came to life. "The program was given a top-secret code name, '*Übermorgen!*' the day after tomorrow."

Osborn's thumb slipped off the control and the picture froze where it was.

His mind flashed to the Jungfrau. He saw Von Holden standing above him, the machine pistol pointed at his chest. He heard himself ask the why of his father's death and then heard Von Holden's reply.

"*Für Übermorgen!*" he said. "For the day after tomorrow!"

If that part of his experience had been a dream, an hallucination, how could he have known those words? By Salettl's admission, they were top secret. Known only to the Organization and zealously guarded. And so the answer was, he wouldn't. Unless—Von Holden had actually told him. And for Von Holden to have told him, Osborn would have had to have experienced a true out-of-body journey.

Remmer had said the dogs found him. And he'd seen Vera in the station after his rescue. Yet, either in dream or reality, he was certain she'd been on the mountain. Could she have gone out there and then come back before the police arrived? And how could she have found Von Holden even if she had? Osborn's mind swirled. Could it have been possible? His thumb touched "replay" and he watched Salettl again. And then again. And again. *Übermorgen* was the deepest secret within the Organization and had been for fifty years. How could he know about it if Von Holden hadn't told him? The more he thought about it, the more things became real and less a dream.

Unnerved and energized, Osborn looked to the screen once more. His thumb hit "play" and again he saw Salettl come to life.

"The rebirth of the Reich from the dead was to be symbolized by our own manipulation of life's process," he continued. "Transplants of human organs had been performed for years. But no one had transplanted a human head. That's what we set out to do. And finally, what we did.

"The critical juncture came in 1963 when eighteen males were selected from thousands unknowingly tested. The criterion was that they be as close a match to the genetic fingerprint of Adolf Hitler as possible—personality characteristics, physical and psychological makeup, et cetera. None had any idea of what was happening to them, some were allowed to rise, as Hitler rose, from obscurity to power, others were left on their own so that we might observe their growth in the natural scheme of things. Their ages spanned more than a decade, thereby giving us time to experiment, to fail and then to make adjustments. Ten days after a subject reached his fifty-sixth birthday, he was injected with a powerful sedative. His head was severed and deep-frozen, his body was cremated. Very soon afterward his family—" Salettl paused, and one could see his personal hurt surface, then he collected himself and went on. "—his family, or anyone closely allied with him, either died in an accident or simply disappeared, thereby removing any connecting traces.

"As I have said, many experiments failed. Then, with the man you know as Elton Lybarger, we were successful. The celebration at Charlottenburg is to be a demonstration of that success. And the faithful of the party. The highest ranking, the most committed, all fully aware of the history of the plan, are to attend.

"To reach this fantastic pinnacle took fifty years. Over that time, many innocent people who unknowingly helped us were put to death because we dared not leave a trail. We hired professional murderers to kill them and then our own security killed the killers. We had an enormous number of ordinary people working for us. Some who peripherally believed in the Aryan cause, others who were bullied or beaten into working for it, still others who were on legitimate business payrolls and had no idea what they were doing. The process, as I have said, took fifty years. And when at last we succeeded, the time was ripe for the second phase of *Übermorgen*.

Second phase? Osborn's heart skipped a beat. He slid his chair closer to the screen.

"We had raised two young men, twin brothers. We sent them to the finest academic institutions and then, in the years just prior to reunification, we sent them to the Eastern sector's elite College for Physical Culture in Leipzig. Genetically engineered, pure Aryan from birth, they are today among the finest physical specimens alive. At age twenty-four, each is ready and eager to make the supreme sacrifice.

"The presentation of Elton Lybarger at Charlottenburg will be a scientific and spiritual affirmation of our intent. Proof of our commitment to the rebirth of the Reich. At the end of the festivity, a second ceremony is scheduled to take place in the mausoleum on the palace grounds in the company of only the most select guests. There, one of the two boys will be chosen to take Lybarger's place and become the messiah for the new Reich. At the moment of choosing, Lybarger is to be killed by the chosen boy who will then be prepared for the surgical operation that will, within two years, make him our leader.

"Myself, Erwin Scholl, Gustav Dortmund and Uta Baur are the elder members of the inner circle. We are the ones who carried on after Nuremberg, after Martin Bormann, Himmler and the rest.

"In fifty years Scholl, Dortmund and Uta Baur have grown rich and powerful, while I have stayed in the background to oversee the experiments. In fifty years they have become old and, as we neared fruition, exceedingly cruel and filled with conceit.

"The success of the Lybarger transplant enabled Scholl to pick a date for his presentation at Charlottenburg. That left seven of those originally selected still alive but no longer needed. It was Scholl's directive to kill them in the manner of the others but instead of cremating the bodies to leave them scattered across Europe. Their families were left unharmed to suffer in anguish, while the media had a field day covering the gruesome murders for the public. It was disdain at its highest flung in the face of the world. Human life became nothing when it no longer served the Organization. To Scholl it was a glorious echo of the past. One, he was certain, that would soon come again.

"In fifty years, I have had time to reflect on what we have done. What we are doing. What the future holds. We attempted the impossible and succeeded. That very fact is testimony to our skills. Working in almost total isolation from the rest of the world we developed a process of atomic surgery utilizing a supercold technology unheard of in modern medicine or modern physics. Its purpose was to show our brilliance. Our ingenuity. That in a world craving more and more technology, no one could match us. Not the Japanese. Not the Americans. The marketplace would be ours without question. And that this was only the beginning."

"But—" Abruptly, as if a shroud had suddenly fallen, Salettl became pensive and somber. In a matter of seconds he seemed to age a decade. "The objective behind what we were doing was the same that led to the death of six million Jews and to the deaths of uncountable millions more on a thousand battlefields and in a thousand towns under falling bombs. The same machination that left the great cities of Europe in ruins.

"I stood in the dock at Nuremberg in 1946 surrounded by many who had caused it. Göring, Hess, Ribbentrop,

Von Papen, Jodl, Raeder, Donitz—once proud and contemptuous, they were now old, dreary and muddled men. Standing with them, I remembered a warning I received not to go to the *Vernichtungslager,* the extermination camps. Don't go because you will not be permitted to describe what you have seen there. Well, I did go. To Auschwitz. And the warning was correct. Not because I was not permitted to describe what I had seen but because I *could not* describe what I had seen. The piles of glasses. The piles of shoes. The piles of bones. The piles of human hair. I thought that I had never seen the kind of thinking that did this, that I had never seen this kind of reality. Not in movies, not in theater. Yet it *was* real.

"And here was I, a key member of a secret underground, plotting, even before its demise, its rebirth. It was hideous. Impossible. But had I spoken out or tried to leave, I would have been shot and it would have gone on anyway. So I decided to say nothing and let it grow into adulthood, at the same time raising myself to a rank above suspicion. Then, at the proper time, I would destroy it.

"The German writer Günter Grass has said that we, as Germans, must understand ourselves. We are perhaps the finest technical craftsmen history has ever known. We are capable of making miracles. But nothing we ever do can escape Auschwitz or Treblinka or Birkenau or Sobibór or any of the others, because they are ours, they belong to us—they are in our soul, and we must know what they are, and understand why, and never—ever—allow it to happen again.

"By the time you view this everything we have created will have been destroyed. The new Reich will have been ended. At Charlottenburg. At *der Garten.* At the station in Switzerland, hidden in the recesses of the glacier beneath Jungfraujoch.

"There will be no *Übermorgen.*"

With that Salettl simply stood, walked past the camera and out of sight. A moment later the screen went black.

159

OSBORN LEFT downtown without remembering it, overwhelmed, his mind and emotions blurred together. He tried to separate them. Reflect on what he had just seen. Focus on the scope and history of what Salettl had revealed. To rage at what the Third Reich had done to the world. And at the audacity of what they had tried to do again! He wanted to shout at the horror of the extermination camps. He wanted to see the faces of the foul men in the dock at Nuremberg and superimpose over them the faces of Scholl and Dortmund and the others he knew only by name. He wanted to know if the Organization's covert incursion into French politics had led directly to the death of François Christian.

In one breath he sought to acknowledge the singular burden Salettl had carried alone for so many years and for the dark heroism of his own "final solution." And in the next, rage furiously at him for giving nothing of the details of the atomic surgery. How the temperatures at, or reaching, absolute zero had been attained. How the surgery had been done! How the recovery process worked! To medicine, to the alleviation of pain and suffering, that disclosure would have been priceless.

At some point it vaguely registered that he was on the Santa Monica Freeway headed toward home. It was rush hour and he was bumper-to-bumper in heavy traffic. But it made no difference, he was driving on autopilot. He had no idea how much time had passed since he'd left police headquarters. He could have turned north or south or east as easily as west. It would have made no difference. Somewhere he sensed he had reached the end of the freeway and was on the s-curves approaching McClure Tunnel. Then he was through it and out onto Pacific Coast Highway. In front of him the Santa Monica Mountains seemed to rise straight out of the sea and the ocean itself disappeared in the V of the setting sun on the horizon.

A sudden affection for McVey came over him. McVey had shown him the tape because he'd hoped it would finally kill the demon and help put his soul to rest. Help make some very real and cognizant sense of what had happened when before there had only been fragments. It had been a kind and decent gesture and he wished he could tell him that. He wished there was a way he could thank him. Even love him, if that were possible. As a son could love a father, even though they might have been at odds most of their lives.

But then his thoughts collapsed against the emotional whirlwind that had swept him as he watched the video. The thing that was sweeping him over the edge.

It was the thing Salettl had left out of his message. The thing forcing him to confront something he did not want to face. It was something McVey didn't know, and never would. Nor would Noble or Remmer, or Vera or anyone else because there was no rational way Osborn could ever talk about it. Maybe Salettl had left it out because he thought he had taken care of it as he had taken care of everything else.

Suddenly Osborn realized traffic was backed up in front of him and he had to hit the brakes hard to avoid hitting the car in front of him. A police car and two tow trucks flew by in the center lane. It meant an accident up ahead. Traffic could be locked up for hours. He couldn't sit there that long, because the only thing he could listen to would be his mind and he would go insane. He had to get out of there. To move and keep moving.

Glancing over his shoulder, he saw the center lane open. Stepping on the accelerator, he swung past the car in front of him, made a U-turn on the highway and roared back the way he had come. A moment later he cut a sharp right and pulled into a beach parking lot. For a moment he sat there staring at the ocean.

Then he got out. Crutches first, then pushing himself up until he was standing. Leaving the door open and the keys in the ignition, he moved out into the sand. The crutches sank in and the going became difficult. It didn't matter. Motion was everything and he kept going, across the beach toward the breakers. His shoes filled with sand and he tore them off and left them. Then his feet touched hard, wet sand and he felt the water. In seconds he was knee deep, leaning forward on the crutches, a gentle surf soaking his trousers.

The audacity of it was that they could even conceive of such a thing, much less do it.

After thirty years, his father's death had been resolved. But it was not a resolution he could have ever imagined or foreseen, not in his darkest hours. And were it not for Salettl's video, it would have remained an extension of that part of his experience on the Jungfrau that he had until now fully accepted as illusion, an hallucinatory dream, filled with the horrors of his own imagination. But now, having seen what he had, there was no doubt whatsoever that what he had experienced had been no dream. It had been real. And it made clear not only the reason behind his father's death but the motivation for Von Holden's journey to the glacier, and the hiding place deep within the ice.

Somewhere he heard Salettl's voice—"We had raised two young men . . . Genetically engineered, pure Aryan from birth . . . among the finest physical specimens alive . . . age twenty-four . . . one of the two boys will be chosen . . . prepared for the surgical operation . . . messiah for the new Reich."

"Hey, mister, you're all wet!" a young boy yelled from the shore. But Osborn didn't hear. He was on the Jungfrau, and Von Holden was falling toward him, the box he had brought with him from Berlin still cradled in his arms.

"*Für Übermorgen!* For the day after tomorrow!" He heard Von Holden scream and then the box slipped from his grasp and Von Holden plunged over the side, swallowed by the icy blackness as if he had been airbrushed out of existence. But the box landed near where Osborn lay in the snow, rolling over with its own weight and momentum. As it did, it came open and what was inside was revealed. And in the instant before it vanished over the edge, Osborn saw clearly what it was. It was the thing Salettl had left out. The thing Osborn could tell no one because no one would believe him. It was the real reason for *Übermorgen.* Its driving essence. Its center core. The severed, deep-frozen head of Adolf Hitler.

Acknowledgments

For technical information and advice I am especially indebted to Detective John "Jigsaw" St. John, Los Angeles Police Department Homicide, retired, Lieutenant John Dunkin of the Los Angeles Police Department, Danny Bacher of the Swiss National Tourist Office, Robert Abrams of San Francisco, Imara of Denver, and James W. Howatt, M.D., Bert R. Mandelbaum, M.D., Robert N. Mohr, D.P.M., Herbert G. Resnick, M.D., and Norton F. Kristy, Ph.D.

For suggestions and corrections to the manuscript, I am indebted to Fredrica S. Friedman, Hilary Hale, and most especially to Frances Jalet-Miller. Further, my deepest appreciation to Marion Rosenberg, and to Aaron Priest, the magician who made it all happen. Finally, my most sincere gratitude to Leon I. Bender, M.D., without whose extraordinary skills this book never would have been written.

attach